J.W. ORR N.Y.

MISS TROTWOOD'S VISIT.

DAVID COPPERFIELD.

BY

CHARLES DICKENS.

LITTLE EMILY.

Philadelphia:

T. B. PETERSON & BROTHERS.

DAVID COPPERFIELD.

BY

CHARLES DICKENS.
("BOZ.")

WITH FORTY ILLUSTRATIONS,

FROM DESIGNS BY H. K. BROWNE.

IN TWO VOLUMES.

VOL. I.

Philadelphia:
T. B. PETERSON, NO. 306 CHESTNUT STREET.

Affectionately Inscribed

TO

THE HON. MR. AND MRS. RICHARD WATSON,

OF

ROCKINGHAM NORTHAMPTONSHIRE.

PREFACE.

I do not find it easy to get sufficiently far away from this Book, in the first sensations of having finished it, to refer to it with the composure which this formal heading would seem to require. My interest in it is so recent and strong; and my mind is so divided between pleasure and regret—pleasure in the achievement of a long design, regret in the separation from many companions—that I am in danger of wearying the reader whom I love, with personal confidences, and private emotions.

Besides which, all that I could say of the Story, to any purpose, I have endeavoured to say in it.

It would concern the reader little, perhaps, to know, how sorrowfully the pen is laid down at the end of a two-years' imaginative task; or how an Author feels as if he were dismissing some portion of himself into the shadowy world, when a crowd of the creatures of his brain are going from him for ever. Yet, I have nothing else to tell; unless, indeed, I were to confess (which might be of less moment still) that no one can ever believe this Narrative, in the reading, more than I have believed it in the writing.

Instead of looking back, therefore, I will look forward. I cannot close this Volume more agreeably to myself, than with a hopeful glance towards the time when I shall again put forth my two green leaves once a month, and with a faithful remembrance of the genial sun and showers that have fallen on these leaves of David Copperfield, and made me happy.

CONTENTS.

LIST OF ILLUSTRATIONS.

THE

PERSONAL HISTORY AND EXPERIENCE

OF

DAVID COPPERFIELD THE YOUNGER.

CHAPTER I.

I AM BORN.

WHETHER I shall turn out to be the hero of my own life, or whether that station will be held by any body else, these pages must show. To begin my life with the beginning of my life, I record that I was born (as I have been informed and believe) on a Friday, at twelve o'clock at night. It was remarked that the clock began to strike, and I began to cry, simultaneously.

In consideration of the day and hour of my birth, it was declared by the nurse, and by some sage women in the neighborhood, who had taken a lively interest in me several months before there was any possibility of our becoming personally acquainted; first, that I was destined to be unlucky in life; and secondly, that I was privileged to see ghosts and spirits—both these gifts inevitably attaching, as they believed, to all unlucky infants, of either gender, born towards the small hours on a Friday night.

I need say nothing here, on the first head, because nothing can show better than my history whether that prediction was verified or falsified by the result. On the second branch of the question, I will only remark, that unless I ran through that part of my inheritance while I was still a baby, I have not come into it yet. But I do not at all complain of having been kept out of this property; and if any body else should be in the present enjoyment of it, he is heartily welcome to keep it.

I was born with a caul, which was advertised for sale, in the newspapers, at the low price of fifteen guineas. Whether sea-going people were short of money about that time, or were short of faith and preferred cork-jackets, I don't know; all I know is, that there was but one solitary bidding, and that was from an attorney connected with the bill-broking business, who offered two pounds in cash, and the balance in Sherry, but declined to be guaranteed from drowning on any higher bargain. Consequently the advertisement was withdrawn at a dead loss—for as to sherry, my poor dear mother's own sherry was in the market then—and ten years afterwards the caul was put up in a raffle down in our part of the country to fifty members at half-a-crown a head, the winner to spend five shillings. I was present myself, and I remember to have felt quite uncomfortable and confused, at a part of myself being disposed of in that way. The caul was won, I recollect, by an old lady with a hand-basket, who, very reluctantly, produced from it the stipulated five shillings, all in halfpence, and twopence halfpenny short; as it took an immense time and a great waste of arithmetic to endeavor without any effect to prove to her. It is a fact which will be long remembered as remarkable down there, that she was never drowned, but died triumphantly in bed, at ninety-two. I have understood that it was, to the last, her proudest boast, that she never had been on the water in her life, except upon a bridge; and that over her tea (to which she was extremely partial) she, to the last, expressed her indignation at the impiety of mariners and others who had the presumption to go "meandering" about the world. It was in vain to represent to her that some conveniences, tea perhaps included, resulted from this objectionable practice. She always returned with greater emphasis and with an instinctive knowledge of the strength of her objection, "Let us have no meandering."

Not to meander, myself, at present, I will go back to my birth.

I was born at Blunderstone, in Suffolk, or "thereby," as they say in Scotland. I was a posthumous child. My father's eyes had closed upon the light of this world six months, when mine opened on it. There is something strange to me, even now, in the reflection that he never saw me, and something stranger yet in the shadowy remembrance that I have of my first childish associations with his white grave-stone in the churchyard, and of the indefinable compassion I used to feel for it lying out alone there in the dark night, when our little parlor was warm and bright with fire and candle, and the doors of our house were—almost cruelly it seemed to me sometimes—bolted and locked against it.

An aunt of my father's, and consequently a great-aunt of mine, of whom I shall have more to relate by and by, was the principal magnate of our family. Miss Trotwood, or Miss Betsey, as my poor mother always called her, when she sufficiently overcame her dread of this formidable personage to mention her at all (which was seldom), had been married to a husband younger than herself, who was very handsome, except in the sense of the homely adage, "handsome is, that handsome does"—for he was strongly suspected of having beaten Miss Betsey, and even of having once, on a disputed question of supplies, made some hasty but determined arrangements to throw her out of a two pair of stairs' window. These evidences of an incompatibility of temper induced Miss Betsey to pay him off, and effect a separation by mutual consent. He went to India with his capital, and there, according to a wild legend in our family, he was once seen riding on an elephant, in company with a Baboon; but I think it must have been a Baboo—or a Begum. Any how, from India tidings of his death reached home, within ten years. How they affected my aunt, nobody knew; for immediately upon the separation, she took her maiden name again, bought a cottage in a hamlet on the sea-coast a long way off, established herself there as a single woman, with one servant, and was understood to live secluded, ever afterwards, in an inflexible retirement.

My father had once been a favorite of hers, I believe, but she was mortally affronted by his marriage, on the ground that my mother was "a wax doll." She had never seen my mother, but she knew her to be not yet twenty. My father and Miss Betsey never met again. He was double my mother's age when he married, and of but a delicate constitution. He died a year afterwards, and, as I have said, six months before I came into the world.

This was the state of matters, on the afternoon of what *I* may be excused for calling, that eventful and important Friday. I can make no claim therefore to have known, at that time, how matters stood, or to have any remembrance, founded upon the evidence of my own senses, of what follows.

My mother was sitting by the fire, but poorly in health, and very low in spirits, looking at it through her tears, and desponding heavily about herself and the fatherless little stranger who was already welcomed by some grosses of prophetic pins in a drawer up-stairs, to a world not at all excited on the subject of his arrival; my mother, I say, was sitting by the fire, that bright, windy March afternoon, very timid and sad, and very doubtful of ever coming alive out of the trial that was before her; when, lifting her eyes as she dried them, to the window opposite, she saw a strange lady coming up the garden.

My mother had a sure foreboding at the second glance, that it was Miss Betsey. The setting sun was glowing on the strange lady, over the garden-fence, and she came walking up to the door with a fell rigidity of figure and composure of countenance that could have belonged to nobody else.

When she reached the house she gave another proof of her identity. My father had often hinted that she seldom conducted herself like any ordinary Christian; and now, instead of ringing the bell, she came and looked in at that identical window, pressing the end of her nose against the glass to that extent, that my poor dear mother used to say it became perfectly flat and white in a moment.

She gave my mother such a turn, that I have always been convinced I am indebted to Miss Betsey for having been born on a Friday.

My mother had left her chair in her agitation, and gone behind it in the corner. Miss Betsey, looking round the room, slowly and inquiringly, began on the other side, and carried her eyes on, like a Saracen's Head in a Dutch clock, until they reached my mother. Then she made a frown and a gesture to my mother, like one who is accustomed to be obeyed, to come and open the door. My mother went.

"Mrs. David Copperfield, I *think*," said Miss Betsey; the emphasis referring, perhaps, to my mother's mourning weeds, and her condition.

"Yes," said my mother, faintly.

"Miss Trotwood," said the visitor. "You have heard of her, I dare say?"

My mother answered she had had that pleasure. And she had a disagreeable consciousness of not appearing to imply that it had been an overpowering pleasure.

"Now you see her," said Miss Betsey. My mother bent her head, and begged her to walk in.

They went into the parlor my mother had come from—the fire in the best room on the other side of the passage not being lighted: not having been lighted, indeed, since my father's funeral—and when they wene both seated, and Miss Betsey said nothing, my mother, after vainly trying to restrain herself, began to cry.

"Oh tut, tut, tut!" said Miss Betsey, in a hurry. "Don't do that! Come, come!"

My mother couldn't help it notwithstanding, so she cried until she had had her cry out.

"Take off your cap, child," said Miss Betsey, "and let me see you."

My mother was too much afraid of her to refuse compliance with this odd request, if she had any disposition to do so. Therefore she did as she was told, and did it with such nervous hands that her hair (whch was luxuriant and beautiful) fell all about her face.

"Why, bless my heart!" exclaimed Miss Betsey. "You are a very Baby!"

My mother was, no doubt, unusually youthful in appearance even for her years; she hung her head, as if it were her fault, poor thing, and said, sobbing, that indeed she was afraid she was but a childish widow, and would be but a childish mother if she fired. In a short pause which ensued, she had a fancy that she felt Miss Betsey touch her hair, and that with no ungentle hand; but, looking at her, in her timid hope, she found that lady sitting with the skirt of her dress tucked up, her hands folded on one knee, and her feet upon the fender, frowning at the fire.

"In the name of Heaven," said Miss Betsey, suddenly, "why Rookery?"

"Do you mean the house, ma'am?" asked my mother.

"Why Rookery?" said Miss Betsey. "Cookery would have been more to the purpose, if you had had any practical ideas of life, either of you."

"The name was Mr. Copperfield's choice," returned my mother. "When he bought the house, he liked to think that there were rooks about it."

The evening wind made such a disturbance just now, among some tall old elm trees at the bottom of the garden, that neither my mother nor Miss Betsey could forbear glancing that way. As the elms bent to one another, like giants who were whispering secrets, and after a few seconds of such repose, fell into a violent flurry, tossing their wild arms about, as if their late confidences were really too wicked for their peace of mind, some weather-beaten ragged old rooks' nests burdening their higher branches, swung like wrecks upon a stormy sea.

"Where are the birds?" asked Miss Betsey.

"The —— ?" My mother had been thinking of something else.

"The rooks—what has become of them?" asked Miss Betsey.

"There have not been any since we have lived here," said my mother. "We thought—Mr. Copperfield thought—it was quite a large rookery, but the nests were very old ones, and the birds have deserted them a long while."

"David Copperfield all over!" cried Miss Betsey. "David Copperfield from head to foot! Calls a house a rookery when there's not a rook near it, and takes the birds on trust, because he sees the nests!"

"Mr. Copperfield," returned my mother, "is dead, and if you dare to speak unkindly of him to me——"

My poor dear mother, I suppose, had some momentary intention of committing an assault and battery upon my aunt, who could easily have settled her with one hand, even if my mother had been in far better training for such an encounter than she was that evening. But it passed with the action of rising from her chair; and she sat down again very meekly, and fainted.

When she came to herself, or when Miss Betsey had restored her, whichever it was, she found the latter standing at the window. The twilight was by this time shading down into darkness; and dimly as they saw each other, they could not have done that, without the aid of the fire.

"Well?" said Miss Betsey, coming back to her chair, as if she had only been taking a casual look at the prospect; "and when do you expect——"

"I am all in a tremble!" faltered my mother. "I don't know what's the matter. I shall die, I am sure!"

"No, no, no," said Miss Betsey. "Have some tea."

"Oh dear me, dear me, do you think it will do me any good?" cried my mother in a helpless manner.

"Of course it will," said Miss Betsey. "It's nothing but fancy. What do you call your girl?"

"I don't know that it will be a girl, yet ma'am," said my mother innocently.

"Bless the Baby!" exclaimed Miss Betsey, unconsciously quoting the second sentiment of the pincushion in the drawer up stairs, but applying it to my mother instead of me. "I on't mean that. I mean your servant-girl."

"Peggotty," said my mother.

"Peggotty," repeated Miss Betsey, with some indignation. "Do you mean to say, child, that any human being has gone into a Christian church, and got herself named Peggotty?"

"It's her surname," said my mother, faintly. "Mr. Copperfield called her by it, because her Christian name was the same as mine."

"Here! Peggotty!" cried Miss Betsey, opening the parlor door. "Tea. Your mistress is a little unwell. Don't dawdle."

Having issued this mandate with as much potentiality as if she had been a recognized authority in the house ever since it had been a house, and having looked out to confront the amazed Peggotty coming along the passage with a candle at the sound of a strange voice, Miss Betsey shut the door again, and sat down as before: with her feet on the fender, the skirt of her dress tucked up, and her hands folded on one knee.

"You were speaking about its being a girl," said Miss Betsey. "I have no doubt it will be a girl. I have a presentiment that it must be a girl. Now child, from the moment of the birth of this girl—"

"Perhaps boy," my mother took the liberty of putting in.

"I tell you I have a presentiment that it must be a girl," returned Miss Betsey. "Don't contradict. From the moment of this girl's birth, child, I intend to be her friend. I intend to be her godmother, and I beg you'll call her Betsey Trotwood Copperfield. There must be no mistakes in life with *this* Betsey Trotwood. There must be no trifling with *her* affections, poor dear. She must be well brought up, and well guarded from reposing any foolish confidences where they are not deserved. I must make that *my* care."

There was a twitch of Miss Betsey's head, after each of these sentences, as if her own old wrongs were working within her, and she repressed any plainer reference to them by strong constraint. So my mother suspected at least, as she observed her by the low glimmer of the fire: too much scared by Miss Betsey, too uneasy in herself, and too subdued and bewildered altogether, to observe any thing very clearly, or to know what to say.

"And was David good to you, child?" asked Miss Betsey, when she had been silent for a little while, and these motions of her head had gradually ceased. "Were you comfortable together?"

"We were very happy," said my mother. "Mr. Copperfield was only too good to me."

"What, he spoilt you, I suppose?" returned Miss Betsey.

"For being quite alone and dependent on myself in this rough world again, yes, I fear he did indeed," sobbed my mother.

"Well! Don't cry!" said Miss Betsey. "You were not equally matched, child—if any two people *can* be equally matched—and so I asked the question. You were an orphan, weren't you?"

"Yes."

"And a governess?"

"I was nursery-governess in a family where Mr. Copperfield came to visit. Mr. Copperfield was very kind to me, and took a great deal of notice of me, and paid me a good deal of attention, and at last proposed to me. And I accepted him. And so we were married," said my mother simply.

"Ha! poor Baby!" mused Miss Betsey, with her frown still bent upon the fire. "Do you know any thing?"

"I beg your pardon ma'am," faltered my mother.

"About keeping house, for instance," said Miss Betsey.

"Not much I fear," returned my mother. "Not so much as I could wish. But Mr. Copperfield was teaching me—"

("Much he knew about it himself!" said Miss Betsey in a parenthesis.)

—"And I hope I should have improved, being very anxious to learn, and he very patient to teach, if the great misfortune of his death"—my mother broke down again here, and could get no farther.

"Well, well!" said Miss Betsey.

—"I kept my Housekeeping-Book regularly and balanced it with Mr. Copperfield every night," cried my mother in another burst of distress, and breaking down again.

"Well, well!" said Miss Betsey. "Don't cry any more."

—"And I am sure we never had a word of difference respecting it, except when Mr. Copperfield objected to my threes and fives being too much like each other, or to my putting curly tails to my sevens and nines," resumed my mother in another burst, and breaking down again.

"You'll make yourself ill," said Miss Betsey, "and you

know that will not be good either for you or for my god-daugnter. Come! You mustn't do it!"

This argument had some share in quieting my mother, though her increasing indisposition perhaps had a larger one. There was an interval of silence, only broken by Miss Betsey's occasionally ejaculating "Ha!" as she sat with her feet upon the fender.

"David had bought an annuity for himself with his money, I know," said she, by and by. "What did he do for you?"

"Mr. Copperfield," said my mother, answering with some difficulty, "was so considerate and good as to secure the reversion of a part of it to me."

"How much?" asked Miss Betsey.

"A hundred and five pounds a year," said my mother.

"He might have done worse," said my aunt.

The word was appropriate to the moment. My mother was so much worse that Peggotty, coming in with the teaboard and candles, and seeing at a glance how ill she was,—as Miss Betsey might have done sooner if there had been light enough,—conveyed her up stairs to her own room with all speed, and immediately dispatched Ham Peggotty, her nephew, who had been, for some days past, secreted in the house, unknown to my mother, as a special messenger in case of emergency, to fetch the nurse and Doctor.

Those allied powers were considerably astonished when they arrived within a few minutes of each other, to find an unknown lady of portentous appearance, sitting before the fire, with her bonnet tied over her left arm, stopping her ears with jewellers' cotton. Peggotty knowing nothing about her, and my mother saying nothing about her, she was quite a Mystery in the parlor; and the fact of her having a magazine of jewellers' cotton in her pocket, and sticking the article in her ears in that way, did not detract from the solemnity of her presence.

The Doctor having been up stairs and come down again, and having satisfied himself, I suppose, that there was a probability of this unknown lady and himself having to sit there, face to face, for some hours, laid himself out to be polite and social.

He was the meekest of his sex, the mildest of little men. He sidled in and out of a room, to take up the less space. He walked as softly as the Ghost in Hamlet—and more slowly. He carried his head on one side, partly in modest depreciation of himself, partly in modest propitiation of every body else. It is nothing to say that he hadn't a word to throw at a dog. He couldn't have *thrown* a word at a mad dog. He might have offered him one gently, or half a one, or a fragment of one ; for he spoke as slowly as he walked ; but he wouldn't have been rude to him, and he couldn't have been quick with him, for any earthly consideration.

Mr. Chillip, looking mildly at my aunt, with his head on one side, and making her a little bow, said, in allusion to the jewellers' cotton, as he softly touched his left ear :

"Some local irritation, ma'am ?"

"What !" replied my aunt, pulling the cotton out of one ear like a cork.

Mr. Chillip was so alarmed by her abrúptness—as he told my mother afterwards—that it was a mercy he didn't lose his presence of mind. But he repeated, sweetly :

"Some local irritation, ma'am."

"Nonsense !" replied my aunt, and corked herself again, at one blow.

Mr. Chillip could do nothing after this, but sit and look at her feebly, as she sat and looked at the fire, until he was called up stairs again. After some quarter of an hour's absence, he returned.

"Well ?" said my aunt, taking the cotton out of the ear nearest to him.

"Well ma'am," returned Mr. Chillip, "we are—we are progressing slowly, ma'am."

"Ba—a—ah !" said my aunt, with a perfect shake on the contemptuous interjection. And corked herself, as before.

Really—really—as Mr. Chillip told my mother, he was almost shocked ; speaking in a professional point of view alone, he was almost shocked. But he sat and looked at her, notwithstanding, for nearly two hours, as she sat looking at the fire, until he was again called out. After another absence, he again returned.

"Well?" said my aunt, taking out the cotton on that side, again.

"Well ma'am," returned Mr. Chillip, "we are—we are progressing slowly, ma'am."

"Ya—a—ah!" said my aunt. With such a snarl at him, that Mr. Chillip absolutely could not bear it. It was really calculated to break his spirit, he said afterwards. He preferred to go and sit upon the stairs, in the dark and a strong draught, until he was again sent for.

Ham Peggotty, who went to the National school, and was a very dragon at his catechism, and who may therefore be regarded as a credible witness, reported next day, that happening to peep in at the parlor-door an hour after this, he was instantly descried by Miss Betsey, then walking to and fro in a state of agitation, and pounced upon before he could make his escape. That there were now occasional sounds of feet and voices overhead which he inferred the cotton did not exclude, from the circumstance of his evidently being clutched by the lady as a victim on whom to expend her superabundant agitation when the sounds were loudest. That, marching him constantly up and down by the collar (as if he had been taking too much laudanum), she, at those times, shook him, rumpled his hair, made light of his linen, stopped *his* ears as if she confounded them with her own, and otherwise touzled and maltreated him. This was in part confirmed by his aunt, who saw him at half-past twelve o'clock, soon after his release, and affirmed that he was then as red as I was.

The mild Mr. Chillip could not possibly bear malice at such a time, if at any time. He sidled into the parlor as soon as he was at liberty, and said to my aunt in his meekest manner:

"Well, ma'am, I am happy to congratulate you."

"What upon?" said my aunt sharply.

Mr. Chillip was fluttered again, by the extreme severity of my aunt's manner; so he made her a little bow and gave her a little smile, to mollify her.

"Mercy on the man, what's he doing!" cried my aunt impatiently. "Can't he speak?"

"Be calm my dear ma'am," said Mr. Chillip, in his softest accents. "There is no longer any occasion for uneasiness, ma'am. Be calm."

It has since been considered almost a miracle that my aunt didn't shake him, and shake what he had to say, out of him, by main force. She only shook her head at him, but in a way that made him quail.

"Well ma'am," resumed Mr. Chillip, as soon as he had courage, "I am happy to congratulate you. All is now over ma'am, and well over."

During the five minutes or so that Mr. Chillip devoted to the delivery of this oration, my aunt eyed him narrowly.

"How is she?" said my aunt, folding her arms with her bonnet still tied on one of them.

"Well ma'am, she will soon be quite comfortable, I hope," returned Mr. Chillip. "Quite as comfortable as we can expect a young mother to be, under these melancholy domestic circumstances. There cannot be any objection to your seeing her presently, ma'am. It may do her good."

"And *she*. How is *she?*" said my aunt sharply.

Mr. Chillip laid his head a little more on one side, and looked at my aunt like an amiable bird.

"The baby," said my aunt. "How is she?"

"Ma'am," returned Mr. Chillip, "I apprehended you had known. It's a boy."

My aunt said never a word, but took her bonnet by the strings, in the manner of a sling, aimed a blow at Mr. Chillip's head with it, put it on bent, walked out, and never came back. She vanished like a discontented fairy, or like one of those supernatural beings, whom it was popularly supposed I was entitled to see; and never came back any more.

No. I lay in my basket, and my mother lay in her bed; but Betsey Trotwood Copperfield was for ever in the land of dreams and shadows, the tremendous region whence I had so lately travelled; and the light upon the window of our room, shone out upon the earthly bourne of all such travellers, and the mound above the ashes and the dust that once was he, without whom I had never been.

CHAPTER II.

I OBSERVE.

THE first objects that assume a distinct presence before me, as I look far back, into the blank of my infancy, are my mother with her pretty hair and youthful shape, and Peggotty with no shape at all, and eyes so dark that they seemed to darken their whole neighborhood in her face, and cheeks and arms so hard and red that I wondered the birds didn't peck her in preference to apples.

I believe I can remember these two at a little distance apart, dwarfed to my sight by stooping down or kneeling on the floor, and I going unsteadily from the one to the other. I have an impression on my mind which I cannot distinguish from actual remembrance, of the touch of Peggotty's fore-finger as she used to hold it out to me, and of its being roughened by needlework, like a pocket nutmeg-grater.

This may be fancy, though I think the memory of most of us can go farther back into such times than many of us suppose. Just as I believe the power of observation in numbers of very young children to be quite wonderful for its closeness and accuracy. Indeed, I think that most grown men who are remarkable in this respect, may with greater propriety be said not to have lost the faculty, than to have acquired it; the rather, as I generally observe such men to retain a certain freshness, and gentleness, and capacity of being pleased, which are also an inheritance they have preserved from their childhood.

I might have a misgiving that I am "meandering" in stopping to say this, but that it brings me to remark that I build these conclusions, in part upon my own experience of myself; and if it should appear from any thing I may set down in this narrative that I was a child of close observation, or that as a man I have a strong memory of my childhood, I undoubtedly lay claim to both of these characteristics.

Looking back, as I was saying, into the blank of my infancy, the first objects I can remember as standing out by themselves from a confusion of things, are my mother and Peggotty. What else do I remember? Let me see.

There comes out of the cloud, our house—not new to me, but quite familiar, in its earliest remembrance. On the ground-floor is Peggotty's kitchen, opening into a back yard; with a pigeon-house on a pole, in the centre, without any pigeons in it; a great dog-kennel in a corner, without any dog; and a quantity of fowls that look terribly tall to me, walking about, in a menacing and ferocious manner. There is one cock who gets upon a post to crow, and seems to take particular notice of me as I look at him through the kitchen window, who makes me shiver, he is so fierce. Of the geese outside the side-gate who come waddling after me with their long necks stretched out when I go that way, I dream at night as a man environed by wild beasts might dream of lions.

Here is a long passage—what an enormous perspective I make of it!—leading from Peggotty's kitchen to the front door. A dark store-room opens out of it, and that is a place to be run past at night; for I don't know what may be among those tubs and jars and old tea chests, when there is nobody in there with a dimly burning light, letting a mouldy air come out at the door, in which there is the smell of soap, pickles, pepper, candles, and coffee, all at one whiff. Then there are the two parlors; the parlor in which we sit of an evening, my mother and I and Peggotty—for Peggotty is quite our companion, when her work is done and we are alone—and the best parlor where we sit on a Sunday: grandly, but not so comfortably. There is something of a doleful air about that room to me, for Peggotty has told me—I don't know when, but apparently ages ago—about my father's funeral, and the company having their black cloaks put on. One Sunday night my mother reads to Peggotty and me in there, how Lazarus was raised up from the dead. And I am so frightened, that they are afterwards obliged to take me out of bed, and show me the quiet churchyard out of the bedroom window, with the dead all lying in their graves at rest, below the solemn moon.

OUR PEW AT CHURCH.

There is nothing half so green that I know any where, as the grass of that churchyard; nothing half so shady as its trees; nothing half so quiet as its tombstones. The sheep are feeding there, when I kneel up, early in the morning, in my little bed in a closet within my mother's room, to look out at it; and I see the red light shining on the sun-dial, and think within myself, "Is the sun-dial glad, I wonder, that it can tell me the time again?"

Here is our pew in the church. What a high-backed pew! With a window near it, out of which our house can be seen—and *is* seen many times during the morning's service by Peggotty, who likes to make herself as sure as she can that it's not being robbed, or is not in flames. But though Peggotty's eye wanders, she is much offended if mine does, and frowns to me, as I stand upon the seat, that I am to look at the clergyman. But I can't always look at him—I know him without that white thing on, and I am afraid of his wondering why I stare so, and perhaps stopping the service to inquire—and what am I do? It's a dreadful thing to gape, but I must do something. I look at my mother, but *she* pretends not to see me. I look at a boy in the aisle, and *he* makes faces at me. I look at the sunlight coming in at the open door through the porch, and there I see a stray sheep—I don't mean a sinner, but mutton—half making up his mind to come into the church. I feel that if I looked at him any longer I might be tempted to say something out loud; and what would become of me then! I look up at the monumental tablets on the wall, and try to think of Mr. Bodgers late of this parish, and what the feelings of Mrs. Bodgers must have been, when affliction sore, long time, Mr. Bodgers bore, and physicians were in vain. I wonder whether they called in Mr. Chillip, and he was in vain, and if so, how he likes to be reminded of it once a week. I look from Mr. Chillip, in his Sunday neckcloth, to the pulpit, and think what a good place it would be to play in, and what a castle it would make, with another boy coming up the stairs to attack it, and having the velvet cushion with the tassels thrown down on his head. In time my eyes gradually shut up, and from seeming to hear the clergyman singing a drowsy song in the heat, I hear nothing, until I fall off the seat with a crash, and am taken out, more dead than alive, by Peggotty.

And now I see the outside of our house, with the latticed bedroom-windows standing open to let in the sweet-smelling air, and the ragged old rooks' nests still dangling in the elm-trees at the bottom of the front garden. Now I am in the garden at the back, beyond the yard where the empty pigeon-house and dog-kennel are—a very preserve of butterflies, as I remember it, with a high fence, and a gate and padlock; where the fruit clusters on the trees, riper and richer than fruit has ever been since, in any other garden, and where my mother gathers some in a basket, while I stand by, bolting furtive gooseberries, and trying to look unmoved. A great wind rises, and the summer is gone in a moment. We are playing in the winter twilight, dancing about the parlor. When my mother is out of breath and rests herself in an elbow chair, I watch her winding her bright curls round her fingers, and straitening her waist, and nobody knows better than I do that she likes to look so well, and is proud of being so pretty.

That is among my very earliest impressions. That, and a sense that we were both a little afraid of Peggotty, and submitted ourselves in most things to her direction, were among the first opinions—if they may be so called—that I ever derived from what I saw.

Peggotty and I were sitting one night by the parlor fire, alone. I had been reading to Peggotty about Crocodiles. I must have read very perspicuously, or the poor soul must have been deeply interested, for I remember she had a cloudy impression after I had done, that they were a sort of vegetable. I was tired of reading, and dead sleepy; but having leave, as a high treat, to sit up until my mother came home from spending the evening at a neighbor's, I would rather have died upon my post (of course) than gone to bed. I had reached that stage of sleepiness when Peggotty seemed to swell and grow immensely large. I propped my eyelids open with my two forefingers, and looked perseveringly at her as she sat at work; at the little bit of wax candle she had got for her thread—how old it looked, being so wrinkled in all directions!—at the little house with a thatched roof, where the yard-measure lived; at her work-box with a sliding lid with a view of Saint Paul's Cathedral (with a pink dome) painted on the top; at the brass thimble on her finger; at herself, whom I thought lovely. I felt so sleepy that I knew if I lost sight of any thing, for a moment, I was gone.

"Peggotty," says I, suddenly, "were you ever married?"

"Lord, Master Davy," replied Peggotty. "What's put marriage in your head!"

She answered with such a start, that it quite awoke me. And then she stopped in her work, and looked at me, with her needle drawn out to its thread's length.

"But *were* you ever married, Peggotty?" says I. "You are a very handsome woman, an't you?"

I thought her in a different style from my mother, certainly; but of another school of beauty, I considered her a perfect example. There was a red velvet footstool in the best parlor on which my mother had painted a nosegay. The groundwork of that stool, and Peggotty's complexion, appeared to me to be one and the same thing. The stool was smooth, and Peggotty was rough, but that made no difference.

"Me handsome, Davy!" said Peggotty. "Lawk, no my dear! But what put marriage in your head?"

"I don't know!—You mustn't marry more than one person at a time, may you, Peggotty?"

"Certainly not," says Peggotty, with the promptest decision.

"But if you marry a person, and the person dies, why then you may marry another person, mayn't you, Peggotty?"

"You MAY," says Peggotty—"if you choose, my dear. That's a matter of opinion."

"But what is your opinion, Peggotty?" said I.

I asked her, and looked curiously at her, because she looked so curiously at me.

"My opinion is," said Peggotty, taking her eyes from me, after a little indecision, and going on with her work, "that I never was married myself, Master Davy, and that I don't expect to be. That's all I know about the subject."

"You an't cross, I suppose, Peggotty, are you?" said I, after sitting quiet for a minute.

I really thought she was, she had been so short with me: but I was quite mistaken; for she laid aside her work (which was a stocking of her own) and opening her arms wide, took my curly head within them, and gave it a good squeeze. I know it was a good squeeze, because, being very plump, whenever she made any little exertion after she was dressed, some of the buttons on the back of her gown, flew off. And I recollect two bursting to the opposite side of the parlor, while she was hugging me.

"Now let me hear some more about the Crorkindills," said Peggotty, who was not quite right in the name yet, "for I an't heard half enough."

I couldn't quite understand why Peggotty looked so queer, or why she was so ready to go back to the crocodiles. However, we returned to those monsters, with fresh wakefulness on my part, and we left their eggs in the sand for the sun to hatch; and we ran away from them and baffled them by constantly turning, which they were unable to do quickly, on account of their unwieldy make; and we went into the water after them, as natives, and put sharp pieces of timber down their throats; and in short we ran the whole crocodile gauntlet. *I* did at least; but I had my doubts of Peggotty, who was thoughtfully sticking her needle into various parts of her face and arms, all the time.

We had exhausted the crocodiles, and begun with the alligators when the garden bell rang. We went out to the door, and there was my mother, looking unusually pretty, I thought, and with her a gentleman with beautiful black hair and whiskers, who had walked home with us from church last Sunday.

As my mother stooped down on the threshold to take me in her arms and kiss me, the gentleman said I was a more highly privileged little fellow than a monarch—or something like that; for my later understanding comes, I am sensible, to my aid here.

"What does that mean?" I asked him over her shoulder.

He patted me on the head; but somehow, I didn't like him or his deep voice, and I was jealous that his hand should touch my mother's in touching me—which it did. I put it away, as well as I could.

"Oh Davy!" remonstrated my mother.

"Dear boy!" said the gentleman. "I cannot wonder at his devotion!"

I never saw such a beautiful color on my mother's face before. She gently chid me for being rude, and keeping me close to her shawl, turned to thank the gentleman for taking so much trouble as to bring her home. She put out her hand to him, as she spoke, and, as he met it with his own she glanced, I thought, at me.

"Let us say 'good night,' my fine boy," said the gentleman, when he had bent his head—*I* saw him!—over my mother's little glove.

"Good night!" said I.

"Come! Let us be the best friends in the world!" said the gentleman, laughing. "Shake hands."

My right hand was in my mother's left, so I gave him the other.

"Why, that's the wrong hand, Davy!" laughed the gentleman.

My mother drew my right hand forward, but I was resolved, for my former reason, not to give it him, and I did not. I gave him the other, and he shook it heartily, and said I was a brave fellow, and went away.

At this minute I see him turn round in the garden, and give us a last look with his ill-omened black eyes, before the door was shut.

Peggotty, who had not said a word or moved a finger, secured the fastenings instantly, and we all went into the parlor. My mother, contrary to her usual habit, instead of coming to the elbow chair by the fire, remained at the other end of the room, and sat singing to herself.

"—Hope you have had a pleasant evening, ma'am," said Peggotty, standing as stiff as a barrel in the centre of the room, with a candlestick in her hand.

"Much obliged to you, Peggotty," returned my mother, in a cheerful voice, "I have had a *very* pleasant evening."

"A stranger or so makes an agreeable change," suggested Peggotty.

"A very agreeable change indeed," returned my mother.

Peggotty continuing to stand motionless in the middle of the room, and my mother resuming her singing, I fell asleep, though I was not so sound asleep but that I could hear voices, without hearing what they said. When I half awoke from this uncomfortable doze, I found Peggotty and my mother both in tears, and both talking.

"Not such a one as this, Mr. Copperfield wouldn't have liked," said Peggotty. "That I say, and that I swear!"

"Good Heavens!" cried my mother. "You'll drive me mad! Was ever any poor girl so ill-used by her servants as I am! Why do I do myself the injustice of calling myself a girl? Have I never been married, Peggotty?"

"God knows you have, ma'am," returned Peggotty.

"Then how can you dare," said my mother—"you know I don't mean how can you dare, Peggotty, but how can you have the heart—to make me so uncomfortable, and say such bitter things to me, when you are well aware that I haven't, out of this place, a single friend to turn to!"

"The more's the reason," returned Peggotty, "for saying that it won't do. No! That it won't do. No! No price could make it do. No!"—I thought Peggotty would have thrown the candlestick away, she was so emphatic with it.

"How can you be so aggravating!" said my mother, shedding more tears than before, "as to talk in such an unjust manner! How can you go on as if it was all settled and arranged, Peggotty, when I tell you over and over again, you cruel thing, that beyond the commonest civilities nothing has passed! You talk of admiration. What am I to do? If people are so silly as to indulge the sentiment, is it my fault? What am I to do, I ask you? Would you wish me to shave my head and black my face, or disfigure myself with a burn, or a scald, or something of that sort? I dare say you would, Peggotty. I dare say you'd quite enjoy it."

Peggotty seemed to take this aspersion very mucn at heart, I thought.

"And my dear boy," cried my mother, coming to the elbow chair in which I was, and caressing me, "my own little Davy! Is it to be hinted to me that I am wanting in affection for my precious treasure, the dearest little fellow that ever was!"

"Nobody never went and hinted no such thing," said Peggotty.

"You did, Peggotty!" returned my mother. "You know you did. What else was it possible to infer from what you said, you unkind creature, when you know as well as I do, that on his account only last quarter I wouldn't buy myself a new parasol, though that old green one is frayed the whole way up, and the fringe is perfectly mangey. You know it is, Peggotty. You can't deny it." Then turning affectionately to me with her cheek against mine; "Am I a naughty mamma to you, Davy? Am I nasty, cruel, selfish, bad mamma? Say I am, my child; say 'yes,' dear boy, and Peggotty will love you, and Peggotty's love is a great deal better than mine, Davy. *I* dont love you at all, do I?"

At this, we all fell a crying together. I think I was the loudest of the party, but I am sure we were all sincere about it. I was quite heart-broken myself, and am afraid that in the first transports of wounded tenderness I called Peggotty a "beast." That honest creature was in deep affliction I remember, and must have become quite buttonless on the occasion; for a little volley of those explosives went off, when, after having made it up with my mother, she kneeled down by the elbow chair, and made it up with me.

We went to bed greatly dejected. My sobs kept waking me for a long time, and when one very strong sob quite hoisted me up in bed, I found my mother sitting on the coverlet, and leaning over me. I fell asleep in her arms, after that, and slept soundly.

Whether it was the following Sunday when I saw the gentleman again, or whether there was any greater lapse of time before he reappeared, I cannot recall. I don't profess to be clear about dates. But there he was, in church, and he walked home with us afterwards. He came in, too, to look at a famous geranium we had in the parlor window. It did not appear to me that he took much notice of it, but before he went he asked my mother to give him a bit of the blossom. She begged him to choose it for himself, but he refused to do that—I could not understand why—so she plucked it for him and gave it into his hand. He said he should never, never part with it any more, and I thought he must be quite a fool not to know that it would fall to pieces in a day or two.

Peggotty began to be less with us of an evening, than she had always been. My mother deferred to her very much—more than usual, it occurred to me—and we were all three excellent friends, still we were different from what we used to be, and were not so comfortable among ourselves. Sometimes I fancied that Peggotty perhaps objected to my mother's wearing all the pretty dresses she had in her drawers, or to her going so often to that neighbor's of an evening; but I couldn't, to my satisfaction, make out how it was.

Gradually I became used to seeing the gentleman with the black whiskers. I liked him no better than at first, and had the same uneasy jealousy of him; but if I had any reason for it beyond a child's instinctive dislike, and a general idea that Peggotty and I could make much of my mother without any help, it certainly was not *the* reason that I might have found if I had been older. No such thing came into my mind or near it. I could observe, in little pieces, as it were; but as to making a net of a number of these pieces, and catching any body in it, that was, as yet, beyond me.

One autumn morning I was with my mother in the front garden, when Mr. Murdstone—I knew him by that name now—came by, on horseback. He reined up his horse to salute my mother, and said he was going to Lowestoft to see some friends who were there with a yacht, and merrily proposed to take me on the saddle before him if I would like the ride.

The air was so clear and pleasant, and the horse seemed to like the idea of the ride so much himself, as he stood snorting and pawing at the garden gate, that I had a great desire to go. So I was sent up stairs to Peggotty to be made spruce, and in the meantime Mr. Murdstone dismounted, and, with his horse's bridle drawn over his arm, walked slowly up and down on the outer side of the sweetbrier fence, while my mother walked slowly up and down on the inner to keep him company. I recollect Peggotty and I peeping out at them from my little window; I recollect how closely they appeared to be examining the sweetbrier between them, as they strolled along; and how, from being in a perfectly angelic temper, Peggotty turned cross in a moment, and brushed my hair the wrong way, excessively hard.

Mr. Murdstone and I were soon off, and trotting along on the green turf by the side of the road. He held me quite easily with one arm, and I don't think I was restless usually; but I could not make up my mind to sit in front of him without turning my head sometimes, and looking up in his face. He had that kind of shallow black eye—I want a better word to express an eye that has no depth in it to be looked into—which, when it is abstracted, seems, from some peculiarity of light, to be disfigured, for a moment at a time, by a cast. Several times when I glanced at him, I observed that appearance with a sort of awe, and wondered what he was thinking about so closely. His hair and whiskers were blacker and thicker, looked at so near, than even I had given them credit for being. A squareness about the lower part of his face, and the dotted indication of the strong black beard he shaved close every day, reminded me of the Wax-work that had travelled into our neighborhood some half a year before. This, his regular eyebrows, and the rich white, and black, and brown, of his complexion—confound his complexion, and his memory!—made me think him, in spite of my misgivings, a very handsome man. I have no doubt that my poor dear mother thought him so too.

We went to a hotel by the sea, where two gentlemen were smoking cigars in a room by themselves. Each of them was lying on at least four chairs, and had a large rough jacket on. In a corner was a heap of coats and boat cloaks, and a flag, all bundled up together.

They both rolled on to their feet in an untidy sort of manner when we came in, and said "Halloa Murdstone! We thought you were dead!"

"Not yet," said Mr. Murdstone.

"And who's this shaver?" said one of the gentlemen, taking hold of me.

"That's Davy," returned Mr. Murdstone.

"Davy who?" said the gentleman, "Jones?"

"Copperfield," said Mr. Murdstone.

"What! Bewitching Mrs. Copperfield's incumbrance?" cried the gentleman. "The pretty little widow?"

"Quinion," said Mr. Murdstone, "take care if you please. Somebody's sharp."

"Who is?" asked the gentleman, laughing.

I looked up, quickly; being curious to know.

"Only Brooks of Sheffield," said Mr. Murdstone.

I was quite relieved to find it was only Brooks of Sheffield; for, at first, I really thought it was I.

There seemed to be something very comical in the reputation of Mr. Brooks of Sheffield, for both the gentlemen laughed heartily when he was mentioned, and Mr. Murdstone was a good deal amused also. After some laughing, the gentleman whom he had called Quinion, said:

"And what is the opinion of Brooks of Sheffield, in reference to the projected business?"

"Why, I don't know that Brooks understands much about it at present," replied Mr. Murdstone; "but he is not generally favorable, I believe."

There was more laughter at this, and Mr. Quinion said, he would ring the bell for some sherry in which to drink to Brooks. This he did, and when the wine came, he made me have a little, with a biscuit, and before I drank it, stand up and say

"Confusion to Brooks of Sheffield!" The toast was received with great applause, and such hearty laughter that it made me laugh too; at which they laughed the more. In short, we quite enjoyed ourselves.

We walked about on the cliff after that, and sat on the grass, and looked at things through a telescope—I could make out nothing myself when it was put to my eye, but I pretended I could—and then we came back to the hotel to an early dinner. All the time we were out the two gentlemen smoked incessantly—which, I thought, if I might judge from the smell of their rough coats, they must have been doing ever since the coats had first come home from the tailors'. I must not forget, that we went on board the yacht, where they all three descended into the cabin, and were busy with some papers—I saw them quite hard at work, when I looked down through the open skylight. They left me, during this time, with a very nice man with a very large head of red hair and a very small shiny hat upon it, who had got a cross-barred shirt or waistcoat on, with "Skylark" in capital letters, across the chest. I thought it was his name, and that, as he lived on board ship and hadn't a street door to put his name on, he put it there instead; but when I called him Mr. Skylark, he said it meant the vessel.

I observed all day that Mr. Murdstone was graver and steadier than the two gentlemen. They were very gay and careless. They joked freely with one another, but seldom with him. It appeared to me that he was more clever and cold than they were, and that they regarded him with some thing of my own feeling. I remarked that once or twice when Mr. Quinion was talking, he looked at Mr. Murdstone sideways, as if to make sure of his not being displeased; and that once when Mr. Jegg (the other gentleman) was in high spirits, he trod upon his foot, and gave him a secret caution with his eyes to observe Mr. Murdstone, who was sitting stern and silent. Nor do I recollect that Mr. Murdstone laughed at all that day, except at the Sheffield joke—and that, by the by, was his own.

We went home, early in the evening. It was a very fine

evening, and my mother and he had another stroll by the sweet-brier while I was sent in to get my tea. When he was gone, my mother asked me all about the day I had had, and what they had said and done. I mentioned what they had said about her, and she laughed, and told me they were impudent fellows who talked nonsense—but I knew it pleased her. I knew it quite as well as I know it now. I took the opportunity of asking if she was at all acquainted with Mr. Brooks of Sheffield, but she answered No, only she supposed he must be a manufacturer in the knife and fork way.

Can I say of her face—altered as I have reason to remember it, perished as I know it is—that it is gone, when here it comes before me at this instant as distinct as any face that I may choose to look on in a crowded street? Can I say of her innocent and girlish beauty, that it faded, and was no more, when its breath falls on my cheek now, as it fell that night? Can I say she ever changed, when my remembrance brings her back to life, thus only, and truer to its loving youth than I have been, or man ever is, still holds fast what it cherished then?

I write of her just as she was when I had gone to bed after this talk, and she came to bid me good night. She kneeled down playfully by the side of the bed, and laying her chin upon her hands, and laughing, said:

"What was it they said, Davy? Tell me again. I can' believe it."

"'Bewitching——'" I began.

My mother put her hands upon her lips to stop me.

"It was never bewitching," she said, laughing. "It never could have been bewitching, Davy. Now I know it wasn't!"

"Yes it was. 'Bewitching Mrs. Copperfield,'" I repeated stoutly. "And 'pretty.'"

"No no, it was never pretty. Not pretty," interposed my mother, laying her fingers on my lips again.

"Yes it was. 'Pretty little widow.'"

"What foolish, impudent creatures!" cried my mother. laughing and covering her face. "What ridiculous men! An't they? Davy dear——"

"Well, Ma."

"Don't tell Peggotty; she might be angry with them. I am dreadfully angry with them myself; but I would rather Peggotty didn't know."

I promised, of course, and we kissed one another over and over again, and I soon fell fast asleep.

It seems to me, at this distance of time, as if it were the next day when Peggotty broached the striking and adventurous proposition I am about to mention; but it was probably about two months afterwards.

We were sitting as before, one evening (when my mother was out as before), in company with the stocking and the yard measure, and the bit of wax, and the box with Saint Paul's on the lid, and the crocodile book, when Peggotty after looking at me several times, and opening her mouth as if she were going to speak, without doing it—which I thought was merely gaping, or I should have been rather alarmed—said coaxingly:

"Master Davy, how should you like to go along with me and spend a fortnight at my brother's at Yarmouth? Wouldn't *that* be a treat?"

"Is your brother an agreeable man, Peggotty?" I inquired, provisionally.

"Oh what an agreeable man he is!" cried Peggotty, holding up her hands. "Then there's the sea; and the boats and ships; and the fishermen; and the beach; and Am to play with—"

Peggotty meant her nephew Ham, mentioned in my first chapter; but she spoke of him as a morsel of English Grammar—first person singular, present tense Indicative, verb neuter To be.

I was flushed by her summary of delights, and replied that it would indeed be a treat, but what would my mother say?

"Why then I'll as good as bet a guinea," said Peggotty, intent upon my face, "that she'll let us go. I'll ask her, if you like, as soon as ever she comes home. There now!"

"But what's she to do while we're away?" said I, putting

my small elbows on the table to argue the point. "She can' live by herself."

If Peggotty were looking for a hole, all of a sudden, in the heel of that stocking, it must have been a very little one indeed, and not worth darning.

"I say! Peggotty: She can't live by herself, you know."

"Oh bless you!" said Peggotty, looking at me again at last. "Don't you know? She's going to stay for a fortnight with Mrs. Grayper. Mrs. Grayper's going to have a lot of company."

Oh! If that was it, I was quite ready to go. I waited, in the utmost impatience until my mother came home from Mrs. Grayper's (for it was that identical neighbor) to ascertain if we could get leave to carry out this great idea. Without being nearly so much surprised as I had expected, my mother entered into it readily, and it was all arranged that night, and my board and lodging during the visit were to be paid for.

The day soon came for our going. It was such an early day that it came soon, even to me, who was in a fever of expectation, and half afraid that an earthquake or a fiery mountain, or some other great convulsion of nature might interpose to stop the expedition. We were to go in a carrier's cart, which departed in the morning after breakfast. I would have given any money to have been allowed to wrap myself up over night, and sleep in my hat and boots.

It touches me nearly now, although I tell it lightly, to recollect how eager I was to leave my happy home; to think how little I suspected what I did leave for ever.

I am glad to recollect that when the carrier's cart was at the gate, and my mother stood there kissing me, a grateful fondness for her and for the old place I had never turned my back upon before, made me cry. I am glad to know that my mother cried too, and that I felt her heart beat against mine.

I am glad to recollect that when the carrier began to move, my mother ran out at the gate, and called to him to stop, that she might kiss me once more. I am glad to dwell upon the earnestness and love with which she lifted up her face to mine, and did so.

As we left her standing in the road, Mr. Murdstone came up to where she was, and seemed to expostulate with her for being so moved. I was looking back round the awning of the cart, and wondered what business it was of his. Peggotty, who was also looking back on the other side, seemed any thing but satisfied; as the face she brought back into the cart denoted.

I sat looking at Peggotty for some time, in a reverie on this supposititious case. Whether, if she were employed to lose me like the boy in the fairy tale, I should be able to track my way home again by the buttons she would shed

CHAPTER III.

I HAVE A CHANGE.

The carrier's horse was the laziest horse in the world, I should hope, and shuffled along with his head down, as if he liked to keep the people waiting to whom the packages were directed. I fancied, indeed, that he sometimes chuckled audibly over this reflection, but the carrier said he was only troubled with a cough.

The carrier had a way of keeping his head down, like his horse, and of drooping sleepily forward as he drove, with one of his arms on each of his knees. I say "drove," but it struck me that the cart would have gone to Yarmouth quite as well without him, for the horse did all that—and as to conversation, he had no idea of it but whistling.

Peggotty had got a basket of refreshments on her knee, which would have lasted us out handsomely, if we had been going to London by the same conveyance. We ate a good deal, and slept a good deal. Peggotty always went to sleep with her chin upon the handle of the basket, her hold of which never relaxed; and I could not have believed unless I had heard her do it, that one defenceless woman could have snored so much.

We made so many deviations up and down lanes, and were such a long time delivering a bedstead at a public house, and calling at other places, that I was quite tired, and very glad, when we saw Yarmouth. It looked rather spongy and soppy, I thought, as I carried my eye over the great dull waste that lay across the river; and I could not help wondering, if the world were really as round as my geography-book said, how any part of it came to be so flat. But I reflected that Yarmouth might be situated at one of the poles; which would account for it.

As we drew a little nearer, and saw the whole adjacent prospect lying a straight low line under the sky, I hinted to

Peggotty that a mound or so might have improved it, and also that if the land had been a little more separated from the sea, and the town and the tide had not been quite so much mixed up, like toast and water, it would have been nicer. But Peggotty said, with greater emphasis than usual, that we must take things as we found them, and that, for her part, she was proud to call herself a Yarmouth Bloater.

When we got into the street (which was strange enough to me) and smelt the fish, and pitch, and oakum, and tar, and saw the sailors walking about, and the carts jingling up and down over the stones, I felt that I had done so busy a place an injustice, and said as much to Peggotty, who heard my expressions of delight with great complacency, and told me it was well known (I suppose to those who had the good fortune to be born Bloaters) that Yarmouth was, upon the whole, the finest place in the universe.

"Here's my Am!" screamed Peggotty, "growed out of knowledge!"

He was waiting for us, in fact, at the public-house, and asked me how I found myself, like an old acquaintance. I did not feel, at first, that I knew him as well as he knew me, because he had never come to our house since the night I was born, and naturally he had the advantage of me. But our intimacy was much advanced by his taking me on his back to carry me home. He was now, a huge, strong fellow of six feet high, broad in proportion, and round-shouldered; but with a simpering boy's face, and curly light hair, that gave him quite a sheepish look. He was dressed in a canvas jacket, and a pair of sucn very stiff trousers that they would have stood quite as well alone, without any legs in them. And you couldn't so properly have said he wore a hat, as that he was covered in a top, like an old building, with something pitchy.

Ham carrying me on his back and a small box of ours under his arm, and Peggotty carrying another small box of ours, we turned down lanes bestrewn with bits of chips and little hillocks of sand, and went past gas-works, rope-walks, boat-builders' yards, shipwrights' yards, ship-breakers' yards, calkers' yards, riggers' lofts, smiths' forges, and a great litter of such places, until we came out upon the dull waste I had already seen at a distance; when Ham said,

"Yon's our house, Master Davy!"

I looked in all directions, as far as I could stare over the wilderness, and away at the sea, and away at the river, but no house could *I* make out. There was a black barge, or some other kind of superannuated boat, not far off, high and dry on the ground, with an iron funnel sticking out of it for a chimney and smoking very cosily, but nothing else in the way of a habitation that was visible to *me*.

"That's not it?" said I, "that ship-looking thing?"

"That's it, Master Davy," returned Ham.

If it had been Aladdin's Palace, roc's egg and all, I suppose I could not have been more charmed with the romantic idea of living in it. There was a delightful door cut in the side, and it was roofed in, and there were little windows in it; but the wonderful charm of it was, that it was a real boat which had no doubt been upon the water hundreds of times, and which had never been intended to be lived in, on dry land. That was the captivation of it to me. If it had ever been meant to be lived in, I might have thought it small, or inconvenient, or lonely, but never having been designed for any such use, it became a perfect abode.

It was beautifully clean inside, and as tidy as possible. There was a table, and a Dutch clock, and a chest of drawers, and on the chest of drawers there was a tea-tray with a painting on it of a lady with a parasol, taking a walk with a military-looking child who was trundling a hoop. The tray was kept from tumbling down, by a Bible, and the tray, if it had tumbled down, would have smashed a quantity of cups and saucers and a teapot that were grouped around the book. On the walls there were some common colored pictures, framed and glazed, of Scripture subjects, such as I have never seen since in the hands of pedlers, without seeing the whole interior of Peggotty's brother's house again, at one view. Abraham in red going to sacrifice Isaac in blue, and Daniel in yellow cast into a den of green lions, were the most prominent of these. Over the little mantel-shelf, was a picture of the Sarah Jane Lugger, built at Sunderland, with a real little wooden stern stuck on to it; a work of art, combining composition with carpentery, which I considered to be one of the most enviable possessions that the world could afford. There were some hooks in the beams of the ceiling, the use of which I did not divine then; and some lockers and boxes and conveniences of that sort, which served for seats, and eked out the chairs.

All this, I saw in the first glance after I crossed the threshold—childlike, according to my theory—and then Peggotty opened a little door and showed me my bedroom. It was the completest and most desirable bedroom ever seen; in the stern of the vessel; with a little window where the rudder used to go through; a little looking-glass, just the right height for me, nailed against the wall, and framed with oyster shells; a little bed which there was just room enough to get into; and a nosegay of seaweed in a blue mug on the table. The walls were whitewashed as white as milk, and the patchwork counterpane made my eyes quite ache with its brightness. One thing I particularly noticed in this delightful house, was the smell of fish; which was so searching that when I took out my pocket-handkerchief to wipe my nose, I found it smelt exactly as if it had wrapped up a lobster. On my imparting this discovery in confidence to Peggotty, she informed me that her brother dealt in lobsters, crabs, and crawfish; and I afterwards found that a heap of these creatures, in a state of wonderful conglomeration with one another, and never leaving off pinching whatever they laid hold of, were usually to be found in a little wooden outhouse where the pots and kettles were kept.

We were welcomed by a very civil woman in a white apron, whom I had seen curtseying at the door when I was on Ham's back, about a quarter of a mile off. Likewise by a most beautiful little girl (or I thought her so) with a necklace of blue beads on, who wouldn't let me kiss her when I offered to, but ran away and hid herself. By and by, when we had dined in a sumptuous manner off boiled dabs, melted butter, and pctatoes, with a chop for me, a hairy man with a very good-natured face, came home. As he called Peggotty "Lass," and gave her a hearty smack on the cheek, I had no doubt, from the general propriety of her conduct, that he was her brother; and so he turned out: being presently introduced to me as Mr. Peggotty, the master of the house.

"Glad to see you, Sir," said Mr. Peggotty. "You'll find us rough, Sir, but you'll find us ready."

I thanked him, and replied that I was sure I should be happy in such a delightful place.

"How's your Ma, Sir," said Mr. Peggotty. "Did you leave her pretty jolly?"

I gave Mr. Peggotty to understand that she was as jolly as I could wish, and that she desired her compliments—which was a polite fiction on my part.

"I'm much obleeged to her, I'm sure," said Mr. Peggotty "Well, Sir, if you can make out here, fur a fortnut, 'long wi' her," nodding at his sister, "and Ham, and little Em'ly, we shall be proud of your company."

Having done the honors of his house in this hospitable manner, Mr. Peggotty went out to wash himself in a kettlefull of hot water, remarking that "cold would never get *his* muck off." He soon returned, greatly improved in appearance, but so rubicund, that I couldn't help thinking his face had this in common with the lobsters, crabs, and crawfish;—that it went into the hot water very black, and came out very red.

After tea, when the door was shut and all was made snug (the nights being cold and misty now) it seemed to me the most delicious retreat that the imagination of man could conceive. To hear the wind getting up out at sea, to know that the fog was creeping over the desolate flat outside, and to look at the fire, and think that there was no house near but this one, and this one a boat, was like enchantment. Little Em'ly had overcome her shyness, and was sitting by my side upon the lowest and least of the lockers, which was just large enough for us two, and just fitted into the chimney corner. Mrs. Peggotty with the white apron, was knitting on the opposite side of

I AM HOSPITABLY RECEIVED BY MR. PEGGOTTY.

the fire. Peggotty at her needle-work was as much at home with Saint Paul's and the bit of wax-candle as if they had never known any other roof. Ham, who had been giving me my first lesson in all-fours, was trying to recollect a scheme of telling fortunes with the dirty cards, and printing off fishy impressions of his thumb on all the cards he turned. Mr. Peggotty was smoking his pipe. I felt it was a time for conversation and confidence.

"Mr. Peggotty!" says I.

"Sir," says he.

"Did you give your son the name of Ham, because you lived in a sort of Ark?"

Mr. Peggotty seemed to think it a deep idea, but answered:

"No, Sir. I never giv him no name."

"Who gave him that name, then?" said I, putting question number two of the catechism to Mr. Peggotty.

"Why, Sir, his father giv it him," said Mr. Peggotty.

"I thought you were his father!"

"My brother Joe was *his* father," said Mr. Peggotty.

"Dead, Mr. Peggotty?" I hinted, after a respectful pause.

"Drowndead," said Mr. Peggotty.

I was very much surprised that Mr. Peggotty was not Ham's father, and began to wonder whether I was mistaken about his relationship to any body else there. I was so curious to know, that I made up my mind to have it out with Mr. Peggotty.

"Little Em'ly," I said, glancing at her. "She is your daughter, isn't she, Mr. Peggotty?"

"No, Sir. My brother-in-law, Tom, was *her* father."

I couldn't help it. "—Dead, Mr. Peggotty?" I hinted, after another respectful silence.

"Drowndead," said Mr. Peggotty.

I felt the difficulty of resuming the subject, but had not got to the bottom of it yet, and must attain the bottom somehow. So I said:

"Haven't you *any* children, Mr. Peggotty?"

"No, master," he answered, with a short laugh. "I'm a bacheldore."

4

"A bachelor!" I said, astonished. "Why, who's that, Mr. Peggotty?" pointing to the person in the apron who was knitting.

"That's Missis Gummidge," said Mr. Peggotty.

"Gummidge, Mr. Peggotty?"

But at this point, Peggotty—I mean my own peculiar Peggotty—made such impressive motions to me not to ask any further questions, that I could only sit and look at all the silent company, until it was time to go to bed. Then, in the privacy of my own little cabin, she informed me that Ham and Em'ly were an orphan nephew and niece, whom my host had at different times adopted in their childhood when they were left destitute; and that Mrs. Gummidge was the widow of his partner in a boat, who had died very poor. He was but a poor man himself, said Peggotty, but as good as gold and as true as steel—those were her similes. The only subject, she informed me, on which he ever showed a violent temper or swore an oath, was this generosity of his; and if it were ever referred to, by any one of them, he struck the table a heavy blow with his right hand (had split it on one such occasion), and swore a dreadful oath that he would be "gormed" if he didn't cut and run for good, if it was ever mentioned again. It appeared, in answer to my inquiries, that nobody had the least idea of the etymology of this terrible verb passive to be gormed; but that they all regarded it as constituting a most solemn imprecation.

I was very sensible of my entertainer's goodness, and listened to the women's going to bed in another little crib like mine at the opposite end of the boat, and to him and Ham hanging up two hammocks for themselves on the hooks I had noticed in the roof, in a very luxurious state of mind, enhanced by my being sleepy. As slumber gradually stole upon me, I heard the wind howling out at sea and coming on across the flat so fiercely, that I had a lazy apprehension of the great deep rising in the night. But I bethought myself that I was in a boat, after all, and that a man like Mr. Peggotty was not a bad person to have on board if any thing did happen.

Nothing happened, however, worse than morning. Almost as soon as it shone upon the oyster-shell frame of my mirror, I was out of bed, and out with little Em'ly, picking up stones upon the beach.

"You're quite a sailor, I suppose?" I said to Em'ly. I don't know that I supposed any thing of the kind, but I felt it an act of gallantry to say something; and a shining sail close to us, made such a pretty little image of itself, at the moment, in her bright eye, that it came into my head to say this.

"No," replied Em'ly, shaking her head. "I'm afraid of the sea."

"Afraid!" I said, with a becoming air of boldness, and looking very big at the mighty ocean. "*I* ain't."

"Ah! but it's cruel," said Em'ly. "I have seen it very cruel to some of our men. I have seen it tear a boat as big as our house, all to pieces."

"I hope it wasn't the boat that ——"

"That father was drownded in?" said Em'ly. "No. Not that one, I never see that boat."

"Nor him?" I asked her.

Little Em'ly shook her head. "Not to remember!"

Here was a coincidence! I immediately went into an explanation how I had never seen my own father, and how my mother and I had always lived by ourselves in the happiest state imaginable, and lived so then, and always meant to live so; and how my father's grave was in the churchyard near our house, and shaded by a tree, beneath the boughs of which I had walked and heard the birds sing many a pleasant morning. But there were some differences between Em'ly's orphanhood and mine, it appeared. She had lost her mother before her father; and where her father's grave was no one knew, except that it was somewhere in the depths of the sea.

"Besides," said Em'ly, as she looked about for shells and pebbles, "your father was a gentleman and your mother is a lady; and my father was a fisherman, and my mother was a fisherman's daughter, and my uncle Dan is a fisherman."

"Dan is Mr. Peggotty, is he?" said I.

"Uncle Dan—yonder," answered Em'ly, nodding at the boat-house.

"Yes. I mean him. He must be very good, I should think?"

"Good?" said Em'ly. "If I was ever to be a lady, I'd give him a sky-blue coat with diamond buttons, nankeen trousers, a red velvet waistcoat, a cocked hat, a large gold watch, a silver pipe, and a box of money."

I said I had no doubt that Mr. Peggotty well deserved these treasures. I must acknowledge that I felt it difficult to picture him quite at his ease in the raiment proposed for him by his grateful little niece, and that I was particularly doubtful of the policy of the cocked hat; but I kept these sentiments to myself.

Little Em'ly had stopped and looked up at the sky in her enumeration of these articles, as if they were a glorious vision. We went on again, picking up shells and pebbles.

"You would like to be a lady?" I said.

Emily looked at me, and laughed, and nodded "yes."

"I should like it very much. We would all be gentlefolks together, then. Me, and uncle, and Ham, and Mrs. Gummidge. We wouldn't mind then, when there come stormy weather. Not for our own sakes, I mean. We would for the poor fishermen's, to be sure, and we'd help 'em with money when they come to any hurt."

This seemed to me to be a very satisfactory, and therefore not at all improbable picture. I expressed my pleasure in the contemplation of it, and little Em'ly was emboldened to say, shyly,

"Don't you think you are afraid of the sea, now?"

It was quiet enough to reassure me, but I have no doubt if I had seen a moderately large wave come tumbling in, I should have taken to my heels, with an awful recollection of her drowned relations. However, I said "No," and I added, "You don't seem to be, either, though you say you are;"—for she was walking much too near the brink of a sort of old jetty or wooden causeway we had strolled upon, and I was afraid of her falling over.

"I'm not afraid in this way," said little Em'ly. "But I wake when it blows, and tremble to think of uncle Dan and Ham, and believe I hear 'em crying out for help. That's why

I should like so much to be a lady. But I'm not afraid in this way. Not a bit. Look here!"

She started from my side, and ran along a jagged timber which protruded from the place we stood upon, and overhung the deep water at some height, without the least defence. The incident is so impressed on my remembrance, that if I were a draughtsman I could draw its form here, I dare say, accurately as it was that day, and Little Em'ly springing forward to her destruction (as it appeared to me), with a look that I have never forgotten, directed out to sea.

The light, bold, fluttering little figure turned and came back safe to me, and I soon laughed at my fears, and at the cry I had uttered; fruitlessly in any case, for there was no one near. But there have been times since, in my manhood, many times there have been, when I have thought, Is it possible, among the possibilities of hidden things, that in the sudden rashness of the child and her wild look so far off, there was any merciful attraction of her into danger, any tempting her towards him permitted on the part of her dead father, that her life might have a chance of ending that day! There has been a time since when I have wondered whether, if the life before her could have been revealed to me at a glance, and so revealed as that a child could fully comprehend it, and if her preservation could have depended on a motion of my hand, I ought to have held it up to save her. There has been a time since—I do not say it lasted long, but it has been—when I have asked myself the question, would it have been better for little Em'ly to have had the waters close above her head that morning in my sight; and when I have answered Yes, it would have been.

This may be premature. I have set it down too soon, perhaps. But let it stand.

We strolled a long way, and loaded ourselves with things that we thought curious, and put some stranded star-fish carefully back into the water—I hardly know enough of the race at this moment to be quite certain whether they had reason to feel obliged to us for doing so, or the reverse—and then made our way home to Mr. Peggotty's dwelling. We stopped under the lee of the lobster-outhouse to exchange an innocent kiss, and went in to breakfast glowing with health and pleasure.

"Like two young Mavishes," Mr. Peggotty said. I knew this meant, in our local dialect, like two young thrushes, and received it as a compliment.

Of course I was in love with little Em'ly. I am sure I loved that baby quite as truly, quite as tenderly, with greater purity, and more disinterestedness, than can enter into the best love of a later time of life, high and ennobling as it is. I am sure my fancy raised up something round that blue-eyed mite of a child, which etherealized, and made a very angel of her. If, any sunny forenoon, she had spread a little pair of wings and flown away before my eyes, I don't think I should have regarded it as much more than I had had reason to expect.

We used to walk about that dim old flat at Yarmouth in a loving manner, hours and hours. The days sported by us, as if Time had not grown up himself yet, but were a child too, and always at play. I told Em'ly I adored her, and that unless she confessed she adored me I should be reduced to the necessity of killing myself with a sword. She said she did, and I have no doubt she did.

As to any sense of inequality, or youthfulness, or other difficulty in our way, little Em'ly and I had no such trouble, because we had no future. We made no more provision for growing older, than we did for growing younger. We were the admiration of Mrs. Gummidge and Peggotty, who used to whisper of an evening when we sat, lovingly, on our little locker side by side, "Lor! wasn't it beautiful!" Mr. Peggotty smiled at us from behind his pipe, and Ham grinned all the evening and did nothing else. They had something of the sort of pleasure in us, I suppose, that they might have had in a toy, or a pocket model of the Colosseum.

I soon found out that Mrs. Gummidge did not always make herself so agreeable as she might have been expected to do, under the circumstances of her residence with Mr. Peggotty. Mrs. Gummidge's was rather a fretful disposition, and she whimpered more sometimes than was comfortable for other par ties in so small an establishment. I was very sorry for her, but there were moments when it would have been more agreeable, I thought, if Mrs. Gummidge had had a convenient apartment of her own to retire to, and had stopped there until her spirits revived.

Mr. Peggotty went occasionally to a public house called The Willing Mind. I discovered this, by his being out on the second or third evening of our visit, and by Mrs. Gummidge's looking up at the Dutch clock, between eight and nine, and saying he was there, and that, what was more, she had known in the morning he would go there.

Mrs. Gummidge had been in a low state all day, and had burst into tears in the forenoon, when the fire smoked. "I am a lone lorn creetur'," were Mrs. Gummidge's words, when that unpleasant occurrence took place, "and every think goes contrairy with me."

"Oh, it 'll soon leave off," said Peggotty—I again mean our Peggotty—"and besides, you know, it's not more disagreeable to you than to us."

"I feel it more," said Mrs. Gummidge.

It was a very cold day, with cutting blasts of wind. Mrs. Gummidge's peculiar corner of the fireside seemed to me to be the warmest and snuggest in the place, as her chair was certainly the easiest, but it didn't suit her that day at all. She was constantly complaining of the cold, and of its occasioning a visitation in her back which she called "the creeps." At last she shed tears on that subject, and said again that she was "a lone lorn creetur' and every think went contrairy with her."

"It is certainly very cold," said Peggotty. "Every body must feel it."

"I feel it more than other people," said Mrs. Gummidge.

So at dinner, when Mrs. Gummidge was always helped immediately after me, to whom the preference was given as a visitor of distinction. The fish were small and bony, and the potatoes were a little burnt. We all acknowledged that we felt this something of a disappointment; but Mrs. Gummidge said she felt it more than we did, and shed tears again, and made that former declaration with great bitterness.

Accordingly, when Mr. Peggotty came home about nine o'clock, this unfortunate Mrs. Gummidge was knitting in her corner in a very wretched and miserable condition. Peggotty had been working cheerfully. Ham had been patching up a great pair of water-boots, and I, with little Em'ly by my side, had been reading to them. Mrs. Gummidge had never made any other remark than a forlorn sigh, and had never raised her eyes since tea.

"Well, Mates," said Mr. Peggotty, taking his seat, "and how are you?"

We all said something, or looked something, to welcome him, except Mrs. Gummidge, who shook her head over her knitting.

"What's amiss?" said Mr. Peggotty, with a clap of his hands. "Cheer up, old Mawther!" (Mr. Peggotty meant old girl.)

Mrs. Gummidge did not appear to be able to cheer up. She took out an old black silk handkerchief and wiped her eyes, but instead of putting it in her pocket, kept it out, and wiped them again, and still kept it out ready for use.

"What's amiss, dame?" said Mr. Peggotty.

"Nothing," returned Mrs. Gummidge. "You've come from The Willing Mind, Dan'l?"

"Why yes, I've took a short spell at The Willing Mind to-night," said Mr. Peggotty.

"I'm sorry I should drive you there," said Mrs. Gummidge.

"Drive! I don't want no driving," returned Mr. Peggotty, with an honest laugh. "I only go too ready."

"Very ready," said Mrs. Gummidge, shaking her head, and wiping her eyes. "Yes, yes, very ready. I am sorry it should be along of me that you're so ready."

"Along o' you? It an't along o' you!" said Mr. Peggotty. "Don't ye believe a bit on it."

"Yes, yes, it is," cried Mrs. Gummidge. "I know what I am. I know that I'm a lone lorn creetur, and not only that every think goes contrairy with me, but that I go contrairy with every body. Yes, yes. I feel more than other people do, and I show it more. It's my misfortun'."

I really couldn't help thinking as I sat taking in all this, that the misfortune extended to some other members of that family besides Mrs. Gummidge. But Mr. Peggotty made no such retort, only answering with another entreaty to Mrs. Gummidge to cheer up.

"I an't what I could wish myself to be," said Mrs. Gummidge. "I am far from it. I know what I am. My troubles has made me contrairy. I feel my troubles, and they make me contrairy. I wish I didn't feel 'em, but I do. I wish I could be hardened to 'em, but I an't. I make the house uncomfortable. I don't wonder at it. I've made your sister so all day, and Master Davy."

Here I was suddenly melted, and roared out, "No, you haven't, Mrs. Gummidge;" in great mental distress.

"It's far from right that I should do it," said Mrs. Gummidge. "It an't a fit return. I had better go into the House and die. I am a lone lorn creetur, and had much better not make myself contrairy here. If thinks must go contrairy with me, and I must go contrairy myself, let me go contrairy in my Parish. Dan'l, I'd better go into the House, and die and be a riddance!"

Mrs. Gummidge retired with these words, and betook herself to bed. When she was gone, Mr. Peggotty, who had not exhibited a trace of any feeling but the profoundest sympathy, looked round upon us, and nodding his head with a lively expression of that sentiment still animating his face, said in a whisper:

"She's been thinking of the old 'un."

I did not quite understand what Old One Mrs. Gummidge was supposed to have fixed her mind upon, until Peggotty, on seeing me to bed, explained that it was the late Mr. Gummidge, and that her brother always took that for a received truth on such occasions, and that it always had a moving effect upon him. Some time after he was in his hammock that night, I heard him myself repeat to Ham, "Poor thing! She's been thinking of the old 'un!" And whenever Mrs. Gummidge was overcome in a similar manner during the remainder of our stay (which happened some few times) he always said the same thing in extenuation of the circumstance, and always with the tenderest commiseration.

So the fortnight slipped away, varied by nothing but the variation of the tide, which altered Mr. Peggotty's times of going out and coming in, and altered Ham's engagements also. When the latter was unemployed, he sometimes walked with us to show us the boats and ships, and once or twice he took us for a row. I don't know why one slight set of impressions should be more particularly associated with a place than another, though I believe this obtains with most people, in reference especially, to the associations of their childhood. I never hear the name, or read the name, of Yarmouth, but I am reminded of a certain Sunday morning on the beach, the bells ringing for church, little Em'ly leaning on my shoulder, Ham lazily dropping stones into the water, and the sun, away at sea, just breaking through the heavy mist, and showing us the ships, like their own shadows.

At last the day came for going home. I bore up against the separation from Mr. Peggotty and Mrs. Gummidge, but my agony of mind at leaving little Em'ly was piercing. We went arm in arm to the public house where the carrier put up, and I promised, on the road, to write to her. (I redeemed that promise afterwards in characters larger than those in which apartments are usually announced in manuscript, as being to let.) We were greatly overcome at parting, and if ever, in my life, I have had a void made in my heart, I had one made that day.

Now, all the time I had been on my visit, I had been ungrateful to my home again, and had thought little or nothing about it. But I was no sooner turned towards it, than my reproachful young conscience seemed to point that way with a steady finger, and I felt, all the more for the sinking of my spirits, that it was my nest, and that my mother was my comforter and friend.

This gained upon me as we went along; so that the nearer we drew, and the more familiar the objects became that we passed, the more excited I was to get there, and to run into her arms. But Peggotty, instead of sharing in these transports, tried to check them (though very kindly) and looked confused and out of sorts.

Blunderstone Rookery would come, however, in spite of her when the carrier's horse pleased—and did. How well I recollect it, on a cold gray afternoon, with a dull sky, threatening rain!

The door opened, and I looked, half laughing and half crying in my pleasant agitation, for my mother. It was not she, but a strange servant.

"Why, Peggotty!" I said ruefully. "Isn't she come home?"

"Yes, yes, Master Davy," said Peggotty. "She's come home. Wait a bit, Master Davy, and I'll—I'll tell you something."

Between her agitation and her natural awkwardness in getting out of the cart, Peggotty was making a most extraordinary festoon of herself, but I felt too blank and strange to tell her so. When she had got down, she took me by the hand; led me, wondering, into the kitchen; and shut the door.

"Peggotty!" said I, quite frightened. "What's the matter?"

"Nothing's the matter, bless you, Master Davy, dear!" she answered, assuming an air of sprightliness.

"Something's the matter, I am sure. Where's mamma?"

"Where's mamma, Master Davy?" repeated Peggotty.

"Yes. Why hasn't she come out of the gate, and what have we come in here for? Oh, Peggotty!" My eyes were full, and I felt as if I were going to tumble down.

"Bless the precious boy!" cried Peggotty, taking hold of me. "What is it? Speak, my pet!"

"Not dead too! Oh, she's not dead, Peggotty?"

Peggotty cried out with an astonishing volume of voice, and then sat down, and began to pant, and said I had given her a turn.

I gave her a hug to take away the turn, or to give her another turn in the right direction, and then stood before her, looking at her in dumb inquiry.

"You see, dear, I should have told you before now," said Peggotty, "but I hadn't an opportunity. I ought to have made it, perhaps, but I couldn't axackly"—that was always the sub stitute for exactly, in Peggotty's militia of words—"bring my mind to it."

"Go on, Peggotty," says I, more frightened than ever.

"Master Davy," said Peggotty, untying her bonnet with a shaking hand, and speaking in a breathless sort of way, "what do you think? You have got a Pa!"

I trembled and turned white. Something—I don't know what, or how—connected with the grave in the churchyard, and the raising of the Dead, seemed to strike me like an unwholesome wind.

"A new one," said Peggotty.

"A new one?" I repeated.

"Peggotty gave a gasp, as if she were swallowing something that was very hard, and, putting out her hand, said:

"Come and see him."

"I don't want to see him."

—"And your mamma," said Peggotty.

I ceased to draw back, and we went straight to the best parlor, where she left me. On one side of the fire sat my mother; on the other, Mr. Murdstone. My mother dropped her work, and arose hurriedly, but timidly I thought.

"Now, Clara, my dear," said Mr. Murdstone. "Recollect! control yourself, always control yourself! Davy boy, how do you do?"

I gave him my hand. After a moment of suspense, I went and kissed my mother; she kissed me, patted me gently on the shoulder, and sat down again to her work. I could not look at her, I could not look at him, I knew quite well that he was looking at us both—and I turned to the window and looked out there, at some shrubs that were drooping their heads in the cold.

As soon as I could creep away, I crept up stairs. My old dear bedroom was changed, and I was to lie a long way off. I rambled down stairs to find any thing that was like itself; so altered it all seemed; and roamed into the yard. I very soon started back from there, for the empty dog-kennel was filled up with a great dog—deep-mouthed and black-haired like Him—and he was very angry at the sight of me, and sprung out to get at me

CHAPTER IV.

I FALL INTO DISGRACE.

If the room to which my bed was removed, were a sentient thing that could give evidence, I might appeal to it at this day—who sleeps there now I wonder!—to bear witness for me what a heavy heart I carried to it. I went up there, hearing the dog in the yard bark after me all the way while I climbed the stairs; and, looking as blank and strange upon the room as the room looked upon me, sat down with my small hands crossed, and thought.

I thought of the oddest things. Of the shape of the room, of the cracks in the ceiling, of the paper on the wall, of the flaws in the window-glass making ripples and dimples on the prospect, of the washing-stand being ricketty on its three legs, and having a discontented something about it, which reminded me of Mrs. Gummidge under the influence of the old one. I was crying all the time, but, except that I was conscious of being cold and dejected, I am sure I never thought why I cried. At last in my desolation I began to consider that I was dreadfully in love with little Em'ly, and had been torn away from her to come here where no one seemed to want me, or to care about me, half as much as she did. This made such a very miserable piece of business of it, that I rolled myself up in a corner of the counterpane, and cried myself to sleep.

I was awoke by somebody saying "Here he is!" and uncovering my hot head. My mother and Peggotty had come to look for me, and it was one of them who had done it.

"Davy," said my mother. "What's the matter?"

I thought it very strange that she should ask me, and answered "Nothing." I turned over on my face, I recollect, to hide my trembling lip, which answered her with greater truth.

"Davy," said my mother. "Davy, my child!"

I dare say no words she could have uttered, would have affected me so much, then, as her calling me her child. I hid my tears in the bedclothes, and pressed her from me with my hand, when she would have raised me up.

"This is your doing, Peggotty, you cruel thing!" said my mother. "I have no doubt at all about it. How can you reconcile it to your conscience, I wonder, to prejudice my own boy against me, or against anybody who is dear to me? What do you mean by it, Peggotty?"

Poor Peggotty lifted up her hands and eyes, and only answered, in a sort of paraphrase of the grace I usually repeated after dinner, "Lord forgive you, Mrs. Copperfield, and for what you have said this minute, may you never be truly sorry!"

"It's enough to distract me," cried my mother. "In my honeymoon, too, when my most inveterate enemy might relent, one would think, and not envy me a little peace of mind and happiness. Davy, you naughty boy! Peggotty, you savage creature! Oh, dear me!" cried my mother, turning from one of us to the other, in her pettish wilful manner, "what a troublesome world this is, when one has the most right to expect it to be as agreeable as possible!"

I felt the touch of a hand that I knew was neither her's nor Peggotty's, and slipped to my feet at the bedside. It was Mr. Murdstone's hand, and he kept it on my arm as he said:

"What's this? Clara, my love, have you forgotten?—Firmness, my dear?"

"I am very sorry, Edward," said my mother. "I meant to be very good, but I am so uncomfortable."

"Indeed!" he answered. "That's a bad hearing, so soon, Clara."

"I say it's very hard I should be made so now," returned my mother, pouting; "and it is—very hard—isn't it?"

He drew her to him, whispered in her ear, and kissed her. I knew as well, when I saw my mother's head lean down upon his shoulder, and her arm touch his neck—I knew as well that he could mould her pliant nature into any form he chose, as I know, now, that he did it.

"Go you below, my love," said Mr. Murdstone. "David and I will come down, together. My friend," turning a darkening face on Peggotty when he had watched my mother out and dismissed her with a nod and a smile: "do you know your mistress's name?"

"She has been my mistress a long time, sir," answered Peggotty. "I ought to it."

"That's true," he answered. "But I thought I heard you, as I came upstairs, address her by a name that is not hers. She has taken mine, you know. Will you remember that?"

Peggotty, with some uneasy glances at me, curtseyed herself out of the room without replying; seeing, I suppose, that she was expected to go, and had no excuse for remaining. When we two were left alone, he shut the door, and sitting on a chair, and holding me standing before him, looked steadily into my eyes. I felt my own attracted, no less steadily, to his. As I recall our being opposed thus, face to face, I seem again to hear my heart beat fast and high.

"David," he said, making his lips thin, by pressing them together, "if I have an obstinate horse or dog to deal with, what do you think I do?"

"I don't know."

"I beat him."

I had answered in a kind of breathless whisper, but I felt, in my silence, that my breath was shorter now.

"I make him wince, and smart. I say to myself, 'I'll conquer that fellow;' and if it were to cost him all the blood he had, I should do it. What is that upon your face?"

"Dirt," I said.

He knew it was the mark of tears as well as I. But if he had asked the question twenty times, each time with twenty blows, I believe my baby heart would have burst before I would have told him so.

"You have a good deal of intelligence for a little fellow," he said, with a grave smile that belonged to him, "and you understood me very well, I see. Wash that face, sir, and come down with me."

He pointed to the washing-stand, which I had made out to be like Mrs. Gummidge, and motioned me with his head to obey him directly. I had little doubt then, and I have less doubt now, that he would have knocked me down without the least compunction, if I had hesitated.

"Clara, my dear," he said, when I had done his bidding, and he walked me into the parlor, with his hand still on my arm, "you will not be made uncomfortable any more, I hope. We shall soon improve our youthful humours."

God help me, I might have been improved for my whole life, I might have been made another creature, perhaps, for life, by a kind word at that season. A word of encouragement and explanation, of pity for my childish ignorance, of welcome home, of reassurance to me that it *was* home, might have made me dutiful to him in my heart henceforth, instead of in my hypocritical outside, and might have made me respect instead of hate him. I thought my mother was sorry to see me standing in the room so scared and strange, and that, presently, when I stole to a chair, she followed me with her eyes more sorrowfully still—missing, perhaps, some freedom in my childish tread—but the word was not spoken, and the time for it was gone.

We dined alone, we three together. He seemed to be very fond of my mother—I am afraid I liked him none the better for that—and she was very fond of him. I gathered from what they said, that an elder sister of his was coming to stay with them, and that she was expected that evening. I am not certain whether I found out then, or afterwards, that, without being actively concerned in any business, he had some share in, or some annual charge upon the profits of, a wine-merchant's house in London, with which his family had been connected from his great-grandfather's time, and in which his sister had a similar interest; but I may mention it in this place, whether or no.

After dinner, when we were sitting by the fire, and I was meditating an escape to Peggotty without having the hardihood to slip away, lest it should offend the master of the house, a coach drove up to the garden gate, and he went out to receive the visitor. My mother followed him. I was timidly following her, when she turned round at the parlor door, in the dusk, and taking me in her embrace as she used to do, whispered me to love my new father and be obedient to him. She did this hurriedly and secretly, as if it were wrong, but tenderly; and, putting out her hand behind her, held mine in it until we came near to where he was standing in the garden, where she let mine go, and drew her's through his arm.

It was Miss Murdstone who was arrived, and a gloomy-looking lady she was; dark, like her brother, whom she greatly resembled in face and voice; and with very heavy eyebrows, nearly meeting over her large nose, as if, being disabled by the wrongs of her sex from wearing whiskers, she had carried them to that account. She brought with her two uncompromising hard black boxes, with her initials on the lids in hard brass nails. When she paid the coachman she took her money out of a hard steel purse, and she kept the purse in a very jail of a bag which hung upon her arm by a heavy chain, and shut up like a bite. I had never, at that time, seen such a metallic lady altogether as Miss Murdstone was.

She was brought into the parlor with many tokens of welcome, and there formally recognised my mother as a new and near relation. Then she looked at me, and said:

"Is that your boy, sister-in-law?"

My mother acknowledged me.

"Generally speaking," said Miss Murdstone, "I don't like boys. How d'ye do, boy?"

Under these encouraging circumstances, I replied that I was very well, and that I hoped she was the same; with such an indifferent grace, that Miss Murdstone disposed of me in two words:

"Wants manner."

Having uttered which, with great distinctness, she begged the favor of being shown to her room, which became to me from that time forth a place of awe and dread, wherein the two black boxes were never seen open or known to be left unlocked, and where (for I peeped in once or twice when she was out) numerous little steel fetters and rivets, with which Miss Murdstone embellished herself when she was dressed, generally hung upon the looking-glass in formidable array.

As well as I could make out, she had come for good, and had no intention of ever going again. She began to "help" my mother next morning, and was in and out of the store-closet all day, putting things to rights, and making havoc in the old arrangements. Almost the first remarkable thing I observed in Miss Murdstone was, her being constantly haunted by a suspicion that the servants had a man secreted somewhere on the premises. Under the influence of this delusion, she dived into the coal-cellar at the most untimely hours, and scarcely ever opened the door of a dark cupboard without clapping it to again, in the belief that she had got him.

Though there was nothing very airy about Miss Murdstone, she was a perfect Lark in point of getting up. She was up (and, as I believe to this hour, looking for that man) before anybody in the house was stirring. Peggotty gave it as her opinion that she even slept with one eye open; but I could not concur in this idea; for I tried it myself after hearing the suggestion thrown out, and found it couldn't be done.

On the very first morning after her arrival she was up and ringing her bell at cock-crow. When my mother came down to breakfast and was going to make the tea, Miss Murdstone gave her a kind of peck on the cheek, which was her nearest approach to a kiss, and said:

"Now, Clara, my dear, I am come here, you know, to relieve you of all the trouble I can. You're much too pretty and thoughtless"—my mother blushed but laughed, and seemed not to dislike this character—"to have any duties imposed upon you that can be undertaken by me. If you'll be so good as to give me your keys, my dear, I'll attend to all this sort of thing in future."

From that time, Miss Murdstone kept the keys in her own little jail all day, and under her pillow all night, and my mother had no more to do with them than I had.

My mother did not suffer her authority to pass from her without a shadow of protest. One night when Miss Murdstone had been developing certain household plans to her brother, of which he signified his approbation, my mother suddenly began to cry, and said she thought she might have been consulted.

"Clara!" said Mr. Murdstone sternly. "Clara! I wonder at you."

"Oh, it's very well to say you wonder, Edward!" cried my mother, "and it's very well for you to talk about firmness, but you wouldn't like it yourself."

Firmness, I may observe, was the grand quality on which both Mr. and Miss Murdstone took their stand. However I might have expressed my comprehension of it at that time, if I had been called upon, I nevertheless did clearly comprehend in my own way, that it was another name for tyranny, and for a certain gloomy, arrogant, devil's humour, that was in them both. The creed, as I should state it now, was this. Mr. Murdstone was firm; nobody in his world was to be so firm as Mr. Murdstone; nobody else in his world was to be firm at all, for everybody was to be bent to his firmness. Miss Murdstone was an exception. She might be firm, but only by relationship, and in an inferior and tributary degree. My mother was another exception. She might be firm, and must be; but only in bearing their firmness, and firmly believing there was no other firmness upon earth.

"It's very hard," said my mother, "that in my own house—"

"*My* own house?" repeated Mr. Murdstone. "Clara?"

"Our own house I mean," faltered my mother, evidently frightened—"I hope you must know what I mean, Edward—it's very hard that in our own house I may not have a word to say about domestic matters. I am sure I managed very well before we were married. There's evidence," said my mother sobbing; "ask Peggotty if I didn't do very well when I wasn't interfered with!"

"Edward," said Miss Murdstone, "let there be an end of this. I go to-morrow."

"Jane Murdstone," said her brother, "be silent! How dare you to insinuate that you don't know my character better than your words imply?"

"I am sure," my poor mother went on, at a grievous disadvantage, and with many tears, "I don't want anybody to go. I should be very miserable and unhappy if anybody was to go. I don't ask much. I am not unreasonable. I only want to be consulted sometimes. I am very much obliged to anybody who assists me, and I only want to be consulted as a mere form, sometimes. I thought you were pleased, once, with my being a little inexperienced and girlish, Edward—I am sure you said so—but you seem to hate me for it now, you are so severe."

"Edward," said Miss Murdstone, again, "let there be an end of this. I go to-morrow."

"Jane Murdstone," thundered Mr. Murdstone. "Will you be silent? How dare you?"

Miss Murdstone made a jail-delivery of her pocket-handkerchief, and held it before her eyes.

"Clara," he continued, looking at my mother, "you surprise me.

You astound me! Yes, I had a satisfaction in the thought of marrying an inexperienced and artless person, and forming her character, and infusing into it some amount of that firmness and decision of which it stood in need. But when Jane Murdstone is kind enough to come to my assistance in this endeavour, and to assume, for my sake, a condition something like a housekeeper's, and when she meets with a base return—"

"Oh pray, pray, Edward," cried my mother, "don't accuse me of being ungrateful. I am sure I am not ungrateful. No one ever said I was, before. I have many faults, but not that. Oh don't, my dear!"

"When Jane Murdstone meets, I say," he went on, after waiting until my mother was silent, "with a base return, that feeling of mine is chilled and altered."

"Don't, my love, say that!" implored my mother, very piteously. "Oh don't, Edward! I can't bear to hear it. Whatever I am, I am affectionate. I know I am affectionate. I wouldn't say it, if I wasn't certain that I am. Ask Peggotty. I am sure she'll tell you I'm affectionate."

"There is no extent of mere weakness, Clara," said Mr. Murdstone in reply, "that can have the least weight with me. You lose breath."

"Pray let us be friends," said my mother. "I couldn't live under coldness or unkindness. I am so sorry. I have a great many defects, I know, and it's very good of you, Edward, with your strength of mind, to endeavour to correct them for me. Jane, I don't object to anything. I should be quite broken-hearted if you thought of leaving—" My mother was too much overcome to go on.

"Jane Murdstone," said Mr. Murdstone to his sister, "any harsh words between us are, I hope, uncommon. It is not my fault that so unusual an occurrence has taken place to-night. I was betrayed into it by another. Nor is it your fault. You were betrayed into it by another. But let us both try to forget it. And as this," he added, after these magnanimous words, "is not a fit scene for the boy—David, go to bed!"

I could hardly find the door, through the tears that stood in my eyes. I was so sorry for my mother's distress; but I groped my way out, and groped my way up to my room in the dark, without even having the heart to say good night to Peggotty, or to get a candle from her. When her coming up to look for me, an hour or so afterwards, awoke me, she said that my mother had gone to bed poorly, and that Mr. and Miss Murdstone were sitting alone.

Going down next morning rather earlier than usual, I paused outside the parlor door, on hearing my mother's voice. She was very earnestly and humbly entreating Miss Murdstone's pardon, which that lady granted, and a perfect reconciliation took place. I never knew my mother afterwards to give an opinion on any matter, without first appealing to Miss Murdstone, or without having first ascertained, by some sure means, what Miss Murdstone's opinion was; and I never saw Miss Murdstone, when out of temper (she was infirm that way), move her hand towards her bag as if she were going to take out the keys and offer to resign them to my mother, without seeing that my mother was in a terrible fright.

The gloomy taint that was in the Murdstone blood, darkened the Murdstone religion, which was austere and wrathful. I have thought, since, that its assuming that character was a necessary consequence of Mr. Murdstone's firmness, which wouldn't allow him to let any body off from the utmost weight of the severest penalties he could find any excuse for. Be this as it may, I well remember the tremendous visages with which we used to go to church, and the changed air of the place. Again, the dreaded Sunday comes round, and I file into the old pew first, like a guarded captive brought to a condemned service. Again, Miss Murdstone, in a black velvet gown, that looks as if it had been made out of a pall, followed close upon me; then my mother; then her husband. There is no Peggotty now, as in the old time. Again, I listen to Miss Murdstone mumbling the responses, and emphasising all the dread words with a cruel relish. Again, I see her dark eyes roll round the church when she says "miserable sinners," as if she were calling all the congregation names. Again, I catch rare glimpses of my mother, moving her lips timidly between the two, with one of them muttering at each ear like low thunder. Again, I wonder with a sudden fear whether it is likely that our good old clergyman can be wrong, and Mr. and Miss Murdstone right, and that all the angels in Heaven can be destroying angels. Again, if I move a finger or relax a muscle of my face, Miss Murdstone pokes me with her prayer-book, and makes my side ache.

Yes, and again, as we walk home, I note some neighbours looking at my mother, and at me, and whispering. Again, as the three go on arm-in-arm, and I linger behind alone, I follow some of those looks, and wonder if my mother's step be really not so light as I have seen it, and if the gaiety of her beauty be really almost worried away. Again, I wonder whether any of the neighbours call to mind, as I do, how we used to walk home together, she and I; and I wonder stupidly about that all the dreary dismal day.

There had been some talk on occasions of my going to a boarding-school. Mr. and Miss Murdstone had originated it, and my mother had of course agreed with them. Nothing, however, was concluded on the subject yet. In the meantime, I learnt lessons at home.

Shall I ever forget those lessons! They were presided over nominally by my mother, but really by Mr. Murdstone and his sister, who were always present, and found them a favourable occasion for giving my mother lessons in that miscalled firmness, which was the bane of both our lives. I believe I was kept at home for that purpose. I had been apt enough to learn, and willing enough, when my mother and I had lived alone together. I can faintly remember learning the alphabet at her knee. To this day, when I look upon the fat black letters in the primer, the puzzling novelty of their shapes, and the easy good-nature of O and Q and S, seem to present themselves again before me as they used to do. But they recall no feeling of disgust or reluctance. On the contrary, I seem to have walked along a path of flowers as far as the crocodile-book, and to have been cheered by the gentleness of my mother's voice and manner all the way. But these solemn lessons which succeeded those, I remember as the death-blow at my peace, and a grievous daily drudgery and misery. They were very long, very numerous, very hard—perfectly unintelligible, some of them, to me—and I was generally as much bewildered by them as I believe my poor mother was herself.

Let me remember how it used to be, and bring one morning back again.

I come into the second-best parlor after breakfast with my books, and an exercise book, and a slate. My mother is ready for me at her writing-desk, but not half so ready as Mr. Murdstone in his easy chair by the window (though he pretends to be reading a book), or as Miss Murdstone, sitting near my mother stringing steel beads. The very sight of these two has such an influence over me, that I begin to feel the words I have been at infinite pains to get into my head, all sliding away, and going I don't know where. I wonder where they *do* go, by-the-bye?

I hand the first book to my mother. Perhaps it is a grammar, perhaps a history, or geography. I take a last drowning look at the page as I give it into her hand, and start off aloud at a racing pace while I have got it fresh. I trip over a word. Mr. Murdstone looks up. I trip over another word. Miss Murdstone looks up. I redden, tumble over half-a-dozen words, and stop. I think my mother would show me the book if she dared, but she does not dare, and she says softly :

"Oh Davy, Davy!"

"Now, Clara," says Mr. Murdstone, "be firm with the boy. Don't say 'Oh Davy, Davy!' That's childish. He knows his lesson, or he does not know it."

"He does *not* know it," Miss Murdstone interposes awfully.

"I am really afraid he does not," says my mother.

"Then you see, Clara," returns Miss Murdstone, "you should just give him the book back, and make him know it."

"Yes, certainly," says my mother; "that's what I intend to do, my dear Jane. Now Davy, try once more, and don't be stupid."

I obey the first clause of the injunction by trying once more, but am not so successful with the second, for I am very stupid. I tumble down before I get to the old place, at a point where I was all right before, and stop to think. But I can't think about the lesson. I think of the number of yards of net in Miss Murdstone's cap, or of the price of Mr. Murdstone's dressing-gown, or any such ridiculous problem that I have no business with, and don't want to have anything at all to do with. Mr. Murdstone makes a movement of impatience which I have been expecting for a long time. Miss Murdstone does the same. My mother glances submissively at them, shuts the book, and lays it by as an arrear to be worked out when my other tasks are done.

There is a pile of these arrears very soon, and it swells like a rolling snowball. The bigger it gets, the more stupid *I* get. The case is so hopeless, and I feel that I am wallowing in such a bog of nonsense, that I give up all idea of getting out, and abandon myself to my fate. The despairing way in which my mother and I look at each other, as I blunder on, is truly melancholy. But the greatest effect in these miserable lessons is when my mother (thinking nobody is observing her) tries to give me the cue by the motion of her lips. At that instant, Miss Murdstone, who has been lying in wait for nothing else all along, says in a deep warning voice:

"Clara!"

My mother starts, colours, and smiles faintly. Mr. Murdstone comes out of his chair, takes the book, throws it at me or boxes my ears with it, and turns me out of the room by the shoulders.

Even when the lessons are done, the worst is yet to happen, in the shape of an appalling sum. This is invented for me, and delivered to me orally by Mr. Murdstone, and begins, "If I go into a cheesemonger's shop, and buy five thousand double-Gloucester cheeses at fourpence-halfpenny each, present payment"—at which I see Miss Murdstone secretly overjoyed. I pore over these cheeses without any result or enlightenment until dinner-time; when, having made a Mulatto of myself by getting the dirt of the slate into the pores of my skin, I have a slice of bread to help me out with the cheeses, and am considered in disgrace for the rest of the evening.

It seems to me, at this distance of time, as if my unfortunate studies generally took this course. I could have done very well if I had been without the Murdstones; but the influence of the Murdstones upon me was like the fascination of two snakes on a wretched young bird. Even when I did get through the morning with tolerable credit, there was not much gained but dinner; for Miss Murdstone never could endure to see me untasked, and if I rashly made any show of being unemployed, called her brother's attention to me by saying, "Clara, my dear, there 's nothing like work—give your boy an exercise;" which caused me to be clapped down to some new labor there and then. As to any recreation with other children of my age, I had very little of that; for the gloomy theology of the Murdstones made all children out to be a swarm of little vipers (though there *was* a child once set in the midst of the Disciples), and held that they contaminated one another.

The natural result of this treatment, continued, I suppose, for some six months, was to make me sullen, dull, and dogged. I was not made the less so, by my sense of being daily more and more shut out and alienated from my mother. I believe I should have been almost stupified but for one circumstance.

It was this. My father had left a small collection of books in a little room up stairs, to which I had access (for it adjoined my own) and which nobody else in our house ever troubled. From that blessed little room, Roderick Random, Peregrine Pickle, Humphrey Clinker, Tom Jones, The Vicar of Wakefield, Don Quixote, Gil Blas, and Robinson Crusoe, came out, a glorious host, to keep me company. They kept alive my fancy, and my hope of something beyond that place and time,—they, and the Arabian Nights, and the Tales of the Genii,—and did me no harm; for whatever harm was in some of them was not there for me; *I* knew nothing of it. It is astonishing to me now, how I found time, in the midst of my porings and blunderings over heavier themes, to read those books as I did. It is curious to me how I could ever have consoled myself under my small troubles (which were great troubles to me), by impersonating my favorite characters in them—as I did—and by putting Mr. and Miss Murdstone into all the bad ones—which I did too. I have been Tom Jones (a child's Tom Jones, a harmless creature) for a week together. I have sustained my own idea of Roderick Random for a month at a stretch, I verily believe. I had a greedy relish for a few volumes of Voyages and Travels—I forget what, now—that were on those shelves; and for days and days I can remember to have gone about my region of our house, armed with the centre-piece out of an old set of boot-trees—the perfect realisation of Captain Somebody, of the Royal British Navy, in danger of being beset by savages, and resolved to sell his life at a great price. The Captain never lost dignity, from having his ears boxed with the Latin Grammar. I did; but the Captain was a Captain and a hero, in despite of all the grammars of all the languages in the world, dead or alive.

This was my only and my constant comfort. When I think of it, the picture always rises in my mind, of a summer evening, the boys at play in the churchyard, and I sitting on my bed, reading as if for life. Every barn in the neighbourhood, every stone in the church, and every foot of the churchyard, had some association of its own, in my mind, connected with these books, and stood for some locality made famous in them. I have seen Tom Pipes go climbing up the church-steeple; I have watched Strap, with the knapsack on his back, stopping to rest himself upon the wicket-gate; and I *know* that Commodore Trunnion held that club with Mr. Pickle, in the parlor of our little village alehouse.

The reader now understands as well as I do, what I was when I came to that point of my youthful history to which I am now coming again.

One morning when I went into the parlor with my books, I found my mother looking anxious, Miss Murdstone looking firm, and Mr. Murdstone binding something round the bottom of a cane—a lithe and limber cane, which he left off binding when I came in, and poised and switched in the air.

"I tell you, Clara," said Mr. Murdstone, "I have been often flogged myself."

"To be sure; of course," said Miss Murdstone.

"Certainly, my dear Jane," faltered my mother, meekly. "But—but do you think it did Edward good?"

"Do you think it did Edward harm, Clara?" asked Mr. Murdstone, gravely.

"That 's the point!" said his sister.

To this my mother returned "Certainly, my dear Jane," and said no more.

I felt apprehensive that I was personally interested in this dialogue, and sought Mr. Murdstone's eye as it lighted on mine.

"Now, David," he said—and I saw that cast again, as he said it—"you must be far more careful to-day than usual." He gave the cane another poise, and another switch; and having finished his preparation of it, laid it down beside him, with an expressive look, and took up his book.

This was a good freshener to my presence of mind, as a beginning. I felt the words of my lesson slipping off, not one by one, or line by line, but by the entire page. I tried to lay hold of them; but they seemed, if I may so express it, to have put skates on, and to skim away from me with a smoothness there was no checking.

We began badly, and went on worse. I had come in, with an

idea of distinguishing myself rather, conceiving that I was very well prepared; but it turned out to be quite a mistake. Book after book was added to the heap of failures, Miss Murdstone being firmly watchful of us all the time. And when we came at last to the five thousand cheeses (canes he made it that day, I remember), my mother burst out crying.

"Clara!" said Miss Murdstone, in her warning voice.

"I am not quite well, my dear Jane, I think," said my mother.

I saw him wink, solemnly, at his sister, as he rose and said, taking up the cane,

"Why, Jane, we can hardly expect Clara to bear, with perfect firmness, the worry and torment that David has occasioned her to-day. That would be stoical. Clara is greatly strengthened and improved, but we can hardly expect so much from her. David, you and I will go up stairs, boy."

As he took me out at the door, my mother ran towards us. Miss Murdstone said, "Clara! are you a perfect fool?" and interfered. I saw my mother stop her ears then, and I heard her crying.

He walked me up to my room slowly and gravely—I am certain he had a delight in that formal parade of executing justice—and when we got there, suddenly twisted my head under his arm.

"Mr. Murdstone! Sir!" I cried to him. "Don't! Pray don't beat me! I have tried to learn, sir, but I can't learn while you and Miss Murdstone are by. I can't indeed!"

"Can't you, indeed, David?" he said. "We'll try that."

He had my head as in a vice, but I twined round him somehow, and stopped him for a moment, entreating him not to beat me. It was only for a moment that I stopped him, for he cut me heavily an instant afterwards, and in the same instant I caught the hand with which he held me in my mouth, between my teeth, and bit it through. It sets my teeth on edge to think of it.

He beat me then, as if he would have beaten me to death. Above all the noise we made, I heard them running up the stairs, and crying out—I heard my mother crying out—and Peggotty. Then he was gone; and the door was locked outside; and I was lying, fevered and hot, and torn, and sore, and raging in my puny way, upon the floor.

How well I recollect, when I became quiet, what an unnatural stillness seemed to reign through the whole house! How well I remember, when my smart and passion began to cool, how wicked I began to feel!

I sat listening for a long while, but there was not a sound. I crawled up from the floor, and saw my face in the glass, so swollen, red, and ugly, that it almost frightened me. My stripes were sore and stiff, and made me cry afresh, when I moved; but they were nothing to the guilt I felt. It lay heavier on my breast than if I had been a most atrocious criminal, I dare say.

It had begun to grow dark, and I had shut the window (I had been lying, for the most part, with my head upon the sill, by turns crying, dozing, and looking listlessly out), when the key was turned, and Miss Murdstone came in with some bread and meat, and milk. These she put down upon the table without a word, glaring at me the while with exemplary firmness, and then retired, locking the door after her.

Long after it was dark I sat there, wondering whether anybody else would come. When this appeared improbable for that night, I undressed, and went to bed; and, there, I began to wonder fearfully what would be done to me. Whether it was a criminal act that I had committed? Whether I should be taken into custody, and sent to prison? Whether I was at all in danger of being hanged?

I never shall forget the waking, next morning; the being cheerful and fresh for the first moment, and then the being weighed down by the stale and dismal oppression of remembrance. Miss Murdstone re-appeared before I was out of bed; told me, in so many words, that I was free to walk in the garden for half an hour and no longer; and retired, leaving the door open, that I might avail myself of that permission.

I did so, and did so every morning of my imprisonment, which lasted five days. If I could have seen my mother alone, I should have gone down on my knees to her and besought her forgiveness; but I saw no one, Miss Murdstone excepted, during the whole time —except at evening prayers in the parlor; to which I was escorted by Miss Murdstone after every body else was placed; where I was stationed, a young outlaw, all alone by myself near the door; and whence I was solemnly conducted by my jailor, before any one arose from the devotional posture. I only observed that my mother was as far off from me as she could be, and kept her face another way so that I never saw it; and that Mr. Murdstone's hand was bound up in a large linen wrapper.

The length of those five days I can convey no idea of to any one. They occupy the place of years in my remembrance. The way in which I listened to all the incidents of the house that made themselves audible to me; the ringing of bells, the opening and shutting of doors, the murmuring of voices, the footsteps on the stairs; to any laughing, whistling, or singing, outside, which seemed more dismal than anything else to me in my solitude and disgrace—the uncertain pace of the hours, especially at night, when I would wake thinking it was morning, and find that the family were not yet gone to bed, and that all the length of night had yet to come—the depressed dreams and nightmares I had—the return of day, noon, afternoon, evening, when the boys played in the churchyard, and I watched them from a distance within the room, being ashamed to show myself at the window lest they should know I was a prisoner—the strange sensation of never hearing myself speak—the fleeting intervals of something like cheerfulness, which came with eating and drinking, and went away with it—the setting in of rain one evening, with a fresh smell, and its coming down faster and faster between me and the church, until it and gathering night seemed to quench me in gloom and fear, and remorse—all this appears to have gone round and round for years instead of days, it is so vividly and strongly stamped on my remembrance.

On the last night of my restraint, I was awakened by hearing my own name spoken in a whisper. I started up in bed, and putting out my arms in the dark, said:

"Is that you, Peggotty?"

There was no immediate answer, but presently I heard my name again, in a tone so very mysterious and awful, that I think I should have gone into a fit, if it had not occurred to me that it must have come through the keyhole.

I groped my way to the door, and putting my own lips to the keyhole, whispered:

"Is that you, Peggotty, dear?"

"Yes, my own precious Davy," she replied. "Be as soft as a mouse, or the Cat 'll hear us."

I understood this to mean Miss Murdstone, and was sensible of the urgency of the case; her room being close by.

"How 's Mama, dear Peggotty? Is she very angry with me?"

I could hear Peggotty crying softly on her side of the keyhole, as I was doing on mine, before she answered. "No. Not very."

"What is going to be done with me, Peggotty dear? Do *you* know?"

"School. Near London," was Peggotty's answer. I was obliged to get her to repeat it, for she spoke it the first time quite down my throat, in consequence of my having forgotten to take my mouth away from the keyhole and put my ear there; and though her words tickled me a good deal, I didn't hear them.

"When, Peggotty?"

"To-morrow."

"Is that the reason why Miss Murdstone took the clothes out of my drawers?" which she had done, though I have forgotten to mention it.

"Yes," said Peggotty. "Box."

"Shan't I see Mama?"

"Yes," said Peggotty. "Morning."

Then Peggotty fitted her mouth close to the keyhole, and delivered these words through it with as much feeling and earnestness as a keyhole has ever been the medium of communicating, I will venture to assert: shooting in each broken little sentence in a convulsive little burst of its own.

"Davy, dear. If I ain't ben azackly as intimate with you. Lately, as I used to be. It ain't becase I don't love you. Just as well and more, my pretty poppet. It's becase I thought it better for you. And for some one else besides. Davy, my darling, are you listening? Can you hear?"

"Ye—ye—ye—yes, Peggotty!" I sobbed.

"My own!" said Peggotty, with infinite compassion. "What I want to say, is. That you must never forget me. For I'll never forget you. And I'll take as much care of your Mama, Davy. As ever I took of you. And I won't leave her. The day may come when she'll be glad to lay her poor head. On her stupid, cross old Peggotty's arm again. And I'll write to you, my dear. Though I ain't no scholar. And I'll—I'll—" Peggotty fell to kissing the keyhole, as she couldn't kiss me.

"Thank you, dear Peggotty!" said I. "Oh, thank you! Thank you! Will you promise me one thing, Peggotty? Will you write and tell Mr. Peggotty and little Em'ly and Mrs. Gummidge and Ham, that I am not so bad as they might suppose, and that I sent 'em all my love—especially to little Em'ly? Will you, if you please, Peggotty?"

The kind soul promised, and we both of us kissed the keyhole with the greatest affection—I patted it with my hand, I recollect, as if it had been her honest face—and parted. From that night there grew up in my breast, a feeling for Peggotty, which I cannot very well define. She did not replace my mother; no one could do that; but she came into a vacancy in my heart, which closed upon her, and I felt towards her something I have never felt for any other human being. It was a sort of comical affection too; and yet if she had died, I cannot think what I should have done, or how I should have acted out the tragedy it would have been to me.

In the morning Miss Murdstone appeared as usual, and told me I was going to school; which was not altogether such news to me as she supposed. She also informed me that when I was dressed, I was to come down stairs into the parlor, and have my breakfast. There, I found my mother, very pale and with red eyes: into whose arms I ran, and begged her pardon from my suffering soul.

"Oh Davy!" she said. "That you could hurt any one I love! Try to be better, pray to be better! I forgive you; but I am so grieved, Davy, that you should have such bad passions in your heart."

They had persuaded her that I was a wicked fellow, and she was more sorry for that, than for my going away. I felt it sorely. I tried to eat my parting breakfast, but my tears dropped upon my bread and butter, and trickled into my tea. I saw my mother look at me sometimes, and then glance at the watchful Miss Murdstone, and then look down, or look away.

"Master Copperfield's box there!" said Miss Murdstone, when wheels were heard at the gate.

I looked for Peggotty, but it was not she; neither she nor Mr

Murdstone appeared. My former acquaintance, the carrier, was at the door; the box was taken out to his cart, and lifted in.

"Clara!" said Miss Murdstone, in her warning note.

"Ready, my dear Jane," returned my mother. "Good bye, Davy. You are going for your own good. Good bye, my child. You will come home in the holidays, and be a better boy."

"Clara!" Miss Murdstone repeated.

"Certainly, my dear Jane," replied my mother, who was holding me. "I forgive you, my dear boy. God bless you!"

"Clara!" Miss Murdstone repeated.

Miss Murdstone was good enough to take me out to the cart, and to say on the way that she hoped I would repent before I came to a bad end; and then I got into the cart, and the lazy horse walked off with it.

CHAPTER V.

I AM SENT AWAY FROM HOME.

We might have gone about half a mile, and my pocket-handkerchief was quite wet through, when the carrier stopped short.

Looking out to ascertain what for, I saw, to my amazement, Peggotty burst from a hedge and climb into the cart. She took me in both her arms, and squeezed me to her stays until the pressure on my nose was extremely painful, though I never thought of that till afterwards when I found it very tender. Not a single word did Peggotty speak. Releasing one of her arms, she put it down in her pocket to the elbow, and brought out some paper-bags of cakes which she crammed into my pockets, and a purse which she put into my hand, but not one word did she say. After another and a final squeeze with both arms, she got down from the cart and ran away; and, my belief is, and has always been, without a solitary button on her gown. I picked up one, of several that were rolling about, and treasured it as a keepsake for a long time.

The carrier looked at me, as if to enquire if she were coming back. I shook my head, and said I thought not. "Then come up," said the carrier to the lazy horse; who came up accordingly.

Having by this time cried as much as I possibly could, I began to think it was of no use crying any more, especially as neither Roderick Random, nor that Captain in the Royal British Navy, had ever cried, that I could remember, in trying situations. The carrier, seeing me in this resolution, proposed that my pocket-handkerchief should be spread upon the horse's back to dry. I thanked him, and assented; and particularly small it looked, under those circumstances.

I had now leisure to examine the purse. It was a stiff leather purse, with a snap, and had three bright shillings in it, which Peggotty had evidently polished up with whitening, for my greater delight. But its most precious contents were two half-crowns folded together in a bit of paper, on which was written, in my mother's hand, "For Davy. With my love." I was so overcome by this, that I asked the carrier to be so good as reach me my pocket-handkerchief again; but he said he thought I had better do without it; and I thought I really had; so I wiped my eyes on my sleeve and stopped myself.

For good, too; though in consequence of my previous emotions, I was still occasionally seized with a stormy sob. After we had jogged on for some little time, I asked the carrier if he was going all the way.

"All the way where?" enquired the carrier.

"There," I said.

"Where's there?" enquired the carrier.

"Near London?" I said.

"Why that horse," said the carrier, jerking the rein to point him out, "would be deader than pork afore he got over half the ground."

"Are you only going to Yarmouth then?" I asked.

"That's about it," said the carrier. "And there I shall take you to the stage-cutch, and the stage-cutch that'll take you to—wherever it is."

As this was a great deal for the carrier (whose name was Mr. Barkis) to say—he being, as I observed in a former chapter, of a phlegmatic temperament, and not at all conversational—I offered him a cake as a mark of attention, which he ate at one gulp, exactly like an elephant, and which made no more impression on his big face than it would have done on an elephant's.

"Did *she* make 'em now?" said Mr. Barkis, always leaning forward, in his slouching way, on the footboard of the cart with an arm on each knee.

"Peggotty, do you mean, sir?"

"Ah!" said Mr. Barkis. "Her."

"Yes. She makes all our pastry, and does all our cooking."

"Do she though?" said Mr. Barkis.

He made up his mouth as if to whistle, but he didn't whistle. He sat looking at the horse's ears, as if he saw something new there; and sat so, for a considerable time. By-and-by, he said:

"No sweethearts, I b'lieve?"

"Sweetmeats did you say, Mr. Barkis?" For I thought he wanted something else to eat, and had pointedly alluded to that description of refreshment.

"Hearts," said Mr. Barkis. "Sweet hearts; no person walks with her!"

"With Peggotty?"

"Ah!" he said. "Her."

"Oh no. She never had a sweetheart."

"Didn't she though!" said Mr. Barkis.

Again he made up his mouth to whistle, and again he didn't whistle, but sat looking at the horse's ears.

"So she makes," said Mr. Barkis after a long interval of reflection, "all the apple parsties, and does all the cooking, do she?"

I replied that such was the fact.

"Well. I'll tell you what," said Mr. Barkis. "P'raps you might be writin' to her?"

"I shall certainly write to her," I rejoined.

"Ah!" he said, slowly turning his eyes towards me. "Well! If you was writin' to her, p'raps you'd recollect to say that Barkis was willin'; would you."

"That Barkis is willing," I repeated, innocently. "Is that all the message?"

"Ye—es," he said, considering. "Ye—s. Barkis is willin'."

"But you will be at Blunderstone again to-morrow, Mr. Barkis," I said, faltering a little at the idea of my being far away from it then, "and could give your own message so much better."

As he repudiated this suggestion, however, with a jerk of his head, and once more confirmed his previous request by saying, with profound gravity, "Barkis is willin'. That's the message," I readily undertook its transmission. While I was waiting for the coach in the Hotel at Yarmouth that very afternoon, I procured a sheet of paper and an inkstand, and wrote a note to Peggotty which ran thus: "My dear Peggotty. I have come here safe. Barkis is willing. My love to Mama. Yours affectionately. P.S. He says he particularly wants you to know—*Barkis is willing.*"

When I had taken this commission on myself, prospectively, Mr. Barkis relapsed into perfect silence; and I, feeling quite worn out by all that had happened lately, lay down on a sack in the cart and fell asleep. I slept soundly until we got to Yarmouth; which was so entirely new and strange to me in the inn yard to which we drove, that I at once abandoned a latent hope I had had of meeting with some of Mr. Peggotty's family there, perhaps even with little Em'ly herself.

The coach was in the yard, shining very much all over, but without any horses to it as yet; and it looked in that state as if nothing was more unlikely than its ever going to London. I was thinking this, and wondering what would ultimately become of my box, which Mr. Barkis had put down on the yard-pavement by the pole (he having driven up the yard to turn his cart), and also what would ultimately become of me, when a lady looked out of a bow-window where some fowls and joints of meat were hanging up, and said:

"Is that the little gentleman from Blunderstone?"

"Yes, ma'am," I said.

"What name?" enquired the lady.

"Copperfield, ma'am," I said.

"That won't do," returned the lady. "Nobody's dinner is paid for here, in that name."

"Is it Murdstone, ma'am?" I said.

"If you're Master Murdstone," said the lady, "why do you go and give another name first?"

I explained to the lady how it was, who then rang a bell, and called out, "William! show the coffee-room!" Upon which a waiter came running out of a kitchen on the opposite side of the yard to show it, and seemed a good deal surprised when he found he was only to show it to me.

It was a large long room with some large maps in it. I doubt if I could have felt much stranger if the maps had been real foreign countries, and I cast away in the middle of them. I felt it was taking a liberty to sit down, with my cap in my hand, on the corner of the chair nearest the door; and when the waiter laid a cloth on purpose for me, and put a set of castors on it, I think I must have turned red all over with modesty.

He brought me some chops, and vegetables, and took the covers off in such a bouncing manner that I was afraid I must have given

MY FRIENDLY WAITER AND I.

him some offence. But he greatly relieved my mind by putting a chair for me at the table, and saying, very affably, "Now six-foot! come on!"

I thanked him, and took my seat at the board; but found it extremely difficult to handle my knife and fork with anything like dexterity, or to avoid splashing myself with the gravy, while he was standing opposite, staring so hard, and making me blush in the most dreadful manner every time I caught his eye. After watching me into the second chop, he said:

"There's half a pint of ale for you. Will you have it now?"

I thanked him, and said Yes. Upon which he poured it out of a jug into a large tumbler, and held it up against the light, and made it look beautiful.

"My eye!" he said. "It seems a good deal, don't it?"

"It does seem a good deal," I answered with a smile. For it was quite delightful to me, to find him so pleasant. He was a twinkling-eyed, pimple-faced man, with his hair standing upright all over his head; and as he stood with one arm a-kimbo, holding up the glass to the light with the other hand, he looked quite friendly.

"There was a gentleman here, yesterday," he said, "a stout gentleman, by the name of Topsawyer—perhaps you know him!"

"No," I said, "I don't think—"

"In breeches and gaiters, broad-brimmed hat, grey coat, speckled choaker," said the waiter.

"No," I said bashfully, "I haven't the pleasure—"

"He came in here," said the waiter, looking at the light through the tumbler, "ordered a glass of this ale—*would* order it—I told him not—drank it, and fell dead. It was too old for him. It oughtn't to be drawn; that's the fact."

I was very much shocked to hear of this melancholy accident, and said I thought I had better have some water.

"Why you see," said the waiter, still looking at the light through the tumbler, with one of his eyes shut up, "our people don't like things being ordered and left. It offends 'em. But *I*'ll drink it, if you like. I'm used to it, and use is everything. I don't think it 'll hurt me, if I throw my head back, and take it off quick. Shall I.

I replied that he would much oblige me by drinking it, if he thought he could do it safely, but by no means otherwise. When he did throw his head back, and take it off quick, I had a horrible fear, I confess, of seeing him meet the fate of the lamented Mr. Topsawyer, and fall lifeless on the carpet. But it didn't hurt him. On the contrary, I thought he seemed the fresher for it.

"What have we got here?" he said, putting a fork into my dish. "Not chops?"

"Chops," I said.

"Lord bless my soul!" he exclaimed, "I didn't know they were chops. Why, a chop's the very thing to take off the bad effects of that beer! Ain't it lucky?"

So he took a chop by the bone in one hand, and a potatoe in the other, and ate away with a very good appetite, to my extreme satisfaction. He afterwards took another chop, and another potatoe; and after that, another chop and another potatoe. When we had done, he brought me a pudding, and having set it before me, seemed to ruminate, and to become absent in his mind for some moments.

"How's the pie?" he said, rousing himself.

"It's a pudding," I made answer.

"Pudding?" he exclaimed. "Why, bless me, so it is! What!" looking at it nearer. "You don't mean to say it's a batter pudding!"

"Yes, it is indeed."

"Why, a batter pudding," he said, taking up a table-spoon, "is my favorite pudding! Ain't that lucky? Come on, little 'un, and let's see who'll get most."

The waiter certainly got most. He entreated me more than once to come in and win, but what with his table-spoon to my tea-spoon, his dispatch to my dispatch, and his appetite to my appetite, I was left far behind at the first mouthful, and had no chance with him. I never saw any one enjoy a pudding so much, I think; and he laughed, when it was all gone, as if his enjoyment of it lasted still.

Finding him so very friendly and companionable, it was then that I asked for the pen and ink and paper, to write to Peggotty. He not only brought it immediately, but was good enough to look over me while I wrote the letter. When I had finished it, he asked me where I was going to school.

I said, "near London," which was all I knew.

"Oh, my eye!" he said, looking very low-spirited, "I am sorry for that."

"Why?" I asked him.

"Oh Lord!" he said, shaking his head, "that's the school where they broke the boy's ribs—two ribs—a little boy he was. I should say he was—let me see—how old are you, about?"

I told him between eight and nine—almost nine.

"That's just his age," he said. "He was eight years and six months old when they broke his first rib; eight years and eight months old when they broke his second, and did for him."

I could not disguise from myself, or from the waiter, that this was an uncomfortable coincidence, and inquired how it was done. His answer was not cheering to my spirits, for it consisted of two dismal words, "With whopping."

The blowing of the coach-horn in the yard was a seasonable diversion, which made me get up and hesitatingly enquire, in the mingled pride and diffidence of having a purse (which I took out of my pocket), if there were anything to pay.

"There's a sheet of letter-paper," he returned. "Did you ever buy a sheet of letter-paper?"

I could not remember that I ever had.

"It's dear," he said, "on account of the duty. Threepence. That's the way we're taxed in this country. There's nothing else, except the waiter. Never mind the ink. *I* lose by that."

"What should you—what should I—how much ought I to—what would it be right to pay the waiter, if you please?" I stammered, blushing.

"If I hadn't a family, and that family hadn't the cowpox," said the waiter, "I wouldn't take a sixpence. If I didn't support a aged pairint, and a lovely sister,"—here the waiter was greatly agitated—"I wouldn't take a farthing. If I had a good place, and was treated well here, I should beg acceptance of a trifle, instead of taking of it. But I live on broken wittles—and I sleep on the coals"—here the waiter burst into tears.

I was very much concerned for his misfortunes, and felt that any recognition short of ninepence would be mere brutality and hardness of heart. Therefore I gave him one of my three bright shillings.

which he received with much humility and veneration, and spun up with his thumb, directly afterwards, to try the goodness of.

It was a little disconcerting to me, to find, when I was being helped up behind the coach, that I was supposed to have eaten all the dinner without any assistance. I discovered this, from overhearing the lady in the bow-window say to the guard: "Take care of that child, George, or he'll burst!" and observing that the women-servants who were about the place came out to look and giggle at me as a young phenomenon. My unfortunate friend the waiter, who had quite recovered his spirits, did not appear to be disturbed by this, but joined in the general admiration without being at all confused. If I had any doubt of him, I suppose this half-awakened it; but I am inclined to believe that with the simple confidence of a child, and the natural reliance of a child upon superior years (qualities I am very sorry any children should prematurely change for worldly wisdom), I had no serious mistrust of him on the whole, even then.

I felt it rather hard, I must own, to be made, without deserving it, the subject of jokes between the coachman and guard as to the coach drawing heavy behind, on account of my sitting there, and as to the greater expediency of my travelling by waggon. The story of my supposed appetite getting wind among the outside passengers, they were merry upon it likewise; and asked me whether I was going to be paid for, at school, as two brothers or three, and whether I was contracted for, or went upon the regular terms; with other pleasant questions. But the worst of it was, that I knew I should be ashamed to eat anything, when an opportunity offered, and that, after a rather light dinner, I should remain hungry all night—for I had left my cakes behind, at the Hotel, in my hurry. My apprehensions were realised. When we stopped for supper I couldn't muster courage to take any, though I should have liked very much, but sat by the fire and said I didn't want anything This did not save me from more jokes, either; for a husky-voiced gentleman with a rough face, who had been eating out of a sandwich-box nearly all the way, except when he had been drinking out of a bottle, said I was like a Boa Constrictor who took enough at one meal to last him a long time; after which, he actually brought a rash out upon himself with boiled beef.

We had started from Yarmouth at three o'clock in the afternoon, and we were due in London about eight next morning. It was Midsummer weather, and the evening was very pleasant. When we passed through a village, I pictured to myself what the insides of the houses were like, and what the inhabitants were about; and when boys came running after us, and got up behind, and swung there for a little way, I wondered whether their fathers were alive, and whether they were happy at home. I had plenty to think of, therefore, besides my mind running continually on the kind of place I was going to—which was an awful speculation. Sometimes, I remember, I resigned myself to thoughts of home and Peggotty; and to endeavouring, in a confused blind way, to recall how I had felt, and what sort of boy I used to be, before I bit Mr. Murdstone: which I couldn't satisfy myself about by any means, I seemed to have bitten him in such a remote antiquity.

The night was not so pleasant as the evening, for it got chilly; and being put between two gentlemen (the rough-faced one and another) to prevent my tumbling off the coach, I was nearly smothered by their falling asleep, and completely blocking me up. They squeezed me so hard sometimes, that I could not help crying out "Oh! if you please!"—which they didn't like at all, because it woke them. Opposite me was an elderly lady in a great fur cloak, who looked in the dark more like a haystack than a lady, she was wrapped up to such a degree. This lady had a basket with her, and she hadn't known what to do with it, for a long time, until she found that on account of my legs being short, it could go underneath me. It cramped and hurt me so, that it made me perfectly miserable; but if I moved in the least, and made a glass that was in the basket rattle against something else (as it was sure to do), she gave me the cruellest poke with her foot, and said, "Come, don't *you* fidget. *Your* bones are young enough, *I*'m sure!"

At last the sun rose, and then my companions seemed to sleep easier. The difficulties under which they had laboured all night, and which had found utterance in the most terrific gasps and snorts, are not to be conceived. As the sun got higher, their sleep became lighter, and so they gradually one by one awoke. I recollect being very much surprised by the feint everybody made, then, of not having been to sleep at all, and by the uncommon indignation with which every one repelled the charge. I labor under the same kind of astonishment to this day, having invariably observed that of all human weaknesses, the one to which our common nature is the least disposed to confess (I cannot imagine why) is the weakness of having gone to sleep in a coach.

What an amazing place London was to me when I saw it in the distance, and how I believed all the adventures of all my favorite heroes to be constantly enacting and re-enacting there, and how I vaguely made it out in my own mind to be fuller of wonders and wickedness than all the cities of the earth, I need not stop here to relate. We approached it by degrees, and got, in due time, to the inn in the Whitechapel district, for which we were bound. I forget whether it was the Blue Bull, or the Blue Boar; but I know it was the Blue Something, and that its likeness was painted up on the back of the coach.

The guard's eye lighted on me as he was getting down, and he said at the booking-office door:

"Is there anybody here for a yoongster booked in the name of Murdstone, from Bloonderstone, Sooffolk, to be left 'till called for?"

Nobody answered.

"Try Copperfield, if you please, sir," said I, looking helplessly down.

"Is there anybody here for a yoongster, booked in the name of Murdstone, from Bloonderstone, Sooffolk, but owning to the name of Copperfield, to be left 'till called for?" said the guard. "Come! *Is* there anybody?"

No. There was nobody. I looked anxiously around; but the enquiry made no impression on any of the bystanders, if I except a man in gaiters, with one eye, who suggested that they had better put a brass collar round my neck, and tie me up in the stable.

A ladder was brought, and I got down after the lady, who was like a haystack: not daring to stir, until her basket was removed. The coach was clear of passengers by that time, the luggage was very soon cleared out, the horses had been taken out before the luggage, and now the coach itself was wheeled and backed off by some hostlers, out of the way. Still, nobody appeared, to claim the dusty youngster from Blunderstone, Suffolk.

More solitary than Robinson Crusoe, who had nobody to look

at him and see that he was solitary, I went into the booking-office, and, by invitation of the clerk on duty, passed behind the counter, and sat down on the scale at which they weighed the luggage. Here, as I sat looking at the parcels, packages, and books, and inhaling the smell of stables (ever since associated with that morning), a procession of most tremendous considerations began to march through my mind. Supposing nobody should ever fetch me, how long would they consent to keep me there? Would they keep me long enough to spend seven shillings? Should I sleep at night in one of those wooden binns with the other luggage, and wash myself at the pump in the yard in the morning; or should I be turned out every night, and expected to come again to be left 'till called for, when the office opened next day? Supposing there was no mistake in the case, and Mr. Murdstone had devised this plan to get rid of me, what should I do? If they allowed me to remain there until my seven shillings were spent, I couldn't hope to remain there when I began to starve. That would obviously be inconvenient and unpleasant to the customers, besides entailing on the Blue Whatever-it-was, the risk of funeral expenses. If I started off at once, and tried to walk back home, how could I ever find my way, how could I ever hope to walk so far, how could I make sure of any one but Peggotty, even if I got back? If I found out the nearest proper authorities, and offered myself to go for a soldier, or a sailor, I was such a little fellow that it was most likely they wouldn't take me in. These thoughts, and a hundred other such thoughts, turned me burning hot, and made me giddy with apprehension and dismay. I was in the height of my fever when a man entered and whispered to the clerk, who presently slanted me off the scale, and pushed me over to him, as if I were weighed, bought, delivered, and paid for.

As I went out of the office, hand in hand with this new acquaintance, I stole a look at him. He was a gaunt, sallow young man, with hollow cheeks, and a chin almost as black as Mr. Murdstone's; but there the likeness ended, for his whiskers were shaved off, and his hair, instead of being glossy, was rusty and dry. He was dressed in a suit of black clothes which were rather rusty and dry too, and rather short in the sleeves and legs; and he had a white neck-kerchief on that was not over-clean. I did not, and do not, suppose that this neck-kerchief was all the linen he wore, but it was all he showed or gave any hint of.

"You 're the new boy?" he said.

"Yes, sir," I said. I supposed I was. I didn't know.

"I'm one of the masters at Salem House," *he* said.

I made him a bow and felt very much overawed. I was so ashamed to allude to a common-place thing like my box, to a scholar and a master at Salem House, that we had gone some little distance from the yard before I had the hardihood to mention it. We turned back, on my humbly insinuating that it might be useful to me hereafter; and he told the clerk that the carrier had instructions to call for it at noon.

"If you please, sir," I said, when we had accomplished about the same distance as before, "is it far?"

"It 's down by Blackheath," he said.

"Is *that* far, sir?" I diffidently asked.

"It 's a good step," he said. "We shall go by the stage-coach. It 's about six miles."

I was so faint and tired, that the idea of holding out for six miles more, was too much for me. I took heart to tell him that I had had nothing all night, and that if he would allow me to buy something to eat, I should be very much obliged to him. He appeared surprised at this—I see him stop and look at me now—and after considering for a few moments, said he wanted to call on an old person who lived not far off, and that the best way would be for me to buy some bread, or whatever I liked best that was wholesome, and make my breakfast at her house, where we could get some milk.

Accordingly we looked in at a baker's window, and after I had made a series of proposals to buy everything that was bilious in the shop, and he had rejected them one by one, we decided in favour of a nice little loaf of brown bread, which cost me threepence. Then, at a grocer's shop, we bought an egg and a slice of streaky bacon; which still left what I thought a good deal of change, out of the second of the bright shillings, and made me consider London a very cheap place. These provisions laid in, we went on through a great noise and uproar that confused my weary head beyond description, and over a bridge which, no doubt, was London Bridge (indeed I think he told me so, but I was half asleep), until we came to the poor person's house, which was a part of some alms-houses, as I knew by their look, and by an inscription on a stone over the gate, which said they were established for twenty-five poor women.

The Master at Salem House lifted the latch of one of a number of little black doors that were all alike, and had each a little diamond-paned window on one side, and another little diamond-paned window above; and we went into the little house of one of these poor old women, who was blowing a fire to make a little saucepan boil. On seeing the master enter, the old woman stopped with the bellows on her knee, and said something that I thought sounded like "My Charley!" but on seeing me come in too, she got up, and rubbing her hands made a confused sort of half curtsey.

"Can you cook this young gentleman's breakfast for him, if you please?" said the Master at Salem House.

"Can I?" said the old woman. "Yes can I, sure!"

"How's Mrs. Fibbitson to-day?" said the Master, looking at another old woman in a large chair by the fire, who was such a bundle of clothes that I feel grateful to this hour for not having sat upon her by mistake.

"Ah, she's poorly," said the first old woman. "It's one of her bad days. If the fire was to go out, through any accident, I verily believe she'd go out too, and never come to life again."

As they looked at her, I looked at her also. Although it was a warm day, she seemed to think of nothing but the fire. I fancied she was jealous even of the saucepan on it; and I have reason to know that she took its impressment into the service of boiling my egg and broiling my bacon, in dudgeon; for I saw her, with my own discomfited eyes, shake her fist at me once, when those culinary operations were going on, and no one else was looking. The sun streamed in at the little window, but she sat with her own back and the back of the large chair towards it, screening the fire as if she were sedulously keeping *it* warm, instead of it keeping her warm, and watching it in a most distrustful manner. The completion of the preparations for my breakfast, by relieving the fire, gave her such extreme joy that she laughed aloud—and a very unmelodious laugh she had, I must say.

I sat down to my brown loaf my egg, and my rasher of bacon

with a bason of milk besides, and made a most delicious meal. While I was yet in the full enjoyment of it, the old woman of the house said to the Master:

"Have you got your flute with you?"

"Yes," he returned.

"Have a blow at it," said the old woman, coaxingly. "Do!"

The Master, upon this, put his hand underneath the skirts of his coat, and brought out his flute in three pieces, which he screwed together, and began immediately to play. My impression is, after many years of consideration, that there never can have been anybody in the world who played worse. He made the most dismal sounds I have ever heard produced by any means, natural or artificial. I don't know what the tunes were—if there were such things in the performance at all, which I doubt—but the influence of the strain upon me was, first, to make me think of all my sorrows until I could hardly keep my tears back; then to take away my appetite; and lastly to make me so sleepy that I couldn't keep my eyes open. They begin to close again, and I begin to nod, as the recollection rises fresh upon me. Once more the little room with its open corner cupboard, and its square-backed chairs, and its angular little staircase leading to the room above, and its three peacock's feathers displayed over the mantelpiece—I remember wondering when I first went in, what that peacock would have thought if he had known what his finery was doomed to come to—fades from before me, and I nod, and sleep. The flute becomes inaudible, the wheels of the coach are heard instead, and I am on my journey. The coach jolts, I wake with a start, and the flute has come back again, and the Master at Salem House is sitting with his legs crossed, playing it dolefully, while the old woman of the house looks on delighted. She fades in her turn, and he fades, and all fades, and there is no flute, no Master, no Salem House, no David Copperfield, no anything but heavy sleep.

I dreamed, I thought, that once while he was blowing into this dismal flute, the old woman of the house, who had gone nearer and nearer to him in her ecstatic admiration, leaned over the back of his chair and gave him an affectionate squeeze round the neck, which stopped his playing for a moment. I was in the middle state between sleeping and waking, either then or immediately afterwards,

MY MUSICAL BREAKFAST.

for, as he resumed—it was a real fact that he had stopped playing—I saw and heard the same old woman ask Mrs. Fibbitson, if it wasn't delicious (meaning the flute), to which Mrs. Fibbitson replied, "Ay, ay! Yes!" and nodded at the fire: to which, I am persuaded, she gave the credit of the whole performance.

When I seemed to have been dozing a long while, the Master at Salem House unscrewed his flute into the three pieces, put them up as before, and took me away. We found the coach very near at hand, and got upon the roof; but I was so dead sleepy, that when we stopped on the road to take up somebody else, they put me inside where there were no passengers, and where I slept profoundly, until I found the coach going at a footpace up a steep hill among green leaves. Presently, it stopped, and had come to its destination.

A short walk brought us—I mean the Master and me—to Salem House, which was enclosed with a high brick wall, and looked very dull. Over a door in this wall was a board with SALEM HOUSE upon it; and through a grating in this door we were surveyed when we rang the bell by a surly face, which I found, on the door being opened, belonged to a stout man with a bull-neck, a wooden leg, overhanging temples, and his hair cut close all round his head.

"The new boy," said the Master.

The man with the wooden leg eyed me all over—it didn't take long, for there was not much of me—and locked the gate behind us, and took out the key. We were going up to the house, among some dark heavy trees, when he called after my conductor.

"Hallo!"

We looked back, and he was standing at the door of a little lodge, where he lived, with a pair of boots in his hand.

"Here! The cobbler's been," he said, "since you've been out, Mr. Mell, and he says he can't mend 'em any more. He says there an't a bit of the original boot left, and he wonders you expect it."

With these words he threw the boots towards Mr. Mell, who went back a few paces to pick them up, and looked at them (very disconsolately, I was afraid), as we went on together. I observed then, for the first time, that the boots he had on were a good deal the worse for wear, and that his stocking was just breaking out in one place, like a bud.

Salem House was a square brick building with wings; of a bare and unfurnished appearance. All about it was so very quiet, that I said to Mr. Mell I supposed the boys were out; but he seemed surprised at my not knowing that it was holiday-time. That all the boys were at their several homes. That Mr. Creakle, the proprietor, was down by the sea-side with Mrs. and Miss Creakle; and that I was sent in holiday-time as a punishment for my misdoing all of which he explained to me as we went along.

I gazed upon the schoolroom into which he took me, as the most forlorn and desolate place I had ever seen. I see it now. A long room with three long rows of desks, and six of forms, and bristling all round with pegs for hats and slates. Scraps of old copy-books and exercises litter the dirty floor. Some silk-worms' houses, made of the same materials, are scattered over the desks. Two miserable white mice, left behind by their owner, are running up and down in a fusty castle made of pasteboard and wire, looking in all the corners with their red eyes for anything to eat. A bird, in a cage a very little bigger than himself, makes a mournful rattle now and then in hopping on his perch, two inches high, or dropping from it; but neither sings nor chirps. There is a strange unwholesome smell upon the room, like mildewed corduroys, sweet apples wanting air, and rotten books. There could not well be more ink splashed about it, if it had been roofless from its first construction, and the skies had rained, snowed, hailed, and blown ink through the varying seasons of the year.

Mr. Mell having left me while he took his irreparable boots upstairs, I went softly to the upper end of the room, observing all this as I crept along. Suddenly I came upon a pasteboard placard, beautifully written, which was lying on the desk, and bore these words—"*Take care of him. He bites.*"

I got upon the desk immediately, apprehensive of at least a great dog underneath. But, though I looked all round with anxious eyes, I could see nothing of him. I was still engaged in peering about, when Mr. Mell came back, and asked me what I did up there.

"I beg your pardon, sir," says I, "if ou please, I'm looking for the dog."

"Dog?" says he. "What dog?"

"Isn't it a dog, sir?'

"Isn't what a dog?"

"That's to be taken care of, sir; that bites."

"No, Copperfield," says he gravely, "that's not a dog. That's a boy. My instructions are, Copperfield, to put this placard on your back. I am sorry to make such a beginning with you, but I must do it."

With that, he took me down, and tied the placard, which was neatly constructed for the purpose, on my shoulders like a knapsack; and wherever I went, afterwards, I had the consolation of carrying it.

What I suffered from that placard, nobody can imagine. Whether it was possible for people to see me or not, I always fancied that somebody was reading it. It was no relief to turn round and find nobody; for wherever my back was, there I imagined somebody always to be. That cruel man with the wooden leg, aggravated my sufferings. He was in authority; and if he ever saw me leaning against a tree, or a wall, or the house, he roared out from his lodge-door in a stupendous voice, "Hallo, you sir! You Copperfield! Show that badge conspicuous, or I'll report you!" The playground was a bare gravelled yard, open to all the back of the house and the offices; and I knew that the servants read it, and the butcher read it, and the baker read it; that everybody, in a word, who came backwards and forwards to the house, of a morning, when I was ordered to walk there, read that I was to be taken care of, for I bit. I recollect that I positively began to have a dread of myself, as a kind of wild boy who did bite.

There was an old door in this playground, on which the boys had a custom of carving their names. It was completely covered with such inscriptions. In my dread of the end of the vacation and their coming back, I could not read a boy's name, without enquiring in what tone and with what emphasis *he* would read, "take care of him. He bites." There was one boy—a certain J. Steerforth—who cut his name very deep and very often, who, I conceived, would read it in a rather strong voice, and afterwards pull my hair. There was another boy, one Tommy Traddles, who I dreaded would make game of it, and pretend to be dreadfully frightened of me. There was a third, George Demple, who I fancied would sing it. I have looked, a little shrinking creature, at that door, until the owners of all the names—there were five-and-forty of them in the school then,

Mr. Mell said—seemed to send me to Coventry by general acclamation, and to cry out, each in his own way, "Take care of him. He bites!"

It was the same with the places at the desks and forms. It was the same with the groves of deserted bedsteads I peeped at, on my way to, and when I was in, my own bed. I remember dreaming night after night, of being with my mother as she used to be, or of going to a party at Mr. Peggotty's, or of travelling outside the stage-coach, or of dining again with my unfortunate friend the waiter, and in all these circumstances making people scream and stare, by the unhappy disclosure that I had nothing on but my little night-shirt, and that placard.

In the monotony of my life, and in my constant apprehension of the re-opening of the school, it was such an insupportable affliction! I had long tasks every day to do with Mr. Mell; but I did them, there being no Mr. and Miss Murdstone here, and got through them without disgrace. Before, and after them, I walked about—supervised, as I have mentioned, by the man with the wooden leg. How vividly I call to mind the damp about the house, the green cracked flag-stones in the court, an old leaky water-butt, and the discolored trunks of some of the grim trees, which seemed to have dripped more in the rain than other trees, and to have blown less in the sun! At one we dined, Mr. Mell and I, at the upper end of a long bare dining-room, full of deal tables, and smelling of fat. Then, we had more tasks until tea, which Mr. Mell drank out of a blue tea-cup, and I out of a tin pot. All day long, and until seven or eight in the evening, Mr. Mell, at his own detached desk in the schoolroom, worked hard with pen, ink, ruler, books, and writing-paper, making out the bills (as I found) for last half-year. When he had put up his things for the night he took out his flute, and blew at it, until I almost thought he would gradually blow his whole being into the large hole at the top, and ooze away at the keys.

I picture my small self in the dimly-lighted rooms, sitting with my head upon my hand, listening to the doleful performance of Mr. Mell, and conning to-morrow's lessons. I picture myself with my books shut up, still listening to the doleful performance of Mr. Mell, and listening through it to what used to be at home, and to the blowing of the wind on Yarmouth flats, and feeling very sad and solitary

I picture myself going up to bed, among the unused rooms, and sitting on my bed-side crying for a comfortable word from Peggotty. I picture myself coming down stairs in the morning, and looking through a long ghastly gash of a staircase-window, at the school-bell hanging on the top of an outhouse, with a weathercock above it; and dreading the time when it shall ring J. Steerforth and the rest to work: which is only second to the time when the man with the wooden leg shall unlock the rusty gate to give admission to the awful Mr. Creakle. I cannot think I was a very dangerous character in any of these aspects, but in all of them I carried the same warning on my back.

Mr. Mell never said much to me, but he was never harsh to me. I suppose we were company to each other, without talking. I forgot to mention that he would talk to himself sometimes, and grin, and clench his fist, and grind his teeth, and pull his hair in an unaccountable manner. But he had these peculiarities: and at first they frightened me, though I soon got used to them.

CHAPTER VI.

I ENLARGE MY CIRCLE OF ACQUAINTANCE.

I HAD led this life about a month, when the man with the wooden leg began to stump about with a mop and a bucket of water, from which I inferred that preparations were making to receive Mr. Creakle and the boys. I was not mistaken; for the mop came into the schoolroom before long, and turned out Mr. Mell and me, who lived where we could, and got on how we could for some days, during which we were always in the way of two or three young women, who had rarely shown themselves before, and were so continually in the midst of dust that I sneezed almost as much as if Salem House had been a great snuff-box.

One day I was informed by Mr. Mell that Mr. Creakle would be home that evening. In the evening, after tea, I heard that he was come. Before bed-time, I was fetched by the man with the wooden leg to appear before him.

Mr. Creakle's part of the house was a good deal more comfortable than ours, and he had a snug bit of garden that looked pleasant after the dusty playground, which was such a desert in miniature, that I thought no one but a camel, or a dromedary, could have felt at home in it. It seemed to me a bold thing even to take notice that the passage looked comfortable, as I went on my way, trembling, to Mr. Creakle's presence: which so abashed me, when I was ushered into it, that I hardly saw Mrs. Creakle or Miss Creakle (who were both there, in the parlor), or anything but Mr. Creakle, a stout gentleman with a bunch of watch-chain and seals, in an arm-chair, with a tumbler and bottle beside him.

"So!" said Mr. Creakle. "This is the young gentleman whose teeth are to be filed! Turn him round."

The wooden-legged man turned me about so as to exhibit the placard; and having afforded time for a full survey of it turned me about again with my face to Mr. Creakle, and posted himself at Mr. Creakle's side. Mr. Creakle's face was fiery, and his eyes were small, and deep in his head: he had thick veins in his forehead, a little nose, and a large chin. He was bald on the top of his head; and had some thin wet-looking hair that was just turning grey, brushed across each temple, so that the two sides interlaced on his forehead. But the circumstance about him which impressed me most, was, that he had no voice, but spoke in a whisper. The exertion this cost him, or the consciousness of talking in that feeble way, made his angry face so much more angry, and his thick veins so much thicker, when he spoke, that I am not surprised, on looking back, at this peculiarity striking me as his chief one.

"Now," said Mr. Creakle. "What's the report of this boy?"

"There's nothing against him yet," returned the man with the wooden leg. "There has been no opportunity."

I thought Mr. Creakle was disappointed. I thought Mrs. and Miss Creakle (at whom I now glanced for the first time, and who were, both, thin and quiet) were not disappointed.

"Come here, sir!" said Mr. Creakle, beckoning to me.

"Come here!" said the man with the wooden leg, repeating the gesture.

"I have the happiness of knowing your father-in-law," whispered Mr. Creakle, taking me by the ear; "and a worthy man he is, and a man of a strong character. He knows me, and I know him. Do *you* know me! Hey?" said Mr. Creakle, pinching my ear with ferocious playfulness.

"Not yet, sir," I said, flinching with the pain.

"Not yet? Hey?" repeated Mr. Creakle. "But you will soon Hey?"

"You will soon. Hey?" repeated the man with the wooden leg. I afterwards found that he generally acted, with his strong voice, as Mr. Creakle's interpreter to the boys.

I was very much frightened, and said, I hoped so, if he pleased. I felt all this while, as if my ear were blazing; he pinched it so hard.

"I'll tell you what I am," whispered Mr. Creakle, letting it go at last, with a screw at parting that brought the water into my eyes. "I'm a Tartar."

"A Tartar," said the man with the wooden leg.

"When I say I'll do a thing, I do it," said Mr. Creakle; "and when I say I will have a thing done, I will have it done."

"—Will have a thing done, I will have it done," repeated the man with the wooden leg.

"I am a determined character," said Mr. Creakle. "That's what I am. I do my duty. That's what *I* do. My flesh and blood"—he looked at Mrs. Creakle as he said this—"when it rises against me, is not my flesh and blood. I discard it. Has that fellow," to the man with the wooden leg, "been here again?"

"No," was the answer.

"No," said Mr. Creakle. "He knows better. He knows me. Let him keep away. I say let him keep away," said Mr. Creakle, striking his hand upon the table, and looking at Mrs. Creakle, "for he knows me. Now you have begun to know me too, my young friend, and you may go. Take him away."

I was very glad to be ordered away, for Mrs. and Miss Creakle were both wiping their eyes, and I felt as uncomfortable for them, as I did for myself. But I had a petition on my mind which concerned me so nearly, that I couldn't help saying, though I wondered at my own courage:

"If you please, sir—"

Mr. Creakle whispered "Hah! What's this?" and bent his eyes upon me, as if he would have burnt me up with them.

"If you please, sir," I faltered, "if I might be allowed (I am very sorry indeed, sir, for what I did) to take this writing off, before the boys come back—"

Whether Mr. Creakle was in earnest, or whether he only did it to frighten me, I don't know, but he made a burst out of his chair, before which I precipitately retreated, without waiting for the escort of the man with the wooden leg, and never once stopped until I reached my own bedroom, where, finding I was not pursued, I went to bed, as it was time, and lay quaking, for a couple of hours.

Next morning Mr. Sharp came back. Mr. Sharp was the first master, and superior to Mr. Mell. Mr. Mell took his meals with the boys, but Mr. Sharp dined and supped at Mr. Creakle's table. He was a limp, delicate-looking gentleman, I thought, with a good deal of nose, and a way of carrying his head on one side, as if it were a little too heavy for him. His hair was very smooth and wavy; but I was informed by the very first boy who came back that it was a wig (a second-hand one *he* said), and that Mr. Sharp went out every Saturday afternoon to get it curled.

It was no other than Tommy Traddles who gave me this piece of intelligence. He was the first boy who returned. He introduced himself by informing me that I should find his name on the right-hand corner of the gate, over the top bolt; upon that I said "Master Traddles?" to which he replied, "the same," and then he asked me for a full account of myself and family.

It was a happy circumstance for me that Traddles came back first. He enjoyed my placard so much, that he saved me from the embarrassment of either disclosure or concealment, by presenting me to every other boy who came back, great or small, immediately on his arrival, in this form of introduction, "Look here! Here's a game!" Happily, too, the greater part of the boys came back low-spirited, and were not so boisterous at my expense as I had expected. Some of them certainly did dance about me like wild Indians, and the greater part could not resist the temptation of pretending that I was a dog, and patting and smoothing me lest I should bite, and saying "Lie down, sir!" and calling me Towzer. This was naturally confusing, among so many strangers, and cost me some tears, but on the whole it was much better than I had anticipated.

I was not considered as being formally received into the school, however, until J. Steerforth arrived. Before this boy, who was reputed to be a great scholar, and was very good-looking, and at least half-a-dozen years my senior, I was carried as before a magistrate. He enquired, under a shed in the playground, into the particulars of my punishment, and was pleased to express his opinion that it was "a jolly shame;" for which I became bound to him ever afterwards.

"What money have you got, Copperfield?" he said, walking side with me when he had disposed of my affair in these terms.

I told him seven shillings.

"You had better give it to me to take care of," he said. "At east, you can if you like. You needn't if you don't like."

I hastened to comply with his friendly suggestion, and opening Peggotty's purse, turned it upside down into his hand.

"Do you want to spend anything now?" he asked me.

"No thank you," I replied.

"You can if you like, you know," said Steerforth. "Say the word."

"No thank you, sir," I repeated.

"Perhaps you'd like to spend a couple of shillings or so, in a bottle of currant wine by-and-by, up in the bedroom?" said Steerforth. "You belong to my bedroom I find."

It certainly had not occurred to me before, but I said, Yes, I should like that.

"Very good," said Steerforth. "You'll be glad to spend another shilling or so, in almond cakes, I dare say?"

I said, Yes, I should like that too.

"And another shilling or so in biscuits, and another in fruit, eh?" said Steerforth. "I say, young Copperfield, you're going it!"

I smiled because he smiled, but I was a little troubled in my mind, too.

"Well!" said Steerforth. "We must make it stretch as far as we can; that's all. I'll do the best in my power for you. I can go out when I like, and I'll smuggle the prog in." With these words he put the money in his pocket, and kindly told me not to make myself uneasy; he would take care it should be all right.

He was as good as his word, if that were all right which I had a secret misgiving was nearly all wrong—for I feared it was a waste of my mother's two half-crowns—though I had preserved the piece of paper they were wrapped in: which was a precious saving.

When we went up stairs to bed, he produced the whole seven shillings worth, and laid it out on my bed in the moonlight, saying:

"There you are, young Copperfield, and a royal spread you 've got!"

I couldn't think of doing the honors of the feast, at my time of life, while he was by; my hand shook at the very thought of it. I begged him to do me the favor of presiding; and my request being seconded by the other boys who were in that room, he acceded to it, and sat upon my pillow, handing round the viands—with perfect fairness I must say—and dispensing the currant wine in a little glass without a foot, which was his own property. As to me, I sat on his left hand, and the rest were grouped about us, on the nearest beds and on the floor.

How well I recollect our sitting there, talking in whispers; or their talking, and my respectfully listening, I ought rather to say; the moonlight falling a little way into the room, through the window, painting a pale window on the floor, and the greater part of us in shadow, except when Steerforth dipped a match into a phosphorus-box, when he wanted to look for anything on the board, and shed a blue glare over us that was gone directly! A certain mysterious feeling, consequent on the darkness, the secresy of the revel, and the whisper in which everything was said, steals over me again, and I listen to all they tell me with a vague feeling of solemnity and awe, which makes me glad that they are all so near, and frightens me (though I feign to laugh) when Traddles pretends to see a ghost in the corner.

I heard all kinds of things about the school and all belonging to it. I heard that Mr. Creakle had not preferred his claim to being a Tartar without reason; that he was the sternest and most severe of masters; that he laid about him, right and left, every day of his life, charging in among the boys like a trooper, and slashing away, unmercifully. That he knew nothing himself, but the art of slashing, being more ignorant (J. Steerforth said) than the lowest boy in the school; that he had been, a good many years ago, a small hop-dealer in the Borough, and had taken to the schooling business after being bankrupt in hops, and making away with Mrs. Creakle's money. With a good deal more of that sort, which I wondered how they knew.

I heard that the man with the wooden leg, whose name was Tungay, was an obstinate barbarian who had formerly assisted in the hop business, but had come into the scholastic line with Mr. Creakle, in consequence, as was supposed among the boys, of his having broken his leg in Mr. Creakle's service, and having done a deal of dishonest work for him, and knowing his secrets. I heard that with *the single* exception of Mr. Creakle, Tungay considered the whole establishment, masters and boys, as his natural enemies, and that the only delight of his life was to be sour and malicious. I heard that Mr. Creakle had a son, who had not been Tungay's friend, and who, assisting in the school, had once held some remonstrance with his father on an occasion when its discipline was very cruelly exercised, and was supposed, besides, to have protested against his father's usage of his mother. I heard that Mr. Creakle had turned him out of doors in consequence, and that Mrs. and Miss Creakle had been in a sad way, ever since.

But the greatest wonder that I heard of Mr. Creakle was, there being one boy in the school on whom he never ventured to lay a hand, and that boy being J. Steerforth. Steerforth himself confirmed this when it was stated, and said that he should like to begin to see him do it. On being asked by a mild boy (not me) how he would proceed if he did begin to see him do it, he dipped a match into his phosphorus box on purpose to shed a glare over his reply, and said he would commence by knocking him down with a blow on the forehead from the seven-and-sixpenny ink-bottle that was always on the mantelpiece. We sat in the dark for some time, breathless.

I heard that Mr. Sharp and Mr. Mell were both supposed to be wretchedly paid; and that when there was hot and cold meat for dinner at Mr. Creakle's table, Mr. Sharp was always expected to say he preferred cold; which was again corroborated by J. Steerforth, the only parlor-boarder. I heard that Mr. Sharp's wig didn't fit him; and that he needn't be so "bounceable"—somebody else said "bumptious"—about it, because his own red hair was very plainly to be seen behind.

I heard that one boy, who was a coal-merchant's son, came as a set-off against the coal bill, and was called on that account "Exchange or Barter"—a name selected from the arithmetic book as expressing this arrangement. I heard that the table beer was a robbery of parents, and the pudding an imposition. I heard that Miss Creakle was regarded by the school in general as being in love with Steerforth; and I am sure, as I sat in the dark, thinking of his nice voice, and his fine face, and his easy manner, and his curling hair, I thought it very likely. I heard that Mr. Mell was not a bad sort of fellow, but hadn't a sixpence to bless himself with; and that there was no doubt that old Mrs. Mell, his mother, was as poor as Job. I thought of my breakfast then, and what had sounded like "My Charley!" but I was, I am glad to remember, as mute as a mouse about it.

The hearing of all this, and a good deal more, outlasted the banquet some time. The greater part of the guests had gone to bed as soon as the eating and drinking were over; and we, who had remained whispering and listening half undressed, at last betook ourselves to bed, too.

"Good night, young Copperfield," said Steerforth, "I'll take care of you."

"You're very kind," I gratefully returned. "I am much obliged to you, indeed."

"You haven't got a sister, have you?" said Steerforth, yawning.

"No," I answered.

"That's a pity," said Steerforth. "If you had one, I should think she would have been a pretty, timid, little, bright-eyed sort of girl. I should have liked to know her. Good night, young Copperfield."

"Good night, sir," I replied.

I thought of him very much after I went to bed, and raised myself, I recollect, to look at him where he lay in the moonlight, with his handsome face turned up, and his head reclining easily on his arm. He was a person of great power in my eyes; that was of course the reason of my mind running on him. No veiled future dimly glanced upon him in the moonbeams. There was no shadowy picture of his footsteps, in the garden that I dreamed of—the garden that I picked up shells and pebbles in, with little Em'ly, all night.

CHAPTER VII.

MY "FIRST HALF" AT SALEM HOUSE.

School began in earnest next day. A profound impression was made upon me, I remember, by the roar of voices in the schoolroom suddenly becoming hushed as death when Mr. Creakle entered after breakfast, and stood in the doorway looking round upon us like a giant in a story-book surveying his captives.

Tungay stood at Mr. Creakle's elbow. He had no occasion, I thought, to cry out "Silence!" so ferociously, for the boys were all struck speechless and motionless.

Mr. Creakle was seen to speak, and Tungay was heard, to this effect.

"Now, boys, this is a new half. Take care what you're about, in this new half. Come fresh up to the lessons, I advise you, for I come fresh up to the punishment. I won't flinch. It will be of no use your rubbing yourselves; you won't rub the marks out that I shall give you. Now get to work, every boy!"

When this dreadful exordium was over, and Tungay had stumped out again, Mr. Creakle came to where I sat, and told me that if I were famous for biting, he was famous for biting, too. He then showed me the cane, and asked me what I thought of *that*, for a tooth? Was it a sharp tooth, hey? Was it a double tooth, hey? Had it a deep prong, hey? Did it bite, hey? Did it bite? At every question he gave me a fleshy cut with it that made me writhe; so I was very soon made free of Salem House (as Steerforth said), and very soon in tears also.

Not that I mean to say these were special marks of distinction, which only I received. On the contrary, a large majority of the boys (especially the smaller ones) were visited with similar instances of notice, as Mr. Creakle made the round of the schoolroom. Half the establishment was writhing and crying, before the day's work began; and how much of it had writhed and cried before the day's work was over. I am really afraid to recollect, lest I should seem to exaggerate.

I should think there never can have been a man who enjoyed his profession more than Mr. Creakle did. He had a delight in cutting at the boys, which was like the satisfaction of a craving appetite. I am confident that he couldn't resist a chubby boy, especially; that there was a fascination in such a subject, which made him restless in his mind, until he had scored and marked him for the day. I was chubby myself, and ought to know. I am sure when I think of the fellow now, my blood rises against him with the disinterested indignation I should feel if I could have known all about him without having ever been in his power; but it rises hotly, because I know him to have been an incapable brute, who had no more right to be possessed of the great trust he held, than to be Lord High Admiral, or Commander-in-chief: in either of which capacities, it is probable that he would have done infinitely less mischief.

Miserable little propitiators of a remorseless Idol, how abject we were to him! what a launch in life I think it now, on looking back, to be so mean and servile to a man of such parts and pretensions!

Here I sit at the desk again, watching his eye—humbly watching his eye, as he rules a cyphering-book for another victim whose hands have just been flattened by that identical ruler, and who is trying to wipe the sting out with a pocket-handkerchief. I have plenty to do. I don't watch his eye in idleness, but because I am morbidly attracted to it, in a dread desire to know what he will do next, and whether it will be my turn to suffer, or somebody else's. A lane of small boys beyond me, with the same interest in his eye, watch it too. I think he knows it, though he pretends he don't. He makes dreadful mouths as he rules the cyphering-book; and now he throws his eye sideways down our lane, and we all droop over our books and tremble. A moment afterwards we are again eyeing him. An unhappy culprit, found guilty of imperfect exercise, approaches at his command. The culprit falters excuses, and professes a determination to do better to-morrow. Mr. Creakle cuts a joke before he beats him, and we laugh at it,—miserable little dogs, we laugh, with our visages as white as ashes, and our hearts sinking into our boots.

Here I sit at the desk again, on a drowsy summer afternoon. A buzz and hum go up around me, as if the boys were so many blue-bottles. A cloggy sensation of the lukewarm fat of meat is upon me (we dined an hour or two ago), and my head is as heavy as so much lead. I would give the world to go to sleep. I sit with my eye on Mr. Creakle, blinking at him like a young owl; when sleep overpowers me for a minute, he still looms through my slumber, ruling those cyphering-books; until he softly comes behind me and wakes me to plainer perception of him, with a red ridge across my back.

Here I am in the playground, with my eye still fascinated by him, though I can't see him. The window at a little distance from which I know he is having his dinner, stands for him, and I eye that instead. If he shows his face near it, mine assumes an imploring and submissive expression. If he looks out through the glass, the boldest boy (Steerforth excepted) stops in the middle of a shout or yell, and becomes contemplative. One day, Traddles (the most unfortunate boy in the world) breaks that window accidentally, with a ball. I shudder at this moment with the tremendous sensation of seeing it done, and feeling that the ball has bounded on to Mr. Creakle's sacred head.

Poor Traddles! In a tight sky-blue suit that made his arms and legs like German sausages, or roly-poly puddings, he was the merriest and most miserable of all the boys. He was always being caned —I think he was caned every day that half-year, except one holiday Monday when he was only ruler'd on both hands—and was always going to write to his uncle about it, and never did. After laying his head on the desk for a little while, he would cheer up, somehow, begin to laugh again, and draw skeletons all over his slate, before his eyes were dry. I used at first to wonder what comfort Traddles found in drawing skeletons; and for some time looked upon him as a sort of hermit, who reminded himself by those symbols of mortality that caning couldn't last for ever. But I believe he only did it because they were easy, and didn't want any features.

He was very honorable, Traddles was; and held it as a solemn duty in the boys to stand by one another. He suffered for this on several occasions; and particularly once, when Steerforth laughed in church, and the Beadle thought it was Traddles, and took him out. I see him now, going away in custody, despised by the congregation. He never said who was the real offender, though he smarted for it next day, and was imprisoned so many hours that he came forth with a whole churchyard-full of skeletons swarming all over his Latin Dictionary. But he had his reward. Steerforth said there was nothing of the sneak in Traddles, and we all felt that to be the highest praise. For my part, I could have gone through a good deal (though I was much less brave than Traddles, and nothing like so old) to have won such a recompense.

To see Steerforth walk to church before us, arm-in-arm with Miss Creakle, was one of the great sights of my life. I didn't think Miss Creakle equal to little Em'ly in point of beauty, and I didn't love her (I didn't dare); but I thought her a young lady of extraordinary attractions, and in point of gentility not to be surpassed. When Steerforth, in white trousers, carried her parasol for her, I felt proud to know him; and believed that she could not choose but adore him with all her heart. Mr. Sharp and Mr. Mell were both notable personages in my eyes; but Steerforth was to them what the sun was to two stars.

Steerforth continued his protection of me, and proved a very useful friend; since nobody dared to annoy one whom he honored with his countenance. He couldn't—or at all events, he didn't—defend me from Mr. Creakle, who was very severe with me; but whenever I had been treated worse than usual, he always told me that I wanted a little of his pluck, and that he wouldn't have stood it himself; which I felt he intended for encouragement, and considered to be very kind of him. There was one advantage, and only one that I knew of, in Mr. Creakle's severity. He found my placard in his way, when he came up or down behind the form on which I sat, and wanted to make a cut at me in passing; for this reason it was soon taken off, and I saw it no more.

An accidental circumstance cemented the intimacy between Steerforth and me, in a manner that inspired me with great pride and satisfaction, though it sometimes led to inconvenience. It happened on one occasion, when he was doing me the honor of talking to me in the playground, that I hazarded the observation that something or somebody—I forget what now—was like something or somebody in Peregrine Pickle. He said nothing at the time; but when I was going to bed at night, asked me if I had got that book.

I told him no, and explained how it was that I had read it, and all those other books of which I have made mention.

"And do you recollect them?" Steerforth said.

"Oh yes," I replied; "I had a good memory, and I believed I recollected them very well."

"Then I tell you what, young Copperfield," said Steerforth, "you shall tell 'em to me. I can't get to sleep very early at night, and I generally wake rather early in the morning. We'll go over 'em one after another. We'll make some regular Arabian Nights of it."

I felt extremely flattered by this arrangement, and we commenced carrying it into execution that very evening. What ravages I committed on my favorite authors in the course of my interpretation of them, I am not in a condition to say, and should be very unwilling to know; but I had a profound faith in them, and I had, to the best of my belief, a simple, earnest manner of narrating what I did narrate; and these qualities went a long way.

The drawback was, that I was often sleepy at night, or out of spirits and indisposed to resume the story; and then it was rather hard work, and it must be done; for to disappoint or displease Steerforth was of course out of the question. In the morning, too, when I felt weary and should have enjoyed another hour's repose very much, it was a tiresome thing to be roused, like the Sultana Scheherazade, and forced into a long story before the getting-up bell rang; but Steerforth was resolute; and as he explained to me, in return, my sums and exercises, and anything in my tasks that was too hard for me, I was no loser by the transaction. Let me do myself justice, however. I was moved by no interested or selfish motive, nor was I moved by fear of him. I admired and loved him, and his approval was return enough. It was so precious to me that I look back on these trifles, now, with an aching heart.

Steerforth was considerate, too; and showed his consideration, in one particular instance, in an unflinching manner that was a little tantalising, I suspect, to poor Traddles and the rest. Peggotty's promised letter—what a comfortable letter it was!—arrived before "the half" was many weeks old; and with it a cake in a perfect nest of oranges, and two bottles of cowslip wine. This treasure, as in duty bound, I laid at the feet of Steerforth, and begged him to dispense.

"Now, I'll tell you what, young Copperfield," said he: "the wine shall be kept to wet your whistle when you are story-telling."

I blushed at the idea, and begged him, in my modesty, not to think of it. But he said he had observed I was sometimes hoarse—a little roopy was his exact expression—and it should be, every drop, devoted to the purpose he had mentioned. Accordingly, it was locked up in his box, and drawn off by himself in a phial, and administered to me through a piece of quill in the cork, when I was supposed to be in want of a restorative. Sometimes, to make it a more sovereign specific, he was so kind as to squeeze orange juice into it, or to stir it up with ginger, or dissolve a peppermint drop in it; and although I cannot assert that the flavour was improved by these experiments, or that it was exactly the compound one would have chosen for a stomachic, the last thing at night and the first thing in the morning, I drank it gratefully and was very sensible of his attention.

We seem, to me, to have been months over Peregrine, and months more over the other stories. The institution never flagged for want of a story, I am certain; and the wine lasted out almost as well as the matter. Poor Traddles—I never think of that boy but with a strange disposition to laugh, and with tears in my eyes—was a sort of chorus, in general; and affected to be convulsed with mirth at the comic parts, and to be overcome with fear when there was any passage of an alarming character in the narrative. This rather put me out, very often. It was a great jest of his, I recollect, to pretend that he couldn't keep his teeth from chattering, whenever mention was made of an Alguazil in connexion with the adventures of Gil Blas; and I remember, when Gil Blas met the captain of the robbers in Madrid, this unlucky joker counterfeited such an ague of terror, that he was overheard by Mr. Creakle, who was prowling about the passage, and handsomely flogged for disorderly conduct in the bedroom.

Whatever I had within me that was romantic and dreamy, was encouraged by so much story-telling in the dark; and in that respect the pursuit may not have been very profitable to me. But the being cherished as a kind of plaything in my room, and the consciousness that this accomplishment of mine was bruited about among the boys, and attracted a good deal of notice to me though

I was the youngest there, stimulated me to exertion. In a school carried on by sheer cruelty, whether it is presided over by a dunce or not, there is not likely to be much learnt. I believe our boys were, generally, as ignorant a set as any schoolboys in existence; they were too much troubled and knocked about to learn; they could no more do that to advantage, than any one can do anything to advantage in a life of constant misfortune, torment, and worry. But my little vanity, and Steerforth's help, urged me on somehow; and without saving me from much, if anything, in the way of punishment, made me, for the time I was there, an exception to the general body, insomuch that I did steadily pick up some crumbs of knowledge.

In this I was much assisted by Mr. Mell, who had a liking for me that I am grateful to remember. It always gave me pain to observe that Steerforth treated him with systematic disparagement, and seldom lost an occasion of wounding his feelings, or inducing others to do so. This troubled me the more for a long time, because I had soon told Steerforth, from whom I could no more keep such a secret than I could keep a cake or any other tangible possession, about the two old women Mr. Mell had taken me to see; and I was always afraid that Steerforth would let it out, and twit him with it.

We little thought any one of us, I dare say, when I ate my breakfast that first morning, and went to sleep under the shadow of the peacock's feathers to the sound of the flute, what consequences would come of the introduction into those alms-houses of my insignificant person. But the visit had its unforeseen consequences; and of a serious sort, too, in their way.

One day when Mr. Creakle kept the house from indisposition, which naturally diffused a lively joy through the school, there was a good deal of noise in the course of the morning's work. The great relief and satisfaction experienced by the boys made them difficult to manage; and though the dreaded Tungay brought his wooden leg in twice or thrice, and took notes of the principal offenders' names, no great impression was made by it, as they were pretty sure of getting into trouble to-morrow do what they would, and thought it wise, no doubt, to enjoy themselves to-day.

It was, properly, a half-holiday; being Saturday. But as the noise in the playground would have disturbed Mr. Creakle, and the weather was not favorable for going out walking, we were ordered into school in the afternoon, and set some lighter tasks than usual, which were made for the occasion. It was the day of the week on which Mr. Sharp went out to get his wig curled; so Mr. Mell, who always did the drudgery, whatever it was, kept school by himself.

If I could associate the idea of a bull or a bear with any one so mild as Mr. Mell, I should think of him, in connexion with that afternoon when the uproar was at its height, as one of those animals, baited by a thousand dogs. I recall him bending his aching head, supported on his bony hand, over the book on his desk, and wretchedly endeavoring to get on with his tiresome work, amidst an uproar that might have made the Speaker of the House of Commons giddy. Boys started in and out of their places, playing at puss in the corner with other boys; there were laughing boys, singing boys, talking boys, dancing boys, howling boys; boys shuffled with their feet, boys whirled about him, grinning, making faces, mimicking him behind his back and before his eyes; mimicking his poverty, his boots, his coat, his mother, everything belonging to him that they should have had consideration for.

"Silence!" cried Mr. Mell, suddenly rising up, and striking his desk with the book. "What does this mean! It's impossible to bear it. It's maddening. How can you do it to me, boys?"

It was my book that he struck his desk with; and as I stood beside him, following his eye as it glanced round the room, I saw the boys all stop, some suddenly surprised, some half afraid, and some sorry perhaps.

Steerforth's place was at the bottom of the school, at the opposite end of the long room. He was lounging with his back against the wall, and his hands in his pockets, and looked at Mr. Mell with his mouth shut up as if he were whistling, when Mr. Mell looked at him.

"Silence, Mr. Steerforth!" said Mr. Mell.

"Silence yourself," said Steerforth, turning red. "Whom are you talking to?"

"Sit down," said Mr. Mell.

"Sit down yourself," said Steerforth, "and mind your business."

There was a titter, and some applause; but Mr. Mell was so

STEERFORTH AND MR. MELL.

white, that silence immediately succeeded; and one boy, who had darted out behind him to imitate his mother again, changed his mind, and pretended to want a pen mended.

"If you think, Steerforth," said Mr. Mell, "that I am not acquainted with the power you can establish over any mind here"—he laid his hand, without considering what he did (as I supposed), upon my head—"or that I have not observed you, within a few minutes, urging your juniors on to every sort of outrage against me, you are mistaken."

"I don't give myself the trouble of thinking at all about you," said Steerforth, coolly; "so I'm not mistaken, as it happens."

"And when you make use of your position of favoritism here, sir," pursued Mr. Mell, with his lip trembling very much, "to insult a gentleman—"

"A what?—where is he?" said Steerforth.

Here somebody cried out, "Shame, J. Steerforth! Too bad!" It was Traddles; whom Mr. Mell instantly discomfited by bidding him hold his tongue.

—"To insult one who is not fortunate in life, sir, and who never gave you the least offence, and the many reasons for not insulting whom you are old enough and wise enough to understand," said Mr. Mell, with his lip trembling more and more, "you commit a mean and base action. You can sit down or stand up as you please, sir. Copperfield, go on."

"Young Copperfield," said Steerforth, coming forward up the room, "stop a bit. I tell you what, Mr. Mell, once for all. When you take the liberty of calling me mean or base, or anything of that sort, you are an impudent beggar. You are always a beggar, you know; but when you do that, you are an impudent beggar."

I am not clear whether he was going to strike Mr. Mell, or Mr. Mell was going to strike him, or there was any such intention on either side. I saw a rigidity come upon the whole school as if they had been turned into stone, and found Mr. Creakle in the midst of us, with Tungay at his side, and Mrs. and Miss Creakle looking in at the door as if they were frightened. Mr. Mell, with his elbows on his desk and his face in his hands, sat, for some moments, quite still.

"Mr. Mell," said Mr. Creakle, shaking him by the arm; and his whisper was so audible now, that Tungay felt it unnecessary to repeat his words; "you have not forgotten yourself, I hope?"

"No, sir, no," returned the Master, showing his face, and shaking his head, and rubbing his hands in great agitation. "No, sir. No. I have remembered myself, I—no, Mr. Creakle, I have not forgotten myself, I—I have remembered myself, sir. I—I—could wish you had remembered me a little sooner, Mr. Creakle. It—it would have been more kind, sir, more just, sir. It would have saved me something, sir."

Mr. Creakle, looking hard at Mr. Mell, put his hand on Tungay's shoulder, and got his feet upon the form close by, and sat upon the desk. After still looking hard at Mr. Mell from his throne, as he shook his head, and rubbed his hands, and remained in the same state of agitation, Mr. Creakle turned to Mr. Steerforth, and said:

"Now, sir, as he don't condescend to tell me, what *is* this?"

Steerforth evaded the question for a little while; looking in scorn and anger on his opponent, and remaining silent. I could not help thinking even in that interval, I remember, what a noble fellow he was in appearance, and how homely and plain Mr. Mell looked opposed to him.

"What did he mean by talking about favorites, then!" said Steerforth at length.

"Favorites?" repeated Mr. Creakle, with the veins in his forehead swelling quickly. "Who talked about favorites?"

"He did," said Steerforth.

"And pray, what did you mean by that, sir?" demanded Mr. Creakle, turning angrily on his assistant.

"I meant, Mr. Creakle," he returned in a low voice, "as I said; that no pupil had a right to avail himself of his position of favoritism to degrade me."

"To degrade *you?*" said Mr. Creakle. "My stars! But give me leave to ask you, Mr. What's-your-name;" and here Mr. Creakle folded his arms, cane and all, upon his chest, and made such a knot of his brows that his little eyes were hardly visible below them; "whether, when you talked about favorites, you showed proper respect to me? To me, sir," said Mr. Creakle, darting his head at him suddenly, and drawing it back again, "the principal of this establishment, and your employer."

"It was not judicious, sir, I am willing to admit," said Mr. Mell. "I should not have done so, if I had been cool."

Here Steerforth struck in.

"Then he said I was mean, and then he said I was base, and then I called him a beggar. If *I* had been cool perhaps I shouldn't have called him a beggar. But I did, and I am ready to take the consequences of it."

Without considering, perhaps, whether there were any consequences to be taken, I felt quite in a glow at this gallant speech. It made an impression on the boys too, for there was a low stir among them, though no one spoke a word.

"I am surprised, Steerforth—although your candor does you honor," said Mr. Creakle, "does you honor, certainly—I am surprised, Steerforth, I must say, that you should attach such an epithet to any person employed and paid in Salem House, sir."

Steerforth gave a short laugh.

"That's not an answer, sir," said Mr. Creakle, "to my remark. I expect more than that from you, Steerforth."

If Mr. Mell looked homely, in my eyes, before the handsome boy, it would be quite impossible to say how homely Mr. Creakle looked.

"Let him deny it," said Steerforth.

"Deny that he is a beggar, Steerforth?" cried Mr. Creakle. "Why, where does he go a begging?"

"If he is not a beggar himself, his near relation's one," said Steerforth. "It's all the same."

He glanced at me, and Mr. Mell's hand gently patted me upon the shoulder. I looked up, with a flush upon my face and remorse in my heart, but Mr. Mell's eyes were fixed on Steerforth. He continued to pat me kindly on the shoulder, but he looked at him.

"Since you expect me, Mr. Creakle, to justify myself," said Steerforth, "and to say what I mean,—what I have to say is, that his mother lives on charity in an alms-house."

Mr. Mell still looked at him, and still patted me kindly on the shoulder, and said to himself, in a whisper, if I heard right: "Yes, I thought so."

Mr. Creakle turned to his assistant, with a severe frown and labored politeness.

"Now, you hear what this gentleman says, Mr Mell. Have the

goodness, if you please, to set him right before the assembled school."

"He is right, sir, without correction," returned Mr. Mell, in the midst of a dead silence; "what he has said, is true."

"Be so good then as declare publicly, will you," said Mr. Creakle, putting his head on one side, and rolling his eyes round the school, "whether it ever came to my knowledge until this moment?"

"I believe not directly," he returned.

"Why, you know not," said Mr. Creakle. "Don't you, man?"

"I apprehend you never supposed my worldly circumstances to be very good," replied the assistant. "You know what my position is, and always has been, here."

"I apprehend, if you come to that," said Mr. Creakle, with his veins swelling again bigger than ever, "that you've been in a wrong position altogether, and mistook this for a charity school. Mr. Mell, we'll part if you please. The sooner the better."

"There is no time," answered Mr. Mell, rising, "like the present."

"Sir, to you!" said Mr. Creakle.

"I take my leave of you. Mr. Creakle, and of all of you," said Mr. Mell, glancing round the room, and again patting me gently on the shoulder. "James Steerforth, the best wish I can leave you is that you may come to be ashamed of what you have done to-day. At present I would prefer to see you anything rather than a friend, to me, or to any one in whom I feel an interest."

Once more he laid his hand upon my shoulder, and then taking his flute and a few books from his desk, and leaving the key in it for his successor, he went out of the school, with his property under his arm. Mr. Creakle then made a speech, through Tungay, in which he thanked Steerforth for asserting (though perhaps too warmly) the independence and respectability of Salem House; and which he wound up by shaking hands with Steerforth, while we gave three cheers—I did not quite know what for, but I supposed for Steerforth, and so joined in them ardently, though I felt miserable. Mr. Creakle then caned Tommy Traddles for being discovered in tears, instead of cheers, on account of Mr. Mell's departure; and went back to his sofa, or his bed, or wherever he had come from.

We were left to ourselves now, and looked very blank, I recollect, on one another. For myself, I felt so much self-reproach and contrition for my part in what had happened, that nothing would have enabled me to keep back my tears but the fear that Steerforth, who often looked at me, I saw, might think it unfriendly—or, I should rather say, considering our relative ages, and the feeling with which I regarded him, undutiful—if I showed the emotion which distressed me. He was very angry with Traddles, and said he was glad he had caught it.

Poor Traddles, who had passed the stage of lying with his head upon the desk, and was relieving himself as usual with a burst of skeletons, said he didn't care. Mr. Mell was ill-used.

"Who has ill-used him, you girl?" said Steerforth.

"Why, you have," returned Traddles.

"What have I done?" said Steerforth.

"What have you done?" retorted Traddles. "Hurt his feelings and lost him his situation."

"His feelings!" repeated Steerforth disdainfully. "His feelings will soon get the better of it, I'll be bound. His feelings are not like yours, Miss Traddles. As to his situation—which was a precious one, wasn't it?—do you suppose I am not going to write home, and take care that he gets some money? Polly?"

We thought this intention very noble in Steerforth, whose mother was a widow, and rich, and would do almost anything, it was said, that he asked her. We were all extremely glad to see Traddles so put down, and exalted Steerforth to the skies: especially when he told us, as he condescended to do, that what he had done had been done expressly for us, and for our cause; and that he had conferred a great boon upon us by unselfishly doing it.

But I must say that when I was going on with a story in the dark that night, Mr. Mell's old flute seemed more than once to sound mournfully in my ears; and that when at last Steerforth was tired, and I lay down in my bed, I fancied it playing so sorrowfully somewhere, that I was quite wretched.

I soon forgot him in the contemplation of Steerforth, who, in an easy amateur way, and without any book (he seemed to me to know everything by heart), took some of his classes until a new master was found. The new master came from a grammar-school; and before he entered on his duties, dined in the parlor one day to be introduced to Steerforth. Steerforth approved of him highly, and told us he was a Brick. Without exactly understanding what learned distinction was meant by this, I respected him greatly for it, and had no doubt whatever of his superior knowledge: though he never took the pains with me—not that I was anybody—that Mr. Mell had taken.

There was only one other event in this half-year, out of the daily school-life, that made an impression on me which still survives. It survives for many reasons.

One afternoon when we were all harassed into a state of dire confusion, and Mr. Creakle was laying about him dreadfully, Tungay came in, and called out in his usual strong way: "Visitors for Copperfield!"

A few words were interchanged between him and Mr. Creakle, as, who the visitors were, and what room they were to be shown into; and then I, who had, according to custom, stood up on the announcement being made, and felt quite faint with astonishment, was told to go by the back stairs and get a clean frill on, before I repaired to the dining-room. These orders I obeyed, in such a flutter and hurry of my young spirits as I had never known before; and when I got to the parlor-door, and the thought came into my head that it might be my mother—I had only thought of Mr. or Miss Murdstone until then—I drew back my hand from the lock, and stopped to have a sob before I went in.

At first I saw nobody; but feeling a pressure against the door, I looked round it, and there, to my amazement, were Mr. Peggotty and Ham, ducking at me with their hats, and squeezing one another against the wall. I could not help laughing; but it was much more in the pleasure of seeing them, than at the appearance they made. We shook hands in a very cordial way; and I laughed and laughed, until I pulled out my pocket-handkerchief and wiped my eyes.

Mr. Peggotty (who never shut his mouth once, I remember, during the visit) showed great concern when he saw me do this, and nudged Ham to say something.

"Cheer up, Mas'r Davy, bo'!" said Ham, in his simpering way. "Why, how you have growed!"

"Am I grown?" I said, drying my eyes. I was not crying at anything particular that I know of; but somehow it made me cry to see old friends.

"Growed, Mas'r Davy, bo'? Ain't he growed?" said Ham.

"Ain't he growed!" said Mr. Peggotty.

They made me laugh again by laughing at each other, and then we all three laughed until I was in danger of crying again.

"Do you know how mama is, Mr. Peggotty?" I said. "And how my dear, dear, old Peggotty is?"

"Oncommon," said Mr. Peggotty.

"And little Em'ly, and Mrs. Gummidge?"

"On—common," said Mr. Peggotty.

There was a silence. Mr. Peggotty, to relieve it, took two prodigious lobsters, and an enormous crab, and a large canvas bag of shrimps, out of his pockets, and piled them up in Ham's arms.

"You see," said Mr. Peggotty, "knowing as you was partial to a little relish with your wittles when you was along with us, we took the liberty. The old Mawther biled 'em, she did. Mrs. Gummidge biled 'em. Yes," said Mr. Peggotty slowly, who I thought appeared to stick to the subject on account of having no other subject ready, "Mrs. Gummidge, I do assure you, she biled 'em."

I expressed my thanks; and Mr. Peggotty, after looking at Ham, who stood smiling sheepishly over the shell-fish, without making any attempt to help him, said:

"We come, you see, the wind and tide making in our favour, in one of our Yarmouth lugs to Gravesen'. My sister she wrote to me the name of this here place, and wrote to me as if ever I chanced to come to Gravesen', I was to come over and enquire for Mas'r Davy and give her dooty, humbly wishing him well and reporting of the fam'ly as they was oncommon to-be-sure. Little Em'ly, you see, she'll write to my sister when I go back, as I see you and as you was similarly oncommon, and so we make it quite a merry-go-rounder."

I was obliged to consider a little before I understood what Mr. Peggotty meant by this figure, expressive of a complete circle of intelligence. I then thanked him heartily; and said, with a consciousness of reddening, that I supposed little Em'ly was altered too, since we used to pick up shells and pebbles on the beach?

"She's getting to be a woman, that's wot's she's getting to be," said Mr. Peggotty. "Ask him."

He meant Ham, who beamed with delight and assent over the bag of shrimps.

"Her pretty face!" said Mr. Peggotty, with his own shining like a light.

"Her learning!" said Ham.

"Her writing!" said Mr. Peggotty. "Why, it's as black as jet! And so large it is, you might see it anywheres."

It was perfectly delightful to behold with what enthusiasm Mr. Peggotty became inspired when he thought of his little favorite. He stands before me again, his bluff hairy face irradiating with a joyful love and pride, for which I can find no description. His honest eyes fire up, and sparkle, as if their depths were stirred by something bright. His broad chest heaves with pleasure. His strong loose hands clench themselves, in his earnestness; and he emphasises what he says with a right arm that shows, in my pigmy view, like a sledge hammer.

Ham was quite as earnest as he. I dare say they would have said much more about her, if they had not been abashed by the unexpected coming in of Steerforth, who, seeing me in a corner speaking with two strangers, stopped in a song he was singing, and said: "I didn't know you were here, young Copperfield!" (for it was not the usual visiting room), and crossed by us on his way out.

I am not sure whether it was in the pride of having such a friend as Steerforth, or in the desire to explain to him how I came to have such a friend as Mr. Peggotty, that I called to him as he was going away. But I said, modestly—Good Heaven, how it all comes back to me this long time afterwards!—

"Don't go, Steerforth, if you please. These are two Yarmouth boatmen—very kind, good people—who are relations of my nurse, and have come from Gravesend to see me."

"Aye, aye?" said Steerforth, returning. "I am glad to see them. How are ye both?"

There was an ease in his manner—a gay and light manner it was, but not swaggering—which I still believe to have borne a kind of enchantment with it. I still believe him, in virtue of this carriage, his animal spirits, his delightful voice, his handsome face and figure, and, for aught I know, of some inborn power of attraction besides (which I think a few people possess), to have carried a spell with him to which it was a natural weakness to yield, and which not many persons could withstand. I could not but see how pleased they were with him, and how they seemed to open their hearts to him in a moment.

"You must let them know at home, if you please, Mr. Peggotty," I said, "when that letter is sent, that Mr. Steerforth is very kind to me, and that I don't know what I should ever do here without him."

"Nonsense!" said Steerforth, laughing, "You mustn't tell them anything of the sort."

"And if Mr. Steerforth ever comes into Norfolk or Suffolk, Mr. Peggotty," I said, "while I am there, you may depend upon it I shall bring him to Yarmouth, if he will let me, to see your house. You never saw such a good house, Steerforth. It's made out of a boat."

"Made out of a boat, is it?" said Steerforth. "It's the right sort of house for such a thorough-built boatman."

"So 'tis, sir, so 'tis, sir," said Ham, grinning. "You're right, young gen'lm'n. Mas'r Davy bo', gen'lm'n's right. A thorough-built boatman! Hor, hor! That's what he is, too!"

Mr. Peggotty was no less pleased than his nephew, though his modesty forbade him to claim a personal compliment so vociferously.

"Well, sir," he said, bowing and chuckling, and tucking in the ends of his neckerchief at his breast, "I thankee, sir, I thankee! I do my endeavours in my line of life, sir."

"The best of men can do no more, Mr. Peggotty," said Steerforth. He had got his name already.

"I'll pound it, it's wot you do yourself, sir," said Mr. Peggotty, shaking his head, "and wot you do well—right well! I thankee, sir. I'm obleeged to you, sir, for your welcoming manner of me. I'm rough, sir, but I'm ready—least ways, I *hope*, I'm ready, you understand. My house ain't much for to see, sir, but it's hearty at your service if ever you should come along with Mas'r Davy to see it. I'm a reg'lar Dodman, I am," said Mr. Peggotty; by which he meant snail, and this was in allusion to his being slow to go, for he had attempted to go after every sentence, and had somehow or other come back again; "but I wish you both well, and I wish you happy!"

Ham echoed this sentiment, and we parted with them in the heartiest manner. I was almost tempted that evening to tell Steerforth about pretty Em'ly, but I was too timid of mentioning her name, and too much afraid of his laughing at me. I remember that I thought a good deal, and in an uneasy sort of way, about Mr. Peggotty having said that she was getting on to be a woman; but I decided that was nonsense.

We transported the shell-fish, or the "relish" as Mr. Peggotty modestly called it, up into our room unobserved, and made a great supper that evening. But Traddles couldn't get happily out of it. He was too unfortunate even to come through a supper like anybody else. He was taken ill in the night—quite prostrate he was—in consequence of Crab; and after being drugged with black draughts and blue pills, to an extent which Demple (whose father was a doctor) said was enough to undermine a horse's constitution, received a caning and six chapters of Greek Testament for refusing to confess.

The rest of the half-year is a jumble in my recollection of the daily strife and struggle of our lives; of the waning summer and the changing season; of the frosty mornings when we were rung out of bed, and the cold, cold smell of the dark nights when we were rung into bed again; of the evening schoolroom dimly lighted and indifferently warmed, and the morning schoolroom which was nothing but a great shivering-machine; of the alternation of boiled beef with roast beef, and boiled mutton with roast mutton; of clods of bread-and-butter, dog's-eared lesson-books, cracked slates, tear-blotted copy-books, canings, rulerings, hair-cuttings, rainy Sundays, suet puddings, and a dirty atmosphere of ink surrounding all.

I well remember though, how the distant idea of the holidays, after seeming for an immense time to be a stationary speck, began to come towards us, and to grow and grow. How, from counting months, we came to weeks, and then to days; and how I then began to be afraid that I should not be sent for, and, when I learned from Steerforth that I *had* been sent for and was certainly to go home, had dim forebodings that I might break my leg first. How the breaking-up day changed its place fast, at last, from the week after next to next week, this week, the day after to-morrow, to-morrow, to-day, to-night—when I was inside the Yarmouth mail, and going home.

I had many a broken sleep inside the Yarmouth mail, and many an incoherent dream of all these things. But when I awoke at intervals, the ground outside the window was not the playground of Salem House, and the sound in my ears was not the sound of Mr. Creakle giving it to Traddles, but the sound of the coachman touching up the horses.

CHAPTER VIII.

MY HOLIDAYS. ESPECIALLY ONE HAPPY AFTERNOON.

When we arrived before day at the inn where the mail stopped, which was not the inn where my friend the waiter lived, I was shown up to a nice little bedroom, with Dolphin painted on the door. Very cold I was I know, notwithstanding the hot tea they had given me before a large fire down-stairs; and very glad I was to turn into the Dolphin's bed, pull the Dolphin's blankets round my head, and go to sleep.

Mr. Barkis the carrier was to call for me in the morning at nine o'clock. I got up at eight, a little giddy from the shortness of my night's rest, and was ready for him before the appointed time. He received me exactly as if not five minutes had elapsed since we were last together, and I had only been into the hotel to get change for sixpence, or something of that sort.

As soon as I and my box were in the cart, and the carrier seated, the lazy horse walked away with us all at his accustomed pace.

"You look very well, Mr. Barkis," I said, thinking he would like to know it.

Mr. Barkis rubbed his cheek with his cuff, and then looked at his cuff as if he expected to find some of the bloom upon it; but made no other acknowledgment of the compliment.

"I gave your message, Mr. Barkis," I said; "I wrote to Peggotty."

"Ah!" said Mr. Barkis.

Mr. Barkis seemed gruff, and answered drily.

"Wasn't it right, Mr. Barkis?" I asked, after a little hesitation.

"Why, no," said Mr. Barkis.

"Not the message?"

"The message was right enough, perhaps," said Mr. Barkis; "but it come to an end there."

Not understanding what he meant, I repeated inquisitively: "Came to an end, Mr. Barkis?"

"Nothing come of it,' he explained, looking at me sideways. "No answer."

"There was an answer expected, was there, Mr. Barkis?" said I, opening my eyes. For this was a new light to me.

"When a man says he's willin'," said Mr. Barkis, turning his glance slowly on me again, "it's as much as to say, that man's a waitin' for a answer."

"Well, Mr. Barkis?"

"Well," said Mr. Barkis, carrying his eyes back to his horse's ears; "that man's been a waitin' for a answer ever since."

"Have you told her so, Mr. Barkis?"

"N—no," growled Mr. Barkis, reflecting about it. "I ain't got no call to go and tell her so. I never said six words to her myself. *I* ain't a goin' to tell her so."

"Would you like me to do it, Mr. Barkis?" said I, doubtfully.

"You might tell her if you would," said Mr. Barkis, with another slow look at me, "that Barkis was a waitin' for a answer. Says you —what name is it?"

"Her name?"

"Ah!" said Mr. Barkis, with a nod of his head.

"Peggotty."

"Chrisen name? Or nat'ral name?" said Mr. Barkis.

"Oh, it's not her christian name. Her christian name is Clara."

"Is it though!" said Mr. Barkis.

He seemed to find an immense fund of reflection in this circumstance, and sat pondering and inwardly whistling for some time.

"Well!" he resumed at length. "Says you, 'Peggotty! Barkis is a waitin' for a answer.' Says she, perhaps, 'Answer to what?' Says you, 'To what I told you.' 'What is that?' says she. 'Barkis is willin',' says you."

This extremely artful suggestion, Mr. Barkis accompanied with a nudge of his elbow that gave me quite a stitch in my side. After that, he slouched over his horse in his usual manner; and made no other reference to the subject except, half an hour afterwards, taking a piece of chalk from his pocket, and writing up, inside the tilt of the cart, "Clara Peggotty" —apparently as a private memorandum.

Ah, wnat a strange feeling it was to be going home when it was not home, and to find that every object I looked at, reminded me of the happy old home, which was like a dream I could never dream again! The days when my mother and I and Peggotty were all in all to one another, and there was no one to come between us, rose up before me so sorrowfully on the road, that I am not sure I was glad to be there—not sure but that I would rather have remained away, and forgotten it in Steerforth's company. But there I was; and soon I was at our house, where the bare old elm trees wrung their many hands in the bleak wintry air, and shreds of the old rooks' nests drifted away upon the wind.

The carrier put my box down at the garden gate, and left me. I walked along the path towards the house, glancing at the windows, and fearing at every step to see Mr. Murdstone or Miss Murdstone lowering out of one of them. No face appeared, however; and being come to the house, and knowing how to open the door, before dark, without knocking, I went in with a quiet, timid step.

God knows how infantine the memory may have been, that was awakened within me by the sound of my mother's voice in the old parlor, when I set foot in the hall. She was singing in a low tone. I think I must have lain in her arms, and heard her singing so to me when I was but a baby. The strain was new to me, and yet it was so old that it filled my heart brim-full; like a friend come back from a long absence.

I believed, from the solitary and thoughtful way in which my mother murmured her song, that she was alone. And I went softly into the room. She was sitting by the fire, suckling an infant, whose tiny hand she held against her neck. Her eyes were looking down upon its face, and she sat singing to it. I was so far right, that she had no other companion.

I spoke to her, and she started, and cried out. But seeing me, she called me her dear Davy, her own boy! and coming half across the room to meet me, kneeled down upon the ground and kissed me, and laid my head down on her bosom near the little creature that was nestling there, and put its hand up to my lips.

I wish I had died. I wish I had died then, with that feeling in my heart! I should have been more fit for Heaven than I ever have been since.

"He is your brother," said my mother, fondling me. "Davy, my pretty boy! My poor child!" Then she kissed me more and more,

CHANGES AT HOME.

and clasped me round the neck. This she was doing when Peggotty came running in, and bounced down on the ground beside us. and went mad about us both for a quarter of an hour.

It seemed that I had not been expected so soon, the carrier being much before his usual time. It seemed, too, that Mr. and Miss Murdstone had gone out upon a visit in the neighbourhood, and would not return before night. I had never hoped for this. I had never thought it possible that we three could be together undisturbed, once more; and I felt, for the time, as if the old days were come back.

We dined together by the fireside. Peggotty was in attendance to wait upon us, but my mother wouldn't let her do it, and made her dine with us. I had my own old plate, with a brown view of a man-of-war in full sail upon it, which Peggotty had hoarded somewhere all the time I had been away, and would not have had broken, she said, for a hundred pounds. I had my own old mug with David on it, and my own old little knife and fork that wouldn't cut.

While we were at table, I thought it a favorable occasion to tell Peggotty about Mr. Barkis, who, before I had finished what I had to tell her, began to laugh, and threw her apron over her face.

"Peggotty!" said my mother. "What's the matter?"

Peggotty only laughed the more, and held her apron tight over her face when my mother tried to pull it away, and sat as if her head were in a bag.

"What are you doing, you stupid creature?" said my mother, laughing.

"O, drat the man!" cried Peggotty. "He wants to marry me."

"It would be a very good match for you; wouldn't it?" said my mother.

"Oh! I don't know," said Peggotty. "Don't ask me. I wouldn't have him if he was made of gold. Nor I wouldn't have anybody."

"Then, why don't you tell him so, you ridiculous thing?" said my mother.

"Tell him so," retorted Peggotty, looking out of her apron. "He has never said a word to me about it. He knows better. If he was to make so bold as say a word to me, I should slap his face."

Her own was as red as ever I saw it, or any other face, I think; but she only covered it again, for a few moments at a time, when she was taken with a violent fit of laughter; and after two or three of those attacks, went on with her dinner.

I remarked that my mother, though she smiled when Peggotty looked at her, became more serious and thoughtful. I had seen at first that she was changed. Her face was very pretty still, but it looked careworn, and too delicate; and her hand was so thin and white that it seemed to me to be almost transparent. But the change to which I now refer was superadded to this: it was in her manner, which became anxious and fluttered. At last she said, putting out her hand, and laying it affectionately on the hand of her old servant,

"Peggotty, dear, you are not going to be married?"

"Me, ma'am?" returned Peggotty, staring. "Lord bless you, no!"

"Not just yet?" said my mother, tenderly.

"Never!" cried Peggotty.

My mother took her hand, and said:

"Don't leave me, Peggotty. Stay with me. It will not be for long, perhaps. What should I ever do without you!"

"Me leave you, my precious!" cried Peggotty. "Not for all the world and his wife. Why, what's put that in your silly little head?" —For Peggotty had been used of old to talk to my mother sometimes like a child.

But my mother made no answer, except to thank her, and Peggotty went running on in her own fashion.

"Me leave you? I think I see myself. Peggotty go away from you? I should like to catch her at it! No, no, no," said Peggotty, shaking her head, and folding her arms; "not she, my dear. It isn't that there ain't some Cats that would be well enough pleased if she did, but they shan't be pleased. They shall be aggravated. I'll stay with you till I am a cross cranky old woman. And when I'm too deaf, and too lame, and too blind, and too mumbly for want of teeth, to be of any use at all, even to be found fault with, then I shall go to my Davy, and ask him to take me in."

"And Peggotty," says I, "I shall be glad to see you, and I'll make you as welcome as a queen."

"Bless your dear heart!" cried Peggotty. "I know you will!" And she kissed me beforehand, in grateful acknowledgment of my hospitality. After that, she covered her head up with her apron again, and had another laugh about Mr. Barkis. After that, she took the baby out of its little cradle, and nursed it. After that, she cleared the dinner-table; after that, she came in with another cap on, and her work-box, and the yard-measure, and the bit of wax candle, all just the same as ever.

We sat round the fire, and talked delightfully. I told them what a hard master Mr. Creakle was, and they pitied me very much. I told them what a fine fellow Steerforth was, and what a patron of mine, and Peggotty said she would walk a score of miles to see him. I took the little baby in my arms when it was awake, and nursed it lovingly. When it was asleep again, I crept close to my mother's side according to my old custom, broken now a long time, and sat with my arms embracing her waist, and my little red cheek on her shoulder, and once more felt her beautiful hair drooping over me—like an angel's wing as I used to think, I recollect—and was very happy indeed.

While I sat thus, looking at the fire, and seeing pictures in the red-hot coals, I almost believed that I had never been away; that Mr. and Miss Murdstone were such pictures, and would vanish when the fire got low; and that there was nothing real in all that I remembered, save my mother, Peggotty, and I.

Peggotty darned away at a stocking as long as she could see, and then sat with it drawn on her left hand like a glove, and her needle in her right, ready to take another stitch whenever there was a blaze. I cannot conceive whose stockings they can have been that Peggotty was always darning, or where such an unfailing supply of stockings in want of darning can have come from. From my earliest infancy she seems to have been always employed in that class of needlework, and never by any chance in any other.

"I wonder," said Peggotty, who was sometimes seized with a fit of wondering on some most unexpected topic, "what's become of Davy's great-aunt?"

"Lor, Peggotty!" observed my mother, rousing herself from a reverie, "what nonsense you talk!"

"Well, but I really do wonder, ma'am," said Peggotty.

"What can have put such a person in your head?" inquired my mother. "Is there nobody else in the world to come there?"

"I don't know how it is," said Peggotty, "unless it's on account of being stupid, but my head never can pick and choose its people. They come and they go, and they don't come and they don't go, just as they like. I wonder what's become of her?"

"How absurd you are, Peggotty," returned my mother. "One would suppose you wanted a second visit from her."

"Lord forbid!" cried Peggotty.

"Well then, don't talk about such uncomfortable things, there's a good soul," said my mother. "Miss Betsey is shut up in her cottage by the sea, no doubt, and will remain there. At all events, she is not likely ever to trouble us again."

"No!" mused Peggotty. "No, that ain't likely at all.—I wonder, if she was to die, whether she'd leave Davy anything?"

"Good gracious me, Peggotty," returned my mother, "what a nonsensical woman you are! when you know that she took offence at the poor dear boy's ever being born at all!"

"I suppose she wouldn't be inclined to forgive him now," hinted Peggotty.

"Why should she be inclined to forgive him now?" said my mother, rather sharply.

"Now that he's got a brother, I mean," said Peggotty.

My mother immediately began to cry, and wondered how Peggotty dared to say such a thing.

"As if this poor little innocent in its cradle had ever done any harm to you or anybody else, you jealous thing!" said she. "You had much better go and marry Mr. Barkis, the carrier. Why don't you?"

"I should make Miss Murdstone happy, if I was to," said Peggotty.

"What a bad disposition you have, Peggotty!" returned my mother. "You are as jealous of Miss Murdstone as it is possible for a ridiculous creature to be. You want to keep the keys yourself, and give out all the things, I suppose? I shouldn't be surprised if you did. When you know that she only does it out of kindness and the best intentions! You know she does, Peggotty—you know it well."

Peggotty muttered something to the effect of "Bother the best intentions!" and something else to the effect that there was a little too much of the best intentions going on.

"I know what you mean, you cross thing," said my mother. "I understand you, Peggotty, perfectly. You know I do, and I wonder you don't color up like fire. But one point at a time. Miss Murdstone is the point now, Peggotty, and you shan't escape from it. Haven't you heard her say, over and over again, that she thinks I am too thoughtless and too—a—a—"

"Pretty," suggested Peggotty.

"Well," returned my mother, half laughing, "and if she is so silly as to say so, can I be blamed for it?"

"No one says you can," said Peggotty.

"No, I should hope not, indeed!" returned my mother. "Haven't you heard her say, over and over again, that on this account she wishes to spare me a great deal of trouble, which she thinks I am not suited for, and which I really don't know myself that I *am* suited for; and isn't she up early and late, and going to and fro continually—and doesn't she do all sorts of things, and grope into all sorts of places, coal-holes and pantries and I don't know where, that can't be very agreeable—and do you mean to insinuate that there is not a sort of devotion in that?"

"I don't insinuate at all," said Peggotty.

"You do, Peggotty," returned my mother. "You never do anything else, except your work. You are always insinuating. You revel in it. And when you talk of Mr. Murdstone's good intentions—"

"I never talked of 'em," said Peggotty.

"No, Peggotty," returned my mother, "but you insinuated. That's what I told you just now. That's the worst of you. You *will* insinuate. I said, at the moment, that I understood you, and you see I did. When you talk of Mr. Murdstone's good intentions, and pretend to slight them (for I don't believe you really do, in your heart, Peggotty), you must be as well convinced as I am how good they are, and how they actuate him in everything. If he seems to have been at all stern with a certain person, Peggotty—you understand, and so I am sure does Davy, that I am not alluding to anybody present—it is solely because he is satisfied that it is for a certain person's benefit. He naturally loves a certain person, on my account; and acts solely for a certain person's good. He is better able to judge of it than I am; for I very well know that I am a weak, light, girlish creature, and that he is a firm, grave, serious man. And he takes," said my mother, with the tears which were engendered in her affectionate nature, stealing down her face, "he takes great pains with me; and I ought to be very thankful to him, and very submissive to him even in my thoughts; and when I am not, Peggotty, I worry and condemn myself, and feel doubtful of my own heart, and don't know what to do."

Peggotty sat with her chin on the foot of the stocking, looking silently at the fire.

"There, Peggotty," said my mother, changing her tone, "don't let us fall out with one another, for I couldn't bear it. You are my true friend, I know, if I have any in the world. When I call you a ridiculous creature, or a vexatious thing, or anything of that sort, Peggotty, I only mean that you are my true friend, and always have been, ever since the night when Mr. Copperfield first brought me home here, and you came out to the gate to meet me."

Peggotty was not slow to respond, and ratified the treaty of friendship by giving me one of her best hugs. I think I had some glimpses of the real character of this conversation at the time; but I am sure, now, that the good creature originated it, and took her part in it, merely that my mother might comfort herself with the little contradictory summary in which she had indulged. The design was efficacious; for I remember that my mother seemed more at ease during the rest of the evening, and that Peggotty observed her less.

When we had had our tea, and the ashes were thrown up, and the candles snuffed, I read Peggotty a chapter out of the Crocodile Book, in remembrance of old times—she took it out of her pocket: I don't know whether she had kept it there ever since—and then we talked about Salem House, which brought me round again to

Steerforth, who was my great subject. We were very happy; and that evening, as the last of its race, and destined evermore to close that volume of my life, will never pass out of my memory.

It was almost ten o'clock before we heard the sound of wheels. We all got up then; and my mother said hurriedly that, as it was so late, and Mr. and Miss Murdstone approved of early hours for young people, perhaps I had better go to bed. I kissed her, and went up stairs with my candle directly, before they came in. It appeared to my childish fancy, as I ascended to the bedroom where I had been imprisoned, that they brought a cold blast of air into the house which blew away the old familiar feeling like a feather.

I felt uncomfortable about going down to breakfast in the morning, as I had never set eyes on Mr. Murdstone since the day when I committed my memorable offence. However, as it must be done, I went down, after two or three false starts half-way, and as many runs back on tip-toe to my own room, and presented myself in the parlor.

He was standing before the fire with his back to it, while Miss Murdstone made the tea. He looked at me steadily as I entered, but made no sign of recognition whatever.

I went up to him, after a moment of confusion, and said: "I beg your pardon, sir. I am very sorry for what I did, and I hope you will forgive me."

"I am glad to hear you are sorry, David," he replied.

The hand he gave me was the hand I had bitten. I could not restrain my eye from resting for an instant on a red spot upon it, but it was not so red as I turned, when I met that sinister expression in his face.

"How do you do, ma'am?" I said to Miss Murdstone.

"Ah, dear me!" sighed Miss Murdstone, giving me the tea-caddy scoop instead of her fingers. "How long are the holidays?"

"A month, ma'am."

"Counting from when?"

"From to-day, ma'am."

"Oh!" said Miss Murdstone. "Then here's *one* day off."

She kept a calendar of the holidays in this way, and every morning checked a day off in exactly the same manner. She did it gloomily until she came to ten, but when she got into two figures she became more hopeful, and, as the time advanced, even jocular.

It was on this very first day that I had the misfortune to throw her, though she was not subject to such weaknesses in general, into a state of violent consternation. I came into the room where she and my mother were sitting; and the baby (who was only a few weeks old) being on my mother's lap, I took it very carefully in my arms. Suddenly Miss Murdstone gave such a scream that I all but dropped it.

"My dear Jane!" cried my mother.

"Good heavens, Clara, do you see?" exclaimed Miss Murdstone.

"See what, my dear Jane?" said my mother; "where?"

"He 's got it!" cried Miss Murdstone. "The boy has got the baby!"

She was limp with horror; but stiffened herself to make a dart at me, and take it out of my arms. Then she turned faint; and was so very ill, that they were obliged to give her cherry-brandy. I was solemnly interdicted by her, on her recovery, from touching my brother any more on any pretence whatever; and my poor mother, who, I could see, wished otherwise, meekly confirmed the interdict, by saying: "No doubt you are right, my dear Jane."

On another occasion, when we three were together, this same dear baby—it was truly dear to me, for our mother's sake—was the innocent occasion of Miss Murdstone's going into a passion. My mother, who had been looking at its eyes as it lay upon her lap, said:

"Davy! come here!" and looked at mine.

I saw Miss Murdstone lay her beads down.

"I declare," said my mother, gently, "they are exactly alike. I suppose they are mine. I think they are the color of mine. But they are wonderfully alike."

"What are you talking about, Clara?" said Miss Murdstone.

"My dear Jane," faltered my mother, a little abashed by the harsh tone of this inquiry, "I find that the baby's eyes and Davy's are exactly alike."

"Clara!" said Miss Murdstone, rising angrily, "you are a positive fool sometimes."

"My dear Jane," remonstrated my mother.

"A positive fool," said Miss Murdstone. "Who else could compare my brother's baby with your boy? They are not at all alike. They are exactly unlike. They are utterly dissimilar in all respects. I hope they will ever remain so. I will not sit here and hear such comparisons made." With that she stalked out, and made the door bang after her.

In short, I was not a favorite with Miss Murdstone. In short, I was not a favorite there with anybody, not even with myself; for those who did like me could not show it, and those who did not, showed it so plainly that I had a sensitive consciousness of always appearing constrained, boorish, and dull.

I felt that I made them as uncomfortable as they made me. If I came into the room where they were, and they were talking together and my mother seemed cheerful, an anxious cloud would steal over her face from the moment of my entrance. If Mr. Murdstone were in his best humor, I checked him. If Miss Murdstone were in her worst, I intensified it. I had perception enough to know that my mother was the victim always; that she was afraid to speak to me or be kind to me, lest she should give them some offence by her manner of doing so, and receive a lecture afterwards; that she was not only ceaselessly afraid of her own offending, but of my offending, and uneasily watched their looks if I only moved. Therefore I resolved to keep myself as much out of their way as I could; and many a wintry hour did I hear the church-clock strike, when I was sitting in my cheerless bedroom, wrapped in my little great-coat, poring over a book.

In the evening, sometimes, I went and sat with Peggotty in the kitchen. There I was comfortable, and not afraid of being myself. But neither of these resources was approved of in the parlor. The tormenting humor which was dominant there stopped them both. I was still held to be necessary to my poor mother's training, and, as one ot her trials, could not be suffered to absent myself.

"David," said Mr. Murdstone, one day after dinner when I was going to leave the room as usual; "I am sorry to observe that you are of a sullen disposition."

"As sulky as a bear!" said Miss Murdstone.

I stood still, and hung my head.

"Now, David," said Mr. Murdstone, "a sullen obdurate disposition is, of all tempers, the worst."

"And the boy's is, of all such dispositions that ever I have seen," remarked his sister, "the most confirmed and stubborn. I think, my dear Clara, even you must observe it?"

"I beg your pardon, my dear Jane," said my mother, "but are you quite sure—I am certain you'll excuse me, my dear Jane—that you understand Davy?"

"I should be somewhat ashamed of myself, Clara," returned Miss Murdstone, "if I could not understand the boy, or any boy. I don't profess to be profound; but I do lay claim to common sense."

"No doubt, my dear Jane," returned my mother, "your understanding is very vigorous—"

"O dear, no! Pray don't say that, Clara," interposed Miss Murdstone, angrily.

"But I am sure it is," resumed my mother; "and everybody knows it is. I profit so much by it myself, in many ways—at least I ought to—that no one can be more convinced of it than myself; and therefore I speak with great diffidence, my dear Jane, I assure you."

"We'll say I don't understand the boy, Clara," returned Miss Murdstone, arranging the little fetters on her wrists. "We'll agree, if you please, that I don't understand him at all. He is much too deep for me. But perhaps my brother's penetration may enable him to have some insight into his character. And I believe my brother was speaking on the subject when we—not very decently—interrupted him."

"I think, Clara," said Mr. Murdstone, in a low, grave voice, "that there may be better and more dispassionate judges of such a question than you."

"Edward," replied my mother, timidly, "you are a far better judge of all questions than I pretend to be. Both you and Jane are. I only said—"

"You only said something weak and inconsiderate," he replied. "Try not to do it again, my dear Clara, and keep a watch upon yourself."

My mother's lips moved, as if she answered, "Yes, my dear Edward," but she said nothing aloud.

"I was sorry, David, I remarked," said Mr. Murdstone, turning his head and his eyes stiffly towards me, "to observe that you are of a sullen disposition. This is not a character that I can suffer to develop itself beneath my eyes without an effort at improvement. You must endeavour, sir, to change it. We must endeavour to change it for you."

"I beg your pardon, sir," I faltered. "I have never meant to be sullen since I came back."

"Don't take refuge in a lie, sir!" he returned so fiercely, that I saw my mother involuntarily put out her trembling hand as if to interpose between us. "You have withdrawn yourself in your sullenness to your own room. You have kept your own room when you ought to have been here. You know now, once for all, that I require you to be here, and not there. Further, that I require you to bring obedience here. You know me, David. I will have it done."

Miss Murdstone gave a hoarse chuckle.

"I will have a respectful, prompt, and ready bearing towards myself," he continued, "and towards Jane Murdstone, and towards your mother. I will not have this room shunned as if it were infected, at the pleasure of a child. Sit down."

He ordered me like a dog, and I obeyed like a dog.

"One thing more," he said. "I observe that you have an attachment to low and common company. You are not to associate with servants. The kitchen will not improve you, in the many respects in which you need improvement. Of the woman who abets you, I say nothing—since you, Clara," addressing my mother in a lower voice, "from old associations and long-established fancies, have a weakness respecting her which is not yet overcome."

"A most unaccountable delusion it is!" cried Miss Murdstone.

"I only say," he resumed, addressing me, "that I disapprove of your preferring such company as Mistress Peggotty, and that it is to be abandoned. Now, David, you understand me, and you know what will be the consequence if you fail to obey me to the letter."

I knew well—better perhaps than he thought, as far as my poor mother was concerned—and I obeyed him to the letter. I retreated to my own room no more; I took refuge with Peggotty no more, but sat wearily in the parlor day after day, looking forward to night, and bed-time.

What irksome constraint I underwent, sitting in the same attitude hours upon hours, afraid to move an arm or a leg lest Miss Murdstone should complain (as she did on the least pretence) of my restlessness, and afraid to move an eye lest it should light on some look of dislike or scrutiny that would find new cause for complaint in mine! What intolerable dulness to sit listening to the ticking of the clock; and watching Miss Murdstone's little shiny steel beads as she strung them; and wondering whether she would ever be married, and if so, to what sort of unhappy man; and counting the divisions in the moulding on the chimney-piece; and wandering away, with my eyes, to the ceiling, among the curls and corkscrews in the paper on the wall!

What walks I took alone, down muddy lanes, in the bad winter weather, carrying that parlor, and Mr. and Miss Murdstone in it, everywhere: a monstrous load that I was obliged to bear, a daymare that there was no possibility of breaking in, a weight that brooded on my wits, and blunted them!

What meals I had in silence and embarrassment, always feeling that there were a knife and fork too many, and that mine; an appetite too many, and that mine; a plate and chair too many, and those mine; a somebody too many, and that I!

What evenings, when the candles came, and I was expected to employ myself, but, not daring to read an entertaining book, pored over some hard-headed, and harder-hearted treatise on arithmetic; when the tables of weights and measures set themselves to tunes, as Rule Britannia, or Away with Melancholy; and wouldn't stand still to be learnt, but would go threading my grandmother's needle through my unfortunate head, in at one ear and out at the other!

What yawns and dozes I lapsed into, in spite of all my care; what starts I came out of concealed sleeps with; what answers I never got, to little observations that I rarely made; what a blank space I seemed, which everybody overlooked, and yet was in everybody's way; what a heavy relief it was to hear Miss Murdstone hail the first stroke of nine at night, and order me to bed!

Thus the holidays lagged away, until the morning came when

Miss Murdstone said: "Here's the last day off!" and gave me the closing cup of tea of the vacation.

I was not sorry to go. I had lapsed into a stupid state; but I was recovering a little and looking forward to Steerforth, albeit Mr. Creakle loomed behind him. Again Mr. Barkis appeared at the gate, and again Miss Murdstone in her warning voice said: "Clara!" when my mother bent over me, to bid me farewell.

I kissed her, and my baby brother, and was very sorry then; but not sorry to go away, for the gulf between us was there, and the parting was there, every day. And it is not so much the embrace she gave me, that lives in my mind, though it was as fervent as could be, as what followed the embrace.

I was in the carrier's cart when I heard her calling to me. I looked out, and she stood at the garden-gate alone, holding her baby up in her arms for me to see. It was cold, still weather; and not a hair of her head, or a fold of her dress, was stirred, as she looked intently at me, holding up her child.

So I lost her. So I saw her afterwards, in my sleep at school—a silent presence near my bed—looking at me with the same intent face—holding up her baby in her arms.

CHAPTER IX.

I HAVE A MEMORABLE BIRTHDAY

I PASS over all that happened at school, until the anniversary of my birthday came round in March. Except that Steerforth was more to be admired than ever, I remember nothing. He was going away at the end of the half-year, if not sooner, and was more spirited and independent than before in my eyes, and therefore more engaging than before; but beyond this I remember nothing. The great remembrance by which that time is marked in my mind, seems to have swallowed up all lesser recollections, and to exist alone.

It is even difficult for me to believe that there was a gap of full two months between my return to Salem House and the arrival of that birthday. I can only understand that the fact was so, because I know it must have been so; otherwise I should feel convinced that there was no interval, and that the one occasion trod upon the other's heels.

How well I recollect the kind of day it was! I smell the fog that hung about the place; I see the hoar frost, ghostly, through it; I feel my rimy hair fall clammy on my cheek; I look along the dim perspective of the schoolroom, with a sputtering candle here and there to light up the foggy morning, and the breath of the boys wreathing and smoking in the raw cold as they blow upon their fingers, and tap their feet upon the floor.

It was after breakfast, and we had been summoned in from the play-ground, when Mr. Sharp entered and said:

"David Copperfield is to go into the parlor."

I expected a hamper from Peggotty, and brightened at the order. Some of the boys about me put in their claim not to be forgotten in the distribution of the good things, as I got out of my seat with great alacrity.

"Don't hurry, David," said Mr. Sharp. "There's time enough, my boy, don't hurry."

I might have been surprised by the feeling tone in which he spoke, if I had given it a thought; but I gave it none until afterwards. I hurried away to the parlor; and there I found Mr. Creakle sitting at his breakfast with the cane and a newspaper before him, and Mrs. Creakle with an opened letter in her hand. But no hamper.

"David Copperfield," said Mrs. Creakle, leading me to a sofa, and sitting down beside me. "I want to speak to you very particularly I have something to tell you, my child."

Mr. Creakle, at whom of course I looked, shook his head without looking at me, and stopped up a sigh with a very large piece of buttered toast.

"You are too young to know how the world changes every day," said Mrs. Creakle, "and how the people in it pass away. But we all have to learn it, David; some of us when we are young, some of us when we are old, some of us at all times of our lives."

I looked at her earnestly.

"When you came away from home at the end of the vacation," said Mrs. Creakle, after a pause, "were they all well?" And after another pause, "Was your mama well?"

I trembled without distinctly knowing why, and still looked at her earnestly, making no attempt to answer.

"Because," said she, "I grieve to tell you that I hear this morning your mama is very ill."

A mist arose between Mrs. Creakle and me, and her figure seemed to move in it for an instant. Then I felt the burning tears run down my face, and it was steady again.

"She is very dangerously ill," she added.

I knew all now.

"She is dead."

There was no need to tell me so. I had already broken out into a desolate cry, and felt an orphan in the wide world.

She was very kind to me. She kept me there all day, and left me alone sometimes; and I cried, and wore myself to sleep, and awoke and cried again. When I could cry no more, I began to think; and then the oppression on my breast was heaviest, and my grief a dull pain that there was no ease for.

And yet my thoughts were idle; not intent on the calamity that weighed upon my heart, but idly loitering near it. I thought of our house shut up and hushed. I thought of the little baby, who,

Mrs. Creakle said, had been pining away for some time, and who, they believed, would die too. I thought of my father's grave in the churchyard, by our house, and of my mother lying there beneath the tree I knew so well. I stood upon a chair when I was left alone, and looked into the glass to see how red my eyes were, and how sorrowful my face. I considered, after some hours were gone, if my tears were really hard to flow now, as they seemed to be, what, in connexion with my loss, it would affect me most to think of when I drew near home—for I was going home to the funeral. I am sensible of having felt that a dignity attached to me among the rest of the boys, and that I was important in my affliction.

If ever child were stricken with sincere grief, I was. But I remember that this importance was a kind of satisfaction to me, when I walked in the playground that afternoon while the boys were in school. When I saw them glancing at me out of the windows, as they went up to their classes, I felt distinguished, and looked more melancholy, and walked slower. When school was over, and they came out and spoke to me, I felt it rather good in myself not to be proud to any of them, and to take exactly the same notice of them all, as before.

I was to go home next night; not by the mail, but by the heavy night-coach, which was called the Farmer, and was principally used by country-people travelling short intermediate distances upon the road. We had no story telling that evening, and Traddles insisted on lending me his pillow. I don't know what good he thought it would do me, for I had one of my own; but it was all he had to lend, poor fellow, except a sheet of letter paper full of skeletons; and that he gave me at parting, as a soother of my sorrows and a contribution to my peace of mind.

I left Salem House upon the morrow afternoon. I little thought then that I left it, never to return. We travelled very slowly all night, and did not get into Yarmouth before nine or ten o'clock in the morning. I looked out for Mr. Barkis, but he was not there; and instead of him a fat, short-winded, merry-looking, little old man in black, with rusty little bunches of ribbons at the knees of his breeches, black stockings, and a broad-brimmed hat, came puffing up to the coach window, and said:

"Master Copperfield?"

"Yes, sir."

"Will you come with me, young sir, if you please," he said, opening the door, "and I shall have the pleasure of taking you home."

I put my hand in his, wondering who he was, and we walked away to a shop in a narrow street, on which was written OMER, DRAPER, TAILOR, HABERDASHER, FUNERAL FURNISHER, &c. It was a close and stifling little shop; full of all sorts of clothing, made and unmade, including one window full of beaver-hats and bonnets. We went into a little back-parlor behind the shop, where we found three young women at work on a quantity of black materials, which were heaped upon the table, and little bits and cuttings of which were littered all over the floor. There was a good fire in the room, and a breathless smell of warm black crape—I did not know what the smell was then, but I know now.

The three young women, who appeared to be very industrious and comfortable, raised their heads to look at me, and then went on with their work. Stitch, stitch, stitch. At the same time there came from a workshop across a little yard outside the window, a regular sound of hammering that kept a kind of tune: RAT—tat-tat, RAT—tat-tat, RAT—tat-tat, without any variation.

"Well," said my conductor to one of the three young women. "How do you get on, Minnie?"

"We shall be ready by the trying-on time," she replied gaily, without looking up. "Don't you be afraid, father."

Mr. Omer took off his broad-brimmed hat, and sat down and panted. He was so fat that he was obliged to pant some time before he could say:

"That's right."

"Father!" said Minnie playfully. "What a porpoise you do grow!"

"Well, I don't know how it is, my dear," he replied, considering about it. "I *am* rather so."

"You are such a comfortable man, you see," said Minnie. "You take things so easy."

"No use taking 'em otherwise, my dear" said Mr. Omer.

"No, indeed," returned his daughter. "We are all pretty gay here, thank Heaven! Ain't we, father?"

"I hope so, my dear," said Mr. Omer. "As I have got my breath now, I think I'll measure this young scholar. Would you walk into the shop, Master Copperfield?"

I preceded Mr. Omer, in compliance with his request; and after showing me a roll of cloth which he said was extra super, and too good mourning for anything short of parents, he took my various dimensions, and put them down in a book. While he was recording them he called my attention to his stock in trade, and to certain fashions which he said had "just come up," and to certain other fashions which he said had "just gone out."

"And by that sort of thing we very often lose a little mint of money," said Mr. Omer. "But fashions are like human beings. They come in, nobody knows when, why, or how; and they go out, nobody knows when, why, or how. Everything is like life, in my opinion, if you look at it in that point of view."

I was too sorrowful to discuss the question, which would possibly have been beyond me under any circumstances; and Mr. Omer took me back into the parlor, breathing with some difficulty on the way.

He then called down a little break-neck range of steps behind a door: "Bring up that tea and bread-and-butter!" which, after some time, during which I sat looking about me and thinking, and listening to the stitching in the room, and the tune that was being hammered across the yard, appeared on a tray, and turned out to be for me.

"I have been acquainted with you," said Mr. Omer, after watching me for some minutes, during which I had not made much impression on the breakfast, for the black things destroyed my appetite, "I have been acquainted with you a long time, my young friend."

"Have you, sir?"

"All your life," said Mr. Omer. "I may say before it. I knew your father before you. He was five foot nine and a half, and he lays in five and twen-ty foot of ground."

"RAT—tat-tat, RAT—tat-tat, RAT—tat-tat," across the yard.

"He lays in five and twen-ty foot of ground, if he lays in a fraction," said Mr. Omer pleasantly. "It was either his request or her direction, I forget which."

"Do you know how my little brother is, sir?" I inquired.

Mr. Omer shook his head.

"RAT—tat-tat, RAT—tat-tat, RAT—tat-tat."

"He is in his mother's arms," said he.

"Oh, poor little fellow! Is he dead?"

"Don't mind it more than you can help," said Mr. Omer. "Yes. The baby's dead."

My wounds broke out afresh at this intelligence. I left the scarcely-tasted breakfast, and went and rested my head on another table in a corner of the little room, which Minnie hastily cleared, lest I should spot the mourning that was lying there with my tears. She was a pretty good-natured girl, and put my hair away from my eyes with a soft kind touch; but she was very cheerful at having nearly finished her work and being in good time, and was so different from me.

Presently the tune left off, and a good-looking young fellow came across the yard into the room. He had a hammer in his hand, and his mouth was full of little nails, which he was obliged to take out before he could speak.

"Well, Joram!" said Mr. Omer. "How do *you* get on?"

"All right," said Joram. "Done, sir."

Minnie colored a little, and the other two girls smiled at one another.

"What! you were at it by candle-light last night, when I was at the club, then? Were you?" said Mr. Omer, shutting up one eye.

"Yes," said Joram. "As you said we could make a little trip of it, and go over together, if it was done, Minnie and me—and you."

"Oh! I thought you were going to leave me out altogether," said Mr. Omer, laughing till he coughed.

"—As you was so good as to say that," resumed the young man, "why I turned to with a will, you see. Will you give me your opinion of it?"

"I will," said Mr. Omer, rising. "My dear;" and he stopped and turned to me; "would you like to see your——"

"No, father," Minnie interposed.

"I thought it might be agreeable, my dear," said Mr. Omer. "But perhaps you're right."

I can't say how I knew it was my dear, dear mother's coffin that they went to look at. I had never heard one making; I had never seen one that I know of: but it came into my mind what the noise was, while it was going on; and when the young man entered, I am sure I knew what he had been doing.

The work being now finished, the two girls, whose names I had not heard, brushed the shreds and threads from their dresses, and went into the shop to put that to rights, and wait for customers. Minnie stayed behind to fold up what they had made, and pack it into baskets. This she did upon her knees, humming a lively little tune the while. Joram, who I had no doubt was her lover, came in and stole a kiss from her while she was busy (he didn't appear to mind me, at all), and said her father was gone for the chaise, and he must make haste and get himself ready. Then he went out again; and then she put her thimble and scissors in her pocket, and stuck a needle threaded with black thread neatly in the bosom of her gown, and put on her outer clothing smartly, at a little glass behind the door, in which I saw the reflection of her pleased face.

All this I observed, sitting at the table in the corner with my head leaning on my hand, and my thoughts running on very different things. The chaise soon came round to the front of the shop, and the baskets being put in first, I was put in next, and those three followed. I remember it as a kind of half chaise-cart, half piano-forte van, painted of a sombre color, and drawn by a black horse with a long tail. There was plenty of room for us all.

I do not think I have ever experienced so strange a feeling in my life (I am wiser now, perhaps) as that of being with them, remembering how they had been employed, and seeing them enjoy the ride. I was not angry with them; I was more afraid of them, as if I were cast away among creatures with whom I had no community of nature. They were very cheerful. The old man sat in front to drive, and the two young people sat behind him, and whenever he spoke to them leaned forward, the one on one side of his chubby face, and the other on the other, and made a great deal of him. They would have talked to me too, but I held back, and moped in my corner; scared by their love-making and hilarity, though it was far from boisterous, and almost wondering that no judgment came upon them for their hardness of heart.

So, when they stopped to bait the horse, and ate and drank and enjoyed themselves, I could touch nothing that they touched, but kept my fast unbroken. So, when we reached home, I dropped out of the chaise behind, as quickly as possible, that I might not be in their company before those solemn windows, looking blindly on me like closed eyes once bright. And oh, how little need I had had to think what would move me to tears when I came back—seeing the window of my mother's room, and next it that which, in the better time, was mine!

I was in Peggotty's arms before I got to the door, and she took me into the house. Her grief burst out when she first saw me; but she controlled it soon, and spoke in whispers, and walked softly, as if the dead could be disturbed. She had not been in bed, I found, for a long time. She sat up at night still, and watched. As long as her poor dear pretty was above the ground, she said, she would never desert her.

Mr. Murdstone took no heed of me when I went into the parlor where he was, but sat by the fireside, weeping silently, and pondering in his elbow-chair. Miss Murdstone, who was busy at her writing-desk, which was covered with letters and papers, gave me her cold finger-nails, and asked me, in an iron whisper, if I had been measured for my mourning.

I said: "Yes."

"And your shirts," said Miss Murdstone; "have you brought 'em home?"

"Yes, ma'am. I have brought home all my clothes."

This was all the consolation that her firmness administered to me. I do not doubt that she had a choice pleasure in exhibiting what she called her self-command, and her firmness, and her strength of mind, and her common sense, and the whole diabolical catalogue of her unamiable qualities, on such an occasion. She was particularly proud of her turn for business; and she showed it now in reducing everything to pen and ink, and being moved by nothing. All the rest of that day, and from morning to night afterwards, she sat at that desk; scratching composedly with a hard pen, speaking in the same imperturbable whisper to everybody; never relaxing a muscle of her face, or softening a tone of her voice, or appearing with an atom of her dress astray.

Her brother took a book sometimes, but never read it that I saw. He would open it and look at it as if he were reading, but would remain for a whole hour without turning the leaf, and then put it down and walk to and fro in the room. I used to sit with folded hands watching him, and counting his footsteps hour after hour He very seldom spoke to her, and never to me. He seemed to be the only restless thing, except the clocks, in the whole motionless house.

In these days before the funeral, I saw but little of Peggotty except that, in passing up or down stairs, I always found her close to the room where my mother and her baby lay, and except that she came to me every night, and sat by my bed's head while I went to sleep. A day or two before the burial—I think it was a day or two before, but I am conscious of confusion in my mind about that heavy time, with nothing to mark its progress—she took me into the room. I only recollect that underneath some white covering on the bed, with a beautiful cleanliness and freshness all around it, there seemed to me to lie embodied the solemn stillness that was in the house; and that when she would have turned the cover gently back, I cried: "Oh no! oh no!" and held her hand.

If the funeral had been yesterday, I could not recollect it better. The very air of the best parlor, when I went in at the door, the bright condition of the fire, the shining of the wine in the decanters, the patterns of the glasses and plates, the faint sweet smell of cake, the odour of Miss Murdstone's dress, and our black clothes. Mr. Chillip is in the room, and comes to speak to me.

"And how is Master David?" he says kindly.

I cannot tell him very well. I give him my hand, which he holds in his.

"Dear me!" says Mr. Chillip, meekly smiling, with something shining in his eye. "Our little friends grow up around us. They grow out of our knowledge, ma'am?"

This is to Miss Murdstone, who makes no reply.

"There is a great improvement here, ma'am!" says Mr. Chillip.

Miss Murdstone merely answers with a frown and a formal bend; Mr. Chillip, discomfited, goes into a corner, keeping me with him, and opens his mouth no more.

I remark this, because I remark everything that happens, not because I care about myself, or have done since I came home. And now the bell begins to sound, and Mr. Omer and another come to make us ready. As Peggotty was wont to tell me, long ago, the followers of my father to the same grave were made ready in the same room.

There are Mr. Murdstone, our neighbour Mr. Grayper, Mr. Chillip, and I. When we go out to the door, the Bearers and their load are in the garden; and they move before us down the path, and past the elms, and through the gate, and into the church-yard where I have so often heard the birds sing on a summer morning.

We stand around the grave. The day seems different to me from every other day, and the light not of the same color—of a sadder color. Now there is a solemn hush, which we have brought from home with what is resting in the mould; and while we stand bare-headed, I hear the voice of the clergyman, sounding remote in the open air, and yet distinct and plain, saying: "I am the Resurrection and the Life, saith the Lord!" Then I hear sobs; and, standing apart among the lookers-on, I see that good and faithful servant, whom of all the people upon earth I love the best, and unto whom my childish heart is certain that the Lord will one day say: "Well done."

There are many faces that I know, among the little crowd; faces that I knew in church, when mine was always wondering there; faces that first saw my mother, when she came to the village in her youthful bloom. I do not mind them—I mind nothing but my grief—and yet I see and know them all; and even in the back ground, far away, see Minnie looking on, and her eye glancing on her sweetheart, who is near me.

It is over, and the earth is filled in, and we turn to come away. Before us stands our house, so pretty and unchanged, so linked in my mind with the young idea of what is gone, that all my sorrow has been nothing to the sorrow it calls forth. But they take me on; and Mr. Chillip talks to me; and when we get home, puts some water to my lips; and when I ask his leave to go up to my room, dismisses me with the gentleness of a woman.

All this, I say, is yesterday's event. Events of later date have floated from me to the shore where all forgotten things will reappear, but this stands like a high rock in the ocean.

I knew that Peggotty would come to me in my room. The Sab

bath stillness of the time (the day was so like Sunday! I have forgotten that) was suited to us both. She sat down by my side upon my little bed; and holding my hand, and sometimes putting it to her lips, and sometimes smoothing it with hers, as she might have comforted my little brother, told me, in her way, all that she had to tell concerning what had happened.

"She was never well," said Peggotty, "for a long time. She was uncertain in her mind, and not happy. When her baby was born, I thought at first she would get better, but she was more delicate, and sunk a little every day. She used to like to sit alone before her baby came, and then she cried; but afterwards she used to sing to it—so soft, that I once thought, when I heard her, it was like a voice up in the air, that was rising away.

"I think she got to be more timid, and more frightened-like, of late; and that a hard word was like a blow to her. But she was always the same to me. She never changed to her foolish Peggotty, didn't my sweet girl."

Here Peggotty stopped, and softly beat upon my hand a little while.

"The last time that I saw her like her own old self, was the night when you came home, my dear. The day you went away, she said to me, 'I never shall see my pretty darling again. Something tells me so, that tells the truth, I know.'

"She tried to hold up after that; and many a time, when they told her she was thoughtless and light-hearted, made believe to be so; but it was all a bygone then. She never told her husband what she had told me—she was afraid of saying it to anybody else—till one night, a little more than a week before it happened, when she said to him: 'My dear, I think I am dying.'

"'It's off my mind now, Peggotty,' she told me, when I laid her in her bed that night. 'He will believe it more and more, poor fellow, every day for a few days to come; and then it will be past. I am very tired. If this is sleep, sit by me while I sleep: don't leave me. God bless both my children! God protect and keep my fatherless boy!'"

"I never left her afterwards," said Peggotty. "She often talked to them two down stairs—for she loved them; she couldn't bear not to love any one who was about her—but when they went away from her bedside, she always turned to me, as if there was rest where Peggotty was, and never fell asleep in any other way.

"On the last night, in the evening, she kissed me, and said: 'If my baby should die too, Peggotty, please let them lay him in my arms, and bury us together.' (It was done; for the poor lamb lived but a day beyond her.) 'Let my dearest boy go with us to our resting-place,' she said, 'and tell him that his mother, when she lay here, blessed him not once, but a thousand times.'"

Another silence followed this, and another gentle beating on my hand.

"It was pretty far in the night," said Peggotty, "when she asked me for some drink; and when she had taken it, gave me such a patient smile, the dear!—so beautiful!—

"Daybreak had come, and the sun was rising, when she said to me, how kind and considerate Mr. Copperfield had always been to her, and how he had borne with her, and told her, when she doubted herself, that a loving heart was better and stronger than wisdom, and that he was a happy man in hers. 'Peggotty, my dear,' she said then, 'put me nearer to you,' for she was very weak. 'Lay your good arm underneath my neck,' she said, 'and turn me to you, for your face is going far off, and I want it to be near.' I put it as she asked; and oh Davy! the time had come when my first parting words to you were true—when she was glad to lay her poor head on her stupid cross old Peggotty's arm—and she died like a child that had gone to sleep!"

Thus ended Peggotty's narration. From the moment of my knowing of the death of my mother, the idea of her as she had been of late had vanished from me. I remembered her, from that instant, only as the young mother of my earliest impressions, who had been used to wind her bright curls round and round her finger, and to dance with me at twilight in the parlor. What Peggotty had told me now, was so far from bringing me back to the later period, that it rooted the earlier image in my mind. It may be curious, but it is true. In her death she winged her way back to her calm untroubled youth, and cancelled all the rest.

The mother who lay in the grave, was the mother of my infancy the little creature in her arms, was myself, as I had once been, hushed for ever on her bosom.

CHAPTER X.

I BECOME NEGLECTED, AND AM PROVIDED FOR.

THE first act of business Miss Murdstone performed when the day of the solemnity was over, and light was freely admitted into the house, was to give Peggotty a month's warning. Much as Peggotty would have disliked such a service, I believe she would have retained it, for my sake, in preference to the best upon earth. She told me we must part, and told me why; and we condoled with one another, in all sincerity.

As to me or my future, not a word was said, or a step taken. Happy they would have been, I dare say, if they could have dismissed me at a month's warning too. I mustered courage once, to ask Miss Murdstone when I was going back to school; and she answered dryly, she believed I was not going back at all. I was told nothing more. I was very anxious to know what was going to be done with me, and so was Peggotty; but neither she nor I could pick up any information on the subject.

There was one change in my condition, which, while it relieved me of a great deal of present uneasiness, might have made me, if I had been capable of considering it closely, yet more uncomfortable about the future. It was this. The constraint that had been put upon me was quite abandoned. I was so far from being required to keep my dull post in the parlor, that on several occasions, when I took my seat there, Miss Murdstone frowned to me to go away. I was so far from being warned off from Peggotty's society, that, provided I was not in Mr. Murdstone's, I was never sought out or inquired for. At first I was in daily dread of his taking my education in hand again, or of Miss Murdstone's devoting herself to it; but I soon began to think that such fears were groundless, and that all I had to anticipate was neglect.

I do not conceive that this discovery gave me much pain then. I was still giddy with the shock of my mother's death, and in a kind of stunned state as to all tributary things. I can recollect, indeed, to have speculated, at odd times, on the possibility of my not being taught any more, or cared for any more; and growing up to be a shabby moody man, lounging an idle life away, about the village; as well as on the feasibility of my getting rid of this picture by going away somewhere, like the hero in a story, to seek my fortune: but these were transient visions, day dreams I sat looking at sometimes, as if they were faintly painted or written on the wall of my room, and which, as they melted away, left the wall blank again.

"Peggotty," I said in a thoughtful whisper, one evening, when I was warming my hands at the kitchen fire, "Mr. Murdstone likes me less than he used to. He never liked me much, Peggotty; but he would rather not even see me now, if he can help it."

"Perhaps it's his sorrow," said Peggotty, stroking my hair.

"I am sure, Peggotty, I am sorry too. If I believed it was his sorrow, I should not think of it at all. But it's not that; oh, no, it's not that."

"How do you know it's not that?" said Peggotty, after a silence.

"Oh, his sorrow is another and quite a different thing. He is sorry at this moment, sitting by the fireside with Miss Murdstone; but if I was to go in, Peggotty, he would be something besides."

"What would he be?" said Peggotty.

"Angry," I answered, with an involuntary imitation of his dark frown. "If he was only sorry, he wouldn't look at me as he does. *I* am only sorry, and it makes me feel kinder."

Peggotty said nothing for a little while; and I warmed my hands, as silent as she.

"Davy," she said at length.

"Yes, Peggotty?"

"I have tried, my dear, all ways I could think of—all the ways there are, and all the ways there ain't, in short—to get a suitable service here, in Blunderstone; but there's no such a thing, my love."

"And what do you mean to do, Peggotty?" says I, wistfully "Do you mean to go and seek your fortune?"

"I expect I shall be forced to go to Yarmouth," replied Peggotty, "and live there."

"You might have gone farther off," I said, brightening a little, "and been as bad as lost. I shall see you sometimes, my dear old Peggotty, there. You won't be quite at the other end of the world, will you?"

"Contrary ways, please God!" cried Peggotty, with great animation. "As long as you are here, my pet, I shall come over every week of my life to see you. One day, every week of my life!"

I felt a great weight taken off my mind by this promise; but even this was not all, for Peggotty went on to say:

"I'm a going, Davy, you see, to my brother's, first, for another fortnight's visit—just till I have had time to look about me, and get to be something like myself again. Now, I have been thinking, that perhaps, as they don't want you here at present, you might be let to go along with me."

If anything, short of being in a different relation to every one about me, Peggotty excepted, could have given me a sense of pleasure at that time, it would have been this project of all others. The idea of being again surrounded by those honest faces, shining welcome on me; of renewing the peacefulness of the sweet Sunday morning, when the bells were ringing, the stones dropping in the water, and the shadowy ships breaking through the mist; of roaming up and down with little Em'ly, telling her my troubles, and finding charms against them in the shells and pebbles on the beach; made a calm in my heart. It was ruffled next moment, to be sure, by a doubt of Miss Murdstone's giving her consent; but even that was set at rest soon, for she came out to take an evening grope in the store-closet while we were yet in conversation, and Peggotty, with a boldness that amazed me, broached the topic on the spot.

"The boy will be idle there," said Miss Murdstone, looking into a pickle-jar, "and idleness is the root of all evil. But, to be sure, he would be idle here—or anywhere, in my opinion."

Peggotty had an angry answer ready, I could see; but she swallowed it for my sake, and remained silent.

"Humph!" said Miss Murdstone, still keeping her eye on the

pickles; "it is of more importance than anything else—it is of paramount importance—that my brother should not be disturbed or made uncomfortable. I suppose I had better say yes."

I thanked her without making any demonstration of joy, lest it should induce her to withdraw her assent. Nor could I help thinking this a prudent course, when she looked at me out of the pickle-jar, with as great an access of sourness as if her black eyes had absorbed its contents. However, the permission was given, and was never retracted; for when the month was out, Peggotty and I were ready to depart.

Mr. Barkis came into the house for Peggotty's boxes. I had never known him to pass the garden-gate before, but on this occasion he came into the house. And he gave me a look, as he shouldered the largest box and went out, which I thought had meaning in it, if meaning could ever be said to find its way into Mr. Barkis's visage.

Peggotty was naturally in low spirits at leaving what had been her home so many years, and where the two strong attachments of her life—for my mother and myself—had been formed. She had been walking in the churchyard, too, very early; and she got into the cart, and sat in it with her handkerchief at her eyes.

So long as she remained in this condition Mr. Barkis gave no sign of life whatever. He sat in his usual place and attitude, like a great stuffed figure. But when she began to look about her, and to speak to me, he nodded his head and grinned several times. I have not the least notion at whom, or what he meant by it.

"It's a beautiful day, Mr. Barkis!" I said, as an act of politeness.

"It ain't bad," said Mr. Barkis, who generally qualified his speech, and rarely committed himself.

"Peggotty is quite comfortable now, Mr. Barkis," I remarked, for his satisfaction.

"Is she, though!" said Mr. Barkis.

After reflecting about it, with a sagacious air, Mr. Barkis eyed her, and said:

"*Are* you pretty comfortable?"

Peggotty laughed, and answered in the affirmative.

"But really and truly, you know. Are you?" growled Mr.

Barkis, sliding nearer to her on the seat, and nudging her with his elbow. "Are you? Really and truly pretty comfortable? Are you? Eh?" At each of these inquiries Mr. Barkis shuffled nearer to her, and gave her another nudge; so that at last we were all crowded together in the left-hand corner of the cart, and I was so squeezed that I could hardly bear it.

Peggotty calling his attention to my sufferings, Mr. Barkis gave me a little more room at once, and got away by degrees. But I could not help observing that he seemed to think he had hit upon a wonderful expedient for expressing himself in a neat, agreeable, and pointed manner, without the inconvenience of inventing conversation. He manifestly chuckled over it for some time. By-and-by he turned to Peggotty again, and repeating, "Are you pretty comfortable though?" bore down upon us as before, until the breath was nearly wedged out of my body. By-and-by he made another descent upon us with the same inquiry, and the same result. At length, I got up whenever I saw him coming, and standing on the foot-board, pretended to look at the prospect; after which I did very well.

He was so polite as to stop at a public-house, expressly on our account, and entertain us with broiled mutton and beer. Even when Peggotty was in the act of drinking, he was seized with one of those approaches, and almost choked her. But as we drew nearer to the end of our journey, he had more to do and less time for gallantry; and when we got on Yarmouth pavement, we were all too much shaken and jolted, I apprehend, to have any leisure for anything else.

Mr. Peggotty and Ham waited for us at the old place. They received me and Peggotty in an affectionate manner, and shook hands with Mr. Barkis, who, with his hat on the very back of his head, and a shame-faced leer upon his countenance, and pervading his very legs, presented but a vacant appearance, I thought. They each took one of Peggotty's trunks, and we were going away, when Mr. Barkis solemnly made a sign to me with his forefinger to come under an archway.

"I say," growled Mr. Barkis, "it was all right."

I looked up into his face, and answered, with an attempt to be very profound: "Oh!"

"It didn't come to a end there," said Mr. Barkis, nodding confidentially. "It was all right."

Again I answered: "Oh!"

"You know who was willin'," said my friend. "It was Barkis and Barkis only."

I nodded assent.

"It's all right," said Mr. Barkis, shaking hands; "I'm a friend of your'n. You made it all right, first. It's all right."

In his attempts to be particularly lucid, Mr. Barkis was so extremely mysterious, that I might have stood looking in his face for an hour, and most assuredly should have got as much information out of it as out of the face of a clock that had stopped, but for Peggotty's calling me away. As we were going along, she asked me what he had said; and I told her he had said it was all right.

"Like his impudence," said Peggotty, "but I don't mind that! Davy dear, what should you think if I was to think of being married?"

"Why—I suppose you would like me as much then, Peggotty, as you do now?" I returned, after a little consideration.

Greatly to the astonishment of the passengers in the street, as well as of her relations going on before, the good soul was obliged to stop and embrace me on the spot, with many protestations of her unalterable love.

"Tell me what should you say, darling?" she asked again, when this was over, and we were walking on.

"If you were thinking of being married—to Mr. Barkis, Peggotty?"

"Yes," said Peggotty.

"I should think it would be a very good thing. For then you know, Peggotty, you would always have the horse and cart to bring you over to see me, and could come for nothing, and be sure of coming."

"The sense of the dear!" cried Peggotty. "What I have been thinking of, this month back! Yes, my precious; and I think I should be more independent altogether, you see; let alone my working with a better heart in my own house, than I could in anybody else's now. I don't know what I might be fit for, now, as a servant to a stranger. And I shall be always near my pretty's resting-place," said Peggotty musing, "and able to see it when I like; and when *I* lie down to rest, I may be laid not far off from my darling girl!"

We neither of us said anything for a little while.

"But I wouldn't so much as give it another thought," said Peggotty, cheerily, "if my Davy was anyways against it—not if I had been asked in church thirty times three times over, and was wearing out the ring in my pocket."

"Look at me, Peggotty," I replied; "and see if I am not really glad, and don't truly wish it!" As indeed I did, with all my heart.

"Well, my life," said Peggotty, giving me a squeeze, "I have thought of it night and day, every way I can, and I hope the right way; but I'll think of it again, and speak to my brother about it, and in the meantime we'll keep it to ourselves, Davy, you and me. Barkis is a good plain creetur'," said Peggotty, "and if I tried to do my duty by him, I think it would be my fault if I wasn't—if I wasn't pretty comfortable," said Peggotty, laughing heartily.

This quotation from Mr. Barkis was so appropriate, and tickled us both so much, that we laughed again and again, and were quite in a pleasant humour when we came within view of Mrs. Peggotty's cottage.

It looked just the same, except that it may, perhaps, have shrunk a little in my eyes; and Mrs. Gummidge was waiting at the door as if she had stood there ever since. All within was the same, down to the seaweed in the blue mug in my bedroom. I went into the out-house to look about me; and the very same lobsters, crabs, and crawfish possessed by the same desire to pinch the world in general, appeared to be in the same state of conglomeration in the same old corner.

But there was no little Em'ly to be seen, so I asked Mr. Peggotty where she was.

"She 's at school, sir," said Mr. Peggotty, wiping the heat con sequent on the porterage of Peggotty's box from his forehead "she 'll be home," looking at the Dutch clock, "in from twenty minutes to half-an-hour's time. We all on us feel the loss of her bless ye!"

Mrs. Gummidge moaned.

"Cheer up, Mawther!" cried Mr. Peggotty.

"I feel it more than anybody else," said Mrs. Gummidge; "I 'm a lone lorn creetur', and she used to be a'most the only think that did'nt go contrairy with me."

Mrs. Gummidge, whimpering and shaking her head, applied herself to blowing the fire. Mr. Peggotty, looking round upon us while she was so engaged, said in a low voice, which he shaded with his hand: "The old 'un!" From this I rightly conjectured that no improvement had taken place since my last visit in the state of Mrs. Gummidge's spirit.

Now, the whole place was, or it should have been, quite as delightful a place as ever; and yet it did not impress me in the same way. I felt rather disappointed with it. Perhaps it was because little Em'ly was not at home. I knew the way by which she would come, and presently found myself strolling along the path to meet her.

A figure appeared in the distance before long, and I soon knew it to be Em'ly, who was a little creature still in stature, though she was grown. But when she drew nearer, and I saw her blue eyes looking bluer, and her dimpled face looking brighter, and her whole self prettier and gayer, a curious feeling came over me that made me pretend not to know her, and pass by as if I were looking at something a long way off. I have done such a thing since in later life, or I am mistaken.

Little Em'ly didn't care a bit. She saw me well enough; but instead of turning round and calling after me, ran away laughing. This obliged me to run after her, and she ran so fast that we were very near the cottage before I caught her.

"Oh, it's you, is it?" said little Em'ly.

"Why, you knew who it was, Em'ly," said I.

"And didn't you know who it was?" said Em'ly. I was going to kiss her but she covered her cherry lips with her hands, and said she wasn't a baby, now, and ran away, laughing more than ever, into the house.

She seemed to delight in teasing me, which was a change in her I wondered at very much. The tea-table was ready, and our little locker was put out in its old place, but instead of coming to sit by me, she went and bestowed her company upon that grumbling Mrs. Gummidge: and on Mr. Peggotty's inquiring why, rumpled her hair all over her face to hide it, and would do nothing but laugh.

"A little puss, it is!" said Mr. Peggotty, patting her with his great hand.

"So sh' is! so sh' is!" cried Ham. "Mas'r Davy bo', so sh' is!" and he sat and chuckled at her for some time in a state of mingled admiration and delight, that made his face a burning red.

Little Em'ly was spoiled by them all, in fact; and by no one more than Mr. Peggotty himself, whom she could have coaxed into anything, by only going and laying her cheek against his rough whisker. That was my opinion, at least, when I saw her do it; and I held Mr. Peggotty to be thoroughly in the right. But she was so affectionate and sweet-natured, and had such a pleasant manner of being both sly and shy at once, that she captivated me more than ever.

She was tender-hearted, too; for when, as we sat round the fire after tea, an allusion was made by Mr. Peggotty over his pipe to the loss I had sustained, the tears stood in her eyes, and she looked at me so kindly across the table, that I felt quite thankful to her.

"Ah!" said Mr. Peggotty, taking up her curls, and running them over his hand like water, "here 's another orphan, you see, sir. And here," said Mr. Peggotty, giving Ham a back-handed knock in the chest, "is another of 'em, though he don't look much like it."

"If I had you for my guardian, Mr. Peggotty," said I, shaking my head, "I don't think I should *feel* much like it."

"Well said, Mas'r Davy bo'!" cried Ham, in an ecstasy. "Hoorah! Well said! Nor more you wouldn't! Hor! Hor!"—Here he returned Mr. Peggotty's back-hander, and little Em'ly got up and kissed Mr. Peggotty.

"And how 's your friend, sir?" said Mr. Peggotty to me.

"Steerforth?" said I.

"That 's the name!" cried Mr. Peggotty, turning to Ham. "I knowed it was something in our way."

"You said it was Rudderford," observed Ham, laughing.

"Well?" retorted Mr. Peggotty. "And ye steer with a rudder, don't ye? It ain't fur off. How is he, sir?"

"He was very well indeed when I came away, Mr. Peggotty."

"There's a friend!" said Mr. Peggotty, stretching out his pipe. "There's a friend, if you talk of friends! Why, Lord love my heart alive, if it ain't a treat to look at him!"

"He is very handsome, is he not?" said I, my heart warming with this praise.

"Handsome!" cried Mr. Peggotty. "He stands up to you like—like a—why I don't know what he *don't* stand up to you like. He's so bold!"

"Yes! That's just his character," said I. "He's as brave as a lion, and you can't think how frank he is, Mr. Peggotty."

"And I do suppose now," said Mr. Peggotty, looking at me through the smoke of his pipe, "that in the way of book-learning he'd take the wind out of a'most anything."

"Yes," said I, delighted; "he knows everything. He is astonishingly clever."

"There's a friend!" murmured Mr. Peggotty, with a grave toss of his head.

"Nothing seems to cost him any trouble," said I. "He knows a task if he only looks at it. He is the best cricketer you ever saw. He will give you almost as many men as you like at draughts, and beat you easily."

Mr. Peggotty gave his head another toss, as much as to say: "Of course he will."

"He is such a speaker," I pursued, "that he can win anybody over; and I don't know what you'd say if you were to hear him sing, Mr. Peggotty."

Mr. Peggotty gave his head another toss, as much as to say: "I have no doubt of it."

"Then, he's such a generous, fine, noble fellow," said I, quite carried away by my favorite theme, "that it's hardly possible to give him as much praise as he deserves. I am sure I can never feel thankful enough for the generosity with which he has protected me, so much younger and lower in the school than himself."

I was running on, very fast indeed, when my eyes rested on little Em'ly's face, which was bent forward over the table, listening with the deepest attention, her breath held, her blue eyes sparkling like jewels, and the colour mantling in her cheeks. She looked so extraordinarily earnest and pretty, that I stopped in a sort of wonder; and they all observed her at the same time, for, as I stopped, they laughed and looked at her.

"Em'ly is like me," said Peggotty, "and would like to see him."

Em'ly was confused by our all observing her, and hung down her head, and her face was covered with blushes. Glancing up presently through her stray curls, and seeing that we were all looking at her still (I am sure, I, for one, could have looked at her for hours), she ran away, and kept away till it was nearly bedtime.

I lay down in the old little bed in the stern of the boat, and the wind came moaning on across the flat as it had done before. But I could not help fancying, now, that it moaned of those who were gone; and instead of thinking that the sea might rise in the night and float the boat away, I thought of the sea that had risen, since I last heard those sounds, and drowned my happy home. I recollect, as the wind and water began to sound fainter in my ears, putting a short clause in my prayers, petitioning that I might grow up to marry little Em'ly, and so dropping lovingly asleep.

The days passed pretty much as they had passed before, except—it was a great exception—that little Em'ly and I seldom wandered on the beach now. She had tasks to learn, and needlework to do; and was absent during a great part of each day. But I felt that we should not have had those old wanderings, even if it had been otherwise. Wild and full of childish whims as Em'ly was, she was more of a little woman than I had supposed. She seemed to have got a great distance away from me, in little more than a year. She liked me, but she laughed at me, and tormented me; and when I went to meet her, stole home another way, and was laughing at the door when I came back disappointed. The best times were when she sat quietly at work in the doorway, and I sat on the wooden step at her feet, reading to her. It seems to me, at this hour, that I have never seen such sunlight as on those bright April afternoons; that I have never seen such a sunny little figure as I used to see, sitting in the doorway of the old boat; that I have never beheld such sky, such water, such glorified ships sailing away into golden air.

On the very first evening after our arrival, Mr. Barkis appeared in an exceedingly vacant and awkward condition, and with a bundle of oranges tied up in a handkerchief. As he made no allusion of any kind to this property, he was supposed to have left it behind him by accident when he went away; until Ham, running after him to restore it, came back with the information that it was intended for Peggotty. After that occasion he appeared every evening at exactly the same hour, and always with a little bundle, to which he never alluded, and which he regularly put behind the door, and left there. These offerings of affection were of a most various and eccentric description. Among them I remember a double set of pig's trotters, a huge pin-cushion, half a bushel or so of apples, a pair of jet earrings, some Spanish onions, a box of dominoes, a canary bird and cage, and a leg of pickled pork.

Mr. Barkis's wooing, as I remember it, was altogether of a peculiar kind. He very seldom said anything; but would sit by the fire in much the same attitude as he sat in, in his cart, and stare heavily at Peggotty, who was opposite. One night, being, as I suppose, inspired by love, he made a dart at the bit of wax-candle she kept for her thread, and put it in his waistcoat-pocket and carried it off. After that, his great delight was to produce it when it was wanted, sticking to the lining of his pocket, in a partially-melted state, and pocket it again when it was done with. He seemed to enjoy himself very much, and not to feel at all called upon to talk. Even when he took Peggotty out for a walk on the flats, he had no uneasiness on that head, I believe; contenting himself with now and then asking her if she was pretty comfortable; and I remember that sometimes, after he was gone, Peggotty would throw her apron over her face, and laugh for half-an-hour. Indeed, we were all more or less amused,

except that miserable Mrs. Gummidge, whose courtship would appear to have been of an exactly parallel nature, she was so continually reminded by these transactions of the old one.

At length, when the term of my visit was nearly expired, it was given out that Peggotty and Mr. Barkis were going to make a day's holiday together, and that little Em'ly and I were to accompany them. I had but a broken sleep the night before, in anticipation of the pleasure of a whole day with Em'ly. We were all astir betimes in the morning; and while we were yet at breakfast, Mr. Barkis appeared in the distance, driving a chaise-cart towards the object of his affections.

Peggotty was drest as usual, in her neat and quiet mourning; but Mr. Barkis bloomed in a new blue coat, of which the tailor had given him such good measure, that the cuffs would have rendered gloves unnecessary in the coldest weather, while the collar was so high that it pushed his hair up on end on the top of his head. His bright buttons, too, were of the largest size. Rendered complete by drab pantaloons and a buff waistcoat, I thought Mr. Barkis a phenomenon of respectability.

When we were all in a bustle outside the door, I found that Mr. Peggotty was prepared with an old shoe, which was to be thrown after us for luck, and which he offered to Mrs. Gummidge for that purpose.

"No. It had better be done by somebody else, Dan'l," said Mrs. Gummidge. "I'm a lone lorn creetur' myself, and everythink that reminds me of creetur's that ain't lone and lorn, goes contrairy with me."

"Come, old gal!" cried Mr. Peggotty. "Take and heave it!"

"No, Dan'l," returned Mrs. Gummidge, whimpering and shaking her head. "If I felt less, I could do more. You don't feel like me, Dan'l; thinks don't go contrairy with you, nor you with them; you had better do it yourself."

But here Peggotty, who had been going about from one to another in a hurried way, kissing everybody, called out from the cart, in which we all were by this time (Em'ly and I on two little chairs, side by side), that Mrs. Gummidge must do it. So Mrs. Gummidge did it; and, I am sorry to relate, cast a damp upon the festive character of our departure, by immediately bursting into tears, and sinking subdued into the arms of Ham, with the declaration that she knowed she was a burden, and had better be carried to the House at once. Which I really thought was a sensible idea, that Ham might have acted on.

Away we went, however, on our holiday excursion: and the first thing we did was to stop at a church, where Mr. Barkis tied the horse to some rails, and went in with Peggotty, leaving little Em'ly and me alone in the chaise. I took that occasion to put my arm round Em'ly's waist, and propose that as I was going away so very soon now, we should determine to be very affectionate to one another, and very happy, all day. Little Em'ly consenting, and allowing me to kiss her, I became desperate; informing her, I recollect, that I never could love another, and that I was prepared to shed the blood of anybody who should aspire to her affections.

How merry little Em'ly made herself about it! With what a demure assumption of being immensely older and wiser than I, the fairly little woman said I was "a silly boy;" and then laughed so charmingly that I forgot the pain of being called by that disparaging name, in the pleasure of looking at her.

Mr. Barkis and Peggotty were a good while in the church, but came out at last, and then we drove away into the country. As we were going along, Mr. Barkis turned to me, and said, with a wink,—by the by, I should hardly have thought, before, that he *could* wink:

"What name was it as I wrote up in the cart?"

"Clara Peggotty," I answered.

"What name would it be as I should write up now, if there was a tilt here?"

"Clara Peggotty, again?" I suggested.

"Clara Peggotty BARKIS!" he returned, and burst into a roar of laughter that shook the chaise.

In a word, they were married, and had gone into the church for no other purpose. Peggotty was resolved that it should be quietly done; and the clerk had given her away, and there had been no witnesses of the ceremony. She was a little confused when Mr. Barkis made this abrupt announcement of their union, and could not hug me enough in token of her unimpaired affection; but she soon became herself again, and said she was very glad it was over.

We drove to a little inn in a bye road, where we were expected, and where we had a very comfortable dinner, and passed the day with great satisfaction. If Peggotty had been married every day for the last ten years, she could hardly have been more at her ease about it; it made no sort of difference in her: she was just the same as ever, and went out for a stroll with little Em'ly and me before tea, while Mr. Barkis philosophically smoked his pipe, and enjoyed himself, I suppose, with the contemplation of his happiness. If so, it sharpened his appetite; for I distinctly call to mind that, although he had eaten a good deal of pork and greens at dinner, and had finished off with a fowl or two, he was obliged to have cold boiled bacon for tea, and disposed of a large quantity without any emotion.

I have often thought, since, what an odd, innocent, out-of-the-way kind of wedding it must have been! We got into the chaise again soon after dark, and drove cosily back, looking up at the stars, and talking about them. I was their chief exponent, and opened Mr. Barkis's mind to an amazing extent. I told him all I knew, but he would have believed anything I might have taken it into my head to impart to him; for he had a profound veneration for my abilities, and informed his wife in my hearing, on that very occasion, that I was "a young Roeshus"—by which I think he meant, prodigy.

When we had exhausted the subject of the stars, or rather when I had exhausted the mental faculties of Mr. Barkis, little Em'ly and I made a cloak of an old wrapper, and sat under it for the rest of the journey. Ah, how I loved her! What happiness (I thought) if we were married, and were going away anywhere to live among the trees and in the fields, never growing older, never growing wiser, children ever, rambling hand in hand through sunshine and among flowery meadows, laying down our heads on moss at night, in a sweet sleep of purity and peace, and buried by the birds when we were dead! Some such picture, with no real world in it, bright with the light of our innocence, and vague as the stars afar off, was in my mind all the way. I am glad to think there were two such guileless hearts at Peggotty's marriage as little Em'ly's and mine. I am glad to think the Loves and Graces took such airy forms in its homely procession.

Well, we came to the old boat again in good time at night; and there Mr. and Mrs. Barkis bade us good bye, and drove away snugly to their own home. I felt then, for the first time, that I had lost Peggotty. I should have gone to bed with a sore heart indeed under any other roof but that which sheltered little Em'ly's head.

Mr. Peggotty and Ham knew what was in my thoughts as wel as I did, and were ready with some supper and their hospitable faces to drive it away. Little Em'ly came and sat beside me on the locker, for the only time in all that visit; and it was altogether a wonderful close to a wonderful day.

It was a night tide; and soon after we went to bed, Mr. Peggotty and Ham went out to fish. I felt very brave at being left alone in the solitary house, the protector of Emily and Mrs. Gummidge, and only wished that a lion or a serpent, or any ill-disposed monster, would make an attack upon us, that I might destroy him, and cover myself with glory. But as nothing of the sort happened to be walking about on Yarmouth flats that night, I provided the best substitute I could by dreaming of dragons until morning.

With morning came Peggotty; who called to me, as usual, under my window as if Mr. Barkis the carrier had been from first to last a dream too. After breakfast she took me to her own home, and a beautiful little home it was. Of all the moveables in it, I must have been most impressed by a certain old bureau of some dark wood in the parlor (the tile-floored kitchen was the general sitting-room), with a retreating top which opened, let down, and became a desk, within which was a large quarto edition of Fox's Book of Martyrs. This precious volume, of which I do not recollect one word, I immediately discovered and immediately applied myself to; and I never visited the house afterwards, but I kneeled on a chair, opened the casket where this gem was enshrined, spread my arms over the desk, and fell to devouring the book afresh. I was chiefly edified, I am afraid, by the pictures, which were numerous, and represented all kinds of dismal horrors; but the Martyrs and Peggotty's house have been inseparable in my mind ever since, and are now.

I took leave of Mr. Peggotty, and Ham, and Mrs. Gummidge, and little Em'ly, that day; and passed the night at Peggotty's, in a little room in the roof (with the crocodile-book on a shelf by the bed's head) which was to be always mine, Peggotty said, and should always be kept for me in exactly the same state.

"Young or old, Davy dear, as long as I am alive and have this house over my head," said Peggotty, "you shall find it as if I expected you here directly every minute. I shall keep it every day, as I used to keep your old little room, my darling; and if you was to go to China, you might think of it as being kept just the same, all the time you were away."

I felt the truth and constancy of my dear old nurse, with all my heart, and thanked her as well as I could. That was not very well, for she spoke to me thus, with her arms round my neck, in the morning, and I was going home in the morning, and I went home in the morning, with herself and Mr. Barkis in the cart. They left me at the gate, not easily or lightly; and it was a strange sight to me to see the cart go on, taking Peggotty away, and leaving me under the old elm-trees looking at the house, in which there was no face to look on mine with love or liking any more.

And now I fell into a state of neglect, which I cannot look back upon without compassion. I fell at once into a solitary condition,—apart from all friendly notice, apart from the society of all other boys of my own age, apart from all companionship but my own spiritless thoughts,—which seems to cast its gloom upon this paper as I write.

What would I have given, to have been sent to the hardest school that ever was kept!—to have been taught something, anyhow, anywhere! No such hope dawned upon me. They disliked me; and they sullenly, sternly, steadily, overlooked me. I think Mr. Murdstone's means were straitened at about this time; but it is little to the purpose. He could not bear me; and in putting me from him he tried, as I believe, to put away the notion that I had any claim upon him—and succeeded.

I was not actively ill-used. I was not beaten, or starved; but the wrong that was done to me had no intervals of relenting, and was done in a systematic, passionless manner. Day after day, week after week, month after month, I was coldly neglected. I wonder sometimes, when I think of it, what they would have done if I had been taken with an illness; whether I should have lain down in my lonely room, and languished through it in my usual solitary way, or whether anybody would have helped me out.

When Mr. and Miss Murdstone were at home, I took my meals with them; in their absence, I ate and drank by myself. At all times I lounged about the house and neighbourhood quite disregarded, except that they were jealous of my making any friends: thinking, perhaps, that, if I did, I might complain to some one. For this reason, though Mr. Chillip often asked me to go and see him (he was a widower, having, some years before that, lost a little light-haired wife, whom I can just remember connecting in my own thoughts with a pale tortoise-shell cat), it was but seldom that I enjoyed the happiness of passing an afternoon in his closet of a surgery; reading some book that was new to me, with the smell of the whole pharmacopœia coming up my nose, or pounding something in a mortar under his mild directions.

For the same reason, added no doubt to the old dislike of her, I was seldom allowed to visit Peggotty. Faithful to her promise, she either came to see me, or met me somewhere near, once every week, and never empty-handed; but many and bitter were the disappointments I had, in being refused permission to pay a visit to her at her house. Some few times, however, at long intervals, I was allowed to go there; and then I found out that Mr. Barkis was something of a miser, or as Peggotty dutifully expressed it, was "a little near," and kept a heap of money in a box under his bed, which he pretended was only full of coats and trousers. In this coffer, his riches hid themselves with such a tenacious modesty, that the smallest instalments could only be tempted out by artifice; so that Peggotty had to prepare a long and elaborate scheme, a very Gunpowder Plot, for every Saturday's expenses.

All this time I was so conscious of the waste of any promise I had given, and of my being utterly neglected, that I should have been perfectly miserable, I have no doubt, but for the old books. They were my only comfort; and I was as true to them as they were to me, and read them over and over I don't know how many times more.

I now approach a period of my life, which I can never lose the remembrance of, while I remember anything; and the recollection of which has often, without my invocation, come before me like a ghost, and haunted happier times.

I had been out, one day, loitering somewhere, in the listless, meditative manner that my way of life engendered, when. turning the corner of a lane near our house, I came upon Mr. Murdstone walking with a gentleman. I was confused, and was going by them, when the gentleman cried:

"What! Brooks!"

"No, sir, David Copperfield," I said.

"Don't tell me. You are Brooks," said the gentleman. "You are Brooks of Sheffield. That's your name."

At these words, I observed the gentleman more attentively. His laugh coming to my remembrance too, I knew him to be Mr. Quinion, whom I had gone over to Lowestoft with Mr. Murdstone to see, before—it is no matter—I need not recall when.

"And how do you get on, and where are you being educated, Brooks?" said Mr. Quinion.

He had put his hand upon my shoulder, and turned me about, to walk with them. I did not know what to reply, and glanced dubiously at Mr. Murdstone.

"He is at home at present," said the latter. "He is not being educated anywhere. I don't know what to do with him. He is a difficult subject."

That old, double look was on me for a moment; and then his eye darkened with a frown, as it turned, in its aversion, elsewhere.

"Humph!" said Mr. Quinion, looking at us both, I thought. "Fine weather!"

Silence ensued, and I was considering how I could best disengage my shoulder from his hand, and go away, when he said:

"I suppose you are a pretty sharp fellow still? Eh, Brooks?"

"Aye! He is sharp enough," said Mr. Murdstone, impatiently. "You had better let him go. He will not thank you for troubling him."

On this hint, Mr. Quinion released me, and I made the best of my way home. Looking back as I turned into the front garden, I saw Mr. Murdstone leaning against the wicket of the churchyard, and Mr. Quinion talking to him. They were both looking after me, and I felt that they were speaking of me.

Mr. Quinion lay at our house that night. After breakfast, the next morning, I had put my chair away, and was going out of the room, when Mr. Murdstone called me back. He then gravely repaired to another table, where his sister sat herself at her desk. Mr. Quinion, with his hands in his pockets, stood looking out of window; and I stood looking at them all.

"David," said Mr. Murdstone, "to the young, this is a world for action; not for moping and droning in."

—"As you do," added his sister.

"Jane Murdstone, leave it to me, if you please. I say, David, to the young, this is a world for action, and not for moping and droning in. It is especially so for a young boy of your disposition, which requires a great deal of correcting; and to which no greater service can be done than to force it to conform to the ways of the working world, and to bend it and break it."

"For stubbornness won't do here," said his sister. "What it wants, is to be crushed. And crushed it must be. Shall be, too!"

He gave her a look, half in remonstrance, half in approval, and went on:

"I suppose you know, David, that I am not rich. At any rate, you know it now. You have received some considerable education already. Education is costly; and even if it were not, and I could afford it, I am of opinion that it would not be at all advantageous to you to be kept at a school. What is before you, is a fight with the world; and the sooner you begin it, the better."

I think it occurred to me that I had already begun it, in my poor way: but it occurs to me now, whether or no.

"You have heard 'the counting-house' mentioned sometimes," said Mr. Murdstone.

"The counting-house, sir?" I repeated.

"Of Murdstone and Grinby, in the wine trade," he replied.

I suppose I looked uncertain, for he went on hastily:

"You have heard the 'counting-house' mentioned, or the business, or the cellars, or the wharf, or something about it."

"I think I have heard the business mentioned, sir," I said, remembering what I vaguely knew of his and his sister's resources. "But I don't know when."

"It does not matter when," he returned. "Mr. Quinion manages that business."

I glanced at the latter deferentially as he stood looking out of window.

"Mr. Quinion suggests that it gives employment to some other boys, and that he sees no reason why it shouldn't, on the same terms, give employment to you."

"He having," Mr. Quinion observed in a low voice, and half turning round, "no other prospect, Murdstone."

Mr. Murdstone, with an impatient, even an angry gesture, resumed, without noticing what he had said:

"Those terms are, that you will earn enough for yourself to provide for your eating and drinking, and pocket-money. Your lodging (which I have arranged for) will be paid by me. So will your washing—"

—"Which will be kept down to my estimate," said his sister.

"Your clothes will be looked after for you, too," said Mr. Murdstone; "as you will not be able, yet awhile, to get them for yourself. So you are now going to London, David, with Mr. Quinion, to begin the world on your own account."

"In short, you are provided for," observed his sister; "and will please to do your duty."

Though I quite understood that the purpose of this announcement was to get rid of me, I have no distinct remembrance whether it pleased or frightened me. My impression is, that I was in a state of confusion about it, and, oscillating between the two points, touched neither. Nor had I much time for the clearing of my thoughts, as Mr. Quinion was to go upon the morrow.

Behold me, on the morrow, in a much-worn little white hat, with a black crape round it for my mother, a black jacket, and a pair of hard, stiff corduroy trousers—which Miss Murdstone considered the best armour for the legs in that fight with the world which was now to come off; behold me so attired, and with my little worldly all before me in a small trunk, sitting, a lone lorn child (as Mrs. Gummidge might have said), in the post-chaise that was carrying Mr. Quinion to the London coach at Yarmouth! See, how our house and church are lessening in the distance; how the grave beneath the tree is blotted out by intervening objects; how the spire points upward from my old playground no more, and the sky is empty

CHAPTER XI.

I BEGIN LIFE ON MY OWN ACCOUNT, AND DON'T LIKE IT

I KNOW enough of the world now, to have almost lost the capacity of being much surprised by anything; but it is matter of some surprise to me, even now, that I can have been so easily thrown away at such an age. A child of excellent abilities, and with strong powers of observation, quick, eager, delicate, and soon hurt bodily or mentally, it seems wonderful to me that nobody should have made any sign in my behalf. But none was made; and I became, at ten years old, a little labouring hind in the service of Murdstone and Grinby.

Murdstone and Grinby's warehouse was at the water side. It was down in Blackfriars. Modern improvements have altered the place; but it was the last house at the bottom of a narrow street, curving down hill to the river, with some stairs at the end, where people took boat. It was a crazy old house with a wharf of its own, abutting on the water when the tide was in, and on the mud when the tide was out, and literally overrun with rats. Its panelled rooms, discolored with the dirt and smoke of a hundred years, I dare say; its decaying floors and staircase; the squeaking and scuffling of the old grey rats down in the cellars; and the dirt and rottenness of the place; are things, not of many years ago, in my mind, but of the present instant. They are all before me, just as they were in the evil hour when I went among them for the first time, with my trembling hand in Mr. Quinion's.

Murdstone and Grinby's trade was among a good many kinds of people, but an important branch of it was the supply of wines and spirits to certain packet ships. I forget now where they chiefly went, but I think there were some among them that made voyages both to the East and West Indies. I know that a great many empty bottles were one of the consequences of this traffic, and that certain men and boys were employed to examine them against the light, and reject those that were flawed, and to rinse and wash them. When the empty bottles ran short, there were labels to be pasted on full ones, or corks to be fitted to them, or seals to be put upon the corks, or finished bottles to be packed in casks. All this work was my work, and of the boys employed upon it I was one.

There were three or four of us, counting me. My working place was established in a corner of the warehouse, where Mr. Quinion could see me, when he chose to stand up on the bottom rail of his stool in the counting-house, and look at me through a window above the desk. Hither, on the first morning of my so auspiciously beginning life on my own account, the oldest of the regular boys was summoned to show me my business. His name was Mick Walker, and he wore a ragged apron and a paper cap. He informed me that his father was a bargeman, and walked, in a black velvet head-dress, in the Lord Mayor's show. He also informed me that our principal associate would be another boy whom he introduced by the—to me—extraordinary name of Mealy Potatoes. I discovered, however, that this youth had not been christened by that name, but that it had been bestowed upon him in the warehouse, on account of his complexion, which was pale or mealy. Mealy's father was a waterman, who had the additional distinction of being a fireman, and was engaged as such at one of the large theatres; where some young relation of Mealy's—I think his little sister—did Imps in the Pantomimes.

No words can express the secret agony of my soul as I sunk into this companionship; compared these henceforth every-day associates with those of my happier childhood—not to say with Steerforth, Traddles, and the rest of those boys; and felt my hopes of growing up to be a learned and distinguished man crushed in my bosom. The deep remembrance of the sense I had, of being utterly without hope now; of the shame I felt in my position; of the misery it was to my young heart to believe that day by day what I had learned, and thought, and delighted in, and raised my fancy and my emulation up by, would pass away from me, little by little, never to be brought back any more; cannot be written. As often as Mick Walker went away in the course of that forenoon, I mingled my tears with the water in which I was washing the bottles; and sobbed as if there were a flaw in my own breast, and it were in danger of bursting.

The counting-house clock was at half-past twelve, and there was general preparation for going to dinner, when Mr. Quinion tapped at the counting-house window, and beckoned to me to go in. I went in, and found there a stoutish, middle-aged person, in a brown surtout and black tights and shoes, with no more hair upon his head (which was a large one, and very shining) than there is upon an egg, and with a very extensive face, which he turned full upon me. His clothes were shabby, but he had an imposing shirt-collar on. He carried a jaunty sort of a stick, with a large pair of rusty tassels to it; and a quizzing-glass hung outside his coat,—for ornament, I afterwards found, as he very seldom looked through it, and couldn't see anything when he did.

"This," said Mr. Quinion, in allusion to myself, "is he."

"This," said the stranger, with a certain condescending roll in his voice, and a certain indescribable air of doing something genteel, which impressed me very much, "is Master Copperfield. I hope I see you well, sir?"

I said I was very well, and hoped he was. I was sufficiently ill at ease, Heaven knows; but it was not in my nature to complain much at that time of my life, so I said I was very well, and hoped he was

"I am," said the stranger, "thank Heaven, quite well. I have received a letter from Mr. Murdstone, in which he mentions that he would desire me to receive into an apartment in the rear of my house, which is at present unoccupied—and is, in short, to be let as a—in short," said the stranger, with a smile and in a burst of confidence, "as a bed-room—the young beginner whom I have now the pleasure to—" and the stranger waved his hand, and settled his chin in his shirt collar.

"This is Mr. Micawber," said Mr. Quinion to me.

"Ahem!" said the stranger, "that is my name."

"Mr. Micawber," said Mr. Quinion, "is known to Mr. Murdstone. He takes orders for us on commission, when he can get any. He has been written to by Mr. Murdstone, on the subject of your lodgings, and he will receive you as a lodger."

"My address," said Mr. Micawber, "is Windsor Terrace, City Road. I—in short," said Mr. Micawber, with the same genteel air and in another burst of confidence—"I live there."

I made him a bow.

"Under the impression," said Mr. Micawber, "that your peregrinations in this metropolis have not as yet been extensive, and that you might have some difficulty in penetrating the arcana of the Modern Babylon in the direction of the City Road—in short," said Mr. Micawber, in another burst of confidence, "that you might lose yourself—I shall be happy to call this evening, and install you in the knowledge of the nearest way."

I thanked him with all my heart, for it was friendly in him to offer to take that trouble.

"At what hour," said Mr. Micawber, "shall I—"

"At about eight," said Mr. Quinion.

"At about eight," said Mr. Micawber. "I beg to wish you good day, Mr. Quinion. I will intrude no longer."

So he put on his hat, and went out with his cane under his arm: very upright, and humming a tune when he was clear of the counting-house.

Mr. Quinion then formally engaged me to be as useful as I could in the warehouse of Murdstone and Grinby, at a salary, I think, of six shillings a week. I am not clear whether it was six or seven. I am inclined to believe, from my uncertainty on this head, that it was six at first and seven afterwards. He paid me a week down (from his own pocket, I believe), and I gave Mealy sixpence out of it to get my trunk carried to Windsor Terrace at night: it being too heavy for my strength, small as it was. I paid sixpence more for my dinner, which was a meat pie and a turn at a neighbouring pump; and passed the hour which was allowed for that meal, in walking about the streets.

At the appointed time in the evening, Mr. Micawber reappeared. I washed my hands and face, to do the greater honour to his gentility, and we walked to our house, as I suppose I must now call it, together; Mr. Micawber impressing the names of streets, and the shapes of corner houses upon me, as we went along, that I might find my way back, easily, in the morning.

Arrived at his house in Windsor Terrace (which I noticed was shabby, like himself, but also, like himself, made all the show it could), he presented me to Mrs. Micawber, a thin and faded lady, not at all young, who was sitting in the parlor (the first floor was altogether unfurnished, and the blinds were kept down to delude the neighbours), with a baby at her breast. This baby was one of twins; and I may remark here that I hardly ever, in all my experience of the family, saw both the twins detached from Mrs. Micawber at the same time. One of them was always taking refreshment.

There were two other children: Master Micawber, aged about four, and Miss Micawber, aged about three. These, and a dark-complexioned young woman, with a habit of snorting, who was servant to the family, and informed me, before half-an-hour had expired, that she was "a Orfling," and came from St. Luke's workhouse in the neighbourhood, completed the establishment. My room was at the top of the house, at the back: a close chamber; stencilled all over with an ornament which my young imagination represented as a blue muffin, and very scantily furnished.

"I never thought," said Mrs. Micawber, when she came up, twin and all, to show me the apartment, and sat down to take breath, "before I was married, when I lived with papa and mama, that I should ever find it necessary to take a lodger. But Mr. Micawber being in difficulties, all considerations of private feeling must give way."

I said: "Yes, ma'am."

"Mr. Micawber's difficulties are almost overwhelming just at present," said Mrs. Micawber; "and whether it is possible to bring him through them, I don't know. When I lived at home with papa and mama, I really should have hardly understood what the word meant, in the sense in which I now employ it, but experientia does it—as papa used to say."

I cannot satisfy myself whether she told me that Mr. Micawber had been an officer in the Marines, or whether I have imagined it. I only know that I believe to this hour that he *was* in the Marines once upon a time, without knowing why. He was a sort of town traveller for a number of miscellaneous houses, now; but made little or nothing of it, I am afraid.

"If Mr. Micawber's creditors *will not* give him time," said Mrs. Micawber, "they must take the consequences; and the sooner they bring it to an issue the better. Blood cannot be obtained from a stone, neither can anything on account be obtained at present (not to mention law expenses) from Mr. Micawber."

I never can quite understand whether my precocious self-dependence confused Mrs. Micawber in reference to my age, or whether she was so full of the subject that she would have talked about it to the very twins if there had been nobody else to communicate with, but this was the strain in which she began, and she went on accordingly all the time I knew her.

Poor Mrs. Micawber! She said she had tried to exert herself; and so, I have no doubt, she had. The centre of the street-door was perfectly covered with a great brass-plate, on which was engraved "Mrs. Micawber's Boarding Establishment for Young Ladies;" but I never found that any young lady had ever been to school there; or that any young lady ever came, or proposed to come: or that the least preparation was ever made to receive any young lady. The only visitors I ever saw or heard of, were creditors. *They* used to come at all hours, and some of them were quite ferocious. One dirty-faced man, I think he was a bootmaker, used to edge himself into the passage as early as seven o'clock in the morning, and call up the stairs to Mr. Micawber—"Come! You ain't out yet, you know. Pay us, will you? Don't hide, you know; that's mean. I wouldn't be mean if I was you. Pay us, will you? You just pay us, d'ye hear? Come!" Receiving no answer to these taunts, he would mount in his wrath to the words "swindlers" and "robbers;" and these being ineffectual too, would sometimes go to the extremity of crossing the street, and roaring up at the windows of the second floor, where he knew Mr. Micawber was. At these times, Mr. Micawber would be transported with grief and mortification, even to the length (as I was once made aware by a scream from his wife) of making motions at himself with a razor; but within half an hour afterwards, he would polish up his shoes with extraordinary pains, and go out, humming a tune with a greater air of gentility than ever. Mrs. Micawber was quite as elastic. I have known her to be thrown into fainting fits by the king's taxes at three o'clock, and to eat lamb chops, breaded, and drink warm ale (paid for with two teaspoons that had gone to the pawnbroker's) at four. On one occasion, when an execution had just been put in, coming home through some chance as early as six o'clock, I saw her lying (of course with a twin) under the grate in a swoon, with her hair all torn about her face; but I never knew her more cheerful than she was, that very same night, over a veal-cutlet before the kitchen fire, telling me stories about her papa and mama, and the company they used to keep.

In this house, and with this family, I past my leisure time. My own exclusive breakfast of a penny loaf and a penny worth of milk, I provided myself. I kept another small loaf, and a modicum of cheese, on a particular shelf of a particular cupboard, to make my supper on when I came back at night. This made a hole in the six or seven shillings, I know well; and I was out at the warehouse all day, and had to support myself on that money all the week. From Monday morning until Saturday night, I had no advice, no counsel, no encouragement, no consolation, no assistance, no support, of any kind, from any one, that I can call to mind, as I hope to go to heaven!

I was so young and childish, and so little qualified—how could I be otherwise?—to undertake the whole charge of my own existence, that often, in going to Murdstone and Grinby's, of a morning, I could not resist the stale pastry put out for sale at half-price at the pastrycook's doors, and spent in that, the money I should have kept for my dinner. Then, I went without my dinner, or bought a roll or a slice of pudding. I remember two pudding-shops, between which I was divided, according to my finances. One was in a court close to St. Martin's Church—at the back of the church—which is now removed altogether. The pudding at that shop was made of currants, and was rather a special pudding, but was dear, twopenny-worth not being larger than a pennyworth of more ordinary pudding. A good shop for the latter was in the Strand—somewhere in that part which has been rebuilt since. It was a stout pale pudding, heavy and flabby, and with great flat raisins in it, stuck in whole at wide distances apart. It came up hot at about my time every day, and many a day did I dine off it. When I dined regularly and handsomely, I had a saveloy and a penny-loaf, or a fourpenny plate of red beef from a cook's shop; or a plate of bread and cheese and a glass of beer, from a miserable old public-house opposite our place of business, called the Lion, or the Lion and something else that I have forgotten. Once, I remember, carrying my own bread (which

I had brought from home in the morning), under my arm, wrapped in a piece of paper, like a book, and going to a famous alamode beef-house near Drury Lane, and ordering a "small plate" of that delicacy to eat with it. What the waiter thought of such a strange little apparition coming in all alone, I don't know; but I can see him now, staring at me as I ate my dinner, and bringing up the other waiter to look. I gave him a halfpenny for himself, and I wish he hadn't taken it.

We had half-an-hour, I think, for tea. When I had money enough, I used to get half-a-pint of ready-made coffee and a slice of bread and butter. When I had none, I used to look at a venison-shop in Fleet-street; or I have strolled, at such a time, as far as Covent Garden Market, and stared at the pine-apples. I was fond of wandering about the Adelphi, because it was a mysterious place, with those dark arches. I see myself emerging one evening from some of these arches, on a little public-house close to the river, with an open space before it, where some coal-heavers were dancing; to look at whom, I sat down upon a bench. I wonder what they thought of me!

I was such a child, and so little, that frequently when I went into the bar of a strange public-house for a glass of ale or porter, to moisten what I had had for dinner, they were afraid to give it me. I remember one hot evening I went into the bar of a public-house, and said to the landlord:

"What is your best—your *very best*—ale a glass?" For it was a special occasion. I don't know what. It may have been my birth-day.

"Twopence-halfpenny," says the landlord, "is the price of the Genuine Stunning ale."

"Then," says I, producing the money, "just draw me a glass of the Genuine Stunning, if you please, with a good head to it."

The landlord looked at me in return over the bar, from head to foot, with a strange smile on his face; and instead of drawing the beer, looked round the screen and said something to his wife. She came out from behind it, with her work in her hand, and joined him in surveying me. Here we stand, all three, before me now. The landlord in his shirt sleeves, leaning against the bar window-frame, his wife looking over the little half-door; and I, in some confusion,

MY MAGNIFICENT ORDER AT THE PUBLIC HOUSE.

looking up at them from outside the partition. They asked me a good many questions; as, what my name was, how old I was, where I lived, how I was employed, and how I came there. To all of which, that I might commit nobody, I invented, I am afraid, appropriate answers. They served me with the ale, though I suspect it was not the Genuine Stunning; and the landlord's wife, opening the little half-door of the bar, and bending down, gave me my money back, and gave me a kiss that was half admiring and half compassionate, but all womanly and good, I am sure.

I know I do not exaggerate, unconsciously and unintentionally, the scantiness of my resources or the difficulties of my life. I know that if a shilling were given me by Mr. Quinion at any time, I spent it in a dinner or a tea. I know that I worked, from morning until night, with common men and boys, a shabby child. I know that I lounged about the streets, insufficiently and unsatisfactorily fed. I know that, but for the mercy of God, I might easily have been, for any care that was taken of me, a little robber or a little vagabond.

Yet I held some station at Murdstone and Grinby's too. Besides that Mr. Quinion did what a careless man so occupied, and dealing with a thing so anomalous, could, to treat me as one upon a different footing from the rest, I never said, to man or boy, how it was that I came to be there, or gave the least indication of being sorry that I was there. That I suffered in secret, and that I suffered exquisitely, no one ever knew but I. How much I suffered, it is, as I have said already, utterly beyond my power to tell. But I kept my own counsel, and I did my work. I knew from the first, that, if I could not do my work as well as any of the rest, I could not hold myself above slight and contempt. I soon became at least as expeditious and as skilful as either of the other boys. Though perfectly familiar with them, my conduct and manner were different enough from theirs to place a space between us. They and the men generally spoke of me as "the little gent," or "the young Suffolker." A certain man named Gregory, who was foreman of the packers, and another named Tipp, who was the carman, and wore a red jacket, used to address me sometimes as "David:" but I think it was mostly when we were very confidential, and when I had made some efforts to entertain them, over our work, with some results of the old readings; which were fast perishing out of my remembrance. Mealy Potatoes uprose once, and rebelled against my being so distinguished; but Mick Walker settled him in no time.

My rescue from this kind of existence I considered quite hopeless, and abandoned, as such, altogether. I am solemnly convinced that I never for one hour was reconciled to it, or was otherwise than miserably unhappy; but I bore it; and even to Peggotty, partly for the love of her and partly for shame, never in any letter (though many passed between us) revealed the truth.

Mr. Micawber's difficulties were an addition to the distressed state of my mind. In my forlorn state I became quite attached to the family, and used to walk about, busy with Mrs. Micawber's calculations of ways and means, and heavy with the weight of Mr. Micawber's debts. On a Saturday night, which was my grand treat,—partly because it was a great thing to walk home with six or seven shillings in my pocket, looking into the shops and thinking what such a sum would buy, and partly because I went home early,—Mrs. Micawber would make the most heart-rending confidences to me; also on a Sunday morning, when I mixed the portion of tea or coffee I had bought over-night, in a little shaving pot, and sat late at my breakfast. It was nothing at all unusual for Mr. Micawber to sob violently at the beginning of one of these Saturday night conversations, and sing about Jack's delight being his lovely Nan, towards the end of it. I have known him to come home to supper with a flood of tears, and a declaration that nothing was now left but a jail; and go to bed making a calculation of the expense of putting bow-windows to the house, "in case anything turned up," which was his favorite expression. And Mrs. Micawber was just the same.

A curious equality of friendship, originating, I suppose, in our respective circumstances, sprung up between me and these people, notwithstanding the ludicrous disparity in our years. But I never allowed myself to be prevailed upon to accept any invitation to eat and drink with them out of their stock (knowing that they got on badly with the butcher and baker, and had often not too much for themselves), until Mrs. Micawber took me into her entire confidence. This she did one evening as follows:

"Master Copperfield," said Mrs. Micawber, "I make no stranger of you, and therefore do not hesitate to say that Mr. Micawber's difficulties are coming to a crisis."

It made me very miserable to hear it, and I looked at Mrs. Micawber's red eyes with the utmost sympathy.

"With the exception of the heel of a Dutch cheese—which is not adapted to the wants of a young family"—said Mrs. Micawber, "there is really not a scrap of anything in the larder. I was accustomed to speak of the larder when I lived with papa and mama, and I use the word almost unconsciously. What I mean to express, is, that there is nothing to eat in the house."

"Dear me!" I said, in great concern.

I had two or three shillings of my week's money in my pocket—from which I presume that it must have been on a Wednesday night when we held this conversation—and I hastily produced them, and with heartfelt emotion begged Mrs. Micawber to accept of them as a loan. But that lady, kissing me, and making me put them back in my pocket, replied that she couldn't think of it.

"No, my dear Master Copperfield," said she, "far be it from my thoughts! But you have a discretion beyond your years, and can render me another kind of service, if you will; and a service I will thankfully accept of."

I begged Mrs. Micawber to name it.

"I have parted with the plate myself," said Mrs. Micawber. "Six tea, two salt, and a pair of sugars, I have at different times borrowed money on, in secret, with my own hands. But the twins are a great tie; and to me, with my recollections of papa and mama, these transactions are very painful. There are still a few trifles tha. we could part with. Mr. Micawber's feelings would never allow *him* to dispose of them; and Clickett"—this was the girl from the workhouse—"being of a vulgar mind, would take painful liberties if so much confidence was reposed in her. Master Copperfield, if I might ask you"—

I understood Mrs. Micawber now, and begged her to make use of me to any extent. I began to dispose of the more portable articles of property that very evening; and went out on a similar expedition almost every morning, before I went to Murdstone and Grinby's.

Mr. Micawber had a few books on a little chiffonier, which he called the library; and those went first. I carried them, one after another, to a bookstall in the City Road—one part of which, near our house, was almost all bookstalls and bird-shops then—and sold them for whatever they would bring. The keeper of this bookstall, who lived in a little house behind it, used to get tipsy every night, and to be violently scolded by his wife every morning. More than once, when I went there early, I had audience of him in a turn-up bedstead, with a cut in his forehead or a black eye, bearing witness to his excesses over night (I am afraid he was quarrelsome in his drink), and he, with a shaking hand, endeavoring to find the needful shillings in one or other of the pockets of his clothes, which lay upon the floor, while his wife, with a baby in her arms and her shoes down at heel, never left off rating him. Sometimes he had lost his money, and then he would ask me to call again; but his wife had always got some—had taken his, I dare say, while he was drunk—and secretly completed the bargain on the stairs, as we went down together.

At the pawnbroker's shop, too, I began to be very well known. The principal gentleman who officiated behind the counter, took a good deal of notice of me; and often got me, I recollect, to decline a Latin noun or adjective, or to conjugate a Latin verb, in his ear, while he transacted my business. After all these occasions Mrs. Micawber made a little treat, which was generally a supper; and there was a peculiar relish in these meals which I well remember.

At last Mr. Micawber's difficulties came to a crisis, and he was arrested early one morning, and carried over to the King's Bench Prison in the Borough. He told me, as he went out of the house, that the God of day had now gone down upon him—and I really thought his heart was broken and mine too. But I heard, afterwards, that he was seen to play a lively game at skittles, before noon.

On the first Sunday after he was taken there, I was to go and see him, and have dinner with him. I was to ask my way to such a place, and just short of that place I should see such another place, and just short of that I should see a yard, which I was to cross, and keep straight on until I saw a turnkey. All this I did; and when at last I did see a turnkey (poor ittle fellow that I was!), and thought how, when Roderick Random was in a debtor's prison, there was a man there with nothing on him but an old rug, the turnkey swam before my dimmed eyes and my beating heart.

Mr. Micawber was waiting for me within the gate, and we went up to his room (top story but one), and cried very much. He solemnly conjured me, I remember, to take warning by his fate; and to observe that if a man had twenty pounds a-year for his income, and spent nineteen pounds nineteen shillings and sixpence, he would be happy, but that if he spent twenty pounds one he would be miserable. After which he borrowed a shilling of me for porter, gave me a written order on Mrs. Micawber for the amount, and put away his pocket-handkerchief, and cheered up.

We sat before a little fire, with two bricks put within the rusted grate, one on each side, to prevent its burning too many coals; until another debtor, who shared the room with Mr. Micawber, came in from the bakehouse with the loin of mutton which was our joint-stock repast. Then I was sent up to "Captain Hopkins" in the room overhead, with Mr. Micawber's compliments, and I was his young friend, and would Captain Hopkins lend me a knife and fork.

Captain Hopkins lent me the knife and fork, with his compliments to Mr. Micawber. There was a very dirty lady in his little room, and two wan girls, his daughters, with shock heads of hair. I thought it was better to borrow Captain Hopkins's knife and fork, than Captain Hopkins's comb. The Captain himself was in the last extremity of shabbiness, with large whiskers, and an old, old brown great-coat with no other coat below it. I saw his bed rolled up in a corner; and what plates and dishes and pots he had, on a shelf; and I divined (God knows how) that though the two girls with the shock heads of hair were Captain Hopkins's children, the dirty lady was not married to Captain Hopkins. My timid station on his threshold was not occupied more than a couple of minutes at most; but I came down again with all this in my knowledge, as surely as the knife and fork were in my hand.

There was something gipsy-like and agreeable in the dinner, after all. I took back Captain Hopkins's knife and fork early in the afternoon, and went home to comfort Mrs. Micawber with an account of my visit. She fainted when she saw me return, and made a little jug of egg-hot afterwards to console us while we talked it over.

I don't know how the household furniture came to be sold for the family benefit, or who sold it, except that *I* did not. Sold it was, however, and carried away in a van · except the bed, a few chairs, and the kitchen-table. With these possessions we encamped, as it were, in the two parlors of the emptied house in Windsor Terrace; Mrs. Micawber, the children, the Orfling, and myself; and lived in those rooms night and day. I have no idea for how long, though it seems to me for a long time. At last Mrs. Micawber resolved to move into the prison, where Mr. Micawber had now secured a room to himself. So I took the key of the house to the landlord, who was very glad to get it; and the beds were sent over to the King's Bench, except mine, for which a little room was hired outside the walls in the neighbourhood of that Institution, very much to my satisfaction, since the Micawbers and I had become too used to one another, in our troubles, to part. The Orfling was likewise accommodated with an inexpensive lodging in the same neighbourhood. Mine was a quiet back garret with a sloping roof, commanding a pleasant prospect of a timber-yard; and when I took possession of it, with the reflection that Mr. Micawber's troubles had come to a crisis at last, I thought it quite a paradise.

All this time I was working at Murdstone and Grinby's in the same common way, and with the same common companions, and with the same sense of unmerited degradation as at first. But I never, happily for me no doubt, made a single acquaintance, or spoke to any of the many boys whom I saw daily in going to the warehouse, in coming from it, and in prowling about the streets at meal times. I led the same secretly unhappy life; but I led it in the same lonely, self-reliant manner. The only changes I am conscious of are, firstly, that I had grown more shabby, and secondly, that I was now relieved of much of the weight of Mr. and Mrs. Micawber's cares; for some relatives or friends had engaged to help them at their present pass, and they lived more comfortably in the prison than they had lived for a long while out of it. I used to breakfast with them now, in virtue of some arrangement, of which I have forgotten the details. I forget, too, at what hour the gates were opened in the morning, admitting of my going in; but I know that I was often up at six o'clock, and that my favorite lounging-place in the interval was old London Bridge, where I was wont to sit in one of the stone recesses, watching the people going by, or to look over the balustrades at the sun shining in the water, and lighting up the golden flame on the top of the Monument. The Orfling met me here sometimes, to be told some astonishing fictions respecting the wharves and the Tower; of which I can say no more than that I hope I believed them myself. In the evening I used to go back to the prison, and walk up and down the parade with Mr. Micawber; or play casino with Mrs. Micawber, and hear reminiscences of her papa and mama. Whether Mr. Murdstone knew where I was, I am unable to say. I never told them at Murdstone and Grinby's.

Mr. Micawber's affairs, although past their crisis, were very much involved by reason of a certain "Deed," of which I used to hear a great deal, and which I suppose, now, to have been some former composition with his creditors, though I was so far from being clear about it then, that I am conscious of having confounded it with those demoniacal parchments which are held to have, once upon a time, obtained to a great extent in Germany. At last this document appeared to be got out of the way, somehow; at all events it ceased to be the rock-ahead it had been; and Mrs. Micawber informed me that "her family" had decided that Mr. Micawber should apply for his release under the Insolvent Debtors Act, which would set him free, she expected, in about six weeks.

"And then," said Mr. Micawber, who was present, "I have no doubt I shall, please Heaven, begin to be beforehand with the world, and to live in a perfectly new manner, if—in short, if anything turns up."

By way of going in for anything that might be on the cards, I call to mind that Mr. Micawber, about this time, composed a petition to the House of Commons, praying for an alteration in the law of imprisonment for debt. I set down this remembrance here, because it is an instance to myself of the manner in which I fitted my old books to my altered life, and made stories for myself out of the streets, and out of men and women; and how some main points in the character I shall unconsciously develope, I suppose, in writing my life, were gradually forming all this while.

There was a club in the prison, in which Mr. Micawber, as a gentleman, was a great authority. Mr. Micawber had stated his idea of this petition to the club, and the club had strongly approved of the same. Wherefore Mr. Micawber (who was a thoroughly good-natured man, and as active a creature about everything but his own affairs as ever existed, and never so happy as when he was busy about something that could never be of any profit to him) set to work at the petition, invented it, engrossed it on an immense sheet of paper, spread it out on a table, and appointed a time for all the club, and all within the walls if they chose, to come up to his room and sign it.

When I heard of this approaching ceremony, I was so anxious to see them all come in, one after another, though I knew the greater part of them already, and they me, that I got an hour's leave of absence from Murdstone and Grinby's, and established myself in a corner for that purpose. As many of the principal members of the club as could be got into the small room without filling it, supported Mr. Micawber in front of the petition, while my old friend Captain Hopkins (who had washed himself, to do honor to so solemn an occasion) stationed himself close to it, to read it to all who were unacquainted with its contents. The door was then thrown open, and the general population began to come in, in a long file: several waiting outside, while one entered, affixed his signature, and went out. To everybody in succession, Captain Hopkins said: "Have you read it?"—"No."—"Would you like to hear it read?" If he weakly showed the least disposition to hear it, Captain Hopkins, in a loud sonorous voice, gave him every word of it. The Captain would have read it twenty thousand times, if twenty thousand people would have heard him, one by one. I remember a certain luscious roll he gave to such phrases as "The people's representatives in Parliament assembled," "Your petitioners therefore humbly approach your honorable house," "His gracious Majesty's unfortunate subjects," as if the words were something real in his mouth, and delicious to taste; Mr. Micawber, meanwhile, listening with a little of an author's vanity, and contemplating (not severely) the spikes on the opposite wall.

As I walked to and fro daily between Southwark and Blackfriars, and lounged about at meal-times in obscure streets, the stones of which may, for anything I know, be worn at this moment by my childish feet, I wonder how many of these people were wanting in the crowd that used to come filing before me in review again, to the echo of Captain Hopkins's voice! When my thoughts go back, now, to that slow agony of my youth, I wonder how much of the histories I invented for such people hangs like a mist of fancy over well-remembered facts! When I tread the old ground, I do not wonder that I seem to see and pity, going on before me, an innocent romantic boy, making his imaginative world out of such strange experiences and sordid things!

CHAPTER XII.

LIKING LIFE ON MY OWN ACCOUNT NO BETTER, I FORM A GREAT RESOLUTION.

In due time, Mr. Micawber's petition was ripe for hearing; and that gentleman was ordered to be discharged under the act, to my great joy. His creditors were not implacable; and Mrs. Micawber informed me that even the revengeful bootmaker had declared in open court that he bore him no malice, but that when money was owing to him he liked to be paid. He said he thought it was human nature.

Mr. Micawber returned to the King's Bench when his case was over, as some fees were to be settled, and some formalities observed, before he could be actually released. The club received him with transport, and held an harmonic meeting that evening in his honor; while Mrs. Micawber and I had a lamb's fry in private, surrounded by the sleeping family.

"On such an occasion I will give you, Master Copperfield," said Mrs. Micawber, "in a little more flip," for we had been having some already, "the memory of my papa and mama."

"Are they dead, ma'am?" I enquired, after drinking the toast in a wine-glass.

"My mama departed this life," said Mrs. Micawber, "before Mr. Micawber's difficulties commenced, or at least before they became pressing. My papa lived to bail Mr. Micawber several times, and then expired, regretted by a numerous circle."

Mrs. Micawber shook her head, and dropped a pious tear upon the twin who happened to be in hand.

As I could hardly hope for a more favourable opportunity of putting a question in which I had a near interest, I said to Mrs. Micawber:

"May I ask, ma'am, what you and Mr. Micawber intend to do, now that Mr. Micawber is out of his difficulties, and at liberty? Have you settled yet?"

"My family," said Mrs. Micawber, who always said those two words with an air, though I never could discover who came under the denomination, "my family are of opinion that Mr. Micawber should quit London, and exert his talents in the country. Mr. Micawber is a man of great talent, Master Copperfield."

I said I was sure of that.

"Of great talent," repeated Mrs. Micawber. "My family are of opinion, that, with a little interest, something might be done for a man of his ability in the Custom House. The influence of my family being local, it is their wish that Mr. Micawber should go down to Plymouth. They think it indispensable that he should be upon the spot."

"That he may be ready?" I suggested.

"Exactly," returned Mrs. Micawber. "That he may be ready—in case of anything turning up."

"And do you go, too, ma'am?"

The events of the day, in combination with the twins, if not with the flip, had made Mrs. Micawber hysterical, and she shed tears as she replied:

"I never will desert Mr. Micawber. Mr. Micawber may have concealed his difficulties from me in the first instance, but his sanguine temper may have led him to expect that he would overcome them. The pearl necklace and bracelets which I inherited from mama, have been disposed of for less than half their value; and the set of coral, which was the wedding gift of my papa, has been actually thrown away for nothing. But I never will desert Mr. Micawber. No!" cried Mrs. Micawber, more affected than before, "I never will do it! It's of no use asking me!"

I felt quite uncomfortable—as if Mrs. Micawber supposed I had asked her to do anything of the sort?—and sat looking at her in alarm.

"Mr. Micawber has his faults. I do not deny that he is improvident. I do not deny that he has kept me in the dark as to his resources and his liabilities, both," she went on, looking at the wall; but I never will desert Mr. Micawber!"

Mrs. Micawber having now raised her voice into a perfect scream, I was so frightened that I ran off to the club-room, and disturbed Mr. Micawber in the act of presiding at a long table, and leading the chorus of

Gee up, Dobbin,
Gee ho, Dobbin,
Gee up, Dobbin,
Gee up, and gee ho—o—o!

—with the tidings that Mrs. Micawber was in an alarming state, upon which he immediately burst into tears, and came away with me with his waistcoat full of the heads and tails of shrimps, of which he had been partaking.

"Emma, my angel!" cried Mr. Micawber, running into the room; "what is the matter?"

"I never will desert you, Micawber!" she exclaimed.

"My life!" said Mr. Micawber, taking her in his arms. "I am perfectly aware of it."

"He is the parent of my children! He is the father of my twins! He is the husband of my affections," cried Mrs. Micawber, struggling; "and I ne—ver—will—desert Mr. Micawber!"

Mr. Micawber was so deeply affected by this proof of her devotion (as to me, I was dissolved in tears), that he hung over her in a passionate manner, imploring her to look up, and to be calm. But the more he asked Mrs. Micawber to look up, the more she fixed her eyes on nothing; and the more he asked her to compose herself, the more she wouldn't. Consequently Mr. Micawber was soon so overcome, that he mingled his tears with hers and mine; until he begged me to do him the favor of taking a chair on the staircase, while he got her into bed. I would have taken my leave for the night, but he would not hear of my doing that until the strangers' bell should ring. So I sat at the staircase window, until he came out with another chair and joined me.

"How is Mrs. Micawber now, sir?"

"Very low," said Mr. Micawber, shaking his head; "re-action. Ah, this has been a dreadful day! We stand alone now—everything is gone from us!"

Mr. Micawber pressed my hand, and groaned, and afterwards shed tears. I was greatly touched, and disappointed too, for I had expected that we should be quite gay on this happy and long-looked for occasion. But Mr. and Mrs. Micawber were so used to their old difficulties, I think, that they felt quite shipwrecked when they came to consider that they were released from them. All their elasticity was departed, and I never saw them half so wretched as on this night; insomuch that when the bell rang, and Mr. Micawber walked with me to the lodge, and parted from me there with a blessing, I felt quite afraid to leave him by himself, he was so profoundly miserable.

But through all the confusion and lowness of spirits in which we had been, so unexpectedly to me, involved, I plainly discerned that Mr. and Mrs. Micawber and their family were going away from London, and that a parting between us was near at hand. It was in my walk home that night, and in the sleepless hours which followed when I lay in bed, that the thought first occurred to me—though I don't know how it came into my head—which afterwards shaped itself into a settled resolution.

I had grown to be so accustomed to the Micawbers, and had been so intimate with them in their distresses, and was so utterly friendless without them, that the prospect of being thrown upon some new shift for a lodging, and going once more among unknown people, was like being that moment turned adrift into my present life, with such a knowledge of it ready made, as experience had given me. All the sensitive feelings it wounded so cruelly, all the shame and misery it kept alive within my breast, became more poignant as I thought of this; and I determined that the life was unendurable.

That there was no hope of escape from it, unless the escape was my own act, I knew quite well. I rarely heard from Miss Murdstone, and never from Mr. Murdstone: but two or three parcels of made or mended clothes had come up for me, consigned to Mr. Quinion, and in each there was a scrap of paper to the effect that J. M. trusted D. C. was applying himself to business, and devoting himself wholly to his duties—not the least hint of my ever being anything else than the common drudge into which I was fast settling down.

The very next day showed me, while my mind was in the first agitation of what it had conceived, that Mrs. Micawber had not spoken of their going away without warrant. They took a lodging in the house where I lived, for a week; at the expiration of which time they were to start for Plymouth. Mr. Micawber himself came down to the counting-house, in the afternoon, to tell Mr. Quinion that he must relinquish me on the day of his departure, and to give me a high character, which I am sure I deserved. And Mr. Quinion, calling in Tipp the carman, who was a married man, and had a room to let, quartered me prospectively on him—by our mutual consent, as he had every reason to think; for I said nothing, though my resolution was now taken.

I passed my evenings with Mr. and Mrs. Micawber, during the remaining term of our residence under the same roof; and I think we became fonder of one another as the time went on. On the last Sunday, they invited me to dinner; and we had a loin of pork and apple sauce, and a pudding. I had bought a spotted wooden horse over-night as a parting gift to little Wilkins Micawber—that was the boy—and a doll for little Emma. I had also bestowed a shilling on the Orfling, who was about to be disbanded.

We had a very pleasant day, though we were all in a tender state about our approaching separation.

"I shall never, Master Copperfield," said Mrs. Micawber, "revert to the period when Mr. Micawber was in difficulties, without thinking of you. Your conduct has always been of the most delicate and obliging description. You have never been a lodger. You have been a friend."

"My dear," said Mr. Micawber; "Copperfield," for so he had been accustomed to call me, of late, "has a heart to feel for the distresses of his fellow creatures when they are behind a cloud, and a head to plan, and a hand to——in short, a general ability to dispose of such available property as could be made away with."

I expressed my sense of this commendation, and said I was very sorry we were going to lose one another.

"My dear young friend," said Mr. Micawber, "I am older than

you; a man of some experience in life, and—and of some experience, in short, in difficulties generally speaking. At present, and until something turns up (which I am, I may say, hourly expecting), I have nothing to bestow but advice. Still my advice is so far worth taking, that—in short, that I have never taken it myself, and am the"—here Mr. Micawber, who had been beaming and smiling, all over his head and face, up to the present moment, checked himself and frowned—"the miserable wretch you behold."

"My dear Micawber!" urged his wife.

"I say," returned Mr. Micawber, quite forgetting himself, and smiling again, "the miserable wretch you behold. My advice is, never do to-morrow what you can to-day. Procrastination is the thief of time. Collar him."

"My poor papa's maxim," Mrs. Micawber observed.

"My dear," said Mr. Micawber, "your papa was very well in his way, and heaven forbid that I should disparage him. Take him for all in all, we ne'er shall—in short, make the acquaintance, probably, of any body else possessing, at his time of life, the same legs for gaiters, and able to read the same description of print, without spectacles. But he applied that maxim to our marriage, my dear; and that was so far prematurely entered into, in consequence, that I never recovered the expense."

Mr. Micawber looked aside, at Mrs. Micawber, and added; "Not that I am sorry for it. Quite the contrary, my love." After which, he was grave for a minute or so.

"My other piece of advice, Copperfield," said Mr. Micawber, "you know. Annual income twenty pounds, annual expenditure nineteen ought and six, result happiness. Annual income, twenty pounds, annual expenditure twenty pounds ought and six, result misery. The blossom is blighted, the leaf is withered, the god of day goes down upon the dreary scene, and—and in short you are forever floored. As I am!"

To make his example the more impressive, Mr. Micawber drank a glass of punch with an air of great enjoyment and satisfaction, and whistled the College Hornpipe.

I did not fail to assure him that I would store these precepts in my mind, though indeed I had no need to do so, for, at the time, they affected me visibly. Next morning I met the whole family at the coach-office, and saw them with a desolate heart, take their places outside, at the back.

"Master Copperfield," said Mrs. Micawber. "God bless you! I never can forget all that, you know, and I never would if I could."

"Copperfield," said Mr. Micawber, "farewell! Every happiness and prosperity! If, in the progress of revolving years, I could persuade myself that my blighted destiny had been a warning to you, I should feel that I had not occupied another man's place in existence altogether in vain. In case of anything turning up (of which I am rather confident), I shall be extremely happy if it should be in my power to improve your prospects."

I think, as Mrs. Micawber sat at the back of the coach, with the children, and I stood in the road looking wistfully at them, a mist cleared from her eyes, and she saw what a little creature I really was. I think so, because she beckoned me to climb up with quite a new and motherly expression in her face, and put her arm round my neck, and gave me just such a kiss as she might have given to her own boy. I had barely time to get down again before the coach started, and I could hardly see the family for the handkerchiefs they waved. It was gone in a minute. The Orfling and I stood looking vacantly at each other in the middle of the road, and then shook hands and said good bye; she going back, I suppose, to Saint Luke's workhouse, as I went to begin my weary day at Murdstone and Grinby's.

But with no intention of passing many more weary days there. No. I had resolved to run away.—To go, by some means or other, down into the country, to the only relation I had in the world, and tell my story to my aunt, Miss Betsey.

I have already observed that I don't know how this desperate idea came into my brain. But, once there, it remained there; and hardened into a purpose than which I have never entertained a more determined purpose in my life. I am far from sure that I believed there was anything hopeful in it, but my mind was thoroughly made up that it must be carried into execution.

Again, and again, and a hundred times again, since the night when the thought had first occurred to me and banished sleep, I had gone over that old story of my poor mother's about my birth, which it had been one of my great delights in the old time to hear her tell and which I knew by heart. My aunt walked into that story, and walked out of it, a dread and awful personage; but there was one little trait in her behavior which I liked to dwell on, and which gave me some faint shadow of encouragement. I could not forget how my mother had thought that she felt her touch her pretty hair with no ungentle hand; and though it might have been altogether my mother's fancy, and might have had no foundation whatever in fact, I made a little picture, out of it, of my terrible aunt relenting towards the girlish beauty that I recollected so well and loved so much, which softened the whole narrative. It is very possible that it had been in my mind a long time, and had gradually engendered my determination.

As I did not even know where Miss Betsey lived, I wrote a long letter to Peggotty, and asked her, incidentally, if she remembered; pretending that I had heard of such a lady living at a certain place I named at random, and had a curiosity to know if it were the same. In the course of that letter, I told Peggotty that I had a particular occasion for half a guinea; and that if she could lend me that sum until I could repay it, I should be very much obliged to her, and would tell her afterwards what I had wanted it for.

Peggotty's answer soon arrived, and was, as usual, full of affectionate devotion. She enclosed the half guinea (I was afraid she must have had a world of trouble to get it out of Mr. Barkis's box), and told me that Miss Betsey lived near Dover, but whether at Dover itself, at Hythe, Sandgate, or Folkstone, she could not say. One of our men, however, informing me on my asking him about these places, that they were all close together, I deemed this enough for my object, and resolved to set out at the end of that week.

Being a very honest little creature, and unwilling to disgrace the memory I was going to leave behind me at Murdstone and Grinby's, I considered myself bound to remain until Saturday night; and, as I had been paid a week's wages in advance when I first came there, not to present myself in the counting-house at the usual hour, to receive my stipend. For this express reason, I had borrowed the half-guinea, that I might not be without a fund for my travelling-expenses. Accordingly, when the Saturday night came, and we were all waiting in the warehouse to be paid, and Tipp the carman, who always took precedence, went in first to draw his money, I shook Mick Walker by the hand; asked him when it came to his turn to be paid, to say to Mr. Quinion that I had gone to move my box to Tipp's; and, bidding a last good night to Mealy Potatoes, ran away.

My box was at my old lodging, over the water, and I had written a direction for it on the back of one of our address cards that we nailed on the casks: "Master David, to be left till called for, at the Coach Office, Dover." This I had in my pocket ready to put on the box, after I should have got it out of the house; and as I went towards my lodging, I looked about me for some one who would help me to carry it to the booking-office.

There was a long-legged young man with a very little empty donkey-cart, standing near the Obelisk, in the Blackfriars Road, whose eye I caught as I was going by, and who addressing me as "Sixpenn'orth of bad ha'pence," hoped "I should know him agin to swear to"—in allusion, I have no doubt, to my staring at him. I stopped to assure him that I had not done so in bad manners, but uncertain whether he might or might not like a job.

"Wot job?" said the long-legged young man.

"To move a box," I answered.

"Wot box?" said the long-legged young man.

I told him mine, which was down that street there, and which I wanted him to take to the Dover coach-office for sixpence.

"Done with you for a tanner!" said the long-legged young man, and directly got upon his cart, which was nothing but a large wooden-tray on wheels, and rattled away at such a rate, that it was as much as I could do to keep pace with the donkey.

There was a defiant manner about this young man, and particularly about the way in which he chewed straw as he spoke to me, that I did not much like; as the bargain was made, however, I took him up-stairs to the room I was leaving, and we brought the box down, and put it on his cart. Now, I was unwilling to put the direction-card on there, lest any of my landlord's family should fathom what I was doing, and detain me; so I said to the young man that I would be glad if he would stop for a minute, when he came to the dead-wall of the King's Bench prison. The words were no sooner out of my mouth, than he rattled away as if he, my box, the cart, and the donkey, were all equally mad; and I was quite out of breath with running and calling after him, when I caught him at the place appointed.

Being much flushed and excited, I tumbled my half-guinea out of my pocket in pulling the card out. I put it in my mouth for safety, and though my hands trembled a good deal, had just tied the card on very much to my satisfaction, when I felt myself violently chucked under the chin by the long-legged young man, and saw my half-guinea fly out of my mouth into his hand.

"Wot!" said the young man, seizing me by my jacket collar, with a frightful grin. "This is a pollis case, is it? You're a going to bolt, are you? Come to the pollis, you young warmin, come to the pollis!"

"You give me my money back, if you please," said I, very much frightened; "and leave me alone."

"Come to the pollis!" said the young man. "You shall prove it yourn to the pollis."

"Give me my box and money, will you," I cried, bursting into tears.

The young man still replied: "Come to the pollis!" and was dragging me against the donkey in a violent manner, as if there were any affinity between that animal and a magistrate, when he changed his mind, jumped into the cart, sat upon my box, and, exclaiming that he would drive to the pollis straight, rattled away harder than ever.

I ran after him as fast as I could, but I had no breath to call out with, and should not have dared to call out, now, if I had. I narrowly escaped being run over, twenty times at least, in half a mile. Now I lost him, now I saw him, now I lost him, now I was cut at with a whip, now shouted at, now down in the mud, now up again, now running into somebody's arms, now running headlong at a post. At length, confused by fright and heat, and doubting whether half London might not by this time be turned out for my apprehension, I left the young man to go where he would with my box and money; and, panting and crying, but never stopping, faced about for Greenwich, which I had understood was on the Dover Road: taking very little more out of the world, towards the retreat of my aunt, Miss Betsey, than I had brought into it, on the night when my arrival gave her so much umbrage.

CHAPTER XIII.

THE SEQUEL OF MY RESOLUTION.

For anything I know, I may have had some wild idea of running all the way to Dover, when I gave up the pursuit of the young man with the donkey cart, and started for Greenwich. My scattered senses were soon collected as to that point, if I had; for I came to a stop in the Kent Road, at a terrace with a piece of water before it, and a great foolish image in the middle, blowing a dry shell. Here I sat down on a door-step, quite spent and exhausted with the efforts I had already made, and with hardly breath enough to cry for the loss of my box and half-guinea.

It was by this time dark; I heard the clocks strike ten, as I sat resting. But it was a summer night, fortunately, and fine weather. When I had recovered my breath, and had got rid of a stifling sensation in my throat, I rose up and went on. In the midst of my distress, I had no notion of going back. I doubt if I should have had any, though there had been a Swiss snow-drift in the Kent Road.

But my standing possessed of only three-halfpence in the world (and I am sure I wonder how *they* came to be left in my pocket on a Saturday night!) troubled me none the less because I went on. I began to picture to myself, as a scrap of newspaper intelligence, my being found dead in a day or two, under some hedge; and I trudged on miserably, though as fast as I could, until I happened to pass a little shop, where it was written up that ladies' and gentlemen's wardrobes were bought, and that the best price was given for rags, bones, and kitchen-stuff. The master of this shop was sitting at the door in his shirt sleeves, smoking; and as there were a great many coats and pairs of trowsers dangling from the low ceiling, and only two feeble candles burning inside to show what they were, I fancied that he looked like a man of a revengeful disposition, who had hung all his enemies, and was enjoying himself.

My late experiences with Mr. and Mrs. Micawber suggested to me that here might be the means of keeping off the wolf for a little while. I went up the next bye-street, took off my waistcoat, rolled it neatly under my arm, and came back to the shop-door. "If you please, sir," I said, "I am to sell this for a fair price."

Mr. Dolloby—Dolloby was the name over the shop-door, at least—took the waistcoat, stood his pipe on its head against the door-post, went into the shop, followed by me, snuffed the two candles with his fingers, spread the waistcoat on the counter, and looked at it there, held it up against the light, and looked at it there, and ultimately said:

"What do you call a price, now, for this here little weskit?"

"Oh! you know best, sir," I returned, modestly.

"I can't be buyer and seller, too," said Mr. Dolloby. "Put a price on this here little weskit."

"Would eighteenpence be"—I hinted, after some hesitation.

Mr. Dolloby rolled it up again, and gave it me back. "I should rob my family," he said, "if I was to offer ninepence for it."

This was a disagreeable way of putting the business; because it imposed upon me, a perfect stranger, the unpleasantness of asking Mr. Dolloby to rob his family on my account. My circumstances being so very pressing, however, I said I would take ninepence for it, if he pleased. Mr. Dolloby, not without some grumbling, gave ninepence. I wished him good night, and walked out of the shop, the richer by that sum, and the poorer by a waistcoat. But when I buttoned my jacket, that was not much.

Indeed, I foresaw pretty clearly that my jacket would go next, and that I should have to make the best of my way to Dover in a shirt and a pair of trowsers, and might deem myself lucky if I got there even in that trim. But my mind did not run so much on this as might be supposed. Beyond a general impression of the distance before me, and of the young man with the donkey-cart having used me cruelly, I think I had no very urgent sense of my difficulties when I once again set off with my ninepence in my pocket.

A plan had occurred to me for passing the night, which I was going to carry into execution. This was, to lie behind the wall at the back of my old school, in a corner where there used to be a haystack. I imagined it would be a kind of company to have the boys, and the bed-room where I used to tell the stories, so near me: although the boys would know nothing of my being there, and the bed-room would yield me no shelter.

I had had a hard day's work, and was pretty well jaded when I came climbing out, at last, upon the level of Blackheath. It cost me some trouble to find out Salem House; but I found it, and I found a haystack in the corner, and I lay down by it; having first walked round the wall, and looked up at the windows, and seen that all was dark and silent within. Never shall I forget the lonely sensation of first lying down, without a roof above my head!

Sleep came upon me as it came on many other outcasts, against whom house-doors were locked, and house-dogs barked, that night—and I dreamed of lying on my old school bed, talking to the boys in my room; and found myself sitting upright, with Steerforth's name upon my lips, looking wildly at the stars that were glistening and glimmering above me. When I remembered where I was at that untimely hour, a feeling stole upon me that made me get up, afraid of I don't know what, and walk about. But the fainter glimmering of the stars, and the pale light in the sky where the day was coming, reassured me: and my eyes being very heavy, I lay down again, and slept—though with a knowledge in my sleep that it was cold—until the warm beams of the sun, and the ringing of the getting-up bell at Salem House, awoke me. If I could have hoped that Steerforth was there, I would have lurked about until he came out alone; but I knew he must have left long since. Traddles still remained, perhaps, but it was very doubtful; and I had not sufficient confidence in his discretion or good luck, however strong my reliance was on his good-nature, to wish to trust him with my situation. So I crept away from the wall as Mr. Creakle's boys were getting up, and struck into the long dusty track which I had first known to be the Dover road when I was one of them, and when I little expected that any eyes would ever see me the wayfarer I was now, upon it.

What a different Sunday morning from the old Sunday morning at Yarmouth! In due time I heard the church-bells ringing, as I plodded on; and I met people who were going to church; and I passed a church or two where the congregation were inside, and the sound of singing came out into the sun-shine, while the beadle sat and cooled himself in the shade of the porch, or stood beneath the yew-tree, with his hand to his forehead, glowering at me going by. But the peace and rest of the old Sunday morning were on everything, except me. That was the difference. I felt quite wicked in my dirt and dust, and with my tangled hair. But for the quiet picture I had conjured up, of my mother in her youth and beauty, weeping by the fire, and my aunt relenting to her, I hardly think I should have had courage to go on until next day. But it always went before me, and I followed.

I got, that Sunday, through three-and-twenty miles on the straight road, though not very easily, for I was new to that kind of toil. I see myself, as evening closes in, coming over the bridge at Rochester, footsore and tired, and eating bread that I had bought for supper. One or two little houses, with the notice, "Lodgings for Travellers," hanging out, had tempted me; but I was afraid of spending the few pence I had, and was even more afraid of the vicious looks of the trampers I had met or overtaken. I sought no shelter, therefore, but the sky; and toiling into Chatham,—which, in that night's aspect, is a mere dream of chalk, and drawbridges, and mastless ships in a muddy river, roofed like Noah's arks,—crept, at last, upon a sort of grass-grown battery overhanging a lane, where a sentry was walking to and fro. Here I lay down, near a cannon; and, happy in the society of the sentry's footsteps, though he knew no more of my being above him than the boys at Salem House had known of my lying by the wall, slept soundly until morning.

Very stiff and sore of foot I was in the morning, and quite dazed by the beating of drums and marching of troops, which seemed to hem me in on every side when I went down towards the long narrow street. Feeling that I could go but a very little way that day, if I were to reserve any strength for getting to my journey's end, I resolved to make the sale of my jacket its principal business. Accordingly, I took the jacket off, that I might learn to do without it; and carrying it under my arm, began a tour of inspection of the various slop-shops.

It was a likely place to sell a jacket in; for the dealers in second-hand clothes were numerous, and were, generally speaking, on the look-out for customers at their shop-doors. But as most of them had, hanging up among their stock, an officer's coat or two, epauletts and all, I was rendered timid by the costly nature of their dealings, and walked about for a long time without offering my merchandize to any one.

This modesty of mine directed my attention to the marine-store shops, and such shops as Mr. Dolloby's, in preference to the regular dealers. At last I found one that I thought looked promising, at the corner of a dirty lane, ending in an inclosure full of stinging nettles, against the palings of which some second-hand sailors' clothes, that seemed to have overflowed the shop, were fluttering among some cots, and rusty guns, and oilskin hats, and certain trays full of so many old rusty keys of so many sizes that they seemed various enough to open all the doors in the world.

Into this shop, which was low and small, and which was darkened rather than lighted by a little window, overhung with clothes, and was descended into by some steps, I went with a palpitating heart; which was not relieved when an ugly old man, with the lower part of his face all covered with a stubbly grey beard, rushed out of a dirty den behind it, and seized me by the hair of my head. He was a dreadful old man to look at, in a filthy flannel waistcoat, and smelling terribly of rum. His bedstead, covered with a tumbled and ragged piece of patchwork, was in the den he had come from, where another little window showed a prospect of more stinging nettles, and a lame donkey.

"Oh, what do you want?" grinned this old man, in a fierce, monotonous whine. "Oh, my eyes and limbs, what do you want? Oh, my lungs and liver, what do you want? Oh, goroo, goroo!"

I was so much dismayed by these words, and particularly by the repetition of the last unknown one, which was a kind of rattle in his throat, that I could make no answer; hereupon the old man, still holding me by the hair, repeated:

"Oh, what do you want? Oh, my eyes and limbs, what do you want? Oh, my lungs and liver, what do you want! Oh, goroo!" —which he screamed out of himself, with an energy that made his eyes start in his head.

"I wanted to know," I said, trembling, "if you would buy a jacket."

"Oh, let's see the jacket!" cried the old man. "Oh, my heart on fire, show the jacket to us! Oh, my eyes and limbs, bring the jacket out!"

With that he took his trembling hands, which were like the claws of a great bird, out of my hair; and put on a pair of spectacles, not at all ornamental to his inflamed eyes.

"Oh, how much for the jacket?" cried the old man, after examining it. "Oh—goroo!—how much for the jacket?"

"Half-a-crown," I answered, recovering myself.

"Oh, my lungs and liver," cried the old man, "no! Oh, my eyes, no! Oh, my limbs, no! Eighteenpence. Goroo!"

Every time he uttered this ejaculation, his eyes seemed to be in danger of starting out; and every sentence he spoke, he delivered in a sort of tune, always exactly the same, and more like a gust of wind, which begins low, mounts up high, and falls again, than any other comparison I can find for it.

"Well," said I, glad to have closed the bargain, "I'll take eighteenpence."

"Oh, my liver!" cried the old man, throwing the jacket on a shelf. "Get out of the shop! Oh, my lungs, get out of the shop! Oh, my eyes and limbs—goroo!—don't ask for money; make it an exchange."

I never was so frightened in my life, before or since; but I told him humbly that I wanted money, and that nothing else was of any use to me, but that I would wait for it, as he desired, outside, and had no wish to hurry him. So I went outside, and sat down in the shade in a corner. And I sat there so many hours, that the shade became sunlight, and the sunlight became shade again, and still I sat there waiting for the money.

There never was such another drunken madman in that line of business, I hope. That he was well known in the neighbourhood and enjoyed the reputation of having sold himself to the devil, I soon understood from the visits he received from the boys, who continually came skirmishing about the shop, shouting that legend, and calling to him to bring out his gold. "You ain't poor, you know, Charley, as you pretend. Bring out your gold. Bring out some of the gold you sold yourself to the devil for. Come! It's in the lining of the mattress, Charley. Rip it open and let's have some!" This, and many offers to lend him a knife for the purpose, exasperated him to such a degree, that the whole day was a succession of rushes on his part, and flights on the part of the boys. Sometimes in his rage he would take me for one of them, and come at me, mouthing as if he were going to tear me in pieces; then, remembering me, just in time, would dive into the shop, and lie upon his bed, as I thought from the sound of his voice, yelling in a frantic way, to his own windy tune, the Death of Nelson; with an Oh! before every line, and innumerable Goroos interspersed. As if this were not bad enough for me, the boys, connecting me with the establishment, on account of the patience and perseverance with which I sat outside, half-dressed, pelted me, and used me very ill all day.

He made many attempts to induce me to consent to an exchange; at one time coming out with a fishing-rod, at another with a fiddle, at another with a cocked hat, at another with a flute. But I resisted all these overtures, and sat there in desperation; each time asking him, with tears in my eyes, for my money or my jacket. At last he began to pay me in halfpence at a time; and was full two hours getting by easy stages to a shilling.

"Oh, my eyes and limbs!" he then cried, peeping hideously out of the shop, after a long pause, "will you go for twopence more?"

"I can't," I said; "I shall be starved."

"Oh, my lungs and liver, will you go for threepence?"

"I would go for nothing, if I could," I said, "but I want the money badly."

"Oh, go—roo!" (it is really impossible to express how he twisted this ejaculation out of himself, as he peeped round the door-post at me, showing nothing but his crafty old head); "will you go for fourpence?"

I was so faint and weary that I closed with this offer; and taking the money out of his claw, not without trembling, went away more hungry and thirsty than I had ever been, a little before sunset. But at an expense of threepence I soon refreshed myself completely; and, being in better spirits then, limped seven miles upon my road.

My bed at night was under another haystack, where I rested comfortably, after having washed my blistered feet in a stream, and dressed them as well as I was able, with some cool leaves. When I took the road again next morning, I found that it lay through a succession of hop-grounds and orchards. It was sufficiently late in the year for the orchards to be ruddy with ripe apples; and in a few places the hop-pickers were already at work. I thought it all extremely beautiful, and made up my mind to sleep among the hops that night: imagining some cheerful companionship in the long perspectives of poles, with the graceful leaves twining round them.

The trampers were worse than ever that day, and inspired me with a dread that is yet quite fresh in my mind. Some of them were most ferocious-looking ruffians, who stared at me as I went by; and stopped, perhaps, and called after me to come back and speak to them; and when I took to my heels, stoned me. I recollect one young fellow—a tinker, I suppose, from his wallet and brazier—who had a woman with him, and who faced about and stared at me thus; and then roared at me in such a tremendous voice to come back, that I halted and looked round.

"Come here, when you 're called," said the tinker, "or I 'll rip your young body open."

I thought it best to go back. As I drew nearer to them, trying to propitiate the tinker by my looks, I observed that the woman had a black eye.

"Where are you going?" said the tinker, griping the bosom of my shirt with his blackened hand.

"I am going to Dover," I said.

"Where do you come from?" asked the tinker, giving his hand another turn in my shirt, to hold me more securely.

"I come from London," I said.

"What lay are you upon?" asked the tinker. "Are you a prig?"

"N—no," I said.

"Ain't you, by G—? If you make a brag of your honesty to me," said the tinker, "I 'll knock your brains out."

With his disengaged hand he made a menace of striking me, and then looked at me from head to foot.

"Have you got the price of a pint of beer about you?" said the tinker. "If you have, out with it, afore I take it away!"

I should certainly have produced it, but that I met the woman's look, and saw her very slightly shake her head, and form "No!" with her lips.

"I am very poor," I said, attempting to smile, "and have got no money."

"Why, what do you mean?" said the tinker, looking so sternly at me, that I almost feared he saw the money in my pocket.

"Sir!" I stammered.

"What do you mean," said the tinker, "by wearing my brother's silk handkercher? Give it over here!" And he had mine off my neck in a moment, and tossed it to the woman.

The woman burst into a fit of laughter, as if she thought this a joke, and tossing it back to me, nodded once, as slightly as before, and made the word "Go!" with her lips. Before I could obey, however, the tinker seized the handkerchief out of my hand with a roughness that threw me away like a feather, and putting it loosely round his own neck, turned upon the woman with an oath, and knocked her down. I never shall forget seeing her fall backward on the hard road, and lie there with her bonnet tumbled off, and her hair all whitened in the dust; nor, when I looked back from a distance, seeing her sitting on the pathway, which was a bank by the roadside, wiping the blood from her face with a corner of her shawl, while he went on ahead.

This adventure frightened me so, that, afterwards, when I saw any of these people coming, I turned back until I could find a hiding-place, where I remained until they had gone out of sight; which happened so often, that I was very seriously delayed. But under this difficulty, as under all the other difficulties of my journey, I seemed to be sustained and led on by my fanciful picture of my mother in her youth, before I came into the world. It always kept me company. It was there, among the hops, when I lay down to sleep; it was with me on my waking in the morning; it went before me all day. I have associated it, ever since, with the sunny street of Canterbury, dozing as it were in the hot light; and with the sight of its old houses and gateways, and the stately, grey Cathedral, with the rooks sailing round the towers. When I came, at last, upon the bare, wide downs near Dover, it relieved the solitary aspect of the scene with hope; and not until I reached that first great aim of my journey, and actually set foot in the town itself, on the sixth day of my flight, did it desert me. But then, strange to say, when I stood with my ragged shoes, and my dusty, sunburnt, half-clothed figure, in the place so long desired, it seemed to vanish like a dream, and to leave me helpless and dispirited.

I inquired about my aunt among the boatmen first, and received various answers. One said she lived in the South Foreland Light, and had singed her whiskers by doing so; another, that she was made fast to the great buoy outside the harbor, and could only be visited at half-tide; a third, that she was locked up in Maidstone Jail for child-stealing; a fourth, that she was seen to mount a broom in the last high wind, and make direct for Calais. The fly-drivers, among whom I inquired next, were equally jocose and equally disrespectful; and the shopkeepers, not liking my appearance, generally replied, without hearing what I had to say, that they had got nothing for me. I felt more miserable and destitute than I had done at any period of my running away. My money was all gone, I had nothing left to dispose of; I was hungry, thirsty, and worn out; and seemed as distant from my end as if I had remained in London.

The morning had worn away in these inquiries, and I was sitting on the step of an empty shop at a street corner, near the market-place, deliberating upon wandering towards those other places which had been mentioned, when a fly-driver, coming by with his carriage, dropped a horsecloth. Something good-natured in the man's face, as I handed it up, encouraged me to ask him if he could tell me where Miss Trotwood lived; though I had asked the question so often, that it almost died upon my lips.

"Trotwood," said he. "Let me see. I know the name, too. Old lady?"

"Yes," I said, "rather."

"Pretty stiff in the back?" said he, making himself upright.

"Yes," I said. "I should think it very likely."

"Carries a bag?" said he—"bag with a good deal of room in it —is gruffish, and comes down upon you, sharp?"

My heart sunk within me as I acknowledged the undoubted accuracy of this description.

"Why then, I tell you what," said he. "If you go up there," pointing with his whip towards the heights, "and keep right on till you come to some houses facing the sea, I think you'll hear of her. My opinion is she won't stand anything, so here's a penny for you."

I accepted the gift thankfully, and bought a loaf with it. Dispatching this refreshment by the way, I went in the direction my friend had indicated, and walked on a good distance without coming to the houses he had mentioned. At length I saw some before me; and approaching them, went into a little shop (it was what we used to call a general shop, at home), and inquired if they could have the goodness to tell me where Miss Trotwood lived. I addressed myself to a man behind the counter, who was weighing some rice for a young woman; but the latter taking the inquiry to herself, turned round quickly.

"My mistress?" she said. "What do you want with her, boy?"

"I want," I replied, "to speak to her, if you please."

"To beg of her, you mean," retorted the damsel.

"No," I said, "indeed." But suddenly remembering that in truth I came for no other purpose, I held my peace in confusion, and felt my face burn.

My aunt's handmaid, as I supposed she was from what she had said, put her rice in a little basket and walked out of the shop; telling me that I could follow her, if I wanted to know where Miss Trotwood lived. I needed no second permission; though I was by this time in such a state of consternation and agitation, that my legs shook under me. I followed the young woman, and we soon came to a very neat little cottage with cheerful bow-windows: in front of it, a small square gravelled court or garden full of flowers, carefully tended, and smelling deliciously.

"This is Miss Trotwood's," said the young woman. "Now you know; and that's all I have got to say." With which words she hurried into the house, as if to shake off the responsibility of my appearance; and left me standing at the garden-gate, looking disconsolately over the top of it towards the parlor window, where a muslin curtain partly undrawn in the middle, a large round green screen or fan fastened on to the window-sill, a small table, and a great chair, suggested to me that my aunt might be at that moment seated in awful state.

My shoes were by this time in a woeful condition. The soles had shed themselves bit by bit, and the upper leathers had broken and burst until the very shape and form of shoes had departed from them. My hat (which had served me for a night-cap, too) was so crushed and bent, that no old battered handle-less saucepan on a dunghill need have been ashamed to vie with it. My shirt and trowsers, stained with heat, dew, grass, and the Kentish soil on which I had slept—and torn besides—might have frightened the birds from my aunt's garden, as I stood at the gate. My hair had known no comb or brush since I left London. My face, neck, and hands, from unaccustomed exposure to the air and sun, were burnt to a berry brown. From head to foot I was powdered almost as white with chalk and dust, as if I had come out of a lime-kiln. In this plight, and with a strong consciousness of it, I waited to introduce myself to, and make my first impression on, my formidable aunt.

The unbroken stillness of the parlor window leading me to infer, after a-while, that she was not there, I lifted up my eyes to the window above it, where I saw a florid, pleasant-looking gentleman, with a grey head, who shut up one eye in a grotesque manner, nodded his head at me several times, shook it at me as often, laughed, and went away.

I had been discomposed enough before; but I was so much the more discomposed by this unexpected behaviour, that I was on the point of slinking off, to think how I had best proceed, when there came out of the house a lady with a handkerchief tied over her cap, and a pair of gardening gloves on her hands, wearing a gardening pocket like a tollman's apron, and carrying a great knife. I knew her immediately to be Miss Betsey, for she came stalking out of the

I MAKE MYSELF KNOWN TO MY AUNT.

house exactly as my poor mother had so often described her stalking up our garden at Blunderstone Rookery.

"Go away!" said Miss Betsey, shaking her head, and making a distant chop in the air with her knife. "Go along! No boys here!"

I watched her, with my heart at my lips, as she marched to a corner of her garden, and stooped to dig up some little root there. Then, without a scrap of courage, but with a great deal of desperation, I went softly in and stood beside her, touching her with my finger.

"If you please, ma'am," I began.

She started, and looked up.

"If you please, aunt."

"EH?" exclaimed Miss Betsey, in a tone of amazement I have never heard approached.

"If you please, aunt, I am your nephew."

"Oh, Lord!" said my aunt. And sat flat down in the garden-path.

"I am David Copperfield, of Blunderstone, in Suffolk—where you came, on the night when I was born, and saw my dear mama. I have been very unhappy since she died. I have been slighted, and taught nothing, and thrown upon myself, and put to work not fit for me. It made me run away to you. I was robbed at first setting out, and have walked all the way, and have never slept in a bed since I began the journey." Here my self-support gave way all at once; and with a movement of my hands, intended to show her my ragged state, and call it to witness that I had suffered something, I broke into a passion of crying, which I suppose had been pent up within me all the week.

My aunt, with every sort of expression but wonder discharged from her countenance, sat on the gravel, staring at me, until I began to cry; when she got up in a great hurry, collared me, and took me into the parlor. Her first proceeding there was to unlock a tall press, bring out several bottles, and pour some of the contents of each into my mouth. I think they must have been taken out at random, for I am sure I tasted aniseed water, anchovy sauce, and salad dressing. When she had administered these restoratives, as I was still quite hysterical, and unable to control my sobs, she put me on the sofa, with a shawl under my head, and the handkerchief from her own head under my feet, lest I should sully the cover; and then, sitting herself down behind the green fan or screen I have already mentioned, so that I could not see her face, ejaculated at intervals, "Mercy on us!" letting those exclamations off like minute guns.

After a time she rang the bell. "Janet," said my aunt, when her servant came in. "Go up stairs, give my compliments to Mr. Dick, and say I wish to speak to him."

Janet looked a little surprised to see me lying stiffly on the sofa (I was afraid to move lest it should be displeasing to my aunt), but went on her errand. My aunt, with her hands behind her, walked up and down the room, until the gentleman who had squinted at me from the upper window came in laughing.

"Mr. Dick," said my aunt, "don't be a fool, because nobody can be more discreet than you can, when you choose. We all know that. So don't be a fool, whatever you are."

The gentleman was serious immediately, and looked at me, I thought, as if he would entreat me to say nothing about the window.

"Mr. Dick," said my aunt, "you have heard me mention David Copperfield? Now don't pretend not to have a memory, because you and I know better."

"David Copperfield?" said Mr. Dick, who did not appear to me to remember much about it. "David Copperfield! O yes, to be sure. David, certainly."

"Well," said my aunt, "this is his boy—his son. He would be as like his father as it's possible to be, if he was not so like his mother, too."

"His son?" said Mr. Dick. "David's son? Indeed!"

"Yes," pursued my aunt, "and he has done a pretty piece of business. He has run away. Ah! His sister, Betsey Trotwood, never would have run away." My aunt shook her head firmly, confident in the character and behaviour of the girl who never was born.

"Oh! you think she wouldn't have run away?" said Mr. Dick.

"Bless and save the man," exclaimed my aunt, sharply, "how he talks! Don't I know she wouldn't? She would have lived with her god-mother, and we should have been devoted to one another. Where, in the name of wonder, should his sister, Betsey Trotwood, have run from, or to?"

"Nowhere," said Mr. Dick.

"Well then," returned my aunt, softened by the reply, "how can you pretend to be wool-gathering, Dick, when you are as sharp as a surgeon's lancet? Now, here you see young David Copperfield, and the question I put to you is, what shall I do with him?"

"What shall you do with him?" said Mr. Dick, feebly, scratching his head. "Oh! do with him?"

"Yes," said my aunt, with a grave look and her forefinger held up. "Come! I want some very sound advice."

"Why, if I was you," said Mr. Dick, considering, and looking vacantly at me, "I should—" The contemplation of me seemed to inspire him with a sudden idea, and he added, briskly, "I should wash him!"

"Janet," said my aunt, turning round with a quiet triumph, which I did not then understand, "Mr. Dick sets us all right. Heat the bath!"

Although I was deeply interested in this dialogue, I could not help observing my aunt, Mr. Dick, and Janet, while it was in progress, and completing a survey I had already been engaged in making of the room.

My aunt was a tall, hard-featured lady, but by no means ill-looking. There was an inflexibility in her face, in her voice, in her gait and carriage, amply sufficient to account for the effect she had made upon a gentle creature like my mother; but her features were rather handsome than otherwise, though unbending and austere. I particularly noticed that she had a very quick, bright, eye. Her hair, which was grey, was arranged in two plain divisions, under what I believe would be called a mob-cap: I mean a cap, much more common then than now, with side-pieces fastening under the chin. Her dress was of a lavender color, and perfectly neat; but scantily made, as if she desired to be as little encumbered as possible. I remember that I thought it, in form, more like a riding-habit with the superfluous skirt cut off, than anything else. She wore at her side a gentleman's gold watch, if I might judge from its size and make, with an appropriate chain and seals; she had some linen at her throat not unlike a shirt-collar, and things at her wrists like little shirt-wristbands.

Mr. Dick, as I have already said, was grey-headed, and florid: I should have said all about him, in saying so, had not his head been curiously bowed—not by age; it reminded me of one of Mr. Creakle's boys' heads after a beating—and his grey eyes prominent and large, with a strange kind of watery brightness in them that made me, in combination with his vacant manner, his submission to my aunt, and his childish delight when she praised him, suspect him of being a little mad; though, if he were mad, how he came to be there puzzled me extremely. He was dressed like any other ordinary gentleman, in a loose grey morning coat and waistcoat, and white trowsers; and had his watch in his fob, and his money in his pockets; which he rattled as if he were very proud of it.

Janet was a pretty blooming girl, of about nineteen or twenty, and a perfect picture of neatness. Though I made no further observation of her at the moment, I may mention here what I did not discover until afterwards, namely, that she was one of a series of protégées whom my aunt had taken into her service expressly to educate in a renouncement of mankind, and who had generally completed their abjuration by marrying the baker.

The room was as neat as Janet or my aunt. As I laid down my pen, a moment since, to think of it, the air from the sea came blowing in again, mixed with the perfume of the flowers; and I saw the old-fashioned furniture brightly rubbed and polished, my aunt's inviolable chair and table by the round green fan in the bow-window, the drugget-covered carpet, the cat, the kettle-holder, the two canaries, the old china, the punchbowl full of dried rose leaves, the tall press guarding all sorts of bottles and pots, and, wonderfully out of keeping with the rest, my dusty self upon the sofa, taking note of everything.

Janet had gone away to get the bath ready, when my aunt, to my great alarm, became in one moment rigid with indignation, and had hardly voice to cry out, "Janet! Donkies!"

Upon which, Janet came running up the stairs as if the house were in flames, darted out on a little piece of green in front, and warned off two saddle-donkeys, lady-ridden, that had presumed to set hoof upon it; while my aunt, rushing out of the house, seized the bridle of a third animal laden with a bestriding child, turned him, led him forth from those sacred precincts, and boxed the ears of the unlucky urchin in attendance who had dared to profane that hallowed ground.

To this hour I don't know whether my aunt had any lawful right of way over that patch of green; but she had settled it in her own mind that she had, and it was all the same to her. The one great outrage of her life, demanding to be constantly avenged, was the passage of a donkey over that immaculate spot. In whatever occupation she was engaged, however interesting to her the conversation in which she was taking part, a donkey turned the current of her ideas in a moment, and she was upon him straight. Jugs of water and watering pots were kept in secret places ready to be discharged on the offending boys; sticks were laid in ambush behind the door; sallies were made at all hours; and incessant war prevailed. Perhaps this was an agreeable excitement to the donkey-boys; or perhaps the more sagacious of the donkeys, understanding how the case stood, delighted with constitutional obstinacy in coming that way. I only know that there were three alarms before the bath was ready; and that on the occasion of the last and most desperate of all, I saw my aunt engage, single-handed, with a sandy-headed lad of fifteen, and bump his sandy head against her own gate, before he seemed to comprehend what was the matter. These interruptions were the more ridiculous to me, because she was giving me broth out of a table-spoon at the time (having firmly persuaded herself that I was actually starving, and must receive nourishment at first in very small quantities), and, while my mouth was yet open to receive the spoon, she would put it back into the basin, cry "Janet! Donkies!" and go out to the assault.

The bath was a great comfort. For I began to be sensible of acute pains in my limbs from lying out in the fields, and was now so tired and low that I could hardly keep myself awake for five minutes together. When I had bathed, they (I mean my aunt and Janet) enrobed me in a shirt and pair of trowsers belonging to Mr

Dick, and tied me up in two or three great shawls. What sort of a bundle I looked like, I don't know, but I felt a very hot one. Feeling also very faint and drowsy, I soon lay down on the sofa again and fell asleep.

It might have been a dream, originating in the fancy which had occupied my mind so long, but I awoke with the impression that my aunt had come and bent over me, and had put my hair away from my face, and laid my head more comfortably, and had then stood looking at me. The words, "Pretty fellow," or, "Poor fellow," seemed to be in my ears, too; but certainly there was nothing else, when I awoke, to lead me to believe that they had been uttered by my aunt, who sat in the bow-window gazing at the sea from behind the green fan, which was mounted on a kind of swivel, and turned any way.

We dined soon after I awoke, off a roast fowl and a pudding; I sitting at table, not unlike a trussed bird myself, and moving my arms with considerable difficulty. But as my aunt had swathed me up, I made no complaint of being inconvenienced. All this time, I was deeply anxious to know what she was going to do with me; but she took her dinner in profound silence, except when she occasionally fixed her eyes on me sitting opposite, and said, "Mercy upon us!" which did not by any means relieve my anxiety.

The cloth being drawn, and some sherry put upon the table, (of which I had a glass,) my aunt sent up for Mr. Dick again, who joined us, and looked as wise as he could when she requested him to attend to my story, which she elicited from me, gradually, by a course of questions. During my recital, she kept her eyes on Mr. Dick, who I thought would have gone to sleep but for that, and who, whensoever he lapsed into a smile, was checked by a frown from my aunt.

"Whatever possessed that poor unfortunate Baby, that she must go and be married again," said my aunt, when I had finished, "*I* can't conceive."

"Perhaps she fell in love with her second husband," Mr. Dick suggested.

"Fell in love!" repeated my aunt. "What do you mean? What business had she to do it?"

"Perhaps," Mr. Dick simpered, after thinking a little, "she did it for pleasure."

"Pleasure, indeed," replied my aunt. "A mighty pleasure for the poor baby to fix her simple faith upon any dog of a fellow, certain to ill-use her in some way or other. What did she propose to herself, I should like to know! She had had one husband. She had seen David Copperfield out of the world, who was always running after wax dolls from his cradle. She had got a baby—oh, there were a pair of babies when she gave birth to this child sitting here, that Friday night!—and what more did she want?"

Mr. Dick secretly shook his head at me, as if he thought there was no getting over this.

"She couldn't even have a baby like anybody else," said my aunt. "Where was this child's sister, Betsey Trotwood. Not forthcoming. Don't tell me!"

Mr. Dick seemed quite frightened.

"That little man of a doctor, with his head on one side," said my aunt, "Jellips, or whatever his name was, what was *he* about? All he could do, was to say to me, like a robin-redbreast—as he *is*—'It's a boy.' A boy! Yah, the imbecility of the whole set of 'em."

The heartiness of the ejaculation startled Mr. Dick exceedingly; and me, too, if I am to tell the truth.

"And then, as if this was not enough, and she had not stood sufficiently in the light of this child's sister, Betsey Trotwood," said my aunt, "she marries a second time—goes and marries a Murderer—or a man with a name like it—and stands in *this* child's light! And the natural consequence is, as anybody but a baby might have foreseen, that he prowls and wanders. He's as like Cain before he was grown up, as he can be."

Mr. Dick looked hard at me, as if to identify me in this character

"And then there's that woman with the Pagan name," said my aunt, "that Peggotty, *she* goes and gets married next. Because she has not seen enough of the evil attending such things, *she* goes and gets married next, as the child relates. I only hope," said my aunt, shaking her head, "that her husband is one of those Poker husbands, who abound in the newspapers, and will beat her well with one."

I could not bear to hear my old nurse so decried, and made the subject of such a wish. I told my aunt that indeed she was mistaken. That Peggotty was the best, the truest, the most faithful, most devoted, and most self-denying friend and servant in the world; who had ever loved me dearly, who had ever loved my mother dearly; who had held my mother's dying head upon her arm, on whose face my mother had imprinted her last grateful kiss. And my remembrance of them both, choking me, I broke down as I was trying to say that her home was my home, and that all she had was mine, and that I would have gone to her for shelter, but for her humble station, which made me fear that I might bring some trouble on her—I broke down, I say, as I was trying to say so, and laid my face in my hands upon the table.

"Well, well!" said my aunt, "the child is right to stand by those who have stood by him—Janet! Donkies!"

I thoroughly believe that but for those unfortunate donkies, we should have come to a good understanding; for my aunt had laid her hand on my shoulder, and the impulse was upon me, thus emboldened, to embrace her and beseech her protection. But the interruption, and the disorder she was thrown into by the struggle outside, put an end to all softer ideas for the present; and kept my aunt indignantly declaiming to Mr. Dick about her determination to appeal for redress to the laws of her country, and to bring actions for trespass against the whole donkey proprietorship of Dover, until tea-time.

After tea, we sat at the window—on the look-out, as I imagined from my aunt's sharp expression of face, for more invaders—until dusk, when Janet set candles, and a backgammon-board, on the table, and pulled down the blinds.

"Now, Mr. Dick," said my aunt, with her grave look, and her fore-finger up as before, "I am going to ask you another question. Look at this child."

"David's son?" said Mr. Dick, with an attentive, puzzled face.

"Exactly so," returned my aunt. "What would you do with him, now?"

"Do with David's son?" said Mr. Dick.

"Ay," replied my aunt, "with David's son."

"Oh!" said Mr. Dick. "Yes. Do with—I should put him to bed."

"Janet!" cried my aunt with the same complacent triumph that I had remarked before. "Mr. Dick sets us all right. If the bed is ready, we'll take him up to it."

Janet reporting it to be quite ready, I was taken up to it; kindly but in some sort like a prisoner; my aunt going in front and Janet bringing up the rear. The only circumstance which gave me any new hope, was my aunt's stopping on the stairs to inquire about a smell of fire that was prevalent there; and Janet's replying that she had been making tinder down in the kitchen, of my old shirt. But there were no other clothes in my room than the old heap of things I wore; and when I was left there, with a little taper which my aunt forewarned me would burn exactly five minutes, I heard them lock my door on the outside. Turning these things over in my mind, I deemed it possible that my aunt, who could know nothing of me, might suspect I had a habit of running away, and took precautions, on that account, to have me in safe keeping.

The room was a pleasant one, at the top of the house, overlooking the sea, on which the moon was shining brilliantly. After I had said my prayers, and the candle had burnt out, I remember how I still sat looking at the moonlight on the water, as if I could hope to read my fortune in it, as in a bright book; or to see my mother with her child, coming from Heaven, along that shining path, to look upon me as she had looked when I last saw her sweet face. I remember how the solemn feeling with which at length I turned my eyes away, yielded to the sensation of gratitude and rest which the sight of the white-curtained bed—and how much more the lying softly down upon it, nestling in the snow-white sheets?—inspired. I remember how I thought of all the solitary places under the night sky where I had slept, and how I prayed that I never might be houseless any more, and never might forget the houseless. I remember how I seemed to float, then, down the melancholy glory of that track upon the sea, away into the world of dreams.

CHAPTER XIV.

MY AUNT MAKES UP HER MIND ABOUT ME.

On going down in the morning, I found my aunt musing so profoundly over the breaefast-table, with her elbow on the tray, that the contents of the urn had overflowed the teapot and were laying the whole table-cloth under water, when my entrance put her meditations to flight. I felt sure that I had been the subject of her reflections, and was more than ever anxious to know her intentions towards me. Yet I dared not express my anxiety, lest it should give her offence.

My eyes, however, not being so much under control as my tongue, were attracted towards my aunt very often during breakfast. I never could look at her for a few moments together but I found her looking at me—in an odd, thoughtful manner, as if I were an immense way off, instead of being on the other side of the small round table. When she had finished her breakfast, my aunt very deliberately leaned back in her chair, knitted her brows, folded her arms, and contemplated me at her leisure, with such a fixedness of attention that I was quite overpowered by embarrassment. Not having as yet finished my own breakfast, I attempted to hide my confusion by proceeding with it; but my knife tumbled over my fork, my fork tripped up my knife, I chipped bits of bacon a surprising height into the air instead of cutting them for my own eating, and choked myself with my tea which persisted in going the wrong way instead of the right one, until I gave in altogether, and sat blushing under my aunt's close scrutiny.

"Hallo!" said my aunt, after a long time.

I looked up, and met her sharp bright glance respectfully.

"I have written to him," said my aunt.

"To —?"

"To your father-in-law," said my aunt. "I have sent him a letter that I'll trouble him to attend to, or he and I will fall out, I can tell him!"

"Does he know where I am, aunt?" I inquired, alarmed.

"I have told him," said my aunt, with a nod.

"Shall I—be—given up to him?" I faltered.

"I don't know," said my aunt. "We shall see."

"Oh! I can't think what I shall do," I exclaimed, "if I have to go back to Mr. Murdstone!"

"I don't know anything about it," said my aunt, shaking her head. "I can't say, I am sure. We shall see."

My spirits sank under these words, and I became very downcast and heavy of heart. My aunt, without appearing to take much heed of me, put on a coarse apron with a bib, which she took out of the press; washed up the teacups with her own hands; and, when everything was washed and set in the tray again, and the cloth folded and put on the top of the whole, rang for Janet to remove it. She next swept up the crumbs with a little broom (putting on a pair of gloves first), until there did not appear to be one microscopic speck left on the carpet; next dusted and arranged the room, which was dusted and arranged to a hair's breadth already. When all these tasks were performed to her satisfaction, she took off the gloves and apron, folded them up, put them in the particular corner of the press from which they had been taken, brought out her work-box to her own table in the open window, and sat down, with the green fan between her and the light, to work.

"I wish you'd go up stairs," said my aunt, as she threaded her needle, "and give my compliments to Mr. Dick, and I'll be glad to know how he gets on with his Memorial."

I rose with alacrity to acquit myself of this commission.

"I suppose," said my aunt, eyeing me as narrowly as she had eyed the needle in threading it, "you think Mr. Dick a short name, eh?"

"I thought it was rather a short name, yesterday," I confessed.

"You are not to suppose that he hasn't got a longer name, if he chose to use it," said my aunt, with a loftier air. "Babley—Mr Richard Babley—that's the gentleman's true name."

I was going to suggest, with a modest sense of my youth and the familiarity I had been already guilty of, that I had better give him the full benefit of that name, when my aunt went on to say:

"But don't you call him by it, whatever you do. He can't bear his name. That's a peculiarity of his. Though I don't know that it's much of a peculiarity, either; for he has been ill-used enough by some that bear it, to have a mortal antipathy for it, Heaven knows. Mr. Dick is his name here, and everywhere else, now—if he ever went anywhere else, which he don't. So take care, child, you don't call him anything *but* Mr. Dick."

I promised to obey, and went up-stairs with my message; thinking, as I went, that if Mr. Dick had been working at his Memorial long, at the same rate as I had seen him working at it, through the open door, when I came down, he was probably getting on very well indeed. I found him still driving at it with a long pen, and his head almost laid upon the paper. He was so intent upon it, that I had ample leisure to observe the large paper kite in the corner, the confusion of bundles of manuscript, the number of pens, and, above all, the quantity of ink (which he seemed to have in, in half-gallon jars by the dozen), before he observed my being present.

"Ha! Phœbus!" said Mr. Dick, laying down his pen. "How does the world go! I'll tell you what," he added, in a lower tone, "I shouldn't wish it to be mentioned, but it's a—" here he beckoned to me, and put his lips close to my ear—"it's a mad world. Mad as Bedlam, boy!" said Mr. Dick, taking snuff from a round box on the table, and laughing heartily.

Without presuming to give my opinion on this question, I delivered my message.

"Well," said Mr. Dick, in answer, "my compliments to her, and I—I believe I have made a start. I think I have made a start," said Mr. Dick, passing his hand among his grey hair, and casting anything but a confident look at his manuscript. "You have been to school?"

"Yes, sir," I answered, "for a short time."

"Do you recollect the date," said Mr. Dick, looking earnestly at me, and taking up his pen to note it down, "when King Charles the First had his head cut off?"

I said I believed it happened in the year sixteen hundred and forty-nine.

"Well," returned Mr. Dick, scratching his ear with his pen, and looking dubiously at me. "So the books say, but I don't see how that can be. Because, if it was so long ago, how could the people about him have made that mistake of putting some of the trouble out of *his* head, after it was taken off, into *mine*?"

I was very much surprised by the inquiry; but could give no information on this point.

"It 's very strange," said Mr. Dick, with a despondent look upon his papers, and with his hand among his hair again, "that I never can get that quite right. I never can make that perfectly clear. But no matter, no matter!" he said cheerfully, and rousing himself, "there's time enough. My compliments to Miss Trotwood, I am getting on very well indeed."

I was going away, when he directed my attention to the kite.

"What do you think of that for a kite?" he said.

I answered that it was a beautiful one. I should think it must have been as much as seven feet high.

"I made it. We 'll go and fly it, you and I," said Mr. Dick. "Do you see this?"

He showed me that it was covered with manuscript, very closely and laboriously written; but so plainly, that as I looked along the lines, I thought I saw some allusion to King Charles the First's head again, in one or two places.

"There's plenty of string," said Mr. Dick, "and when it flies high, it takes the facts a long way. That's my manner of diffusing 'em. I don't know where they may come down. It's according to circumstances, and the wind, and so forth; but I take my chance of that."

His face was so very mild and pleasant, and had something so reverend in it, though it was hale and hearty, that I was not sure but that he was having a good humoured jest with me. So I laughed, and he laughed, and we parted the best friends possible.

"Well, child," said my aunt, when I went down stairs. "And what of Mr. Dick, this morning?"

I informed her that he sent his compliments, and was getting on very well indeed.

"What do you think of him?" said my aunt.

I had some shadowy idea of endeavouring to evade the question, by replying that I thought him a very nice gentleman; but my aunt was not to be so put off, for she laid her work down in her lap, and said, folding her hands upon it:

"Come! Your sister Betsey Trotwood would have told me what she thought of any one, directly. Be as like your sister as you can, and speak out!"

"Is he—is Mr. Dick—I ask because I don't know, aunt—is he at all out of his mind, then?" I stammered; for I felt I was on dangerous ground.

"Not a morsel," said my aunt.

"Oh, indeed," I observed faintly.

"If there is anything in the world," said my aunt, with great decision and force of manner, "that Mr. Dick is not, it's that."

I had nothing better to offer, than another timid "Oh, indeed!"

"He has been *called* mad," said my aunt. "I have a selfish pleasure in saying he has been called mad, or I should not have had the benefit of his society and advice for these last ten years and upwards—in fact, ever since your sister, Betsey Trotwood, disappointed me."

"So long as that?" I said.

"And nice people they were, who had the audacity to call him mad," pursued my aunt. "Mr. Dick is a sort of distant connexion of mine—it doesn't matter how; I needn't enter into that. If it hadn't been for me, his own brother would have shut him up for life. That's all."

I am afraid it was hypocritical in me, but seeing that my aunt felt strongly on the subject, I tried to look as if I felt strongly too.

"A proud fool!" said my aunt. "Because his brother was a little eccentric—though he is not half so eccentric as a good many people—he didn't like to have him visible about his house, and sent him away to some private asylum-place; though he had been left to his particular care by their deceased father, who thought him almost a natural. And a wise man *he* must have been to think so! Mad himself, no doubt."

Again, as my aunt looked quite convinced, I endeavored to look quite convinced also.

"So I stepped in," said my aunt, "and made him an offer. I said, Your brother's sane—a great deal more sane than you are, or ever will be, it is to be hoped. Let him have his little income, and come and live with me. *I* am not afraid of him, *I* am not proud, *I* am ready to take care of him, and shall not ill-treat him as some people (besides the asylum folks) have done. After a good deal of squabbling," said my aunt, "I got him; and he has been here ever since. He is the most friendly and amenable creature in existence; and as for advice!—but nobody knows what that man's mind is, except myself."

My aunt smoothed her dress and shook her head, as if she smoothed defiance of the whole world out of the one, and shook it out of the other.

"He had a favorite sister," said my aunt, "a good creature, and very kind to him. But she did what they all do—took a husband. And *he* did what they all do—made her wretched. It had such an effect upon the mind of Mr. Dick (*that's* not madness I hope!) that, combined with his fear of his brother, and his sense of his unkindness, it threw him into a fever. That was before he came to me, but the recollection of it is oppressive to him even now. Did he say anything to you about King Charles the First, child?"

"Yes, aunt."

"Ah!" said my aunt, rubbing her nose as if she were a little vexed. "That's his allegorical way of expressing it. He connects his illness with great disturbance and agitation, naturally, and that's the figure, or the simile, or whatever it's called, which he chooses to use. And why shouldn't he, if he thinks proper!"

I said: "Certainly, aunt."

"It's not a business-like way of speaking," said my aunt, "nor a worldly way. I am aware of that; and that's the reason why I insist upon it, that there shan't be a word about it in his Memorial."

"Is it a Memorial about his own history that he is writing, aunt?"

"Yes, child," said my aunt, rubbing her nose again. "He is memorializing the Lord Chancellor, or the Lord Somebody or other—one of those people, at all events, who are paid to *be* memorialised—

about his affairs. I suppose it will go in, one of these days. He hasn't been able to draw it up yet, without introducing that mode of expressing himself; but it don't signify; it keeps him employed."

In fact, I found out afterwards that Mr. Dick had been for upwards of ten years endeavouring to keep King Charles the First out of the Memorial; but he had been constantly getting into it, and was there now.

"I say again," said my aunt, "nobody knows what that man's mind is except myself; and he's the most amenable and friendly creature in existence. If he likes to fly a kite sometimes, what of that! Franklin used to fly a kite. He was a Quaker, or something of that sort, if I am not mistaken. And a Quaker flying a kite is a much more ridiculous object than any body else."

If I could have supposed that my aunt had recounted these particulars for my especial behoof, and as a piece of confidence in me, I should have felt very much distinguished, and should have augured favourably from such a mark of her good opinion. But I could hardly help observing that she had launched into them, chiefly because the question was raised in her own mind, and with very little reference to me, though she had addressed herself to me in the absence of anybody else.

At the same time, I must say that the generosity of her championship of poor harmless Mr. Dick, not only inspired my young breast with some selfish hope for myself, but warmed it unselfishly towards her. I believe I began to know that there was something about my aunt, notwithstanding her many eccentricities and odd humours, to be honoured and trusted in. Though she was just as sharp that day, as on the day before, and was in and out about the donkeys just as often, and was thrown into a tremendous state of indignation, when a young man, going by, ogled Janet at a window (which was one of the gravest misdemeanors that could be committed against my aunt's dignity), she seemed to me to command more of my respect, if not less of my fear.

The anxiety I underwent, in the interval which necessarily elapsed before a reply could be received to her letter to Mr. Murdstone, was extreme; but I made an endeavour to suppress it, and to be as agreeable as I could in a quiet way, both to my aunt and Mr. Dick. The latter and I would have gone out to fly the great kite; but that I had still no other clothes than the anything but ornamental garments with which I had been decorated on the first day, and which confined me to the house, except for an hour after dark, when my aunt, for my health's sake, paraded me up and down on the cliff outside, before going to bed. At length the reply from Mr. Murdstone came, and my aunt informed me, to my infinite terror, that he was coming to speak to her himself on the next day. On the next day, still bundled up in my curious habiliments, I sat counting the time, flushed and heated by the conflict of sinking hopes and rising fears within me; and waiting to be startled by the sight of the gloomy face, whose non-arrival startled me every minute.

My aunt was a little more imperious and stern than usual, but I observed no other token of her preparing herself to receive the visitor so much dreaded by me. She sat at work in the window, and I sat by, with my thoughts running astray on all possible and impossible results of Mr. Murdstone's visit, until pretty late in the afternoon. Our dinner had been indefinitely postponed; but it was growing so late, that my aunt had ordered it to be got ready, when she gave a sudden alarm of donkeys, and to my consternation and amazement, I beheld Miss Murdstone, on a side-saddle, ride deliberately over the sacred piece of green, and stop in front of the house, looking about her.

"Go along with you!" cried my aunt, shaking her head and her fist at the window. "You have no business there. How dare you trespass? Go along! Oh, you bold-faced thing!"

My aunt was so exasperated by the coolness with which Miss Murdstone looked about her, that I really believe she was motionless, and unable for the moment to dart out according to custom. I seized the opportunity to inform her who it was; and that the gentleman now coming near the offender (for the way up was very steep, and he had dropped behind), was Mr. Murdstone himself.

"I don't care who it is!" cried my aunt, still shaking her head, and gesticulating anything but welcome from the bow-window. "I won't be trespassed upon. I won't allow it. Go away! Janet, turn him round. Lead him off!" and I saw, from behind my aunt, a sort of hurried battle-piece, in which the donkey stood resisting everybody, with all his four legs planted different ways, while Janet tried to pull him round by the bridle, Mr. Murdstone tried to lead him on, Miss Murdstone struck at Janet with a parasol, and several boys, who had come to see the engagement, shouted vigorously. But my aunt, suddenly descrying among them the young malefactor who was the donkey's guardian, and who was one of the most inveterate offenders against her, though hardly in his teens, rushed out to the scene of action, pounced upon him, captured him, dragged him, with his jacket over his head, and his heels grinding the ground, into the garden, and, calling upon Janet to fetch the constables and justices that he might be taken, tried, and executed on the spot, held him at bay there. This part of the business, however, did not last long; for the young rascal, being expert at a variety of feints and dodges, of which my aunt had no conception, soon went whooping away, leaving some deep impressions of his nailed boots in the flower-beds, and taking his donkey in triumph with him.

Miss Murdstone, during the latter portion of the contest, had dismounted, and was now waiting with her brother at the bottom of the steps, until my aunt should be at leisure to receive them. My aunt, a little ruffled by the combat, marched past them into the house, with great dignity, and took no notice of their presence, until they were announced by Janet.

"Shall I go away, aunt?" I asked, trembling.

"No, sir," said my aunt. "Certainly not!" With which she pushed me into a corner near her, and fenced me in with a chair, as if it were a prison or a bar of justice. This position I continued to occupy during the whole interview, and from it I now saw Mr. and Miss Murdstone enter the room.

"Oh!" said my aunt, "I was not aware at first to whom I had the pleasure of objecting. But I don't allow anybody to ride over that turf. I make no exceptions. I don't allow anybody to do it."

"Your regulation is rather awkward to strangers," said Miss Murdstone.

"Is it!" said my aunt.

Mr. Murdstone seemed afraid of a renewal of hostilities, and interposing began:

THE MOMENTOUS INTERVIEW.

"Miss Trotwood!"

"I beg your pardon," observed my aunt with a keen look. "You are the Mr. Murdstone who married the widow of my late nephew, David Copperfield, of Blunderstone Rookery?—Though why Rookery, *I* don't know!"

"I am," said Mr. Murdstone.

"You'll excuse my saying, sir," returned my aunt, "that I think it would have been a much better and happier thing if you had left that poor child alone."

"I so far agree with what Miss Trotwood has remarked," observed Miss Murdstone, bridling, "that I consider our lamented Clara to have been, in all essential respects, a mere child."

"It is a comfort to you and to me, ma'am," said my aunt, "who are getting on in life, and are not likely to be made unhappy by our personal attractions, that nobody can say the same of us."

"No doubt!" returned Miss Murdstone, though, I thought, not with a very ready or gracious assent. "And it certainly might have been, as you say, a better and happier thing for my brother if he had never entered into such a marriage. I have always been of that opinion."

"I have no doubt you have," said my aunt. "Janet," ringing the bell, "my compliments to Mr. Dick, and beg him to come down."

Until he came, my aunt sat perfectly upright and stiff, frowning at the wall. When he came, my aunt performed the ceremony of introduction.

"Mr. Dick. An old and intimate friend. On whose judgment," said my aunt, with emphasis, as an admonition to Mr. Dick, who was biting his forefinger and looking rather foolish, "I rely."

Mr. Dick took his finger out of his mouth, on this hint, and stood among the group, with a grave and attentive expression of face. My aunt inclined her head to Mr. Murdstone, who went on:

"Miss Trotwood: on the receipt of your letter, I considered it an act of greater justice to myself, and perhaps of more respect to you—"

"Thank you," said my aunt, still eyeing him keenly. "You needn't mind me."

"To answer it in person, however inconvenient the journey," pursued Mr. Murdstone, "rather than by letter. This unhappy boy who has run away from his friends and his occupation—"

"And whose appearance," interposed his sister, directing general attention to me in my indefinable costume, "is perfectly scandalous and disgraceful."

"Jane Murdstone," said her brother, "have the goodness not to interrupt me. This unhappy boy, Miss Trotwood, has been the occasion of much domestic trouble and uneasiness; both during the lifetime of my late dear wife, and since. He has a sullen, rebellious spirit; a violent temper; and an untoward, intractable disposition. Both my sister and myself have endeavoured to correct his vices, but ineffectually. And I have felt—we both have felt, I may say; my sister being fully in my confidence—that it is right you should receive this grave and dispassionate assurance from our lips."

"It can hardly be necessary for me to confirm anything stated by my brother," said Miss Murdstone; "but I beg to observe that, of all the boys in the world, I believe this is the worst boy."

"Strong!" said my aunt, shortly.

"But not at all too strong for the facts," returned Miss Murdstone.

"Ha!" said my aunt. "Well, sir?"

"I have my own opinions," resumed Mr. Murdstone, whose face darkened more and more, the more he and my aunt observed each other, which they did very narrowly, "as to the best mode of bringing him up; they are founded, in part, on my knowledge of him, and in part on my knowledge of my own means and resources. I am responsible for them to myself, I act upon them, and I say no more about them. It is enough that I place this boy under the eye of a friend of my own, in a respectable business; that it does not please him; that he runs away from it; makes himself a common vagabond about the country; and comes here, in rags, to appeal to you, Miss Trotwood. I wish to set before you, honorably, the exact consequences—so far as they are within my knowledge—of your abetting him in this appeal."

"But about the respectable business first," said my aunt. "If he had been your own boy, you would have put him to it, just the same, I suppose?"

"If he had been my brother's own boy," returned Miss Murdstone, striking in, "his character, I trust, would have been altogether different."

"Or if the poor child, his mother, had been alive, he would still have gone into the respectable business, would he?" said my aunt.

"I believe," said Mr. Murdstone, with an inclination of his head, "that Clara would have disputed nothing, which myself and my sister Jane Murdstone were agreed was for the best."

Miss Murdstone confirmed this, with an audible murmur.

"Umph!" said my aunt. "Unfortunate baby!"

Mr. Dick, who had been rattling his money all this time, was rattling it so loudly now, that my aunt felt it necessary to check him with a look, before saying:

"The poor child's annuity died with her?"

"Died with her," replied Mr. Murdstone.

"And there was no settlement of the little property—the house and garden—the what's-its-name Rookery without any rooks in it—upon her boy."

"It had been left to her, unconditionally, by her first husband," Mr. Murdstone began, when my aunt caught him up with the greatest irascibility and impatience.

"Good Lord, man, there's no occasion to say that. Left to her unconditionally! I think I see David Copperfield looking forward to any condition of any sort or kind, though it stared him point-blank in the face! Of course it was left to her unconditionally. But when she married again—when she took that most disastrous step of marrying you, in short," said my aunt, "to be plain—did no one put in a word for the boy at that time?"

"My late wife loved her second husband, madam," said Mr. Murdstone, "and trusted implicitly in him."

"Your late wife, sir, was a most unworldly, most unhappy, most unfortunate baby," returned my aunt, shaking her head at him. "That's what *she* was. And now, what have you got to say next?"

"Merely this, Miss Trotwood," he returned. "I am here to take David back—to take him back unconditionally, to dispose of him as I think proper, and to deal with him as I think right. I am not here to make any promise, or give any pledge to anybody. You may possibly have some idea, Miss Trotwood, of abetting him in his running away, and in his complaints to you. Your manner, which I must say does not seem intended to propitiate, induces me to think it possible. Now I must caution you that if you abet him once, you abet him for good and all; if you step in between him and me now, you must step in, Miss Trotwood, for ever. I cannot trifle, or be trifled with. I am here, for the first and last time, to take him away. Is he ready to go? If he is not—and you tell me he is not; on any pretence; it is indifferent to me what—my doors are shut against him henceforth, and yours, I take it for granted, are open to him."

To this address, my aunt had listened with the closest attention, sitting perfectly upright, with her hands folded on one knee, and looking grimly on the speaker. When he had finished, she turned her eyes so as to command Miss Murdstone, without otherwise disturbing her attitude, and said:

"Well, ma'am, have *you* got anything to remark?"

"Indeed, Miss Trotwood," said Miss Murdstone, "all that I could say has been so well said by my brother, and all that I know to be the fact has been so plainly stated by him, that I have nothing to add except my thanks for your politeness. For your very great politeness, I am sure," said Miss Murdstone; with an irony which no more affected my aunt, than it discomposed the cannon I had slept by at Chatham.

"And what does the boy say?" said my aunt. "Are you ready to go, David?"

I answered no, and entreated her not to let me go. I said that neither Mr. nor Miss Murdstone had ever liked me, or had ever been kind to me. That they had made my mama, who always loved me dearly, unhappy about me, and that I knew it well, and that Peggotty knew it. I said that I had been more miserable than I thought anybody could believe, who only knew how young I was. And I begged and prayed my aunt—I forget in what terms now, but I remember that they affected me very much then—to befriend and protect me, for my father's sake.

"Mr. Dick," said my aunt, "what shall I do with this child?"

Mr. Dick considered, hesitated, brightened, and rejoined, "Have him measured for a suit of clothes directly."

"Mr. Dick," said my aunt, triumphantly, "give me your hand, for your common sense is invaluable." Having shaken it with great cordiality, she pulled me towards her, and said to Mr. Murdstone:

"You can go when you like; I'll take my chance with the boy. If he's all you say he is, at least I can do as much for him then, as you have done. But I don't believe a word of it."

"Miss Trotwood," rejoined Mr. Murdstone, shrugging his shoulders, as he rose, "if you were a gentleman——"

"Bah! stuff and nonsense!" said my aunt. "Don't talk to me!"

"How exquisitely polite!" exclaimed Miss Murdstone, rising. "Overpowering, really!"

"Do you think I don't know," said my aunt, turning a deaf ear to the sister, and continuing to address the brother, and to shake her head at him with infinite expression, "what kind of life you must have led that poor, unhappy, misdirected baby? Do you think I don't know what a woful day it was for the soft little creature, when *you* first came in her way—smirking and making great eyes at her, I'll be bound, as if you couldn't say boh! to a goose!"

"I never heard anything so elegant!" said Miss Murdstone.

"Do you think I can't understand you as well as if I had seen you," pursued my aunt, "now that I *do* see and hear you—which, I tell you candidly, is anything but a pleasure to me? Oh yes, bless us! who so smooth and silky as Mr. Murdstone at first! The poor, benighted innocent had never seen such a man. He was made of sweetness. He worshipped her. He doted on her boy—tenderly doted on him! He was to be another father to him, and they were all to live together in a garden of roses, weren't they? Ugh! Get along with you, do!" said my aunt.

"I never heard anything like this person in my life!" exclaimed Miss Murdstone.

"And when you had made sure of the poor little fool," said my aunt—"God forgive me that I should call her so, and she gone where *you* won't go in a hurry—because you had not done wrong enough to her and hers, you must begin to train her, must you? begin to break her, like a poor caged bird, and wear her deluded life away, in teaching her to sing *your* notes?"

"This is either insanity or intoxication," said Miss Murdstone, in a perfect agony at not being able to turn the current of my aunt's address towards herself; "and my suspicion is, that it 's intoxication."

Miss Betsey, without taking the least notice of the interruption, continued to address herself to Mr. Murdstone as if there had been no such thing.

"Mr. Murdstone," she said, shaking her finger at him, "you were a tyrant to the simple baby, and you broke her heart. She was a loving baby—I know that; I knew it, years before *you* ever saw her—and through the best part of her weakness, you gave her the wounds she died of. There is the truth for your comfort, however you like it. And you and your instruments may make the most of it."

"Allow me to inquire, Miss Trotwood," interposed Miss Murdstone, "whom you are pleased to call, in a choice of words in which I am not experienced, my brother's instruments?"

Still stone-deaf to the voice, and utterly unmoved by it, Miss Betsey pursued her course.

"It was clear enough, as I have told you, years before *you* ever saw her—and why, in the mysterious dispensations of Providence, you ever did see her, is more than humanity can comprehend—it was clear enough that the poor soft little thing would marry somebody, at some time or other; but I did hope it wouldn't have been as bad as it has turned out. That was the time, Mr. Murdstone, when she gave birth to her boy here," said my aunt; "to the poor child you sometimes tormented her through afterwards, which is a disagreeable remembrance, and makes the sight of him odious now. Ay, ay! you needn't wince!" said my aunt, "I know it 's true without that."

He had stood by the door, all this while, observant of her with a smile upon his face, though his black eyebrows were heavily contracted. I remarked now, that, though the smile was on his face still, his colour had gone in a moment, and he seemed to breathe as if he had been running.

"Good day, sir!" said my aunt, "and good bye! Good day to you too, ma'am," said my aunt, turning suddenly upon his sister. "Let me see you ride a donkey over *my* green again, and as sure as you have a head upon your shoulders, I'll knock your bonnet off, and tread upon it!"

It would require a painter, and no common painter too, to depict my aunt's face as she delivered herself of this very unexpected sentiment, and Miss Murdstone's face as she heard it. But the manner of the speech, no less than the matter, was so fiery, that Miss Murdstone, without a word in answer, discreetly put her arm through her brother's, and walked haughtily out of the cottage; my aunt remaining in the window looking after them; prepared, I have no doubt, in case of the donkey's reappearance, to carry her threat into instant execution.

No attempt at defiance being made, however, her face gradually relaxed, and became so pleasant, that I was emboldened to kiss and thank her; which I did with great heartiness, and with both my arms clasped round her neck. I then shook hands with Mr. Dick, who shook hands with me a great many times, and hailed this happy close of the proceedings with repeated bursts of laughter.

"You'll consider yourself guardian, jointly with me, of this child, Mr. Dick," said my aunt.

"I shall be delighted," said Mr. Dick, "to be the guardian of David's son."

"Very good," returned my aunt, "*that's* settled. I have been thinking, do you know, Mr. Dick, that I might call him Trotwood?"

"Certainly, certainly. Call him Trotwood, certainly," said Mr. Dick. "David's son's Trotwood."

"Trotwood Copperfield, you mean," returned my aunt.

"Yes, to be sure. Yes. Trotwood Copperfield," said Mr. Dick, a little abashed.

My aunt took so kindly to the notion, that some ready-made clothes, which were purchased for me that afternoon, were marked "Trotwood Copperfield," in her own handwriting, and in indelible marking-ink, before I put them on; and it was settled that all the other clothes which were ordered to be made for me (a complete outfit was bespoke that afternoon) should be marked in the same way.

Thus I began my new life, in a new name, and with every thing new about me. Now that the state of doubt was over I felt, for many days, like one in a dream. I never thought that I had a curious couple of guardians, in my aunt and Mr. Dick. I never thought of anything about myself, distinctly. The two things clearest in my mind were, that a remoteness had come upon the old Blunderstone life—which seemed to lie in a haze of an immeasurable distance; and that a curtain had for ever fallen on my life at Murdstone and Grinby's. No one has ever raised that curtain since. I have lifted it for a moment, even in this narrative, with a reluctant hand, and dropped it gladly. The remembrance of that life is fraught with so much pain to me, with so much mental suffering and want of hope, that I have never had the courage even to examine how long I was doomed to lead it. Whether it lasted for a year, or more, or less, I do not know. I only know that it was, and ceased to be; and that I have written, and there I leave it.

CHAPTER XV.

I MAKE ANOTHER BEGINNING.

Mr. Dick and I soon became the best of friends, and very often, when his day's work was done, went out together to fly the great kite. Every day of his life he had a long sitting at the Memorial, which never made the least progress, however hard he labored, for King Charles the First always strayed into it, sooner or later, and then it was thrown aside, and another one begun. The patience and hope with which he bore these perpetual disappointments, the mild perception he had that there was something wrong about King Charles the First, the feeble efforts he made to keep him out, and the certainty with which he came in, and tumbled the Memorial out of all shape, made a deep impression on me. What Mr. Dick supposed would come of the Memorial, if it were completed; where he thought it was to go, or what he thought it was to do; he knew no more than anybody else, I believe. Nor was it at all necessary that he should trouble himself with such questions, for if anything were certain under the sun, it was certain that the Memorial never would be finished.

It was quite an affecting sight, I used to think, to see him with the kite when it was up a great height in the air. What he had told me, in his room, about his belief in its disseminating the statements pasted on it, which were nothing but old leaves of abortive Memorials, might have been a fancy with him sometimes; but not when he was out, looking up at the kite in the sky, and feeling it pull and tug at his hand. He never looked so serene as he did then. I used to fancy, as I sat by him of an evening on a green slope, and saw him watch the kite high in the quiet air, that it lifted his mind out of its confusion, and bore it (such was my boyish thought) into the skies. As he wound the string in, and it came lower and lower down out of the beautiful light, until it fluttered to the ground and lay there like a dead thing, he seemed to wake gradually out of a dream; and I remember to have seen him take it up, and look about him in a lost way, as if they had both come down together, so that I pitied him with all my heart.

While I advanced in friendship and intimacy with Mr. Dick, I did not go backward in the favor of his staunch friend, my aunt. She took so kindly to me, that, in the course of a few weeks, she shortened my adopted name of Trotwood into Trot; and even encouraged me to hope that if I went on as I had begun, I might take equal rank in her affections with my sister Betsey Trotwood.

"Trot," said my aunt one evening, when the backgammon-board was placed as usual for herself and Mr. Dick, "we must not forget your education."

This was my only subject of anxiety, and I felt quite delighted by her referring to it.

"Should you like to go to school at Canterbury?" said my aunt.

I replied that I should like it very much, as it was so near her.

"Good," said my aunt. "Should you like to go to-morrow?"

Being already no stranger to the general rapidity of my aunt's evolutions, I was not surprised by the suddenness of the proposal, and said: "Yes."

"Good," said my aunt again. "Janet, hire the grey pony and chaise to-morrow morning at ten o'clock, and pack up Master Trotwood's clothes to-night."

I was greatly elated by these orders; but my heart smote me for my selfishness, when I witnessed their effect on Mr. Dick, who was so low-spirited at the prospect of our separation, and played so ill in consequence, that my aunt, after giving him several admonitory raps on the knuckles with her dice-box, shut up the board, and declined to play with him any more. But, on hearing from my aunt that I should sometimes come over on a Saturday, and that he could sometimes come and see me on a Wednesday, he revived; and vowed to make another kite for those occasions, of proportions greatly surpassing the present one. In the morning he was downhearted again, and would have sustained himself by giving me all the money he had in his possession, gold and silver too, if my aunt had not interposed, and limited the gift to five shillings, which, at his earnest petition, were afterwards increased to ten. We parted at the garden-gate in a most affectionate manner, and Mr. Dick did not go into the house until my aunt had driven me out of sight of it.

My aunt, who was perfectly indifferent to public opinion, drove the grey pony through Dover in a masterly manner; sitting high and stiff like a state coachman, keeping a steady eye upon him wherever he went, and making a point of not letting him have his own way in any respect. When we came into the country road, she permitted him to relax a little, however; and looking at me down in a valley of cushion by her side, asked me whether I was happy.

"Very happy indeed, thank you, aunt," I said.

She was much gratified; and both her hands being occupied, patted me on the head with her whip.

"Is it a large school, aunt?" I asked.

"Why, I don't know," said my aunt. "We are going to Mr Wickfield's first."

"Does *he* keep a school?" I asked.

"No, Trot," said my aunt. "He keeps an office."

I asked for no more information about Mr. Wickfield, as she offered none, and we conversed on other subjects until we came to Canterbury, where, as it was market-day, my aunt had a great opportunity of insinuating the grey pony among carts, baskets, vegetables, and hucksters' goods. The hair-breadth turns and twists we made, drew down upon us a variety of speeches from the people standing about, which were not always complimentary; but my aunt drove on with perfect indifference, and I dare say would have taken her own way with as much coolness through an enemy's country.

At length we stopped before a very old house bulging out over the road; a house with long low lattice-windows bulging out still farther, and beams with carved heads on the ends bulging out too, so that I fancied the whole house was leaning forward, trying to see who was passing on the narrow pavement below. It was quite spotless in its cleanliness. The old-fashioned brass knocker on the low arched door, ornamented with carved garlands of fruit and flowers, twinkled like a star; the two stone steps descending to the door were as white as if they had been covered with fair linen; and all the angles and corners, and carvings and mouldings, and quaint little panes of glass, and quainter little windows, though as old as the hills, were as pure as any snow that ever fell upon the hills.

When the pony-chaise stopped at the door, and my eyes were intent upon the house, I saw a cadaverous face appear at a small window on the ground floor (in a little round tower that formed one side of the house), and quickly disappear. The low arched door then opened, and the face came out. It was quite as cadaverous as it had looked in the window, though in the grain of it there was that tinge of red which is sometimes to be observed in the skins of red-haired people. It belonged to a red-haired person—a youth of fifteen, as I take it now, but looking much older—whose hair was cropped as close as the closest stubble; who had hardly any eyebrows, and no eyelashes, and eyes of a red-brown; so unsheltered and unshaded, that I remember wondering how he went to sleep. He was high-shouldered and bony; dressed in decent black, with a white wisp of a neckcloth; buttoned up to the throat; and had a long, lank, skeleton hand, which particularly attracted my attention, as he stood at the pony's head, rubbing his chin with it, and looking up at us in the chaise.

"Is Mr. Wickfield at home, Uriah Heep?" said my aunt.

"Mr. Wickfield's at home, ma'am," said Uriah Heep, "if you'll please to walk in there"—pointing with his long hand to the room he meant.

We got out; and leaving him to hold the pony, went into a long low parlor looking towards the street, from the window of which I caught a glimpse, as I went in, of Uriah Heep breathing into the pony's nostrils, and immediately covering them with his hand, as if he were putting some spell upon him. Opposite to the tall old chimney-piece, were two portraits: one of a gentleman with grey hair (though not by any means an old man) and black eyebrows, who was looking over some papers tied together with red tape; the other, of a lady, with a very placid and sweet expression of face, who was looking at me.

I believe I was turning about in search of Uriah's picture, when, a door at the farther end of the room opening, a gentleman entered, at sight of whom I turned to the first-mentioned portrait again, to make quite sure that it had not come out of its frame. But it was stationary; and as the gentleman advanced into the light, I saw that he was some years older than when he had had his picture painted.

"Miss Betsey Trotwood," said the gentleman, "pray walk in. I was engaged for the moment, but you'll excuse my being busy. You know my motive. I have but one in life."

Miss Betsey thanked him, and we went into his room, which was furnished as an office, with books, papers, tin boxes, and so forth. It looked into a garden, and had an iron safe let into the wall; so immediately over the mantel-shelf, that I wondered, as I sat down, how the sweeps got round it when they swept the chimney.

"Well, Miss Trotwood," said Mr. Wickfield; for I soon found that it was he, and that he was a lawyer, and steward of the estates of a rich gentleman of the county; "what wind blows you here? Not an ill wind, I hope?"

"No," replied my aunt, "I have not come for any law."

"That's right, ma'am," said Mr. Wickfield. "You had better come for anything else."

His hair was quite white now, though his eyebrows were still black. He had a very agreeable face, and, I thought, was handsome. There was a certain richness in his complexion, which I had been long accustomed, under Peggotty's tuition, to connect with port wine; and I fancied it was in his voice too, and referred his growing corpulency to the same cause. He was very cleanly dressed, in a blue coat, striped waistcoat, and nankeen trowsers; and his fine frilled shirt and cambric neckcloth looked unusually soft and white, reminding my strolling fancy (I call to mind) of the plumage on the breast of a swan.

"This is my nephew," said my aunt.

"Wasn't aware you had one, Miss Trotwood," said Mr. Wickfield.

"My grand-nephew, that is to say," observed my aunt.

"Wasn't aware you had a grand-nephew, I give you my word," said Mr. Wickfield.

"I have adopted him," said my aunt, with a wave of her hand, importing that his knowledge and his ignorance were all one to her, "and I have brought him here, to put him to a school where he may be thoroughly well taught, and well treated. Now tell me where that school is, and what it is, and all about it."

"Before I can advise you properly," said Mr. Wickfield,—"the old question, you know. What 's your motive in this?"

"Deuce take the man!" exclaimed my aunt. "Always fishing for motives, when they 're on the surface! Why, to make the child happy and useful."

"It must be a mixed motive, I think," said Mr. Wickfield, shaking his head and smiling incredulously.

"A mixed fiddlestick!" returned my aunt. "You claim to have one plain motive in all you do yourself. You don't suppose, I hope, that you are the only plain dealer in the world?"

"Ay, but I have only one motive in life, Miss Trotwood," he rejoined, smiling. "Other people have dozens, scores, hundreds. I have only one. There's the difference. However, that's beside the question. The best school? Whatever the motive, you want the best?"

My aunt nodded assent.

"At the best we have," said Mr. Wickfield, considering, "your nephew couldn't board just now."

"But he could board somewhere else, I suppose," suggested my aunt.

Mr. Wickfield thought I could. After a little discussion, he proposed to take my aunt to the school, that she might see it and judge for herself; also, to take her, with the same object, to two or three houses where he thought I could be boarded. My aunt embracing the proposal, we were all three going out together, when he stopped and said:

"Our little friend here might have some motive, perhaps, for objecting to the arrangements. I think we had better leave him behind."

My aunt seemed disposed to contest the point; but to facilitate matters I said I would gladly remain behind, if they pleased; and returned into Mr. Wickfield's office, where I sat down again, in the chair I had first occupied, to await their return.

It so happened that this chair was opposite a narrow passage, which ended in the little circular room where I had seen Uriah Heep's pale face looking out of window. Uriah, having taken the pony to a neighboring stable, was at work at a desk in this room, which had a brass frame on the top to hang papers upon, and on which the writing he was making a copy of was then hanging. Though his face was towards me, I thought, for some time, the writing being between us, that he could not see me; but looking that way more attentively, it made me uncomfortable to observe that, every now and then, his sleepless eyes would come below the writing, like two red suns, and stealthily stare at me for I dare say a whole minute at a time, during which his pen went, or pretended to go, as cleverly as ever. I made several attempts to get out of their way —such as standing on a chair to look at a map on the other side of the room, and poring over the columns of a Kentish newspaper—but they always attracted me back again; and whenever I looked towards those two red suns, I was sure to find them, either just rising or just setting.

At length, much to my relief, my aunt and Mr. Wickfield came back, after a pretty long absence. They were not so successful as I could have wished; for though the advantages of the school were undeniable, my aunt had not approved of any of the boarding-houses proposed for me.

"It's very unfortunate," said my aunt. "I don't know what to do, Trot."

"It *does* happen unfortunately," said Mr. Wickfield. "But I'll tell you what you can do, Miss Trotwood."

"What's that?" inquired my aunt.

"Leave your nephew here, for the present. He's a quiet fellow. He won't disturb me at all. It's a capital house for study. As quiet as a monastery, and almost as roomy. Leave him here."

My aunt evidently liked the offer, though she was delicate of accepting it. So did I.

"Come, Miss Trotwood," said Mr. Wickfield. "This is the way out of the difficulty. It's only a temporary arrangement, you know If it don't act well, or don't quite accord with our mutual convenience, he can easily go to the right about. There will be time to find some better place for him in the meanwhile. You had better determine to leave him here for the present!"

"I am very much obliged to you," said my aunt; "and so is he, I see; but—"

"Come! I know what you mean," cried Mr. Wickfield. "You shall not be oppressed by the receipt of favors, Miss Trotwood. You may pay for him if you like. We won't be hard about terms, but you shall pay if you will."

"On that understanding," said my aunt, "though it doesn't lessen the real obligation, I shall be very glad to leave him."

"Then come and see my little housekeeper," said Mr. Wickfield.

We accordingly went up a wonderful old staircase; with a balustrade so broad that we might have gone up that, almost as easily; and into a shady old drawing-room, lighted by some three or four of the quaint windows I had looked up at from the street: which had old oak seats in them, that seemed to have come of the same trees as the shining oak floor, and the great beams in the ceiling. It was a prettily furnished room, with a piano and some lively furniture in red and green, and some flowers. It seemed to be all old nooks and corners; and in every nook and corner there was some queer little table, or cupboard, or bookcase, or seat, or something or other, that made me think there was not such another good corner in the room; until I looked at the next one, and found it equal to it, if not better. On everything there was the same air of retirement and cleanliness that marked the house outside.

Mr. Wickfield tapped at a door in a corner of the paneled wall, and a girl of about my own age came quickly out and kissed him. On her face, I saw immediately the placid and sweet expression of the lady whose picture had looked at me down-stairs. It seemed to my imagination as if the portrait had grown womanly, and the original remained a child. Although her face was quite bright and happy, there was a tranquillity about it, and about her—a quiet, good, calm spirit—that I never have forgotten; that I never shall forget.

This was his little housekeeper, his daughter Agnes, Mr. Wickfield said. When I heard how he said it, and saw how he held her hand, I guessed what the one motive of his life was.

She had a little basket-trifle hanging at her side, with keys in it; and looked as staid and as discreet a housekeeper as the old house could have. She listened to her father as he told her about me, with a pleasant face; and when he had concluded, proposed to my aunt that we should go up stairs and see my room. We all went together; she before us: and a glorious old room it was, with more oak beams, and diamond panes; and the broad balustrade going all the way up to it.

I cannot call to mind where or when, in my childhood, I had seen a stained glass window in a church. Nor do I recollect its subject. But I know that when I saw her turn round, in the grave light of the old staircase, and wait for us, above, I thought of that window; and that I associated something of its tranquil brightness with Agnes Wickfield ever afterwards.

My aunt was as happy as I was, in the arrangement made for me; and we went down to the drawing-room again, well pleased and gratified. As she would not hear of staying to dinner, lest she should by any chance fail to arrive at home with the grey pony before dark; and as I apprehend Mr. Wickfield knew her too well, to argue any point with her; some lunch was provided for her there, and Agnes went back to her governess, and Mr. Wickfield to his office. So we were left to take leave of one another without any restraint.

She told me that everything would be arranged for me by Mr. Wickfield, and that I should want for nothing, and gave me the kindest words and the best advice.

"Trot," said my aunt in conclusion, "be a credit to yourself, to me, and Mr. Dick, and Heaven be with you!"

I was greatly overcome, and could only thank her, again and again, and send my love to Mr. Dick.

"Never," said my aunt, "be mean in anything; never be false; never be cruel. Avoid those three vices, Trot, and I can always be hopeful of you."

I promised, as well as I could, that I would not abuse her kindness or forget her admonition.

"The pony's at the door," said my aunt, "and I am off! Stay here."

With these words she embraced me hastily, and went out of the room, shutting the door after her. At first I was startled by so abrupt a departure, and almost feared I had displeased her; but when I looked into the street, and saw how dejectedly she got into the chaise, and drove away without looking up, I understood her better, and did not do her that injustice.

By five o'clock, which was Mr. Wickfield's dinner hour, I had mustered up my spirits again, and was ready for my knife and fork. The cloth was only laid for us two; but Agnes was waiting in the drawing-room before dinner, went down with her father, and sat opposite to him at table. I doubted whether he could have dined without her.

We did not stay there after dinner, but came up-stairs into the drawing-room again: in one snug corner of which, Agnes set glasses for her father, and a decanter of port wine. I thought he would have missed its usual flavor, if it had been put there for him by any other hands.

There he sat, taking his wine, and taking a good deal of it, for two hours; while Agnes played on the piano, worked, and talked to him and me. He was, for the most part, gay and cheerful with us; but sometimes his eyes rested on her, and he fell into a brooding state, and was silent. She always observed this quickly, as I thought, and always roused him with a question or a caress. Then he came out of his meditation, and drank more wine.

Agnes made the tea and presided over it; and the time passed away after it, as after dinner, until she went to bed; when her father took her in his arms and kissed her, and, she being gone, ordered candles in his office. Then I went to bed too.

But in the course of the evening I had rambled down to the door, and a little way along the street, that I might have another peep at the old houses, and the gray Cathedral; and might think of my coming through that old city on my journey, and of my passing the very house I lived in, without knowing it. As I came back, I saw Uriah Heep shutting up the office; and feeling friendly towards every body, went in and spoke to him, and at parting, gave him my hand. But oh, what a clammy hand his was! as ghostly to the touch as to the sight! I rubbed mine afterwards to warm it, *and to rub his off.*

It was such an uncomfortable hand, that, when I went to my room, it was still cold and wet upon my memory. Leaning out of window, and seeing one of the faces on the beam-ends looking at me sideways, I fancied it was Uriah Heep got up there somehow, and shut him out in a hurry.

CHAPTER XVI.

I AM A NEW BOY IN MORE SENSES THAN ONE.

NEXT morning, after breakfast, I entered on school life again. I went, accompanied by Mr. Wickfield, to the scene of my future studies—a grave building in a court-yard, with a learned air about it that seemed very well suited to the stray rooks and jackdaws who came down from the Cathedral towers to walk with a clerkly bearing on the grass-plot—and was introduced to my new master, Doctor Strong.

Doctor Strong looked almost as rusty, to my thinking, as the tall iron rails and gates outside the house; and almost as stiff and heavy as the great stone urns that flanked them, and were set up, on the top of the red-brick wall, at regular distances all round the court, like sublimated skittles, for Time to play at. He was in his library (I mean Doctor Strong was), with his clothes not particularly well brushed, and his hair not particularly well combed; his knee-smalls unbraced; his long black gaiters unbuttoned; and his shoes yawning like two caverns on the hearth-rug. Turning upon me a lustreless eye, that reminded me of a long-forgotten blind old horse who once used to crop the grass, and tumble over the graves, in Blunderstone churchyard, he said he was glad to see me: and then he gave me his hand; which I didn't know what to do with, as it did nothing for itself.

But, sitting at work, not far off from Doctor Strong, was a very pretty young lady—whom he called Annie, and who was his daughter, I supposed—who got me out of my difficulty by kneeling down to put Doctor Strong's shoes on, and button his gaiters, which she did with great cheerfulness and quickness. When she had finished, and we were going out to the school-room, I was much surprised to hear Mr. Wickfield, in bidding her good morning, address her as

"Mrs. Strong;" and I was wondering could she be Doctor Strong's son's wife, or could she be Mrs. Doctor Strong, when Doctor Strong himself unconsciously enlightened me.

"By the bye, Wickfield," he said, stopping in a passage with his hand on my shoulder; "you have not found any suitable provision for my wife's cousin yet?"

"No," said Mr. Wickfield. "No. Not yet."

"I could wish it done as soon as it *can* be done, Wickfield," said Doctor Strong, "for Jack Maldon is needy, and idle; and of those two bad things, worse things sometimes come. What does Doctor Watts say," he added, looking at me, and moving his head to the time of his quotation, "'Satan finds some mischief still, for idle hands to do.'"

"Egad, doctor," returned Mr. Wickfield, "if Doctor Watts knew mankind, he might have written, with as much truth, 'Satan finds some mischief still, for busy hands to do.' The busy people achieve their full share of mischief in the world, you may rely upon it. What have the people been about, who have been the busiest in getting money, and in getting power, this century or two? No mischief?"

"Jack Maldon will never be very busy in getting either, I expect," said Doctor Strong, rubbing his chin thoughtfully.

"Perhaps not," said Mr. Wickfield; "and you bring me back to the question, with an apology for digressing. No, I have not been able to dispose of Mr. Jack Maldon yet. I believe," he said this with some hesitation, "I penetrate your motive, and it makes the thing more difficult."

"My motive," returned Dr. Strong, "is to make some suitable provision for a cousin, and an old playfellow, of Annie's."

"Yes, I know," said Mr. Wickfield; "at home or abroad."

"Aye!" replied the Doctor, apparently wondering why he emphasised these words so much. "At home or abroad."

"Your own expression, you know," said Mr. Wickfield. "Or abroad."

"Surely," the Doctor answered. "Surely. One or other."

"One or other? Have you no choice?" asked Mr. Wickfield.

"No," returned the Doctor.

"No?" with astonishment.

"Not the least."

"No motive," said Mr. Wickfield, "for meaning abroad, and not at home?"

"No," returned the Doctor.

"I am bound to believe you, and of course I do believe you," said Mr. Wickfield. "It might have simplified my office very much, if I had known it before. But I confess I entertained another impression."

Doctor Strong regarded him with a puzzled and doubting look, which almost immediately subsided into a smile that gave me great encouragement; for it was full of amiability and sweetness, and there was a simplicity in it, and indeed in his whole manner, when the studious, pondering frost upon it was got through, very attractive and hopeful to a young scholar like me. Repeating "no," and "not the least," and other short assurances to the same purport, Doctor Strong jogged on before us, at a queer, uneven pace; and we followed: Mr. Wickfield looking grave, I observed, and shaking his head to himself, without knowing that I saw him.

The school-room was a pretty large hall, on the quietest side of the house, confronted by the stately stare of some half-dozen of the great urns, and commanding a peep of an old secluded garden belonging to the Doctor, where the peaches were ripening on the sunny south wall. There were two great aloes, in tubs, on the turf outside the windows; the broad hard leaves of which plant (looking as if they were made of painted tin) have ever since, by association, been symbolical to me of silence and retirement. About five-and-twenty boys were studiously engaged at their books when we went in, but they rose to give the Doctor good morning, and remained standing when they saw Mr. Wickfield and me.

"A new boy, young gentlemen," said the Doctor; "Trotwood Copperfield."

One Adams, who was the head-boy, then stepped out of his place and welcomed me. He looked like a young clergyman, in his white cravat, but he was very affable and good-humored; and he showed me my place, and presented me to the masters, in a gentlemanly way that would have put me at my ease, if anything could.

It seemed to me so long, however, since I had been among such boys, or among any companions of my own age, except Mick Walker and Mealey Potatoes, that I felt as strange as I ever have done in all my life. I was so conscious of having passed through scenes of which they could have no knowledge, and of having acquired experiences foreign to my age, appearance, and condition, as one of them, that I half believed it was an imposture to come there as an ordinary little schoolboy. I had become, in the Murdstone and Grinby time, however short or long it may have been, so unused to the sports and games of boys, that I knew I was awkward and inexperienced in the commonest things belonging to them. Whatever I had learnt, had so slipped away from me in the sordid cares of my life from day to night, that now, when I was examined about what I knew, I knew nothing, and was put into the lowest form of the school. But, troubled as I was, by my want of boyish skill, and of book-learning too, I was made infinitely more uncomfortable by the consideration, that, in what I did know, I was much farther removed from my companions than in what I did not. My mind ran upon what they would think, if they knew of my familiar acquaintance with the King's Bench Prison? Was there anything about me which would reveal my proceedings in connexion with the Micawber family—all those pawnings, and sellings, and suppers—in spite of myself? Suppose some of the boys had seen me coming through Canterbury, wayworn and ragged, and should find me out? What would they say, who made so light of money, if they could know how I had scraped my halfpence together, for the purchase of my daily saveloy and beer, or my slices of pudding? How would it affect them, who were so innocent of London life, and London streets, to discover how knowing I was (and was ashamed to be) in some of the meanest phases of both? All this ran in my head so much, on that first day at Doctor Strong's, that I felt distrustful of my slightest look and gesture; shrunk within myself whensoever I was approached by one of my new schoolfellows; and hurried off the minute school was over, afraid of committing myself in my response to any friendly notice or advance.

But there was such an influence in Mr. Wickfield's old house, that when I knocked at it, with my new school-books under my arm, I began to feel my uneasiness softening away. As I went up to my airy old room, the grave shadow of the staircase seemed to fall upon my doubts and fears, and to make the past more indistinct. I sat there, sturdily conning my books, until dinner time (we were out of school for good at three); and went down, hopeful of becoming a passable sort of boy yet.

Agnes was in the drawing-room, waiting for her father, who was detained by some one in his office. She met me with her pleasant smile, and asked me how I liked the school. I told her I should like it very much, I hoped; but I was a little strange to it at first.

"You have never been to school," I said, "have you?"

"Oh, yes! Every day."

"Ah, but you mean here, at your own home?"

"Papa couldn't spare me to go anywhere else," she answered, smiling and shaking her head. "His housekeeper must be in his house, you know."

"He is very fond of you, I am sure," I said.

She nodded "Yes," and went to the door to listen for his coming up, that she might meet him on the stairs. But, as he was not there, she came back again.

"Mama has been dead ever since I was born," she said, in her quiet way. "I only know her picture, down stairs. I saw you looking at it yesterday. Did you think whose it was?"

I told her yes, because it was so like herself.

"Papa says so, too," said Agnes, pleased. "Hark! That's papa now!"

Her bright calm face lighted up with pleasure as she went to meet him, and as they came in, hand in hand. He greeted me cordially; and told me I should certainly be happy under Doctor Strong, who was one of the gentlest of men.

"There may be some, perhaps—I don't know that there are—who abuse his kindness," said Mr. Wickfield. "Never be one of those, Trotwood, in anything. He is the least suspicious of mankind; and whether that's a merit, or whether it 's a blemish, it deserves consideration in all dealings with the Doctor, great or small."

He spoke, I thought as if he were weary, or dissatisfied with something; but I did not pursue the question in my mind, fo ner was just then announced, and we went down and took the ame seats as before.

We had scarcely done so, when Uriah Heep put in his red head and his lank hand at the door, and said:

"Here's Mr. Maldon begs the favor of a word, sir."

"I am but this moment quit of Mr. Maldon," said his master.

"Yes, sir," returned Uriah; "but Mr. Maldon has come back, and he begs the favor of a word."

As he held the door open with his hand, Uriah looked at me, and looked at Agnes, and looked at the dishes, and looked at the plates, and looked at every object in the room, I thought,—yet seemed to look at nothing; he made such an appearance all the while of keeping his red eyes dutifully on his master.

"I beg your pardon. It's only to say, on reflection," observed a voice behind Uriah, as Uriah's head was pushed away, and the speaker's substituted—"pray excuse me for this intrusion—that as it seems I have no choice in the matter, the sooner I go abroad, the better. My cousin Annie did say, when we talked of it, that she liked to have her friends within reach rather than to have them banished, and the old Doctor—"

"Doctor Strong, was that?" Mr. Wickfield interposed, gravely.

"Doctor Strong of course," returned the other; "I call him the old Doctor—it's all the same, you know."

"I don't know," returned Mr. Wickfield.

"Well, Doctor Strong," said the other—"Doctor Strong was of the same mind, I believed. But as it appears from the course you take with me that he has changed his mind, why there's no more to be said, except that the sooner I am off, the better. Therefore, I thought I'd come back and say, that the sooner I am off, the better. When a plunge is to be made into the water, it's of no use lingering on the bank."

"There shall be as little lingering as possible, in your case, Mr. Maldon, you may depend upon it," said Mr. Wickfield.

"Thank'ee," said the other. "Much obliged. I don't want to look a gift-horse in the mouth, which is not a gracious thing to do; otherwise, I dare say, mycous in Annie could easily arrange it in her own way. I suppose Annie would only have to say to the old Doctor—"

"Meaning that Mrs. Strong would only have to say to her husband—do I follow you?" said Mr. Wickfield.

"Quite so," returned the other, "—would only have to say, that she wanted such and such a thing to be so and so; and it would be so and so, as a matter of course."

"And why as a matter of course, Mr. Maldon?" asked Mr. Wickfield, sedately eating his dinner.

"Why, because Annie 's a charming young girl, and the old Doctor—Doctor Strong, I mean—is not quite a charming young boy," said Mr. Jack Maldon, laughing. "No offence to anybody, Mr. Wickfield. I only mean that I suppose some compensation is fair and reasonable, in that sort of marriage."

"Compensation to the lady, sir?" asked Mr. Wickfield gravely.

"To the lady, sir," Mr. Jack Maldon answered, laughing. But appearing to remark that Mr. Wickfield went on with his dinner in the same sedate, immoveable manner, and that there was no hope of making him relax a muscle of his face, he added:

"However, I have said what I came back to say, and, with an other apology for this intrusion, I may take myself off. Of course I shall observe your directions, in considering the matter as one to be arranged between you and me solely, and not to be referred to, up at the Doctor's."

"Have you dined?" asked Mr. Wickfield, with a motion of his hand towards the table.

"Thank'ee. I am going to dine," said Mr. Maldon, "with my cousin Annie. Good bye!"

Mr. Wickfield, without rising, looked after him thoughtfully as he went out. He was rather a shallow sort of young gentleman, I thought, with a handsome face, a rapid utterance, and a confident, bold air. And this was the first I ever saw of Mr. Jack Maldon; whom I had not expected to see so soon, when I heard the Doctor speak of him that morning.

When we had dined, we went up-stairs again, where everything went on exactly as on the previous day. Agnes set the glasses and decanters in the same corner, and Mr. Wickfield sat down to drink, and drank a good deal. Agnes played the piano to him, sat by him, and worked and talked, and played some games at dominoes with me. In good time she made tea; and afterwards, when I brought down my books, looked into them, and showed me what she knew of them (which was no slight matter, though she said it was), and what was the best way to learn and understand them. I see her, with her modest, orderly, placid manner, and I hear her beautiful calm voice, as I write these words. The influence for all good, which she came to exercise over me at a later time, begins already to descend upon my breast. I love little Em'ly, and I don't love Agnes—no, not at all in that way—but I feel that there are goodness, peace, and truth, wherever Agnes is; and that the soft light of the colored window in the church, seen long ago, falls on her always, and on me when I am near her, and on everything around.

The time having come for her withdrawal for the night, and she having left us, I gave Mr. Wickfield my hand, preparatory to going away myself. But he checked me and said: "Should you like to stay with us, Trotwood, or to go elsewhere?"

"To stay," I answered, quickly.

"You are sure?"

"If you please. If I may!"

"Why, it 's but a dull life that we lead here, boy, I am afraid," he said.

"Not more dull for me than Agnes, sir. Not dull at all!"

"Than Agnes," he repeated, walking slowly to the great chimney piece, and leaning against it. "Than Agnes!"

He had drunk wine that evening (or I fancied it) until his eyes were bloodshot. Not that I could see them now, for they were cast down, and shaded by his hand; but I had noticed them a little while before.

"Now I wonder," he muttered, "whether my Agnes tires of me. When should I ever tire of her! But that 's different—that 's quite different."

He was musing—not speaking to me; so I remained quiet.

"A dull old house," he said, "and a monotonous life; but I must have her near me. I must keep her near me. If the thought that

I may die and leave my darling, or that my darling may die and leave me, comes, like a spectre, to distress my happiest hours, and is only to be drowned in ——"

He did not supply the word; but pacing slowly to the place where he had sat, and mechanically going through the action of pouring wine from the empty decanter, set it down and paced back again.

"If it is miserable to bear, when she is here," he said, "what would it be, and she away? No, no, no. I can not try that."

He leaned against the chimney-piece, brooding so long that I could not decide whether to run the risk of disturbing him by going, or to remain quietly where I was, until he should come out of his reverie. At length he aroused himself, and looked about the room until his eyes encountered mine.

"Stay with us, Trotwood, eh?" he said, in his usual manner, and as if he were answering something I had just said. "I am glad of it. You are company to us both. It is wholesome to have you here. Wholesome for me, wholesome for Agnes, wholesome perhaps for all of us."

"I am sure it is for me, sir," I said. "I am so glad to be here."

"That 's a fine fellow!" said Mr. Wickfield. "As long as you are glad to be here, you shall stay here." He shook hands with me upon it, and clapped me on the back; and told me that when I had anything to do at night after Agnes had left us, or when I wished to read for my own pleasure, I was free to come to his room, if he were there and if I desired it for company's sake, and to sit with him. I thanked him for his consideration; and, as he went down soon afterwards, and I was not tired, went down too, with a book in my hand, to avail myself, for half-an-hour, of his permission.

But, seeing a light in the little round office, and immediately feeling myself attracted towards Uriah Heep, who had a sort of fascination for me, I went in there instead. I found Uriah reading a great fat book, with such demonstrative attention, that his lank fore-finger followed up every line as he read, and made clammy tracks along the page (or so I fully believed) like a snail.

"You are working late to-night, Uriah," says I.

"Yes, Master Copperfield," says Uriah.

As I was getting on the stool opposite, to talk to him more conveniently, I observed that he had not such a thing as a smile about him, and that he could only widen his mouth and make two hard creases down his cheeks, one on each side, to stand for one.

"I am not doing office-work, Master Copperfield," said Uriah.

"What work, then?" I asked.

"I am improving my legal knowledge, Master Copperfield," said Uriah. "I am going through Tidd's Practice. Oh, what a writer Mr. Tidd is, Master Copperfield!"

My stool was such a tower of observation, that as I watched him reading on again, after this rapturous exclamation, and following up the lines with his fore-finger, I observed that his nostrils, which were thin and pointed with sharp dints in them, had a singular and most uncomfortable way of expanding and contracting themselves—that they seemed to twinkle, instead of his eyes, which hardly ever twinkled at all.

"I suppose you are quite a great lawyer?" I said after looking at him for some time.

"Me, Master Copperfield?" said Uriah. "Oh, no! I'm a very umble person."

It was no fancy of mine about his hands, I observed; for he frequently ground the palms against each other as if to squeeze them dry and warm, besides often wiping them, in a stealthy way, on his pocket-handkerchief.

"I am well aware that I am the umblest person going," said Uriah Heep, modestly; "let the other be where he may. My mother is likewise a very umble person. We live in a numble abode, Master Copperfield, but have much to be thankful for. My father's former calling was umble. He was a sexton."

"What is he now?" I asked.

"He is a partaker of glory at present, Master Copperfield," said Uriah Heep. "But we have much to be thankful for. How much have I to be thankful for, in living with Mr. Wickfield!"

I asked Uriah if he had been living with Mr. Wickfield long?

"I have been with him, going on four year, Master Copperfield," said Uriah; shutting up his book, after carefully marking the place where he had left off. "Since a year after my father's death. How much have I to be thankful for, in that! How much have I to be thankful for, in Mr. Wickfield's kind intention to give me my articles, which would otherwise not lay within the umble means of mother and self!"

"Then, when your articled time is over, you'll be a regular lawyer, I suppose?" said I.

"With the blessing of Providence, Master Copperfield," returned Uriah.

"Perhaps you'll be a partner in Mr. Wickfield's business, one of these days," I said, to make myself agreeable; "and it will be Wickfield and Heep, or Heep, late Wickfield."

"Oh, no, Master Copperfield," returned Uriah, shaking his head. "I am much too umble for that!"

He certainly did look uncommonly like the carved face on the beam outside my window, as he sat, in his humility, eyeing me sideways, with his mouth widened, and the creases in his cheeks.

"Mr. Wickfield is a most excellent man, Master Copperfield," said Uriah. "If you have known him long, you know it, I am sure, much better than I can inform you."

I replied that I was certain he was; but that I had not known him long myself, though he was a friend of my aunt's.

"Oh, indeed, Master Copperfield," said Uriah. "Your aunt is a sweet lady, Master Copperfield!"

He had a way of writhing when he wanted to express enthusiasm, which was very ugly; and which diverted my attention from the compliment he had paid my relation, to the snaky twistings of his throat and body.

"A sweet lady, Master Copperfield!" said Uriah Heep. "She has a great admiration for Miss Agnes, Master Copperfield, I believe?"

I said "Yes," boldly; not that I knew anything about it, Heaven forgive me!

"I hope you have, too, Master Copperfield," said Uriah. "But I am sure you must have."

"Everybody must have," I returned.

"Oh, thank you, Master Copperfield," said Uriah Heep, "for that remark! It is so true! Umble as I am, I know it is *so* true! Oh, thank you, Master Copperfield!"

He writhed himself quite off his stool in the excitement of his feelings, and being off, began to make arrangements for going home.

"Mother will be expecting me," he said, referring to a pale, inexpressive-faced watch in his pocket, "and getting uneasy; for though we are very umble, Master Copperfield, we are much attached to one another. If you would come and see us, any afternoon, and take a cup of tea at our lowly dwelling, mother would be as proud of your company as I should be."

I said I should be glad to come.

"Thank you, Master Copperfield," returned Uriah, putting his book away upon a shelf.—"I suppose you stop here, some time, Master Copperfield?"

I said I was going to be brought up there, I believed, as long as I remained at school.

"Oh, indeed!" exclaimed Uriah. "I should think *you* would come into the business at last, Master Copperfield!"

I protested that I had no views of that sort, and that no such scheme was entertained in my behalf by anybody; but Uriah insisted on blandly replying to all my assurances, "Oh, yes, Master Copperfield, I should think you would, indeed!" and, "Oh, indeed, Master Copperfield, I should think you would, certainly!" over and over again. Being, at last, ready to leave the office for the night, he asked me if it would suit my convenience to have the light put out; and on my answering "Yes," instantly extinguished it. After shaking hands with me—his hand felt like a fish, in the dark—he opened the door into the street a very little, and crept out, and shut it, leaving me to grope my way back into the house: which cost me some trouble and a fall over his stool. This was the proximate cause, I suppose, of my dreaming about him, for what appeared to me to be half the night; and dreaming, among other things, that he had launched Mr. Peggotty's house on a piratical expedition, with a black flag at the mast-head, bearing the inscription "Tidd's Practice," under which diabolical ensign he was carrying me and little Em'ly to the Spanish Main to be drowned.

I got a little the better of my uneasiness when I went to school next day, and a good deal the better next day, and so shook it off by degrees that in less than a fortnight I was quite at home, and happy, among my new companions. I was awkward enough in their games, and backward enough in their studies; but custom would improve me in the first respect, I hoped, and hard work in the second. Accordingly, I went to work very hard, both in play and in earnest, and gained great commendation. And, in a very little while, the Murdstone and Grinby life became so strange to me that I hardly believed in it, while my present life grew so familiar, that I seemed to have been leading it a long time.

Doctor Strong's was an excellent school; as different from Mr. Creakle's as good is from evil. It was very gravely and decorously ordered, and on a sound system; with an appeal, in everything, to the honour and good faith of the boys, and an avowed intention to rely on their possession of those qualities unless they proved themselves unworthy of it, which worked wonders. We all felt that we had a part in the management of the place, and in sustaining its character and dignity. Hence, we soon became warmly attached to it—I am sure I did for one, and I never knew, in all my time, of any other boy being otherwise—and learnt with a good will, desiring to do it credit. We had noble games out of hours, and plenty of liberty; but even then, as I remember, we were well spoken of in the town, and rarely did any disgrace, by our appearance or manner, to the reputation of Doctor Strong and Doctor Strong's boys.

Some of the higher scholars boarded in the Doctor's house, and through them I learnt, at second hand, some particulars of the Doctor's history—as how he had not yet been married twelve months to the beautiful young lady I had seen in the study, whom he had married for love; as she had not a sixpence, and had a world of poor relations (so our fellows said) ready to swarm the Doctor out of house and home. Also, how the Doctor's cogitating manner was attributable to his being always engaged in looking out for Greek roots; which, in my innocence and ignorance, I supposed to be a botanical furor on the Doctor's part, especially as he always looked at the ground when he walked about—until I understood that they were roots of words, with a view to a new Dictionary.

which he had in contemplation. Adams, our head-boy, who had a turn for mathematics, had made a calculation, I was informed, of the time this Dictionary would take in completing, on the Doctor's plan, and at the Doctor's rate of going. He considered that it might be done in one thousand six hundred and forty-nine years, counting from the Doctor's last, or sixty-second, birthday.

But the Doctor himself was the idol of the whole school; and it must have been a badly composed school if he had been anything else, for he was the kindest of men; with a simple faith in him that might have touched the stone hearts of the very urns upon the wall. As he walked up and down that part of the court-yard which was at the side of the house, with the stray rooks and jackdaws looking after him with their heads cocked slyly, as if they knew how much more knowing they were in worldly affairs than he, if any sort of vagabond could only get near enough to his creaking shoes to attract his attention to one sentence of a tale of distress, that vagabond was made for the next two days. It was so notorious in the house, that the masters and head-boys took pains to cut these marauders off at angles, and to get out of windows, to turn them out of the court-yard, before they could make the Doctor aware of their presence; which was sometimes happily effected within a few yards of him, without his knowing anything of the matter, as he jogged to and fro. Outside his own domain, and unprotected, he was a very sheep for the shearers. He would have taken his gaiters off his legs, to give away. In fact, there was a story current among us (I have no idea, and never had, on what authority, but I have believed it for so many years that I feel quite certain it is true), that on a frosty day, one winter time, he actually did bestow his gaiters on a beggar-woman, who occasioned some scandal in the neighbourhood by exhibiting a fine infant from door to door, wrapped in those garments, which were universally recognised, being as well known in the vicinity as the Cathedral. The legend added that the only person who did not identify them was the Doctor himself, who, when they were shortly afterwards displayed at the door of a little second-hand shop of no very good repute, where such things were taken in exchange for gin, was more than once observed to handle them approvingly, as if admiring some curious novelty in the pattern, and considering them an improvement on his own.

It was very pleasant to see the Doctor with his pretty young wife. He had a fatherly, benignant way of showing his fondness for her, which seemed in itself to express a good man. I often saw them walking in the garden where the peaches were, and I sometimes had a nearer observation of them in the study or the parlor. She appeared to me to take great care of the Doctor, and to like him very much, though I never thought her vitally interested in the Dictionary: some cumbrous fragments of which work the Doctor always carried in his pockets, and in the lining of his hat, and generally seemed to be expounding to her as they walked about.

I saw a good deal of Mrs. Strong, both because she had taken a liking for me on the morning of my introduction to the Doctor, and was always afterwards kind to me, and interested in me; and because she was very fond of Agnes, and was often backwards and forwards at our house. There was a curious constraint between her and Mr. Wickfield, I thought (of whom she seemed to be afraid), that never wore off. When she came there of an evening, she always shrunk from accepting his escort home, and ran away with me instead. And sometimes, as we were running gaily across the Cathedral yard together, expecting to meet nobody, we would meet Mr. Jack Maldon, who was always surprised to see us.

Mrs. Strong's mama was a lady I took great delight in. Her name was Mrs. Markleham; but our boys used to call her the Old Soldier, on account of her generalship, and the skill with which she marshalled great forces of relations against the Doctor. She was a little, sharp-eyed woman, who used to wear, when she was dressed, one unchangeable cap, ornamented with some artificial flowers, and two artificial butterflies supposed to be hovering above the flowers. There was a superstition among us that this cap had come from France, and could only originate in the workmanship of that ingenious nation: but all I certainly know about it, is, that it always made its appearance of an evening, wheresoever Mrs. Markleham made *her* appearance; that it was carried about to friendly meetings in a Hindoo basket; that the butterflies had the gift of trembling constantly; and that they improved the shining hours at Doctor Strong's expense, like busy bees.

I observed the Old Soldier—not to adopt the name disrespectfully

—to pretty good advantage, on a night which is made memorable to me by something else I shall relate. It was the night of a little party at the Doctor's, which was given on the occasion of Mr. Jack Maldon's departure for India, whither he was going as a cadet, or something of that kind: Mr. Wickfield having at length arranged the business. It happened to be the Doctor's birthday, too. We had a holiday, had made presents to him in the morning, had made a speech to him through the head-boy, and had cheered him until we were hoarse, and until he had shed tears. And now, in the evening, Mr. Wickfield, Agnes, and I, went to have tea with him in his private capacity.

Mr. Jack Maldon was there, before us. Mrs. Strong, dressed in white, with cherry-colored ribbons, was playing the piano, when we went in; and he was leaning over her to turn the leaves. The clear red and white of her complexion was not so blooming and flower-like as usual, I thought, when she turned round; but she looked very pretty, wonderfully pretty.

"I have forgotten, Doctor," said Mrs. Strong's mama, when we were seated, "to pay you the compliments of the day—though they are, as you may suppose, very far from being mere compliments in my case. Allow me to wish you many happy returns."

"I thank you, ma'am," replied the Doctor.

"Many, many, many, happy returns," said the Old Soldier. "Not only for your own sake, but for Annie's, and John Maldon's, and many other people's. It seems but yesterday to me, John, when you were a little creature, a head shorter than Master Copperfield, making baby-love to Annie behind the gooseberry bushes in the back-garden."

"My dear mama," said Mrs. Strong, "never mind that now."

"Annie, don't be absurd," returned her mother. "If you are to blush to hear of such things, now you are an old married woman, when are you not to blush to hear of them?"

"Old?" exclaimed Mr. Jack Maldon. "Annie? Come!"

"Yes, John," returned the Soldier. "Virtually, an old married woman. Although not old by years—for when did you ever hear me say, or who has ever heard me say, that a girl of twenty was old by years!—your cousin is the wife of the Doctor, and, as such, what

I have described her. It is well for you, John, that your cousin *is* the wife of the Doctor. You have found in him an influential and kind friend, who will be kinder yet, I venture to predict, if you deserve it. I have no false pride. I never hesitate to admit, frankly, that there are some members of our family who want a friend. You were one yourself, before your cousin's influence raised up one for you."

The Doctor, in the goodness of his heart, waved his hand as if to make light of it, and save Mr. Jack Maldon from any further reminder. But Mrs. Markleham changed her chair for one next the Doctor's, and putting her fan on his coat-sleeve, said:

"No, really, my dear Doctor, you must excuse me if I appear to dwell on this rather, because I feel so very strongly. I call it quite my monomania, it is such a subject of mine. You are a blessing to us. You really are a Boon, you know."

"Nonsense, nonsense," said the Doctor.

"No, no, I beg your pardon," retorted the Old Soldier. "With nobody present, but our dear and confidential friend Mr. Wickfield, I cannot consent to be put down. I shall begin to assert the privileges of a mother-in-law, if you go on like that, and scold you. I am perfectly honest and out-spoken. What I am saying, is what I said when you first overpowered me with surprise—you remember how surprised I was?—by proposing for Annie. Not that there was anything so very much out of the way, in the mere act of the proposal —it would be ridiculous to say that!—but because, you having known her poor father, and having known her from a baby six months old, I hadn't thought of you in such a light at all, or indeed as a marrying man in any way,—simply that, you know."

"Aye, aye," returned the Doctor, good-humoredly. "Never mind."

"But I *do* mind," said the Old Soldier, laying her fan upon his lips. "I mind very much. I recal these things that I may be contradicted if I am wrong. Well! Then I spoke to Annie, and I told her what had happened. I said, 'My dear, here's Doctor Strong has positively been and made you the subject of a handsome declaration and an offer.' Did I press it in the least? No. I said, 'Now, Annie, tell me the truth this moment; is your heart free?' 'Mama, she said, crying, 'I am extremely young'—which was perfectly true—'and I hardly know if I have a heart at all.' 'Then, my dear,' I said, 'you may rely upon it, it's free.' 'At all events, my love,' said I, 'Doctor Strong is in an agitated state of mind, and must be answered. He cannot be kept in his present state of suspense.' 'Mama,' said Annie, still crying, 'would he be unhappy without me? If he would, I honor and respect him so much, that I think I will have him.' So it was settled. And then, and not till then, I said to Annie, 'Annie, Doctor Strong will not only be your husband, but he will represent your late father: he will represent the head of our family, he will represent the wisdom and station, and I may say the means, of our family; and will be, in short, a Boon to it.' I used the word at the time, and I have used it again, to-day. If I have any merit, it is consistency."

The daughter had sat quite silent and still during this speech, with her eyes fixed on the ground; her cousin standing near her, and looking on the ground too. She now said very softly, in a trembling voice:

"Mama, I hope you have finished?"

"No, my dear Annie," returned the Soldier, "I have not quite finished. Since you ask me, my love, I reply that I have *not.* I complain that you really are a little unnatural towards your own family; and, as it is of no use complaining to you, I mean to complain to your husband. Now, my dear Doctor, do look at that silly wife of yours."

As the Doctor turned his kind face, with its smile of simplicity and gentleness, towards her, she drooped her head more. I noticed that Mr. Wickfield looked at her steadily.

"When I happened to say to that naughty thing, the other day," pursued her mother, shaking her head and her fan at her, playfully, "that there was a family circumstance she might mention to you—indeed, I think, was bound to mention—she said, that to mention it was to ask a favor; and that, as you were too generous, and as for her to ask was always to have, she wouldn't."

"Annie, my dear," said the Doctor. "That was wrong. It robbed me of a pleasure."

"Almost the very words I said to her!" exclaimed her mother.

"Now really, another time, when I know what she would tell you but for this reason, and won't, I have a great mind, my dear Doctor, to tell you myself."

"I shall be glad if you will," returned the Doctor.

"Shall I?"

"Certainly."

"Well, then, I will!" said the Old Soldier. "That's a bargain." And having, I suppose, carried her point, she tapped the Doctor's hand several times with her fan (which she kissed first), and returned triumphantly to her former station.

Some more company coming in, among whom were the two masters and Adams, the talk became general; and it naturally turned on Mr. Jack Maldon, and the voyage, and the country he was going to, and his various plans and prospects. He was to leave that night, after supper, in a postchaise, for Gravesend; where the ship, in which he was to make the voyage, lay; and was to be gone—unless he came home on leave, or for his health—I don't know how many years. I recollect it was settled by general consent that India was quite a misrepresented country, and had nothing objectionable in it, but a tiger or two, and a little heat in the warm part of the day. For my own part, I looked on Mr. Jack Maldon as a modern Sinbad, and pictured him the bosom friend of all the Rajahs in the east, sitting under canopies, smoking curly golden pipes—a mile long, if they could be straightened out.

Mrs. Strong was a very pretty singer; as I knew, who often heard her singing by herself. But whether she was afraid of singing before people, or was out of voice that evening, it was certain that she couldn't sing at all. She tried a duet, once, with her cousin Maldon, but could not so much as begin; and afterwards, when she tried to sing by herself, although she began sweetly, her voice died away on a sudden, and left her quite distressed, with her head hanging down over the keys. The good Doctor said she was nervous, and, to relieve her, proposed a round game at cards; of which he knew as much as of the art of playing the trombone. But I remarked that the Old Soldier took him into custody directly, for her partner; and instructed him, as the first preliminary of initiation, to give her all the silver he had in his pocket.

We had a merry game, not made the less merry by the Doctor's mistakes, of which he committed an innumerable quantity, in spite of the watchfulness of the butterflies, and to their great aggravation. Mrs. Strong had declined to play, on the ground of not feeling very well; and her cousin Maldon had excused himself because he had some packing to do. When he had done it, however, he returned, and they sat together, talking, on the sofa. From time to time she came and looked over the Doctor's hand, and told him what to play She was very pale, as she bent over him, and I thought her finger trembled as she pointed out the cards; but the Doctor was quite happy in her attention, and took no notice of this, if it were so.

At supper, we were hardly so gay. Every one appeared to feel that a parting of that sort was an awkward thing, and that the nearer it approached, the more awkward it was. Mr. Jack Maldon tried to be very talkative, but was not at his ease, and made matters worse. And they were not improved, as it appeared to me, by the Old Soldier: who continually recalled passages of Mr. Jack Maldon's youth.

The Doctor, however, who felt, I am sure, that he was making everybody happy, was well pleased, and had no suspicion, but that we were all at the utmost height of enjoyment.

"Annie, my dear," said he, looking at his watch, and filling his glass, "it is past your cousin Jack's time, and we must not detain him, since time and tide—both concerned in this case—wait for no man. Mr. Jack Maldon, you have a long voyage, and a strange country before you; but many men have had both, and many men will have both, to the end of time. The winds you are going to tempt, have wafted thousands upon thousands to fortune, and brought thousands upon thousands happily back."

"It is an affecting thing," said Mrs. Markleham—"however it's viewed, it's affecting—to see a fine young man one has known from an infant, going away to the other end of the world, leaving all he knows behind, and not knowing what's before him. A young man really well deserves constant support and patronage," looking at the Doctor, "who makes such sacrifices."

"Time will go fast with you, Mr. Jack Maldon," pursued the Doctor, "and fast with all of us. Some of us can hardly expect, perhaps, in the natural course of things, to greet you on your return.

The next best thing is to hope to do it, and that's my case. I shall not weary you with good advice. You have long had a good model before you, in your cousin Annie. Imitate her virtues as nearly as you can."

Mrs. Markleham fanned herself, and shook her head.

"Farewell, Mr. Jack," said the Doctor, standing up; on which we all stood up. "A prosperous voyage out, a thriving career abroad, and a happy return home!"

We all drank the toast, and all shook hands with Mr. Jack Maldon; after which he hastily took leave of the ladies who were there, and hurried to the door, where he was received, as he got into the chaise, with a tremendous broadside of cheers discharged by our boys, who had assembled on the lawn for the purpose. Running in among them to swell the ranks, I was very near the chaise when it rolled away; and I had a lively impression made upon me, in the midst of the noise and dust, of having seen Mr. Jack Maldon rattle past with an agitated face, and something cherry-colored in his hand.

After another broadside for the Doctor, and another for the Doctor's wife, the boys dispersed, and I went back into the house, where I found the guests all standing in a group about the Doctor, discussing how Mr. Jack Maldon had gone away, and how he had borne it, and how he had felt it, and all the rest of it. In the midst of these remarks, Mrs. Markleham cried: "Where's Annie?"

No Annie was there; and when they called to her, no Annie replied. But all pressing out of the room, in a crowd, to see what was the matter, we found her lying on the hall floor. There was great alarm at first, until it was found that she was in a swoon, and that the swoon was yielding to the usual means of recovery; when the Doctor, who had lifted her head upon his knee, put her curls aside with his hand, and said, looking around:

"Poor Annie! She's so faithful and tender-hearted! It's the parting from her old playfellow and friend—her favorite cousin—that has done this. Ah! It's a pity! I am very sorry!"

When she opened her eyes, and saw where she was, and that we were all standing about her, she arose with assistance: turning her head, as she did so, to lay it on the Doctor's shoulder—or to hide it, I don't know which. We went into the drawing-room, to leave her with the Doctor and her mother; but she said, it seemed, that she was better than she had been since morning, and that she would rather be brought among us; so they brought her in, looking very white and weak, I thought, and sat her on a sofa.

"Annie, my dear," said her mother, doing something to her dress, "See here! You have lost a bow. Will any body be so good as find a ribbon; a cherry-colored ribbon?"

It was the one she had worn at her bosom. We all looked for it—I myself looked everywhere, I am certain—but nobody could find it.

"Do you recollect where you had it last, Annie?" said her mother.

I wondered how I could have thought she looked white, or anything but burning red, when she answered that she had had it safe, a little while ago, she thought, but it was not worth looking for.

Nevertheless, it was looked for again, and still not found. She entreated that there might be no more searching; but it was still sought for, in a desultory way, until she was quite well, and the company took their departure.

We walked very slowly home, Mr. Wickfield, Agnes, and I—Agnes and I admiring the moonlight, and Mr. Wickfield scarcely raising his eyes from the ground. When we, at last, reached our own door, Agnes discovered that she had left her little reticule behind. Delighted to be of any service to her, I ran back to fetch it.

I went into the supper-room, where it had been left, which was deserted and dark. But a door of communication between that and the Doctor's study, where there was a light, being open, I passed on there, to say what I wanted, and to get a candle.

The Doctor was sitting in his easy chair by the fireside, and his young wife was on a stool at his feet. The Doctor, with a complacent smile, was reading aloud some manuscript explanation or statement of a theory out of that interminable Dictionary, and she was looking up at him. But with such a face as I never saw. It was so beautiful in its form, it was so ashy pale, it was so fixed in its abstraction, it was so full of a wild, sleep-walking, dreamy horror of I don't know what. The eyes were wide open. and her brown hair fell in two rich clusters on her shoulders, and on her white dress, disordered by the want of the lost ribbon. Distinctly as I recollect

I RETURN TO THE DOCTOR'S AFTER THE PARTY.

her look, I cannot say of what it was expressive. I cannot even say of what it is expressive to me now, rising again before my older judgment. Penitence, humiliation, shame, pride, love, and trustfulness—I see them all; and in them all, I see that horror of I don't know what.

My entrance, and my saying what I wanted, roused her. It disturbed the Doctor too, for when I went back to replace the candle I had taken from the table, he was patting her head, in his fatherly way, and saying he was a merciless drone to let her tempt him into reading on; and he would have her go to bed.

But she asked him, in a rapid, urgent manner, to let her stay—to let her feel assured (I heard her murmur some broken words to this effect) that she was in his confidence that night. And, as she turned again towards him, after glancing at me as I left the room and went out at the door, I saw her cross her hands upon his knee, and look up at him with the same face, something quieted, as he resumed his reading.

It made a great impression on me, and I remembered it a long time afterwards; as I shall have occasion to narrate when the time comes.

CHAPTER XVII.

SOMEBODY TURNS UP.

It has not occurred to me to mention Peggotty since I ran away; but, of course, I wrote her a letter almost as soon as I was housed at Dover, and another, and a longer letter, containing all particulars fully related, when my aunt took me formally under her protection. On my being settled at Doctor Strong's I wrote to her again, detailing my happy condition and prospects. I never could have derived any thing like the pleasure from spending the money Mr. Dick had given me, that I felt in sending a gold half-guinea to Peggotty, per post, inclosed in this last letter, to discharge the sum I had borrowed of her: in which epistle, not before, I mentioned about the young man with the donkey-cart.

To these communications Peggotty replied as promptly, if not as concisely, as a merchant's clerk. Her utmost powers of expression (which were certainly not great in ink) were exhausted in the attempt to write what she felt on the subject of my journey. Four sides of incoherent and interjectional beginnings of sentences, that had no end, except blots, were inadequate to afford her any relief. But the blots were more expressive to me than the best composition, for they showed me that Peggotty had been crying all over the paper, and what could I have desired more?

I made out, without much difficulty, that she could not take quite kindly to my aunt yet. The notice was too short after so long a prepossession the other way. We never knew a person, she wrote; but to think that Miss Betsey should seem to be so different from what she had been thought to be, was a Moral!—that was her word. She was evidently still afraid of Miss Betsey, for she sent her grateful duty to her but timidly; and she was evidently afraid of me, too, and entertained the probability of my running away again soon: if I might judge from the repeated hints she threw out, that the coach-fare to Yarmouth was always to be had of her for the asking.

She gave me one piece of intelligence which affected me very much, namely, that there had been a sale of the furniture at our old home, and that Mr. and Miss Murdstone were gone away, and the house was shut up, to be let or sold. God knows I had had no part in it while they remained there, but it pained me to think of the dear old place as altogether abandoned; of the weeds growing tall in the garden, and the fallen leaves lying thick and wet upon the paths. I imagined how the winds of winter would howl round it, how the cold rain would beat upon the window-glass, how the moon would make ghosts on the walls of the empty rooms, watching their solitude all night. I thought afresh of the grave in the churchyard, underneath the tree: and it seemed as if the house were dead too, now, and all connected with my father and mother were faded away.

There was no other news in Peggotty's letters. Mr. Barkis was an excellent husband, she said, though still a little near; but we all had our faults, and she had plenty (though I am sure I don't know what they were); and he sent his duty, and my little bedroom was always ready for me. Mr. Peggotty was well, and Ham was well, and Mrs. Gummidge was but poorly, and little Em'ly wouldn't send her love, but said that Peggotty might send it, if she liked.

All this intelligence I dutifully imparted to my aunt, only reserving to myself the mention of little Em'ly, to whom I instinctively felt that she would not very tenderly incline. While I was yet new at Doctor Strong's, she made several excursions over to Canterbury to see me, and always at unseasonable hours: with the view, I suppose, of taking me by surprise. But, finding me well employed, and bearing a good character, and hearing on all hands that I rose fast in the school, she soon discontinued these visits. I saw her on a Saturday, every third or fourth week, when I went over to Dover for a treat; and I saw Mr. Dick every alternate Wednesday, when he arrived by stage-coach at noon, to stay until next morning.

On these occasions Mr. Dick never travelled without a leathern writing-desk, containing a supply of stationery and the Memorial; in relation to which document he had a notion that time was beginning to press now, and that it really must be got out of hand.

Mr. Dick was very partial to gingerbread. To render his visits the more agreeable, my aunt had instructed me to open a credit for him at a cake-shop, which was hampered with the stipulation that he should not be served with more than one shilling's-worth in the course of any one day. This, and the reference of all his little bills at the county inn where he slept, to my aunt, before they were paid, induced me to suspect that he was only allowed to rattle his money, and not to spend it. I found on further investigation that this was so, or at least there was an agreement between him and my aunt that he should account to her for all his disbursements. As he had no idea of deceiving her, and always desired to please her, he was thus made chary of launching into expense. On this point, as well as on all other possible points, Mr. Dick was convinced that my aunt was the wisest and most wonderful of women; as he repeatedly told me with infinite secresy, and always in a whisper.

"Trotwood," said Mr. Dick, with an air of mystery, after imparting this confidence to me, one Wednesday; "who's the man that hides near our house and frightens her?"

"Frightens my aunt, sir?"

Mr. Dick nodded. "I thought nothing would have frightened

her," he said, "for she's—" here he whispered softly, "don't mention it—the wisest and most wonderful of women." Having said which, he drew back, to observe the effect which this description of her made upon me.

"The first time he came," said Mr. Dick, "was—let me see—sixteen hundred and forty-nine was the date of King Charles's execution. I think you said sixteen hundred and forty-nine?"

"Yes, sir."

"I don't know how it can be," said Mr. Dick, sorely puzzled and shaking his head. "I don't think I'm as old as that."

"Was it in that year that the man appeared, sir?" I asked.

"Why, really," said Mr. Dick, "I don't see how it can have been in that year, Trotwood. Do you get that date out of history?"

"Yes, sir."

"I suppose history never lies, does it?" said Mr. Dick, with a gleam of hope.

"O dear, no, sir!" I replied, most decisively. I was ingenuous and young, and I thought so.

"I can't make it out," said Mr. Dick, shaking his head. "There's something wrong, somewhere. However, it was very soon after the mistake was made of putting some of the trouble out of King Charles's head into my head, that the man first came. I was walking out with Miss Trotwood after tea, just at dark, and there he was, close to our house."

"Walking about?" I inquired.

"Walking about?" repeated Mr. Dick. "Let me see. I must recollect a bit. N—no, no; he was not walking about."

I asked, as the shortest way to get at it, what he *was* doing.

"Well, he wasn't there at all," said Mr. Dick, "until he came up behind her, and whispered. Then she turned round and fainted and I stood still and looked at him, and he walked away; but that he should have been hiding ever since (in the ground or somewhere) is the most extraordinary thing!"

"*Has* he been hiding ever since?" I asked.

"To be sure he has," retorted Mr. Dick, nodding his head gravely "Never came out, till last night! We were walking last night, and he came up behind her again, and I knew him again."

"And did he frighten my aunt again?"

"All of a shiver," said Mr. Dick, counterfeiting that affection and making his teeth chatter. "Held by the palings. Cried. But Trotwood, come here," getting me close to him, that he might whisper very softly; "why did she give him money, boy, in the moonlight?"

"He was a beggar, perhaps."

Mr. Dick shook his head, as utterly renouncing the suggestion; and having replied a great many times, and with great confidence, "No beggar, no beggar, no beggar, sir!" went on to say, that from his window he had afterwards, and late at night, seen my aunt give this person money outside the garden rails in the moonlight, who then slunk away—into the ground again, as he thought probable—and was seen no more; while my aunt came hurriedly and secretly back into the house, and had, even that morning, been quite different from her usual self: which preyed on Mr. Dick's mind.

I had not the least belief, in the outset of the story, that the unknown was anything but a delusion of Mr. Dick's, and one of the line of that ill-fated Prince who occasioned him so much difficulty; but after some reflection I began to entertain the question whether an attempt, or threat of an attempt, might have been twice made to take poor Mr. Dick himself from under my aunt's protection, and whether my aunt, the strength of whose kind feeling towards him I knew from herself, might have been induced to pay a price for his peace and quiet. As I was already much attached to Mr. Dick, and very solicitous for his welfare, my fears favored this supposition; and for a long time his Wednesday hardly ever came round, without my entertaining a misgiving that he would not be on the coach-box as usual. There he always appeared, however, grey-headed, laughing, and happy; and he never had anything more to tell of the man who could frighten my aunt.

These Wednesdays were the happiest days of Mr. Dick's life; they were far from being the least happy of mine. He soon became known to every boy in the school; and though he never took an active part in any game but kite-flying, was as deeply interested in all our sports as any one among us. How often have I seen him, intent upon a match at marbles or pegtop, looking on with a face of unutterable interest, and hardly breathing at the critical times! How often, at hare and hounds, have I seen him mounted on a little knoll, cheering the whole field on to action, and waving his hat above his grey head, oblivious of King Charles the Martyr's head, and all belonging to it! How many a summer-hour have I known to be but blissful minutes to him in the cricket-field! How many winter days have I seen him, standing blue-nosed in the snow and east wind, looking at the boys going down the long slide, and clapping his worsted gloves in rapture!

He was an universal favorite, and his ingenuity in little things was transcendant. He could cut oranges into such devices as none of us had an idea of. He could make a boat out of anything, from a skewer upwards. He could turn crampbones into chessmen; fashion Roman chariots from old court cards; make spoked wheels out of cotton reels, and birdcages of old wire. But he was greatest of all, perhaps, in the articles of string and straw; with which we were all persuaded he could do anything that could be done by hands.

Mr. Dick's renown was not long confined to us. After a few Wednesdays, Doctor Strong himself made some inquiries of me about him, and I told him all my aunt had told me; which interested the Doctor so much that he requested, on the occasion of his next visit, to be presented to him. This ceremony I performed; and the Doctor begging Mr. Dick, whensoever he should not find me at the coach-office, to come on there, and rest himself until our morning's work was over, it soon passed into a custom for Mr. Dick to come on as a matter of course, and, if we were a little late, as often happened on a Wednesday, to walk about the court-yard, waiting for me. Here he made the acquaintance of the Doctor's beautiful young wife (paler than formerly, all this time; more rarely seen by me or any one, I think; and not so gay but not less beautiful), and so became more and more familiar by degrees, until, at last, he would come into the school and wait. He always sat in a particular corner, on a particular stool, which was called "Dick," after him; here he would sit, with his grey head bent forward, attentively listening to whatever might be going on, with a profound veneration for the learning he had never been able to acquire.

This veneration Mr. Dick extended to the Doctor, whom he thought the most subtle and accomplished philosopher of any age. It was long before Mr. Dick ever spoke to him otherwise than bare-headed; and even when he and the Doctor had struck up quite a friendship, and would walk together by the hour, on that side of the court-yard which was known among us as The Doctor's Walk, Mr. Dick would pull off his hat at intervals to show his respect for wisdom and knowledge. How it ever came about, that the Doctor began to read out scraps of the famous Dictionary, in these walks, I never knew; perhaps he felt it all the same, at first, as reading to himself. However, it passed into a custom too; and Mr. Dick, listening with a face shining with pride and pleasure, in his heart of hearts believed the Dictionary to be the most delightful book in the world.

As I think of them going up and down before those school-room windows—the Doctor reading with his complacent smile, an occasional flourish of the manuscript, or grave motion of his head; and Mr. Dick listening, enchained by interest, with his poor wits calmly wandering God knows where, upon the wings of hard words—I think of it as one of the pleasantest things, in a quiet way, that I have ever seen. I feel as if they might go walking to and fro for ever, and the world might somehow be the better for it—as if a thousand things it makes a noise about, were not one-half so good for it, or me.

Agnes was one of Mr. Dick's friends, very soon; and in often coming to the house, he made acquaintance with Uriah. The friendship between himself and me increased continually, and it was maintained on this odd footing: that, while Mr. Dick came professedly to look after me as my guardian, he always consulted me in any little matter of doubt that arose, and invariably guided himself by my advice; not only having a high respect for my native sagacity, but considering that I had inherited a good deal from my aunt.

One Thursday morning, when I was about to walk with Mr. Dick from the hotel to the coach-office before going back to school (for we had an hour's school before breakfast), I met Uriah in the street, who reminded me of the promise I had made to take tea with himself and his mother: adding, with a writhe, "But I didn't expect you to keep it, Master Copperfield, we're so very umble."

I really had not yet been able to make up my mind whether I liked Uriah or detested him; and I was very doubtful about it still, as I stood looking him in the face in the street. But I felt it quite an affront to be supposed proud, and said I only wanted to be asked.

"Oh, if that's all, Master Copperfield," said Uriah, "and it really isn't our umbleness that prevents you, will you come this evening? But if it is our umbleness, I hope you won't mind owning to it, Master Copperfield; for we are well aware of our condition."

I said I would mention it to Mr. Wickfield, and if he approved, as I had no doubt he would, I would come with pleasure. So, at six o'clock that evening, which was one of the early office evenings, I announced myself as ready, to Uriah.

"Mother will be proud indeed," he said, as we walked away together. "Or she would be proud, if it wasn't sinful, Master Copperfield."

"Yet you didn't mind supposing *I* was proud this morning," I returned.

"Oh dear no, Master Copperfield!" returned Uriah. "Oh, believe me, no! Such a thought never came into my head! I shouldn't have deemed it at all proud if you had thought *us* too umble for you. Because we are so very umble."

"Have you been studying much law lately?" I asked, to change the subject.

"Oh, Master Copperfield," he said, with an air of self-denial, "my reading is hardly to be called study. I have passed an hour or two in the evening, sometimes, with Mr. Tidd."

"Rather hard, I suppose?" said I.

"He is hard to *me* sometimes," returned Uriah. "But I don't know what he might be, to a gifted person."

After beating a little tune on his chin as we walked on, with the two fore-fingers of his skeleton right hand, he added:

"There are expressions, you see, Master Copperfield—Latin words and terms—in Mr. Tidd, that are trying to a reader of my umble attainments."

"Would you like to be taught Latin?" I said, briskly. "I will teach it you with pleasure, as I learn it."

"Oh, thank you, Master Copperfield," he answered, shaking his head. "I am sure it's very kind of you to make the offer, but I am much too umble to accept it."

"What nonsense, Uriah!"

"Oh, indeed you must excuse me, Master Copperfield! I am greatly obliged, and I should like it of all things, I assure you; but I am far too umble. There are people enough to tread upon me in my lowly state, without my doing outrage to their feelings by possessing learning. Learning ain't for me. A person like myself had better not aspire. If he is to get on in life, he must get on umbly, Master Copperfield."

I never saw his mouth so wide, or the creases in his cheeks so deep, as when he delivered himself of these sentiments; shaking his head all the time, and writhing modestly.

"I think you are wrong, Uriah," I said. "I dare say there are several things that I could teach you, if you would like to learn them."

"Oh, I don't doubt that, Master Copperfield," he answered; "not in the least. But not being umble yourself, you don't judge well, perhaps, for them that are. I won't provoke my betters with knowledge, thank you. I'm much too umble. Here is my umble dwelling, Master Copperfield!"

We entered a low, old-fashioned room, walked straight into from the street, and found there, Mrs. Heep, who was the dead image of Uriah, only short. She received me with the utmost humility, and apologised to me for giving her son a kiss, observing that, lowly as they were, they had their natural affections, which they hoped would give no offence to any one. It was a perfectly decent room, half parlor and half kitchen, but not at all a snug room. The tea-things were set upon the table, and the kettle was boiling on the hob. There was a chest of drawers with an escrutoire top, for Uriah to read or write at of an evening; there was Uriah's blue bag lying down and vomiting papers; there was a company of Uriah's books, commanded by Mr. Tidd; there was a corner cupboard; and there were the usual articles of furniture. I don't remember that any individual object had a bare, pinched, spare look; but I do remember that the whole place had.

It was perhaps a part of Mrs. Heep's humility, that she still wore weeds. Notwithstanding the lapse of time that had occurred since Mr. Heep's decease, she still wore weeds. I think there was some compromise in the cap; but otherwise she was as weedy as in the early days of her mourning.

"This is a day to be remembered, my Uriah, I am sure," said Mrs. Heep, making the tea, "when Master Copperfield pays us a visit."

"I said you'd think so, mother," said Uriah.

"If I could have wished father to remain among us for any reason," said Mrs. Heep, "it would have been, that he might have known his company this afternoon."

I felt embarrassed by these compliments; but I was sensible, too, of being entertained as an honored guest, and I thought Mrs. Heep an agreeable woman.

"My Uriah," said Mrs. Heep, "has looked forward to this, sir, a long while. He had his fears that our umbleness stood in the way, and I joined in them myself. Umble we are, umble we have been, umble we shall ever be," said Mrs. Heep.

"I am sure you have no occasion to be so, ma'am," I said, "unless you like."

"Thank you, sir," retorted Mrs. Heep. "We know our station and are thankful in it."

I found that Mrs. Heep gradually got nearer to me, and that Uriah gradually got opposite to me, and that they respectfully plied me with the choicest of the eatables on the table. There was nothing particularly choice there, to be sure; but I took the will for the deed, and felt that they were very attentive. Presently they began to talk about aunts, and then I told them about mine; and about fathers and mothers, and then I told them about mine; and then Mrs. Heep began to talk about fathers-in-law, and then I began to tell her about mine—but stopped, because my aunt had advised to observe a silence on that subject. A tender young cork, however, would have had no more chance against a pair of cork screws, or a tender young tooth against a pair of dentists, or a little

SOMEBODY TURNS UP

shuttlecock against two battledores, than I had against Uriah and Mrs. Heep. They did just what they liked with me; and wormed things out of me that I had no desire to tell, with a certainty I blush to think of: the more especially as, in my juvenile frankness, I took some credit to myself for being so confidential, and felt that I was quite the patron of my two respectful entertainers.

They were very fond of one another: that was certain. I take it that had its effect upon me, as a touch of nature; but the skill with which the one followed up whatever the other said, was a touch of art which I was still less proof against. When there was nothing more to be got out of me about myself (for on the Murdstone and Grinby life, and on my journey, I was dumb), they began about Mr. Wickfield and Agnes. Uriah threw the ball to Mrs. Heep, Mrs. Heep caught it and threw it back to Uriah, Uriah kept it up a little while, then sent it back to Mrs. Heep, and so they went on tossing it about until I had no idea who had got it, and was quite bewildered. The ball itself was always changing too. Now it was Mr. Wickfield, now Agnes, now the excellence of Mr. Wickfield, now my admiration of Agnes; now the extent of Mr. Wickfield's business and resources, now our domestic life after dinner; now the wine that Mr. Wickfield took, the reason why he took it, and the pity that it was he took so much; now one thing, now another, then every thing at once; and all the time, without appearing to speak very often, or to do anything but sometimes encourage them a little, for fear they should be overcome by their humility and the honor of my company, I found myself perpetually letting out something or other that I had no business to let out, and seeing the effect of it in the twinkling of Uriah's dinted nostrils.

I had begun to be a little uncomfortable, and to wish myself well out of the visit, when a figure coming down the street passed the door—it stood open to air the room, which was warm, the weather being close for the time of year—came back again, looked in, and walked in, exclaiming loudly, "Copperfield! Is it possible?"

It was Mr. Micawber! It was Mr. Micawber, with his eye-glass, and his walking-stick, and his shirt-collar, and his genteel air, and the condescending roll in his voice, all complete!

"My dear Copperfield," said Mr. Micawber, putting out his hand, "this is indeed a meeting which is calculated to impress the mind with a sense of the instability and uncertainty of all human—in short, it is a most extraordinary meeting. Walking along the street, reflecting upon the probability of something turning up (of which I am at present rather sanguine), I find a young, but valued friend turn up, who is connected with the most eventful period of my life; I may say, with the turning point of my existenee. Copperfield, my dear fellow, how do you do?"

I cannot say—I really *cannot* say—that I was glad to see Mr. Micawber there; but I was glad to see him too, and shook hands with him heartily, inquiring how Mrs. Micawber was.

"Thank you," said Mr. Micawber, waving his hand as of old, and settling his chin in his shirt-collar. "She is tolerably convalescent. The twins no longer derive their sustenance from Nature's founts—in short," said Mr. Micawber, in one of his bursts of confidence, "they are weaned—and Mrs. Micawber is, at present, my travelling companion. She will be rejoiced, Copperfield, to renew her acquaintance with one who has proved himself in all respects a worthy minister at the sacred altar of friendship."

I said I should be delighted to see her.

"You are very good," said Mr. Micawber.

Mr. Micawber then smiled, settled his chin again, and looked about him.

"I have discovered my friend Copperfield," said Mr. Micawber genteelly, and without addressing himself particularly to any one, "not in solitude, but partaking of a social meal in company with a widow lady, and one who is apparently her offspring—in short," said Mr. Micawber, in another of his bursts of confidence, "her son. I shall esteem it an honor to be presented."

I could do no less, under these circumstances, than make Mr. Micawber known to Uriah Heep and his mother; which I accordingly did. As they abased themselves before him, Mr. Micawber took a seat, and waved his hand in his most courtly manner.

"Any friend of my friend Copperfield's," said Mr. Micawber, "has a personal claim upon myself."

"We are too umble, sir," said Mrs. Heep, "my son and me, to be the friends of Master Copperfield. He has been so good as to take his tea with us, and we are thankful to him for his company: also to you, sir, for your notice."

"Ma'am," returned Mr. Micawber, with a bow, "you are very obliging: and what are you doing, Copperfield? Still in the wine trade?"

I was excessively anxious to get Mr. Micawber away; and replied, with my hat in my hand, and a very red face I have no doubt, that I was a pupil at Dr. Strong's.

"A pupil?" said Mr. Micawber, raising his eyebrows. "I am extremely happy to hear it. Although a mind like my friend Copperfield's,"—to Uriah and Mrs. Heep—"does not require that cultivation which, without his knowledge of men and things, it would require, still it is a rich soil teeming with latent vegetation—in short," said Mr. Micawber, smiling, in another burst of confidence, "it is an intellect capable of getting up the classics to any extent."

Uriah, with his long hands slowly twining over one another, made a ghastly writhe from the waist upwards, to express his concurrence in this estimation of me.

"Shall we go and see Mrs. Micawber, sir?" I said, to get Mr. Micawber away.

"If you will do her that favor, Copperfield," replied Mr. Micawber, rising. "I have no scruple in saying, in the presence of our friends here, that I am a man who has, for some years, contended against the pressure of pecuniary difficulties." I knew he was certain to say something of this kind; he always would be so boastful about his difficulties. "Sometimes I have risen superior to my difficulties. Sometimes my difficulties have—in short, have floored me. There have been times when I have administered a succession of facers to them; there have been times when they have been too many for me, and I have given in, and said to Mrs. Micawber in the words of Cato, 'Plato, thou reasonest well. It's all up now. I can show fight no more.' But at no time of my life," said Mr. Micawber, "have I enjoyed a higher degree of satisfaction than in pouring my griefs (if I may describe difficulties chiefly arising out of warrants of attorney and promissory notes at two and four months, by that word) into the bosom of my friend Copperfield."

Mr. Micawber closed this handsome tribute by saying, "Mr. Heep! Good evening. Mrs Heep! Your servant," and then walking out with me in his most fashionable manner, making a good deal of noise on the pavement with his shoes, and humming a tune as we went.

It was a little inn where Mr. Micawber put up, and he occupied a little room in it, partitioned off from the commercial room, and strongly flavored with tobacco smoke. I think it was over the kitchen, because a warm greasy smell appeared to come up through the chinks in the floor, and there was a flabby perspiration on the walls. I know it was near the bar, on account of the smell of spirits and jingling of glasses. Here, recumbent on a small sofa, underneath a picture of a race-horse, with her head close to the fire, and her feet pushing the mustard off the dumb-waiter at the other end of the room, was Mrs. Micawber, to whom Mr. Micawber entered first, saying, "My dear, allow me to introduce to you a pupil of Doctor Strong's."

I noticed, by-the-by, that although Mr. Micawber was just as much confused as ever about my age and standing, he always remembered, as a genteel thing, that I was a pupil of Doctor Strong's.

Mrs. Micawber was amazed, but very glad to see me. I was very glad to see her too, and after an affectionate greeting on both sides, sat down on the small sofa near her.

"My dear," said Mr. Micawber, "if you will mention to Copperfield what our present position is, which I have no doubt he will like to know, I will go and look at the paper the while, and see whether anything turns up among the advertisements."

"I thought you were at Plymouth, ma'am," I said to Mrs. Micawber, as he went out.

"My dear Master Copperfield," she replied, "we went to Plymouth."

"To be on the spot," I hinted.

"Just so," said Mrs. Micawber. "To be on the spot. But, the truth is, talent is not wanted in the Custom House. The local influence of my family was quite unavailing to obtain any employment in that department, for a man of Mr. Micawber's abilities. They would rather *not* have a man of Mr. Micawber's abilities. He would only show the deficiency of the others. Apart from which," said Mrs. Micawber, "I will not disguise from you, my dear Master Copperfield, that when that branch of my family which is settled in

Plymouth became aware that Mr. Micawber was accompanied by myself, and by little Wilkins and his sister, and by the twins, they did not receive him with that ardor which he might have expected, being so newly released from captivity. In fact," said Mrs. Micawber, lowering her voice,—"this is between ourselves—our reception was cool."

"Dear me!" I said.

"Yes," said Mrs. Micawber. "It is truly painful to contemplate mankind in such an aspect, Master Copperfield, but our reception was decidedly cool. There is no doubt about it. In fact, that branch of my family which is settled in Plymouth became quite personal to Mr. Micawber, before we had been there a week."

I said, and thought, that they ought to be ashamed of themselves.

"Still, so it was," continued Mrs. Micawber. "Under such circumstances, what could a man of Mr. Micawber's spirit do? But one obvious course was left. To borrow, of that branch of my family, the money to return to London, and to return at any sacrifice."

"Then you all came back again, ma'am?" I said.

"We all came back again," replied Mrs. Micawber. "Since then, I have consulted other branches of my family on the course which it is most expedient for Mr. Micawber to take—for I maintain that he must take some course, Master Copperfield," said Mr. Micawber, argumentatively. "It is clear that a family of six, not including a domestic, cannot live upon air."

"Certainly, ma'am," said I.

"The opinion of those other branches of my family," pursued Mrs. Micawber, "is, that Mr. Micawber should immediately turn his attention to coals."

"To what, ma'am?"

"To coals," said Mrs. Micawber. "To the coal trade. Mr. Micawber was induced to think, on inquiry, that there might be an opening for a man of his talent in the Medway Coal Trade. Then, as Mr. Micawber very properly said, the first step to be taken clearly was, to come and *see* the Medway. Which we came and saw. I say 'we,' Master Copperfield; for I never will," said Mrs. Micawber with emotion, "I never will desert Mr. Micawber."

I murmured my admiration and approbation.

"We came," repeated Mrs Micawber, "and saw the Medway. My opinion of the coal trade on that river is, that it may require talent, but that it certainly requires capital. Talent, Mr. Micawber has; capital, Mr. Micawber has not. We saw, I think, the greater part of the Medway; and that is my individual conclusion. Being so near here, Mr. Micawber was of opinion that it would be rash not to come on, and see the Cathedral. Firstly, on account of its being so well worth seeing, and our never having seen it; and secondly, on account of the great probability of something turning up in a cathedral town. We have been here," said Mrs. Micawber, "three days. Nothing has, as yet, turned up; and it may not surprise you, my dear Master Copperfield, so much as it would a stranger, to know that we are at present waiting for a remittance from London, to discharge our pecuniary obligations at this hotel. Until the arrival of that remittance," said Mrs. Micawber, with much feeling, "I am cut off from my home (I allude to lodgings in Pentonville), from my boy and girl, and from my twins."

I felt the utmost sympathy for Mr. and Mrs. Micawber in this anxious extremity, and said as much to Mr. Micawber, who now returned: adding that I only wished I had money enough, to lend them the amount they needed. Mr. Micawber's answer expressed the disturbance of his mind. He said, shaking hands with me, "Copperfield, you are a true friend; but when the worst comes to the worst, no man is without a friend who is possessed of shaving materials." At this dreadful hint, Mrs. Micawber threw her arms around Mr. Micawber's neck and entreated him to be calm. He wept; but so far recovered, almost immediately, as to ring the bell for the waiter, and bespeak a hot kidney pudding and a plate of shrimps for breakfast in the morning.

When I took my leave of them, they both pressed me so much to come and dine before they went away, that I could not refuse. But, as I knew I could not come next day, when I should have a good deal to prepare in the evening, Mr. Micawber arranged that he would call at Doctor Strong's in the course of the morning (having a presentiment that the remittance would arrive by that post), and propose the day after, if it would suit me better. Accordingly I was called out of school next forenoon, and found Mr. Micawber in the parlor; who had called to say that the dinner would take place as proposed. When I asked him if the remittance had come, he pressed my hand and departed.

As I was looking out of window that same evening, it surprised me, and made me rather uneasy, to see Mr. Micawber and Uriah Heep walk past, arm in arm: Uriah humbly sensible of the honor that was done him, and Mr. Micawber taking a bland delight in extending his patronage to Uriah. But I was still more surprised, when I went to the little hotel next day at the appointed dinner hour, which was four o'clock, to find, from what Mr. Micawber said, that he had gone home with Uriah, and had drunk brandy-and-water at Mrs. Heep's.

"And I'll tell you what, my dear Copperfield," said Mr. Micawber, "your friend Heep is a young fellow who might be attorney-general. If I had known that young man, at the period when my difficulties came to a crisis, all I can say is, that I believe my creditors would have been a great deal better managed than they were."

I hardly understood how this could have been, seeing that Mr. Micawber had paid them nothing at all as it was; but I did not like to ask. Neither did I like to say, that I hoped he had not been too communicative to Uriah; or to inquire if they had talked much about me. I was afraid of hurting Mr. Micawber's feelings, or, at all events, Mrs. Micawber's, she being very sensitive; but I was uncomfortable about it, too, and often thought about it afterwards.

We had a beautiful little dinner. Quite an elegant dish of fish; the kidney-end of a loin of veal, roasted; fried sausage-meat; a partridge, and a pudding. There was wine, and there was strong ale; and after dinner Mrs. Micawber made us a bowl of hot punch with her own hands.

Mr. Micawber was uncommonly convivial. I never saw him such good company. He made his face shine with the punch, so that it looked as if it had been varnished all over. He got cheerfully sentimental about the town, and proposed success to it; observing, that Mrs. Micawber and himself had been extremely snug and comfortable there, and that he never should forget the agreeable hours they had passed in Canterbury. He proposed me afterwards;

and he, and Mrs. Micawber, and I, took a review of our past acquaintance, in the course of which we sold the property all over again. Then I proposed Mrs. Micawber; or, at least, said modestly, "If you'll allow me, Mrs. Micawber, I shall now have the pleasure of drinking *your* health, ma'am." On which Mr. Micawber delivered an eulogium on Mrs. Micawber's character, and said that she had ever been his guide, philosopher, and friend, and he would recommend me, when I came to a marrying time of life, to marry such another woman, if such another woman could be found.

As the punch disappeared, Mr. Micawber became still more friendly and convivial. Mrs. Micawber's spirits becoming elevated, too, we sang "Auld Lang Syne." When we came to "Here 's a hand, my trusty frere," we all joined hands round the table; and when we declared we would "take a right gude Willie Waught," and hadn't the least idea what it meant, we were really affected.

In a word, I never saw any body so thoroughly jovial as Mr. Micawber was, down to the very last moment of the evening, when I took a hearty farewell of himself and his amiable wife. Consequently, I was not prepared, at seven o'clock next morning, to receive the following communication, dated half-past nine in the evening; a quarter of an hour after I had left him.

"My dear Young Friend,

"The die is cast—all is over. Hiding the ravages of care with a sickly mask of mirth, I have not informed you, this evening, that there is no hope of the remittance! Under these circumstances, alike humiliating to endure, humiliating to contemplate, and humiliating to relate, I have discharged the pecuniary liability contracted at this establishment, by giving a note of hand, made payable fourteen days after date, at my residence, Pentonville, London. When it becomes due, it will not be taken up. The result is destruction. The bolt is impending, and the tree must fall.

"Let the wretched man who now addresses you, my dear Copperfield, be a beacon to you through life. He writes with that intention, and in that hope. If he could think himself of so much use, one gleam of day might, by possibility, penetrate into the cheerless dungeon of his remaining existence—though his longevity is, at present (to say the least of it), extremely problematical.

"This is the last communication, my dear Copperfield, you will ever receive "From
"The
"Beggared Outcast,
"WILKINS MICAWBER."

I was so shocked by the contents of this heart-rending letter, that I ran off directly towards the little hotel with the intention of taking it on my way to Doctor Strong's, and trying to soothe Mr. Micawber with a word of comfort. But, half-way there, I met the London coach with Mr. and Mrs. Micawber up behind; Mr. Micawber, the very picture of tranquil enjoyment, smiling at Mrs. Micawber's conversation, eating walnuts out of a paper bag, with a bottle sticking out of his breast pocket. As they did not see me, I thought it best, all things considered, not to see them. So, with a great weight taken off my mind, I turned into a by-street that was the nearest way to school, and felt, upon the whole, relieved that they were gone; though I still liked them very much, nevertheless.

CHAPTER XVIII.

A RETROSPECT.

MY school-days! The silent gliding on of my existence—the unseen, unfelt progress of my life—from childhood up to youth! Let me think, as I look back upon that flowing water, now a dry channel overgrown with leaves, whether there are any marks along its course, by which I can remember how it ran.

A moment, and I occupy my place in the Cathedral, where we all went together, every Sunday morning, assembling first at school for that purpose. The earthy smell, the sunless air, the sensation of the world being shut out, the resounding of the organ through the black and white arched galleries and aisles, are wings that take me back, and hold me hovering above those days, in a half-sleeping and half-waking dream.

I am not the last boy in the school. I have risen, in a few

months, over several heads. But the first boy seems to me a mighty creature, dwelling afar off, whose giddy height is unattainable. Agnes says "No," but I say "Yes," and tell her that she little thinks what stores of knowledge have been mastered by the wonderful Being, at whose place she thinks I, even I, weak aspirant, may arrive in time. He is not my private friend and public patron, as Steerforth was, but I hold him in a reverential respect. I chiefly wonder what he'll be, when he leaves Doctor Strong's, and what mankind will do to maintain any place against him.

But who is this that breaks upon me? This is Miss Shepherd, whom I love.

Miss Shepherd is a boarder at the Misses Nettingalls' establishment. I adore Miss Shepherd. She is a little girl, in a spencer, with a round face and curly flaxen hair. The Misses Nettingalls' young ladies come to the Cathedral too. I cannot look upon my book, for I must look upon Miss Shepherd. When the choristers chaunt, I hear Miss Shepherd. In the service I mentally insert Miss Shepherd's name—I put her in among the Royal Family. At home, in my own room, I am sometimes moved to cry out, "Oh, Miss Shepherd!" in a transport of love.

For some time, I am doubtful of Miss Shepherd's feelings, but, at length, Fate being propitious, we meet at the dancing-school. I have Miss Shepherd for my partner. I touch Miss Shepherd's glove, and feel a thrill go up the right arm of my jacket, and come out at my hair. I say nothing tender to Miss Shepherd, but we understand each other. Miss Shepherd and myself live but to be united.

Why do I secretly give Miss Shepherd twelve Brazil nuts for a present, I wonder? They are not expressive of affection, they are difficult to pack into a parcel of any regular shape, they are hard to crack, even in room doors, and they are oily when cracked; yet I feel that they are appropriate to Miss Shepherd. Soft, seedy biscuits, also, I bestow upon Miss Shepherd; and oranges innumerable. Once, I kiss Miss Shepherd in the cloak room. Ecstacy! What are my agony and indignation next day, when I hear a flying rumour that the Misses Nettingall have stood Miss Shepherd in the stocks for turning in her toes!

Miss Shepherd being the one pervading theme and vision of my life, how do I ever come to break with her? I can't conceive. And yet a coolness grows between Miss Shepherd and myself. Whispers reach me of Miss Shepherd having said she wished I wouldn't stare so, and having avowed a preference for Master Jones—for Jones! a boy of no merit whatever! The gulf between me and Miss Shepherd widens. At last, one day, I meet the Misses Nettingalls' establishment out walking. Miss Shepherd makes a face as she goes by, and laughs to her companion. All is over. The devotion of a life—it seems a life, it is all the same—is at an end; Miss Shepherd comes out of the morning service, and the Royal Family know her no more.

I am higher in the school, and no one breaks my peace. I am not at all polite now, to the Misses Nettingalls' young ladies, and shouldn't dote on any of them, if they were twice as many and twenty times as beautiful. I think the dancing-school a tiresome affair, and wonder why the girls can't dance by themselves and leave us alone. I am growing great in Latin verses, and neglect the laces of my boots. Doctor Strong refers to me in public as a promising young scholar. Mr. Dick is wild with joy, and my aunt remits me a guinea by the next post.

The shade of a young butcher rises, like the apparition of an armed head in Macbeth. Who is this young butcher? He is the terror of the youth of Canterbury. There is a vague belief abroad, that the beef suet with which he anoints his hair gives him unnatural strength, and that he is a match for a man. He is a broad-faced, bull-necked young butcher, with rough red cheeks, an ill-conditioned mind, and an injurious tongue. His main use of this tongue, is, to disparage Doctor Strong's young gentlemen. He says, publicly, that if they want anything he'll give it 'em. He names individuals among them (myself included), whom he could undertake to settle with one hand, and the other tied behind him. He waylays the smaller boys to punch their unprotected heads, and calls challenges after me in the open streets. For these sufficient reasons I resolve to fight the butcher.

It is a summer evening, down in a green hollow, at the corner of a wall. I meet the butcher by appointment. I am attended by a select body of our boys; the butcher, by two other butchers, a young publican, and a sweep. The preliminaries are adjusted, and the butcher and myself stand face to face. In a moment the butcher lights ten thousand candles out of my left eyebrow. In another moment, I don't know where the wall is, or where I am, or where anybody is. I hardly know which is myself and which the butcher, we are always in such a tangle and tustle, knocking about upon the trodden grass. Sometimes I see the butcher, bloody but confident; sometimes I see nothing, and sit gasping on my second's knee; sometimes I go in at the butcher madly, and cut my knuckles open against his face, without appearing to discompose him at all. At last I awake, very queer about the head, as from a giddy sleep, and see the butcher walking off, congratulated by the two other butchers and the sweep and publican, and putting on his coat as he goes; from which I augur, justly, that the victory is his.

I am taken home in a sad plight, and I have beef-steaks put to my eyes, and am rubbed with vinegar and brandy, and find a great white puffy place bursting out on my upper lip, which swells immoderately. For three or four days I remain at home, a very ill-looking subject, with a green shade over my eyes; and I should be very dull, but that Agnes is a sister to me, and condoles with me, and reads to me, and makes the time light and happy. Agnes has my confidence completely, always; I tell her all about the butcher, and the wrongs he has heaped upon me; and she thinks I couldn't have done otherwise than fight the butcher, while she shrinks and trembles at my having fought him.

Time has stolen on unobserved, for Adams is not the head-boy in the days that are come now, nor has he been this many and many a day. Adams has left the school so long, that when he comes back, on a visit to Doctor Strong, there are not many there, besides myself, who know him. Adams is going to be called to the bar almost directly, and is to be an advocate, and to wear a wig. I am surprised to find him a meeker man than I had thought, and less imposing in appearance. He has not staggered the world yet, either; for it goes on (as well as I can make out) pretty much the same as if he had never joined it.

A blank, through which the warriors of poetry and history march on in stately hosts that seem to have no end—and what comes next! I am the head boy, now; and look down on the line of boys below me, with a condescending interest in such of them as bring to my mind the boy I was myself, when I first came there. That little fellow seems to be no part of me; I remember him as something left behind upon the road of life—as something I have passed, rather than have actually been—and almost think of him as of some one else.

And the little girl I saw on that first day at Mr. Wickfield's, where is she? Gone also. In her stead, the perfect likeness of the picture, a child likeness no more, moves about the house; and Agnes—my sweet sister, as I call her in my thoughts, my counsellor and friend, the better angel of the lives of all who come within her calm, good, self-denying influence—is quite a woman.

What other changes have come upon me, besides the changes in my growth and looks, and in the knowledge I have garnered all this while? I wear a gold watch and chain, a ring upon my little finger, and a long-tailed coat; and I use a great deal of bear's grease—which, taken in conjunction with the ring, looks bad. Am I in love again? I am. I worship the eldest Miss Larkins.

The eldest Miss Larkins is not a little girl. She is a tall, dark, black-eyed, fine figure of a woman. The eldest Miss Larkins is not a chicken; for the youngest Miss Larkins is not that, and the eldest must be three or four years older. Perhaps the eldest Miss Larkins may be about thirty. My passion for her is beyond all bounds.

The eldest Miss Larkins knows officers. It is an awful thing to bear. I see them speaking to her in the street. I see them cross the way to meet her, when her bonnet (she has a bright taste in bonnets) is seen coming down the pavement, accompanied by her sister's bonnet. She laughs and talks, and seems to like it. I spend a good deal of my own spare time in walking up and down to meet her. If I can bow to her once in the day (I know her to bow to, knowing Mr. Larkins), I am happier. I deserve a bow now and then. The raging agonies I suffer on the night of the Race Ball, where I know the eldest Miss Larkins will be dancing with the military, ought to have some compensation, if there be even-handed justice in the world.

My passion takes away my appetite, and makes me wear my newest silk neck-kerchief continually. I have no relief but in putting on my best clothes, and having my boots cleaned over and over again. I seem, then, to be worthier of the eldest Miss Larkins. Everything that belongs to her, or is connected with her, is precious to me. Mr. Larkins (a gruff old gentleman with a double chin, and one of his eyes immovable in his head) is fraught with interest to me. When I can't meet his daughter, I go where I am likely to meet him. To say "How do you do, Mr. Larkins? Are the young ladies and all the family quite well?" seems so pointed, that I blush.

I think continually about my age. Say I am seventeen, and say that seventeen is young for the eldest Miss Larkins, what of that? Besides, I shall be one-and-twenty in no time almost. I regularly take walks outside Mr. Larkins's house in the evening, though it cuts me to the heart to see the officers go in, or to hear them up in the drawing-room, where the eldest Miss Larkins plays the harp. I even walk, on two or three occasions, in a sickly, spoony manner, round and round the house after the family are gone to bed, wondering which is the eldest Miss Larkins's chamber (and pitching, I dare say now, on Mr. Larkins's instead); wishing that a fire would burst out; that the assembled crowd would stand appalled; that I, dashing through them with a ladder, might rear it against her window, save her in my arms, go back for something she had left behind, and perish in the flames. For I am generally disinterested in my love, and think I could be content to make a figure before Miss Larkins, and expire.

—Generally, but not always. Sometimes brighter visions rise before me. When I dress (the occupation of two hours), for a great ball given at the Larkins's (the anticipation of three weeks), I indulge my fancy with pleasing images. I picture myself taking courage to make a declaration to Miss Larkins. I picture Miss Larkins sinking her head upon my shoulder, and saying, "Oh, Mr. Copperfield, can I believe my ears!" I picture Mr. Larkins waiting on me next morning and saying, "My dear Copperfield, my daughter has told me all. Youth is no objection. Here are twenty thousand pounds. Be happy!" I picture my aunt relenting and blessing us; and Mr. Dick and Doctor Strong being present at the marriage ceremony. I am a sensible fellow, I believe—I believe, on looking back, I mean —and modest I am sure; but all this goes on notwithstanding.

I repair to the enchanted house, where there are lights, chattering, music, flowers, officers (I am sorry to see), and the eldest Miss Larkins, a blaze of beauty. She is dressed in blue, with blue flowers in her hair—forget-me-nots—as if *she* had any need to wear forget-me-nots! It is the first really grown-up party that I have ever been invited to, and I am a little uncomfortable; for I appear not to belong to anybody, and nobody appears to have anything to say to me, except Mr. Larkins, who asks me how my schoolfellows are, which he needn't do, as I have not come there to be insulted. But after I have stood in the doorway for some time, and feasted my eyes upon the goddess of my heart, she approaches me—she, the eldest Miss Larkins!—and asks me, pleasantly, if I dance.

I stammer, with a bow, "With you, Miss Larkins."

"With no one else?" enquires Miss Larkins.

"I should have no pleasure in dancing with any one else."

Miss Larkins laughs and blushes (or I think she blushes), and says, "Next time but one, I shall be very glad."

The time arrives. "It is a waltz, I think," Miss Larkins doubtfully observes, when I present myself. "Do you waltz? If not, Captain Bailey —"

But I do waltz (pretty well, too, as it happens), and I take Miss Larkins out. I take her sternly from the side of Captain Bailey. He is wretched, I have no doubt; but he is nothing to me. I have been wretched, too. I waltz with the eldest Miss Larkins! I don't know where, among whom, or how long. I only know that I swim about in space, with a blue angel, in a state of blissful delirium, until I find myself alone with her in a little room, resting on a sofa. She admires a flower (pink camelia japonica, price half-a-crown), in my button hole. I give it her, and say:

"I ask an inestimable price for it, Miss Larkins."

"Indeed! What is that?" returns Miss Larkins.

"A flower of yours, that I may treasure it as a miser does gold."

"You 're a bold boy," says Miss Larkins. "There."

She gives it me, not displeased; and I put it to my lips, and then into my breast. Miss Larkins, laughing, draws her hand through my arm, and says, "Now take me back to Captain Bailey."

I am lost in the recollection of this delicious interview, and the waltz, when she comes to me again, with a plain elderly gentleman, who has been playing whist all night, upon her arm, and says:

"O! here is my bold friend! Mr. Chestle wants to know you, Mr. Copperfield."

I feel at once that he is a friend of the family, and am much gratified.

"I admire your taste, sir," said Mr. Chestle. "It does you credit. I suppose you don't take much interest in hops; but I am a pretty large grower myself; and if you ever like to come over to our neighbourhood—neighbourhood of Ashford—and take a run about our place, we shall be glad for you to stop as long as you like."

I thank Mr. Chestle warmly, and shake hands. I think I am in a happy dream. I waltz with the eldest Miss Larkins once again—she says I waltz so well! I go home in a state of unspeakable bliss, and waltz, in imagination, all night long, with my arm round the blue waist of my dear divinity. For some days afterwards, I am lost in rapturous reflections; but I neither see her in the street, nor when I call. I am imperfectly consoled for this disappointment by the sacred pledge, the perished flower.

"Trotwood," says Agnes, one day after dinner. "Who do you think is going to be married to-morrow? Some one you admire."

"Not you, I suppose, Agnes?"

"Not me!" raising her cheerful face from the music she is copying. "Do you hear him, Papa?—The eldest Miss Larkins."

"To—to Captain Bailey?" I have just power enough to ask.

"No; to no Captain. To Mr. Chestle, a hop-grower."

I am terribly dejected for about a week or two. I take off my ring, I wear my worst clothes, I use no bear's grease, and I frequently lament over the late Miss Larkins's faded flower. Being, by that time, rather tired of this kind of life, and having received new provocation from the butcher, I throw the flower away, go out with the butcher, and gloriously defeat him.

This, and the resumption of my ring, as well as of the bear's grease in moderation, are the last marks I can discern, now, in my progress to seventeen.

CHAPTER XIX.

I LOOK ABOUT ME, AND MAKE A DISCOVERY.

I AM doubtful whether I was at heart glad or sorry, when my school-days drew to an end, and the time came for my leaving Doctor Strong's. I had been very happy there, I had a great attachment for the Doctor, and I was eminent and distinguished in that little world. For these reasons I was sorry to go; but for other reasons, unsubstantial enough, I was glad. Misty ideas of being a young man at my own disposal, of the importance attaching to a young man at his own disposal, of the wonderful things to be seen and done by that magnificent animal, and the wonderful effects he could not fail to make upon society, lured me away. So powerful were these visionary considerations in my boyish mind, that I seem, according to my present way of thinking, to have left school without natural regret. The separation has not made the impression on me, that other separations have. I try in vain to recal how I felt about it, and what its circumstances were; but it is not momentous in my recollection. I suppose the opening prospect confused me. I know that my juvenile experiences went for little or nothing then; and that life was more like a great fairy story, which I was just about to begin to read, than anything else.

My aunt and I had held many grave deliberations on the calling to which I should be devoted. For a year or more I had endeavoured to find a satisfactory answer to her often-repeated question, "What I would like to be?" But I had no particular liking, that I could discover, for anything. If I could have been inspired with a knowledge of the science of navigation, taken the command of a fast-sailing expedition, and gone round the world on a triumphant voyage of discovery, I think I might have considered myself completely suited. But, in the absence of any such miraculous provision, my desire was to apply myself to some pursuit that would not lie too heavily upon her purse; and to do my duty in it, whatever it might bĕ.

Mr. Dick had regularly assisted at our councils, with a meditative and sage demeanour. He never made a suggestion but once; and on that occasion (I don't know what put it in his head), he suddenly proposed that I should be "a Brazier." My aunt received this proposal so very ungraciously, that he never ventured on a second; but ever afterwards confined himself to looking watchfully at her for her suggestions, and rattling his money.

"Trot, I tell you what, my dear," said my aunt, one morning, in the Christmas season when I left school; "as this knotty point is still unsettled, and as we must not make a mistake in our decision if we can help it, I think we had better take a little breathing-time. In the meanwhile, you must try to look at it from a new point of view, and not as a schoolboy."

"I will, aunt."

"It has occurred to me," pursued my aunt, "that a little change, and a glimpse of life out of doors, may be useful, in helping you to know your own mind, and form a cooler judgment. Suppose you were to take a little journey now. Suppose you were to go down into the old part of the country again, for instance, and see that—that out-of-the-way woman with the savagest of names," said my aunt, rubbing her nose, for she could never thoroughly forgive Peggotty for being so called.

"Of all things in the world, aunt, I should like it best!"

"Well," said my aunt, "that's lucky, for I should like it too. But it's natural and rational that you should like it. And I am very well persuaded that whatever you do, Trot, will always be natural and rational."

"I hope so, aunt."

"Your sister, Betsey Trotwood," said my aunt, "would have been as natural and rational a girl as ever breathed. You'll be worthy of her, won't you?"

"I hope I shall be worthy of you, aunt. That will be enough for me."

"It's a mercy that poor dear baby of a mother of yours didn't live," said my aunt, looking at me approvingly, "or she'd have been so vain of her boy by this time, that her soft little head would have been completely turned, if there was anything of it left to turn." (My aunt always excused any weakness of her own in my behalf, by transferring it in this way to my poor mother.) "Bless me, Trotwood, how you do remind me of her?"

"Pleasantly, I hope, aunt?" said I.

"He 's as like her, Dick," said my aunt, emphatically, "he 's as like her, as she was that afternoon, before she began to fret—bless my heart he 's as like her, as he can look at me out of his two eyes!"

"Is he indeed?" said Mr. Dick.

"And he 's like David, too," said my aunt, decisively.

"He is very like David!" said Mr. Dick.

"But what I want you to be, Trot," resumed my aunt —"I don't mean physically, but morally; you are very well physically—is, a firm fellow. A fine firm fellow, with a will of your own. With resolution," said my aunt, shaking her cap at me, and clenching her hand. "With determination. With character, Trot—with strength of character that is not to be influenced, except on good reason, by anybody, or by anything. That 's what I want you to be. That 's what your father and mother might both have been, Heaven knows, and been the better for it."

I intimated that I hoped I should be what she described.

"That you may begin, in a small way, to have a reliance upon yourself, and to act for yourself," said my aunt, "I shall send you upon your trip, alone. I did think, once, of Mr. Dick's going with you; but, on second thoughts, I shall keep him to take care of me."

Mr. Dick, for a moment, looked a little disappointed; until the honor and dignity of having to take care of the most wonderful woman in the world, restored the sunshine to his face.

"Besides," said my aunt, "there 's the Memorial—"

"Oh, certainly," said Mr. Dick, in a hurry, "I intend, Trotwood, to get that done immediately—it really must be done immediately! And then it will go in, you know—and then," said Mr. Dick, after checking himself, and pausing a long time, "there 'll be a pretty kettle of fish!"

In pursuance of my aunt's kind scheme, I was shortly afterwards fitted out with a handsome purse of money, and a portmanteau, and tenderly dismissed upon my expedition. At parting, my aunt gave me some good advice, and a good many kisses; and said that as her object was that I should look about me, and should think a little, she would recommend me to stay a few days in London, if I liked it, either on my way down into Suffolk, or in coming back. In a word, I was at liberty to do what I would, for three weeks or a month; and no other conditions were imposed upon my freedom than the before-mentioned thinking and looking about me, and a pledge to write three times a week and faithfully report myself.

I went to Canterbury first, that I might take leave of Agnes and Mr. Wickfield (my old room in whose house I had not yet relinquished), and also of the good Doctor. Agnes was very glad to see me, and told me that the house had not been like itself since I had left it.

"I am sure I am not like myself when I am away," said I. "I seem to want my right hand, when I miss you. Though that's not saying much; for there's no head in my right hand, and no heart. Every one who knows you consults with you, and is guided by you, Agnes."

"Every one who knows me, spoils me, I believe," she answered, smiling.

"No. It's because you are like no one else. You are so good, and so sweet-tempered. You have such a gentle nature, and you are always right."

"You talk," said Agnes, breaking into a pleasant laugh, as she sat at work, "as if I were the late Miss Larkins."

"Come! It's not fair to abuse my confidence," I answered, reddening at the recollection of my blue enslaver. "But I shall confide in you, just the same, Agnes. I can never grow out of that. Whenever I fall into trouble, or fall in love, I shall always tell you, if you'll let me—even when I come to fall in love in earnest."

"Why, you have always been in earnest!" said Agnes, laughing again.

"Oh! that was as a child, or a school-boy," said I, laughing in my turn, not without being a little shame-faced. "Times are alter ing now, and I suppose I shall be in a terrible state of earnestness one day or other. My wonder is, that you are not in earnest yourself, by this time, Agnes."

Agnes laughed again, and shook her head.

"Oh, I know you are not!" said I; "because, if you had been, you would have told me. Or at least,"—for I saw a faint blush in her face,—"you would have let me find it out for myself. But there is no one that I know of, who deserves to love *you*, Agnes. Some one of a nobler character, and more worthy altogether than any one I have ever seen here, must rise up, before I give *my* consent. In the time to come, I shall have a wary eye on all admirers; and shall exact a great deal from the successful one, I assure you."

We had gone on, so far, in a mixture of confidential jest and earnest, that had long grown naturally out of our familiar relations, begun as mere children. But Agnes, now suddenly lifting up her eyes to mine, and speaking in a different manner, said:

"Trotwood, there is something that I want to ask you, and that I may not have another opportunity of asking for a long time, perhaps—something I would ask, I think, of no one else. Have you observed any gradual alteration in Papa?"

I had observed it, and had often wondered whether she had too. I must have shown as much now, in my face; for her eyes were in a moment cast down, and I saw tears in them.

"Tell me what it is," she said, in a low voice.

"I think—shall I be quite plain, Agnes, liking him so much?"

"Yes," she said.

"I think he does himself no good by the habit that has increased upon him since I first came here. He is often very nervous—or I fancy so."

"It is not fancy," said Agnes, shaking her head.

"His hand trembles, his speech is not plain, and his eyes look wild. I have remarked that at those times, and when he is least like himself, he is most certain to be wanted on some business."

"By Uriah," said Agnes.

"Yes; and the sense of being unfit for it, or of not having understood it, or of having shown his condition in spite of himself, seems to make him so uneasy, that next day he is worse, and next day worse, and so he becomes jaded and haggard. Do not be alarmed by what I say, Agnes, but in this state I saw him, only the other evening, lay down his head upon his desk, and shed tears like a child."

Her hand passed softly before my lips while I was yet speaking, and in a moment she had met her father at the door of the room, and was hanging on his shoulder. The expression of her face, as they both looked towards me, I felt to be very touching. There was such deep fondness for him, and gratitude to him for all his love and care, in her beautiful look; and there was such a fervent appeal to me to deal tenderly by him, even in my inmost thoughts, and to let no harsh construction find any place against him; she was, at once, so proud of him and devoted to him, yet so compassionate and sorry, and so reliant upon me to be so, too; that nothing she could have said would have expressed more to me, or moved me more.

We were to drink tea at the Doctor's. We went there at the usual hour, and round the study-fireside found the Doctor, and his young wife, and her mother. The Doctor, who made as much of my going away as if I were going to China, received me as an honored guest, and called for a log of wood to be thrown on the fire, that he might see the face of his old pupil reddening in the blaze.

"I shall not see many more new faces in Trotwood's stead, Wickfield," said the Doctor, warming his hands; "I am getting lazy, and want ease. I shall relinquish all my young people in another six months, and lead a quieter life."

"You have said so, any time these ten years, Doctor," Mr. Wickfield answered.

"But now I mean to do it," returned the Doctor. "My first master will succeed me—I am in earnest at last—so you'll soon have to arrange our contracts, and to bind us firmly to them, like a couple of knaves."

"And to take care," said Mr. Wickfield, "that you're not imposed on, eh?—as you certainly would be, in any contract you should make for yourself. Well! I am ready. There are worse tasks than that, in my calling."

"I shall have nothing to think of then," said the Doctor, with a smile, "but my Dictionary; and this other contract-bargain—Annie."

As Mr. Wickfield glanced towards her, sitting at the tea-table by Agnes, she seemed to me to avoid his look with such unwonted hesitation and timidity, that his attention became fixed upon her, as if something were suggested to his thoughts.

"There is a post come in from India, I observe," he said, after a short silence.

"By-the-by! and letters from Mr. Jack Maldon!" said the Doctor.

"Indeed?"

"Poor dear Jack!" said Mrs. Markleham, shaking her head. "That trying climate!—like living, they tell me, on a sand-heap, underneath a burning-glass! He looked strong, but he wasn't. My dear Doctor, it was his spirit, not his constitution, that he ventured on so boldly. Annie, my dear, I am sure you must perfectly recollect that your cousin never was strong—not what can be called *robust*, you know," said Mrs. Markleham, with emphasis, and looking round upon us generally—"from the time when my daughter and himself were children together, and walking about, arm in arm, the livelong day."

Annie, thus addressed, made no reply.

"Do I gather from what you say, ma'am, that Mr. Maldon is ill?" asked Mr. Wickfield.

"Ill?" replied the Old Soldier. "My dear sir, he is all sorts of things."

"Except well?" said Mr. Wickfield.

"Except well, indeed!" said the Old Soldier. "He has had dreadful strokes of the sun, no doubt, and jungle fevers and agues, and every kind of thing you can mention. As to his liver," said the Old Soldier resignedly, "that, of course, he gave up altogether, when he first went out!"

"Does he say all this?" asked Mr. Wickfield.

"Say? My dear sir," returned Mrs. Markleham, shaking her head and her fan, "you little know my poor Jack Maldon when you ask that question. Say? Not he. You might drag him at the heels of four wild horses first."

"Mama!" said Mrs. Strong.

"Annie, my dear," returned her mother, "once for all, I must really beg that you will not interfere with me, unless it is to confirm what I say. You know as well as I do, that your cousin Maldon would be dragged at the heels of any number of wild horses—why should I confine myself to four! I *won't* confine myself to four—eight, sixteen, two-and-thirty, rather than say anything calculated to overturn the Doctor's plans."

"Wickfield's plans," said the Doctor, stroking his face, and looking penitently at his adviser. "That is to say, our joint plans for him. I said myself, abroad or at home."

"And I said," added Mr. Wickfield gravely, "abroad. I was the means of sending him abroad. It's my responsibility."

"Oh! Responsibility!" said the Old Soldier. "Everything was done for the best, my dear Mr. Wickfield; everything was done for the kindest and best, we know. But if the dear fellow can't live there, he can't live there. And if he can't live there, he'll die there, sooner than he'll overturn the Doctor's plans. I know him," said the Old Soldier, fanning herself, in a sort of calm prophetic agony, "and I know he'll die there, sooner than he'll overturn the Doctor's plans."

"Well, well, ma'am," said the Doctor, cheerfully, "I am not bigoted to my plans, and I can overturn them myself. I can substitute some other plans. If Mr. Jack Maldon comes home on account of ill health, he must not be allowed to go back, and we must endeavour to make some more suitable and fortunate provision for him in this country."

Mrs. Markleham was so overcome by this generous speech—which, I need not say, she had not at all expected or led up to—that she could only tell the Doctor it was like himself, and go several times through that operation of kissing the sticks of her fan, and then tapping his hand with it. After which she gently chid her daughter Annie, for not being more demonstrative when such kindnesses were showered, for her sake, on her old playfellow; and entertained us with some particulars concerning other deserving members of her family, whom it was desirable to set on their deserving legs.

All this time, her daughter Annie never once spoke, or lifted up her eyes. All this time, Mr. Wickfield had his glance upon her as she sat by his own daughter's side. It appeared to me that he never thought of being observed by any one; but was so intent upon her, and upon his own thoughts in connexion with her, as to be quite absorbed. He now asked what Mr. Jack Maldon had actually written in reference to himself, and to whom he had written it?

"Why, here," said Mrs. Markleham, taking a letter from the chimney-piece above the Doctor's head, "the dear fellow says to the Doctor himself—where is it? Oh!—'I am sorry to inform you that my health is suffering severely, and that I fear I may be reduced to the necessity of returning home for a time, as the only hope of restoration.' That's pretty plain, poor fellow! His only hope of restoration! But Annie's letter is plainer still. Annie, show me that letter again."

"Not now, mama," she pleaded in a low tone.

"My dear, you absolutely are, on some subjects, one of the most ridiculous persons in the world," returned her mother, "and perhaps the most unnatural to the claims of your own family. We never should have heard of the letter at all, I believe, unless I had asked for it myself. Do you call that confidence, my love, towards Doctor Strong? I am surprised. You ought to know better."

The letter was reluctantly produced; and as I handed it to the old lady, I saw how the unwilling hand from which I took it, trembled.

"Now let us see," said Mrs. Markleham, putting her glass to her eye, "where the passage is. 'The remembrance of old times, my dearest Annie—and so forth—it's not there. 'The amiable old Proctor'—who's he? Dear me, Annie, how illegibly your cousin Maldon writes, and how stupid I am! 'Doctor,' of course. Ah! amiable indeed!" Here she left off, to kiss her fan again, and shake it at the Doctor, who was looking at us in a state of placid satisfaction. "Now I have found it. '*You* may not be surprised to hear, Annie'—no, to be sure, knowing that he never was really strong; what did I say just now?—'that I have undergone so much in this distant place, as to have decided to leave it at all hazards; on sick leave, if I can; on total resignation, if that is not to be obtained. What I have endured, and do endure here, is insupportable.' And but for the promptitude of that best of creatures," said Mrs. Markleham, telegraphing the Doctor as before, and refolding the letter, "it would be insupportable to me to think of."

Mr. Wickfield said not one word, though the old lady looked to him as if for his commentary on this intelligence; but sat severely silent, with his eyes fixed on the ground. Long after the subject was dismissed, and other topics occupied us, he remained so; seldom raising his eyes, unless to rest them for a moment, with a thoughtful frown, upon the Doctor, or his wife, or both.

The Doctor was very fond of music. Agnes sang with great sweetness and expression, and so did Mrs. Strong. They sang together, and played duets together, and we had quite a little concert. But I remarked two things: first, that though Annie soon recovered her composure, and was quite herself, there was a blank between her and Mr. Wickfield which separated them wholly from each other; secondly, that Mr. Wickfield seemed to dislike the intimacy between her and Agnes, and to watch it with uneasiness. And now, I must confess, the recollection of what I had seen on that night when Mr. Maldon went away, first began to return upon me with a meaning it had never had, and to trouble me. The innocent beauty of her face was not as innocent to me as it had been; I mistrusted the natural grace and charm of her manner; and when I looked at Agnes by her side, and thought how good and true Agnes was, suspicions arose within me that it was an ill-assorted friendship.

She was so happy in it herself, however, and the other was so happy too, that they made the evening fly away as if it were but an hour. It closed in an incident which I well remember. They were taking leave of each other, and Agnes was going to embrace her and kiss her, when Mr. Wickfield stepped between them, as if by accident, and drew Agnes quickly away. Then I saw, as though all the intervening time had been cancelled, and I were still standing in the doorway on the night of the departure, the expression of that night in the face of Mrs. Strong, as it confronted his.

I cannot say what an impression this made upon me, or how impossible I found it, when I thought of her afterwards, to separate her from this look, and remember her face in its innocent loveliness again. It haunted me when I got home. I seemed to have left the Doctor's roof with a dark cloud lowering on it. The reverence that I had for his grey head, was mingled with commiseration for his faith in those who were treacherous to him, and with resentment against those who injured him. The impending shadow of a great affliction, and a great disgrace that had no distinct form in it yet, fell like a stain upon the quiet place where I had worked and played as a boy, and did it a cruel wrong. I had no pleasure in thinking, any more, of the grave old broad-leaved aloe-trees which remained shut up in themselves a hundred years together, and of the trim, smooth grass-plot, and the stone urns, and the Doctor's walk, and the congenial sound of the Cathedral bell hovering above them all. It was as if the tranquil sanctuary of my boyhood had been sacked before my face, and its peace and honor given to the winds.

But morning brought with it my parting from the old house, which Agnes had filled with her influence; and that occupied my mind sufficiently. I should be there again soon, no doubt; I might sleep again—perhaps often—in my old room; but the days of my inhabiting there were gone, and the old time was past. I was heavier at heart when I packed up such of my books and clothes as still remained there to be sent to Dover, than I cared to show to Uriah Heep: who was so officious to help me, that I uncharitably thought him mighty glad that I was going.

I got away from Agnes and her father, somehow, with an indifferent show of being very manly, and took my seat upon the box of the London coach. I was so softened and forgiving, going through the town, that I had half a mind to nod to my old enemy the butcher, and throw him five shillings to drink. But he looked such a very obdurate butcher as he stood scraping the great block in the shop, and moreover, his appearance was so little improved by the loss of a front tooth which I had knocked out, that I thought it best to make no advances.

The main object on my mind, I remember, when we got fairly on the road, was to appear as old as possible to the coachman, and to speak extremely gruff. The latter point I achieved at great personal inconvenience; but I stuck to it, because I felt it was a grown-up sort of thing.

"You are going through, sir?" said the coachman.

"Yes, William," I said, condescendingly (I knew him); "I am going to London. I shall go down into Suffolk afterwards."

"Shooting, sir?" said the coachman.

He knew as well as I did that it was just as likely, at that time f year, I was going down there whaling; but I felt complimented, too.

"I don't know," I said, pretending to be undecided, "whether I shall take a shot or not."

"Birds is got wery shy, I 'm told," said William.

"So I understand," said I.

"Is Suffolk your county, sir?" asked William.

"Yes," I said, with some importance, "Suffolk 's my county."

"I 'm told the dumplings is uncommon fine down there," said William.

I was not aware of it myself, but I felt it necessary to uphold the institutions of my county, and to evince a familiarity with them; so I shook my head, as much as to say "I believe you!"

"And the Punches," said William. "There 's cattle! A Suffolk Punch, when he 's a good un, is worth his weight in gold. Did you ever breed any Suffolk Punches yourself, sir?"

"N—no," I said, "not exactly."

"Here 's a gen'lm'n behind me, I 'll pound it," said William, "as has bred 'em by wholesale."

The gentleman spoken of was a gentleman with a very unpromising squint, and a prominent chin, who had a tall white hat on with a narrow flat brim, and whose close-fitting drab trousers seemed to button all the way up outside his legs from his boots to his hips. His chin was cocked over the coachman's shoulder, so near to me, that his breath quite tickled the back of my head; and as I looked round at him, he leered at the leaders with the eye with which he didn't squint, in a very knowing manner.

"Ain't you?" said William.

"Ain't I what?" asked the gentleman behind.

"Bred them Suffolk Punches by wholesale?"

"I should think so," said the gentleman. "There ain't no sort of orse that I ain't bred, and no sort of dorg. Orses and dorgs is some men's fancy. They're wittles and drink to me—lodging, wife,

MY FIRST FALL IN LIFE.

and children—reading, writing, and 'rithmetic—snuff, tobacker, and sleep."

"That ain't a sort of man to see sitting behind a coach-box, is it though?" said William in my ear, as he handled the reins.

I construed this remark into an indication of a wish that he should have my place, so I blushingly offered to resign it.

"Well, if you don't mind, sir," said William, "I think it *would* be more correct."

I have always considered this as the first fall I had in life. When I booked my place at the coach-office, I had had "Box Seat" written against the entry, and had given the book-keeper half-a-crown. I was got up in a special great coat and shawl, expressly to do honour to that distinguished eminence; had glorified myself upon it a good deal; and had felt that I was a credit to the coach. And here, in the very first stage, I was supplanted by a shabby man with a squint, who had no other merit than smelling like a livery-stables, and being able to walk across me, more like a fly than a human being, while the horses were at a canter!

A distrust of myself, which has often beset me in life on small occasions, when it would have been better away, was assuredly not stopped in its growth by this little incident outside the Canterbury coach. It was in vain to take refuge in gruffness of speech. I spoke from the pit of my stomach for the rest of the journey, but I felt completely extinguished, and dreadfully young.

It was curious and interesting, nevertheless, to be sitting up there, behind four horses: well educated, well dressed, and with plenty of money in my pocket: and to look out for the places where I had slept on my weary journey. I had abundant occupation for my thoughts, in every conspicuous landmark on the road. When I looked down at the trampers whom we passed, and saw that well-remembered style of face turned up, I felt as if the tinker's blackened hand were in the bosom of my shirt again. When we clattered through the narrow street of Chatham, and I caught a glimpse, in passing, of the lane where the old monster lived who had bought my jacket, I stretched my neck eagerly to look for the place where I had sat, in the sun and in the shade, waiting for my money. When we came, at last, within a stage of London, and passed the veritable Salem House where Mr. Creakle had laid about him with a heavy hand, I would have given all I had, for lawful permission to get down and thrash him, and let all the boys out like so many caged sparrows.

We went to the Golden Cross at Charing Cross, then a mouldy sort of establishment in a close neighbourhood. A waiter showed me into the coffee-room; and a chambermaid introduced me to my small bedchamber, which smelt like a hackney-coach, and was shut up like a family vault. I was still painfully conscious of my youth, for nobody stood in any awe of me at all: the chambermaid being utterly indifferent to my opinions on any subject, and the waiter being familiar with me, and offering advice to my inexperience.

"Well now," said the waiter, in a tone of confidence, "what would you like for dinner? Young gentlemen likes poultry in general, have a fowl!"

I told him, as majestically as I could, that I wasn't in the humour for a fowl.

"Ain't you!" said the waiter. "Young gentlemen is generally tired of beef and mutton, have a weal cutlet!"

I assented to this proposal, in default of being able to suggest anything else.

"Do you care for taters?" said the waiter, with an insinuating smile, and his head on one side. "Young gentlemen generally has been over-dosed with taters."

I commanded him in my deepest voice, to order a veal cutlet and potatoes, and all things fitting; and to inquire at the bar if there were any letters for Trotwood Copperfield, Esquire—which I knew there were not, and couldn't be, but thought it manly to appear to expect.

He soon came back to say that there were none (at which I was much surprised), and began to lay the cloth for my dinner in a box by the fire. While he was so engaged he asked me what I would take with it; and on my replying "Half a pint of sherry," thought it a favourable opportunity, I am afraid, to extract that measure of wine from the stale leavings at the bottoms of several small decanters. I am of this opinion, because, while I was reading the newspaper, I observed him behind a low wooden partition, which was his private apartment, very busy pouring out of a number of those vessels into one, like a chemist and druggist making up a prescription. When the wine came, too, I thought it flat; and it certainly had more English crumbs in it, than were to be expected in a foreign wine in anything like a pure state; but I was bashful enough to drink it, and say nothing.

Being, then, in a pleasant frame of mind (from which I infer that poisoning is not always disagreeable in some stages of the process), I resolved to go to the play. It was Covent Garden Theatre that I chose; and there, from the back of a centre box, I saw Julius Cæsar and the new Pantomime. To have all those noble Romans alive before me, and walking in and out for my entertainment, instead of being the stern taskmasters they had been at school, was a most novel and delightful effect. But the mingled reality and mystery of the whole show, the influence upon me of the poetry, the lights, the music, the company, the smooth stupendous changes of glittering and brilliant scenery, were so dazzling, and opened up such illimitable regions of delight, that when I came out into the rainy street, at twelve o'clock at night, I felt as if I had come from the clouds, where I had been leading a romantic life for ages, to a bawling, splashing, link-lighted, umbrella-struggling, hackney-coach-jostling, patten-clinking, muddy, miserable world.

I had emerged by another door, and stood in the street for a little while, as if I really were a stranger upon earth: but the unceremonious pushing and hustling that I received, soon recalled me to myself, and put me in the road back to the hotel; whither I went, revolving the glorious vision all the way; and where, after some porter and oysters, I sat revolving it still, at past one o'clock, with my eyes on the coffee-room fire.

I was so filled with the play, and with the past—for it was, in a manner, like a shining transparency, through which I saw my earlier life moving along—that I don't know when the figure of a handsome well-formed young man, dressed with a tasteful easy negligence which I have reason to remember very well, became a real presence to me. But I recollect being conscious of his company without having noticed his coming in—and my still sitting, musing, over the coffee-room fire.

At last I rose to go to bed, much to the relief of the sleepy waiter, who had got the fidgets in his legs, and was twisting them, and hitting them, and putting them through all kinds of contortions in his small pantry. In going towards the door, I passed the person who had come in, and saw him plainly. I turned directly, came back, and looked again. He did not know me, but I knew him in a moment.

At another time I might have wanted the confidence or the decision to speak to him, and might have put it off until next day, and might have lost him. But, in the then condition of my mind, where the play was still running high, his former protection of me appeared so deserving of my gratitude, and my old love for him overflowed my breast so freshly and spontaneously, that I went up to him at once, with a fast-beating heart, and said:

"Steerforth! won't you speak to me?"

He looked at me—just as he used to look, sometimes—but I saw no recognition in his face.

"You don't remember me, I am afraid," said I.

"My God!" he suddenly exclaimed. "It's little Copperfield!"

I grasped him by both hands, and could not let them go. But for very shame, and the fear that it might displease him, I could have held him round the neck and cried.

"I never, never, never was so glad! My dear Steerforth, I am so overjoyed to see you!"

"And I am rejoiced to see you, too!" he said, shaking my hands heartily. "Why, Copperfield, old boy, don't be overpowered!" And yet he was glad, too, I thought, to see how the delight I had in meeting him affected me.

I brushed away the tears that my utmost resolution had not been able to keep back, and I made a clumsy laugh of it, and we sat down together, side by side.

"Why, how do you come to be here?" said Steerforth, clapping me on the shoulder.

"I came here by the Canterbury coach, to-day. I have been adopted by an aunt down in that part of the country, and have just finished my education there. How do *you* come to be here, Steerforth?"

"Well, I am what they call an Oxford man," he returned; "that is to say, I get bored to death down there, periodically—and I am on my way now to my mother's. You 're a devilish amiable-looking fellow, Copperfield. Just what you used to be, now I look at you! Not altered in the least!"

"I knew *you* immediately," I said; "but you are more easily remembered."

He laughed as he ran his hand through the clustering curls of his hair, and said gaily:

"Yes, I am on an expedition of duty. My mother lives a little way out of town; and the roads being in a beastly condition, and our house tedious enough, I remained here to-night instead of going on. I have not been in town half-a-dozen hours, and those I have been dozing and grumbling away at the play."

"I have been at the play, too," said I. "At Covent Garden. What a delightful and magnificent entertainment, Steerforth."

Steerforth laughed heartily.

—"My dear young Davy," he said, clapping me on the shoulder again, "you are a very Daisy. The daisy of the field, at sunrise, is not fresher than you are! I have been at Covent Carden, too, and there never was a more miserable business!—Holloa, you, sir!"

This was addressed to the waiter, who had been very attentive to our recognition, at a distance, and now came forward deferentially.

"Where have you put my friend, Mr. Copperfield?" said Steerforth.

"Beg your pardon, sir?"

"Where does he sleep? What's his number? You know what I mean," said Steerforth.

"Well, sir," said the waiter, with an apologetic air. "Mr. Copperfield is at present in forty-four, sir."

"And what the devil do you mean," retorted Steerforth, "by putting Mr. Copperfield into a little loft over the stable?"

"Why, you see we wasn't aware, sir," returned the waiter, still apologetically, "as Mr. Copperfield was anyways particular. We can give Mr. Copperfield seventy-two, sir, if it would be preferred Next you, sir."

"Of course it would be preferred," said Steerforth. "And do it at once."

The waiter immediately withdrew to make the exchange. Steerforth, very much amused at my having been put into forty-four, laughed again, and clapped me on the shoulder again, and invited me to breakfast with him next morning at ten o'clock—an invitation I was only too proud and happy to accept. It being now pretty late, we took our candles and went up-stairs, where we parted with friendly heartiness at his door, and where I found my new room a great improvement on my old one, it not being at all musty, and having an immense four-post bedstead in it, which was quite a little landed estate. Here, among pillows enough for six, I soon fell asleep in a blissful condition, and dreamed of ancient Rome, Steerforth, and friendship, until the early morning coaches, rumbling out of the archway underneath, made me dream of thunder and the gods.

CHAPTER XX.

STEERFORTH'S HOME.

When the chambermaid tapped at my door at eight o'clock, and informed me that my shaving-water was outside, I felt severely the having no occasion for it, and blushed in my bed. The suspicion that she laughed too, when she said it, preyed upon my mind all the time I was dressing; and gave me, I was conscious, a sneaking and guilty air when I passed her on the staircase, as I was going down to breakfast. I was so sensitively aware, indeed, of being younger than I could have wished, that for some time I could not make up my mind to pass her at all, under the ignoble circumstances of the case; but, hearing her there with a broom, stood peeping out of window at King Charles on horseback, surrounded by a maze of hackney-coaches, and looking anything but regal in a drizzling rain and a dark-brown fog, until I was admonished by the waiter that the gentleman was waiting for me.

It was not in the coffee-room that I found Steerforth expecting me, but in a snug private apartment, red-curtained and Turkey-carpeted, where the fire burnt bright, and a fine hot breakfast was set forth on a table covered with a clean cloth; and a cheerful miniature of the room, the fire, the breakfast, Steerforth, and all, was shining in the little round mirror over the sideboard. I was rather bashful at first, Steerforth being so self-possessed, and elegant, and superior to me in all respects (age included); but his easy patronage soon put that to rights, and made me quite at home. I could not enough admire the change he had wrought in the Golden Cross; or compare the dull forlorn state I had held yesterday, with this morning's comfort and this morning's entertainment. As to the waiter's familiarity, it was quenched as if it had never been. He attended on us, as I may say, in sackcloth and ashes.

"Now, Copperfield," said Steerforth, when we were alone, "I should like to hear what you are doing, and where you are going, and all about you. I feel as if you were my property."

Glowing with pleasure to find that he had still this interest in me, I told him how my aunt had proposed the little expedition that I had before me, and whither it tended.

"As you are in no hurry, then," said Steerforth, "come home with me to Highgate, and stay a day or two. You will be pleased with my mother—she is a little vain and prosy about me, but that you can forgive her—and she will be pleased with you."

"I should like to be as sure of that, as you are kind enough to say you are," I answered, smiling.

"Oh!" said Steerforth, "every one who likes me, has a claim on her that is sure to be acknowledged."

"Then I think I shall be a favourite," said I.

"Good!" said Steerforth. "Come and prove it. We will go and see the lions for an hour or two—it's something to have a fresh fellow like you to show them to, Copperfield—and then we'll journey out to Highgate by the coach."

I could hardly believe but that I was in a dream, and that I should wake presently in number forty-four, to the solitary box in the coffee-room and the familiar waiter again. After I had written to my aunt and told her of my fortunate meeting with my admired old school-fellow, and my acceptance of his invitation, we went out in a hackney-chariot, and saw a Panorama and some other sights, and took a walk through the Museum, where I could not help observing how much Steerforth knew, on an infinite variety of subjects, and of how little account he seemed to make his knowledge.

"You'll take a high degree at college, Steerforth," said I, "if you have not done so already; and they will have good reason to be proud of you."

"*I* take a degree!" cried Steerforth. "Not I! my dear Daisy—will you mind my calling you Daisy?"

"Not at all!" said I.

"That's a good fellow! My dear Daisy," said Steerforth, laughing, "I have not the least desire or intention to distinguish myself in that way. I have done quite sufficient for my purpose. I find that I am heavy company enough for myself, as I am."

"But the fame——" I was beginning.

"You romantic Daisy!" said Steerforth, laughing still more heartily; "why should I trouble myself, that a parcel of heavy-headed fellows may gape and hold up their hands? Let them do it at some other man. There's fame for him, and he's welcome to it."

I was abashed at having made so great a mistake, and was glad to change the subject. Fortunately it was not difficult to do, for Steerforth could always pass from one subject to another with a carelessness and lightness that were his own.

Lunch succeeded to our sight-seeing, and the short winter day wore away so fast, that it was dusk when the stage-coach stopped with us at an old brick house at Highgate on the summit of the hill. An elderly lady, though not very far advanced in years, with a proud carriage and a handsome face, was in the doorway as we alighted; and greeting Steerforth as "My dearest James," folded him in her arms. To this lady he presented me as his mother, and she gave me a stately welcome.

It was a genteel old-fashioned house, very quiet and orderly. From the windows of my room I saw all London lying in the distance like a great vapor, with here and there some lights twinkling through it. I had only time, in dressing, to glance at the solid furniture, the framed pieces of work (done, I supposed, by Steerforth's mother when she was a girl), and some pictures in crayons of ladies with powdered hair and boddices, coming and going on the walls, as the newly-kindled fire crackled and sputtered, when I was called to dinner.

There was a second lady in the dining-room, of a slight short figure, dark, and not agreeable to look at, but with some appearance of good looks too, who attracted my attention: perhaps because I had not expected to see her; perhaps because I found myself sitting opposite to her; perhaps because of something really remarkable in her. She had black hair and eager black eyes, and was thin, and had a scar upon her lip. It was an old scar—I should rather call it seam, for it was not discolored, and had healed years ago—which had once cut through her mouth, downward towards the chin, but was now barely visible across the table, except above and on her upper lip, the shape of which it had altered. I concluded in my own mind that she was about thirty years of age, and that she wished to be married. She was a little dilapidated—like a house—with having been so long to let; yet had, as I have said, an appearance of good looks. Her thinness seemed to be the effect of some wasting fire within her, which found a vent in her gaunt eyes.

She was introduced as Miss Dartle, and both Steerforth and his mother called her Rosa. I found that she lived there, and had been for a long time Mrs. Steerforth's companion. It appeared to me that she never said anything she wanted to say, outright; but hinted it, and made a great deal more of it by this practice. For example, when Mrs. Steerforth observed, more in jest than earnest, that she feared her son led but a wild life at college, Miss Dartle put in thus:

"Oh, really? You know how ignorant I am, and that I only asked for information, but isn't it always so? I thought that kind of life was on all hands understood to be—eh?"

"It is education for a very grave profession, if you mean that, Rosa," Mrs. Steerforth answered with some coldness.

"Oh! Yes! That's very true," returned Miss Dartle. "But isn't it, though?—I want to be put right if I am wrong—isn't it really?"

"Really what?" said Mrs. Steerforth.

"Oh! You mean it's *not!*" returned Miss Dartle. "Well, I'm very glad to hear it! Now, I know what to do. That's the advantage of asking. I shall never allow people to talk before me about wastefulness and profligacy, and so forth, in connection with that life, any more."

"And you will be right," said Mrs. Steerforth. "My son's tutor is a conscientious gentleman; and if I had not implicit reliance on my son, I should have reliance on him."

"Should you?" said Miss Dartle. "Dear me! Conscientious is he? Really conscientious, now?"

"Yes, I am convinced of it," said Mrs. Steerforth.

"How very nice! exclaimed Miss Dartle. "What a comfort! Really conscientious? Then he's not—but of course he can't be, if he's really conscientious. Well, I shall be quite happy in my opimon of him, from this time. You can't think how it elevates him in my opinion, to know for certain that he's really conscientious!"

Her own views of every question, and her correction of everything that was said to which she was opposed, Miss Dartle insinuated in the same way: sometimes, I could not conceal from myself, with great power, though in contradiction even of Steerforth. An instance happened before dinner was done. Mrs. Steerforth speaking to me about my intention of going down into Suffolk, I said at hazard how glad I should be, if Steerforth would only go there with me; and explaining to him that I was going to see my old nurse, and Mr. Peggotty's family, I reminded him of the boatman whom he had seen at school.

"Oh! That bluff fellow!" said Steerforth. "He had a son with him, hadn't he?"

"No. That was his nephew," I replied; "whom he adopted, though, as a son. He has a very pretty little niece too, whom he adopted as a daughter. In short, his house (or rather his boat, for he lives in one, on dry land) is full of people who are objects of his generosity and kindness. You would be delighted to see that household."

"Should I?" said Steerforth. "Well, I think I should. I must see what can be done. It would be worth a journey—not to mention the pleasure of a journey with you, Daisy,—to see that sort of people together, and to make one of 'em."

My heart leaped with a new hope of pleasure. But it was in reference to the tone in which he had spoken of "that sort of people," that Miss Dartle, whose sparkling eyes had been watchful of us, now broke in again.

"Oh, but, really? Do tell me. Are they, though?" she said.

"Are they what? And are who what?" said Steerforth.

"That sort of people.—Are they really animals and clods, and beings of another order? I want to know *so* much."

"Why, there's a pretty wide separation between them and us," said Steerforth, with indifference. "They are not to be expected to be as sensitive as we are. Their delicacy is not to be shocked, or hurt very easily. They are wonderfully virtuous, I dare say—some people contend for that, at least; and I am sure I don't want to contradict them—but they have not very fine natures, and they may be thankful that, like their coarse rough skins, they are not easily wounded."

"Really!" said Miss Dartle. "Well, I don't know, now, when I have been better pleased than to hear that. It's so consoling! It's such a delight to know that, when they suffer, they don't feel! Sometimes I have been quite uneasy for that sort of people; but now I shall just dismiss the idea of them, altogether. Live and learn. I had my doubts, I confess, but now they're cleared up. I didn't know, and now I do know; and that shows the advantage of asking—don't it?"

I believed that Steerforth had said what he had, in jest, or to draw Miss Dartle out; and I expected him to say as much when she was gone, and we two were sitting before the fire. But he merely asked me what I thought of her.

"She is very clever, is she not?" I asked.

"Clever! She brings everything to a grindstone," said Steerforth, "and sharpens it, as she has sharpened her own face and figure these years past. She has worn herself away by constant sharpening. She is all edge."

"What a remarkable scar that is upon her lip!" I said.

Steerforth's face fell, and he paused a moment.

"Why, the fact is," he returned, "—*I* did that."

"By an unfortunate accident!"

"No. I was a young boy, and she exasperated me, and I threw a hammer at her. A promising young angel I must have been!"

I was deeply sorry to have touched on such a painful theme, but that was useless now.

"She has borne the mark ever since, as you see," said Steerforth; "and she'll bear it to her grave, if she ever rests in one—though I can hardly believe she will ever rest anywhere. She was the motherless child of a sort of cousin of my father's. He died one day. My mother, who was then a widow, brought her here to be company to her. She has a couple of thousand pounds of her own, and saves the interest of it every year, to add to the principal. There's the history of Miss Rosa Dartle for you."

"And I have no doubt she loves you like a brother," said I.

"Humph!" retorted Steerforth, looking at the fire. "Some brothers are not loved overmuch; and some love—but help yourself, Copperfield! We 'll drink the daisies of the field, in compliment to you; and the lilies of the valley that toil not, neither do they spin, in compliment to me—the more shame for me!" A moody smile that had overspread his features cleared off as he said this merrily, and he was his own frank winning self again.

I could not help glancing at the scar with a painful interest when we went in to tea. It was not long before I observed that it was the most susceptible part of her face, and that, when she turned pale, that mark altered first, and became a dull, lead-coloured streak, lengthening out to its full extent, like a mark in invisible ink brought to the fire. There was a little altercation between her and Steerforth about a cast of the dice at backgammon—when I thought her, for one moment, in a storm of rage; and then I saw it start forth like the old writing on the wall.

It was no matter of wonder to me to find Mrs. Steerforth devoted to her son. She seemed to be able to speak or think about nothing else. She showed me his picture as an infant, in a locket, with some of his baby-hair in it; she showed me his picture as he had been when I first knew him; and she wore at her breast his picture as he was now. All the letters he had ever written to her, she kept in a cabinet near her own chair by the fire; and she would have read me some of them, and I should have been very glad to hear them too, if he had not interposed, and coaxed her out of the design.

"It was at Mr. Creakle's, my son tells me, that you first became acquainted," said Mrs. Steerforth, as she and I were talking at one table, while they played backgammon at another. "Indeed, I recollect his speaking, at that time, of a pupil younger than himself who had taken his fancy there; but your name, as you may suppose, has not lived in my memory."

"He was very generous and noble to me in those days, I assure you, ma'am," said I, "and I stood in need of such a friend. I should have been quite crushed without him.

"He is always generous and noble," said Mrs. Steerforth, proudly.

I subscribed to this with all my heart, God knows. She knew I did; for the stateliness of her manner already abated towards me, except when she spoke in praise of him, and then her air was always lofty.

"It was not a fit school generally for my son," said she; "far from it; but there were particular circumstances to be considered at the time, of more importance even than that selection. My son's high spirit made it desirable that he should be placed with some man who felt its superiority, and would be content to bow himself before it; and we found such a man there."

I knew that, knowing the fellow. And yet I did not despise him the more for it, but thought it a redeeming quality in him—if he could be allowed any grace for not resisting one so irresistible as Steerforth.

"My son's great capacity was tempted on, there, by a feeling of voluntary emulation and conscious pride," the fond lady went on to say. "He would have risen against all constraint; but he found himself the monarch of the place, and he haughtily determined to be worthy of his station. It was like himself."

I echoed with all my heart and soul, that it was like himself.

"So my son took, of his own will, and on no compulsion, to the course in which he can always, when it is his pleasure, outstrip every competitor," she pursued. "My son informs me, Mr. Copperfield, that you were quite devoted to him, and that when you met yesterday you made yourself known to him with tears of joy. I should be an affected woman if I made any pretence of being surprised by my son's inspiring such emotions; but I cannot be indifferent to any one who is so sensible of his merit, and I am very glad to see you here, and can assure you that he feels an unusual friendship for you, and that you may rely on his protection."

Miss Dartle played backgammon as eagerly as she did everything else. If I had seen her, first, at the board, I should have fancied that her figure had got thin, and her eyes had got large, over that pursuit, and no other in the world. But I am very much mistaken if she missed a word of this, or lost a look of mine as I received it with the utmost pleasure, and, honoured by Mrs. Steerforth's confidence, felt older than I had done since I left Canterbury.

When the evening was pretty far spent, and a tray of glasses and decanters came in, Steerforth promised, over the fire, that he would seriously think of going down into the country with me. There was no hurry, he said; a week hence would do; and his mother hospitably said the same. While we were talking, he more than once called me Daisy; which brought Miss Dartle out again.

"But really, Mr. Copperfield," she asked, "is it a nick-name? And why does he give it you? Is it—eh?—because he thinks you young and innocent? I am so stupid in these things."

I coloured in replying that I believed it was.

"Oh," said Miss Dartle. "Now I am glad to know that! I ask for information, and I am glad to know it. He thinks you young and innocent; and so you are his friend. Well, that 's quite delightful!"

She went to bed soon after this, and Mrs. Steerforth retired too. Steerforth and I, after lingering for half an hour over the fire, talking about Traddles and all the rest of them at old Salem House, went up-stairs together. Steerforth's room was next to mine, and I went in to look at it. It was a picture of comfort, full of easy chairs, cushions and footstools, worked by his mother's hand, and with no sort of thing omitted that could help to render it complete. Finally, her handsome features looked down on her darling from a portrait on the wall, as if it were even something to her that her likeness should watch him while he slept.

I found the fire burning clear enough in my room by this time, and the curtains drawn before the windows and round the bed, giving it a very snug appearance. I sat down in a great chair upon the hearth to meditate on my happiness; and had enjoyed the contemplation of it for some time, when I found a likeness of Miss Dartle looking eagerly at me from above the chimney-piece.

It was a startling likeness, and necessarily had a startling look. The painter hadn't made the scar, but *I* made it; and there it was, coming and going; now confined to the upper lip as I had seen it at dinner, and now showing the whole extent of the wound inflicted by the hammer, as I had seen it when she was passionate.

I wondered peevishly why they couldn't put her anywhere else instead of quartering her on me. To get rid of her, I undressed quickly, extinguished my light, and went to bed. But, as I fell asleep, I could not forget that she was still there looking, "Is it really, though? I want to know;" and when I awoke in the night, I found that I was uneasily asking all sorts of people in my dreams whether it really was or not—without knowing what I meant.

CHAPTER XXI.

LITTLE EM'LY.

THERE was a servant in that house, a man who, I understood, was usually with Steerforth, and had come into his service at the University, who was in appearance a pattern of respectability. I believe there never existed in his station a more respectable-looking man. He was taciturn, soft-footed, very quiet in his manner, deferential, observant, always at hand when wanted, and never near when not wanted; but his great claim to consideration was his respectability. He had not a pliant face, he had rather a stiff neck, rather a tight smooth head with short hair clinging to it at the sides, a soft way of speaking, with a peculiar habit of whispering the letter S so distinctly, that he seemed to use it oftener than any other man; but every peculiarity that he had he made respectable. If his nose had been upside-down, he would have made that respectable. He surrounded himself with an atmosphere of respectability, and walked secure in it. It would have been next to impossible to suspect him of anything wrong, he was so thoroughly respectable. Nobody could have thought of putting him in a livery, he was so highly respectable. To have imposed any derogatory work upon him, would have been to inflict a wanton insult on the feelings of a most respectable man. And of this, I noticed the women-servants in the household were so intuitively conscious, that they always did such work themselves, and generally while he read the paper by the pantry fire.

Such a self-contained man I never saw. But in that quality, as in every other he possessed, he only seemed to be the more respectable. Even the fact that no one knew his Christian name, seemed to form a part of his respectability. Nothing could be objected against his surname Littimer, by which he was known. Peter might have been hanged, or Tom transported; but Littimer was perfectly respectable.

It was occasioned, I suppose, by the reverend nature of respectability in the abstract, but I felt particularly young in this man's presence. How old he was himself I could not guess—and that again went to his credit on the same score; for in the calmness of respectability he might have numbered fifty years as well as thirty.

Littimer was in my room in the morning before I was up, to bring me that reproachful shaving-water, and to put out my clothes. When I undrew the curtains and looked out of bed, I saw him, in an equable temperature of respectability, unaffected by the east wind of January, and not even breathing frostily, standing my boots right and left in the first dancing position, and blowing specks of dust off my coat as he laid it down like a baby.

I gave him good morning, and asked him what o'clock it was. He took out of his pocket the most respectable hunting-watch I ever saw, and preventing the spring with his thumb from opening far, looked in at the face, as if he were consulting an oracular oyster shut it up again, and said, if I pleased, it was half-past eight.

"Mr. Steerforth will be glad to hear how you have rested, sir."

"Thank you," said I, "very well indeed. Is Mr. Steerforth quite well?"

"Thank you, sir, Mr. Steerforth is tolerably well." Another of his characteristics,—no use of superlatives. A cool calm medium always.

"Is there anything more I can have the honour of doing for you, sir? The warning-bell will ring at nine; the family take breakfast at half-past nine."

"Nothing, I thank you."

"I thank *you*, sir, if you please;" and with that, and with a little inclination of his head when he passed the bedside, as an apology for correcting me, he went out, shutting the door as delicately as if I had just fallen into a sweet sleep on which my life depended.

Every morning we had exactly this conversation; never any more, and never any less; and yet, invariably, however far I might have been lifted out of myself over-night, and advanced towards maturer years, by Steerforth's companionship, or Mrs. Steerforth's confidence, or Miss Dartle's conversation, in the presence of this most respectable man I became, as our smaller poets sing, "a boy again."

He got horses for us; and Steerforth, who knew every thing, gave me lessons in riding. He provided foils for us, and Steerforth gave me lessons in fencing—gloves, and I began, of the same master, to improve in boxing. It gave me no manner of concern that Steerforth should find me a novice in these sciences, but I never could bear to show my want of skill before the respectable Littimer. I had no reason to believe that Littimer understood such arts himself; he never led me to suppose anything of the kind, by so much as the vibration of one of his respectable eyelashes; yet whenever he was by, while we were practising, I felt myself the greenest and most inexperienced of mortals.

I am particular about this man, because he made a particular effect on me at that time, and because of what took place thereafter.

The week passed away in a most delightful manner. It passed rapidly, as may be supposed, to one entranced as I was; and yet it gave me so many occasions for knowing Steerforth better, and admiring him more in a thousand respects, that at its close I seemed to have been with him for a much longer time. A dashing way he had of treating me like a play-thing, was more agreeable to me than any behaviour he could have adopted. It reminded me of our old acquaintance; it seemed the natural sequel of it; it showed me that he was unchanged; it relieved me of any uneasiness I might have felt, in comparing my merits with his, and measuring my claims upon his friendship by any equal standard; above all, it was a familiar, unrestrained, affectionate demeanour that he used towards no one else. As he had treated me at school differently from all the rest, I joyfully believed that he treated me in life unlike any other friend he had. I believed that I was nearer to his heart than any other friend, and my own heart warmed with attachment to him.

He made up his mind to go with me into the country, and the

day arrived for our departure. He had been doubtful at first whether to take Littimer or not, but decided to leave him at home. The respectable creature, satisfied with his lot whatever it was, arranged our portmanteaus on the little carriage that was to take us into London, as if they were intended to defy the shocks of ages; and received my modestly proffered donation with perfect tranquillity.

We bade adieu to Mrs. Steerforth and Miss Dartle, with many thanks on my part, and much kindness on the devoted mother's. The last thing I saw was Littimer's unruffled eye; fraught, as I fancied, with the silent conviction that I was very young indeed.

What I felt, in returning so auspiciously to the old familiar places, I shall not endeavour to describe. We went down by the Mail. I was so concerned, I recollect, even for the honour of Yarmouth, that when Steerforth said, as we drove through its dark streets to the inn, that, as well as he could make out, it was a good, queer, out-of-the-way kind of hole, I was highly pleased. We went to bed on our arrival (I observed a pair of dirty shoes and gaiters in connexion with my old friend the Dolphin as we passed that door), and breakfasted late in the morning. Steerforth, who was in great spirits, had been strolling about the beach before I was up, and had made acquaintance, he said, with half the boatmen in the place. Moreover he had seen, in the distance, what he was sure must be the identical house of Mr. Peggotty, with smoke coming out of the chimney; and had had a great mind, he told me, to walk in and swear he was myself grown out of knowledge.

"When do you propose to introduce me there, Daisy?" he said, "I am at your disposal. Make your own arrangements."

"Why, I was thinking that this evening would be a good time, Steerforth, when they are all sitting round the fire. I should like you to see it when it's snug, it's such a curious place."

"So be it!" returned Steerforth. "This evening."

"I shall not give them any notice that we are here, you know," said I, delighted. "We must take them by surprise."

"Oh, of course! It's no fun," said Steerforth, "unless we take them by surprise. Let us see the natives in their aboriginal condition."

"Though they *are* that sort of people that you mentioned," I returned

"Aha! What! you recollect my skirmishes with Rosa, do you?" he exclaimed with a quick look. "Confound the girl, I am half afraid of her. She's like a goblin to me. But never mind her. Now what are you going to do? You are going to see your nurse, I suppose?"

"Why, yes," I said, "I must see Peggotty first of all."

"Well," replied Steerforth, looking at his watch. "Suppose I deliver you up to be cried over for a couple of hours. Is that long enough?"

I answered, laughing, that I thought we might get through it in that time, but that he must come also; for he would find that his renown had preceded him, and that he was almost as great a personage as I was.

"I'll come anywhere you like," said Steerforth, "or do anything you like. Tell me where to come to; and in two hours I'll produce myself in any state you please, sentimental or comical."

I gave him minute directions for finding the residence of Mr Barkis, carrier to Blunderstone and elsewhere, and, on this understanding, went out alone. There was a sharp bracing air; the ground was dry; the sea was crisp and clear; the sun was diffusing abundance of light, if not much warmth; and everything was fresh and lively. I was so fresh and lively myself, in the pleasure of being there, that I could have stopped the people in the streets and shaken hands with them.

The streets looked small, of course. The streets that we have only seen as children, always do, I believe, when we go back to them. But I had forgotten nothing in them, and found nothing changed, until I came to Mr. Omer's shop. OMER AND JORAM was now written up, where OMER used to be; but the inscription, DRAPER, TAILOR, HABERDASHER, FUNERAL FURNISHER, &c., remained as it was.

My footsteps seemed to tend so naturally to the shop-door, after I had read these words from over the way, that I went across the road and looked in. There was a pretty woman at the back of the shop, dancing a little child in her arms, while another little fellow clung to her apron. I had no difficulty in recognising either Minnie or Minnie's children. The glass-door of the parlor was not open but in the workshop across the yard I could faintly hear the old tune playing, as if it had never left off.

"Is Mr. Omer at home?" said I, entering. "I should like to see him, for a moment, if he is."

"Oh yes, sir, he is at home," said Minnie; "this weather don't suit his asthma out of doors. Joe, call your grandfather!"

The little fellow, who was holding her apron, gave such a lusty shout, that the sound of it made him bashful, and he buried his face in her skirts, to her great admiration. I heard a heavy puffing and blowing coming towards us, and soon Mr. Omer, shorter-winded than of yore, but not much older-looking, stood before me.

"Servant, sir," said Mr. Omer. "What can I do for you, sir?"

"You can shake hands with me, Mr. Omer, if you please," said I, putting out my own. "You were very good-natured to me once, when I am afraid I didn't show that I thought so."

"Was I though?" returned the old man. "I'm glad to hear it, but I don't remember when. Are you sure it was me?"

"Quite."

"I think my memory has got as short as my breath," said Mr. Omer, looking at me and shaking his head; "for I don't remember you."

"Don't you remember your coming to the coach to meet me, and my having breakfast here, and our riding out to Blunderstone together: you, and I, and Mrs. Joram, and Mr. Joram too—who wasn't her husband then?"

"Why, Lord bless my soul!" exclaimed Mr. Omer, after being thrown by his surprise into a fit of coughing, "you don't say so! Minnie, my dear, you recollect? Dear me, yes—the party was a lady, I think?"

"My mother," I rejoined.

"To—be—sure," said Mr. Omer, touching my waistcoat with his forefinger, "and there was a little child too! There was two parties. The little party was laid along with the other party. Over at Blunderstone it was, of course. Dear me! And how have you been since?"

Very well, I thanked him, as I hoped he had been too.

"Oh! nothing to grumble at, you know," said Mr. Omer. "I

find my breath gets short, but it seldom gets longer as a man gets older. I take it as it comes, and make the most of it. That's the best way, ain't it?"

Mr. Omer coughed again, in consequence of laughing, and was assisted out of his fit by his daughter, who now stood close beside us, dancing her smallest child on the counter.

"Dear me!" said Mr. Omer. "Yes, to be sure. Two parties! Why, in that very ride, if you'll believe me, the day was named for my Minnie to marry Joram. 'Do name it, sir,' says Joram. 'Yes, do, father,' said Minnie. And now he's come into the business. And look here! The youngest!"

Minnie laughed, and stroked her banded hair upon her temples, as her father put one of his fat fingers into the hand of the child she was dancing on the counter.

"Two parties, of course!" said Mr. Omer, nodding his head retrospectively. "Ex-actly so! And Joram's at work, at this minute, on a grey one with silver nails, not this measurement"—the measurement of the dancing child upon the counter—"by a good two inches.—Will you take something?"

I thanked him, but declined.

"Let me see," said Mr. Omer. "Barkis's the carrier's wife—Peggotty's the boatman's sister—she had something to do with your family? She was in service there, sure?"

My answering in the affirmative gave him great satisfaction.

"I believe my breath will get long next, my memory's getting so much so," said Mr. Omer. "Well, sir, we've got a young relation of hers here under articles to us, that has as elegant a taste in the dress-making business—I assure you I don't believe there's a Duchess in England can touch her."

"Not little Em'ly?" said I, involuntarily.

"Em'ly's her name," said Mr. Omer, "and she's little too. But if you'll believe me, she has such a face of her own that half the women in this town are mad against her."

"Nonsense, father!" cried Minnie.

"My dear," said Mr. Omer, "I don't say it's the case with you," winking at me, "but I say that half the women in Yarmouth—ah! and in five miles round—are mad against that girl."

"Then she should have kept to her own station in life, father," said Minnie, "and not have given them any hold to talk about her and then they couldn't have done it."

"Couldn't have done it, my dear!" retorted Mr. Omer. "Couldn't have done it! Is that *your* knowledge of life? What is there that any woman couldn't do, that she shouldn't do—especially on the subject of another woman's good looks?"

I really thought it was all over with Mr. Omer, after he had uttered this libellous pleasantry. He coughed to that extent, and his breath eluded all his attempts to recover it with that obstinacy, that I fully expected to see his head go down behind the counter, and his little black breeches, with the rusty little bunches of ribbons at the knees, come quivering up in a last ineffectual struggle. At length, however, he got better, though he still panted hard, and was so exhausted that he was obliged to sit on the stool of the shop-desk.

"You see," he said, wiping his head, and breathing with difficulty, "she hasn't taken much to any companions here; she hasn't taken kindly to any particular acquaintances and friends, not to mention sweethearts. In consequence, an ill-natured story got about, that Em'ly wanted to be a lady. Now my opinion is, that it came into circulation principally on account of her sometimes saying, at the school, that if she was a lady she would like to do so and so for her uncle—don't you see?—and buy him such and such fine things."

"I assure you, Mr. Omer, she has said so to me," I returned eagerly, "when we were both children."

Mr. Omer nodded his head and rubbed his chin. "Just so. Then out of a very little, she could dress herself, you see, better than most others could out of a deal, and *that* made things unpleasant. More over, she was rather what might be called wayward—I'll go so far as to say what I should call wayward myself," said Mr. Omer,—"didn't know her own mind quite—a little spoiled—and couldn't, at first, exactly bind herself down. No more than that was ever said against her, Minnie?"

"No, father," said Mrs. Joram. "That's the worst, I believe."

"So when she got a situation," said Mr. Omer, "to keep a fractious old lady company, they didn't very well agree, and she didn't stop. At last she came here, apprenticed for three years. Nearly two of 'em are over, and she has been as good a girl as ever was. Worth any six! Minnie, is she worth any six, now?"

"Yes, father," replied Minnie. "Never say *I* detracted from her!"

"Very good," said Mr. Omer. "That's right. And so, young gentleman," he added, after a few moments' further rubbing of his chin, "that you may not consider me long-winded as well as short-breathed, I believe that's all about it."

As they had spoken in a subdued tone, while speaking of Em'ly, I had no doubt that she was near. On my asking now, if that were not so, Mr. Omer nodded yes, and nodded towards the door of the parlor. My hurried inquiry if I might peep in, was answered with a free permission; and, looking through the glass, I saw her sitting at her work. I saw her, a most beautiful little creature, with the cloudless blue eyes, that had looked into my childish heart, turned laughingly upon another child of Minnie's who was playing near her; with enough of wilfulness in her bright face to justify what I had heard; with much of the old capricious coyness lurking in it; but with nothing in her pretty looks, I am sure, but what was meant for goodness and for happiness, and what was on a good and happy course.

The tune across the yard that seemed as if it never had left off—alas! it was the tune that never *does* leave off—was beating, softly, all the while.

"Wouldn't you like to step in," said Mr. Omer, "and speak to her! Walk in and speak to her, sir! Make yourself at home!"

I was too bashful to do so then—I was afraid of confusing her, and I was no less afraid of confusing myself: but I informed myself of the hour at which she left of an evening, in order that our visit might be timed accordingly; and taking leave of Mr. Omer, and his pretty daughter, and her little children, went away to my dear old Peggotty's.

Here she was, in the tiled kitchen, cooking dinner! The moment I knocked at the door she opened it, and asked me what I pleased to want. I looked at her with a smile, but she gave me no smile in return. I had never ceased to write to her, but it must have been seven years since we had met.

"Is Mr. Barkis at home, ma'am?" I said, feigning to speak roughly to her.

"He 's at home, sir," returned Peggotty, "but he 's bad abed with the rheumatics."

"Don't he go over to Blunderstone now?" I asked.

"When he 's well, he do," she answered.

"Do *you* ever go there, Mrs. Barkis?"

She looked at me more attentively, and I noticed a quick movement of her hands towards each other.

"Because I want to ask a question about a house there, that they call the—what is it?—the Rookery," said I.

She took a step backwards, and put out her hands in an undecided frightened way, as if to keep me off.

"Peggotty!" I cried to her.

She cried, "My darling boy!" and we both burst into tears, and were locked in one another's arms.

What extravagances she committed; what laughing and crying over me; what pride she showed, what joy, what sorrow that she whose pride and joy I might have been, could never hold me in a fond embrace; I have not the heart to tell. I was troubled with no misgiving that it was young in me to respond to her emotions. I had never laughed and cried in all my life, I dare say—not even to her—more freely than I did that morning.

"Barkis will be so glad," said Peggotty, wiping her eyes with her apron, "that it 'ill do him more good than pints of liniment. May I go and tell him you are here? Will you come up and see him, my dear?"

Of course I would. But Peggotty could not get out of the room as easily as she meant to, for as often as she got to the door and looked round at me, she came back again to have another laugh and another cry upon my shoulder. At last, to make the matter easier, I went up-stairs with her; and having waited outside for a minute, while she said a word of preparation to Mr. Barkis, presented myself before that invalid.

He received me with absolute enthusiasm. He was too rheumatic to be shaken hands with, but he begged me to shake the tassel on the top of his nightcap, which I did most cordially. When I sat down by the side of the bed, he said that it did him [illegible] of good to feel as if he was driving me on the Blunderstone road again. As he lay in bed, face upward, and so covered, with that exception, that he seemed to be nothing but a face—like a conventional cherubim,—he looked the queerest object I ever beheld.

"What name was it, as I wrote up in the cart, sir?" said Mr. Barkis, with a slow rheumatic smile.

"Ah! Mr. Barkis, we had some grave talks about that matter, hadn't we?"

"I was willin' a long time, sir?" said Mr. Barkis.

"A long time," said I.

"And I don't regret it," said Mr. Barkis. "Do you remember what you told me once, about her making all the apple pasties and doing all the cooking?"

"Yes very well," I returned.

"It was as true," said Mr. Barkis, "as turnips is. It was as true," said Mr. Barkis, nodding his nightcap, which was his only means of emphasis, "as taxes is. And nothing 's truer than them."

Mr. Barkis turned his eyes upon me, as if for my assent to this result of his reflections in bed; and I gave it.

"Nothing 's truer than them," repeated Mr. Barkis; "a man as poor as I am finds that out in his mind when he 's laid up. I 'm a very poor man, sir."

"I am sorry to hear it, Mr. Barkis."

"A very poor man, indeed I am," said Mr. Barkis.

Here his right hand came slowly and feebly from under the bed-clothes, and with a purposeless uncertain grasp took hold of a stick which was loosely tied to the side of the bed. After some poking about with this instrument, in the course of which his face assumed a variety of distracted expressions, Mr. Barkis poked it against a box, an end of which had been visible to me all the time. Then his face became composed.

"Old clothes," said Mr. Barkis.

"Oh!" said I.

"I wish it was Money, sir," said Mr. Barkis.

"I wish it was, indeed," said I.

"But it AIN'T," said Mr. Barkis, opening both his eyes as wide as he possibly could.

I expressed myself quite sure of that, and Mr. Barkis, turning his eyes more gently to his wife, said :

" She's the usefullest and best of women, C. P. Barkis. All the praise that any one can give to C. P. Barkis, she deserves, and more! My dear, you'll get a dinner to-day, for company ; something good to eat and drink, will you ?"

I should have protested against this unnecessary demonstration in my honour, but that I saw Peggotty, on the opposite side of the bed, extremely anxious that I should not. So I held my peace.

" I have got a trifle of money somewhere about me, my dear," said Mr. Barkis, " but I'm a little tired. If you and Mr. David will leave me for a short nap, I'll try and find it when I wake."

We left the room, in compliance with this request. When we got outside the door, Peggotty informed me that Mr. Barkis, being now " a little nearer" than he used to be, always resorted to this same device before producing a single coin from his store ; and that he endured unheard-of agonies in crawling out of bed alone, and taking it from that unlucky box. In effect, we presently heard him uttering suppressed groans of the most dismal nature, as this magpie proceeding racked him in every joint ; but while Peggotty's eyes were full of compassion for him, she said his generous impulse would do him good, and it was better not to check it. So he groaned on, until he had got into bed again, suffering, I have no doubt, a martyrdom ; and then called us in, pretending to have just woke up from a refreshing sleep, and to produce a guinea from under his pillow. His satisfaction in which happy imposition on us, and in having preserved the impenetrable secret of the box, appeared to be a sufficient compensation to him for all his tortures.

I prepared Peggotty for Steerforth's arrival, and it was not long before he came. I am persuaded she knew no difference between his having been a personal benefactor of hers, and a kind friend to me, and that she would have received him with the utmost gratitude and devotion in any case. But his easy, spirited, good humour ; his genial manner, his handsome looks, his natural gift of adapting himself to whomsoever he pleased, and making direct, when he cared to do it, to the main point of interest in anybody's heart ; bound her to him wholly in five minutes. His manner to me, alone, would have won her. But, through all these causes combined, I sincerely believe she had a kind of adoration for him before he left the house that night.

He stayed there with me to dinner—if I were to say willingly, I should not half express how readily and gaily. He went into Mr. Barkis's room like light and air, brightening and refreshing it as if he were healthy weather. There was no noise, no effort, no consciousness, in anything he did; but in everything an indescribable lightness, a seeming impossibility of doing anything else, or doing anything better, which was so graceful, so natural, and agreeable, that it overcomes me, even now, in the remembrance.

We made merry in the little parlor, where the Book of Martyrs, unthumbed since my time, was laid out upon the desk as of old, and where I now turned over its terrific pictures, remembering the old sensations they had awakened, but not feeling them. When Peggotty spoke of what she called my room, and of its being ready for me at night, and of her hoping I would occupy it, before I could so much as look at Steerforth, hesitating, he was possessed of the whole case.

"Of course," he said, "you'll sleep here, while we stay, and I shall sleep at the hotel."

"But to bring you so far," I returned, "and to separate, seems bad companionship, Steerforth."

"Why, in the name of Heaven, where do you naturally belong!" he said. "What is 'seems,' compared to that!" It was settled at once.

He maintained all his delightful qualities to the last, until we started forth, at eight o'clock, for Mr. Peggotty's boat. Indeed, they were more and more brightly exhibited as the hours went on; for I thought even then, and I have no doubt now, that the consciousness of success in his determination to please, inspired him with a new delicacy of perception, and made it, subtle as it was, more easy to him. If any one had told me, then, that all this was a brilliant game, played for the excitement of the moment, for the employment of high spirits, in the thoughtless love of superiority, in a mere wasteful careless course of winning what was worthless to him, and next minute thrown away—I say, if any one had told me such a lie

WE WERE UNEXPECTEDLY AT MR PEGGOTTY'S FIRESIDE.

that night, I wonder in what manner of receiving it my indignation would have found a vent!

Probably only in an increase, had that been possible, of the romantic feelings of fidelity and friendship with which I walked beside him, over the dark wintry sands, towards the old boat; the wind sighing around us even more mournfully, than it had sighed and moaned upon the night when I first darkened Mr. Peggotty's door.

"This is a wild kind of place, Steerforth, is it not?"

"Dismal enough in the dark," he said; "and the sea roars as if it were hungry for us. Is that the boat, where I see a light yonder?"

"That's the boat," said I.

"And it's the same I saw this morning," he returned. "I came straight to it, by instinct, I suppose."

We said no more as we approached the light, but made softly for the door. I laid my hand upon the latch; and whispering Steerforth to keep close to me, went in.

A murmur of voices had been audible on the outside, and, at the moment of our entrance, a clapping of hands: which latter noise, I was surprised to see, proceeded from the generally disconsolate Mrs. Gummidge. But Mrs. Gummidge was not the only person there, who was unusually excited. Mr. Peggotty, his face lighted up with uncommon satisfaction, and laughing with all his might, held his rough arms wide open, as if for little Em'ly to run into them; Ham, with a mixed expression in his face of admiration, exultation, and a lumbering sort of bashfulness that sat upon him very well, held little Em'ly by the hand, as if he were presenting her to Mr. Peggotty; little Em'ly herself, blushing and shy, but delighted with Mr. Peggotty's delight, as her joyous eyes expressed, was stopped by our entrance (for she saw us first) in the very act of springing from Ham to nestle in Mr. Peggotty's embrace. In the first glimpse we had of them all, and at the moment of our passing from the dark cold night into the warm light room, this was the way in which they were all employed: Mrs. Gummidge in the back ground, clapping her hands like a madwoman.

The little picture was so instantaneously dissolved by our going in, that one might have doubted whether it had ever been. I was in the midst of the astonished family, face to face with Mr. Peggotty, and holding out my hand to him, when Ham shouted :

"Mas'r Davy! It's Mas'r Davy!"

In a moment we were all shaking hands with one another, and asking one another how we did, and telling one another how glad we were to meet, and all talking at once. Mr. Peggotty was so proud and overjoyed to see us, that he did not know what to say or do, but kept over and over again shaking hands with me, and then with Steerforth, and then with me, and then ruffling his shaggy hair all over his head, and laughing with such glee and triumph, that it was a treat to see him.

"Why, that you two gent'lmen—gent'lmen growed—should come to this here roof to-night, of all nights in my life," said Mr. Peggotty, "is such a thing as never happened afore, I do rightly believe! Em'ly, my darling, come here! Come here, my little witch! There's Mas'r Davy's friend, my dear! There's the gent'lman as you've heerd on, Em'ly. He comes to see you, along with Mas'r Davy, on the brightest night of your uncle's life as ever was or will be, Gorm the t'other one, and horroar for it!"

After delivering this speech all in a breath, and with extraordinary animation and pleasure, Mr. Peggotty put one of his large hands rapturously on each side of his niece's face, and kissing it a dozen times, laid it with a gentle pride and love upon his broad chest, and patted it as if his hand had been a lady's. Then he let her go; and as she ran into the little chamber where I used to sleep, looked round upon us, quite hot and out of breath with his uncommon satisfaction.

"If you two gent'lmen—gentl'men growed now, and such gent'lmen—" said Mr. Peggotty.

"So th'are, so th'are!" cried Ham. "Well said! So th'are. Mas'r Davy bor—gent'lmen growed—so th'are!"

"If you two gent'lmen, gent'lmen growed," said Mr. Peggotty, "don't ex-cuse me for being in a state of mind, when you understand matters, I'll arsk your pardon Em'ly, my dear!—She knows

I'm a going to tell," here his delight broke out again, "and has made off. Would you be so good as look arter her, Mawther, for a minute?"

Mrs. Gummidge nodded and disappeared.

"If this ain't," said Mr. Peggotty, sitting down among us by the fire, "the brightest night o' my life, I'm a shellfish—biled too—and more I can't say. This here little Em'ly, sir," in a low voice to Steerforth, "—her as you see a blushing here just now—"

Steerforth only nodded; but with such a pleased expression of interest, and of participation in Mr. Peggotty's feelings, that the latter answered him as if he had spoken.

"To be sure," said Mr. Peggotty. "That's her, and so she is. Thankee, sir."

Ham nodded to me several times, as if he would have said so too.

"This here little Em'ly of ours," said Mr. Peggotty, "has been, in our house, what I suppose (I'm a ignorant man, but that's my belief) no one but a little bright-eyed creetur *can* be in a house. She ain't my child; I never had one; but I couldn't love her more. You understand! I couldn't do it!"

"I quite understand," said Steerforth.

"I know you do, sir," returned Mr. Peggotty, "and thankee again. Mas'r Davy, he can remember what she was; you may judge for your own self what she is; but neither of you can't fully know what she has been, is, and will be, to my loving art. I am rough, sir," said Mr. Peggotty, "I am as rough as a Sea Porkypine; but no one, unless, mayhap, it is a woman, can know, I think, what our little Em'ly is to me. And betwixt ourselves," sinking his voice lower yet, "*that* woman's name ain't Missis Gummidge neither, though she has a world of merits."

Mr. Peggotty ruffled his hair again with both hands, as a further preparation for what he was going to say, and went on with a hand upon each of his knees.

"There was a certain person as had know'd our Em'ly, from the time when her father was drownded; as had seen her constant; when a babby, when a young gal, when a woman. Not much of a person to look at, he warn't," said Mr. Peggotty, "something o' my own build—rough—a good deal o' the sou-wester in him—wery salt—but, on the whole, a honest sort of a chap, with his art in the right place."

I thought I had never seen Ham grin to anything like the extent to which he sat grinning at us now.

"What does this here blessed tarpaulin go and do," said Mr. Peggotty, with his face one high noon of enjoyment, "but he loses that there art of his to our little Em'ly. He follers her about, he makes hisself a sort o' servant to her, he loses in a great measure his relish for his wittles, and in the long run he makes it clear to me wot's amiss. Now I could wish myself, you see, that our little Em'ly was in a fair way of being married. I could wish to see her, at all ewents, under articles to a honest man as had a right to defend her. I don't know how long I may live, or how soon I may die; but I know that if I was capsized, any night, in a gale of wind in Yarmouth Roads here, and was to see the town-lights shining for the last time over the rollers as I couldn't make no head against, I could go down quieter for thinking 'There's a man ashore there, iron-true to my little Em'ly, God bless her, and no wrong can touch my Em'ly while so be as that man lives!'"

Mr. Peggotty, in simple earnestness, waved his right arm, as if he were waving it at the town-lights for the last time, and then, exchanging a nod with Ham, whose eye he caught, proceeded as before.

"Well! I counsels him to speak to Em'ly. He 's big enough, but he 's bashfuller than a little un, and he don't like. So *I* speak. 'What! *Him!*' says Em'ly. '*Him* that I 've know'd so intimate so many years, and like so much! Oh, Uncle! I never can have *him*. He 's such a good fellow!' I gives her a kiss, and I says no more to her than 'My dear, you 're right to speak out, you 're to choose for yourself, you 're as free as a little bird.' Then I aways to him, and I says, 'I wish it could have been so, but it can't. But you can both be as you was, and wot I say to you is, Be as you was with her, like a man.' He says to me, a shaking of my hand, 'I will!' he says. And he was—honorable and manful—for two year going on, and we was just the same at home here as afore."

Mr. Peggotty's face, which had varied in its expression with the various stages of his narrative, now resumed all its former triumphant delight, as he laid a hand upon my knee and a hand upon Steerforth's (previously wetting them both, for the greater emphasis of the action), and divided the following speech between us:

"All of a sudden, one evening—as it might be to-night—comes little Em'ly from her work, and him with her! There ain't so much in *that*, you'll say. No, because he takes care on her, like a brother, arter dark, and indeed afore dark, and at all times. But this tarpaulin chap, he takes hold of her hand, and he cries out to me, joyful, 'Look here! This is to be my little wife!' And she says, half bold and half shy, and half a laughing and half a crying, 'Yes, uncle! If you please.'—If I please!" cried Mr. Peggotty, rolling his head in an ecstacy at the idea; "Lord, as if I should do anythink else!—'If you please, I am steadier now, and I have thought better of it, and I'll be as good a little wife as I can to him, for he's a dear good fellow!' Then Missis Gummidge, she claps her hands like a play, and you come in. There! the murder's out!" said Mr. Peggotty—"You come in! It took place this here present hour; and here's the man that'll marry her, the minute she's out of her time."

Ham staggered, as well he might, under the blow Mr. Peggotty dealt him in his unbounded joy, as a mark of confidence and friendship; but feeling called upon to say something to us, he said, with much faltering and great difficulty:

"She warn't no higher than you was, Mas'r Davy—when you first come—when I thought what she'd grow up to be. I see her grow up—gent'lmen—like a flower. I'd lay down my life for her—Mas'r Davy—Oh! most content and cheerful! She's more to me—gent'lmen—than—she's all to me that ever I can want, and more than ever I—than ever I could say. I—I love her true. There ain't a gent'lman in all the land—nor yet sailing upon all the sea—that can love his lady more than I love her, though there's many a common man—would say better—what he meant."

I thought it affecting to see such a sturdy fellow as Ham was now trembling in the strength of what he felt for the pretty little creature who had won his heart. I thought the simple confidence reposed in us by Mr. Peggotty and by himself, was, in itself, affecting. I was affected by the story altogether. How far my emotions were influenced by the recollections of my childhood, I don't know. Whether I had come there with any lingering fancy that I was still to love little Em'ly, I don't know. I know that I was filled with pleasure by all this; but, at first, with an indescribably sensitive pleasure, that a very little would have changed to pain.

Therefore, if it had depended upon me to touch the prevailing chord among them with any skill, I should have made a poor hand of it. But it depended upon Steerforth: and he did it with such address, that in a few minutes we were all as easy and as happy as it was possible to be.

"Mr. Peggotty," he said, "you are a thoroughly good fellow, and deserve to be as happy as you are to-night. My hand upon it! Ham, I give you joy, my boy. My hand upon that, too! Daisy, stir the fire, and make it a brisk one! and Mr. Peggotty, unless you can induce your gentle niece to come back (for whom I vacate this seat in the corner,) I shall go. Any gap at your fireside on such a night—such a gap least of all—I wouldn't make, for the wealth of the Indies!"

So Mr. Peggotty went into my old room to fetch little Em'ly. At first little Em'ly didn't like to come, and then Ham went. Presently they brought her to the fireside, very much confused, and very shy,—but she soon became more assured when she found how gently and respectfully Steerforth spoke to her; how skilfully he avoided anything that would embarrass her; how he talked to Mr. Peggotty of boats, and ships, and tides, and fish; how he referred to me about the time when he had seen Mr. Peggotty at Salem House; how delighted he was with the boat and all belonging to it; how lightly and easily he carried on, until he brought us, by degrees, into a charmed circle, and we were all talking away without any reserve.

Em'ly, indeed, said little all the evening; but she looked, and listened, and her face got animated, and she was charming. Steerforth told a story of a dismal shipwreck (which arose out of his talk with Mr. Peggotty), as if he saw it all before him—and little Em'ly's eyes were fastened on him all the time, as if she saw it too. He told us a merry adventure of his own, as a relief to that, with as much gaiety as if the narrative were as fresh to him as it was to us—and little Em'ly laughed until the boat rang with the musical sounds, and we all laughed (Steerforth too), in irresistible sympathy with what was so pleasant and light-hearted. He got Mr. Peggotty to sing, or rather to roar, "When the stormy winds do blow, do blow, do blow;" and he sang a sailor's song himself, so pathetically and beautifully, that I could have almost fancied that the real wind creeping sorrowfully round the house, and murmuring low through our unbroken silence, was there to listen.

As to Mrs. Gummidge, he roused that victim of despondency with a success never attained by any one else (so Mr. Peggotty informed me) since the decease of the old one. He left her so little leisure for being miserable that she said the next day she thought she must have been bewitched.

But he set up no monopoly of the general attention, or the conversation. When little Em'ly grew more courageous, and talked (but still bashfully) across the fire to me, of our old wanderings upon the beach, to pick up shells and pebbles; and when I asked her if she recollected how I used to be devoted to her; and when we both laughed and reddened, casting these looks back on the pleasant old times, so unreal to look at now; he was silent and attentive, and observed us thoughtfully. She sat, at this time, and all the evening, on the old locker in her old little corner by the fire—Ham beside her, where I used to sit. I could not satisfy myself whether it was in her own little tormenting way, or in a maidenly reserve before us, that she kept quite close to the wall, and away from him; but I observed that she did so, all the evening.

As I remember, it was almost midnight when we took our leave. We had had some biscuit and dried fish for supper, and Steerforth had produced from his pocket a full flask of Hollands, which we men (I may say we men, now, without a blush) had emptied. We parted merrily; and as they all stood crowded round the door to light us as far as they could upon our road, I saw the sweet blue eyes of little Em'ly peeping after us, from behind Ham, and heard her soft voice calling to us to be careful how we went.

"A most engaging little Beauty!" said Steerforth, taking my arm. "Well! It's a quaint place, and they are quaint company, and it's quite a new sensation to mix with them."

"How fortunate we are, too," I returned, "to have arrived to witness their happiness in that intended marriage! I never saw people so happy. How delightful to see it, and to be made the sharers in their honest joy, as we have been!"

"That's rather a chuckle-headed fellow for the girl; isn't he?" said Steerforth.

He had been so hearty with him, and with them all, that I felt a shock in this unexpected and cold reply. But turning quickly upon him, and seeing a laugh in his eyes, I answered, much relieved:

"Ah, Steerforth! It's well for you to joke about the poor! You may skirmish with Miss Dartle, or try to hide your sympathies in jest from me, but I know better. When I see how perfectly you understand them, how exquisitely you can enter into happiness like this plain fisherman's, or humour a love like my old nurse's, I know that there is not a joy or sorrow, not an emotion, of such people, that can be indifferent to you. And I admire and love you for it, Steerforth, twenty times the more!"

He stopped, and, looking in my face, said, "Daisy, I believe you are in earnest, and are good. I wish we all were!" Next moment he was gaily singing Mr. Peggotty's song, as we walked at a round pace back to Yarmouth.

CHAPTER XXII.

SOME OLD SCENES, AND SOME NEW PEOPLE.

Steerforth and I stayed for more than a fortnight in that part of the country. We were very much together, I need not say; but occasionally we were asunder for some hours at a time. He was a good sailor, and I was but an indifferent one; and when he went out boating with Mr. Peggotty, which was a favorite amusement of his, I generally remained ashore. My occupation of Peggotty's spare-room put a constraint upon me, from which he was free: for, knowing how assiduously she attended on Mr. Barkis all day, I did not like to remain out late at night; whereas Steerforth, lying at the Inn, had nothing to consult but his own humour. Thus it came about, that I heard of his making little treats for the fishermen at Mr. Peggotty's house of call, "The Willing Mind," after I was in bed, and of his being afloat, wrapped in fisherman's clothes, whole moonlight nights, and coming back when the morning tide was at flood. By this time, however, I knew that his restless nature and bold spirits delighted to find a vent in rough toil and hard weather, as in any other means of excitement that presented itself freshly to him; so none of his proceedings surprised me.

Another cause of our being sometimes apart, was, that I had naturally an interest in going over to Blunderstone, and revisiting the old familiar scenes of my childhood; while Steerforth, after being there once, had naturally no great interest in going there again. Hence, on three or four days that I can at once recal, we went our several ways after an early breakfast, and met again at a late dinner. I had no idea how he employed his time in the interval, beyond a general knowledge that he was very popular in the place, and had twenty means of actively diverting himself where another man might not have found one

For my own part, my occupation in my solitary pilgrimages was to recal every yard of the old road as I went along it, and to haunt the old spots, of which I never tired. I haunted them, as my memory had often done, and lingered among them as my younger thoughts had lingered when I was far away. The grave beneath the tree, where both my parents lay—on which I had looked out, when it was my father's only, with such curious feelings of compassion, and by which I had stood, so desolate, when it was opened to receive my pretty mother and her baby—the grave which Peggotty's own faithful care had ever since kept neat, and made a garden of, I walked near, by the hour. It lay a little off the church-yard path, in a quiet corner, not so far removed but I could read the names upon the stone as I walked to and fro, startled by the sound of the church-bell when it struck the hour, for it was like a departed voice to me. My reflections at these times were always associated with the figure I was to make in life, and the distinguished things I was to do. My echoing footsteps went to no other tune, but were as constant to that as if I had come home to build my castles in the air at a living mother's side.

There were great changes in my old home. The ragged nests, so long deserted by the rooks, were gone; and the trees were lopped and topped out of their remembered shapes. The garden had run wild, and half the windows of the house were shut up. It was occupied, but only by a poor lunatic gentleman, and the people who took care of him. He was always sitting at my little window, looking out into the church-yard; and I wondered whether his rambling thoughts ever went upon any of the fancies that used to occupy mine, on the rosy mornings when I peeped out of that same little window in my night-clothes, and saw the sheep quietly feeding in the light of the rising sun.

Our old neighbours, Mr. and Mrs. Grayper, were gone to South America, and the rain had made its way through the roof of their empty house, and stained the outer walls. Mr. Chillip was married again to a tall, raw-boned, high-nosed wife; and they had a weazen little baby, with a heavy head that it couldn't hold up, and two weak staring eyes, with which it seemed to be always wondering why it had ever been born.

It was with a singular jumble of sadness and pleasure that I used to linger about my native place, until the reddening winter sun admonished me that it was time to start on my returning walk. But, when the place was left behind, and especially when Steerforth and I were happily seated over our dinner by a blazing fire, it was delicious to think of having been there. So it was, though in a softened degree, when I went to my neat room at night; and, turning over the leaves of the crocodile-book (which was always there, upon a little table), remembered with a grateful heart how blest I was in having such a friend as Steerforth, such a friend as Peggotty, and such a substitute for what I had lost as my excellent and generous aunt.

My nearest way to Yarmouth, in coming back from these long walks, was by a ferry. It landed me on the flat between the town and the sea, which I could make straight across, and so save myself a considerable circuit by the high road. Mr. Peggotty's house being on that waste-place, and not a hundred yards out of my track, I always looked in as I went by. Steerforth was pretty sure to be there expecting me, and we went on together through the frosty air and gathering fog towards the twinkling lights of the town.

One dark evening, when I was later than usual—for I had that day been making my parting visit to Blunderstone, as we were now about to return home—I found him alone in Mr. Peggotty's house, sitting thoughtfully before the fire. He was so intent upon his own reflections that he was quite unconscious of my approach. This, indeed, he might easily have been if he had been less absorbed, for footsteps fell noiselessly on the sandy ground outside; but even my entrance failed to rouse him. I was standing close to him, looking at him; and still, with a heavy brow, he was lost in his meditations.

He gave such a start when I put my hand upon his shoulder, that he made me start too.

"You come upon me," he said, almost angrily, "like a reproachful ghost."

"I was obliged to announce myself somehow," I replied. "Have I called you down from the stars?"

"No," he answered. "No."

"Up from anywhere, then?" said I taking my seat near him.

"I was looking at the pictures in the fire," he returned.

"But you are spoiling them for me," said I, as he stirred it quickly with a piece of burning wood, striking out of it a train of red-hot sparks that went careering up the little chimney, and roaring out into the air.

"You would not have seen them," he returned. "I detest this mongrel time, neither day nor night. How late you are! Where have you been?"

"I have been taking leave of my usual walk," said I.

"And I have been sitting here," said Steerforth, glancing round the room, "thinking that all the people we found so glad on the night of our coming down, might—to judge from the present wasted air of the place—be dispersed, or dead, or come to I don't know what harm. David, I wish to God I had had a judicious father these last twenty years!"

"My dear Steerforth, what is the matter?"

"I wish with all my soul I had been better guided!" he exclaimed. "I wish with all my soul I could guide myself better!"

There was a passionate dejection in his manner that quite amazed me. He was more unlike himself than I could have supposed possible.

"It would be better to be this poor Peggotty, or his lout of a nephew," he said, getting up and leaning moodily against the chimney-piece, with his face towards the fire, "than to be myself, twenty times richer and twenty times wiser, and be the torment to myself that I have been, in this Devil's bark of a boat, within the last half hour!"

I was so confounded by the alteration in him, that at first I could only observe him in silence, as he stood leaning his head upon his hand, and looking gloomily down at the fire. At length I begged him, with all the earnestness I felt, to tell me what had occurred to cross him so unusually, and to let me sympathise with him, if I could not hope to advise him. Before I had well concluded, he began to laugh—fretfully at first, but soon with returning gaiety.

"Tut, it's nothing, Daisy! nothing!" he replied. "I told you, at the inn in London, I am heavy company for myself sometimes. I have been a nightmare to myself, just now—must have had one, I think. At odd dull times, nursery tales come up into the memory, unrecognised for what they are. I believe I have been confounding myself with the bad boy who 'didn't care,' and became food for lions—a grander kind of going to the dogs, I suppose. What old women call the horrors, have been creeping over me from head to foot. I have been afraid of myself."

"You are afraid of nothing else, I think," said I.

"Perhaps not, and yet may have enough to be afraid of too," he answered. "Well! So it goes by! I am not about to be hipped again, David; but I tell you, my good fellow, once more, that it would have been well for me (and for more than me) if I had had a steadfast and judicious father!"

His face was always full of expression, but I never saw it express such a dark kind of earnestness as when he said these words, with his glance bent on the fire.

"So much for that!" he said, making as if he tossed something light into the air with his hand,

"'Why, being gone, I am a man again,'

like Macbeth. And now for dinner! If I have not (Macbeth-like) broken up the feast with most admired disorder, Daisy."

"But where are they all, I wonder!" said I.

"God knows," said Steerforth. "After strolling to the ferry looking for you, I strolled in here and found the place deserted. That set me thinking, and you found me thinking."

The advent of Mrs. Gummidge, with a basket, explained how the house happened to be empty. She had hurried out to buy something that was needed, against Mr. Peggotty's return with the tide; and had left the door open in the meanwhile, lest Ham and little Em'ly, with whom it was an early night, should come home while she was gone. Steerforth, after very much improving Mrs. Gummidge's spirits by a cheerful salutation, and a jocose embrace, took my arm, and hurried me away.

He had improved his own spirits, no less than Mrs. Gummidge's, for they were again at their usual flow, and he was full of vivacious conversation as we went along.

"And so," he said, gaily, "we abandon this buccaneer life to-morrow, do we?"

"So we agreed," I returned. "And our places by the coach are taken, you know."

"Ay! there's no help for it, I suppose," said Steerforth. "I have almost forgotten that there is anything to do in the world but to go out tossing on the sea here. I wish there was not."

"As long as the novelty should last," said I, laughing.

"Like enough," he returned; "though there's a sarcastic meaning in that observation for an amiable piece of innocence like my young friend. Well! I dare say I am a capricious fellow, David. I know I am; but while the iron *is* hot, I can strike it vigorously too. I could pass a reasonably good examination already, as a pilot in these waters, I think."

"Mr. Peggotty says you are a wonder," I returned.

"A nautical phenomenon, eh?" laughed Steerforth.

"Indeed he does, and you know how truly; knowing how ardent you are in any pursuit you follow, and how easily you can master it. And that amazes me most in you, Steerforth—that you should be contented with such fitful uses of your powers."

"Contented?" he answered, merrily. "I am never contented, except with your freshness, my gentle Daisy. As to fitfulness, I have never learnt the art of binding myself to any of the wheels on which the Ixions of these days are turning round and round. I missed it somehow in a bad apprenticeship, and now don't care about it. You know I have bought a boat down here?"

"What an extraordinary fellow you are, Steerforth!" I exclaimed, stopping—for this was the first I had heard of it. "When you may never care to come near the place again!"

"I don't know that," he returned. "I have taken a fancy to the place. At all events," walking me briskly on, "I have bought a boat that was for sale—a clipper, Mr. Peggotty says; and so she is—and Mr. Peggotty will be master of her in my absence."

"Now I understand you, Steerforth!" said I, exultingly. "You pretend to have bought it for yourself, but you have really done so to confer a benefit on him. I might have known as much at first, knowing you. My dear kind Steerforth, how can I tell you what I think of your generosity?"

"Tush!" he answered, turning red. "The less said, the better."

"Didn't I know?" cried I, "didn't I say that there was not a joy, or sorrow, or any emotion of such honest hearts that was indifferent to you?"

"Aye, aye," he answered, "you told me all that. There let it rest. We have said enough!"

Afraid of offending him by pursuing the subject when he made so light of it, I only pursued it in my thoughts as we went on at even a quicker pace than before.

"She must be newly rigged," said Steerforth, "and I shall leave Littimer behind to see it done, that I may know she is quite complete. Did I tell you Littimer had come down?"

"No."

"Oh, yes! came down this morning, with a letter from my mother."

As our looks met, I observed that he was pale even to his lips, though he looked very steadily at me. I feared that some difference between him and his mother might have led to his being in the frame of mind in which I had found him at the solitary fireside. I hinted so.

"Oh, no!" he said, shaking his head, and giving a slight laugh. "Nothing of the sort! Yes. He is come down, that man of mine."

"The same as ever?" said I.

"The same as ever," said Steerforth. "Distant and quiet as the North Pole. He shall see to the boat being fresh named. She's the Stormy Petrel now. What does Mr. Peggotty care for Stormy Petrels! I'll have her christened again."

"By what name?" I asked.

"The Little Em'ly."

As he had continued to look steadily at me, I took it as a reminder that he objected to being extolled for his consideration. I could not help showing in my face how much it pleased me, but I said little, and he resumed his usual smile, and seemed relieved.

"But see here," he said, looking before us, "where the original little Em'ly comes! And that fellow with her, eh? Upon my soul, he's a true knight. He never leaves her!"

Ham was a boat-builder in these days, having improved a natural ingenuity in that handicraft, until he had become a skilled workman. He was in his working-dress, and looked rugged enough, but manly withal, and a very fit protector for the blooming little creature at his side. Indeed, there was a frankness in his face, an honesty, and an undisguised show of his pride in her, and his love for her which were, to me, the best of good looks. I thought, as they came towards us, that they were well matched even in that particular.

She withdrew her hand timidly from his arm as we stopped to speak to them, and blushed as she gave it to Steerforth and to me. When they passed on, after we had exchanged a few words, she did not like to replace that hand, but, still appearing timid and constrained, walked by herself. I thought all this very pretty and engaging, and Steerforth seemed to think so too, as we looked after them fading away in the light of a young moon.

Suddenly there passed us—evidently following them—a young woman whose approach we had not observed, but whose face I saw as she went by, and thought I had a faint remembrance of. She was lightly dressed; looked bold, and haggard, and flaunting, and poor; but seemed, for the time, to have given all that to the wind which was blowing, and to have nothing in her mind but going after them. As the dark distant level, absorbing their figures into itself, left but itself visible between us and the sea and clouds, her figure disappeared in like manner, still no nearer to them than before.

"That is a black shadow to be following the girl," said Steerforth, standing still; "what does it mean?"

He spoke in a low voice that sounded almost strange to me.

"She must have it in her mind to beg of them, I think," said I.

"A beggar would be no novelty," said Steerforth, "but it is a strange thing that the beggar should take that shape to-night."

"Why?" I asked him.

"For no better reason, truly, than because I was thinking," he said, after a pause, "of something like it, when it came by. Where the Devil did it come from, I wonder!"

"From the shadow of this wall, I think," said I, as we emerged upon a road on which a wall abutted.

"It's gone!" he returned looking over his shoulder. "And all ill go with it. Now for our dinner!"

But, he looked again over his shoulder towards the sea-line glimmering afar off; and yet again. And he wondered about it, in some broken expressions, several times, in the short remainder of our walk; and only seemed to forget it when the light of fire and candle shone upon us, seated warm and merry, at table.

Littimer was there, and had his usual effect upon me. When I said to him that I hoped Mrs. Steerforth and Miss Dartle were well, he answered respectfully (and of course respectably), that they were tolerably well, he thanked me, and had sent their compliments. This was all, and yet he seemed to me to say as plainly as a man could say: "You are very young, sir; you are exceedingly young."

We had almost finished dinner, when taking a step or two towards the table, from the corner where he kept watch upon us, or rather upon me, as I felt, he said to his master:

"I beg your pardon, sir. Miss Mowcher is down here."

"Who?" cried Steerforth, much astonished.

"Miss Mowcher, sir."

"Why, what on earth does *she* do here?" said Steerforth.

"It appears to be her native part of the country, sir. She informs me that she makes one of her professional visits here, every year, sir. I met her in the street this afternoon, and she wished to know if she might have the honor of waiting on you after dinner, sir."

"Do you know the Giantess in question, Daisy?" inquired Steerforth.

I was obliged to confess—I felt ashamed, even of being at this disadvantage before Littimer—that Miss Mowcher and I were wholly unacquainted.

"Then you shall know her," said Steerforth, "for she is one of the seven wonders of the world. When Miss Mowcher comes, show her in."

I felt some curiosity and excitement about this lady, especially as Steerforth burst into a fit of laughing when I referred to her, and positively refused to answer any question of which I made her the subject. I remained, therefore, in a state of considerable expectation until the cloth had been removed some half an hour, and we were sitting over our decanter of wine before the fire, when the door opened, and Littimer, with his habitual serenity quite undisturbed, announced:

"Miss Mowcher!"

I looked at the doorway and saw nothing. I was still looking at the doorway, thinking that Miss Mowcher was a long while making her appearance, when, to my infinite astonishment, there came waddling round a sofa which stood between me and it, a pursy dwarf, of about forty or forty-five, with a very large head and face, a pair of roguish grey eyes, and such extremely little arms, that, to enable herself to lay a finger archly against her snub nose, as she ogled Steerforth, she was obliged to meet the finger half-way, and lay her nose against it. Her chin, which was what is called a double-chin, was so fat that it entirely swallowed up the strings of her bonnet, bow and all. Throat she had none; waist she had none; legs she had none, worth mentioning; for though she was more than full-sized down to where her waist would have been, if she had had any, and though she terminated, as human beings generally do, in a pair of feet, she was so short that she stood at a common-sized chair as at a table, resting a bag she carried on the seat. This lady; dressed in an off-hand, easy style; bringing her nose and her forefinger together, with the difficulty I have described; standing with her head necessarily on one side, and, with one of her sharp eyes shut up, making an uncommonly knowing face; after ogling Steerforth for a few moments, broke into a torrent of words.

"What! My flower!" she pleasantly began, shaking her large head at him. "You 're there, are you! Oh, you naughty boy, fie for shame, what do you do so far away from home? Up to mischief, I 'll be bound. Oh, you 're a downy fellow, Steerforth, so you are, and I 'm another, ain't I? Ha, ha, ha! You 'd have betted a hundred pound to five, now, that you wouldn't have seen me here, wouldn't you? Bless you, man alive, I 'm everywhere. I 'm here and there, and where not, like the conjuror's half-crown in the lady's hankercher. Talking of hankerchers—*and* talking of ladies—what a comfort you are to your blessed mother, ain't you, my dear boy, over one of my shoulders, and I don't say which!"

Miss Mowcher untied her bonnet, at this passage of her discourse, threw back the strings, and sat down, panting, on a footstool in front of the fire—making a kind of arbor of the dining-table, which spread its mahogany shelter above her head.

"Oh my stars and what's-their-names!" she went on, clapping a hand on each of her little knees, and glancing shrewdly at me, "I 'm of too full a habit, that 's the fact, Steerforth. After a flight of stairs, it gives me as much trouble to draw every breath I want, as if it was a bucket of water. If you saw me looking out of an upper window, you 'd think I was a fine woman, wouldn't you?"

"I should think that wherever I saw you," replied Steerforth.

"Go along, you dog, do!" cried the little creature, making a whisk at him with the handkerchief with which she was wiping her face, "and don't be impudent! But I give you my word and honor I was at Lady Mithers's last week—*there's* a woman! How *she* wears!—and Mithers himself came into the room where I was waiting for her—*there's* a man! How *he* wears! and his wig too, for he 's had it these ten years—and he went on at that rate in the complimentary line, that I began to think that I should be obliged to ring the bell. Ha! ha! ha! He 's a pleasant wretch, but he wants principle."

"What were you doing for Lady Mithers?" asked Steerforth.

"That's tellings, my blessed infant," she retorted, tapping her nose again, screwing up her face, and twinkling her eyes like an imp of supernatural intelligence. "Never *you* mind! You 'd like to know whether I stop her hair from falling off, or dye it, or touch up her complexion, or improve her eyebrows, wouldn't you? And so you shall, my darling—when I tell you! Do you know what my great grandfather's name was?"

"No," said Steerforth.

"It was Walker, my sweet pet," replied Miss Mowcher, "and he came of a long line of Walkers, that I inherit all the Hookey estates from."

I never beheld anything approaching to Miss Mowcher's wink, except Miss Mowcher's self-possession. She had a wonderful way too, when listening to what was said to her, or when waiting for an answer to what she had said herself, of pausing with her head cunningly on one side, and one eye turned up like a magpie's. Altogether I was lost in amazement, and sat staring at her, quite oblivious, I am afraid, of the laws of politeness.

She had by this time drawn the chair to her side, and was busily engaged in producing from the bag (plunging in her short arm to the shoulder at every dive) a number of small bottles, sponges, combs, brushes, bits of flannel, little pairs of curling irons, and other instruments, which she tumbled in a heap upon the chair. From this employment she suddenly desisted, and said to Steerforth, much o my confusion:

"Who 's your friend?"

"Mr. Copperfield," said Steerforth; "he wants to know you."

"Well, then, he shall! I thought he looked as if he did!" re turned Miss Mowcher, waddling up to me, bag in hand, and laughing on me as she came. "Face like a peach!" standing on tiptoe to pinch my cheek as I sat. "Quite tempting! I 'm very fond of peaches. Happy to make your acquaintance, Mr. Copperfield, I 'm sure."

I said that I congratulated myself on having the honor to make hers, and that the happiness was mutual.

"Oh my goodness, how polite we are!" exclaimed Miss Mowcher, making a preposterous attempt to cover her large face with her morsel of a hand. "What a world of gammon and spinage it is, though, ain't it!"

This was addressed confidentially to both of us, as the morsel of a hand came away from the face, and buried itself, arm and all, in the bag again.

"What do you mean, Miss Mowcher?" said Steerforth.

"Ha! ha! ha! What a refreshing set of humbugs we are, to be sure, ain't we, my sweet child?" replied that morsel of a woman, feeling in the bag with her head on one side, and her eye in the air. "Look here!" taking something out. "Scraps of the Russian Prince's nails! Prince Alphabet turned topsy-turvy, *I* call him, for his name's got all the letters in it, higgledy-piggledy."

"The Russian Prince is a client of yours, is he?" said Steerforth.

"I believe you, my pet," replied Miss Mowcher. "I keep his nails in order for him. Twice a week! Fingers *and* toes!"

"He pays well, I hope?" said Steerforth.

"Pays as he speaks, my dear child—through the nose," replied Miss Mowcher. "None of your close shavers the Prince ain't.

You'd say so, if you saw his mustachios. Red by nature, black by art."

"By your art, of course," said Steerforth.

Miss Mowcher winked assent. "Forced to send for me. Couldn't help it. The climate affected *his* dye; it did very well in Russia, but it was no go here. You never saw such a rusty Prince in all your born days as he was. Like old iron!"

"Is that why you called him a humbug, just now?" inquired Steerforth.

"Oh, you're a broth of a boy, ain't you?" returned Miss Mowcher, shaking her head violently. "I said, what a set of humbugs we were in general, and I showed you the scraps of the Prince's nails to prove it. The Prince's nails do more for me, in private families of the genteel sort, than all my talents put together. I always carry 'em about. They're the best introduction. If Miss Mowcher cuts the Prince's nails, she *must* be all right. I give 'em away to the young ladies. They put 'em in albums, I believe. Ha! ha! ha! Upon my life, 'the whole social system' (as the men call it when they make speeches in Parliament) is a system of Prince's nails!" said this least of women, trying to fold her short arms, and nodding her large head.

Steerforth laughed heartily, and I laughed too. Miss Mowcher continuing all the time to shake her head (which was very much on one side), and to look into the air with one eye, and to wink with the other.

"Well, well!" she said, smiting her small knees, and rising, "this is not business. Come, Steerforth, let's explore the polar regions, and have it over."

She then selected two or three of the little instruments, and a little bottle, and asked (to my surprise) if the table would bear. On Steerforth's replying in the affirmative, she pushed a chair against it, and begging the assistance of my hand, mounted up, pretty nimbly, to the top, as if it were a stage.

"If either of you saw my ankles," she said, when she was safely elevated, "say so, and I'll go home and destroy myself."

"*I* did not," said Steerforth.

"*I* did not," said I.

"Well then," cried Miss Mowcher, "I'll consent to live. Now, ducky, ducky, ducky, come to Mrs. Bond and be killed!"

This was an invitation to Steerforth to place himself under her hands; who, accordingly, sat himself down, with his back to the table, and his laughing face towards me, and submitted his head to her inspection, evidently for no other purpose than our entertainment. To see Miss Mowcher standing over him, looking at his rich profusion of brown hair through a large round magnifying glass, which she took out of her pocket, was a most amazing spectacle.

"*You're* a pretty fellow!" said Miss Mowcher, after a brief inspection. "You'd be as bald as a friar on the top of your head in twelve months, but for me. Just half-a-minute, my young friend, and we'll give you a polishing that shall keep your curls on for the next ten years!"

With this, she tilted some of the contents of the little bottle on to one of the little bits of flannel, and, again imparting some of the virtues of that preparation to one of the little brushes, began rubbing and scraping away with both on the crown of Steerforth's head in the busiest manner I ever witnessed, talking all the time.

"There's Charley Pyegrave, the duke's son," she said. "You know Charley?" peeping round into his face.

"A little," said Steerforth.

"What a man *he* is! *There's* a whisker! As to Charley's legs, if they were only a pair (which they ain't), they'd defy competition. Would you believe he tried to do without me—in the Life-Guards, too?"

"Mad!" said Steerforth.

"It looks like it. However, mad or sane, he tried," returned Miss Mowcher. "What does he do, but, lo and behold you, he goes into a perfumer's shop, and wants to buy a bottle of the Madagascar Liquid?"

"Charley does?" said Steerforth.

"Charley does. But they haven't got any of the Madagascar Liquid."

"What is it? Something to drink?" asked Steerforth.

"To drink?" returned Miss Mowcher, stopping to slap his cheek. "To doctor his own moustachios with, you *know*. There was a

I MAKE THE ACQUAINTANCE OF MISS MOWCHER.

woman in the shop—elderly female—quite a Griffin—who had never even heard of it by name. 'Begging pardon, sir,' said the Griffin to Charley, 'it's not—not—not ROUGE, is it?' 'Rouge,' said Charley to the Griffin. 'What the unmentionable to ears polite, do you think I want with rouge?' 'No offence, sir,' said the Griffin; 'we have it asked for by so many names, I thought it might be.' Now that, my child," continued Miss Mowcher, rubbing all the time as busily as ever, "is another instance of the refreshing humbug I was speaking of. *I* do something in that way myself—perhaps a good deal—perhaps a little—sharp 's the word, my dear boy—never mind!"

"In what way do you mean? In the rouge way?" said Steerforth.

"Put this and that together, my tender pupil," returned the wary Mowcher, touching her nose, "work it by the rule of Secrets in all trades, and the product will give you the desired result. I say *I* do a little in that way myself. One Dowager, *she* calls it lip-salve. Another, *she* calls it gloves. Another, *she* calls it tucker-edging. Another, *she* calls it a fan. *I* call it whatever *they* call it. I supply it for 'em, but we keep up the trick so, to one another, and make believe with such a face, that they'd as soon think of laying it on before a whole drawing-room as before me. And when I wait upon 'em, they'll say to me sometimes—*with it on*—thick, and no mistake—'How am I looking, Mowcher? Am I pale?' Ha! ha! ha! ha! Isn't *that* refreshing, my young friend?"

I never did in my days behold anything like Mowcher as she stood upon the dining-table, intensely enjoying this refreshment, rubbing busily at Steerforth's head, and winking at me over it.

"Ah!" she said. "Such things are not much in demand hereabouts. That sets me off again! I haven't seen a pretty woman since I've been here, Jemmy."

"No?" said Steerforth.

"Not the ghost of one," replied Miss Mowcher.

"We could show her the substance of one, I think?" said Steerforth, addressing his eyes to mine. "Eh, Daisy?"

"Yes, indeed," said I.

"Aha?" cried the little creature, glancing sharply at my face, and then peeping round at Steerforth's. "Umph?"

The first exclamation sounded like a question put to both of us, and the second like a question put to Steerforth only. She seemed to have found no answer to either, but continued to rub, with her head on one side and her eye turned up, as if she were looking for an answer in the air, and were confident of its appearing presently.

"A sister of yours, Mr. Copperfield?" she cried, after a pause, and still keeping the same look out. "Aye, aye?"

"No," said Steerforth, before I could reply. "Nothing of the sort. On the contrary, Mr. Copperfield used—or I am much mistaken—to have a great admiration for her."

"Why, hasn't he now?" returned Miss Mowcher. "Is he fickle? oh, for shame! Did he sip every flower, and change every hour, until Polly his passion requited?—Is her name Polly?"

The Elfin suddenness with which she pounced upon me with this question, and a searching look, quite disconcerted me for a moment.

"No, Miss Mowcher," I replied. "Her name is Emily."

"Aha?" she cried exactly as before. "Umph? What a rattle I am! Mr. Copperfield, ain't I volatile?"

Her tone and look implied something that was not agreeable to me in connexion with the subject. So I said, in a graver manner than any of us had yet assumed:

"She is as virtuous as she is pretty. She is engaged to be married to a most worthy and deserving man in her own station of life. I esteem her for her good sense, as much as I admire her for her good looks."

"Well said!" cried Steerforth. "Hear, hear, hear! Now I'll quench the curiosity of this little Fatima, my dear Daisy, by leaving her nothing to guess at. She is at present apprenticed, Miss Mowcher, or articled, or whatever it may be, to Omer and Joram, Haberdashers, Milliners, and so forth, in this town. Do you observe? Omer and Joram. The promise of which my friend has spoken, is made and entered into with her cousin; Christian name, Ham; surname, Peggotty; occupation, boat-builder; also of this town. She lives with a relative; Christian name, unknown; surname, Peggotty; occupation, seafaring; also of this town. She is the prettiest and most engaging little fairy in the world. I admire her—as my friend does—exceedingly. If it were not that I might appear to disparage her Intended, which I know my friend would not like, I would add, that to *me* she seems to be throwing herself away; that I am sure she might do better; and that I swear she was born to be a lady."

Miss Mowcher listened to these words, which were very slowly and distinctly spoken, with her head on one side, and her eye in the air as if she were still looking for that answer. When he ceased, she became brisk again in an instant, and rattled away with surprising volubility.

"Oh! And that's all about it, is it?" she exclaimed, trimming his whiskers with a little restless pair of scissors, that went glancing round his head in all directions. "Very well: *very* well! Quite a long story. Ought to end, 'and they lived happy ever afterwards;' oughtn't it? Ah! What's that game at forfeits? I love my love with an E, because she's enticing; I hate her with an E, because she's engaged. I took her to the sign of the exquisite, and treated her with an elopement, her name's Emily, and she lives in the east? Ha! ha! ha! Mr. Copperfield, ain't I volatile?"

Merely looking at me with extravagant slyness, and not waiting for any reply, she continued, without drawing breath:

"There! If ever any scapegrace was trimmed and touched up to perfection, you are, Steerforth. If I understand any noddle in the world, I understand yours. Do you hear me when I tell you that, my darling? I understand yours," peeping down into his face. "Now you may mizzle, Jemmy (as we say at Court), and if Mr. Copperfield will take the chair I'll operate on him."

"What do you say, Daisy?" inquired Steerforth, laughing, and resigning his seat. "Will you be improved?"

"Thank you, Miss Mowcher, not this evening."

"Don't say no," returned the little woman, looking at me with the aspect of a connoisseur; "a little bit more eyebrow?"

"Thank you," I returned, "some other time."

"Have it carried half a quarter of an inch towards the temple," said Miss Mowcher. "We can do it in a fortnight."

"No, I thank you. Not at present."

"Go in for a tip," she urged. "No? Let's get the scaffolding up, then, for a pair of whiskers. Come!"

I could not help blushing as I declined, for I felt we were on my weak point, now. But Miss Mowcher, finding that I was not at present disposed for any decoration within the range of her art, and that I was, for the time being, proof against the blandishments of the small bottle which she held up before one eye to enforce her persuasions, said we would make a beginning on an early day, and requested the aid of my hand to descend from her elevated station. Thus assisted, she skipped down with much agility, and began to tie her double chin into her bonnet.

"The fee," said Steerforth, "is ——"

"Five bob," replied Miss Mowcher, "and dirt-cheap, my chicken. Ain't I volatile, Mr. Copperfield?"

I replied politely: "Not at all." But I thought she was rather so, when she tossed up his two half-crowns like a goblin pieman, caught them, dropped them in her pocket, and gave it a loud slap.

"That's the Till!" observed Miss Mowcher, standing at the chair again, and replacing in the bag the miscellaneous collection of little objects she had emptied out of it. "Have I got all my traps? It seems so. It won't do to be like long Ned Beadwood, when they took him to church 'to marry him to somebody,' as he says, and left the bride behind. Ha! ha! ha! A wicked rascal, Ned, but droll! Now, I know I'm going to break your hearts, but I am forced to leave you. You must call up all your fortitude, and try to bear it. Good bye, Mr. Copperfield! Take care of yourself, Jockey of Norfolk! How I *have* been rattling on! It's all the fault of you two wretches. *I* forgive you! 'Bob swore!'—as the Englishman said for 'Good night,' when he first learnt French, and thought it so like English. 'Bob swore,' my ducks!"

With the bag slung over her arm, and rattling as she waddled away, she waddled to the door; where she stopped to inquire if she should leave us a lock of her hair. "Ain't I volatile?" she added, as a commentary on this offer, and, with her finger on her nose, departed.

Steerforth laughed to that degree, that it was impossible for me to help laughing too; though I am not sure I should have done so, but for this inducement. When we had had our laugh quite out, which was after some time, he told me that Miss Mowcher had quite an extensive connexion, and made herself useful to a variety of people in a variety of ways. Some people trifled with her as a mere oddity, he said; but she was as shrewdly and sharply observant as any one he knew, and as long-headed as she was short-armed. He told me that what she had said of being here, and there, and everywhere, was true enough; for she made little darts into the provinces, and seemed to pick up customers everywhere, and to know everybody. I asked him what her disposition was: whether it was at all mischievous, and if her sympathies were generally on the right side of things: but, not succeeding in attracting his attention to these questions after two or three attempts, I forbore or forgot to repeat them. He told me instead, with much rapidity, a good deal about her skill, and her profits; and about her being a scientific cupper, if I should ever have occasion for her services in that capacity.

She was the principal theme of our conversation during the evening: and when we parted for the night Steerforth called after me over the bannisters, "Bob swore!" as I went down stairs.

I was surprised when I came to Mr. Barkis's house to find Ham walking up and down in front of it, and still more surprised to learn from him that little Em'ly was inside. I naturally inquired why he was not there too, instead of pacing the street by himself?

"Why, you see, Mas'r Davy," he rejoined, in a hesitating manner, "Em'ly, she's talking to some 'un in here."

"I should have thought," said I smiling, "that that was a reason for your being in here too, Ham."

"Well, Mas'r Davy, in a general way, so 't would be," he returned; "but look'ee here, Mas'r Davy," lowering his voice, and speaking very gravely. "It's a young woman, sir—a young woman that Em'ly knowed once, and doen't ought to know no more."

When I heard these words, a light began to fall upon the figure I had seen following them, some hours ago.

"It's a poor wurem, Mas'r Davy," said Ham, "as is trod under foot by all the town. Up street and down street. The mowld o the church-yard don't hold any that the folk shrink away from more."

"Did I see her to-night, Ham, on the sands, after we met you?"

"Keeping us in sight?" said Ham. "It's like you did, Mas'r Davy. Not that I know'd, then, she was theer, sir, but along of her creeping soon arterwards under Em'ly's little winder, when she see the light come, and whisp'ring 'Em'ly, Em'ly, for Christ's sake have a woman's heart towards me. I was once like you!' Those was solemn words, Mas'r Davy, for to hear!"

"They were indeed, Ham. What did Em'ly do?"

"Says Em'ly, 'Martha, is it you? Oh, Martha, can it be you!'—for they had sat at work together, many a day, at Mr. Omer's."

"I recollect her now!" cried I, recalling one of the two girls I had seen when I first went there. "I recollect her quite well!"

"Martha Endell," said Ham. "Two or three year older than Em'ly, but was at the school with her."

"I never heard her name," said I. "I didn't mean to interrupt you."

"For the matter o' that, Mas'r Davy," replied Ham, "all's told a'most in them words, 'Em'ly, Em'ly, for Christ's sake have a woman's heart towards me. I was once like you!' She wanted to speak to Em'ly. Em'ly couldn't speak to her theer, for her loving uncle was come home, and he wouldn't—no, Mas'r Davy," said Ham, with great earnestness, "he couldn't, kind-naturd, tender-hearted as he is, see them two together, side by side, for all the treasures that's wrecked in the sea."

I felt how true this was. I knew it on the instant, quite as well as Ham.

"So Em'ly writes in pencil on a bit of paper," he pursued, "and gives it to her out o' winder to bring here. 'Show that,' she says, 'to my aunt, Mrs. Barkis, and she'll set you down by her fire, for the love of me, till uncle is gone out, and I can come.' By-and-by she tells me what I tells you, Mas'r Davy, and asks me to bring her. What can I do? She doen't ought to know any such, but I can't deny her, when the tears is on her face."

He put his hand into the breast of his shaggy jacket, and took out with great care a pretty little purse.

MARTHA.

"And if I could deny her when the tears was on her face, Mas'r Davy," said Ham, tenderly adjusting it on the rough palm of his hand, "how could I deny her when she give me this to carry for her—knowing what she brought it for? Such a toy as it is!" said Ham, thoughtfully looking on it. "With such a little money in it, Em'ly my dear!"

I shook him warmly by the hand when he had put it away again—for that was more satisfactory to me than saying anything—and we walked up and down for a minute or two, in silence. The door opened then, and Peggotty appeared, beckoning to Ham to come in. I would have kept away, but she came after me, entreating me to come in too. Even then, I would have avoided the room where they all were, but for its being the neat-tiled kitchen I have mentioned more than once. The door opening immediately into it, I found myself among them, before I considered whither I was going.

The girl—the same I had seen upon the sands—was near the fire. She was sitting on the ground, with her head and one arm lying on a chair. I fancied, from the disposition of her figure, that Em'ly had but newly risen from the chair, and that the forlorn head might perhaps have been lying on her lap. I saw but little of the girl's face, over which her hair fell loose and scattered, as if she had been disordering it with her own hands; but I saw that she was young, and of a fair complexion. Peggotty had been crying. So had little Em'ly. Not a word was spoken when we first went in; and the Dutch clock by the dresser seemed, in the silence, to tick twice as loud as usual.

Em'ly spoke first.

"Martha wants," she said to Ham, "to go to London."

"Why to London?" returned Ham.

He stood between them, looking on the prostrate girl with a mixture of compassion for her, and of jealousy of her holding any companionship with her whom he loved so well, which I have always remembered distinctly. They both spoke as if she were ill; in a soft, suppressed tone that was plainly heard, although it hardly rose above a whisper.

"Better there than here," said a third voice aloud—Martha's, though she did not move. "No one knows me there. Everybody knows me here."

"What will she do there?" inquired Ham.

She lifted up her head, and looked darkly round at him for a moment; then laid it down again, and curved her right arm about her neck, as a woman in a fever, or in an agony of pain from a shot, might twist herself.

"She will try to do well," said little Em'ly. "You don't know what she has said to us. Does he—do they—aunt?"

Peggotty shook her head compassionately.

"I'll try," said Martha, "if you'll help me away. I never can do worse than I have done here. I may do better. Oh!" with a dreadful shiver, "take me out of these streets, where the whole town knows me from a child!"

As Em'ly held out her hand to Ham, I saw him put in it a little canvas bag. She took it, as if she thought it were her purse, and made a step or two forward; but finding her mistake, came back to where he had retired near me, and showed it to him.

"It's all yourn, Em'ly," I could hear him say. "I haven't nowt in all the wureld that ain't yourn, my dear. It ain't of no delight to me, except for you!"

The tears rose freshly in her eyes, but she turned away, and went to Martha. What she gave her, I don't know. I saw her stooping over her, and putting money in her bosom. She whispered something, and asked was that enough? "More than enough," the other said, and took her hand and kissed it.

Then Martha arose, and gathering her shawl about her, covering her face with it, and weeping aloud, went slowly to the door. She stopped a moment before going out, as if she would have uttered something or turned back; but no word passed her lips. Making the same low, dreary, wretched moaning in her shawl, she went away.

As the door closed, little Em'ly looked at us three in a hurried manner, and then hid her face in her hands, and fell to sobbing.

"Doen't, Em'ly!" said Ham, tapping her gently on the shoulder "Doen't, my dear! You doen't ought to cry so, pretty!"

"Oh, Ham!" she exclaimed, still weeping pitifully, "I am not as good a girl as I ought to be! I know I have not the thankful heart, sometimes, I ought to have!"

"Yes, yes, you have, I'm sure," said Ham.

"No! no! no!" cried little Em'ly, sobbing, and shaking her head, "I am not as good a girl as I ought to be. Not near! not near!" and still she cried, as if her heart would break.

"I try your love too much I know I do!" she sobbed. "I'm often cross to you, and changeable with you, when I ought to be far different. You are never so to me. Why am I ever so to you, when I should think of nothing but how to be grateful, and to make you happy!"

"You always make me so," said Ham, "my dear! I am happy in the sight of you. I am happy all day long, in the thoughts of you."

"Ah! that's not enough!" she cried. "That is because you are good; not because I am! Oh, my dear, it might have been a better fortune for you, if you had been fond of some one else—of some one steadier and much worthier than me, who was all bound up in you, and never vain and changeable like me!"

"Poor little tender-heart," said Ham, in a low voice. "Martha has overset her, altogether."

"Please, aunt," sobbed Em'ly, "come here, and let me lay my head upon you. Oh, I am very miserable to-night, aunt! Oh, I am not as good a girl as I ought to be. I am not, I know!"

Peggotty had hastened to the chair before the fire. Em'ly, with her arms around her neck, kneeled by her, looking up most earnestly into her face.

"Oh, pray, aunt, try to help me! Ham, dear, try to help me! Mr. David, for the sake of old times, do, please, try to help me! I want to be a better girl than I am. I want to feel a hundred times more thankful than I do. I want to feel more, what a blessed thing it is to be the wife of a good man, and to lead a peaceful life. Oh me, oh me! Oh, my heart, my heart!"

She dropped her face on my old nurse's breast, and, ceasing this supplication, which in its agony and grief was half a woman's, half a child's, as all her manner was (being, in that, more natural, and better suited to her beauty, as I thought, than any other manner could have been), wept silently, while my old nurse hushed her like an infant.

She got calmer by degrees, and then we soothed her; now talking encouragingly, and now jesting a little with her, until she began to raise her head and speak to us. So we got on, until she was able to smile, and then to laugh, and then to sit up, half ashamed; while Peggotty recalled her stray ringlets, dried her eyes, and made her neat again, lest her uncle should wonder, when she got home, why his darling had been crying.

I saw her do, that night, what I had never seen her do before I saw her innocently kiss her chosen husband on the cheek, and creep close to his bluff form as if it were her best support. When they went away together, in the waning moonlight, and I looked after them, comparing their departure in my mind with Martha's, I saw that she held his arm with both her hands, and still kept close to him.

CHAPTER XXIII.

I CORROBORATE MR. DICK, AND CHOOSE A PROFESSION.

When I awoke in the morning I thought very much of little Em'ly, and her emotion last night, after Martha had left. I felt as if I had come into the knowledge of those domestic weaknesses and tendernesses in a sacred confidence, and that to disclose them, even to Steerforth, would be wrong. I had no gentler feeling towards any one than towards the pretty creature who had been my playmate, and whom I have always been persuaded, and shall always be persuaded, to my dying day, I then devotedly loved. The repetition to any ears—even to Steerforth's—of what she had been unable to repress when her heart lay open to me by an accident, I felt, would be a rough deed, unworthy of myself, unworthy of the light of our pure childhood, which I always saw encircling her head. I made a resolution, therefore, to keep it in my own breast; and there it gave her image a new grace.

While we were at breakfast, a letter was delivered to me from my aunt. As it contained matter on which I thought Steerforth could advise me as well as any one, and on which I knew I should be delighted to consult him, I resolved to make it a subject of discussion on our journey home. For the present we had enough to do, in taking leave of all our friends. Mr. Barkis was far from being the last among them, in his regret at our departure; and I believe would even have opened the box again, and sacrificed another guinea, if it would have kept us eight-and-forty hours in Yarmouth. Peggotty, and all her family, were full of grief at our going. The whole house of Omer and Joram turned out to bid us good bye; and there were so many seafaring volunteers in attendance on Steerforth, when our portmanteaus went to the coach, that if we had had the baggage of a regiment with us, we should hardly have wanted porters to carry it. In a word, we departed to the regret and admiration of all concerned, and left a great many people very sorry behind us.

"Do you stay long here, Littimer?" said I, as he stood waiting to see the coach start.

"No, sir," he replied; "probably not very long, sir."

"He can hardly say just now," observed Steerforth, carelessly. "He knows what he has to do, and he 'll do it."

"That I am sure he will," said I.

Littimer touched his hat in acknowledgement of my good opinion, and I felt about eight years old. He touched it once more, wishing us a good journey, and we left him standing on the pavement, as respectable a mystery as any pyramid in Egypt.

For some little time we held no conversation, Steerforth being unusually silent, and I being sufficiently engaged in wondering, within myself, when I should see the old places again, and what new changes might happen to me or them in the meanwhile. At length Steerforth, becoming gay and talkative in a moment, as he could become anything he liked at any moment, pulled me by the arm:

"Find a voice, David. What about the letter you were speaking of at breakfast?"

"Oh!" said I, taking it out of my pocket. "It 's from my aunt."

"And what does she say, requiring consideration?"

"Why, she reminds me, Steerforth," said I, "that I came out on this expedition to look about me, and to think a little."

"Which, of course, you have done?"

"Indeed, I can't say I have, particularly. To tell you the truth, I am afraid I had forgotten it."

"Well! look about you now, and make up for your negligence," said Steerforth. "Look to the right, and you'll see a flat country, with a good deal of marsh in it; look to the left, and you'll see the same. Look to the front, and you'll find no difference; look to the rear, and there it is still."

I laughed, and replied that I saw no suitable profession in the whole prospect; which was perhaps to be attributed to its flatness.

"What says our aunt on the subject?" inquired Steerforth, glancing at the letter in my hand. "Does she suggest anything?"

"Why, yes," said I. "She asks me, here, if I think I should like to be a proctor? What do you think of it?"

"Well, I don't know," replied Steerforth, coolly. "You may as well do that as anything else, I suppose."

I could not help laughing again, at his balancing all callings and professions so equally, and I told him so.

"What *is* a proctor, Steerforth?" said I.

"Why, he is a sort of monkish attorney," said Steerforth. "He is, to some faded courts held in Doctors' Commons—a lazy old nook near St. Paul's Churchyard—what solicitors are to the courts of law and equity. He is a functionary whose existence, in the natural course of things, would have terminated about two hundred years ago. I can tell you best what he is, by telling you what Doctors' Commons is. It 's a little out-of-the-way place, where they administer what is called ecclesiastical law, and play all kinds of tricks with obsolete old monsters of acts of Parliament, which three-fourths of the world know nothing about, and the other fourth supposes to have been dug up, in a fossil state, in the days of the Edwards. It 's a place that has an ancient monopoly in suits about people's wills, and people's marriages, and disputes among ships and boats."

"Nonsense, Steerforth!" I exclaimed. "You don't mean to say

that there is any affinity between nautical matters and ecclesiastical matters?"

"I don't, indeed, my dear boy," he returned; "but I mean to say that they are managed and decided by the same set of people, down in that same Doctors' Commons. You shall go there one day, and find them blundering through half the nautical terms in Young's Dictionary, apropos of the 'Nancy' having run down the 'Sarah Jane,' or Mr. Peggotty and the Yarmouth boatmen having put off in a gale of wind with an anchor and cable to the 'Nelson' Indiaman in distress; and you shall go there another day, and find them deep in the evidence, pro and con, respecting a clergyman who has misbehaved himself; and you shall find the judge in the nautical case, the advocate in the clergyman case, or contrariwise. They are like actors; now a man's judge, and now he is not a judge: now he 's one thing, now he 's another; now he 's something else, change and change about; but it 's always a very pleasant, profitable, little affair of private theatricals, presented to an uncommonly select audience."

"But advocates and proctors are not one and the same?" said I, a little puzzled. "Are they?"

"No," returned Steerforth, "the advocates are civilians—men who have taken a doctor's degree at college—which is the first reason of my knowing anything about it. The proctors employ the advocates. Both get very comfortable fees, and altogether they make a mighty snug little party. On the whole, I would recommend you to take to Doctors' Commons kindly, David. They plume themselves on their gentility there, I can tell you, if that's any satisfaction."

I made allowance for Steerforth's light way of treating the subject, and, considering it with reference to the staid air of gravity and antiquity which I associated with that "lazy old nook near St. Paul's Churchyard," did not feel indisposed towards my aunt's suggestion, which she left to my free decision, making no scruple of telling me that it had occurred to her, on her lately visiting her own proctor in Doctors' Commons for the purpose of settling her will in my favor.

"That's a laudable proceeding on the part of our aunt, at all events," said Steerforth, when I mentioned it; and one deserving of all encouragement. Daisy, my advice is that you take kindly to Doctors' Commons."

I quite made up my mind to do so. I then told Steerforth that my aunt was in town awaiting me (as I found from her letter) and that she had taken lodgings for a week at a kind of private hotel in Lincoln's Inn Fields, where there was a stone staircase, and a convenient door in the roof; my aunt being firmly persuaded that every house in London was going to be burnt down every night.

We achieved the rest of our journey pleasantly, sometimes recurring to Doctors' Commons, and anticipating the distant days when I should be a proctor there, which Steerforth pictured in a variety of humorous and whimsical lights, that made us both merry. When we came to our journey's end, he went home, engaging to call upon me next day but one: and I drove to Lincoln's Inn Fields, where I found my aunt up, and waiting supper.

If I had been round the world since we parted, we could hardly have been better pleased to meet again. My aunt cried outright as she embraced me; and said, pretending to laugh, that if my poor mother had been alive, that silly little creature would have shed tears, she had no doubt.

"So you have left Mr. Dick behind, aunt?" said I. "I am sorry for that. Ah, Janet, how do you do?"

As Janet curtsied, hoping I was well, I observed my aunt's visage lengthen very much.

"I am very sorry for it, too," said my aunt, rubbing her nose. "I have had no peace of mind, Trot, since I have been here."

Before I could ask why, she told me.

"I am convinced," said my aunt; laying her hand with melancholy firmness on the table, "that Dick's character is not a character to keep the donkies off. I am confident he wants strength of purpose. I ought to have left Janet at home, instead, and then my mind might perhaps have been at ease. If ever there was a donkey trespassing on my green," said my aunt, with emphasis, "there was one this afternoon at four o'clock. A cold feeling came over me from head to foot, and I *know* it was a donkey!"

I tried to comfort her on this point, but she rejected consolation.

"It was a donkey," said my aunt; "and it was the one with the stumpy tail which that Murdering sister of a woman rode, when she came to my house." This had been, ever since, the only name my aunt knew for Miss Murdstone. "If there is any donkey in Dover, whose audacity it is harder to me to bear than another's, that," said my aunt, striking the table, "is the animal!"

Janet ventured to suggest that my aunt might be disturbing herself unnecessarily, and that she believed the donkey in question was then engaged in the sand and gravel line of business, and was not available for purposes of trespass. But my aunt wouldn't hear it.

Supper was comfortably served and hot, though my aunt's rooms were very high up—whether that she might have more stone stairs for her money, or might be nearer to the door in the roof, I don't know—and consisted of a roast fowl, a steak, and some vegetables, to all of which I did ample justice, and which were all excellent. But my aunt had her own ideas concerning London provision, and ate but little.

"I suppose this unfortunate fowl was born and brought up in a cellar," said my aunt, "and never took the air except on a hackney coach-stand. I *hope* the steak may be beef, but I don't believe it. Nothing's genuine in the place, in my opinion, but the dirt."

"Don't you think the fowl may have come out of the country, aunt?" I hinted.

"Certainly not," returned my aunt. "It would be no pleasure to a London tradesman to sell anything which was what he pretended it was."

I did not venture to controvert this opinion, but I made a good supper, which it greatly satisfied her to see me do. When the table was cleared, Janet assisted her to arrange her hair, to put on her nightcap, which was of a smarter construction than usual ("in case of fire," my aunt said), and to fold her gown back over her knees, these being her usual preparations for warming herself before going to bed. I then made her, according to certain established regulations from which no deviation, however slight, could ever be permitted, a glass of hot white wine and water, and a slice of toast cut into long thin strips. With these accompaniments we were left alone to finish the evening, my aunt sitting opposite to me drinking her wine and water; soaking her strips of toast in it, one by one, before eating them; and looking benignantly on me, from among the borders of her nightcap.

"Well, Trot," she began, "what do you think of the proctor plan? Or have you not begun to think about it yet?"

"I have thought a good deal about it, my dear aunt, and I have talked a good deal about it with Steerforth. I like it very much indeed. I like it exceedingly."

"Come!" said my aunt. "That's cheering!"

"I have only one difficulty, aunt."

"Say what it is, Trot," she returned.

"Why, I want to ask, aunt, as this seems, from what I under stand, to be a limited profession, whether my entrance into it would not be very expensive?"

"It will cost," returned my aunt, "to article you, just a thousand pounds."

"Now, my dear aunt," said I, drawing my chair nearer, "I am uneasy in my mind about that. It's a large sum of money. You have expended a great deal on my education, and have always been as liberal to me in all things as it was possible to be. You have been the soul of generosity. Surely there are some ways in which I might begin life with hardly any outlay, and yet begin with a good hope of getting on by resolution and exertion. Are you sure that it would not be better to try that course? Are you certain that you can afford to part with so much money, and that it is right it should be so expended? I only ask you, my second mother, to consider. Are you certain?"

My aunt finished eating the piece of toast on which she was then engaged, looking me full in the face all the while; and then setting her glass on the chimney-piece, and folding her hands upon her folded skirts, replied as follows:

"Trot, my child, if I have any object in life, it is to provide for your being a good, sensible, and a happy man. I am bent upon it—so is Dick. I should like some people that I know to hear Dick's conversation on the subject. Its sagacity is wonderful. But no one knows the resources of that man's intellect, except myself!"

She stopped for a moment to take my hand between hers, and went on:

"It's in vain, Trot, to recall the past, unless it works some influence upon the present. Perhaps I might have been better friends with your poor father. Perhaps I might have been better friends with that poor child your mother, even after your sister Betsey Trotwood disappointed me. When you came to me, a little runaway boy, all dusty and wayworn, perhaps I thought so. From that time until now, Trot, you have ever been a credit to me and a pride and pleasure. I have no other claim upon my means; at least"—here to my surprise she hesitated, and was confused—" no, I have *no* other claim upon my means—and you are my adopted child. Only be a loving child to me in my age, and bear with my whims and fancies; and you will do more for an old woman whose prime of life was not so happy or conciliating as it might have been, than ever that old woman did for you."

It was the first time I had heard my aunt refer to her past history. There was a magnanimity in her quiet way of doing so, and of dismissing it, which would have exalted her in my respect and affection, if any thing could.

"All is agreed and understood between us now, Trot," said my aunt, "and we need talk of this no more. Give me a kiss, and we'll go to the Commons after breakfast to-morrow."

We had a long chat by the fire before we went to bed. I slept in a room on the same floor with my aunt's, and was a little disturbed in the course of the night by her knocking at my door, as often as she was agitated by a distant sound of hackney-coaches or market-carts, and inquiring "If I heard the engines?" But towards morning she slept better, and suffered me to do so too.

At about mid-day, we set out for the offices of Messrs. Spenlow and Jorkins in Doctors' Commons. My aunt, who had this other general opinion in reference to London, that every man she saw was a pickpocket, gave me her purse to carry for her, which had ten guineas in it and some silver.

We made a pause at the toy-shop in Fleet-street, to see the giants of Saint Dunstan's strike upon the bells—we had timed our going, so as to catch them at it, at twelve o'clock—and then went on towards Ludgate Hill, and St. Paul's Churchyard. We were crossing to the former place, when I found that my aunt greatly accelerated her speed, and looked frightened. I observed, at the same time, that a lowering ill-dressed man who had stopped and stared at us in passing, a little before, was coming so close after us, as to brush against her.

"Trot! my dear Trot!" cried my aunt, in a terrified whisper, and pressing my arm. "I don't know what I am to do."

"Don't be alarmed," said I. "There's nothing to be afraid of. Step into a shop, and I'll soon get rid of this fellow."

"No, no, child!" she returned. "Don't speak to him for the world. I entreat, I order you!"

"Good Heaven, aunt!" said I. "He is nothing but a sturdy beggar."

"You don't know what he is!" replied my aunt. "You don't know who he is! You don't know what you say!"

We had stopped in an empty doorway, while this was passing, and he had stopped too.

"Don't look at him!" said my aunt, as I turned my head indignantly, "but get me a coach, my dear, and wait for me in St. Paul's Churchyard."

"Wait for you?" I repeated.

"Yes," rejoined my aunt, "I must go alone. I must go with him."

"With him, aunt? This man?"

"I am in my senses," she replied, "and I tell you I *must*. Get me a coach!"

However much astonished I might be, I was sensible that I had no right to refuse compliance with such a peremptory command. I hurried away a few paces, and called a hackney chariot which was passing empty. Almost before I could let down the steps, my aunt sprang in, I don't know how, and the man followed. She waved her hand to me to go away, so earnestly, that, all confounded as I was, I turned from them at once. In doing so I heard her say to the coachman, "Drive anywhere! Drive straight on!" and presently the chariot passed me, going up the hill.

What Mr. Dick had told me, and what I had supposed to be a delusion of his, now came into my mind. I could not doubt that this person was the person of whom he had made such mysterious mention, though what the nature of his hold upon my aunt could possibly be, I was quite unable to imagine. After half an hour's cooling in the churchyard, I saw the chariot coming back. The driver stopped beside me, and my aunt was sitting in it alone.

She had not yet sufficiently recovered from her agitation to be quite prepared for the visit we had to make. She desired me to get into the chariot, and tell the coachman to drive slowly up and down a little while. She said no more, except, "My dear child, never ask me what it was, and don't refer to it," until she had perfectly regained her composure, when she told me she was quite herself now, and we might get out. On her giving me her purse, to pay the driver, I found that all the guineas were gone, and only the loose silver remained.

Doctors' Commons was approached by a little low archway. Before we had taken many paces down the street beyond it, the noise of the city seemed to melt, as if by magic, into a softened distance. A few dull courts, and narrow ways, brought us to the sky-lighted offices of Spenlow and Jorkins; in the vestibule of which temple, accessible to pilgrims without the ceremony of knocking, three or four clerks were at work as copyists. One of these, a little dry man, sitting by himself, who wore a stiff brown wig that looked as if it were made of gingerbread, rose to receive my aunt, and show us into Mr. Spenlow's room.

"Mr. Spenlow's in Court, ma'am," said the dry man; "it's an Arches day; but it's close by, and I'll send for him directly."

As we were left to look about us while Mr. Spenlow was fetched, I availed myself of the opportunity. The furniture of the room was old-fashioned and dusty; and the green baize on the top of the writing-table had lost all its color, and was as withered and pale as an old pauper. There were a great many bundles of papers on it, some indorsed as Allegations, and some (to my surprise) as Libels, and some as being in the Consistory Court, and some in the Arches Court, and some in the Prerogative Court, and some in the Admiralty Court, and some in the Delegates' Court; giving me occasion to wonder much, how many Courts there might be in the gross, and how long it would take to understand them all. Besides these, there were sundry immense manuscript Books of Evidence taken on affidavit, strongly bound, and tied together in massive sets, a set to each cause, as if every cause were a history in ten or twenty volumes. All this looked tolerably expensive, I thought, and gave me an agreeable notion of a proctor's business. I was casting my eyes with increasing complacency over these and many similar objects, when hasty footsteps were heard in the room outside, and Mr. Spenlow, in a black gown trimmed with white fur, came hurrying in, taking off his hat as he came.

He was a little light-haired gentleman, with undeniable boots and the stiffest of white cravats and shirt-collars. He was buttoned up, mighty trim and tight, and must have taken a great deal of pains with his whiskers, which were accurately curled. His gold watch-chain was so massive, that a fancy came across me that he ought to have a sinewy golden arm, to draw it out with, like those which are put up over the gold-beaters' shops. He was got up with such care, and was so stiff, that he could hardly bend himself; being obliged, when he glanced at some papers on his desk, after sitting down in his chair, to move his whole body, from the bottom of his spine, like Punch.

I had previously been presented by my aunt, and had been courteously received. He now said:

"And so, Mr. Copperfield, you think of entering into our profession? I casually mentioned to Miss Trotwood, when I had the pleasure of an interview with her the other day,"—with another inclination of his body—Punch again—"that there was a vacancy here. Miss Trotwood was good enough to mention that she had a nephew who was her peculiar care, and for whom she was seeking to provide genteelly in life. That nephew, I believe, I have now the pleasure of"—Punch again.

I bowed my acknowledgments, and said, my aunt had mentioned to me that there was that opening, and that I believed I should like it very much. That I was strongly inclined to like it, and had taken immediately to the proposal. That I could not absolutely pledge myself to like it, until I knew something more about it. That although it was little else than a matter of form, I presumed I should have an opportunity of trying how I liked it, before I bound myself to it irrevocably.

"Oh surely! surely!" said Mr. Spenlow. "We always, in this house, propose a month—an initiatory month. I should be happy, myself, to propose two months—three—an indefinite period, in fact,—but I have a partner. Mr. Jorkins."

"And the premium, sir," I returned, "is a thousand pounds?"

"And the premium, Stamp included, is a thousand pounds," said Mr. Spenlow. "As I have mentioned to Miss Trotwood, I am actuated by no mercenary considerations; few men less so, I believe; but Mr. Jorkins has his opinions on these subjects, and I am bound to respect Mr. Jorkins's opinions. Mr. Jorkins thinks a thousand pounds too little, in short."

"I suppose, sir," said I, still desiring to spare my aunt, "that it is not the custom here, if an articled clerk were particularly useful, and made himself a perfect master of his profession—" I could not help blushing, this looked so like praising myself—"I suppose it is not the custom, in the later years of his time, to allow him any—"

Mr. Spenlow, by a great effort, just lifted his head far enough out of his cravat to shake it, and answered, anticipating the word "salary:"

"No. I will not say what consideration I might give to that point myself, Mr. Copperfield, if I were unfettered. Mr. Jorkins is immovable."

I was quite dismayed by the idea of this terrible Jorkins. But I found out afterwards that he was a mild man, of a heavy temperament, whose place in the business was to keep himself in the background, and be constantly exhibited by name as the most obdurate and ruthless of men. If a clerk wanted his salary raised, Mr. Jorkins wouldn't listen to such a proposition. If a client were slow to settle his bill of costs, Mr. Jorkins was resolved to have it paid; and however painful these things might be (and always were) to the feelings of Mr. Spenlow, Mr. Jorkins would have his bond. The heart and hand of the good angel Spenlow would have been always open, but for the restraining demon Jorkins. As I have grown older, I think I have had the experience of some other houses doing business on the principle of Spenlow and Jorkins.

It was settled that I should begin my month's probation as soon as I pleased, and that my aunt need neither remain in town nor return at its expiration, as the articles of agreement, of which I wa. to be the subject, could easily be sent to her at home for her signature. When we had got so far, Mr. Spenlow offered to take me into Court then and there, and show me what sort of place it was. As I was willing enough to know, we went out with this object, leaving my aunt behind; who would trust herself, she said, in no such place, and who, I think, regarded all Courts of Law as a sort of powder-mills that might blow up at any time.

Mr. Spenlow conducted me through a paved courtyard formed of grave brick houses, which I inferred, from the Doctors' names upon the doors, to be the official abiding-places of the learned advocates of whom Steerforth had told me; and into a large dull room, not unlike a chapel to my thinking, on the left hand. The upper part of this room was fenced off from the rest; and there, on the two sides of a raised platform of the horse-shoe form, sitting on easy old-fashioned dining-room chairs, were sundry gentlemen in red gowns and grey wigs, whom I found to be the Doctors aforesaid. Blinking over a little desk like a pulpit-desk, in the curve of the horse-shoe, was an old gentleman, whom, if I had seen him in an aviary, I should certainly have taken for an owl, but who I learned was the presiding judge. In the space within the horse-shoe, lower than these, that is to say, on about the level of the floor, were sundry other gentlemen of Mr. Spenlow's rank, and dressed like him in black gowns with white fur upon them, sitting at a long green table. Their cravats were in general stiff, I thought, and their looks haughty; but in this last respect I presently conceived I had done them an injustice, for when two or three of them had to rise and answer a question of the presiding dignitary, I never saw anything more sheepish. The public, represented by a boy with a comforter, and a shabby-genteel man secretly eating crumbs out of his coat pocket, was warming itself at a stove in the centre of the Court. The languid stillness of the place was only broken by the chirping of this fire and by the voice of one of the Doctors, who was wandering slowly through a perfect library of evidence, and stopping to put up, from time to time, at little roadside inns of argument on the journey Altogether, I have never, on any occasion, made one at such a cosey, dosey, old-fashioned, time-forgotten, sleepy-headed little family-party in all my life; and I felt it would be quite a soothing opiate to belong to it in any character—except perhaps as a suitor.

Very well satisfied with the dreamy nature of this retreat, I informed Mr. Spenlow that I had seen enough for that time, and we rejoined my aunt; in company with whom I presently departed from the Commons, feeling very young when I went out of Spenlow and Jorkins's, on account of the clerks poking one another with their pens to point me out.

We arrived at Lincoln's Inn Fields without any new adventures, except encountering an unlucky donkey in a costermonger's cart, who suggested painful associations to my aunt. We had another long talk about my plans, when we were safely housed; and as I knew she was anxious to get home, and, between fire, food, and pickpockets, could never be considered at her ease for half an hour in London, I urged her not to be uncomfortable on my account, but to leave me to take care of myself.

"I have not been here a week to-morrow, without considering that too, my dear," she returned. "There is a furnished little set of chambers to be let in the Adelphi, Trot, which ought to suit you to a marvel."

With this brief introduction, she produced from her pocket an advertisement, carefully cut out of a newspaper, setting forth that in Buckingham Street in the Adelphi, there was to be let, furnished, with a view of the river, a singularly desirable and compact set of chambers, forming a genteel residence for a young gentleman, a member of one of the Inns of Court, or otherwise, with immediate possession. Terms moderate, and could be taken for a month only if required.

"Why, this is the very thing, aunt!" said I, flushed with the possible dignity of living in chambers.

"Then come," replied my aunt, immediately resuming the bonnet she had a minute before laid aside. "We'll go and look at 'em."

Away we went. The advertisement directed us to apply to Mrs. Crupp on the premises, and we rung the area bell, which we supposed to communicate with Mrs. Crupp. It was not until we had rung three or four times that we could prevail on Mrs. Crupp to communicate with us, but at last she appeared, being a stout lady with a flounce of flannel petticoat below a nankeen gown.

"Let us see these chambers of yours, if you please, ma'am," said my aunt.

"For this gentleman?" said Mrs. Crupp, feeling in her pocket for her keys.

"Yes, for my nephew," said my aunt.

"And a sweet set they is for sich!" said Mrs. Crupp.

So we went up stairs.

They were on the top of the house—a great point with my aunt, being near the fire-escape—and consisted of a little half-blind entry, where you could see hardly anything, a little stone-blind pantry, where you could see nothing at all, a sitting room, and a bedroom. The furniture was rather faded, but quite good enough for me; and, sure enough, the river was outside the windows.

As I was delighted with the place, my aunt and Mrs. Crupp withdrew into the pantry to discuss the terms, while I remained on the sitting-room sofa, hardly daring to think it possible that I could be destined to live in such a noble residence. After a single combat of some duration they returned, and I saw, to my joy, both in Mrs. Crupp's countenance and in my aunt's, that the deed was done.

"Is it the last occupant's furniture?" inquired my aunt.

"Yes it is, ma'am," said Mrs. Crupp.

"What's become of him?" asked my aunt.

Mrs. Crupp was taken with a troublesome cough, in the midst of which she articulated with much difficulty. "He was took ill here, ma'am, and—ugh! ugh! ugh! dear me!—and he died."

"Hey! What did he die of?" asked my aunt.

"Well, ma'am, he died of drink," said Mrs. Crupp, in confidence. "And smoke."

"Smoke? You don't mean chimneys?" said my aunt.

"No, ma'am," returned Mrs. Crupp. "Cigars and pipes."

"*That's* not catching, Trot, at any rate," remarked my aunt, turning to me.

"No, indeed," said I.

In short, my aunt, seeing how enraptured I was with the premises, took them for a month, with leave to remain for twelve months when that time was out. Mrs. Crupp was to find linen, and to cook; every other necessary was already provided; and Mrs. Crupp expressly intimated that she should always yearn towards me as a son. I was to take possession the day after to-morrow, and Mrs. Crupp said thank Heaven she had now found summun she could care for!

On our way back, my aunt informed me how she confidently trusted that the life I was now to lead would make me firm and self-reliant, which was all I wanted. She repeated this several times the next day, in the intervals of our arranging for the transmission of my clothes and books from Mr. Wickfield's; relative to which, and to all my late holiday, I wrote a long letter to Agnes, of which my aunt took charge, as she was to leave on the succeeding day. Not to lengthen these particulars, I need only add, that she made a handsome provision for all my possible wants during my month of trial; that Steerforth, to my great disappointment and hers too, did not make his appearance before she went away; that I saw her safely seated in the Dover coach, exulting in the coming discomfiture of the vagrant donkeys, with Janet at her side; and that when the coach was gone, I turned my face to the Adelphi, pondering on the old days when I used to roam about its subterranean arches, and on the happy changes which had brought me to the surface.

CHAPTER XXIV.

MY FIRST DISSIPATION.

It was a wonderfully fine thing to have that lofty castle to myself, and to feel, when I shut my outer door, like Robinson Crusoe, when he had got into his fortification, and pulled his ladder up after him. It was a wonderfully fine thing to walk about town with the key of my house in my pocket, and to know that I could ask any fellow to come home, and make quite sure of its being inconvenient to nobody, if it were not so to me. It was a wonderfully fine thing to let myself in and out, and to come and go without a word to any one, and to ring Mrs. Crupp up, gasping, from the depths of the earth, when I wanted her—and when she was disposed to come. All this, I say, was wonderfully fine; but I must say, too, that there were times when it was very dreary.

It was fine in the morning, particularly in the fine mornings. It looked a very fresh, free life, by daylight: still fresher, and more free, by sunlight. But as the day declined, the life seemed to go down too. I don't know how it was; it seldom looked well by candle-light. I wanted somebody to talk to, then. I missed Agnes. I found a tremendous blank, in the place of that smiling repository of my confidence. Mrs. Crupp appeared to be a long way off. I thought about my predecessor, who had died of drink and smoke; and I could have wished he had been so good as to live, and not bother me with his decease.

After two days and nights, I felt as if I had lived there for a year, and yet I was not an hour older, but was quite as much tormented by my own youthfulness as ever.

Steerforth not yet appearing, which induced me to apprehend that he must be ill, I left the Commons early on the third day, and walked out to Highgate. Mrs. Steerforth was very glad to see me, and said that he had gone away with one of his Oxford friends to see another who lived near St. Albans, but that she expected him to return to-morrow. I was so fond of him that I felt quite jealous of his Oxford friends.

As she pressed me to stay to dinner, I remained, and I believe we talked about nothing but him all day. I told her how much the people liked him at Yarmouth, and what a delightful companion he had been. Miss Dartle was full of hints and mysterious questions, but took a great interest in all our proceedings there, and said, "Was it really, though?" and so forth, so often, that she got everything out of me she wanted to know. Her appearance was exactly what I have described it, when I first saw her; but the society of the two ladies was so agreeable, and came so natural to me, that I felt myself falling a little in love with her. I could not help thinking, several times in the course of the evening, and particularly when I walked home at night, what delightful company she would be in Buckingham Street.

I was taking my coffee and roll in the morning, before going to the Commons—and I may observe in this place that it is surprising how much coffee Mrs. Crupp used, and how weak it was, considering—when Steerforth himself walked in, to my unbounded joy.

"My dear Steerforth," cried I, "I began to think I should never see you again!"

"I was carried off, by force of arms," said Steerforth, "the very next morning after I got home. Why, Daisy, what a rare old Bachelor you are here!"

I showed him over the establishment, not omitting the pantry, with no little pride, and he commended it highly. "I tell you what, old boy," he added, "I shall make quite a town-house of this place, unless you give me notice to quit."

This was a delightful hearing. I told him if he waited for that, he would have to wait till doomsday.

"But you shall have some breakfast!" said I, with my hand on the bell-rope, "and Mrs. Crupp shall make you some fresh coffee, and I'll toast you some bacon in a bachelor's Dutch-oven that I have got here."

"No, no!" said Steerforth. "Don't ring! I can't. I am going

to breakfast with one of these fellows who is at the Piazza Hotel, in Covent Garden."

"But you'll come back to dinner?" said I.

"I can't, upon my life. There's nothing I should like better, but I *must* remain with these two fellows. We are all three off together to-morrow morning."

"Then bring them here to dinner," I returned. "Do you think they would come?"

"Oh! they would come fast enough," said Steerforth; "but we should inconvenience you. You had better come and dine with us somewhere."

I would not by any means consent to this, for it occurred to me that I really ought to have a little housewarming, and that there never could be a better opportunity. I had a new pride in my rooms after his approval of them, and burned with a desire to develop their utmost resources. I therefore made him promise positively in the names of his two friends, and we appointed six o'clock as the dinner-hour.

When he was gone, I rang for Mrs. Crupp, and acquainted her with my desperate design. Mrs. Crupp said, in the first place, of course it was well known she couldn't be expected to wait, but she knew a handy young man, who she thought could be prevailed upon to do it, and whose terms would be five shillings, and what I pleased. I said, certainly, we would have him. Next, Mrs. Crupp said it was clear she couldn't be in two places at once (which I felt to be reasonable), and that "a young gal" stationed in the pantry with a bedroom candle, there never to desist from washing plates, would be indispensable. I said, what would be the expense of this young female, and Mrs. Crupp said she supposed eighteen-pence would neither make me nor break me. I said I supposed not; and *that* was settled. Then Mrs. Crupp said, Now about the dinner.

It was a remarkable instance of want of forethought on the part of the ironmonger who had made Mrs. Crupp's kitchen fire-place, that it was capable of cooking nothing but chops and mashed potatoes. As to a fish-kettle, Mrs. Crupp said, well! would I only come and look at the range. She couldn't say fairer than that. Would I come and look at it? As I should not have been much the wiser if I *had* looked at it, I declined, and said, "Never mind fish." But Mrs. Crupp said, Don't say that; oysters was in, and why not them? So *that* was settled. Mrs. Crupp then said what she would recommend would be this. A pair of hot roast fowls—from the pastry-cook's; a dish of stewed beef, with vegetables—from the pastry-cook's; two little corner things, as a raised pie and a dish of kidneys—from the pastry-cook's; a tart, and (if I liked) a shape of jelly—from the pastry-cook's. This, Mrs. Crupp said, would leave her at full liberty to concentrate her mind on the potatoes, and to serve up the cheese and celery as she could wish to see it done.

I acted on Mrs. Crupp's opinion, and gave the order at the pastry-cook's myself. Walking along the Strand, afterwards, and observing a hard mottled substance in the window of a ham and beef shop, which resembled marble, but was labelled "Mock Turtle," I went in and bought a slab of it, which I have since seen reason to believe would have sufficed for fifteen people. This preparation, Mrs. Crupp, after some difficulty, consented to warm up; and it shrunk so much in a liquid state, that we found it what Steerforth called "rather a tight fit" for four.

These preparations happily completed, I bought a little dessert in Covent Garden Market, and gave a rather extensive order at a retail wine-merchant's in that vicinity. When I came home in the afternoon, and saw the bottles drawn up in a square on the pantry-floor, they looked so numerous (though there were two missing which made Mrs. Crupp very uncomfortable), that I was absolutely frightened at them.

One of Steerforth's friends was named Grainger, and the other Markham. They were both very gay and lively fellows; Grainger, something older than Steerforth; Markham, youthful-looking, and I should say not more than twenty. I observed that the latter always spoke of himself indefinitely, as "a man," and seldom or never in the first person singular.

"A man might get on very well here, Mr. Copperfield," said Markham—meaning himself.

"It 's not a bad situation," said I, "and the rooms are really commodious."

"I hope you have both brought appetites with you?" said Steerforth.

"Upon my honour," returned Markham, "town seems to sharpen a man's appetite. A man is hungry all day long. A man is perpetually eating."

Being a little embarrassed at first, and feeling much too young to preside, I made Steerforth take the head of the table when dinner was announced, and seated myself opposite to him. Everything was very good; we did not spare the wine; and he exerted himself so brilliantly to make the thing pass off well, that there was no pause in our festivity. I was not quite such good company during dinner, as I could have wished to be, for my chair was opposite the door, and my attention was distracted by observing that the handy young man went out of the room very often, and that his shadow always presented itself, immediately afterwards, on the wall of the entry, with a bottle at its mouth. The "young girl" likewise occasioned me some uneasiness: not so much by neglecting to wash the plates, as by breaking them. For being of an inquisitive disposition, and unable to confine herself (as her positive instructions were) to the pantry, she was constantly peering in at us, and constantly imagining herself detected; in which belief, she several times retired upon the plates (with which she had carefully paved the floor), and did a great deal of destruction.

These, however, were small drawbacks, and easily forgotten when the cloth was cleared, and the dessert put on the table; at which period of the entertainment the handy young man was discovered to be speechless. Giving him private directions to seek the society of Mrs. Crupp, and to remove the "young gal" to the basement also, I abandoned myself to enjoyment.

I began, by being singularly cheerful and light-hearted; all sorts of half-forgotten things to talk about, came rushing into my mind, and made me hold forth in a most unwonted manner. I laughed heartily at my own jokes, and everybody else's; called Steerforth to order for not passing the wine; made several engagements to go to Oxford; announced that I meant to have a dinner party exactly like that, once a week until further notice; and madly took so much snuff out of Grainger's box, that I was obliged to go into the pantry, and have a private fit of sneezing ten minutes long.

I went on, by passing the wine faster and faster yet, and continually starting up with a corkscrew to open more wine, long before any was needed. I proposed Steerforth's health. I said he was my dearest friend, the protector of my boyhood, and the companion of my prime. I said I was delighted to propose his health. I said I owed him more obligation than I could ever repay, and held him in a higher admiration than I could ever express. I finished by saying "I'll give you Steerforth! God bless him! Hurrah!" We gave him three times three, and another, and a good one to finish with. I broke my glass in going round the table to shake hands with him, and I said (in two words) "Steerforth you'retheguidingstarofmyexistence."

I went on, by finding suddenly that somebody was in the middle of a song. Markham was the singer, and he sang "When the heart of a man is depressed with care." He said, when he had sung it, he would give us "Woman." I took objection to that, and I couldn't allow it. I said it was not a respectful way of proposing the toast, and I would never permit that toast to be drunk in my house otherwise than as "The Ladies!" I was very high with him, mainly I think because I saw Steerforth and Grainger laughing at me—or at him—or at both of us. He said a man was not to be dictated to. I said a man *was*. He said a man was not to be insulted, then. I said he was right there—never under my roof, where the Lares were sacred, and the laws of hospitality paramount. He said it was no derogation from a man's dignity to confess that I was a devilish good fellow. I instantly proposed his health.

Somebody was smoking. We were all smoking. *I* was smoking, and trying to suppress a rising tendency to shudder. Steerforth had made a speech about me, in the course of which I had been affected almost to tears. I returned thanks, and hoped the present company would dine with me to-morrow, and the day after—each day at five o'clock, that we might enjoy the pleasures of conversation and society through a long evening. I felt called upon to propose an individual. I would give them my aunt. Miss Betsey Trotwood, the best of her sex!

Somebody was leaning out of my bed-room window, refreshing his forehead against the cool stone of the parapet, and feeling the air upon his face. It was myself. I was addressing myself as "Copperfield," and saying, "Why did you try to smoke? You might have known you couldn't do it." Now, somebody was unsteadily contemplating his features in the looking-glass. That was I too. I was very pale in the looking-glass; my eyes had a vacant appearance; and my hair—only my hair, nothing else—looked drunk.

Somebody said to me, "Let us go to the Theatre, Copperfield!" There was no bed-room before me, but again the jingling table covered with glasses; the lamp; Grainger on my right hand, Markham on my left, and Steerforth opposite—all sitting in a mist, and a long way off. The Theatre? To be sure. The very thing! Come along! But they must excuse me if I saw everybody out first, and turned the lamp off—in case of fire.

Owing to some confusion in the dark, the door was gone. I was feeling for it in the window-curtains, when Steerforth, laughing, took me by the arm and led me out. We went down stairs, one behind another. Near the bottom, somebody fell, and rolled down. Somebody else said it was Copperfield. I was angry at that false report, until finding myself on my back in the passage, I began to think there might be some foundation for it.

A very foggy night, with great rings round the lamps in the streets! There was an indistinct talk of its being wet. *I* considered it frosty. Steerforth dusted me under a lamp-post, and put my hat into shape, which somebody produced from somewhere in a most extraordinary manner, for I hadn't had it on before. Steerforth then said, "You are all right, Copperfield, are you not?" and I told him, "Neverberrer."

A man, sitting in a pigeon-hole-place, looked out of the fog, and took money from somebody, inquiring if I was one of the gentlemen paid for, and appearing rather doubtful (as I remember in the glimpse I had of him) whether to take the money from me or not. Shortly afterwards, we were very high up in a very hot theatre, looking down into a very large pit, that seemed to me to smoke; the people with whom it was crammed were so indistinct. There was a great stage, too, looking very clean and smooth after the streets; and there were people upon it, talking about something or other, but not at all intelligibly. There was an abundance of bright lights, and there was music, and there were ladies down in the boxes, and I don't know what more. The whole building looked to me, as if it were learning to swim; it conducted itself in such an unaccountable manner, when I tried to steady it.

On somebody's motion, we resolved to go down-stairs to the dress-boxes, where the ladies were. A gentleman lounging, full dressed, on a sofa, with an opera-glass in his hand, passed before my view, and also my own figure at full length in a glass. Then I was being ushered into one of these boxes, and found myself saying something as I sat down, and people about me crying "Silence!" to somebody, and ladies casting indignant glances at me, and—what! yes!—Agnes, sitting on the seat before me, in the same box, with a lady and gentleman beside her, whom I didn't know. I see her face now, better than I did then I dare say, with its indelible look of regret and wonder turned upon me.

"Agnes!" I said thickly, "Lorblessmer! Agnes!"

"Hush! Pray!" she answered, I could not conceive why. "You disturb the company. Look at the stage!"

I tried, on her injunction, to fix it, and to hear something of what was going on there, but quite in vain. I looked at her again by-and-by, and saw her shrink into her corner, and put her gloved hand to her forehead.

"Agnes!" I said. "I'mafraidyou'renorwell."

"Yes, yes. Do not mind me, Trotwood," she returned. "Listen! Are you going away soon?"

"Amigoarawaysoo?" I repeated.

"Yes."

I had a stupid intention of replying that I was going to wait, to hand her down stairs. I suppose I expressed it, somehow; for, after she had looked at me attentively for a little while, she appeared to understand, and replied in a low tone:

"I know you will do as I ask you, if I tell you I am very earnest in it. Go away now, Trotwood, for my sake, and ask your friends to take you home."

She had so far improved me, for the time, that though I was angry with her, I felt ashamed, and with a short "Goori!" (which I intended for "Good night!") got up and went away. They followed, and I stepped at once out of the box-door into my bedroom, where only Steerforth was with me, helping me to undress, and where I was by turns telling him that Agnes was my sister, and adjuring him to bring the corkscrew, that I might open another bottle of wine.

How somebody, lying in my bed, lay saying and doing all this over again, at cross-purposes, in a feverish dream all night—the bed a rocking sea that was never still. How, as that somebody slowly settled down into myself, did I begin to parch, and feel as if my outer covering of skin were a hard board; my tongue the bottom of an empty kettle, furred with long service, and burning up over a slow fire; the palms of my hands, hot plates of metal, which no ice could cool!

But the agony of mind, the remorse, and shame I felt, when I became conscious next day! My horror of having committed a thousand offences I had forgotten, and which nothing could ever expiate—my recollection of that indelible look which Agnes had given me—the torturing impossibility of communicating with her, not knowing, Beast that I was, how she came to be in London, or where she stayed—my disgust of the very sight of the room where the revel had been held—my racking head—the smell of smoke, the sight of glasses, the impossibility of going out, or even getting up! Oh, what a day it was!

Oh, what an evening, when I sat down by the fire to a basin of mutton broth, dimpled all over with fat, and thought I was going the way of my predecessor, and should succeed to his dismal story as well as to his chambers, and had half a mind to rush express to Dover and reveal all! What an evening, when Mrs. Crupp, coming in to take away the broth-basin, produced one kidney on a cheese-plate as the entire remains of yesterday's feast, and I was really inclined to fall upon her nankeen breast, and say, in heartfelt penitence, "Oh, Mrs. Crupp, Mrs. Crupp, never mind the broken meats! I am very miserable!"—only that I doubted, even at that pass, if Mrs. Crupp were quite the sort of woman to confide in!

CHAPTER XXV.

GOOD AND BAD ANGELS.

I WAS going out at my door on the morning after that deplorable day of headache, sickness, and repentance, with an odd confusion in my mind, relative to the date of my dinner-party, as if a body of Titans had taken an enormous lever and pushed the day before yesterday some months back, when I saw a ticket-porter coming up-stairs, with a letter in his hand. He was taking his time about his errand, then; but when he saw me at the top of the staircase, looking at him over the bannisters, he swung into a trot, and came up panting as if he had run himself into a state of exhaustion.

"T. Copperfield, Esquire," said the ticket-porter, touching his hat with his little cane.

I could scarcely lay claim to the name: I was so disturbed by the conviction that the letter came from Agnes. However, I told him I was T. Copperfield, Esquire, and he believed it, and gave me the letter, which he said required an answer. I shut him out on the landing to wait for the answer, and went into my chambers again, in such a nervous state that I was fain to lay the letter down on my breakfast-table, and familiarise myself with the outside of it a little, before I could resolve to break the seal.

I found, when I did open it, that it was a very kind note, containing no reference to my condition at the theatre. All it said, was, "My dear Trotwood. I am staying at the house of papa's agent, Mr. Waterbrook, in Ely-place, Holborn. Will you come and see me to-day, at any time you like to appoint? Ever yours affectionately, AGNES."

It took me such a long time to write an answer at all to my satis faction, that I don't know what the ticket-porter can have thought, unless he thought I was learning to write. I must have written half a dozen answers at least. I began one, "How can I ever hope, my dear Agnes, to efface from your remembrance the disgusting impression"—there I didn't like it, and then I tore it up. I began another, "Shakspeare has observed, my dear Agnes, how strange it is that a man should put an enemy into his mouth"—that reminded me of Markham, and it got no farther. I even tried poetry. I began one note, in a six-syllable line, "Oh do not remember"—but that associated itself with the 5th of November, and became an absurdity. After many attempts, I wrote, "My dear Agnes. Your letter is like you, and what could I say of it that would be higher praise than that? I will come at four o'clock. Affectionately and sorrowfully, T. C." With this missive (which I was in twenty minds at once about recalling, as soon as it was out of my hands) the ticket-porter at last departed.

If the day were half as tremendous to any other professional gentleman in Doctors' Commons as it was to me, I sincerely believe he made some expiation for his share in that rotten old ecclesiastical cheese. Although I left the office at half-past three, and was prowling about the place of appointment within a few minutes afterwards, the appointed time was exceeded by a full quarter of an hour, according to the clock of St. Andrew's, Holborn, before I could muster up sufficient desperation to pull the private bell-handle let into the left-hand door-post of Mr. Waterbrook's house.

The professional business of Mr. Waterbrook's establishment was done on the ground-floor, and the genteel business (of which there was a good deal) in the upper part of the building. I was shown into a pretty but rather close drawing-room, and there sat Agnes, netting a purse.

She looked so quiet and good, and reminded me so strongly of my airy fresh school days at Canterbury, and the sodden, smoky, stupid wretch I had been the other night, that, nobody being by, I yielded to my self-reproach and shame, and—in short, made a foo. of myself. I cannot deny that I shed tears. To this hour I am undecided whether it was upon the whole the wisest thing I could have done, or the most ridiculous.

"If it had been any one but you, Agnes," said I, turning away my head, "I should not have minded it half so much. But that it should have been you who saw me! I almost wish I had been dead first."

She put her hand—its touch was like no other hand—upon my arm for a moment; and I felt so befriended and comforted, that I could not help moving it to my lips, and gratefully kissing it.

"Sit down," said Agnes, cheerfully. "Don't be unhappy, Trotwood. If you cannot confidently trust me, whom will you trust?"

"Ah, Agnes!" I returned. "You are my good Angel!"

She smiled rather sadly, I thought, and shook her head.

"Yes, Agnes, my good Angel! Always my good angel!"

"If I were, indeed, Trotwood," she returned, "there is one thing that I should set my heart on very much."

I looked at her inquiringly; but already with a foreknowledge of her meaning.

"On warning you," said Agnes, with a steady glance, "against your bad Angel."

"My dear Agnes," I began, "if you mean Steerforth—"

"I do, Trotwood," she returned.

"Then, Agnes, you wrong him very much. He my bad Angel, or any one's! He, anything but a guide, a support, and a friend to me! My dear Agnes! Now, is it not unjust, and unlike you, to judge him from what you saw of me the other night?"

"I do not judge him from what I saw of you the other night," she quietly replied.

"From what, then?"

"From many things—trifles in themselves, but they do not seem to me to be so, when they are put together. I judge him, partly from your account of him, Trotwood, and your character, and the influence he has over you."

There was always something in her modest voice that seemed to touch a chord within me, answering to that sound alone. It was always earnest; but when it was very earnest, as it was now, there was a thrill in it that quite subdued me. I sat looking at her as she cast her eyes down on her work; I sat seeming still to listen to her; and Steerforth, in spite of all my attachment to him, darkened in that tone.

"It is very bold in me," said Agnes, looking up again, "who

have lived in such seclusion, and can know so little of the world, to give you my advice so confidently, or even to have this strong opinion. But I know in what it is engendered, Trotwood,—in how true a remembrance of our having grown up together, and in how true an interest in all relating to you. It is that which makes me bold. I am certain that what I say is right. I am quite sure it is. I feel as if it were some one else speaking to you, and not I, when I cautioned you that you have made a dangerous friend."

Again I looked at her, again I listened to her after she was silent, and again his image, though it was still fixed in my heart, darkened.

"I am not so unreasonable as to expect," said Agnes, resuming her usual tone, after a little while, "that you will, or that you can, at once, change any sentiment that has become a conviction to you; least of all a sentiment that is rooted in your trusting disposition. You ought not hastily to do that. I only ask you, Trotwood, if you ever think of me—I mean," with a quiet smile, for I was going to interrupt her, and she knew why, "as often as you think of me—to think of what I have said. Do you forgive me for all this?"

"I will forgive you, Agnes," I replied, "when you come to do Steerforth justice, and to like him as well as I do."

"Not until then?" said Agnes.

I saw a passing shadow on her face when I made this mention of him, but she returned my smile, and we were again as unreserved in our mutual confidence as of old.

"And when, Agnes," said I, "will you forgive me the other night?"

"When I recall it," said Agnes.

She would have dismissed the subject so, but I was too full of it to allow that, and insisted on telling her how it happened that I had disgraced myself, and what chain of accidental circumstances had had the theatre for its final link. It was a great relief to me to do this, and to enlarge on the obligation that I owed to Steerforth for his care of me when I was unable to take care of myself.

"You must not forget," said Agnes, calmly changing the conversation as soon as I had concluded, "that you are always to tell me, not only when you fall into trouble, but when you fall in love. Who has succeeded to Miss Larkins, Trotwood?"

"No one, Agnes."

"Some one, Trotwood," said Agnes, laughing, and holding up her finger.

"No, Agnes, upon my word! There is a lady, certainly, at Mrs. Steerforth's house, who is very clever, and whom I like to talk to—Miss Dartle—but I don't adore her."

Agnes laughed again at her own penetration, and told me that if I were faithful to her in my confidence she thought she should keep a little register of my violent attachments, with the date, duration, and termination of each, like the table of the reigns of the kings and queens, in the History of England. Then she asked me if I had seen Uriah.

"Uriah Heep?" said I. "No. Is he in London?"

"He comes to the office down-stairs, every day," returned Agnes. "He was in London a week before me. I am afraid on disagreeable business, Trotwood."

"On some business that makes you uneasy, Agnes, I see," said I. "What can that be?"

Agnes laid aside her work, and replied, folding her hands upon one another, and looking pensively at me out of those beautiful soft eyes of hers:

"I believe he is going to enter into partnership with papa."

"What? Uriah? That mean, fawning fellow, worm himself into such promotion?" I cried, indignantly. "Have you made no remonstrance about it, Agnes? Consider what a connexion it is likely to be. You must speak out. You must not allow your father to take such a mad step. You must prevent it, Agnes, while there's time."

Still looking at me, Agnes shook her head while I was speaking with a faint smile at my warmth: and then replied:

"You remember our last conversation about papa? It was not long after that—not more than two or three days—when he gave me the first intimation of what I tell you. It was sad to see him struggling between his desire to represent it to me as a matter of choice on his part, and his inability to conceal that it was forced upon him. I felt very sorry."

"Forced upon him, Agnes! Who forces it upon him?"

"Uriah," she replied, after a moment's hesitation, "has made himself indispensable to papa. He is subtle and watchful. He has mastered papa's weaknesses, fostered them, and taken advantage of them, until—to say all that I mean in a word, Trotwood, until papa is afraid of him."

There was more that she might have said; more that she knew or that she suspected; I clearly saw. I could not give her pain by asking what it was, for I knew that she withheld it from me, to spare her father. It had long been going on to this, I was sensible: yes, I could not but feel, on the least reflection, that it had been going on to this for a long time. I remained silent.

"His ascendency over papa," said Agnes, "is very great. He professes humility and gratitude—with truth, perhaps: I hope so—but his position is really one of power, and I fear he makes a hard use of his power."

I said he was a hound, which, at the moment, was a great satisfaction to me.

"At the time I speak of, as the time when papa spoke to me," pursued Agnes, "he had told papa that he was going away; that he was very sorry, and unwilling to leave, but that he had better prospects. Papa was very much depressed then, and more bowed down by care than ever you or I have seen him; but he seemed relieved by this expedient of the partnership, though at the same time he seemed hurt by it and ashamed of it."

"And how did you receive it, Agnes?"

"I did, Trotwood," she replied, "what I hope was right. Feeling sure that it was necessary for papa's peace that the sacrifice should be made, I entreated him to make it. I said it would lighten the load of his life—I hope it will! and that it would give me increased opportunities of being his companion. Oh, Trotwood!" cried Agnes, putting her hands before her face, as her tears started on it, "I almost feel as if I had been papa's enemy, instead of his loving child. For I know how he has altered, in his devotion to me. I know how he has narrowed the circle of his sympathies and duties, in the concentration of his whole mind upon me. I know what a multitude of things he has shut out for my sake, and how his anxious thoughts of me have shadowed his life, and weakened his strength and energy, by turning them always upon one idea. If I could ever set this right! If I could ever work out his restoration, as I have so innocently been the cause of his decline!"

I had never before seen Agnes cry. I had seen tears in her eyes when I had brought new honours home from school, and I had seen them there when we last spoke about her father, and I had seen her turn her gentle head aside when we took leave of one another; but I had never seen her grieve like this. It made me so sorry that I could only say, in a foolish, helpless manner, "Pray, Agnes, don't! Don't, my dear sister!"

But Agnes was too superior to me in character and purpose, as I know well now, whatever I might know or not know then, to be long in need of my entreaties. The beautiful, calm manner, which makes her so different in my remembrance from everybody else, came back again, as if a cloud had passed from a serene sky.

"We are not likely to remain alone much longer," said Agnes, "and while I have an opportunity, let me earnestly entreat you, Trotwood, to be friendly to Uriah. Don't repel him. Don't resent (as I think you have a general disposition to do) what may be uncongenial to you in him. He may not deserve it, for we know no certain ill of him. In any case, think first of papa and me!"

Agnes had no time to say more, for the room-door opened, and Mrs. Waterbrook, who was a large lady—or who wore a large dress: I don't exactly know which, for I don't know which was dress and which was lady—came sailing in. I had a dim recollection of having seen her at the theatre, as if I had seen her in a pale magic lantern; but she appeared to remember me perfectly, and still to suspect me of being in a state of intoxication.

Finding by degrees, however, that I was sober, and (I hope) that I was a modest young gentleman, Mrs. Waterbrook softened towards me considerably, and inquired, firstly, if I went much into the parks, and secondly, if I went much into society. On my replying to both these questions in the negative, it occurred to me that I fell again in her good opinion; but she concealed the fact gracefully, and invited me to dinner next day. I accepted the invitation, and took my leave; making a call on Uriah in the office as I went out, and leaving a card for him in his absence.

When I went to dinner next day, and, on the street-door being opened, plunged into a vapour-bath of haunch of mutton, I divined that I was not the only guest: for I immediately identified the ticket-porter in disguise, assisting the family servant, and waiting at the foot of the stairs to carry up my name. He looked, to the best of his ability, when he asked me for it confidentially, as if he had never seen me before; but well did I know him, and well did he know me. Conscience made cowards of us both.

I found Mr. Waterbrook to be a middle-aged gentleman, with a short throat, and a good deal of shirt-collar, who only wanted a black nose to be the portrait of a pug-dog. He told me he was happy to have the honour of making my acquaintance; and when I had paid my homage to Mrs. Waterbrook, presented me, with much ceremony, to a very awful lady in a black velvet dress, and a great black velvet hat, whom I remember as looking like a near relation of Hamlet's—say his aunt.

Mrs. Henry Spiker was this lady's name; and her husband was there too: so cold a man, that his head, instead of being grey, seemed to be sprinkled with hoar-frost. Immense deference was shown to the Henry Spikers, male and female; which Agnes told me was on account of Mr. Henry Spiker being solicitor to something or to somebody, I forget what or which, remotely connected with the Treasury.

I found Uriah Heep among the company, in a suit of black, and in deep humility. He told me, when I shook hands with him, that he was proud to be noticed by me, and that he really felt obliged to me for my condescension. I could have wished he had been less obliged to me, for he hovered about me in his gratitude all the rest of the evening: and whenever I said a word to Agnes, was sure, with his shadowless eyes and cadaverous face, to be looking gauntly down upon us from behind.

There were other guests—all iced for the occasion, as it struck me, like the wine. But, there was one who attracted my attention before he came in, on account of my hearing him announced as Mr. Traddles! My mind flew back to Salem House; and could it be Tommy, I thought, who used to draw the skeletons!

I looked for Mr. Traddles with unusual interest. He was a sober steady-looking young man of retiring manners, with a comic head of hair, and eyes that were rather wide open; and he got into an obscure corner so soon, that I had some difficulty in making him out. At length I had a good view of him, and either my vision deceived me, or it was the old unfortunate Tommy.

I made my way to Mr. Waterbrook, and said, that I believed I had the pleasure of seeing an old schoolfellow there.

"Indeed?" said Mr. Waterbrook, surprised. "You are too young to have been at school with Mr. Henry Spiker?"

"Oh, I don't mean him!" I returned. "I mean the gentleman named Traddles."

"Oh! Aye, aye! Indeed!" said my host, with much diminished interest. "Possibly."

"If it's really the same person," said I, glancing towards him, "it was at a place called Salem House where we were together, and he was an excellent fellow."

"Oh yes. Traddles is a good fellow," returned my host, nodding his head with an air of toleration. "Traddles is quite a good fellow."

"It's a curious coincidence," said I.

"It is really," returned my host, "quite a coincidence, that Traddles should be here at all: as Traddles was only invited this morning, when the place at table, intended to be occupied by Mrs. Henry Spiker's brother, became vacant, in consequence of his indisposition. A very gentlemanly man, Mrs. Henry Spiker's brother, Mr. Copperfield."

I murmured an assent, which was full of feeling, considering that I knew nothing at all about him; and I inquired what Mr. Traddles was by profession.

"Traddles," returned Mr. Waterbrook, "is a young man reading for the bar. Yes. He is quite a good fellow—nobody's enemy but his own."

"Is he his own enemy?" said I, sorry to hear this.

"Well," returned Mr. Waterbrook, pursing up his mouth, and playing with his watch-chain, in a comfortable, prosperous sort of way. "I should say he was one o those men who stand in their own light. Yes, I should say he would never, for example, be worth five hundred pound. Traddles was recommended to me, by a professional friend. Oh yes. Yes. He has a kind of talent for drawing briefs and stating a case in writing plainly. I am able to throw something in Traddles's way in the course of the year; something—for him—considerable. Oh yes. Yes."

I was much impressed by the extremely comfortable and satisfied manner in which Mr. Waterbrook delivered himself of this little word "Yes," every now and then. There was wonderful expression in it. It completely conveyed the idea of a man who had been born, not to say with a silver spoon, but with a scaling-ladder, and had gone on mounting all the heights of life one after another, until now he looked from the top of the fortifications with the eye of a philosopher and a patron on the people down in the trenches.

My reflections on this theme were still in progress when dinner was announced. Mr. Waterbrook went down with Hamlet's aunt. Mr. Henry Spiker took Mrs. Waterbrook. Agnes, whom I should have liked to take myself, was given to a simpering fellow with weak legs. Uriah, Traddles, and I, as the junior part of the company, went down last how we could. I was not so vexed at losing Agnes as I might have been, since it gave me an opportunity of making myself known to Traddles on the stairs, who greeted me with great fervor: while Uriah writhed with such obtrusive satisfaction and self-abasement, that I could gladly have pitched him over the bannisters.

Traddles and I were separated at table, being billeted in two remote corners: he in the glare of a red velvet lady; I, in the gloom of Hamlet's aunt. The dinner was very long, and the conversation was about the Aristocracy—and Blood. Mrs. Waterbrook repeatedly told us, that if she had a weakness, it was Blood.

It occurred to me several times that we should have got on better if we had not been quite so genteel. We were so exceedingly genteel, that our scope was very limited. A Mr. and Mrs. Gulpidge were of the party, who had something to do at second-hand (at least, Mr. Gulpidge had) with the law business of the Bank; and what with the Bank, and what with the Treasury, we were as exclusive as the Court Circular. To mend the matter, Hamlet's aunt had the family failing of indulging in soliloquy, and held forth in a desultory manner, by herself, on every topic that was introduced. These were few enough to be sure; but as we always fell back upon Blood, she had as wide a field for abstract speculation as her nephew himself.

We might have been a party of Ogres, the conversation assumed such a sanguine complexion.

"I confess I am of Mrs. Waterbrook's opinion," said Mr. Waterbrook, with his wine-glass at his eye. "Other things are all very well in their way, but give me Blood!"

"Oh! There is nothing," observed Hamlet's aunt, "so satisfactory to one! There is nothing that is so much one's *beau-ideal* of—of all that sort of thing, speaking generally. There are some low minds (not many, I am happy to believe, but there are *some*) that would prefer to do what *I* should call bow down before idols. Positively Idols! Before services, intellect, and so on. But these are intangible points. Blood is not so. We see Blood in a nose, and we know it. We meet with it in a chin, and we say, 'There it is! That's Blood!' It is an actual matter of fact. We point it out. It admits of no doubt."

The simpering fellow with the weak legs, who had taken Agnes down, stated the question more decisively yet, I thought.

"Oh, you know, deuce take it," said this gentleman, looking round the board with an imbecile smile, "we can't forego Blood, you know. We must have Blood, you know. Some young fellows, you know, may be a little behind their station, perhaps, in point of education and behaviour, and may go a little wrong, you know, and get themselves and other people into a variety of fixes—and all that—but deuce take it, it's delightful to reflect that they've got Blood in 'em! Myself, I'd rather at any time be knocked down by a man who had got Blood in him, than I'd be picked up by a man who hadn't!"

This sentiment, as compressing the general question into a nutshell, gave the utmost satisfaction, and brought the gentleman into great notice until the ladies retired. After that, I observed that Mr. Gulpidge and Mr. Henry Spiker, who had hitherto been very distant, entered into a defensive alliance against us, the common enemy, and exchanged a mysterious dialogue across the table for our defeat and overthrow.

"That affair of the first bond for four thousand five hundred pounds has not taken the course that was expected, Gulpidge," said Mr. Henry Spiker.

"Do you mean the D. of A.'s?" said Mr. Spiker.

"The C. of B.'s," said Mr. Gulpidge.

Mr. Spiker raised his eye-brows, and looked much concerned.

"When the question was referred to Lord—I needn't name him," said Mr. Gulpidge, checking himself.

"I understand," said Mr. Spiker, "N."

Mr. Gulpidge darkly nodded—"was referred to him, his answer was, 'Money, or no release.'"

"Lord bless my soul!" cried Mr. Spiker.

"'Money, or no release,'" repeated Mr. Gulpidge firmly. "The next in reversion—you understand me?"

"K.," said Mr. Spiker, with an ominous look.

"—K. then positively refused to sign. He was attended at Newmarket for that purpose, and he point-blank refused to do it."

Mr. Spiker was so interested that he became quite stony.

"So the matter rests at this hour," said Mr. Gulpidge, throwing himself back in his chair. "Our friend Waterbrook will excuse me if I forbear to explain myself generally, on account of the magnitude of the interests involved."

Mr. Waterbrook was only too happy, as it appeared to me, to have such interests and such names even hinted at across his table. He assumed an expression of gloomy intelligence (though I am persuaded he knew no more about the discussion than I did), and highly approved of the discretion that had been observed. Mr. Spiker, after the receipt of such a confidence, naturally desired to favor his friend with a confidence of his own; therefore the foregoing dialogue was succeeded by another, in which it was Mr. Gulpidge's turn to be surprised, and that by another, in which the surprise came round to Mr. Spiker's turn again, and so on, turn and turn about. All this time we, the outsiders, remained oppressed by the tremendous interests involved in the conversation; and our host regarded us with pride, as the victims of a salutary awe and astonishment.

I was very glad indeed to get up-stairs to Agnes, and to talk with her in a corner, and to introduce Traddles to her, who was shy, but agreeable, and the same good-natured creature still. As he was obliged to leave early, on account of going away next morning for a month, I had not nearly so much conversation with him as I could have wished; but we exchanged addresses, and promised ourselves the pleasure of another meeting when he should come back to town. He was greatly interested to hear that I knew Steerforth, and spoke of him with such warmth that I made him tell Agnes what he thought of him. But Agnes only looked at me the while, and very slightly shook her head when only I observed her.

As she was not among people with whom I believed she could be very much at home, I was almost glad to hear that she was going away within a few days, though I was sorry at the prospect of parting from her again so soon. This caused me to remain until all the company were gone. Conversing with her, and hearing her sing, was such a delightful reminder to me of my happy life in the grave old house she had made so beautiful, that I could have remained there half the night; but, having no excuse for staying any longer, when the lights of Mr. Waterbrook's society were all snuffed out, I took my leave very much against my inclination. I felt then, more than ever, that she was my better Angel; and if I thought of her sweet face and placid smile, as though they had shone on me from some removed being, like an Angel, I hope I thought no harm.

I have said that the company were all gone; but I ought to have excepted Uriah, whom I don't include in that denomination, and who had never ceased to hover near us. He was close behind me when I went down-stairs. He was close beside me, when I walked away from the house, slowly fitting his long skeleton fingers into the still longer fingers of a great Guy Fawkes pair of gloves.

It was in no disposition for Uriah's company, but in the remembrance of the entreaty Agnes had made to me, that I asked him if he would come home to my rooms, and have some coffee.

"Oh, really, Master Copperfield," he rejoined,—"I beg your pardon, Mister Copperfield, but the other comes so natural,—I don't like that you should put a constraint upon yourself to ask a numble person like me to your ouse."

"There is no constraint in the case," said I. "Will you come?"

"I should like to, very much," replied Uriah, with a writhe.

"Well, then, come along!" said I.

I could not help being rather short with him, but he appeared not to mind it. We went the nearest way, without conversing much upon the road; and he was so humble in respect of those scarecrow gloves, that he was still putting them on, and seemed to have made no advance in that labour, when we got to my place.

I led him up the dark stairs, to prevent his knocking his head against anything, and really his damp cold hand felt so like a frog in mine, that I was tempted to drop it and run away. Agnes and hospitality prevailed, however, and I conducted him to my fireside. When I lighted my candles, he fell into meek transports with the room that was revealed to him; and when I heated the coffee in an unassuming block-tin vessel, in which Mrs. Crupp delighted to prepare it (chiefly, I believe, because it was not intended for the purpose, being a shaving-pot, and because there was a patent invention of great price mouldering away in the pantry), he professed so much emotion, that I could joyfully have scalded him.

"Oh, really, Master Copperfield,—I mean Mister Copperfield," said Uriah, "to see you waiting upon me is what I never could have expected! But, one way and another, so many things happen to me which I never could have expected, I am sure, in my umble station, that it seems to rain blessings on my ed. You have heard something, I des-say, of a change in my expectations, Master Copperfield, *I* should say, Mister Copperfield?"

As he sat on my sofa, with his long knees drawn up under his coffee-cup, his hat and gloves upon the ground close to him, his spoon going softly round and round, his shadowless red eyes, which looked as if they had scorched their lashes off, turned towards me without looking at me, the disagreeable dints I have formerly described in his nostrils coming and going with his breath, and a snaky undulation pervading his frame from his chin to his boots, I decided in my own mind that I disliked him intensely. It made me very uncomfortable to have him for a guest, for I was young then, and unused to disguise what I so strongly felt.

"You have heard something, I des-say, of a change in my expectations, Master Copperfield,—I should say Mister Copperfield?" observed Uriah.

"Yes," said I, "something."

"Ah! I thought Miss Agnes would know of it!" he quietly returned. "I'm glad to find Miss Agnes knows of it. Oh, thank you, Master—Mister Copperfield!"

I could have thrown my bootjack at him (it lay ready on the rug), for having entrapped me into the disclosure of anything concerning Agnes, however immaterial. But I only drank my coffee.

"What a prophet you have shown yourself, Mister Copperfield!" pursued Uriah. "Dear me, what a prophet you have proved yourself to be! Don't you remember saying to me once, that perhaps I should be a partner in Mr. Wickfield's business, and perhaps it might be Wickfield and Heep! *You* may not recollect it; but when a person is umble, Master Copperfield, a person treasures such things up!"

"I recollect talking about it," said I, "though I certainly did not think it very likely then."

"Oh! who *would* have thought it likely, Mister Copperfield!" returned Uriah, enthusiastically, "I am sure I didn't myself. I recollect saying with my own lips that I was much too umble. So I considered myself really and truly."

He sat, with that carved grin on his face, looking at the fire, as I looked at him.

"But the umblest persons, Master Copperfield," he presently resumed, "may be the instruments of good. I am glad to think I have been the instrument of good to Mr. Wickfield, and that I may be more so. Oh what a worthy man he is, Mister Copperfield, but how imprudent he has been!"

"I am sorry to hear it," said I. I could not help adding, rather pointedly, "on all accounts."

"Decidedly so, Mister Copperfield," replied Uriah. "On all accounts. Miss Agnes's above all! You don't remember your own eloquent expressions, Master Copperfield; but *I* remember how you said one day that everybody must admire her, and how I thanked you for it! You have forgot that, I have no doubt, Master Copperfield?"

"No," said I, dryly.

"Oh how glad I am, you have not!" exclaimed Uriah. "To think that you should be the first to kindle the sparks of ambition in my umble breast, and that you've not forgot it! Oh!—Would you excuse me asking for a cup more coffee?"

Something in the emphasis he laid upon the kindling of those sparks, and something in the glance he directed at me as he said it, had made me start as if I had seen him illuminated by a blaze of light. Recalled by his request, preferred in quite another tone of voice, I did the honors of the shaving-pot; but I did them with an unsteadiness of hand, a sudden sense of being no match for him, and a perplexed suspicious anxiety as to what he might be going to say next, which I felt could not escape his observation.

He said nothing at all. He stirred his coffee round and round, he sipped it, he felt his chin softly with his grisly hand, he looked at the fire, he looked about the room, he gasped rather than smiled at me, he writhed and undulated about, in his deferential servility, he stirred and sipped again, but he left the renewal of the conversation to me.

"So, Mr. Wickfield," said I, at last, "who is worth five hundred of you—or me;" for my life, I think I could not have helped dividing that part of the sentence with an awkward jerk; "has been imprudent, has he, Mr. Heep?"

"Oh very imprudent indeed, Master Copperfield," returned Uriah, sighing modestly. "Oh very much so! But I wish you'd call me Uriah, if you please. It's like old times."

"Well! Uriah," said I, bolting it out with some difficulty.

"Thank you!" he returned, with fervor. "Thank you, Master Copperfield! It's like the blowing of old breezes, or the ringing of old bellses, to hear *you* say Uriah! I beg your pardon. Was I making any observation?"

"About Mr. Wickfield," I suggested.

"Oh! Yes, truly," said Uriah. "Ah! Great imprudence, Master Copperfield! It's a topic that I wouldn't touch upon, to any soul but you. Even to you I can only touch upon it, and no more. If any one else had been in my place during the last few years, by this time he would have had Mr. Wickfield (oh, what a worthy man he is, Master Copperfield, too!) under his thumb. Un--der—his thumb," said Uriah, very slowly, as he stretched out his cruel-looking hand above my table, and pressed his own thumb down upon it, until it shook, and shook the room.

If I had been obliged to look at him with his splay foot on Mr Wickfield's head, I think I could scarcely have hated him more.

"Oh dear, yes, Master Copperfield," he proceeded, in a soft voice, most remarkably contrasting with the action of his thumb, which did not diminish its hard pressure in the least degree, "there's no doubt of it. There would have been loss, disgrace, I don't know what all. Mr. Wickfield knows it. I am the umble instrument of umbly serving him, and he puts me on an eminence I hardly could have hoped to reach. How thankful should I be!" With his face turned towards me, as he finished, but without looking at me, he took his crooked thumb off the spot where he had planted it, and slowly and thoughtfully scraped his lank jaw with it, as if he were shaving himself.

I recollect well how indignantly my heart beat as I saw his crafty face, with the appropriately red light of the fire upon it, preparing for something else.

"Master Copperfield," he began—"but am I keeping you up?"

"You are not keeping me up. I generally go to bed late."

"Thank you, Master Copperfield! I have risen from my umble station since first you used to address me, it is true; but I am umble still. I hope I never shall be otherwise than umble. You will not think the worse of my umbleness, if I make a little confidence to you, Master Copperfield? Will you?"

"Oh, no," said I, with an effort.

"Thank you!" He took out his pocket-handkerchief, and began wiping the palms of his hands. "Miss Agnes, Master Copperfield—"

"Well, Uriah?"

"Oh, how pleasant to be called Uriah, spontaneously," he cried; and gave himself a jerk, like a convulsive fish. "You thought her looking very beautiful to-night, Master Copperfield?"

"I thought her looking as she always does: superior, in all respects, to every one around her," I returned.

"Oh, thank you! It's so true!" he cried. "Oh, thank you very much for that!"

"Not at all," I said, loftily. "There is no reason why you should thank me."

"Why that, Master Copperfield," said Uriah, "is, in fact, the confidence that I am going to take the liberty of reposing. Umble as I am," he wiped his hands harder, and looked at them and at the fire by turns, "umble as my mother is, and lowly as our poor but honest roof has ever been, the image of Miss Agnes (I don't mind trusting you with my secret, Master Copperfield, for I have always overflowed towards you since that first moment I had the pleasure of beholding you in a pony-shay) has been in my breast for years. Oh, Master Copperfield, with what a pure affection do I love the ground my Agnes walks on!"

I believe I had a delirious idea of seizing the red-hot poker out of the fire, and running him through with it. It went from me with a shock, like a ball fired from a rifle; but the image of Agnes, outraged by so much as a thought of this red-headed animal's, remained in my mind when I looked at him, sitting all awry as if his mean soul griped his body, and made me giddy. He seemed to swell and grow before my eyes; the room seemed full of the echoes of his voice; and the strange feeling (to which, perhaps, no one is quite a stranger) that all this had occurred before, at some indefinite time, and that I knew what he was going to say next, took possession of me.

A timely observation of the sense of power that there was in his face, did more to bring back to my remembrance the entreaty of Agnes, in its full force, than any effort I could have made. I asked him, with a better appearance of composure than I could have thought possible a minute before, whether he had made his feelings known to Agnes.

"Oh, no, Master Copperfield!" he returned; "oh dear, no! Not to any one but you. You see I am only just emerging from my lowly station. I rest a good deal of hope on her observing how useful I am to her father (for I trust to be very useful to him, indeed, Master Copperfield), and how I smooth the way for him, and keep him straight. She's so much attached to her father, Master Copperfield (oh what a lovely thing it is in a daughter!), that I think she may come, on his account, to be kind to me."

I fathomed the depth of the rascal's whole scheme, and understood why he laid it bare.

"If you 'll have the goodness to keep my secret, Master Copperfield," he pursued, "and not, in general, to go against me, I shall take it as a particular favor. You wouldn't wish to make unpleasantness. I know what a friendly heart you 've got; but having only known me on my umble footing (on my umblest, I should say, for I am very umble still), you might, unbeknown, go against me rather, with my Agnes. I call her mine, you see, Master Copperfield. There's a song that says, 'I 'd crowns resign, to call her mine!' I hope to do it, one of these days."

Dear Agnes! So much too loving and too good for any one that I could think of, was it possible that she was reserved to be the wife of such a wretch as this!

"There's no hurry at present, you know, Master Copperfield," Uriah proceeded, in his slimy way, as I sat gazing at him, with this thought in my mind. "My Agnes is very young still; and mother and me will have to work our way upards, and make a good many new arrangements, before it would be quite convenient. So I shall have time gradually to make her familiar with my hopes, as opportunities offer. Oh, I'm so much obliged to you for this confidence! Oh, it 's such a relief, you can't think, to know that you understand our situation, and are certain (as you wouldn't wish to make unpleasantness in the family) not to go against me!"

He took the hand which I dared not withhold, and having given it a damp squeeze, referred to his pale-faced watch.

"Dear me!" he said, "it 's past one. The moments slip away so, in the confidence of old times, Master Copperfield, that it 's almost half-past one!"

I answered that I had thought it was later. Not that I had really thought so, but because my conversational powers were effectually scattered.

"Dear me!" he said, considering. "The ouse that I am stopping at—a sort of a private hotel and boarding ouse, Master Copperfield, near the New River ed—will have gone to bed these two hours."

"I am sorry," I returned, "that there is only one bed here, and that I—"

"Oh, don't think of mentioning beds, Master Copperfield!" he rejoined ecstatically, drawing up one leg. "But *would* you have any objections to my laying down before the fire?"

"If it comes to that," I said, "pray take my bed, and I'll lie down before the fire."

His repudiation of this offer was almost shrill enough, in the excess of its surprise and humility, to have penetrated to the ears of Mrs. Crupp, then sleeping, I suppose, in a distant chamber, situated at about the level of low water mark, soothed in her slumbers by the ticking of an incorrigible clock, to which she always referred me when we had any little difference on the score of punctuality, and which was never less than three quarters of an hour too slow, and had always been put right in the morning by the best authorities. As no arguments I could urge, in my bewildered condition, had the least effect upon his modesty in inducing him to accept my bedroom, I was obliged to make the best arrangements I could, for his repose before the fire. The mattress of the sofa (which was a great deal too short for his lank figure), the sofa pillows, a blanket, the table-cover, a clean breakfast-cloth, and a great coat, made him a bed and covering, for which he was more than thankful. Having lent him a night-cap, which he put on at once, and in which he made such an awful figure that I have never worn one since, I left him to his rest.

I never shall forget that night. I never shall forget how I turned and tumbled; how I wearied myself with thinking about Agnes and this creature; how I considered what could I do, and what ought I to do; how I could come to no other conclusion than that the best course for her peace, was to do nothing, and to keep to myself what I had heard. If I went to sleep for a few moments, the image of Agnes with her tender eyes, and of her father looking fondly on her, as I had so often seen him look, arose before me with appealing faces, and filled me with vague terrors. When I awoke, the recollection that Uriah was lying in the next room sat heavy on me like a waking night-mare; and oppressed me with a leaden dread, as if I had had some meaner quality of devil for a lodger.

The poker got into my dozing thoughts besides, and wouldn't

come out. I thought, between sleeping and waking, that it was still red hot, and I had snatched it out of the fire, and run him through the body. I was so haunted at last by the idea, though I knew there was nothing in it, that I stole into the next room to look at him. There I saw him, lying on his back, with his legs extending to I don't know where, gurglings taking place in his throat, stoppages in his nose, and his mouth open like a post-office. He was so much worse in reality than in my distempered fancy, that afterwards I was attracted to him in very repulsion, and could not help wandering in and out every half hour or so, and taking another look at him. Still, the long, long night seemed heavy and hopeless as ever, and no promise of day was in the murky sky.

When I saw him going down stairs early in the morning (for, thank Heaven! he would not stay to breakfast), it appeared to me as if the night was going away in his person. When I went out to the Commons, I charged Mrs. Crupp with particular directions to leave the windows open, that my sitting-room might be aired, and purged of his presence.

CHAPTER XXVI.

I FALL INTO CAPTIVITY.

I SAW no more of Uriah Heep, until the day when Agnes left town. I was at the coach-office to take leave of her and see her go; and there was he, returning to Canterbury by the same conveyance. It was some small satisfaction to me to observe his spare, short-waisted, high-shouldered, mulberry-coloured great-coat perched up, in company with an umbrella like a small tent, on the edge of the back seat on the roof, while Agnes was, of course, inside; but what I underwent in my efforts to be friendly with him, while Agnes looked on, perhaps deserved that little recompense. At the coach-window, as at the dinner-party, he hovered about us without a moment's intermission, like a great vulture: gorging himself on every syllable that I said to Agnes, or Agnes said to me.

In the state of trouble into which his disclosure by my fire had thrown me, I had thought very much of the words Agnes had used in reference to the partnership. "I did what I hope was right. Feeling sure that it was necessary for papa's peace that the sacrifice should be made, I entreated him to make it." A miserable foreboding that she would yield to, and sustain herself by, the same feeling in reference to any sacrifice for his sake, had oppressed me ever since. I knew how she loved him. I knew what the devotion of her nature was. I knew from her own lips that she regarded herself as the innocent cause of his errors, and as owing him a great debt she ardently desired to pay. I had no consolation in seeing how different she was from this detestable Rufus, with the mulberry-coloured great-coat, for I felt that in the very difference between them, in the self-denial of her pure soul and the sordid baseness of his, the greatest danger lay. All this, doubtless, he knew thoroughly, and had, in his cunning, considered well.

Yet, I was so certain that the prospect of such a sacrifice afar off must destroy the happiness of Agnes; and I was so sure, from her manner, of its being unseen by her then, and having cast no shadow on her yet; that I could as soon have injured her, as given her any warning of what impended. Thus it was that we parted without explanation: she waving her hand and smiling farewell from the coach-window; her evil genius writhing on the roof, as if he had her in his clutches and triumphed.

I could not get over this farewell glimpse of them for a long time. When Agnes wrote to tell me of her safe arrival, I was as miserable as when I saw her going away. Whenever I fell into a thoughtful state, this subject was sure to present itself, and all my uneasiness was sure to be redoubled. Hardly a night passed without my dreaming of it. It became a part of my life, and as inseparable from my life as my own head.

I had ample leisure to refine upon my uneasiness: for Steerforth was at Oxford, as he wrote to me, and when I was not at the Commons, I was very much alone. I believe I had at this time some lurking distrust of Steerforth. I wrote to him most affectionately in reply to his, but I think I was glad, upon the whole, that he could not come to London just then. I suspect the truth to be, that the influence of Agnes was upon me, undisturbed by the sight of him;

and that it was the more powerful with me, because she had so large a share in my thoughts and interests.

In the meantime, days and weeks slipped away. I was articled to Spenlow and Jorkins. I had ninety pounds a year (exclusive of my house-rent and sundry collateral matters) from my aunt. My rooms were engaged for twelve months certain: and though I still found them dreary of an evening and the evenings long, I could settle down into a state of equable low spirits, and resign myself to coffee; which I seem, on looking back, to have taken by the gallon at about this period of my existence. At about this time, too, I made three discoveries: first, that Mrs. Crupp was a martyr to a curious disorder called "the spazzums," which was generally accompanied with inflammation of the nose, and required to be constantly treated with peppermint; secondly, that something peculiar in the temperature of my pantry, made the brandy-bottles burst; thirdly, that I was alone in the world, and much given to record that circumstance in fragments of English versification.

On the day when I was articled, no festivity took place, beyond my having sandwiches and sherry into the office for the clerks, and going alone to the theatre at night. I went to see "The Stranger" as a Doctors' Commons sort of play, and was so dreadfully cut up, that I hardly knew myself in my own glass when I got home. Mr. Spenlow remarked, on this occasion, when we concluded our business, that he should have been happy to have seen me at his house at Norwood to celebrate our becoming connected, but for his domestic arrangements being in some disorder, on account of the expected return of his daughter from finishing her education at Paris. But he intimated, that when she came home he should hope to have the pleasure of entertaining me. I knew that he was a widower, with one daughter, and expressed my acknowledgments.

Mr. Spenlow was as good as his word. In a week or two he referred to this engagement, and said that if I would do him the favor to come down next Saturday, and stay till Monday, he would be extremely happy. Of course I said I *would* do him the favor; and he was to drive me down in his phæton, and to bring me back.

When the day arrived, my very carpet-bag was an object of veneration to the stipendiary clerks, to whom the house at Norwood was a sacred mystery. One of them informed me that he had heard that Mr. Spenlow ate entirely off plate and china; and another hinted at champagne being constantly on draught, after the usual custom of table beer. The old clerk with the wig, whose name was Mr. Tiffey, had been down on business several times in the course of his career, and had on each occasion penetrated to the breakfast-parlor. He described it as an apartment of the most sumptuous nature, and said that he had drunk brown East India sherry there, of a quality so precious as to make a man wink.

We had an adjourned cause in the Consistory that day—about excommunicating a baker who had been objecting in a vestry to a paving rate—and as the evidence was just twice the length of Robinson Crusoe, according to a calculation I made, it was rather late in the day before we finished. However, we got him excommunicated for six weeks, and sentenced in no end of costs; and then the baker's proctor, and the judge, and the advocates on both sides (who were all nearly related), went out of town together, and Mr. Spenlow and I drove away in the phaeton.

The phaeton was a very handsome affair; the horses arched their necks and lifted up their legs as if they knew they belonged to Doctors' Commons. There was a good deal of competition in the Commons on all points of display, and it turned out some very choice equipages then; though I have always considered, and always shall consider, that in my time the great article of competition there was starch: which I think was worn among the proctors to as great an extent as it is in the nature of man to bear.

We were very pleasant going down, and Mr. Spenlow gave me some hints in reference to my profession. He said it was the genteelest profession in the world, and must on no account be confounded with the profession of a solicitor: being quite another sort of thing, infinitely more exclusive, less mechanical, and more profitable. We took things much more easily in the Commons than they could be taken anywhere else, he observed, and that set us, as a privileged class, apart. He said it was impossible to conceal the disagreeable fact, that we were chiefly employed by solicitors; but he gave me to understand that they were an inferior race of men, universally looked down upon by all proctors of any pretensions.

I asked Mr. Spenlow what he considered the best sort of professional business? He replied, that a good case of a disputed will, where there was a neat little estate of thirty or forty thousand pounds, was, perhaps, the best of all. In such a case, he said, not only were there very pretty pickings in the way of arguments at every stage of the proceedings, and mountains upon mountains of evidence on interrogatory and counter-interrogatory (to say nothing of an appeal lying, first to the Delegates, and then to the Lords); but, the costs being pretty sure to come out of the estate at last, both sides went at it in a lively and spirited manner, and expense was no consideration. Then, he launched into a general eulogium on the Commons. What was to be particularly admired (he said) in the Commons, was its compactness. It was the most conveniently organized place in the world. It was the complete idea of snugness. It lay in a nut-shell. For example: You brought a divorce case, or a restitution case, into the Consistory. Very good. You tried it in the Consistory. You made a quiet little round game of it, among a family group, and you played it out at leisure. Suppose you were not satisfied with the Consistory, what did you do then? Why, you went into the Arches. What was the Arches? The same court, in the same room, with the same bar, and the same practitioners, but another judge, for there the Consistory judge could plead any court-day as an advocate. Well, you played your round game out again. Still you were not satisfied. Very good. What did you do then? Why, you went to the Delegates. Who were the Delegates? Why, the Ecclesiastical Delegates were the advocates without any business, who had looked on at the round game when it was playing in both courts, and had seen the cards shuffled, and cut, and played, and had talked to all the players about it, and now came fresh, as judges, to settle the matter to the satisfaction of everybody! Discontented people might talk of corruption in the Commons, closeness in the Commons, and the necessity of reforming the Commons, said Mr. Spenlow solemnly, in conclusion; but when the price of wheat per bushel had been highest, the Commons had been busiest; and a man might lay his hand upon his heart, and say this to the whole world,—"Touch the Commons, and down comes the country!"

I listened to all this with attention; and though, I must say, I had my doubts whether the country was quite as much obliged to the Commons as Mr. Spenlow made out, I respectfully deferred to his opinion. That about the price of wheat per bushel, I modestly felt was too much for my strength, and quite settled the question. I have never, to this hour, got the better of that bushel of wheat. It has re-appeared to annihilate me, all through my life, in connexion with all kinds of subjects. I don't know now, exactly, what it has to do with me, or what right it has to crush me, on an infinite variety of occasions; but whenever I see my old friend the bushel brought in by the head and shoulders (as he always is, I observe), I give up a subject for lost.

This is a digression. *I* was not the man to touch the Commons, and bring down the country. I submissively expressed, by my silence, my acquiescence in all I had heard from my superior in years and knowledge; and we talked about "The Stranger" and the Drama, and the pair of horses, until we came to Mr. Spenlow's gate.

There was a lovely garden to Mr. Spenlow's house; and though that was not the best time of the year for seeing a garden, it was so beautifully kept, that I was quite enchanted. There was a charming lawn, there were clusters of trees, and there were perspective walks that I could just distinguish in the dark, arched over with trellis-work, on which shrubs and flowers grew in the growing season. "Here Miss Spenlow walks by herself," I thought. "Dear me!"

We went into the house, which was cheerfully lighted up, and into a hall where there were all sorts of hats, caps, great-coats, plaids, gloves, whips, and walking-sticks. "Where is Miss Dora?" said Mr. Spenlow to the servant. "Dora!" I thought. "What a beautiful name!"

We turned into a room near at hand, (I think it was the identical breakfast-room, made memorable by the brown East Indian Sherry), and I heard a voice say, "Mr. Copperfield, my daughter Dora, and my daughter Dora's confidential friend!" It was, no doubt, Mr. Spenlow's voice, but I didn't know it, and I didn't care whose it was. All was over in a moment. I had fulfilled my destiny. I was a captive and a slave. I loved Dora Spenlow to distraction!

She was more than human to me. She was a Fairy, a Sylph, I

I FALL INTO CAPTIVITY.

don't know what she was—anything that no one ever saw, and everything that everybody ever wanted. I was swallowed up in an abyss of love in an instant. There was no pausing on the brink; no looking down, or looking back; I was gone, headlong, before I had sense to say a word to her.

"*I*," observed a well-remembered voice, when I had bowed and murmured something, "have seen Mr. Copperfield before."

The speaker was not Dora. No; the confidential friend. Miss Murdstone!

I don't think I was much astonished. To the best of my judgment, no capacity of astonishment was left in me. There was nothing worth mentioning in the material world, but Dora Spenlow, to be astonished about. I said, "How do you do, Miss Murdstone? I hope you are well." She answered, "Very well." I said, "How is Mr. Murdstone?" She replied, "My brother is robust, I am obliged to you."

Mr. Spenlow, who, I suppose, had been surprised to see us recognise each other, then put in his word.

"I am glad to find," he said, "Copperfield, that you and Miss Murdstone are already acquainted."

"Mr. Copperfield and myself," said Miss Murdstone, with severe composure, "are connexions. We were once slightly acquainted. It was in his childish days. Circumstances have separated us since. I should not have known him."

I replied that I should have known her, any where. Which was true enough.

"Miss Murdstone has had the goodness," said Mr. Spenlow to me, "to accept the office—if I may so describe it—of my daughter Dora's confidential friend. My daughter Dora having, unhappily, no mother, Miss Murdstone is obliging enough to become her companion and protector."

A passing thought occurred to me that Miss Murdstone, like the pocket instrument called a life-preserver, was not so much designed for purposes of protection as of assault. But as I had none but passing thoughts for any subject save Dora, I glanced at her, directly afterwards, and was thinking that I saw, in her prettily pettish manner, that she was not very much inclined to be particularly confidential to her companion and protector, when a bell rang, which Mr. Spenlow said was the first dinner-bell, and so carried me off to dress.

The idea of dressing one's self, or doing any thing in the way of action, in that state of love, was a little too ridiculous. I could only sit down before my fire, biting the key of my carpet-bag, and thinking of the captivating, girlish, bright-eyed lovely Dora. What a form she had, what a face she had, what a graceful, variable, enchanting manner!

The bell rang again so soon that I made a mere scramble of my dressing, instead of the careful operation I could have wished under the circumstances, and went down stairs. There was some company. Dora was talking to an old gentleman with a grey head. Grey as he was—and a great-grandfather into the bargain, for he said so—I was madly jealous of him.

What a state of mind I was in! I was jealous of everybody. I couldn't bear the idea of anybody knowing Mr. Spenlow better than I did. It was torturing to me to hear them talk of occurrences in which I had had no share. When a most amiable person, with a highly polished bald head, asked me across the dinner-table, if that were the first occasion of my seeing the grounds, I could have done anything to him that was savage and revengeful.

I don't remember who was there, except Dora. I have not the least idea what we had for dinner, besides Dora. My impression is, that I dined off Dora, entirely, and sent away half-a-dozen plates untouched. I sat next to her. I talked to her. She had the most delightful little voice, the gayest little laugh, the pleasantest and most fascinating little ways, that ever led a lost youth into hopeless slavery. She was rather diminutive altogether. So much the more precious, I thought.

When she went out of the room with Miss Murdstone (no other ladies were of the party), I fell into a reverie, only disturbed by the cruel apprehension that Miss Murdstone would disparage me to her. The amiable creature with the polished head told me a long story, which I think was about gardening. I think I heard him say, "my gardener," several times. I seemed to pay the deepest attention to him, but I was wandering in a garden of Eden all the while, with Dora.

My apprehensions of being disparaged to the object of my engrossing affection were revived when we went into the drawing-room, by the grim and distant aspect of Miss Murdstone. But I was relieved of them in an unexpected manner.

"David Copperfield," said Miss Murdstone, beckoning me aside into a window. "A word."

I confronted Miss Murdstone alone.

"David Copperfield," said Miss Murdstone, "I need not enlarge upon family circumstances. They are not a tempting subject."

"Far from it, ma'am," I returned.

"Far from it," assented Miss Murdstone. "I do not wish to revive the memory of past differences, or of past outrages. I have received outrages from a person—a female I am sorry to say, for the credit of my sex—who is not to be mentioned without scorn and disgust; and therefore I would rather not mention her."

I felt very fiery on my aunt's account; but I said it would certainly be better, if Miss Murdstone pleased, *not* to mention her. I could not hear her disrespectfully mentioned, I added, without expressing my opinion in a decided tone.

Miss Murdstone shut her eyes, and disdainfully inclined her head; then, slowly opening her eyes, resumed:

"David Copperfield, I shall not attempt to disguise the fact, that I formed an unfavorable opinion of you in your childhood. It may have been a mistaken one, or you may have ceased to justify it. That is not in question between us now. I belong to a family remarkable, I believe, for some firmness; and I am not the creature of circumstance or change. I may have my opinion of you. You may have your opinion of me."

I inclined my head, in my turn.

"But it is not necessary," said Miss Murdstone, "that these opinions should come into collision here. Under existing circumstances, it is as well on all accounts that they should not. As the chances of life have brought us together again, and may bring us together on other occasions, I would say let us meet here as distant acquaintances. Family circumstances are a sufficient reason for our only meeting on that footing, and it is quite unnecessary that either of us should make the other the subject of remark. Do you approve of this?"

"Miss Murdstone," I returned, "I think you and Mr. Murdstone used me very cruelly, and treated my mother with great unkindness. I shall always think so, as long as I live. But I quite agree in what you propose."

Miss Murdstone shut her eyes again, and bent her head. Then, just touching the back of my hand with the tips of her cold, stiff fingers, she walked away, arranging the little fetters on her wrists and round her neck; which seemed to be the same set, in exactly the same state, as when I had seen her last. These reminded me, in reference to Miss Murdstone's nature, of the fetters over a jail-door; suggesting on the outside, to all beholders, what was to be expected within.

All I know of the rest of the evening is, that I heard the empress of my heart sing enchanted ballads in the French language, generally to the effect that, whatever was the matter, we ought always to dance, Ta ra la, Ta ra la! accompanying herself on a glorified instrument, resembling a guitar. That I was lost in blissful delirium. That I refused refreshment. That my soul recoiled from punch particularly. That when Miss Murdstone took her into custody and led her away, she smiled and gave me her delicious hand. That I caught a view of myself in a mirror, looking perfectly imbecile and idiotic. That I retired to bed in a most maudlin state of mind, and got up in a crisis of feeble infatuation.

It was a fine morning, and early, and I thought I would go and take a stroll down one of those wire-arched walks, and indulge my passion by dwelling on her image. On my way through the hall, I encountered her little dog, who was called Jip—short for Gipsy. I approached him tenderly, for I loved even him; but he showed his whole set of teeth, got under a chair expressly to snarl, and wouldn't hear of the least familiarity.

The garden was cool and solitary. I walked about, wondering what my feelings of happiness would be, if I could ever become engaged to this dear wonder. As to marriage, and fortune, and all that, I believe I was almost as innocently undesigning then, as when I loved little Em'ly. To be allowed to call her "Dora," to write to her, to dote upon and worship her, to have reason to think that when she was with other people she was yet mindful of me, seemed to me the summit of human ambition—I am sure it was the summit of mine. There is no doubt whatever that I was a lackadaisical young spooney; but there was a purity of heart in all this still, that prevents my having quite a contemptuous recollection of it, let me laugh as I may.

I had not been walking long, when I turned a corner, and met her. I tingle again from head to foot as my recollection turns that corner, and my pen shakes in my hand.

"You—are—out early, Miss Spenlow," said I.

"It's so stupid at home," she replied, "and Miss Murdstone is so absurd! She talks such nonsense about its being necessary for the day to be aired, before I come out. Aired!" (She laughed here in the most melodious manner.) "On a Sunday morning, when I don't practise, I must do something. So I told papa last night I *must* come out. Besides, it's the brightest time of the whole day. Don't you think so?"

I hazarded a bold flight, and said (not without stammering) that it was very bright to me then, though it had been very dark to me a minute before.

"Do you mean a compliment," said Dora, "or that the weather has really changed?"

I stammered worse than before, in replying that I meant no compliment, but the plain truth; though I was not aware of any change having taken place in the weather. It was in the state of my own feelings, I added, bashfully: to clench the explanation.

I never saw such curls—how could I, for there never were such curls!—as those she shook out to hide her blushes. As to the straw hat and blue ribbons which was on the top of the curls, if I could only have hung it up in my room in Buckingham Street, what a priceless possession it would have been!

"You have just come home from Paris," said I.

"Yes," said she. "Have you ever been there?"

"No."

"Oh! I hope you'll go soon. You would like it so much!"

Traces of deep-seated anguish appeared in my countenance. That she should hope I would go, that she should think it possible I *could* go, was insupportable. I depreciated Paris; I depreciated France. I said I wouldn't leave England, under existing circumstances, for any earthly consideration. Nothing should induce me. In short, she was shaking the curls again, when the little dog came running along the walk to our relief.

He was mortally jealous of me, and persisted in barking at me. She took him up in her arms—oh, my goodness!—and caressed him, but he insisted upon barking still. He wouldn't let me touch him, when I tried; and then she beat him. It increased my sufferings greatly to see the pats she gave him for punishment on the bridge of his blunt nose, while he winked his eyes, and licked her hand, and still growled within himself like a little double-bass. At length he was quiet—well he might be with her dimpled chin upon his head!—and we walked away to look at a greenhouse.

"You are not very intimate with Miss Murdstone, are you?" said Dora.—"My pet!"

(The two last words were to the dog. Oh, if they had only been to me!)

"No," I replied. "Not at all so."

"She is a tiresome creature," said Dora, pouting. "I can't think what papa can have been about, when he chose such a vexatious thing to be my companion. Who wants a protector! I am sure *I* don't want a protector. Jip can protect me a great deal better than Miss Murdstone,—can't you, Jip dear?"

He only winked lazily, when she kissed his ball of a head.

"Papa calls her my confidential friend, but I am sure she is no such thing—is she, Jip? We are not going to confide in any such cross people, Jip and I. We mean to bestow our confidence where we like, and to find out our own friends, instead of having them found out for us—don't we, Jip?"

Jip made a comfortable noise, in answer, a little like a tea-kettle when it sings. As for me, every word was a new heap of fetters, riveted above the last.

"It is very hard, because we have not a kind Mama, that we are to have, instead, a sulky, gloomy old thing like Miss Murdstone, always following us about—isn't it, Jip? Never mind, Jip. We won't be confidential, and we'll make ourselves as happy as we can in spite of her, and we'll teaze her, and not please her,—won't we, Jip?"

If it had lasted any longer, I think I must have gone down on my knees on the gravel, with the probability before me of grazing them, and of being presently ejected from the premises besides. But, by good fortune, the greenhouse was not far off, and these words brought us to it.

It contained quite a show of beautiful geraniums. We loitered along in front of them, and Dora often stopped to admire this one or that one, and I stopped to admire the same one, and Dora, laughing, held the dog up, childishly, to smell the flowers; and if we were not all three in Fairyland, certainly *I* was. The scent of a geranium leaf, at this day, strikes me with a half comical, half serious wonder as to what change has come over me in a moment; and then I see a straw hat and blue ribbons, and a quantity of curls, and a little black dog being held up, in two slender arms, against a bank of blossoms and bright leaves.

Miss Murdstone had been looking for us. She found us here; and presented her uncongenial cheek, the little wrinkles in it filled with hair powder, to Dora to be kissed. Then she took Dora's arm in hers, and marched us in to breakfast as if it were a soldier's funeral.

How many cups of tea I drank, because Dora made it, I don't know. But, I perfectly remember that I sat swilling tea until my whole nervous system, if I had had any in those days, must have gone by the board. By-and-by we went to church. Miss Murdstone was between Dora and me in the pew; but I heard her sing, and the congregation vanished. A sermon was delivered—about Dora, of course—and I am afraid that is all I know of the service.

We had a quiet day. No company, a walk, a family dinner of four, and an evening of looking over books and pictures; Miss Murdstone with a homily before her, and her eye upon us, keeping guard vigilantly. Ah! little did Mr. Spenlow imagine, when he sat opposite to me after dinner that day, with his pocket-handkerchief over his head, how fervently I was embracing him, in my fancy, as his son-in-law! Little did he think, when I took leave of him at night, that he had just given his full consent to my being engaged to Dora, and that I was invoking blessings on his head!

We departed early in the morning, for we had a Salvage case coming on in the Admiralty Court, requiring a rather accurate knowledge of the whole science of navigation, in which (as we couldn't be expected to know much about those matters in the Commons) the judge had entreated two old Trinity Masters, for charity's sake, to come and help him out. Dora was at the breakfast-table to make the tea again, however; and I had the melancholy pleasure of taking off my hat to her in the phaeton, as she stood on the door-step with Jip in her arms.

What the Admiralty was to me that day; what nonsense I made of our case in my mind, as I listened to it; how I saw "DORA" engraved upon the blade of the silver oar which they lay upon the table, as the emblem of that high jurisdiction; and how I felt, when Mr. Spenlow went home without me (I had had an insane hope that he might take me back again), as if I were a mariner myself, and the ship to which I belonged had sailed away and left me on a desert island; I shall make no fruitless effort to describe. If that sleepy old court could rouse itself, and present in any visible form the day dreams I have had in it about Dora, it would reveal my truth.

I don't mean the dreams that I dreamed on that day alone, but day after day, from week to week, and term to term. I went there, not to attend to what was going on, but to think about Dora. If I ever bestowed a thought upon the cases, as they dragged their slow length before me, it was only to wonder, in the matrimonial cases (remembering Dora), how it was that married people could ever be otherwise than happy; and, in the Prerogative cases, to consider, if the money in question had been left to me, what were the foremost steps I should immediately have taken in regard to Dora. Within the first week of my passion, I bought four sumptuous waistcoats—not for myself; *I* had no pride in them; for Dora—and took to wearing straw-colored kid gloves in the streets, and laid the foundations of all the corns I have ever had. If the boots I wore at that period could only be produced and compared with the natural size of my feet, they would show what the state of my heart was, in a most affecting manner.

And yet, wretched cripple as I made myself by this act of homage to Dora, I walked miles upon miles daily in the hope of seeing her. Not only was I soon as well known on the Norwood Road as the postmen on that beat, but I pervaded London likewise. I walked about the streets where the best shops for ladies were, I haunted the

Bazaar like an unquiet spirit, I fagged through the park again and again, long after I was quite knocked up. Sometimes, at long intervals and on rare occasions, I saw her. Perhaps I saw her glove wave in a carriage window; perhaps I met her, walked with her and Miss Murdstone a little way, and spoke to her. In the latter case I was always very miserable afterwards, to think that I had said nothing to the purpose; or that she had no idea of the extent of my devotion, or that she cared nothing about me. I was always looking out, as may be supposed, for another invitation to Mr. Spenlow's house. I was always being disappointed, for I got none.

Mrs. Crupp must have been a woman of penetration; for when this attachment was but a few weeks old, and I had not had the courage to write more explicitly even to Agnes, than that I had been to Mr. Spenlow's house, "whose family," I added, "consists of one daughter;"—I say Mrs. Crupp must have been a woman of penetration, for even in that early stage, she found it out. She came up to me one evening, when I was very low, to ask (she being then afflicted with the disorder I have mentioned) if I could oblige her with a little tincture of cardamums mixed with rhubarb, and flavored with seven drops of the essence of cloves, which was the best remedy for her complaint;—or, if I had not such a thing by me, with a little brandy which was the next best. It was not, she remarked, so palatable to her, but it was the next best. As I had never even heard of the first remedy, and always had the second in the closet, I gave Mrs. Crupp a glass of the second, which (that I might have no suspicion of its being devoted to any improper use) she began to take in my presence.

"Cheer up, sir," said Mrs. Crupp, "I can't abear to see you so, sir, I'm a mother myself."

I did not quite perceive the application of this fact to *my*self, but I smiled on Mrs. Crupp, as benignly as was in my power.

"Come, sir," said Mrs. Crupp. "Excuse me. I know what it is, sir. There's a young lady in the case."

"Mrs. Crupp?" I returned, reddening.

"Oh, bless you! Keep a good heart, sir!" said Mrs. Crupp, nodding encouragement. "Never say die, sir! If she don't smile upon you there's a many as will. You're a young gentleman to *be* smiled on, Mr. Copperfull, and you must learn your walue, sir."

Mrs. Crupp always called me Mr. Copperfull: firstly, no doubt, because it was not my name; and secondly, I am inclined to think, in some indistinct association with a washing-day.

"What makes you suppose there is any young lady in the case, Mrs. Crupp?" said I.

"Mr. Copperfull," said Mrs. Crupp, with a great deal of feeling, "I'm a mother myself."

For some time Mrs. Crupp could only lay her hand upon her nankeen bosom, and fortify herself against returning pain with sips of her medicine. At length she spoke again.

"When the present set were took for you by your dear aunt, Mr. Copperfull," said Mrs. Crupp, "my remark were, I had now found summun I could care for. 'Thank Ev'in!' were the expression, 'I have now found summun I can care for!'—You don't eat enough, sir, nor yet drink."

"Is that what you found your supposition on, Mrs. Crupp?" said I.

"Sir," said Mrs. Crupp, in a tone approaching to severity, "I've laundressed other young gentlemen besides yourself. A young gentleman may be over-careful of himself, or he may be under-careful of himself. He may brush his hair too regular, or too unregular. He may wear his boots much too large for him, or much too small. That is according as the young gentleman has his original character formed. But let him go to which extreme he may, sir, there's a young lady in both of 'em."

Mrs. Crupp shook her head in such a determined manner, that I had not an inch of 'vantage ground left.

"It was but the gentleman which died here before yourself," said Mrs. Crupp, "that fell in love—with a barmaid—and had his waistcoats took in directly, though much swelled by drinking."

"Mrs. Crupp," said I, "I must beg you not to connect the young lady in my case with a barmaid, or anything of that sort, if you please."

"Mr. Copperfull," returned Mrs. Crupp, "I'm a mother myself, and not likely. I ask your pardon, sir, if I intrude. I should never wish to intrude where I were not welcome. But you are a young gentleman, Mr. Copperfull, and my adwice to you is, to cheer up, sir, to keep a good heart, and to know your own walue. If you was to take to something, sir," said Mrs. Crupp, "if you was to take to skittles, now, which is healthy, you might find it divert your mind, and do you good."

With these words, Mrs. Crupp, affecting to be very careful of the brandy—which was all gone—thanked me with a majestic curtsey, and retired. As her figure disappeared into the gloom of the entry, this counsel certainly presented itself to my mind in the light of a slight liberty on Mrs. Crupp's part; but, at the same time, I was content to receive it, in another point of view, as a word to the wise, and a warning in future to keep my secret better.

CHAPTER XXVII.

TOMMY TRADDLES.

It may have been in consequence of Mrs. Crupp's advice, and, perhaps, for no better reason than because there was a certain similarity in the sound of the words skittles and Traddles, that it came into my head, next day, to go and look after Traddles. The time he had mentioned was more than out, and he lived in a little street near the Veterinary College at Camden Town, which was principally tenanted, as one of our clerks who lived in that direction informed me, by gentlemen students, who bought live donkeys, and made experiments on those quadrupeds in their private apartments. Having obtained from this clerk a direction to the academic grove in question, I set out, the same afternoon, to visit my old school-fellow.

I found that the street was not as desirable a one as I could have wished it to be, for the sake of Traddles. The inhabitants appeared to have a propensity to throw any little trifles they were not in want of, into the road; which not only made it rank and sloppy, but untidy too, on account of the cabbage-leaves. The refuse was not wholly vegetable either, for I myself saw a shoe, a doubled-up saucepan, a black bonnet, and an umbrella, in various stages of decomposition, as I was looking out for the number I wanted.

The general air of the place reminded me forcibly of the days when I lived with Mr. and Mrs. Micawber. An indescribable character of faded gentility that attached to the house I sought, and made it unlike all the other houses in the street—though they were all built on one monotonous pattern, and looked like the early copies of a blundering boy who was learning to make houses, and had not yet got out of his cramped brick and mortar pothooks—reminded me still more of Mr. and Mrs. Micawber. Happening to arrive at the door as it was opened to the afternoon milkman, I was reminded of Mr. and Mrs. Micawber more forcibly yet.

"Now," said the Milkman to a very youthful servant girl. "Has that there little bill of mine been heerd on?"

"Oh master says he'll attend to it immediate," was the reply.

"Because," said the milkman, going on as if he had received no answer, and speaking, as I judged from his tone, rather for the edification of somebody within the house, than of the youthful servant—an impression which was strengthened by his manner of glaring down the passage—"Because that there little bill has been running so long, that I begin to believe it's run away altogether, and never won't be heerd of. Now, I'm not a going to stand it, you know!" said the milkman, still throwing his voice into the house, and glaring down the passage.

As to his dealing in the mild article of milk, by-the-by, there never was a greater anomaly. His deportment would have been fierce in a butcher or a brandy merchant.

The voice of the youthful servant became faint, but she seemed to me, from the action of her lips, again to murmur that it would be attended to immediate.

"I tell you what," said the milkman, looking hard at her for the first time, and taking her by the chin, "are you fond of milk?"

"Yes, I likes it," she replied.

"Good," said the milkman. "Then you won't have none to-morrow. D'ye hear? Not a fragment of milk you won't have to-morrow."

I thought she seemed, upon the whole, relieved, by the prospect of having any to-day. The milkman, after shaking his head at her, darkly, released her chin, and with anything rather than good will opened his can, and deposited the usual quantity in the family jug. This done, he went away, muttering, and uttered the cry of his trade next door, in a vindictive shriek.

"Does Mr. Traddles live here?" I then enquired.

A mysterious voice from the end of the passage replied 'Yes." Upon which the youthful servant replied "Yes."

"Is he at home?" said I.

Again the mysterious voice replied in the affirmative, and again the servant echoed it. Upon this, I walked in, and in pursuance of the servant's directions walked up-stairs; conscious, as I passed the back parlor-door, that I was surveyed by a mysterious eye, probably belonging to the mysterious voice.

When I got to the top of the stairs—the house was only a story high above the ground floor—Traddles was on the landing to meet me. He was delighted to see me, and gave me welcome, with great heartiness, to his little room. It was in the front of the house, and extremely neat, though sparely furnished. It was his only room, I saw; for there was a sofa-bedstead in it, and his blacking-brushes and blacking were among his books—on the top shelf, behind a dictionary. His table was covered with papers, and he was hard at work in an old coat. I looked at nothing, that I know of, but I saw everything, even to the prospect of a church upon his china inkstand, as I sat down—and this, too, was a faculty confirmed in me in the old Micawber times. Various ingenious arrangements he had made, for the disguise of his chest of drawers, and the accommodation of his boots, his shaving-glass, and so forth, particularly impressed themselves upon me, as evidences of the same Traddles who used to make models of elephants' dens in writing paper to put flies in; and to comfort himself, under ill usage, with the memorable works of art I have so often mentioned.

In a corner of the room was something neatly covered up with a large white cloth. I could not make out what that was.

"Traddles," said I, shaking hands with him again, after I had sat down. "I am delighted to see you."

"I am delighted to see *you*, Copperfield," he returned. "I am very glad indeed to see you. It was because I was thoroughly glad to see you when we met in Ely Place, and was sure you were thoroughly glad to see me, that I gave you this address instead of my address at chambers."

"Oh! You have chambers?" said I.

"Why, I have the fourth of a room and a passage, and the fourth of a clerk," returned Traddles. "Three others and myself unite to have a set of chambers—to look business-like—and we quarter the clerk too. Half-a-crown a week he costs me."

His old simple character and good temper, and something of his old unlucky fortune also, I thought, smiled at me in the smile with which he made this explanation.

"It's not because I have the least pride, Copperfield, you understand," said Traddles, "that I don't usually give my address here. It's only on account of those who come to me, who might not like to come here. For myself, I am fighting my way on in the world against difficulties, and it would be ridiculous if I made a pretence of doing any thing else."

"You are reading for the bar, Mr. Waterbrook informed me?" said I.

"Why, yes," said Traddles, rubbing his hands slowly over one another, "I am reading for the bar. The fact is, I have just begun to keep my terms, after rather a long delay. It's some time since I was articled, but the payment of that hundred pounds was a great pull. A great pull!" said Traddles, with a wince, as if he had had a tooth out.

"Do you know what I can't help thinking of, Traddles, as I sit here looking at you?" I asked him.

"No," said he.

"That sky-blue suit you used to wear."

"Lord, to be sure!" cried Traddles, laughing. "Tight in the arms and legs, you know? Dear me! Well! Those were happy times, weren't they?"

"I think our schoolmaster might have made them happier, without doing any harm to any of us, I acknowledge," I returned.

"Perhaps he might," said Traddles. "But dear me, there was a good deal of fun going on. Do you remember the nights in the bed-room? When we used to have the suppers? And when you used to tell the stories? Ha, ha, ha! And do you remember when I got caned for crying about Mr. Mell? Old Creakle! I should like to see him again, too!"

"He was a brute to you, Traddles," said I, indignantly; for his good humour made me feel as if I had seen him beaten but yesterday.

"Do you think so?" returned Traddles. "Really? Perhaps he was, rather. But it's all over, a long while. Old Creakle!"

"You were brought up by an uncle, then?" said I.

"Of course I was!" said Traddles. "The one I was always going to write to. And always didn't, eh! Ha, ha, ha! Yes, I had an uncle then. He died soon after I left school."

"Indeed!"

"Yes. He was a retired—what do you call it!—draper—cloth-merchant—and had made me his heir. But he didn't like me when I grew up."

"Do you really mean that?" said I. He was so composed, that I fancied he must have some other meaning.

"O dear yes, Copperfield! I mean it," replied Traddles. "It was an unfortunate thing, but he didn't like me at all. He said I wasn't at all what he expected, and so he married his housekeeper."

"And what did you do?" I asked.

"I didn't do anything in particular," said Traddles. "I lived with them, waiting to be put out in the world, until his gout unfortunately flew to his stomach—and so he died, and so she married a young man, and so I wasn't provided for."

"Did you get nothing, Traddles, after all?"

"Oh dear yes!" said Traddles. "I got fifty pounds. I had never been brought up to any profession, and at first I was at a loss what to do for myself. However, I began, with the assistance of the son of a professional man, who had been to Salem House—Yawler, with his nose on one side. Do you recollect him?"

"No. He had not been there with me; all the noses were straight, in my day."

"It don't matter," said Traddles. "I began, by means of his assistance, to copy law writings. That didn't answer very well; and then I began to state cases for them, and make abstracts, and do that sort of work. For I am a plodding kind of fellow, Copperfield, and had learnt the way of doing such things pithily. Well! that put it in my head to enter myself as a law student; and that ran away with all that was left of the fifty pounds. Yawler recommended me to one or two other offices, however—Mr. Waterbrook's for one—and I got a good many jobs. I was fortunate enough, too, to become acquainted with a person in the publishing way, who was getting up an Encyclopædia, and he set me to work; and, indeed" (glancing at his table), "I am at work for him at this minute. I am not a bad compiler, Copperfield," said Traddles, preserving the same air of cheerful confidence in all he said, "but I have no invention at all; not a particle. I suppose there never was a young man with less originality than I have."

As Traddles seemed to expect that I should assent to this as a matter of course, I nodded; and he went on, with the same sprightly patience—I can find no better expression—as before.

"So, by little and little, and not living high, I managed to scrape up the hundred pounds at last," said Traddles; "and thank Heaven that's paid—though it was—though it certainly was," said Traddles, wincing again as if he had had another tooth out, "a pull. I am living by the sort of work I have mentioned, still, and I hope, one of these days, to get connected with some newspaper: which would almost be the making of my fortune. Now, Copperfield, you are so exactly what you used to be, with that agreeable face, and it's so pleasant to see you, that I shan't conceal anything. Therefore you must know that I am engaged."

Engaged! Oh Dora!

"She is a curate's daughter," said Traddles; "one of ten, down in Devonshire. Yes!" For he saw me glance, involuntarily, at the prospect on the inkstand. "That's the church! You come round here, to the left, out of this gate," tracing his finger along the inkstand, "and exactly where I hold this pen, there stands the house—facing, you understand, towards the church."

The delight with which he entered into these particulars did not fully present itself to me until afterwards; for my selfish thoughts were making a ground-plan of Mr. Spenlow's house and garden at the same moment.

"She is such a dear girl!" said Traddles; "a little older than me, but the dearest girl! I told you I was going out of town? I have been down there. I walked there, and I walked back, and I had the most delightful time! I dare say ours is likely to be a rather long engagement, but our motto is 'Wait and hope!' We always ay that. 'Wait and hope,' we always say. And she would wait, Copperfield, till she was sixty—any age you can mention—for me!"

Traddles rose from his chair, and, with a triumphant smile, put his hand upon the white cloth I had observed.

"However," he said, "it's not that we haven't made a beginning towards housekeeping. No, no; we have begun. We must get on by degrees, but we have begun. Here," drawing the cloth off with great pride and care, "are two pieces of furniture to commence with. This flower-pot and stand, she bought herself. You put that in a parlor-window," said Traddles, falling a little back from it to survey it with the greater admiration, "with a plant in it, and—there you are! This little round table with the marble top (it's two feet ten in circumference), *I* bought. You want to lay a book down, you know, or somebody comes to see you or your wife, and wants a place to stand a cup of tea upon, and—and there you are again!" said Traddles. "It's an admirable piece of workmanship—firm as a rock!"

I praised them both, highly, and Traddles replaced the covering as carefully as he had removed it.

"It's not a great deal towards the furnishing," said Traddles, "but it's something. The table-cloths and pillow-cases, and articles of that kind, are what discourage me most, Copperfield. So does the ironmongery—candle-boxes and gridirons, and that sort of necessaries—because those things tell, and mount up. However, 'wait and hope!' And I assure you she's the dearest girl!"

"I am quite certain of it," said I.

"In the mean time," said Traddles, coming back to his chair; "and this is the end of my prosing about myself, I get on as well as I can. I don't make much, but I don't spend much. In general, I board with the people down-stairs, who are very agreeable people indeed. Both Mr. and Mrs. Micawber have seen a good deal of life, and are excellent company."

"My dear Traddles!" I quickly exclaimed. "What are you talking about?"

Traddles looked at me, as if he wondered what *I* was talking about.

"Mr. and Mrs. Micawber!" I repeated. "Why, I am intimately acquainted with them!"

An opportune double knock at the door, which I knew well from old experience in Windsor Terrace, and which nobody but Mr. Micawber could ever have knocked at that door, resolved any doubt in my mind as to their being my old friends. I begged Traddles to ask his landlord to walk up. Traddles accordingly did so, over the bannister; and Mr. Micawber, not a bit changed—his tights, his stick, his shirt-collar, and his eye-glass, all the same as ever—came into the room with a genteel and youthful air.

"I beg your pardon, Mr. Traddles," said Mr. Micawber, with the old roll in his voice, as he checked himself in humming a soft tune. "I was not aware that there was any individual, alien to this tenement, in your sanctum."

Mr. Micawber slightly bowed to me, and pulled up his shirt-collar.

"How do you do, Mr. Micawber?" said I.

"Sir," said Mr. Micawber, "you are exceedingly obliging. I am *in statu quo.*"

"And Mrs. Micawber?" I pursued.

"Sir," said Mr. Micawber, "she is also, thank God, *in statu quo.*"

"And the children, Mr. Micawber?"

"Sir," said Mr. Micawber, "I rejoice to reply that they are, likewise, in the enjoyment of salubrity."

All this time, Mr. Micawber had not known me in the least, though he had stood face to face with me. But, now, seeing me smile, he examined my features with more attention, fell back, cried, "Is it possible! Have I the pleasure of again beholding Copperfield?" and shook me by both hands with the utmost fervor.

"Good Heaven, Mr. Traddles!" said Mr. Micawber, "to think that I should find you acquainted with the friend of my youth, the companion of earlier days! My dear!" calling over the bannisters to Mrs. Micawber, while Traddles looked (with reason) not a little amazed at this description of me. "Here is a gentleman in Mr.

Traddles's apartment, whom he wishes to have the pleasure of presenting to you, my love!"

Mr. Micawber immediately reappeared, and shook hands with me again.

"And how is our good friend the Doctor, Copperfield?" said Mr. Micawber, "and all the circle at Canterbury?"

"I have none but good accounts of them," said I.

"I am most delighted to hear it," said Mr. Micawber. "It was at Canterbury where we last met. Within the shadow, I may figuratively say, of that religious edifice, immortalized by Chaucer, which was anciently the resort of Pilgrims from the remotest corners of—in short," said Mr. Micawber, "in the immediate neighborhood of the Cathedral."

I replied that it was. Mr. Micawber continued talking as volubly as he could; but not, I thought, without showing, by some marks of concern in his countenance, that he was sensible of sounds in the next room, as of Mrs. Micawber washing her hands, and hurriedly opening and shutting drawers that were uneasy in their action.

"You find us, Copperfield," said Mr. Micawber, with one eye on Traddles, "at present established, on what may be designated as a small and unassuming scale; but, you are aware that I have, in the course of my career, surmounted difficulties, and conquered obstacles. You are no stranger to the fact, that there have been periods of my life, when it has been requisite that I should pause, until certain expected events should turn up; when it has been necessary that I should fall back, before making what I trust I shall not be accused of presumption in terming—a spring. The present is one of those momentous stages in the life of man. You find me, fallen back, *for* a spring; and I have every reason to believe that a vigorous leap will shortly be the result."

I was expressing my satisfaction, when Mrs. Micawber came in; a little more slatternly than she used to be, or so she seemed now, to my unaccustomed eyes, but still with some preparation of herself for company, and with a pair of brown gloves on.

"My dear," said Mr. Micawber, leading her towards me. "Here is a gentleman of the name of Copperfield, who wishes to renew his acquaintance with you."

It would have been better, as it turned out, to have led gently up to his announcement, for Mrs. Micawber, being in a delicate state of health, was overcome by it, and was taken so unwell, that Mr. Micawber was obliged, in great trepidation, to run down to the water-butt in the back yard, and draw a basinful to lave her brow with. She presently revived, however, and was really pleased to see me. We had half-an-hour's talk, all together; and I asked her about the twins, who, she said, were "grown great creatures;" and after Master and Miss Micawber, whom she described as "absolute giants," but they were not produced on that occasion.

Mr. Micawber was very anxious that I should stay to dinner. I should not have been averse to do so, but that I imagined I detected trouble, and calculation relative to the extent of the cold meat, in Mrs. Micawber's eye. I therefore pleaded another engagement; and observing that Mrs. Micawber's spirits were immediately lightened, I resisted all persuasion to forego it.

But I told Traddles, and Mr. and Mrs. Micawber, that before I could think of leaving, they must appoint a day when they would come and dine with me. The occupations to which Traddles stood pledged, rendered it necessary to fix a somewhat distant one; but an appointment was made for the purpose, that suited us all, and then I took my leave.

Mr. Micawber, under pretence of showing me a nearer way than that by which I had come, accompanied me to the corner of the street; being anxious (he explained to me) to say a few words to an old friend, in confidence.

"My dear Copperfield," said Mr. Micawber, "I need hardly tell you that to have beneath our roof, under existing circumstances, a mind like that which gleams—if I may be allowed the expression—which gleams—in your friend Traddles, is an unspeakable comfort. With a washerwoman, who exposes hard-bake for sale in her parlor-window, dwelling next door, and a Bow-street officer residing over the way, you may imagine that his society is a source of consolation to myself and to Mrs. Micawber. I am at present, my dear Copperfield, engaged in the sale of corn upon commission. It is not an avocation of a remunerative description—in other words it does *not* pay—and some temporary embarrassments of a pecuniary nature have been the consequence. I am, however, delighted to add that I have now an immediate prospect of something turning up (I am not at liberty to say in what direction), which I trust will enable me to provide, permanently, both for myself and for your friend Traddles, in whom I have an unaffected interest. You may, perhaps, be prepared to hear that Mrs. Micawber is in a state of health which renders it not wholly improbable that an addition may be ultimately made to those pledges of affection which—in short, to the infantine group. Mrs. Micawber's family have been so good as to express their dissatisfaction with this state of things. I have merely to observe, that I am not aware it is any business of theirs, and that I repel that exhibition of feeling with scorn, and with defiance!"

Mr. Micawber then shook hands with me again, and left me.

CHAPTER XXVIII.

MR. MICAWBER'S GAUNTLET.

Until the day arrived on which I was to entertain my newly-found old friends, I lived principally on Dora and coffee. In my love-lorn condition, my appetite languished; and I was glad of it, for I felt as though it would have been an act of perfidy towards Dora to have a natural relish for my dinner. The quantity of walking exercise I took, was not in this respect attended with its usual consequence, as the disappointment counteracted the fresh air. I have my doubts, too, founded on the acute experience acquired at this period of my life, whether a sound enjoyment of animal food can develop itself freely in any human subject who is always in torment from tight boots. I think the extremities require to be at peace before the stomach will conduct itself with vigour.

On the occasion of this domestic little party, I did not repeat my former extensive preparations. I merely provided a pair of soles, a small leg of mutton, and a pigeon-pie. Mrs. Crupp broke out into rebellion on my first bashful hint in reference to the cooking of the fish and joint, and said, with a dignified sense of injury, "No! no, sir! You will not ask me sich a thing, for you are better acquainted with me than to suppose me capable of doing what I cannot do with ampial satisfaction to my own feelings!" But, in the end, a compromise was effected; and Mrs. Crupp consented to achieve this feat, on condition that I dined from home for a fortnight afterwards.

And here I may remark, that what I underwent from Mrs. Crupp, in consequence of the tyranny she established over me, was dreadful. I never was so much afraid of any one. We made a compromise of everything. If I hesitated, she was taken with that wonderful disorder which was always lying in ambush in her system, ready, at the shortest notice, to prey upon her vitals. If I rang the bell impatiently, after half-a-dozen unavailing modest pulls, and she appeared at last—which was not by any means to be relied upon—she would appear with a reproachful aspect, sink breathless on a chair near the door, lay her hand upon her nankeen bosom, and become so ill, that I was glad, at any sacrifice of brandy or anything else, to get rid of her. If I objected to having my bed made at five o'clock in the afternoon—which I *do* still think an uncomfortable arrangement—one motion of her hand towards the same nankeen region of wounded sensibility was enough to make me falter an apology. In short, I would have done anything in an honorable way rather than give Mrs. Crupp offence; and she was the terror of my life.

I bought a second-hand dumb-waiter for this dinner-party, in preference to re-engaging the handy young man; against whom I had conceived a prejudice, in consequence of meeting him in the Strand, one Sunday morning, in a waistcoat remarkably like one of mine, which had been missing since the former occasion. The "young gal" was re-engaged; but on the stipulation that she should only bring in the dishes, and then withdraw to the landing-place, beyond the outer door; where a habit of sniffing she had contracted would be lost upon the guests, and where her retiring on the plates would be a physical impossibility.

Having laid in the materials for a bowl of punch, to be compounded by Mr. Micawber; having provided a bottle of lavender-water, two wax candles, a paper of mixed pins, and a pincushion, to assist Mrs. Micawber in her toilette, at my dressing-table; having also caused the fire in my bed-room to be lighted for Mrs. Micawber's convenience; and having laid the cloth with my own hands, I awaited the result with composure.

At the appointed time, my three visitors arrived together. Mr. Micawber with more shirt-collar than usual, and a new ribbon to his eye-glass; Mrs. Micawber with her cap in a whitey-brown paper parcel; Traddles carrying the parcel, and supporting Mrs. Micawber on his arm. They were all delighted with my residence. When I conducted Mrs. Micawber to my dressing-table, and she saw the scale on which it was prepared for her, she was in such raptures, that she called Mr. Micawber to come in and look.

"My dear Copperfield," said Mr. Micawber, "this is luxurious. This is a way of life which reminds me of the period when I was myself in a state of celibacy, and Mrs. Micawber had not yet been solicited to plight her faith at the hymeneal altar."

"He means solicited by him, Mr. Copperfield," said Mrs. Micawber archly. "He cannot answer for others."

"My dear," returned Mr. Micawber with sudden seriousness, "I have no desire to answer for others. I am too well aware that when, in the inscrutable decrees of Fate, you were reserved for me, it is possible you may have been reserved for one, destined, after a protracted struggle, at length to fall a victim to pecuniary involvements of a complicated nature. I understand your allusion, love. I regret it, but I can bear it."

"Micawber!" exclaimed Mrs. Micawber, in tears. "Have I deserved this! I, who never have deserted you; who never *will* desert you, Micawber!"

"My love," said Mr. Micawber, much affected, "you will forgive, and our old and tried friend Copperfield will, I am sure, forgive, the momentary laceration of a wounded spirit, made sensitive by a recent collision with the Minion of Power—in other words, with a ribald Turncock attached to the water-works—and will pity, not condemn, its excesses."

Mr. Micawber then embraced Mrs. Micawber, and pressed my hand; leaving me to infer from this broken allusion that his domestic supply of water had been cut off that afternoon, in consequence of default in the payment of the company's rates.

To divert his thoughts from this melancholy subject, I informed Mr. Micawber that I relied upon him for a bowl of punch, and led him to the lemons. His recent despondency, not to say despair, was gone in a moment. I never saw a man so thoroughly enjoy himself amid the fragrance of lemon-peel and sugar, the odor of burning rum, and the steam of boiling water, as Mr. Micawber did that afternoon. It was wonderful to see his face shining at us out of a thin cloud of these delicate fumes, as he stirred, and mixed, and tasted, and looked as if he were making, instead of punch, a fortune for his family down to the latest posterity. As to Mrs. Micawber, I don't know whether it was the effect of the cap, or the lavender-water, or the pins, or the fire, or the wax candles, but she came out of my room, comparatively speaking, lovely. And the lark was never gayer than that excellent woman.

I suppose—I never ventured to inquire, but I suppose—that Mrs. Crupp, after frying the soles, was taken ill. Because we broke down at that point. The leg of mutton came up very red within, and very pale without: besides having a foreign substance of a gritty nature sprinkled over it, as if it had had a fall into the ashes of that remarkable kitchen fire-place. But we were not in a condition to judge of this fact from the appearance of the gravy, forasmuch as the "young gal" had dropped it all upon the stairs—where it remained, by-the-by, in a long train, until it was worn out. The pigeon-pie was not bad, but it was a delusive pie: the crust being like a disappointing head, phrenologically speaking: full of lumps and bumps, with nothing particular underneath. In short, the banquet was such a failure that I should have been quite unhappy—about the failure, I mean, for I was always unhappy about Dora—if I had not been relieved by the great good-humour of my company, and by a bright suggestion from Mr. Micawber.

"My dear friend Copperfield," said Mr. Micawber, "accidents will occur in the best regulated families; and in families not regulated by that pervading influence which sanctifies while it enhances the—a—I would say, in short, by the influence of Woman, in the lofty character of Wife, they may be expected with confidence, and must be borne with philosophy. If you will allow me to take the liberty of remarking that there are few comestibles better, in their way, than a Devil, and that I believe, with a little division of labour, we could accomplish a good one if the young person in attendance could produce a gridiron, I would put it to you, that this little misfortune may be easily repaired."

There was a gridiron in the pantry, on which my morning rasher of bacon was cooked. We had it in, in a twinkling, and immediately applied ourselves to carrying Mr. Micawber's idea into effect. The division of labour to which he had referred was this:—Traddles cut the mutton into slices; Mr. Micawber (who could do anything of this sort to perfection) covered them with pepper, mustard, salt, and cayenne; I put them on the gridiron, turned them with a fork, and took them off, under Mr. Micawber's directions; and Mrs. Micawber heated, and continually stirred, some mushroom ketchup in a little saucepan. When we had slices enough done to begin upon, we fell-to, with our sleeves still tucked up at the wrists, more slices sputtering and blazing on the fire, and our attention divided between the mutton on our plates, and the mutton then preparing.

What with the novelty of this cookery, the excellence of it, the bustle of it, the frequent starting up to look after it, the frequent sitting down to dispose of it as the crisp slices came off the gridiron hot and hot, the being so busy, so flushed with the fire, so amused, and in the midst of such a tempting noise and savour, we reduced the leg of mutton to the bone. My own appetite came back miraculously. I am ashamed to record it, but I really believe I forgot Dora for a little while. I am satisfied that Mr. and Mrs. Micawber could not have enjoyed the feast more if they had sold a bed to provide it. Traddles laughed as heartily, almost the whole time, as he ate and worked. Indeed we all did, all at once; and I dare say there never was a greater success.

We were at the height of our enjoyment, and were all busily engaged, in our several departments, endeavouring to bring the last batch of slices to a state of perfection that should crown the feast, when I was aware of a strange presence in the room, and my eyes encountered those of the staid Littimer, standing hat in hand before me.

"What's the matter?" I involuntarily asked.

"I beg your pardon, sir, I was directed to come in. Is my master not here, sir?"

"No."

"Have you not seen him, sir?"

"No; don't you come from him?"

"Not immediately so, sir."

"Did he tell you you would find him here?"

"Not exactly so, sir. But I should think he might be here to-morrow, as he has not been here to-day."

"Is he coming up from Oxford?"

"I beg, sir," he returned respectfully, "that you will be seated, and allow me to do this." With which he took the fork from my unresisting hand, and bent over the gridiron, as if his whole attention were concentrated on it.

We should not have been much discomposed, I dare say, by the appearance of Steerforth himself, but we became in a moment the meekest of the meek before his respectable serving-man. Mr. Micawber, humming a tune, to show that he was quite at ease, subsided into his chair, with the handle of a hastily-concealed fork sticking out of the bosom of his coat, as if he had stabbed himself. Mrs. Micawber put on her brown gloves, and assumed a genteel languor. Traddles ran his greasy hands through his hair, and stood it bold upright, and stared in confusion at the table-cloth. As for me I was a mere infant at the head of my own table; and hardly ventured to glance at the respectable phenomenon, who had come from Heaven knows where, to put my establishment to rights.

Meanwhile he took the mutton off the gridiron, and gravely handed it round. We all took some, but our appreciation of it was gone, and we merely made a show of eating it. As we severally pushed away our plates, he noiselessly removed them, and set on the cheese. He took that off, too, when it was done with; cleared the table; piled everything on the dumb-waiter; gave us our wine-glasses; and of his own accord wheeled the dumb-waiter into the pantry. All this was done in a perfect manner, and he never raised his eyes from what he was about. Yet his very elbows, when he had his back towards me, seemed to teem with the expression of his fixed opinion that I was extremely young.

"Can I do anything more, sir?"

I thanked him and said, No; but would he take no dinner himself?

"None, I am obliged to you, sir."

"Is Mr. Steerforth coming from Oxford?"

"I beg your pardon, sir?"

"Is Mr. Steerforth coming from Oxford?"

"I should imagine that he might be here to-morrow, sir. I rather thought he might have been here to-day, sir. The mistake is mine, no doubt, sir."

"If you should see him first—" said I.

"If you'll excuse me, sir, I don't think I shall see him first."

"In case you do," said I, "pray say that I am sorry he was not here to-day, as an old schoolfellow of his was here."

"Indeed, sir!" and he divided a bow between me and Traddles, with a glance at the latter.

He was moving softly to the door, when, in a forlorn hope of saying something naturally—which I never could, to this man—I said:

"Oh! Littimer!"

"Sir!"

"Did you remain long at Yarmouth, that time?"

"Not particularly so, sir."

"You saw the boat completed?"

"Yes, sir. I remained behind on purpose to see the boat completed."

"I know!" He raised his eyes to mine respectfully. "Mr. Steerforth has not seen it yet, I suppose?"

"I really can't say, sir. I think—but I really can't say, sir. I wish you good night, sir."

He comprehended everybody present, in the respectful bow with which he followed these words, and disappeared. My visitors seemed to breathe more freely when he was gone; but my own relief was very great, for besides the constraint, arising from that extraordinary sense of being at a disadvantage which I always had in this man's presence, my conscience had embarrassed me with whispers that I had mistrusted his master, and I could not repress a vague uneasy dread that he might find it out. How was it, having so little in reality to conceal, that I always *did* feel as if this man were finding me out?

Mr. Micawber roused me from this reflection, which was blended with a certain remorseful apprehension of seeing Steerforth himself, by bestowing many encomiums on the absent Littimer as a most respectable fellow, and a thoroughly admirable servant. Mr. Micawber, I may remark, had taken his full share of the general bow, and had received it with infinite condescension.

"But punch, my dear Copperfield," said Mr. Micawber, tasting it, "like time and tide, waits for no man. Ah! it is at the present moment in high flavor. My love, will you give me your opinion?"

Mrs. Micawber pronounced it excellent.

"Then I will drink," said Mr. Micawber, "if my friend Copperfield will permit me to take that social liberty, to the days when my friend Copperfield and myself were younger, and fought our way in the world side by side. I may say, of myself and Copperfield, in words we have sung together before now, that

> We twa' hae run about the braes
> And pu'd the gowans fine

—in a figurative point of view—on several occasions. I am not exactly aware," said Mr. Micawber, with the old roll in his voice, and the old indescribable air of saying something genteel, "what gowans may be, but I have no doubt that Copperfield and myself would frequently have taken a pull at them, if it had been feasible."

Mr. Micawber, at the then present moment, took a pull at his punch. So we all did: Traddles evidently lost in wondering at what distant time Mr. Micawber and I could possibly have been comrades in the battle of the world.

"Ahem!" said Mr. Micawber, clearing his throat, and warming with the punch and with the fire. "My dear, another glass?"

Mrs. Micawber said it must be very little, but we couldn't allow that, so it was a glassful.

"As we are quite confidential here, Mr. Copperfield," said Mrs. Micawber, sipping her punch, "Mr. Traddles being a part of our domesticity, I should much like to have your opinion on Mr. Micawber's prospects. For corn," said Mrs. Micawber argumentatively, "as I have repeatedly said to Mr. Micawber, may be gentlemanly, but it is not remunerative. Commission to the extent of two and ninepence in a fortnight cannot, however limited our ideas, be considered remunerative."

We were all agreed upon that.

"Then," said Mrs. Micawber, who prided herself on taking a clear view of things, and keeping Mr. Micawber straight by her woman's wisdom, when he might otherwise go a little crooked, "then I ask myself this question. If corn is not to be relied upon, what is? Are coals to be relied upon? Not at all. We have turned our attention to that experiment, on the suggestion of my family, and we find it fallacious."

Mr. Micawber, leaning back in his chair, with his hands in his pockets, eyed us aside, and nodded his head, as much as to say that the case was very clearly put.

"The articles of corn and coals," said Mrs. Micawber, still more argumentatively, "being equally out of the question, Mr. Copperfield, I naturally look round the world, and say, 'What is there in which a person of Mr. Micawber' talent is likely to succeed?' And I exclude the doing anything on commission, because commission is not a certainty. What is best suited to a person of Mr. Micawber's peculiar temperament, is, I am convinced, a certainty."

Traddles and I both expressed, by a feeling murmur, that this great discovery was no doubt true of Mr. Micawber, and that it did him much credit.

"I will not conceal from you, my dear Mr. Copperfield," said Mrs. Micawber, "that *I* have long felt the Brewing business to be particularly adapted to Mr. Micawber. Look at Barclay and Perkins! Look at Truman, Hanbury, and Buxton! It is on that extensive footing that Mr. Micawber, I know from my own knowledge of him, is calculated to shine; and the profits, I am told, are e-NOR—mous! But if Mr. Micawber cannot get into those firms—which decline to answer his letters, when he offers his services, even in an inferior capacity—what is the use of dwelling upon that idea? None. I may have a conviction that Mr. Micawber's manners"—

"Hem! Really, my dear," interposed Mr. Micawber.

"My love, be silent," said Mrs. Micawber, laying her brown glove on his hand. "I may have a conviction, Mr. Copperfield, that Mr. Micawber's manners peculiarly qualify him for the Banking business. I may argue within myself, that if *I* had a deposit at a banking-house, the manners of Mr. Micawber, as representing that banking-house, would inspire confidence, and must extend the connexion. But if the various banking-houses refuse to avail themselves of Mr. Micawber's abilities, or receive the offer of them with contumely, what is the use of dwelling upon *that* idea? None. As to originating a banking-business, I may know that there are members of my family who, if they chose to place their money in Mr. Micawber's hands, might found an establishment of that description. But if they do *not* choose to place their money in Mr. Micawber's hands—

which they don't—what is the use of that? Again I contend that we are no farther advanced than we were before."

I shook my head, and said, "Not a bit." Traddles also shook his head, and said, "Not a bit."

"What do I deduce from this?" Mrs. Micawber went on to say, still with the same air of putting a case lucidly. "What is the conclusion, my dear Mr. Copperfield, to which I am irresistibly brought? Am I wrong in saying, it is clear that we must live?"

I answered, "Not at all!" and Traddles answered, "Not at all!" and I found myself afterwards sagely adding, alone, that a person must either live or die.

"Just so," returned Mrs. Micawber. "It is precisely that. And the fact is, my dear Mr. Copperfield, that we can *not* live without something widely different from existing circumstances shortly turning up. Now I am convinced, myself, and this I have pointed out to Mr. Micawber several times of late, that things cannot be expected to turn up of themselves. We must, in a measure, assist to turn them up. I may be wrong, but I have formed that opinion."

Both Traddles and I applauded it highly.

"Very well," said Mrs. Micawber. "Then what do I recommend? Here is Mr. Micawber, with a variety of qualifications—with great talent—"

"Really, my love," said Mr. Micawber.

"Pray, my dear, allow me to conclude. Here is Mr. Micawber, with a variety of qualifications, with great talent—*I* should say, with genius, but that may be the partiality of a wife—"

Traddles and I both murmured "No."

"And here is Mr. Micawber without any suitable position or employment. Where does that responsibility rest? Clearly on society. Then I would make a fact so disgraceful known, and boldly challenge society to set it right. It appears to me, my dear Mr. Copperfield," said Mrs. Micawber, forcibly, "that what Mr Micawber has to do, is to throw down the gauntlet to society, and say, in effect, 'Show me who will take that up. Let the party immediately step forward.'"

I ventured to ask Mrs. Micawber how this was to be done.

"By advertising," said Mrs. Micawber—"in all the papers. It

appears to me, that what Mr. Micawber has to do, in justice to himself, in justice to his family, and I will even go so far as to say in justice to society, by which he has been hitherto overlooked, is to advertise in all the papers ; to describe himself plainly as so and so, with such and such qualifications, and to put it thus : '*Now* employ me, on remunerative terms, and address, post-paid, to *W. M.*, Post Office, Camden Town.' "

"This idea of Mrs. Micawber's, my dear Copperfield," said Mr. Micawber, making his shirt-collar meet in front of his chin, and glancing at me sideways, "is, in fact, the Leap to which I alluded, when I last had the pleasure of seeing you."

"Advertising is rather expensive," I remarked, dubiously.

"Exactly so!" said Mrs. Micawber, preserving the same logical air. "Quite true, my dear Mr. Copperfield! I have made the identical observation to Mr. Micawber. It is for that reason especially, that I think Mr. Micawber ought (as I have already said, in justice to himself, in justice to his family, and in justice to society) to raise a certain sum of money—on a bill."

Mr. Micawber, leaning back in his chair, trifled with his eye-glass, and cast his eyes up at the ceiling; but I thought him observant of Traddles too, who was looking at the fire.

"If no member of my family," said Mrs. Micawber, "is possessed of sufficient natural feeling to negotiate that bill—I believe there is a better business-term to express what I mean—"

Mr. Micawber, with his eyes still cast up at the ceiling, suggested "Discount."

"To discount that bill," said Mrs. Micawber, "then my opinion is, that Mr. Micawber should go into the City, should take that bill into the Money Market, and should dispose of it for what he can get. If the individuals in the Money Market oblige Mr. Micawber to sustain a great sacrifice, that is between themselves and their consciences. I view it, steadily, as an investment. I recommend Mr. Micawber, my dear Mr. Copperfield, to do the same; to regard it as an investment which is sure of return, and to make up his mind to *any* sacrifice."

I felt, but I am sure I don't know why, that this was self-denying and devoted in Mrs. Micawber, and I uttered a murmur to that effect. Traddles, who took his tone from me, did likewise, still looking at the fire.

"I will not," said Mrs. Micawber, finishing her punch, and gathering her scarf about her shoulders, preparatory to her withdrawal to my bed-room: "I will not protract these remarks on the subject of Mr. Micawber's pecuniary affairs. At your fireside, my dear Mr. Copperfield, and in the presence of Mr. Traddles, who, though not so old a friend, is quite one of ourselves, I could not refrain from making you acquainted with the course I advise Mr Micawber to take. I feel that the time is arrived when Mr. Micawber should exert himself and—I will add—assert himself, and it appears to me that these are the means. I am aware that I am merely a female, and that a masculine judgment is usually considered more competent to the discussion of such questions; still I must not forget that, when I lived at home with my papa and mama, my papa was in the habit of saying, 'Emma's form is fragile, but her grasp of a subject is inferior to none.' That my papa was too partial, I well know; but that he was an observer of character in some degree, my duty and my reason equally forbid me to doubt."

With these words, and resisting our entreaties that she would grace the remaining circulation of the punch with her presence, Mrs. Micawber retired to my bed-room. And really I felt that she was a noble woman—the sort of woman who might have been a Roman matron, and done all manner of heroic things, in times of public trouble.

In the fervor of this impression, I congratulated Mr. Micawber on the treasure he possessed. So did Traddles. Mr. Micawber extended his hand to each of us in succession, and then covered his face with his pocket-handkerchief, which I think had more snuff upon it than he was aware of. He then returned to the punch, in the highest state of exhilaration.

He was full of eloquence. He gave us to understand that in our children we lived again, and that, under the pressure of pecuniary difficulties, any accession to their number was doubly welcome. He said that Mrs. Micawber had latterly had her doubts on this point, but that he had dispelled them, and reassured her. As to her family, they were totally unworthy of her, and their sentiments were utterly indifferent to him, and they might—I quote his own expression—go to the Devil.

Mr. Micawber then delivered a warm eulogy on Traddles. He said Traddles's was a character, to the steady virtues of which he (Mr. Micawber) could lay no claim, but which, he thanked Heaven, he could admire. He feelingly alluded to the young lady, unknown, whom Traddles had honored with his affection, and who had reciprocated that affection by honoring and blessing Traddles with *her* affection. Mr. Micawber pledged her. So did I. Traddles thanked us both, by saying, with a simplicity and honesty I had sense enough to be quite charmed with, "I am very much obliged to you indeed. And I do assure you, she's the dearest girl!—"

Mr. Micawber took an early opportunity, after that, of hinting, with the utmost delicacy and ceremony, at the state of *my* affections. Nothing but the serious assurance of his friend Copperfield to the contrary, he observed, could deprive him of the impression that his friend Copperfield loved and was beloved. After feeling very hot and uncomfortable for some time, and after a good deal of blushing, stammering, and denying, I said, having my glass in my hand, "Well! I would give them D.!" which so excited and gratified Mr. Micawber, that he ran with a glass of punch into my bed-room, in order that Mrs. Micawber might drink D., who drank it with enthusiasm, crying from within, in a shrill voice, "Hear, hear! My dear Mr. Copperfield, I am delighted. Hear!" and tapping at the wall, by way of applause.

Our conversation, afterwards, took a more worldly turn; Mr. Micawber telling us that he found Camden Town inconvenient, and that the first thing he contemplated doing, when the advertisement should have been the cause of something satisfactory turning up, was to move. He mentioned a terrace at the western end of Oxford Street, fronting Hyde Park, on which he had always had his eye, but which he did not expect to attain immediately, as it would require a large establishment. There would probably be an interval, he explained, in which he should content himself with the upper part of a house, over some respectable place of business,—say in Piccadilly,—which would be a cheerful situation for Mrs. Micawber; and where, by throwing out a bow window, or carrying up the roof another story, or making some little alteration of that sort, they might live, comfortably and reputably, for a few years. Whatever was reserved for him, he expressly said, or wherever his abode might be, we might rely on this—there would always be a room for Traddles, and a knife and fork for me. We acknowledged his kindness; and he begged us to forgive his having launched into these practical and business-like details, and to excuse it as natural in one who was making entirely new arrangements in life.

Mrs. Micawber, tapping at the wall again, to know if tea were ready, broke up this particular phase of our friendly conversation. She made tea for us in a most agreeable manner; and, whenever I went near her, in handing about the tea-cups and bread-and-butter, asked me, in a whisper, whether D. was fair, or dark, or whether she was short, or tall: or something of that kind; which I think I liked. After tea, we discussed a variety of topics before the fire; and Mrs. Micawber was good enough to sing us (in a small, thin, flat voice, which I remember to have considered, when I first knew her, the very table-beer of acoustics) the favorite ballads of "The Dashing White Serjeant," and "Little Tafflin." For both of these songs Mrs. Micawber had been famous when she lived at home with her papa and mama. Mr. Micawber told us, than when he heard her sing the first one, on the first occasion of his seeing her beneath the parental roof, she had attracted his attention in an extraordinary degree; but that when it came to Little Tafflin, he had resolved to win that woman or perish in the attempt.

It was between ten and eleven o'clock when Mrs. Micawber rose to replace her cap in the whitey-brown paper parcel, and to put on her bonnet. Mr. Micawber took the opportunity of Traddles putting on his great coat, to slip a letter into my hand, with a whispered request that I would read it at my leisure. I also took the opportunity of my holding a candle over the bannisters to light them down, when Mr. Micawber was going first, leading Mrs. Micawber, and Traddles was following with the cap, to detain Traddles for a moment on the top of the stairs.

"Traddles," said I, "Mr. Micawber don't mean any harm, poor fellow; but, if I were you, I wouldn't lend him anything."

"My dear Copperfield," returned Traddles, smiling, "I haven't got anything to lend."

"You have got a name, you know," said I.

"Oh! You call *that* something to lend?" returned Traddles, with a thoughtful look.

"Certainly."

"Oh!" said Traddles. "Yes, to be sure! I am very much obliged to you, Copperfield; but—I am afraid I have lent him that already."

"For the bill that is to be a certain investment?" I inquired.

"No," said Traddles. "Not for that one. This is the first I have heard of that one. I have been thinking that he will most likely propose that one, on the way home. Mine's another."

"I hope there will be nothing wrong about it," said I.

"I hope not," said Traddles. "I should think not, though, because he told me, only the other day, that it was provided for. That was Mr. Micawber's expression. 'Provided for.'"

Mr. Micawber looking up at this juncture to where we were standing, I had only time to repeat my caution. Traddles thanked me, and descended. But I was much afraid, when I observed the good-natured manner in which he went down with the cap in his hand, and gave Mrs. Micawber his arm, that he would be carried into the Money Market neck and heels.

I returned to my fireside, and was musing, half gravely and half laughing, on the character of Mr. Micawber and the old relations between us, when I heard a quick step ascending the stairs. At first, I thought it was Traddles coming back for something Mrs. Micawber had left behind; but as the step approached, I knew it, and felt my heart beat high, and the blood rush to my face, for it was Steerforth's.

I was never unmindful of Agnes, and she never left that sanctuary in my thoughts—if I may call it so—where I had placed her from the first. But when he entered, and stood before me with his hand out, the darkness that had fallen on him changed to light, and I felt confounded and ashamed of having doubted one I loved so heartily. I loved her none the less; I thought of her as the same benignant, gentle angel in my life; I reproached myself, not her, with having done him an injury; and I would have made him any atonement if I had known what to make, and how to make it.

"Why, Daisy, old boy, dumb-foundered!" laughed Steerforth,

shaking my hand heartily, and throwing it gaily away. "Have I detected you in another feast, you Sybarite! These Doctors' Commons fellows are the gayest men in town, I believe, and beat us sober Oxford people all to nothing!" His bright glance went merrily round the room, as he took the seat on the sofa opposite to me, which Mrs. Micawber had recently vacated, and stirred the fire into blaze.

"I was so surprised at first," said I, giving him welcome with all the cordiality I felt, "that I had hardly breath to greet you with, Steerforth."

"Well, the sight of me *is* good for sore eyes, as the Scotch say," replied Steerforth, "and so is the sight of you, Daisy, in full bloom. How are you, my Bacchanal?"

"I am very well," said I; "and not at all Bacchanalian to-night, though I confess to another party of three."

"All of whom I met in the street, talking loud in your praise," returned Steerforth. "Who's our friend in the tights?"

I gave him the best idea I could, in a few words, of Mr. Micawber. He laughed heartily at my feeble portrait of that gentleman, and said he was a man to know, and he must know him.

"But who do you suppose our other friend is?" said I, in my turn.

"Heaven knows," said Steerforth. "Not a bore, I hope? I thought he looked a little like one."

"Traddles!" I replied triumphantly.

"Who's he?" asked Steerforth, in his careless way.

"Don't you remember Traddles? Traddles in our room at Salem House?"

"Oh! That fellow?" said Steerforth, beating a lump of coal on the top of the fire, with the poker. "Is he as soft as ever? And where the deuce did you pick *him* up?"

I extolled Traddles in reply, as highly as I could; for I felt that Steerforth rather slighted him. Steerforth, dismissing the subject with a light nod, and a smile, and the remark that he would be glad to see the old fellow too, for he had always been an odd fish, inquired if I could give him any thing to eat? During most of this short dialogue, when he had not been speaking in a wild vivacious manner, he had sat idly beating on the lump of coal with the poker. I observed that he did the same thing while I was getting out the remains of the pigeon-pie, and so forth.

"Why, Daisy, here's a supper for a king!" he exclaimed, starting out of his silence with a burst, and taking his seat at the table. "I shall do it justice, for I have come from Yarmouth."

"I thought you came from Oxford?" I returned.

"Not I," said Steerforth. "I have been seafaring—better employed."

"Littimer was here to-day, to inquire for you," I remarked, "and I understood him that you were at Oxford; though, now I think of it, he certainly did not say so."

"Littimer is a greater fool than I thought him, to have been inquiring for me at all," said Steerforth, jovially pouring out a glass of wine, and drinking to me. "As to understanding him, you are a cleverer fellow than most of us, Daisy, if you can do that."

"That's true, indeed," said I, moving my chair to the table. "So you have been at Yarmouth, Steerforth!" interested to know all about it. "Have you been there long?"

"No," he returned. "An *escapade* of a week or so."

"And how are they all? Of course, little Em'ly is not married yet?"

"Not yet. Going to be, I believe—in so many weeks, or months, or something or other. I have not seen much of 'em. By-the-by;" he laid down his knife and fork, which he had been using with great diligence, and began feeling in his pockets; "I have a letter for you."

"From whom?"

"Why, from your old nurse," he returned, taking some papers out of his breast pocket. "'J.Steerforth, Esquire, debtor, to the Willing Mind;' that's not it. Patience, and we'll find it presently. Old what's-his-name's in a bad way, and it's about that, I believe."

"Barkis, do you mean?"

"Yes!" still feeling in his pockets, and looking over their contents: "it's all over with poor Barkis, I am afraid. I saw a little apothecary there—surgeon, or whatever he is—who brought your worship into the world. He was mighty learned about the case, to me; but the upshot of his opinion was, that the carrier was making his last journey rather fast.—Put your hand into the breast pocket of my great coat on the chair yonder, and I think you'll find the letter. Is it there?"

"Here it is!" said I.

"That's right!"

It was from Peggotty; something less legible than usual, and brief. It informed me of her husband's hopeless state, and hinted at his being "a little nearer" than heretofore, and consequently more difficult to manage for his own comfort. It said nothing of her weariness and watching, and praised him highly. It was written with a plain, unaffected, homely piety, that I knew to be genuine, and ended with "my duty to my ever darling"—meaning myself.

While I deciphered it, Steerforth continued to eat and drink.

"It is a bad job," he said, when I had done; "but the sun sets every day, and people die every minute, and we mustn't be scared by the common lot. If we failed to hold our own, because that equal foot at all men's doors was heard knocking somewhere, every object in this world would slip from us. No! Ride on! Rough-shod if need be, smooth-shod if that will do, but ride on! Ride over all obstacles, and win the race!"

"And win what race?" said I.

"The race that one has started in," said he. "Ride on!"

I noticed, I remember, as he paused, looking at me with his handsome head a little thrown back, and his glass raised in his hand, that, though the freshness of the sea-wind was on his face, and it was ruddy, there were traces in it, made since I last saw it, as if he had applied himself to some habitual strain of the fervent energy which, when roused, was so passionately roused within him. I had it in my thoughts to remonstrate with him upon his desperate way of pursuing any fancy that he took—such as this buffeting of rough seas, and braving of hard weather, for example—when my mind glanced off to the immediate subject of our conversation again, and pursued that instead.

"I tell you what, Steerforth," said I, "if your high spirits will listen to me"—

"They are potent spirits, and will do whatever you like," he answered, moving from the table to the fireside again.

"Then I tell you what, Steerforth. I think I will go down and see my old nurse. It is not that I can do her any good, or render her any real service; but she is so attached to me that my visit will have as much effect on her, as if I could do both. She will take it so kindly that it will be a comfort and support to her. It is no great effort to make, I am sure, for such a friend as she has been to me. Wouldn't you go a day's journey, if you were in my place?"

His face was thoughtful, and he sat considering a little before he answered, in a low voice, "Well! Go. You can do no harm."

"You have just come back," said I, "and it would be in vain to ask you to go with me?"

"Quite," he returned. "I am for Highgate to-night. I have not seen my mother this long time, and it lies upon my conscience, for it's something to be loved as she loves her prodigal son.—Bah! Nonsense!—You mean to go to-morrow, I suppose?" he said, holding me out at arm's length, with a hand on each of my shoulders.

"Yes, I think so."

"Well, then, don't go till next day. I wanted you to come and stay a few days with us. Here I am, on purpose to bid you, and you fly off to Yarmouth!"

"You are a nice fellow to talk of flying off, Steerforth, who are always running wild on some unknown expedition or other!"

He looked at me for a moment without speaking, and then rejoined, still holding me as before, and giving me a shake:

"Come! Say the next day, and pass as much of to-morrow as you can with us! Who knows when we may meet again, else? Come! Say the next day! I want you to stand between Rosa Dartle and me, and keep us asunder."

"Would you love each other too much without me!"

"Yes; or hate," laughed Steerforth; "no matter which. Come! Say the next day!"

I said the next day; and he put on his great-coat, and lighted his cigar, and set off to walk home. Finding him in this intention, I put on my own great-coat (but did not light my own cigar, having had enough of that for one while) and walked with him as far as the open road: a dull road, then, at night. He was in great spirits all the way; and when we parted, and I looked after him going so gallantly and airily homeward, I thought of his saying "Ride on over all obstacles, and win the race!" and wished, for the first time, that he had some worthy race to run.

I was undressing in my own room, when Mr. Micawber's letter tumbled on the floor. Thus reminded of it, I broke the seal and read as follows. It was dated an hour and a half before dinner. I am not sure whether I have mentioned that, when Mr. Micawber was at any particularly desperate crisis, he used a sort of legal phraseology: which he seemed to think equivalent to winding up his affairs.

"Sir—for I dare not say, my dear Copperfield.

"It is expedient that I should inform you that the undersigned is Crushed. Some flickering efforts to spare you the premature knowledge of his calamitous position, you may observe in him this day; but hope has sunk beneath the horizon, and the undersigned is Crushed.

"The present communication is penned within the personal range (I cannot call it the society) of an individual, in a state closely bordering on intoxication, employed by a broker. That individual is in legal possession of the premises, under a distress for rent. His inventory includes, not only the chattels and effects of every description belonging to the undersigned, as yearly tenant of this habitation, but also those appertaining to Mr. Thomas Traddles, lodger, a member of the Honourable Society of the Inner Temple.

"If any drop of gloom were wanting in the overflowing cup, which is now 'commended' (in the language of an immortal Writer) to the lips of the undersigned, it would be found in the fact, that a friendly acceptance granted to the undersigned, by the before-mentioned Mr. Thomas Traddles, for the sum of £23 4*s.* 9½*d.* is over due, and is NOT provided for. Also, in the fact, that the living responsibilities clinging to the undersigned, will, in the course of nature, be increased by the sum of one more helpless victim; whose miserable appearance may be looked for—in round numbers—at the expiration of a period not exceeding six lunar months from the present date.

"After premising thus much, it would be a work of supererogation to add, that dust and ashes are for ever scattered

"On
"The
"Head
"Of
"WILKINS MICAWBER."

Poor Traddles! I knew enough of Mr. Micawber by this time, to foresee that *he* might be expected to recover the blow; but my night's rest was sorely distressed by thoughts of Traddles, and of the curate's daughter, who was one of ten, down in Devonshire, and who was such a dear girl, and who would wait for Traddles (ominous phrase!) until she was sixty or any age that could be mentioned.

CHAPTER XXIX.

I VISIT STEERFORTH AT HIS HOME AGAIN.

I MENTIONED to Mr. Spenlow in the morning, that I wanted leave of absence for a short time; and as I was not in the receipt of any salary, and consequently was not obnoxious to the implacable Jorkins, there was no difficulty about it. I took that opportunity, with my voice sticking in my throat, and my sight failing as I uttered the words, to express my hope that Miss Spenlow was quite well; to which Mr. Spenlow replied, with no more emotion than if he had been speaking of an ordinary human being, that he was much obliged to me, and she was very well.

We articled clerks, as germs of the patrician order of proctors, were treated with so much consideration, that I was almost my own master at all times. As I did not care, however, to get to Highgate before one or two o'clock in the day, and as we had another little excommunication case in court that morning, which was called The office of the Judge promoted by Tipkins against Bullock for his soul's correction, I passed an hour or two in attendance on it with Mr. Spenlow very agreeably. It arose out of a scuffle between two churchwardens, one of whom was alleged to have pushed the other against a pump; the handle of which pump projecting into a school-house, which school-house was under a gable of the church roof, made the push an ecclesiastical offence. It was an amusing case; and sent me up to Highgate, on the box of the stage-coach, thinking about the Commons, and what Mr. Spenlow had said about touching the Commons and bringing down the country.

Mrs. Steerforth was pleased to see me, and so was Rosa Dartle. I was agreeably surprised to find that Littimer was not there, and that we were attended by a modest little parlor-maid, with blue ribbons in her cap, whose eye it was much more pleasant, and much less disconcerting, to catch by accident, than the eye of that respectable man. But what I particularly observed, before I had been half an hour in the house, was the close and attentive watch Miss Dartle kept upon me; and the lurking manner in which she seemed to compare my face with Steerforth's, and Steerforth's with mine, and to lie in wait for something to come out between the two So surely as I looked towards her, did I see that eager visage, with its gaunt black eyes and searching brow, intent on mine; or passing suddenly from mine to Steerforth's; or comprehending both of us at once. In this lynx-like scrutiny she was so far from faltering when she saw I observed it, that at such a time she only fixed her piercing look upon me with a more intent expression still. Blameless as I was, and knew that I was, in reference to any wrong she could possibly suspect me of, I shrunk before her strange eyes, quite unable to endure their angry lustre.

All day, she seemed to pervade the whole house. If I talked to Steerforth in his room, I heard her dress rustle in the little gallery outside. When he and I engaged in some of our old exercises on the lawn behind the house, I saw her face pass from window to window, like a wandering light, until it fixed itself in one, and watched us. When we all four went out walking in the afternoon, she closed her thin hand on my arm like a spring, to keep me back, while Steerforth and his mother went on out of hearing: and then spoke to me.

"You have been a long time," she said, "without coming here. Is your profession really so engaging and interesting as to absorb your whole attention? I ask because I always want to be informed, when I am ignorant. Is it really, though?"

I replied that I liked it well enough, but that I certainly could not claim so much for it.

"Oh! I am glad to know that, because I always like to be put right when I am wrong," said Rosa Dartle. "You mean it is a little dry, perhaps?"

Well, I replied; perhaps it *was* a little dry.

"Oh! and that 's a reason why you want relief and change—excitement, and all that?" said she. "Ah! very true! But isn't it a little——Eh?—for him; I don't mean you?"

A quick glance of her eye towards the spot where Steerforth was walking, with his mother leaning on his arm, showed me whom she meant; but beyond that I was quite lost. And I looked so, I have no doubt.

"Don't it—I don't say that it *does*, mind I want to know—don't it rather engross him? Don't it make him, perhaps, a little more remiss than usual in his visits to his blindly doting—eh?" With another quick glance at them, and such a glance at me as seemed to look into my innermost thoughts.

"Miss Dartle," I returned, "pray do not think—"

"I don't!" she said. "Oh, dear me, don't suppose that I think anything! I am not suspicious. I only ask a question. I don't state any opinion. I want to found an opinion on what you tell me. Then, it's not so? Well! I am very glad to know it."

"It certainly is not the fact," said I, perplexed, "that I am accountable for Steerforth's having been away from home longer than usual—if he has been: which I really don't know at this moment, unless I understand it from you. I have not seen him this long while, until last night."

"No?"

"Indeed, Miss Dartle, no."

As she looked full at me, I saw her face grow sharper and paler, and the marks of the old wound lengthened out until it cut through the disfigured lip, and deep into the nether lip, and slanted down the face. There was something positively awful to me in this, and in the brightness of her eyes, as she said, looking fixedly at me:

"What is he doing?"

I repeated the words, more to myself than her, being so amazed.

"What is he doing?" she said, with an eagerness that seemed enough to consume her like a fire. "In what is that man assisting him, who never looks at me without an inscrutable falsehood in his eyes? If you are honorable and faithful, I don't ask you to betray your friend. I ask you only to tell me, is it anger, is it hatred, is it pride, is it restlessness, is it some wild fancy, is it love, *what is it*, that is leading him?"

"Miss Dartle," I returned, "how shall I tell you, so that you will believe me, that I know of nothing in Steerforth different from what there was when I first came here. I can think of nothing. I firmly believe there is nothing. I hardly understand, even, what you mean."

As she still looked fixedly at me, a twitching or throbbing, from which I could not dissociate the idea of pain, came into that cruel mark; and lifted up the corner of her lip as if with scorn, or with a pity that despised its object. She put her hand upon it hurriedly—a hand so thin and delicate, that when I had seen her hold it up before the fire to shade her face, I had compared it in my thoughts to fine porcelain—and saying, in a quick, fierce, passionate way, "I swear you to secresy about this!" said not a word more.

Mrs. Steerforth was particularly happy in her son's society, and Steerforth was, on this occasion, particularly attentive and respectful to her. It was very interesting to me to see them together, not only on account of their mutual affection, but because of the strong personal resemblance between them, and the manner in which what was haughty or impetuous in him was softened by age and sex, in her, to a gracious dignity. I thought, more than once, that it was well no serious cause of division had ever come between them; or two such natures—I ought rather to express it, two such shades of the same nature—might have been harder to reconcile than the two extremest opposites in creation. The idea did not originate in my own discernment, I am bound to confess, but in a speech of Rosa Dartle's.

She said at dinner:

"Oh, but do tell me, though, somebody, because I have been thinking about it all day, and I want to know."

"You want to know what, Rosa?" returned Mrs. Steerforth "Pray, pray, Rosa, do not be mysterious."

"Mysterious!" she cried. "Oh! really? Do you consider me so?"

"Do I constantly entreat you," said Mrs. Steerforth, "to speak plainly, in your own natural manner?"

"Oh! then, this is *not* my natural manner?" she rejoined. "Now you must really bear with me, because I ask for information. We never know ourselves."

"It has become a second nature," said Mrs. Steerforth, without any displeasure; "but I remember,—and so must you, I think,—when your manner was different, Rosa; when it was not so guarded, and was more trustful."

"I am sure you are right," she returned; "and so it is that bad habits grow upon one! Really? Less guarded and more trustful? How *can* I, imperceptibly, have changed, I wonder! Well, that's very odd! I must study to regain my former self."

"I wish you would," said Mrs. Steerforth, with a smile.

"Oh! I really will, you know!" she answered. "I will learn frankness from—let me see—from James."

"You cannot learn frankness, Rosa," said Mrs. Steerforth, quickly—for there was always some effect of sarcasm in what Rosa Dartle said, though it was said, as this was, in the most unconscious manner in the world—"in a better school."

"That I am sure of," she answered, with uncommon fervour. "If I am sure of anything, of course, you know, I am sure of that."

Mrs. Steerforth appeared to me to regret having been a little nettled; for she presently said, in a kind tone:

"Well, my dear Rosa, we have not heard what it is that you want to be satisfied about?"

"That I want to be satisfied about?" she replied, with provoking coldness. "Oh! It was only whether people, who are like each other in their moral constitution—is that the phrase?"

"It's as good a phrase as another," said Steerforth.

"Thank you:—whether people, who are like each other in their moral constitution, are in greater danger than people not so circumstanced, supposing any serious cause of variance to rise between them, of being divided angrily and deeply?"

"I should say yes," said Steerforth.

"Should you?" she retorted. "Dear me! Supposing then, for instance,—any unlikely thing will do for a supposition—that you and your mother were to have a serious quarrel."

"My dear Rosa," interposed Mrs. Steerforth, laughing good-naturedly, "suggest some other supposition! James and I know our duty to each other better, I pray Heaven!"

"Oh!" said Miss Dartle, nodding her head thoughtfully. "To be sure. *That* would prevent it? Why, of course it would. Ex-actly.

Now, I am glad I have been so foolish as to put the case, for it is so very good to know that your duty to each other would prevent it! Thank you very much."

One other little circumstance connected with Miss Dartle I must not omit; for I had reason to remember it thereafter, when all the irremediable past was rendered plain. During the whole of this day, but especially from this period of it, Steerforth exerted himself with his utmost skill, and that was with his utmost ease, to charm this singular creature into a pleasant and pleased companion. That he should succeed, was no matter of surprise to me. That she should struggle against the fascinating influence of his delightful art—delightful nature I thought it then—did not surprise me either; for I knew that she was sometimes jaundiced and perverse. I saw her features and her manner slowly change; I saw her look at him with growing admiration; I saw her try, more and more faintly, but always angrily, as if she condemned a weakness in herself, to resist the captivating power that he possessed; and finally I saw her sharp glance soften, and her smile become quite gentle, and I ceased to be afraid of her as I had really been all day, and we all sat about the fire, talking and laughing together, with as little reserve as if we had been children.

Whether it was because we had sat there so long, or because Steerforth was resolved not to lose the advantage he had gained, I do not know; but we did not remain in the dining-room more than five minutes after her departure. "She is playing her harp," said Steerforth, softly, at the drawing-room door, "and nobody but my mother has heard her do that, I believe, these three years." He said it with a curious smile, which was gone directly; and we went into the room and found her alone.

"Don't get up!" said Steerforth (which she had already done); "my dear Rosa, don't! Be kind for once, and sing us an Irish song."

"What do you care for an Irish song?" she returned.

"Much!" said Steerforth. "Much more than for any other. Here is Daisy, too, loves music from his soul. Sing us an Irish song, Rosa! and let me sit and listen as I used to do."

He did not touch her, or the chair from which she had risen, but sat himself near the harp. She stood beside it for some little while, in a curious way, going through the motion of playing with her right hand, but not sounding it. At length she sat down, and drew it to her with one sudden action, and played and sang.

I don't know what it was, in her touch or voice, that made that song the most unearthly I have ever heard in my life, or can imagine. There was something fearful in the reality of it. It was as if it had never been written, or set to music, but sprung out of the passion within her; which found imperfect utterance in the low sounds of her voice, and crouched again when all was still. I was dumb when she leaned beside the harp again, playing it, but not sounding it, with her right hand.

A minute more, and this had roused me from my trance:—Steerforth had left his seat, and gone to her, and had put his arm laughingly about her, and had said, "Come, Rosa, for the future we will love each other very much!" And she had struck him, and had thrown him off with the fury of a wild cat, and had burst out of the room.

"What is the matter with Rosa?" said Mrs. Steerforth, coming in.

"She has been an angel, mother," returned Steerforth, "for a little while; and has run into the opposite extreme, since, by way of compensation."

"You should be careful not to irritate her, James. Her temper has been soured, remember, and ought not to be tried."

Rosa did not come back; and no other mention was made of her, until I went with Steerforth into his room to say, Good night. Then he laughed about her, and asked me if I had ever seen such a fierce little piece of incomprehensibility.

I expressed as much of my astonishment as was then capable of expression, and asked if he could guess what it was that she had taken so much amiss, so suddenly.

"Oh, Heaven knows," said Steerforth. "Anything you like—or nothing! I told you she took everything, herself included, to a grindstone, and sharpened it. She is an edge-tool, and requires great care in dealing with. She is always dangerous. Good night!"

"Good night!" said I, "my dear Steerforth! I shall be gone before you wake in the morning. Good night!"

He was unwilling to let me go; and stood, holding me out, with a hand on each of my shoulders, as he had done in my own room.

"Daisy," he said, with a smile—"for though that's not the name your Godfathers and Godmothers gave you, it's the name I like best to call you by—and I wish, I wish, I wish, you could give it to me!"

"Why so I can, if I choose," said I.

"Daisy, if anything should ever separate us, you must think of me at my best, old boy. Come! Let us make that bargain. Think of me at my best, if circumstances should ever part us!"

"You have no best to me, Steerforth," said I, "and no worst. You are always equally loved and cherished in my heart."

So much compunction for having ever wronged him, even by a shapeless thought, did I feel within me, that the confession of having done so was rising to my lips. But for the reluctance I had, to betray the confidence of Agnes, but for my uncertainty how to approach the subject with no risk of doing so, it would have reached them before he said, "God bless you, Daisy, and good night!" In my doubt, it did *not* reach them; and we shook hands, and we parted.

I was up with the dull dawn, and, having dressed as quietly as I could, looked into his room. He was fast asleep; lying, easily, with his head upon his arm, as I had often seen him lie at school.

The time came in its season, and that was very soon, when I almost wondered that nothing troubled his repose, as I looked at him. But he slept—let me think of him so again—as I had often seen him sleep at school; and thus, in this silent hour, I left him.

—Never more, oh God forgive you, Steerforth! to touch that passive hand in love and friendship. Never, never, more!

CHAPTER XXX.

A LOSS.

I GOT down to Yarmouth in the evening, and went to the inn. I knew that Peggotty's spare room—my room—was likely to have occupation enough in a little while, if that great Visitor, before whose presence all the living must give place, were not already in the house; so I betook myself to the inn, and dined there, and engaged my bed.

It was ten o'clock when I went out. Many of the shops were shut, and the town was dull. When I came to Omer and Joram's, I found the shutters up, but the shop door standing open. As I could obtain a perspective view of Mr. Omer inside, smoking his pipe by the parlor-door, I entered, and asked him how he was.

"Why, bless my life and soul!" said Mr. Omer, "how do you find yourself? Take a seat.—Smoke not disagreeable, I hope?"

"By no means," said I. "I like it—in somebody else's pipe."

"What, not in your own, eh?" Mr. Omer returned, laughing. "All the better, sir. Bad habit for a young man. Take a seat. I smoke, myself, for the asthma."

Mr. Omer had made room for me, and placed a chair. He now sat down again, very much out of breath, gasping at his pipe as if it contained a supply of that necessary, without which he must perish.

"I am sorry to have heard bad news of Mr. Barkis," said I.

Mr. Omer looked at me, with a steady countenance, and shook his head.

"Do you know how he is to-night?" I asked.

"The very question I should have put to you, sir," returned Mr. Omer, "but on account of delicacy. It's one of the drawbacks of our line of business. When a party 's ill, we *can't* ask how the party is."

The difficulty had not occurred to me; though I had had my apprehensions too, when I went in, of hearing the old tune. On its being mentioned, I recognised it, however, and said as much.

"Yes, yes, you understand," said Mr. Omer, nodding his head.—"We durstn't do it. Bless you, it would be a shock that the generality of parties mightn't recover, to say 'Omer and Joram's compliments, and how do you find yourself this morning'—or this afternoon—as it may be."

Mr. Omer and I nodded at each other, and Mr. Omer recruited his wind by the aid of his pipe.

"It 's one of the things that cut the trade off from attentions they could often wish to show," said Mr. Omer. "Take myself.—If I have known Barkis a year, to move to as he went by, I have known him forty year. But *I* can't go and say 'how is he?'"

I felt it was rather hard on Mr. Omer, and I told him so.

"I 'm not more self-interested, I hope, than another man," said Mr. Omer. "Look at me! My wind may fail me at any moment, and it ain't likely that, to my own knowledge, I 'd be self-interested under such circumstances. I say it ain't likely, in a man who knows his wind will go, when it *does* go, as if a pair of bellows was cut open; and that man a grandfather," said Mr. Omer.

I said "Not at all."

"It ain't that I complain of my line of business," said Mr. Omer. "It ain't that. Some good and some bad goes, no doubt, to all callings. What I wish, is, that parties were brought up stronger-minded."

Mr. Omer, with a very complacent and amiable face, took several puffs in silence; and then said, resuming his first point.

"Accordingly we 're obleeged, in ascertaining how Barkis goes on, to limit ourselves to Em'ly. She knows what our real objects are, and she don't have any more alarms or suspicions about us, than if we were so many lambs. Minnie and Joram have just stepped down to the house, in fact (she 's there, after hours, helping her aunt a bit), to ask her how he is to-night; and if you was to please to wait till they come back, they 'd give you full partic'lers. Will you take something? A glass of srub and water, now? I smoke on srub and water, myself," said Mr. Omer, taking up his glass, "because it's considered softening to the passages, by which this troublesome breath of mine gets into action. But, Lord bless you," said Mr. Omer, huskily, "it ain't the passages that 's out of order? 'Give me breath enough,' said I to my daughter Minnie, 'and *I'll* find passages, my dear.'"

He really had no breath to spare, and it was very alarming to see him laugh. When he was again in a condition to be talked to, I thanked him for the proffered refreshment, which I declined, as I had just had dinner; and, observing that I would wait, since he was so good as to invite me, until his daughter and his son-in-law came back, I inquired how little Em'ly was?

"Well, sir," said Mr. Omer, removing his pipe, that he might rub his chin; "I tell you truly, I shall be glad when her marriage has taken place."

"Why so?" I inqnired.

"Well, she's unsettled at present," said Mr. Omer. "It ain't that she's not as pretty as ever, for she's prettier—I do assure you she is prettier. It ain't that she don't work as well as ever, for she does. She *was* worth any six, and she *is* worth any six. But somehow she wants heart. If you understand," said Mr. Omer, after rubbing his chin again, and smoking a little, "what I mean in a general way by the expression, 'A long pull, and a strong pull, and a pull altogether, my hearties, hurrah!' I should say to you, that *that* was—in a general way—what I miss in Em'ly."

Mr. Omer's face and manner went for so much, that I could conscientiously nod my head, as divining his meaning. My quickness of apprehension seemed to please him, and he went on.

"Now, I consider this is principally on account of her being in an unsettled state, you see. We have talked it over a good deal, her uncle and myself, and her sweetheart and myself, after business; and I consider it is principally on account of her being unsettled. You must always recollect of Em'ly," said Mr. Omer, shaking his head gently, "that she's a most extraordinary affectionate little thing. The proverb says, 'You can't make a silk purse out of a sow's ear.' Well, I don't know about that. I rather think you may, if you begin early in life. She has made a home out of that old boat, sir, that stone and marble couldn't beat."

"I am sure she has!" said I.

"To see the clinging of that pretty little thing to her uncle," said Mr. Omer; "to see the way she holds on to him, tighter and tighter, and closer and closer, every day, is to see a sight. Now, you know, there's a struggle going on when that's the case. Why should it be made a longer one than is needful?"

I listened attentively to the good old fellow, and acquiesced, with all my heart, in what he said.

"Therefore, I mentioned to them," said Mr. Omer, in a comfortable, easy-going tone, "this. I said, 'Now, don't consider Em'ly nailed down in point of time, at all. Make it your own time. Her services have been more valuable than was supposed; her learning has been quicker than was supposed; Omer and Joram can run their pen through what remains; and she's free when you wish. If she likes to make any little arrangement, afterwards, in the way of doing any little thing for us at home, very well. If she don't, very well still. We're no losers, anyhow.' For—don't you see," said Mr. Omer, touching me with his pipe, "it ain't likely that a man so short of breath as myself, and a grandfather too, would go and strain points with a little bit of a blue-eyed blossom, like *her?*"

"Not at all, I am certain," said I.

"Not at all! You're right!" said Mr. Omer. "Well, sir, her cousin—you know it's a cousin she's going to be married to?"

"Oh yes," I replied. "I know him well."

"Of course you do," said Mr. Omer. "Well, sir! Her cousin being, as it appears, in good work, and well to do, thanked me in a very manly sort of manner for this (conducting himself altogether, I must say, in a way that gives me a high opinion of him), and went and took as comfortable a little house as you or I could wish to clap eyes on. That little house is now furnished, right through, as neat and complete as a doll's parlor; and but for Barkis's illness having taken this bad turn, poor fellow, they would have been man and wife—I dare say, by this time. As it is, there's a postponement."

"And Em'ly, Mr. Omer?" I inquired. "Has she become more settled?"

"Why that, you know," he returned, rubbing his double chin again, "can't naturally be expected. The prospect of the change and separation, and all that, is, as one may say, close to her and far away from her, both at once. Barkis's death needn't put it off much, but his lingering might. Anyway, it's an uncertain state of matters, you see."

"I see," said I.

"Consequently," pursued Mr. Omer, "Em'ly's still a little down, and a little fluttered; perhaps, upon the whole, she's more so than she was. Every day she seems to get fonder and fonder of her uncle, and more loth to part from all of us. A kind word from me brings the tears into her eyes; and if you was to see her with my daughter Minnie's little girl, you'd never forget it. Bless my heart alive!" said Mr. Omer, pondering, "how she loves that child!"

Having so favourable an opportunity, it occurred to me to ask Mr. Omer, before our conversation should be interrupted by the return of his daughter and her husband, whether he knew anything of Martha.

"Ah!" he rejoined, shaking his head, and looking very much dejected. "No good. A sad story, sir, however you come to know it. I never thought there was harm in the girl. I wouldn't wish to mention it before my daughter Minnie—for she'd take me up directly—but I never did. None of us ever did."

Mr. Omer hearing his daughter's footstep before I heard it, touched me with his pipe, and shut up one eye, as a caution. She and her husband came in immediately afterwards.

Their report was, that Mr. Barkis was "as bad as bad could be;" that he was quite unconscious; and that Mr. Chillip had mournfully said in the kitchen, on going away just now, that the College of Physicians, the College of Surgeons, and Apothecaries' Hall, if they were all called in together, couldn't help him. He was past both Colleges, Mr. Chillip said, and the Hall could only poison him.

Hearing this, and learning that Mr. Peggotty was there, I determined to go to the house at once. I bade good night to Mr. Omer, and to Mr. and Mrs. Joram; and directed my steps thither, with a solemn feeling, which made Mr. Barkis quite a new and different creature.

My low tap at the door was answered by Mr. Peggotty. He was not so much surprised to see me as I had expected. I remarked this in Peggotty, too, when she came down; and I have seen it since; and I think, in the expectation of that dread surprise, all other changes and surprises dwindle into nothing.

I shook hands with Mr. Peggotty, and passed into the kitchen, while he softly closed the door. Little Em'ly was sitting by the fire, with her hands before her face. Ham was standing near her.

We spoke in whispers; listening between whiles, for any sound in the room above. I had not thought of it on the occasion of my last visit, but how strange was it to me now, to miss Mr. Barkis out of the kitchen!

"This is very kind of you, Mas'r Davy," said Mr. Peggotty.

"It is oncommon kind," said Ham.

"Em'ly, my dear," cried Mr. Peggotty. "See here! Here's Mas'r Davy come! What, cheer up, pretty! Not a wured to Mas'r Davy?"

There was a trembling upon her, that I can see now. The coldness of her hand when I touched it, I can feel yet. Its only sign of animation was to shrink from mine; and then she glided from the chair, and, creeping to the other side of her uncle, bowed herself, silently and trembling still, upon his breast.

"It's such a loving art," said Mr. Peggotty, smoothing her rich hair with his great hard hand, "that it can't abear the sorrer of this. It's nat'ral in young folk, Mas'r Davy, when they're new to these here trials, and timid, like my little bird,—it's nat'ral."

She clung the closer to him, but neither lifted up her face, nor spoke a word.

"It's getting late, my dear," said Mr. Peggotty, "and here's Ham come fur to take you home. Theer! Go along with t'other loving art! What, Em'ly? Eh, my pretty?"

The sound of her voice had not reached me, but he bent his head as if he listened to her, and then said:

"Let you stay with your uncle? Why, you doen't mean to ask me that! Stay with your uncle, Moppet? When your husband that'll be so soon, is here fur to take you home? Now a person wouldn't think it, fur to see this little thing alongside a rough-weather chap like me," said Mr. Peggotty, looking round at bo.h o. us, with infinite pride; "but the sea ain't more salt in it than she has fondness in her for her uncle—a foolish little Em'ly!"

"Em'ly's in the right in that, Mas'r Davy!" said Ham. "Lookee here! As Em'ly wishes of it, and as she's hurried and frightened, like, besides, I'll leave her till morning. Let me stay too!"

"No, no," said Mr. Peggotty. "You doen't ought—a married man like you—or what's as good—to take and hull away a day's work. And you doen't ought to watch and work both. That won't do. You go home and turn in. You ain't afeerd of Em'ly not being took good care on, *I* know."

Ham yielded to this persuasion, and took his hat to go. Even when he kissed her,—and I never saw him approach her, but I felt that nature had given him the soul of a gentleman,—she seemed to cling closer to her uncle, even to the avoidance of her chosen husband. I shut the door after him, that it might cause no disturbance of the quiet that prevailed; and when I turned back, I found Mr. Peggotty still talking to her.

"Now, I'm a going up-stairs to tell your aunt as Mas'r Davy's here, and that'll cheer her up a bit," he said. "Sit ye down by the fire, the while, my dear, and warm these mortal cold hands. You don't need to be so fearsome, and take on so much. What? You'll go along with me?—Well! come along with me—come! If her uncle was turned out of house and home, and forced to lay down in the dyke, Mas'r Davy," said Mr. Peggotty, with no less pride than before, "it's my belief she'd go along with him, now! But there'll be some one else, soon,—some one else, soon, Em'ly!"

Afterwards, when I went up-stairs, as I passed the door of my little chamber, which was dark, I had an indistinct impression of her being within it, cast down upon the floor. But, whether it was really she, or whether it was a confusion of the shadows in the room, I don't know now.

I had leisure to think, before the kitchen fire, of pretty little Em'ly's dread of death—which, added to what Mr. Omer had told me, I took to be the cause of her being so unlike herself—and I had leisure, before Peggotty came down, even to think more leniently of the weakness of it: as I sat counting the ticking of the clock, an

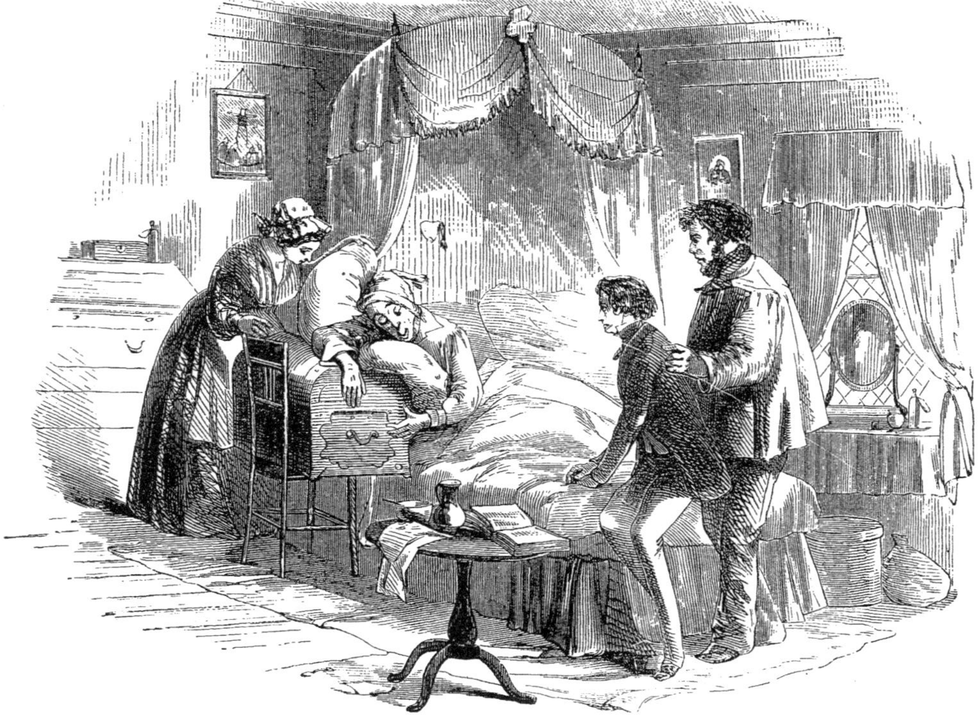

I FIND MR. BARKIS "GOING OUT WITH THE TIDE."

deepening my sense of the solemn hush around me. Peggotty took me in her arms, and blessed and thanked me over and over again for being such a comfort to her (that was what she said) in her distress. She then entreated me to come up-stairs, sobbing that Mr. Barkis had always liked me and admired me; that he had often talked of me, before he fell into a stupor; and that she believed, in case of his coming to himself again, he would brighten up at sight of me, if he could brighten up at any earthly thing.

The probability of his ever doing so appeared to me, when I saw him, to be very small. He was lying with his head and shoulders out of bed, in an uncomfortable attitude, half resting on the box which had cost him so much pain and trouble. I learned, that, when he was past creeping out of bed to open it, and past assuring himself of its safety by means of the divining rod I had seen him use, he had required to have it placed on the chair at the bed-side, where he had ever since embraced it, night and day. His arm lay on it now. Time and the world were slipping from beneath him, but the box was there; and the last words he had uttered were (in an explanatory tone) "Old Clothes!"

"Barkis, my dear!" said Peggotty, almost cheerfully: bending over him, while her brother and I stood at the bed's foot. "Here's my dear boy—my dear boy, Master Davy, who brought us together, Barkis! That you sent messages by, you know! Won't you speak to Master Davy?"

He was as mute and senseless as the box, from which his form derived the only expression it had.

"He's a going out with the tide," said Mr. Peggotty to me, behind his hand.

My eyes were dim, and so were Mr. Peggotty's; but I repeated in a whisper "With the tide?"

"People can't die, along the coast," said Mr. Peggotty, "except when the tide's pretty nigh out. They can't be born, unless it's pretty nigh in—not properly born, till flood. He's a going out with the tide. It's ebb at half arter three, slack water half-an-hour. If he lives till it turns, he'll hold his own till past the flood, and go out with the next tide."

We remained there, watching him, a long time—hours. What

mysterious influence my presence had upon him in that state of his senses, I shall not pretend to say; but when he at last began to wander feebly, it is certain he was muttering about driving me to school.

"He's coming to himself," said Peggotty.

Mr. Peggotty touched me, and whispered with much awe and reverence, "They are both a going out fast."

"Barkis, my dear!" said Peggotty.

"C. P. Barkis," he cried faintly. "No better woman anywhere!"

"Look! Here's Master Davy!" said Peggotty. For he now opened his eyes.

I was on the point of asking him if he knew me, when he tried to stretch out his arm, and said to me, distinctly, with a pleasant smile:

"Barkis is willin'!"

And, it being low water, he went out with the tide.

CHAPTER XXXI.

A GREATER LOSS.

It was not difficult for me, on Peggotty's solicitation, to resolve to stay where I was, until after the remains of the poor carrier should have made their last journey to Blunderstone. She had long ago bought, out of her own savings, a little piece of ground in our old churchyard near the grave "of her sweet girl," as she always called my mother; and there they were to rest.

In keeping Peggotty company, and doing all I could for her (little enough at the utmost), I was as grateful, I rejoice to think, as even now I could wish myself to have been. But I am afraid I had a supreme satisfaction, of a personal and professional nature, in taking charge of Mr. Barkis's will, and expounding its contents.

I may claim the merit of having originated the suggestion that the will should be looked for in the box. After some search, it was found in the box, at the bottom of a horse's nose-bag; wherein (besides hay) there was discovered an old gold watch, with chain and seals, which Mr. Barkis had worn on his wedding-day, and which had never been seen before or since; a silver tobacco-stopper, in the form of a leg; an imitation lemon, full of minute cups and saucers, which I have some idea Mr. Barkis must have purchased to present to me when I was a child, and afterwards found himself unable to part with; eighty-seven guineas and a half, in guineas and half guineas; two hundred and ten pounds, in perfectly clean Bank notes; certain receipts for Bank of England stock; an old horse-shoe, a bad shilling, a piece of camphor, and an oyster-shell. From the circumstance of the latter article having been much polished, and displaying prismatic colors on the inside, I conclude that Mr. Barkis had some general ideas about pearls, which never resolved themselves into anything definite.

For years and years, Mr. Barkis had carried this box, on all his journeys, every day. That it might the better escape notice, he had invented a fiction that it belonged to "Mr. Blackboy," and was "to be left with Barkis till called for;" a fable he had elaborately written on the lid, in characters now scarcely legible.

He had hoarded, all these years, I found, to good purpose. His property in money amounted to nearly three thousand pounds. Of this he bequeathed the interest of one thousand to Mr. Peggotty for his life; on his decease, the principal to be equally divided between Peggotty, little Em'ly, and me, or the survivor or survivors of us, share and share alike. All the rest he died possessed of, he bequeathed to Peggotty; whom he left residuary legatee, and sole executrix of that his last will and testament.

I felt myself quite a proctor when I read this document aloud with all possible ceremony, and set forth its provisions, any number of times, to those whom they concerned. I began to think there was more in the Commons than I had supposed. I examined the will with the deepest attention, pronounced it perfectly formal in all respects, made a pencil-mark or so on the margin, and thought it rather extraordinary that I knew so much.

In this abstruse pursuit; in making an account for Peggotty of all the property into which she had come; in arranging all the affairs in an orderly manner; and in being her referee and adviser on every point, to our joint delight; I passed the week before the funeral. I did not see little Em'ly in that interval, but they told me she was to be quietly married in a fortnight.

I did not attend the funeral in character, if I may venture to say so. I mean I was not dressed up in a black cloak and a streamer, to frighten the birds; but I walked over to Blunderstone early in the morning, and was in the churchyard when it came, attended only by Peggotty and her brother. The mad gentleman looked on, out of my little window; Mr. Chillip's baby wagged its heavy head, and rolled its goggle eyes, at the clergyman, over its nurse's shoulder; Mr. Omer breathed short in the background; no one else was there; and it was very quiet. We walked about the churchyard for an hour, after all was over; and pulled some young leaves from the ree above my mother's grave.

A dread falls on me here. A cloud is lowering on the distant town, towards which I retraced my solitary steps. I fear to approach it. I cannot bear to think of what did come, upon that memorable night; of what must come again, if I go on.

It is no worse, because I write of it. It would be no better, if I stopped my most unwilling hand. It is done. Nothing can undo it; nothing can make it otherwise than as it was.

My old nurse was to go to London with me next day, on the business of the will. Little Em'ly was passing that day at Mr. Omer's. We were all to meet in the old boathouse that night. Ham would bring Em'ly at the usual hour. I would walk back at my leisure. The brother and sister would return as they had come, and be expecting us, when the day closed in, at the fireside.

I parted from them at the wicket-gate, where visionary Straps had rested with Roderick Random's knapsack in the days of yore; and, instead of going straight back, walked a little distance on the road to Lowestoft. Then I turned, and walked back towards Yarmouth. I stayed to dine at a decent alehouse, some mile or two from the Ferry I have mentioned before; and thus the day wore away, and it was evening when I reached it. Rain was falling heavily by that time, and it was a wild night; but there was a moon behind the clouds, and it was not dark.

I was soon within sight of Mr. Peggotty's house, and of the light within it shining through the window. A little floundering across the sand, which was heavy, brought me to the door, and I went in.

It looked very comfortable indeed. Mr. Peggotty had smoked his evening pipe, and there were preparations for some supper by-and-by. The fire was bright, the ashes were thrown up, the locker was ready for little Em'ly in her old place. In her own old place sat Peggotty, once more, looking (but for her dress) as if she had never left it. She had fallen back, already, on the society of the work-box with Saint Paul's upon the lid, the yard-measure in the cottage, and the bit of wax-candle: and there they all were, just as if they had never been disturbed. Mrs. Gummidge appeared to be fretting a little, in her old corner; and consequently looked quite natural, too.

"You're first of the lot, Mas'r Davy!" said Mr. Peggotty, with a happy face. "Doen't keep in that coat, sir, if it's wet."

"Thank you, Mr. Peggotty," said I, giving him my outer coat to hang up. "It's quite dry."

"So 'tis!" said Mr. Peggotty, feeling my shoulders. "As a chip! Sit ye down, sir. It ain't o' no use saying welcome to you, but you're welcome, kind and hearty."

"Thank you, Mr. Peggotty, I am sure of that. Well, Peggotty!" said I, giving her a kiss. "And how are you, old woman?"

"Ha, ha!" laughed Mr. Peggotty, sitting down beside us, and rubbing his hands in his sense of relief from recent trouble, and in the genuine heartiness of his nature; "there's not a woman in the wureld, sir—as I tell her—that need to feel more easy in her mind than her! She done her dooty by the departed, and the departed know'd it; and the departed done what was right by her, as she done what was right by the departed; and—and—and it's *all* right!"

Mrs. Gummidge groaned.

"Cheer up, my pretty mawther!" said Mr. Peggotty. (But he shook his head aside at us, evidently sensible of the tendency of the late occurrences to recal the memory of the old one.) "Doen't be down! Cheer up, for your own self, on'y a little bit, and see if a good deal more doen't come nat'ral!"

"Not to me, Dan'l," returned Mrs. Gummidge. "Nothink's nat'ral to me but to be lone and lorn."

"No, no," said Mr. Peggotty, soothing her sorrows.

"Yes, yes, Dan'l!" said Mrs. Gummidge. "I ain't a person to live with them as has had money left. Thinks go too contrairy with me. I had better be a riddance."

"Why, how should I ever spend it without you?" said Mr. Peggotty, with an air of serious remonstrance. "What are you a talking on? Doen't I want you more now, than ever I did?"

"I know'd I was never wanted before!" cried Mrs. Gummidge, with a pitiable whimper, "and now I'm told so! How could I expect to be wanted, being so lone and lorn, and so contrairy!"

Mr. Peggotty seemed very much shocked at himself for having

made a speech capable of this unfeeling construction, but was prevented from replying, by Peggotty's pulling his sleeve, and shaking her head. After looking at Mrs. Gummidge for some moments, in sore distress of mind, he glanced at the Dutch clock, rose, snuffed the candle, and put it in the window.

"Theer!" said Mr. Peggotty, cheerily. "Theer we are, Missis Gummidge!" Mrs. Gummidge slightly groaned. "Lighted up, accordin' to custom! You 're a wonderin' what that's fur, sir! Well, it's fur our little Em'ly. You see, the path ain't over light or cheerful arter dark; and when I'm here at the hour as she's comin' home, I puts the light in the winder. That, you see," said Mr. Peggotty, bending over me with great glee, "meets two objects. She says, says Em'ly, 'Theer's home!' she says. And likewise, says Em'ly, 'My uncle's theer!' Fur if I ain't theer, I never have no light showed."

"You 're a baby!" said Peggotty; very fond of him for it, if she thought so.

"Well," returned Mr. Peggotty, standing with his legs pretty wide apart, and rubbing his hands up and down them in his comfortable satisfaction, as he looked alternately at us and at the fire, "I doen't know but I am. Not, you see, to look at."

"Not azackly," observed Peggotty.

"No," laughed Mr. Peggotty, "not to look at, but to—to consider on, you know. *I* doen't care, bless you! Now I tell you. When I go a looking and looking about that theer pritty house of our Em'ly's, I'm—I'm Gormed," said Mr. Peggotty, with sudden emphasis—"theer! I can't say more—if I doen't feel as if the littlest things was her, a'most. I takes 'em up, and I puts 'em down, and I touches of 'em as delicate as if they was our Em'ly. So 'tis with her little bonnets and that. I couldn't see one on 'em rough used a purpose—not fur the wureld. There's a babby fur you, in the form of a great Sea Porkypine!" said Mr. Peggotty, relieving his earnestness with a roar of laughter.

Peggotty and I both laughed, but not so loud.

"It's my opinion, you see," said Mr. Peggotty, with a delighted face, after some further rubbing of his legs "as this is along of my havin' played with her so much, and made believe as we was Turks, and French, and sharks, and every wariety of forinners—bless you, yes; and lions and whales, and I don't know what all!—when she warn't no higher than my knee. I've got into the way on it, you know. Why, this here candle, now!" said Mr. Peggotty, gleefully holding out his hand towards it, "*I* know wery well that arter she's married and gone, I shall put that candle theer, just the same as now. I know wery well that when I'm here o' nights (and where else should *I* live, bless your arts, whatever fortun' I come into!) and she ain't here, or I ain't theer, I shall put the candle in the winder, and sit afore the fire, pretending I'm expecting of her, like I'm a doing now. *There's* a babby for you," said Mr. Peggotty, with another roar, "in the form of a Sea Porkypine! Why, at the present minute, when I see the candle sparkle up, I says to myself, 'She's a looking at it! Em'ly 's a coming!' *There's* a babby for you, in the form of a Sea Porkypine! Right for all that," said Mr. Peggotty stopping in his roar, and smiting his hands together; "fur here she is!"

It was only Ham. The night should have turned more wet since I came in, for he had a large sou'wester hat on, slouched over his face.

"Where's Em'ly?" said Mr. Peggotty.

Ham made a motion with his head, as if she were outside. Mr. Peggotty took the light from the window, trimmed it, put it on the table, and was busily stirring the fire, when Ham, who had not moved, said:

"Mas'r Davy, will you come out a minute, and see what Em'ly and me has got to show you?"

We went out. As I passed him at the door, I saw, to my astonishment and fright, that he was deadly pale. He pushed me hastily into the open air, and closed the door upon us. Only upon us two.

"Ham! what's the matter!"

"Mas'r Davy!"— Oh, for his broken heart, how dreadfully he wept!

I was paralyzed by the sight of such grief. I don't know what I thought, or what I dreaded. I could only look at him.

"Ham! Poor good fellow! For heaven's sake tell me what's the matter!"

"My love, Mas'r Davy—the pride and hope of my art—her that I'd have died for, and would die for now—she's gone!"

"Gone?"

"Em'ly 's run away! Oh, Mas'r Davy, think *how* she's run away, when I pray my good and gracious God to kill her (her that is so dear above all things) sooner than let her come to ruin and disgrace!"

The face he turned up to the troubled sky, the quivering of his clasped hands, the agony of his figure, remain associated with that lonely waste, in my remembrance, to this hour. It is always night there, and he is the only object in the scene.

"You're a scholar," he said, hurriedly, "and know what's right and best. What am I to say, in-doors? How am I ever to break it to him, Mas'r Davy?"

I saw the door move, and instinctively tried to hold the latch on the outside, to gain a moment's time. It was too late. Mr. Peggotty thrust forth his face; and never could I forget the change that came upon it when he saw us, if I were to live five hundred years.

I remember a great wail and cry, and the women hanging about him, and we all standing in the room; I with a paper in my hand, which Ham had given me; Mr. Peggotty, with his vest torn open, his hair wild, his face and lips quite white, and blood trickling down his bosom (it had sprung from his mouth, I think), looking fixedly at me.

"Read it, sir," he said, in a low shivering voice. "Slow, please. I doen't know as I can understand."

In the midst of the silence of death, I read thus, from a blotted letter.

"'When you, who love me so much better than I ever have deserved, even when my mind was innocent, see this, I shall be far away.'"

"I shall be fur away," he repeated slowly. "Stop! Em'ly fur away. Well!"

'When I leave my dear home—my dear home—oh, my dear home!—in the morning,'

the letter bore date on the previous night:

'—it will be never to come back, unless he brings me back a lady. This will be found at night, many hours after, instead of me. Oh, if you knew how my heart is torn. If even you, that I have wronged so much, that never can forgive me, could only know what I suffer! I am too wicked to write about myself. Oh, take comfort in thinking that I am so bad. Oh, for mercy's sake, tell uncle that I never loved him half so dear as now. Oh, don't remember how affectionate and kind you have all been to me—don't remember we were ever to be married—but try to think as if I died when I was little, and was buried somewhere. Pray Heaven that I am going away from, have compassion on my uncle! Tell him that I never loved him half so dear. Be his comfort. Love some good girl, that will be what I was once to uncle, and be true to you, and worthy of you, and know no shame but me. God bless all! I'll pray for all, often, on my knees. If he don't bring me back a lady, and I don't pray for my own self, I'll pray for all. My parting love to uncle. My last tears, and my last thanks, for uncle!'"

That was all.

He stood, long after I had ceased to read, still looking at me. At length I ventured to take his hand, and to entreat him, as well as I could, to endeavour to get some command of himself. He replied, "I thankee, sir, I thankee!" without moving.

Ham spoke to him. Mr. Peggotty was so far sensible of *his* affliction, that he wrung his hand; but, otherwise, he remained in the same state, and no one dared to disturb him.

Slowly, at last, he moved his eyes from my face, as if he were waking from a vision, and cast them round the room. Then he said, in a low voice:

"Who's the man? I want to know his name."

Ham glanced at me, and suddenly I felt a shock that struck me back.

"There's a man suspected," said Mr. Peggotty. "Who is it?"

"Mas'r Davy!" implored Ham. "Go out a bit, and let me tell him what I must. You doen't ought to hear it, sir."

I felt the shock again. I sank down in a chair, and tried to utter some reply; but my tongue was fettered, and my sight was weak.

"I want to know his name!" I heard said, once more.

"For some time past," Ham faltered, "there's been a servant about here, at odd times. There's been a gen'lm'n too. Both of 'em belonged to one another."

Mr. Peggotty stood fixed as before, but now looking at him.

"The servant," pursued Ham, "was seen along with—our poor girl—last night. He's been in hiding about here, this week or over. He was thought to have gone, but he was hiding. Doen't stay, Mas'r Davy, doen't!"

I felt Peggotty's arm round my neck, but I could not have moved if the house had been about to fall upon me.

"A strange chay and horses was outside town, this morning, on the Norwich road, a'most afore the day broke," Ham went on. "The servant went to it, and come from it, and went to it again. When he went to it again, Em'ly was nigh him. The t'other was inside. He's the man."

"For the Lord's love," said Mr. Peggotty, falling back, and putting out his hand, as if to keep off what he dreaded. "Doen't tell me his name's Steerforth!"

"Mas'r Davy," exclaimed Ham, in a broken voice, "it ain't no fault of yourn—and I am far from laying of it to you—but his name is Steerforth, and he's a damned villain!"

Mr. Peggotty uttered no cry, and shed no tear, and moved no more, until he seemed to wake again, all at once, and pulled down his rough coat from its peg in a corner.

"Bear a hand with this! I'm struck of a heap, and can't do it," he said, impatiently. "Bear a hand, and help me. Well!" when somebody had done so. "Now give me that theer hat!"

Ham asked him whither he was going.

"I'm a going to seek my niece. I'm a going to seek my Em'ly. I'm a going, first, to stave in that theer boat, and sink it where I would have drownded *him*, as I'm a livin' soul, if I had had one thought of what was in him! As he sat afore me," he said, wildly, holding out his clenched right hand, "as he sat afore me, face to face, strike me down dead, but I'd have drownded him, and thought it right!—I'm a going to seek my niece."

"Where?" cried Ham, interposing himself before the door.

"Anywhere! I'm a going to seek my niece through the wureld.

I'm a going to find my poor niece in her shame, and bring her back. No one stop me! I tell you I'm a going to seek my niece!"

"No, no!" cried Mrs. Gummidge, coming between them, in a fit of crying. "No, no, Dan'l, not as you are now. Seek her in a little while, my lone lorn Dan'l, and that'll be but right; but not as you are now. Sit ye down, and give me your forgiveness for having ever been a worrit to you, Dan'l—what have *my* contrairies ever been to this!—and let us speak a word about them times when she was first an orphan, and when Ham was too, and when I was a poor widder woman, and you took me in. It 'll soften your poor heart, Dan'l," laying her head upon his shoulder, "and you'll bear your sorrow better; but you know the promise, Dan'l, 'As you have done it unto one of the least of these, you have done it unto me;' and that can never fail under this roof, that's been our shelter for so many, many year!"

He was quite passive now; and when I heard him crying, the impulse that had been upon me to go down upon my knees, and ask their pardon for the desolation I had caused, and curse Steerforth, yielded to a better feeling. My overcharged heart found the same relief, and I cried too.

www.ingramcontent.com/pod-product-compliance
Lightning Source LLC
LaVergne TN
LVHW021301110826
845150LV00003B/455

* 9 7 8 1 4 2 5 5 5 9 9 3 9 *